A dragon slayer's tale

I0642405

Copyright©2017 Anne Olga Vea/Skogtrollet forlag.
Publisher: Skogtrollet forlag/Anne Olga Vea
ISBN: **978-82-93355-36-6**
First edition.

This book is not suitable for minors due to : Nasty language, violence and situations of a sexual nature.

Chapter 1: Good old days

He was swearing to himself, trying to hold the goddamn nag still while he got the last nail in. The horse had been refusing to stand still the entire time and by now his patience was wearing thin. At last he managed to get the nail in and could let go of the leg, sweat was pouring of him and he felt how his shirt had started to stick to his back. If the owner didn't pay well he would face the evening in a very foul mood indeed. The horse was the type who is likely to try to take a piece out of you so he didn't go near the head, to the dark with such high strung thoroughbreds. He usually only got ordinary riding horses and some plow horses and he had rarely put shoes on something this expensive but he did his job well and he was the only farrier in this village. The noble man had stayed at the local inn when he discovered a lose shoe and wanted all four replaced by new ones. The job could have been a swift and easy one if the Akhi cursed gelding hadn't been plain vicious.

The owner waited outside and he smiled widely. "You are done, excellent. You are fast indeed, my usual farrier uses half a day when this horse needs shoes"

The farrier sort of smiled but was thinking that it would have been nice if the owner had informed him of this beforehand. The noble man opened his purse and pulled out some gold coins and the farrier immediately felt better, five coins were placed in his palm and that was the best payment he had received in years. This area was quite poor and some copper shillings were the most he could ask for from the locals. The nobleman was a rather young fellow, perhaps in his early thirties and he had a rather sweet face which was clean shaven, it made him look like a half grown boy and perhaps he was used to exploiting that. "I am very grateful, I am in a bit of a hurry you see, a wedding"

The farrier smiled again, he was way taller than the nobleman and most believed that he was an apprentice, not a trained farrier and blacksmith. "Well he is good to go now"

The nobleman smiled and pulled on his riding gloves. "Brilliant, he is my fastest horse, a handful no doubt but valuable. I would hate it if he went lame"

The nobleman got the horse by the reins and brought it outside of the smithy. The animal looked as if it was contemplating taking a bite out of its master too but the noble man gave it a solid punch to the chest and the horse looked like a sulking kid. The farrier liked this man, he knew how to handle horses for sure. "The work looks excellent my good man, by which name should I remember you?"

The farrier sent the noble man a swift smile. "I am Phraan, just that"

The noble man did look puzzled for a few moments. "Phraan? Hmm, I could have sworn I have heard that name before, anyhow, I better be on my way!"

Phraan bowed and the noble man turned the horse and rode out of the yard in a rather brisk pace, it was very clear that he was impatient. Phraan put the coins into a secret little compartment in the very forge itself, nobody would look there but he kept one in his purse. He needed an evening off and the inn had excellent beer and wine. The autumn was setting in and there wasn't that much to do anymore, just smaller repairs and farrier work. He made sure that there couldn't be any fires and returned inside. His living quarters was in the same building as the forge and the stable and he had a tiny room with a narrow bed, a table and a small closet. That was all he needed. He got a bucket of water from a container built into

4

the wall on the other side of the forge, it would keep the water hot at all times and he stripped down and washed himself thoroughly. He didn't have a mirror but he did know how he looked these days.

He was way more scarred than before, and he was perhaps leaner than he once had been. But he was still showing his mixed heritage and he sighed and pulled on some clean clothes. He didn't look much like his mother at all, that was the truth. Most times when a child was born of a human mother and an elven father it would be simply elven, but creatures like him were extremely rare. There was barely a trace of human in him except from the fact that he was broader and more muscular than most full blooded elven males. Children born of elven females and male humans were more common, but it was very special when a human female got pregnant by an elf and then survived the pregnancy. The reason was simply that an elven pregnancy last for a whole year and with an elven father the mother would have to endure at least two extra months and in most cases that became fatal. A human body couldn't support an elven fetus since its demands were way greater than that of a human one.

He could remember his mother, she had been a huge woman with wide hips and she had been strong as an ox. Perhaps that had been the reason why she had made it when many others hadn't.

The noble man had almost remembered his name and he had to grin again, a somewhat melancholic smile. Once his name had been on everybody's tongue but that was decades ago. Now he was just a common blacksmith and perhaps it was for the best. They had been too good at what they had been doing and they had ruined their own business. Back then nobody had believed that it was a bad thing, but it was. The balance of nature had been disturbed and he had seen the results with his own eyes. Too bad the humans didn't see it that way. Most had forgotten. What had been a frightening reality was now just bed time stories for children. He took a peek into the stable before he went to the inn, put some hay into the stall where his horse stood. He owned just one horse now, an ageing mare. She was of good breeding and had been very valuable once but now she was way past her best years, she was limping and thin and only old habit had made him keep her. At least she was company. Once he would have ridden great destriers, born and bred for their job and worth more money than the entire village but these days he had very little and didn't need much neither. The mare whinnied and he petted her white coat, soon she would be too old to move and then he would have to put her down but he feared the day.

He was welcomed into the inn by the keeper, everybody knew him and he was given a jug of ale and sat down by the hearth. A traveler had placed himself on a solid table and he was telling everybody of the things which happened in the wide world. This place was isolated and some news was always welcome. The innkeeper shouted to the guy, he was probably a travelling salesman for he carried a huge sack with ribbons and cloth and he wore a silly cloak in so many colors it hurt looking at it. "How about old King Vhandar, is he still around?"

The salesman shook his head. "Unfortunately no, he went to his forefathers two years ago, during the wedding of his youngest daughter, peace be with him."

The innkeeper scoffed. "At his daughter's wedding? What happened?"

The salesman did swing his cup. "Oh everybody knows that the old bloke loved his ale, and his beer, and mead and wine and liquor. Heck, if it could be ingested and contained alcohol he would drink it. He got into a drinking game with one of the groom's knights and didn't want to lose, so he kept chugging them down. When you are more than seventy winters old that is rarely a good idea"

The innkeeper chuckled and some of the guests there laughed. "My old man lived until he was ninety and five and he drank to his last day, never harmed him"

The man who spoke was the local baker and he sat there with his arms across his formidable chest and looked very important. The traveler nodded. "I am sure he was strong as the very mountains themselves, but these born of noble blood are more...fragile!"

That last word made everybody there burst into laughter, everybody knew that the noble families were fond of marrying their children off to relatives and the results could be horrifying at times. A woman spoke up. "Are there any news from the north? I have heard that the king has ordered more troops up towards the mountains?"

The salesman nodded eagerly. "Yes, that is correct madam, he has ordered more troops into the northern territory. There have been some problems up there, dragons some say"

Phraan tensed up, dragons? That was impossible! One of the younger men there stared at the salesman with wide eyes. "Are you sure? Everybody says that dragons went extinct fifty years ago, there haven't been any sightings since then. They just disappeared all of a sudden."

The salesman smiled widely. "I am sure, believe me, there are dragons up north once more. Not many I think but the king is always such a careful man who likes to take care of a problem before it grows into a big one"

Phraan held his breath. He didn't really know what to feel right now, a part of him was relieved that they hadn't wiped an entire species off the face of the earth and another part of him felt that his old instincts came back to life. "Have anyone said anything about the type of dragons?"

He kept his voice low and almost indifferent and the salesman shrugged. "A soldier I spoke to claimed that they were greybacks, but surely nobody knows for certain"

Phraan swallowed hard. Greybacks? He remembered that subspecies, they were flightless and very vicious, capable of transforming a herd of cattle into a heap of bones in a very short time. If there were greybacks alive the army could be in trouble, nobody knew how to slay dragons these days. Well, very few did. He felt a sudden urge to get up and leave, borrow a horse and ride to the city to ask if his skills would be needed but he decided against it just as fast. He had once sworn to live a peaceful life, he wasn't gonna break that promise just because of a silly whim. The king had skilled men, and it was probably just a small pack, perhaps not more than two or three dragons. No, no need for him this time. The salesman started talking about the type of gowns the ladies of the courts wore these days and Phraan listened with half an ear. He got another jug of ale and a plate with some good stew and he enjoyed the food. Afterwards he enjoyed flirting with the barmaid and then he walked home in the night, half drunk and a wee bit lonely and he fell asleep as soon as he let his head touch the hard pillow.

The next days were busy, the miller needed a new mechanism for the mill and had to replace a lot of the parts he had ordered from the city with better ones and Phraan was a very good blacksmith. He managed to make the pieces needed and felt a sting of real pride. He had been trained as a blacksmith by his mother's father, a strict and harsh man who did have a good heart behind the brusque façade and he had been taught well too. He did take great pride in his work. He used an entire week finishing the mill and then there were a dozen or more smaller jobs which needed to be done. Housewives needed their kettles mended, some plowshares had to be fixed before the winter came and he kept his mind busy the whole time. He had forgotten about the salesman and his tales.

He was standing by the forge hammering out some pieces of raw metal when he heard hooves and he put down the hammer and dried the sweat from his brow. He always wore a sort of hood while he was working with heat, he didn't want his hair scorched and it got very hot sometimes. Sweat was pouring from him and he turned around, wiped his face with a wet cloth. The forge work always left him looking rather dirty, covered with sooth and he didn't want to scare off a potential customer. He straightened his back and saw that a very tall brown horse trotted into the yard. It was ridden by a man wearing the uniform of the king's personal guard and he frowned. What the hell? Nobody that high ranking had ever come to this forsaken place? The rider dismounted the very fine horse and turned around and Phraan gasped, he stared with huge eyes at the man.

"Fastonar?!"

The man grinned widely and stepped forth, before Phraan really had time to react he was pulled into a hug and had to gasp for air, Fastonar was just as strong as he had been. "Yes old friend, it is me! Not some phantom."

Phraan had to swallow, he hadn't seen his old partner for decades, not since their group had been dissolved. Fastonar had gotten a few grey hairs but he did look almost unchanged. He was a so called soul-sworn, a priest as much as a warrior and it kept him young way longer than normal. He was about a hundred by now but didn't look as if he was a day over thirty. He could probably live for as long as a dwarf if nothing got to him first. "Ah, I am glad to see you, but what in the name of all the gods are you doing here?!"

Fastonar grinned again and petted Phraan across the back, the half elf cringed, his friend had hands the size of hams and he didn't know his own strength. "That is a question which is easy to answer, the king wants us to gather the group once more. They have a huge problem up north"

Phraan frowned. "Huge? I have heard of a few greybacks?"

9

Fastonar scoffed. "A few? Call it the second coming of the plague, there are swarms of beasts streaming into the valleys and over the plains, all sorts of types."

Phraan didn't understand. "How is that even possible? I though all dragons were extinct? Where do they come from?"

Fastonar smiled. "Now there is the mystery, the king wants us to find out. Isn't it exciting? It will be like the good old days"

Phraan did look as if he had his doubts. "Really? I remember those good old days, when we almost got killed and had to spend weeks and months out in the wild, hungry, scared and sick. It was great fun indeed, just as much fun as dancing in a field of thistles."

Fastonar had to laugh. "You are the same old pessimistic fool Phraan, you always see problems where we others see possibilities. Hear, remember that inn, by the lake? Remember that bar maiden you were so fascinated with? She really found the title dragon slayer thrilling didn't she? Or the ladies of the courts? They were all over us like bees"

Phraan grimaced. "Oh yes, and quite a sting they had too some of them. But seriously, the king wants us to return to duty?"

Fastonar put an arm around Phraan's neck. "Yes, as of immediately. Of course you can decline the offer but I think you want to find out where those pesky dragons come from now don't you? Come on, you were the best, you were the one true dragon slayer among us, our leader, our idol. It won't be the same without you"

Phraan took a deep breath, it did tempt him, it truly did. "So the dragons are a nuisance?"

Fastonar rolled his eyes. "Nuisance? You can say that again, they have leveled two villages already"

Phraan stiffened. "What? But...!"

Fastonar nodded. "I know, dragons usually don't attack settlements but now they do, the death toll is great, men women and children alike, and cattle of course. People are losing everything they have, and the troops are helpless. They have no idea of how to bring down such a creature, the reports I have read claim that more than a hundred soldiers are either dead, severely burned or injured in other ways"

Phraan moaned. "Morons, that is what they are, they have no clue about what they are doing right?"

Fastonar nodded sternly. "Exactly, they sort of think that they know everything and the soldiers have officers who weren't even born the last time there were dragons around. And they think they are oh so skilled when in reality they are dumb fuckers too nervous about getting stains on their uniforms to even follow their men into the field."

Phraan took a deep breath, stared at the smithy and its surroundings. It had been some good decades and a part of him still didn't want to be involved but he did know what carnage a whole pack of dragons can unleash. People were defenseless, even more so now than back then, it was a bit unnerving to say the least. "I will do it, but first, who is left of the group? Have you contacted everybody?"

Fastonar nodded. "I have, we have lost Ulbar and Aishrin but that is expected, they were both normal humans and both above their best age too. Ulbar died just four years after we quit in a bar fight but Aishrin lived to the ripe age of eighty."

Phraan had to sigh, the mortality of humans made them fade so fast, like shining gems that were there and then gone, they had been the groups healer and mage. "The others?"

Fastonar smiled, a wry smile. "Dhokay was ecstatic when I asked him, he said yes right away, Kapha too, he couldn't wait. It took some time finding Vitile and she almost declined but then she agreed and Shaluun did join the group again too."

Phraan sighed. "With us two that makes six, that is too few goddamn it. We need at least four more, and we do need a healer, and a mage too!"

Fastonar nodded and leaned against the door. "The king has promised us a healer and a mage, and I think he will find some good ones. Vitile too had a couple of trackers who may want to join us and the mayor did promise to hand over a couple of convicted criminals. They are suitable as bait I guess."

Phraan had to scoff. "Yeah, if they don't run away first that is, well, we can make it, but like I said, we do really need a healer. I do hope the king has one available, and a mage who knows how to ward off fire. Where do we meet up?"

Fastonar made a grimace. "In the city, tomorrow. I have been given quite a lot of money from his majesty so the others are already out shopping for equipment. You are the last one so I guess you can pick whatever you like. I bet the king already is busy trying to find someone who can step in as a healer, he has lots and lots of people available."

Phraan took a deep breath. "Great, tomorrow. You will stay here in this village I recon?"

Fastonar nodded and straightened his cloak. "Yes, so get your stuff ready, we leave at sunrise"

Phraan took a deep breath, he had to think. "Alright, I recon you are staying at the inn? I have things to take care off before I leave"

He saw that Fastonar understood and the tall officer left the yard and Phraan leaned against the wall, feeling strangely torn apart. This had been his home now for decades, the life there had been peaceful and built on routines. Maybe it really was time he moved forth again, challenged himself once more. The people needed him, that was the truth which made him change his mind. He went over to the neighbor, an elderly man who made a living from painting stuff and managed to convince him that taking care of the old mare would be a good thing to do. Then he found the only other man in the village capable of being a blacksmith and let him know that he could use the smithy until Phraan returned. In fact he wasn't sure he would return at all, anything could happen out there. Phraan didn't own much, he had a casket under the bed with his most precious belongings and he pulled it out and stared at it, then he took a deep breath and opened it for the first time in many years. It didn't contain much, a pouch containing a necklace which had belonged to his mother, a few drawings a friend of his had made, some coins and a cloak with his own insignia on it, embroidered in red upon black. A kneeling dragon, it was fitting back then, now he didn't know anymore.

He pulled out the last objects, two long dirks forged from a very special alloy, almost priceless and so sharp they would cut a falling hair. A long knife, made the same way. An elegant set of throwing axes and some spearheads and then at the bottom his old swords. He lifted them out of the crate with reverence, stared at the still shiny black leather covering the sheaths and let a hand glide along the handles. These were elven swords, elegant and lethal, slightly curved and with a sort of almost vibrant energy in them. He pulled them free, the blades stainless and shiny, almost glowing in the faint light. These were among the best blades ever forged and their origins had been lost in the sea of time but he knew of few other blades like these. They were unique and very dear to him. He put his stuff into a bag and pushed the crate back under the bed, then he found some bread and cheese and sat down to eat.

His mind was already preoccupied with the things he had heard, scores of dragons? So suddenly? That could mean that there had been some sort of hidden breeding area up north, somewhere unknown and now the beasts had started migrating south to find food. It could mean that this was just the beginning and he felt a sort of eager nervous energy building up inside. He finished his work, let the forge cool down before the night and then he went to bed. He did fall asleep rather fast, in spite of it all.

The next morning he did awake rather late, he got up, ate some, washed himself and put on his best clothes. Then he gathered his stuff, locked the door and left. The neighbor had already come for the old mare and he knew she would be well taken care off. He walked to the inn and Fastonar was up already, grinning widely. He smacked the behind of the barmaid as she scurried by him and he did look very eager to go. "Have you eaten? Yes? Good, then we can go right away"

He gave the innkeeper a very generous amount of money and then he whistled as they went outside. The brown horse was there but so was a long legged grey mare too and Phraan frowned. "Have you bought that horse?"

Fastonar shook his head. "No, it belongs to the army, I borrowed her when I realized that I had to go and fetch you. Hurry up"

Phraan sent the tall man a swift glance. "What's the hurry?"

Fastonar smiled and got in the saddle of the brown one. "We have to get to the horse market outside of the city early, before the best horses are sold"

Phraan frowned. "Fastonar, how much money did the King give you?"

Fastonar just made a gesture with his hand, "Enough, I know you want to pick out your own horses so let's go, before our butts grow moldy"

Phraan got in the saddle and they rode off, it felt odd being on a horse again after so long but he soon got used to it once more and relaxed. The city was a couple of hours ride away and these horses were fast so there wasn't much chance of talking. Phraan just hung onto the saddle and let the mare pick her own pace. They slowed down when the massive walls of the city started appearing behind the trees and hills. Here the road was packed with people travelling to and fro and Fastonar pointed towards the area to the west of the city where the markets were being held. The city itself was huge, the largest city in this part of the realm and also its capital. They said that the population was too large to be counted but the more educated minds guessed that about half a million souls had a home there, or at least something resembling a home.

The city had its own smell and Phraan sort of felt a wee bit disgusted by it, he would get used to it soon enough but right now it was too overwhelming and he sneezed and felt like an idiot. He wore such old fashioned clothes and looked like a vagabond compared with Fastonar. His friend grinned. "Worry not, we will get you an armor soon enough, and some clothes too. The King doesn't spare any expenses now, we have free hands."

They rode down towards the market, it was a large area filled with paddocks and you could find all sorts of animals there. Fastonar smiled. "We are early, good, I bet we can find a good destrier for you here"

Phraan felt a bit excited again, a good horse, he had missed that a lot. They did take a round and found the part of the market reserved for horses, there were plenty of salesmen there and Phraan knew that some did try to fool their customers. It was against the law of course but often there were no evidence that the animal in question had been tampered with. He had to use his eyes well to be able to find a horse brave enough to do what he would ask of it. They sort of rode through the area, using every trick they had learned to determine whether or not the animals were healthy, of good behavior and were well broken. There were destriers there, many in fact and they were excellent animals but Phraan didn't like any of them. Most were too young and inexperienced or too hot blooded. And some were way too old or too docile to be useful in a fight. He was ready to give up and tell Fastonar that they could go meet the others when he heard the sound of whinnying coming from outside of the market area. It was more a scream than a whinny and he heard shouts and screams from people too. He spurred the mare and rode towards the racket, something was going on and he wanted to find out what it was.

He reached the outer fence and rode through a gate and there he saw more paddocks, people who had been too late to buy access to the main marketplace. The sound came from one of the smaller paddocks and he clenched his teeth. It was a scream in anger and he rode forth again, the mare tensed up but he got her to move. The paddock was a cheap one and a rather obese man stood in it, trying to control a giant of a horse. Phraan had seen that race just once before, when he had visited the south coast. These horses came from the continent to the southeast of this and they were very hard to come by. He had to stare, the stallion was a blue roan with a white blaze and socks and it was exquisite, why a horse like that was taken to a cheap market like this was beyond him until he saw that the horse clearly wasn't easy to handle. It was trying to attack the man and it reminded Phraan of an angry dragon more than a horse. He had to grin, he had found his perfect mount. He got off the mare and walked to the fence, the man did notice him and waved his hand. "Take care sir, this animal is mad!"

Phraan stared at the horse, it had to be more than twenty hands in height with long hard legs and a majestic appearance. The tall arched neck and the short back told of great strength and he saw that this was one animal which never would surrender. "Where is he from?"

The fat man panted. "South, I was told to sell him on behalf of his former owner, apparently this beast have killed three men already. How am I to sell something like this ha? Not even the butcher wants him, he cannot sell the meat of a horse that has killed people!"

Phraan smiled, a slow grin. "I will take him off your hands, how much?"

The fat man blinked, looked a bit dumbfounded. "Ha? You want to buy him? Well, it will be your funeral I fear but ten gold coins, not a shilling less, and that is by my mother's sideburns cheap!"

Phraan nodded. "Very cheap, a horse like that is usually worth a thousand times that much."

Fastonar had caught up with him now and sat on his gelding, just staring with huge eyes. Phraan jumped into the paddock and the stallion bared his teeth and threw his head, a threatening gesture. This horse had been abused for sure, and Phraan started speaking to him in elvish, soothing melodic words that made the long ears clip and move and the stallion snorted and pawed at the ground. Phraan grasped the rope from the fat man and handed over ten coins, that was all he had but he knew he would get refunded by the King now. The stallion nickered and started dancing around him, tried to figure him out and Phraan stayed calm, the horse was proud and spirited and very intelligent and he was also very brave. He could see that on its body language, this one wouldn't shy away from anything and Phraan smiled and let the stallion get close enough to sniff him. "You are a beauty, but have been treated like a beast. That will change from now on, I promise you that."

The stallion just sniffed him and Phraan adjusted the halter and stroked the mighty neck. He was so tall he had no problems handling such a huge animal but others would need a ladder to mount him. The fat guy looked as if lightening had struck him. "Damn, that was…impressive"

Fastonar chuckled. "Oh you haven't seen anything yet, you are looking at a man who kept a dreklugnin as a pet for two whole years so yes, he knows how to deal with animals"

Phraan had to make a grimace. It was true, he had managed to tame on of the small dragons of that species but after two years he had let the beast run off, he couldn't stand the job of cleaning up after it and it did stink too, like few other things. The stallion had calmed down and Phraan made a swift movement and was on its back with a jump. He grinned to himself, the horse was loaded with power and he petted the neck and turned it around. "You will serve me well I am sure"

Fastonar opened the gate to let them out. "What will you name him?"

Phraan smiled, a somewhat crooked smile. "Drake, what else?"

Fastonar got back in the saddle and tied the mare to his own horse, Phraan waved the fat man goodbye and he felt that the newly named Drake had to have been well trained. The horse did obey as long as you didn't push it. They rode into the city and stopped by a tack shop, bought a new saddle and equipment for the destrier and Phraan made sure that everything was of the best quality available. He was starting to feel proud of the horse and Fastonar made them stop by the royal armories to get armor and clothes. When they were done Phraan was dressed in black and red as back in the days, carrying a light armor and he now wore his blades on his back, like he had back then. It felt weird but good too and when he had visited the barber and had a small haircut he did look pretty much the same way he had. It felt like stepping through a wall and into the past. Fastonar grasped his shoulder. "So, are you ready to meet the old gang?"

Phraan nodded. "Ready as ever"

Fastonar smiled and he did look very happy indeed. They rode towards the merchant's area of the city, that was where taverns and shops were and Phraan looked at his friend. "So, what have you been up to since the group was dissolved?"

Fastonar sighed, a very deep sigh. "Well, for the first decade I was of course regarded as something rather special, war hero you know. All the nobles wanted to be seen with me, and I was popular, hell, I was more popular than a piece of fresh dung to flies"

Phraan tilted his head. "That didn't last?"

Fastonar made a nasty grimace. "You can say that again, no, it didn't last at all to be honest. People started to forget and soon I was back to square one. Guarding the citadel, training recruits and doing my duties at the temple. By every deity, it was boring as fuck!"

Phraan had to grin widely, Fastonar hadn't changed at all, he had always preferred the heat of battle to the tranquility of the temples. "So there wasn't much action to be found?"

Fastonar shook his head with a bit too much energy. "Exactly, except from when some young fool tried to sneak out of the training camp at night, or someone managed to insult the high priests"

Phraan smiled to himself, Fastonar had always been the one with the strongest faith of them all, he had never doubted their mission even once nor had he ever doubted that they would emerge from the war victorious. For it had been a war back then, one fought with tooth and nail and every available resource and the outcome had always been uncertain. The packs of dragons of every size and sub species had threatened to ruin the northern areas completely and people had fled by the thousands. Back then he had been proud to be a part of the army fighting to eradicate the threat, no he wasn't so sure anymore. It had taken less than a decade for the farmers to rebuild the farms and regrow their herds but the damage had become visible not long afterwards. The once thriving herds of wild animals gradually dwindled and disease and other problems had brought many herds to near extinction. And the livestock too became ill since there weren't any wild animals grazing the hills, removing all the toxic plants. It was a rather terrible effect of having removed the top predator from the food chain. There had of course been way too many dragons back then but the hunters had taken it to the other extreme, none at all and look what they had gotten. The small dragons had been hunted mercilessly and the larger ones had simply vanished into thin air, some said that they had fought each other to extinction, that the aggressive males had ended up killing each other. And with no males left there would be no more dragons. The few dragons which had been living up north before had been dangerous but no more of a problem than the occasional bear or wolf pack, people respected them but didn't fear them.

The fertile areas weren't fertile anymore for the herds of deer and other grazing beasts had exploded and then eaten themselves into a rapid decline and now there were dry and sandy hills and meadows where once it had been lush and green. Some said that the northern areas had become cursed after the dragons disappeared, that the loss of life force had been forced through by dark magic but the king's counselors meant that it was just natural, some sort of cycle and that the fertile years would return soon enough.

The city streets were crowded as always but people did move out of the way and Fastonar did lead them to the tavern where the others waited. He was humming and looked incredibly jolly and Phraan guessed that he had disliked the last decades intensely. As a soul-sworn he was gifted with long life and great strength but there was little use for that here in the city and Fastonar had never been the type of person who is fond of routines. He craved excitement and drama and Phraan had to snicker. "So, any fair ladies in your path?"

Fastonar laughed out loud, a rather deep and full laughter. "Oh Phraan, you ought to see them all, high born or not. I have met plenty of fair ladies my friend, and some who cannot be called ladies at all. But I have had my fun, it has made life worth living for sure. How about you?"

Phraan blushed slightly. "Oh, not many ladies out there, I have made my living as a blacksmith remember? Sooty, dirty, smelly and not very wealthy, that doesn't attract the females very well"

Fastonar scoffed. "Are you telling me you have lived in celibacy this entire time? Akhi burn you man, you used to roll in the hay almost every night if I don't remember it wrong"

Phraan swore under his breath. "I can hardly remember it thus my friend, yes, I was lucky a few times but..."

Fastonar scoffed loudly. "A few times?! Phraan, you got laid more often than the whores at old Bilaum's brothel, don't try to deny it, you were damn popular back then"

Phraan sighed and rolled his eyes. "Fine, okay, I was popular but that type of lifestyle never suited me, not truly"

Fastonar almost giggled. "No, of course not, for you are the romantic type right? Who dreams of finding your one true love and settle down and have a dozen or more kids and just sit there and let your swords rust"

Phraan sighed, he felt a sting of anger and tried not to show it. Fastonar had probably forgotten that people like Phraan rarely were able to reproduce, it was like trying to mate a mule, it simply wouldn't happen. His friend stopped his horse in front of a rather huge tavern which appeared to be among the more posh ones. He nodded. "I hope we aren't too early, and I do hope that Vitile has managed to find those trackers she spoke of."

Phraan nodded, without proper trackers they didn't really stand much of a chance, they had to be able to determine the number of dragons if they attacked in a pack, and the species. The tavern was indeed one of the more expensive where the customers were mostly people who were rather wealthy, the fine furniture and lack of grease stains and dirt told that very clearly. Phraan saw the four former members of their group right away, they sat by the huge fireplace and he saw that none had changed that much. He felt a lump in his throat, it felt good to see them again, and to see that they all were alright.

Vitile got up and ran over, hugged him firmly and Phraan returned the hug. She was a wood elf, of the shures race and not very tall but slender and agile and very brave. She had long brown hair braided tightly and wore leather and wool like most of her kindred. Vitile was an archer and lethal with any bow, she was rather phenomenal with a blade too and Phraan knew she had felled more dragons than any other of her profession. Dhokay too got up, he was of the luptay race, a species of elf like very tall beings with a set of elegantly curved horns which indicated status and age. He was very muscular and most people found his race to be pretty but frightening too. Right now he had his thick bluish hair pulled back into a pony tail and he was grinning so Phraan saw all the sharp teeth. He hugged Dhokay and the warrior returned the hug with glee. "You have gotten more tattoos since I saw you last"

Dhokay nodded. "Yes, at least ten. It is good to see you Phraan"

The next to greet him was Kapha, he was a half dwarf half human hybrid and he looked as if he could run through a brick wall unharmed. He was short but not as short as a dwarf and he was the most lighthearted person Phraan had ever met. He didn't appear to have changed for he laughed and gave Phraan a smack across the bottom. "You do still favor the ladies ha? Too bad, I have dreamt of that pert little rear of yours"

Phraan blushed and Vitile giggled. "Kapha, don't you dare scaring him off, go find yourself someone else to seduce. Phraan has no interest in you and you know it!"

The half elf had to grin, they were the same and it felt wonderful really. Shaluun was the last one to get up, the tall mountain elf was impressive as always, three inches taller than Phraan, not as muscular but very wiry and extremely tough. He carried his twin axes across his back and bowed deeply to show his respect. His people were very polite and very quiet, they hardly ever spoke but when they did you listened. A mountain elf rarely wasted a single word. He had a deep dark tan and long flaxen hair and was clad in leather and furs. Phraan was glad he had agreed to return to the group, Shaluun was the one they all relied upon when they had to bring down larger dragons. He was strong enough to cleave the skull of almost anything as long as he managed to get up onto the head.

Vitile gave Fastonar a quick grin. "I found the trackers, both agreed upon joining us, and I did find two others too, they have some experience hunting dreklugnins and both have fought in several battles against the red creek orcs"

Fastonar smiled, a wide and relieved grin. "Excellent, who are they?"

Vitile crossed her arms across her chest. "Dwarves, tough as stone and probably a very good addition to the group. Their names are Dabin and Rhuk."

Phraan lifted his head. "Rhuk? That is a name from the Dabhak dwarves yes?"

She nodded. "Any problems with that?"

Phraan shook his head vigorously. "Nope, they are fierce, just a wee bit odd at times"

Vitile made a wry grin and Fastonar rolled his eyes. "As long as said dwarf is able to swing an axe I don't care how odd he might be"

Vitile leaned against the wall. "The trackers are of my tribe, their names are Taurin and Thiana, I trust them with my life. Both are very experienced"

Kapha nodded slowly. "Elven trackers, cannot find any better than that. Are we good to go then?"

Fastonar shook his head. "Not quite yet, the king has promised us some extra hands, I guess he has some criminals locked away in some dungeon who would rather volunteer than face the hangman. They may be useful"

Shaluun just shook his head but Dhokay made a grimace. "As bait then, I cannot see that convicts would be useful for anything else than that"

Phraan had to snicker, he guessed that the idea of being pardoned in exchange for serving the group could be tempting but the poor bastards wouldn't know what they were getting themselves into. Fastonar cleaned his fingernails with his dagger, sometimes his manners were a bit affected by his life in barracks and army tents. "When do the trackers and the two dwarves arrive?"

Vitile smiled again, she did look eager. "Tomorrow morning, I told them all to get horses and ponies. We cannot wait for them to shop tomorrow"

Fastonar nodded. "We are to meet the king's primary counsellor tomorrow too, after noon. He is to give is a quick briefing and we are to pick up the gear I have ordered. Worry not, I have asked for just top quality and we all know that there aren't that many dragon slayers left so the king won't spare the expenses this time"

Phraan nodded, he remembered when he started hunting dragons, they had been many back then, at least twenty groups and in the beginning they had to make it with just what they had. Understandably the death toll had been insane back then and as the number of people brave enough to hunt the beasts did dwindle the king and his men realized that they had to give the hunters a helping hand financially. Phraan had to grin when he thought of all the insane errors people had made back then, the first and most spectacular one was using ordinary armor. Many a knight came to the northern territories wearing the same armor they would use on the battle field or in tournaments and most of it was solid plate armor and very well made too. Phraan remembered many of them, cocky young men with a lot of self-confidence and a feeling of being invincible. He had seen many of them getting literally cooked inside of their armor and he knew that the military academy trained knights for battle but not for dragon hunting. Armor was good against the species of dragons which couldn't spew fire but some of them spewed ice or even acid instead and then you had another problem. A knight in armor, frozen stiff was just a tasty snack for a hungry dragon, a roasted one was too when he thought of it.

"You have used the same lists as before I recon?"

Fastonar nodded. "Yes, but I have added some stuff I missed back in the old days"

Kapha frowned. "Not to interrupt but a healer? Do we have a healer?"

Fastonar sighed. "Not yet, but I asked the king for one, he has got to have some extra healers don't you think?"

Vitile cringed. "Oh Fastonar, there are few healers these days, the old powers are slowly seeping away, most these days can barely heal a blister on their own."

Fastonar rolled his eyes and shrugged. "I know alright? But we do need one so I just hope the king sends us one of those who still has the power"

Kapha snorted. "Wouldn't bet on it"

Dhokay grinned. "Oh, do you remember that young one we got right at the end? The one with the braid and the pox marks? He knew only two healing spells, one against toothache and one used to heal trench foot!"

Phraan had to laugh. "Oh yes, he pissed himself the first time he saw a dragon, and passed out"

Vitile giggled. "And it was a dead one too, a very small greyback. Oh I remember, he was useless"

Kapha raised an eyebrow. "No he was not, what if someone had caught a toothache? Then he would be very useful indeed"

Phraan remembered that the healer in question had died barely a week after he joined them, he got trampled by a spooked horse and bye bye to him. Phraan hadn't exactly missed the fellow for he was a sad example of the fact that good people had been almost impossible to find back then. Nobody wanted to hunt dragons after the first few years for everybody knew that the chance of surviving was slim to say the least.

Phraan stared at the group, he felt slightly proud. Their group had been the one with the greatest success and they had lost only three group members in ten years. That was almost unbelievable and it spoke volumes of their skills. Fastonar went over and patted Phraan on the back. "And I did find our boss yesterday, working as a smith just like before. But worry not my friends, with Phraan back at the helm we are gonna clear the north of this plague in no time!"

Phraan felt himself blush once more, he had been the leader, that was right. He had been a soldier before he became a dragon slayer, and before that a smith. It had been the war against the orcs of the north east which had lead him onto the path towards dragon hunting, he had never been a very violent person before and he had been terrified when he first had to fight. As a half elf he was large and strong enough to fight even a mountain orc and the king's men had recruited everybody they thought of as possible fighters. He had been recruited as the first in his village and the trainers had discovered that he had a very uncanny ability, one which set him apart from the others. He seemed to know exactly how to deliver the most lethal blow possible and he was so fast and unpredictable beating him soon became almost impossible. Before long he was among the elite warriors who were sent ahead of the armies to clear the path and he got a name for himself. He didn't like to kill, but that in turn made him so much more efficient. He never got carried away in the heat of battle, never went too far just to satisfy the need for a thrill and thus he managed to think strategically and attack with almost surgical precision no matter what.

They said that he fought with a complete lack of passion, as if he was a gardener cutting down weeds, doing a rather boring chore. And yet it had been a lethal ballet, a veritable dance of swift steel and spilled blood. He had barely even gotten wounded and when the war ended and the dragons became a problem the king promptly sent him to the territories to fight them. There he discovered that his gift was just as useful against dragons and his old nickname resurfaced. The orcs had called him Thalak-bhar which meant death's lover, they believed that he was blessed by the death Gods to be able to do that much damage alone. Now he became death for so many dragons and other beasts and he did find some pride in it. He would steer the others like a general commands his troops and make sure that they attacked at just the right moment, at the right target. Without his gift the job would have been almost impossible for the dragons were very different and some could be much stronger than others.

Fastonar waved at the keeper of the tavern. "Get us some wine and a good meal, the king does pay. And a room for my friend here"

The tall and somewhat fat man just nodded and ran off and Fastonar sat down. "I have made sure that we have many carriages, plenty of supplies and the best weapons available too. This time around we do know what we may need"

Vitile nodded. "That is good, the king haven't managed to find any other slayers?"

Fastonar shook his head. "Nope, not even one!"

Dhokay tilted his head, the elegantly bowed horns did shine in the lamp light. "But I remember several?"

Fastonar nodded and put his feet up on a bench, he stretched his legs and yawned. "Yes but remember, it is a lifetime ago. Some were ordinary humans and died of old age or disease decades ago while others have perished due to other reasons. We are the only professionals left but heed my words, we are gonna meet some amateurs for sure, that is pretty darn guaranteed"

Phraan and Kapha both cringed visibly and Vitile spat. Dhokay almost sneered. "That will be nothing but a waste of lives, if the problem is as bad as they say it is. Amateurs have no business trying to hunt dragons, they will perish"

Phraan sighed and the host came with some jugs of ale and wine while a barmaid carried cups and glasses. "Of course they will, but we do remember what happened the last time right? Being a dragon slayer was what every poor sod wanted, and I cannot count how many graves the wanderers had to dig. And it lasted for several years, before they realized that yes, people do really die when hunting dragons."

Vitile took a deep breath. "Do not let us worry before we have a reason to, tonight I suggest that we celebrate this reunion, and have a good time."

Kapha lifted his cup and smiled. "Hear, hear! Now that is a sound suggestion!"

Phraan filled his glass with wine and found that it was a good one, he hadn't had really good wine for a long time and drank slowly to really savor the taste. Of course he didn't get drunk, to get anyone of elven blood drunk you would need something so strong it would be toxic to all other races but he could get tipsy if he drank a lot fast and as the food was brought forth and the atmosphere got more and more relaxed he realized that he had missed this. The camaraderie and the trust, the feeling of being among equals. He just hoped that the king had gotten them what they needed.

As the evening ended he found himself singing along with the others and the songs were almost forgotten by everybody else but they were typical drinking songs and not at all decent. Kapha ended up with one of the servants sitting on his knees and the poor man did look rather shocked. Fastonar disappeared upstairs with one of the bar maids and Dhokay sat by the fireplace and recited poems to someone only he saw. Vitile was grinning and she was a bit tipsy too, her eyes were shining. She sat down next to Phraan and smiled. "I have missed you, I didn't think I would ever say this but I have."

Phraan had to look back at her. "I have missed you too, heck, I have missed you all"

Vitile giggled. "Even Kapha?"

Phraan nodded solemnly" Even Kapha yes"

Vitile leaned back and closed her eyes, an expression of melancholic longing on her face. "I know he can be a bit much at times but he is good as gold"

Phraan grinned. "I know, he hasn't changed. He still thinks he can tempt me into bedding him"

Vitile almost snorted wine. "And?"

Phraan sent her a wicked grin. "It will never happen, not that I have anything against his preferences but he isn't my type"

Vitile leaned closer in, her face a bit flushed. "No, for your type is more like…?"

He smiled. "You for an example"

She licked her lips. "Care to find out if we are a match?"

He felt his heart beating faster. "Oh but I do know we are a match, I don't think that has changed"

She pouted. "Don't be so sure of that, many years have passed by"

He breathed in her scent and knew that she was trying to talk him into bedding her, what the heck, why not? It had been decades since the last time he had been in bed with anyone except his own right hand and he and Vitile had in fact been lovers many times. As a matter of fact he had almost popped the great question back in the old days. He got up and sent her an inviting grin. "Then let's find out shall we?"

She too got onto her feet and let a hand slide up the inside of his thigh, very suggestively. He had to moan, the mere idea of her had already made him react and his pants had become uncomfortably tight. She grabbed him by his braid and almost dragged him with her upstairs.

When Phraan woke up the next morning it was with a bit of a headache and he felt rather confused until he remembered the last days. Vitile slept by his side, nude as the day she was born and her long hair had escaped the braid and covered her rather well. He had to stare at her, she was a nice view to wake up to and he grinned and knew they had to get up. They had spent the time well last night and both had fallen asleep both sated and exhausted. He had needed this, he felt as if he now was able to throw away the blacksmith and become the warrior once more. He shook her gently and Vitile grunted and opened one hazel eye, she didn't appear to be too happy about the situation, she swore softly. "Damn it Phraan, why can't we stay in bed a little longer?"

He smacked her across the ass. "You know why, but if it is any comfort I can tell you that I too would wish to stay in bed today. "

She almost growled and got up, pulled her clothes back on and braided her hair quickly. She was humming while she did it so her mood wasn't all that bad in spite of it all. Phraan felt famished and thirsty and he almost ran down to the dining hall where Fastonar and Dhokay already were having a breakfast consisting of mostly bacon. Fastonar skewered a huge piece on his knife and stared at it with a sigh. "I think we'd better enjoy this while we can, there won't be much food like this when we are out there"

Phraan sat down and the cook placed a huge plate in front of him, covered with bacon and eggs. The half elf rolled his eyes and sighed, he wouldn't be able to eat very much of it, this cook obviously believed that elves ate half a pig in one sitting. The thin ale he was given in a huge mug was a whole different matter and he emptied the whole mug in one go, he was truly thirsty. Fastonar chuckled. "You look as if she almost drained you completely last night"

Phraan just blushed and saw that Fastonar too looked slightly disheveled. Dhokay threw his head backwards and laughed. "You both look as if you have had a really good tumble, well, good for you. The bath is ready by the way, you ought to scrub yourselves rather well, you reek!"

Fastonar just grimaced and sighed and Phraan blushed. But Dhokay was right, they ought to look good when they were to meet the king's counsellor. Phraan managed to eat most of the food and Vitile who entered the hall yawning so widely you could count her teeth took the rest. She too was thirsty and did look a bit sweaty. They both visited the bath and it felt good getting clean again, Phraan combed and braided his hair back and then they got their stuff and by now the trackers and the two dwarves had arrived. Phraan was very pleased with what he saw, the two trackers wore almost the same clothes as Vitile and they were both dark blond with soft brown eyes and a slender body. Both carried a bow and long knives and they moved with the fleeting elegance of the wood elves. He had no doubt that these two could become valuable for sure. The two dwarves stood there and looked a bit cranky, both carried twin axes and there was no doubt about their skills for they wore visible tattoos telling of their skills in battle but Phraan did notice that they refused to look at each other. They were of different tribes, Dabin were of the Boithan tribe which meant that he was a bit taller and more elegant than Rhuk, and he wore very elaborate braids and clothing. Rhuk on the other hand did look rather uncouth and his clothes and armor did look like something he had pulled out of a garbage pile somewhere. Phraan knew that the Dhabak dwarves had a very different culture from the Boithan dwarves and it could spell trouble, he just hoped that there wouldn't be any hostility between the two of them. Both clans were known as capable fighters and the Dhabak dwarves in special were known for their tenacity and their stubbornness. They refused to back down even in the face of overwhelming odds.

Vitile greeted her friends with a sort of shrill sound Phraan knew the forest elves used to express joy and both answered in the same manner, it made his ears hurt a bit. Fastonar stared at the two dwarves. "So, you have volunteered for this, dragon slaying is no easy dance, it may be your last fight"

Both dwarves just bowed their heads and Dabin smiled, the elaborate pattern of braids told Phraan that this dwarf was someone of importance and status. "We fear naught, and we wish to serve"

Fastonar stared at Rhuk, looking at the two dwarves was like comparing a huge sleek and well-groomed hound with a shaggy looking shepherd. "And you agree on this Rhuk?"

Rhuk raised a fist and bumped it against his chest, the leather armor creaked. "I do, I wish for honor"

Shaluun had entered the hall and he wore better clothes today, he looked a bit more civilized but the wild expression upon his face was giving away his nature. The mountain elves were known for being savages and Phraan had seen this many times, Shaluun was a very dangerous being. Fastonar clapped once. "Alright then, we are all ready? Good, then let's go. I don't think the good Sir Aphalber likes to wait"

Phraan walked behind Fastonar out of the door and the group found their way towards the palace. The two dwarves looked very calm and collected but the two trackers were obviously not accustomed to the things they saw there and were wide eyed and in obvious awe. The palace was a huge area and they entered through one of the side gates. The counsellor had agreed upon meeting them within the area of the palace where supplies were brought in and it was the least posh part of the huge complex of buildings. There were several thick walls separating the palace area and they were heavily guarded and could be used as a last line of defense in case of an attack. The palace was like a city of its own and Phraan saw that little had changed since he was there the last time.

They entered a huge open yard and he had to raise an eyebrow, several carriages were ready with good horses ready to go, and there was a herd of riding horses there as well, and some huge stocky mules. Fastonar almost purred, he was grinning from one ear to the other. "Like I said, the king spares no expenses this time. His father tried to do that and see how far that got him in the end"

The carriages were filled with equipment, tents, food, weapons, clothing, all sorts of equipment, medicine, armors and even wine. Phraan started to feel optimistic, if only ever so slightly.

A very tall but extremely thin man walked out of the shades towards them, he did look as if he was trying to suck the last little drop of juice out of a very sour lemon and he wore a robe made from exquisite silk and some pants Phraan guessed was made from genuine Rhuk'sal leather, the huge herbivores which lived in and by the rivers to the far south were rare and their hide became the most expensive leather there is, as smooth and silky as a baby's bottom. This man was wealthy and he loved to show it off too, Phraan could see it very well. The well-groomed and braided hair was adorned with at least two combs with real rubies in them and he carried a small writing board which had to be made from the heart wood of Goldflower trees. Fastonar bowed his head politely and the man clicked with his tongue and didn't look too impressed by what he saw. "So, this is the king's new dragon slayers? You look like a travelling menagerie!"

Rhuk almost growled and Dhokay whispered something to the dwarf which made him snicker and turn slightly red in the face. Fastonar managed to smile and he did look rather calm but Phraan knew him and the sudden dark glimpse within his eyes told the half elf that this counsellor had insulted Fastonar by insulting the group, and you didn't do that unpunished! "Sir Aphalber, I can assure you, the king won't find finer warriors anywhere within the five regions."

Aphalber just snorted and stared at Vitile with obvious disdain, the forest elf pretended to ignore the glare but she made a gesture behind her back and the two others saw it and turned red. It was very obscene, the forest elves had a sort of sign language which was extremely elaborate and they used it when they couldn't risk making any sort of noise, it could of course also be used to communicate when they didn't want others to understand what they were saying. "The king has spent good money on this…project of his. Our good lord Ropherto is way too naïve for his own good, this dragon problem is just a minor nuisance and hardly worth spending even a handful of gold over."

Phraan felt his head starting to feel hot, and Fastonar sent him a warning glance, they didn't need an explosion now. The warrior just smiled very sweetly. "Oh, I think our dear king is very wise, and he is thinking ahead instead of lagging behind the whole time, the way his father did. When old Vhandar finally reacted the last time dragons came down from the mountains an entire region was laid to waste before anybody even tried to stop it."

Aphalber sneered. "Oh nonsense, it cannot have been that bad, what are a few dragons to a fully armed unit of knights?"

Dhokay smiled, the sharp teeth were shining and the golden eyes were flaring. "I will tell you what a dragon is to a knight, a blowtorch! Imagine the armor as a kettle and the knight as the stew within that kettle and the dragon as a very impatient cook!"

Aphalber just stared, slightly shaken out of balance by this outburst. "A knight of from our king's guard would surely not fail in such a manner"

Shaluun shook his head. "Know what, we saw many knights back in the old days, hundreds of them if I don't recall it wrong and I don't. Fires are bad, frost too but guess what is worse? Acid! Some species of dragons spew acid and it makes you melt you see, both you and the armor you are wearing. The man and the metal merge, and we have seen men survive for hours with most of their bodies dissolved. The screams are amazing, you will never forget it once you have heard it."

Aphalber swallowed and Dhokay shook his head slowly. "I remember one fellow in special, big guy, one of Vhandar's best knights. He had won every tournament you can name and several battles too. They believed that he was invincible, blessed by the gods. He died the first evening after he arrived at the camp, tried to attack a greyback all by himself and the beast got him good. There wasn't even enough left of him to bury the remains properly. Instead of a coffin they used a hat box"

Aphalber was slightly green. "You are jesting for sure"

Phraan shook his head. "Nope, a dragon can transform a living breathing man to ashes or mosh in less time than it would take you to walk from here to that fountain over there."

The counsellor still looked as if he believed that they were lying and Fastonar went over to the nearest wagon and pulled the tarp aside. He stared into it and smiled. "Wonderful, just what I wanted."

He pulled out a roll of rope and Phraan let out a small shout of excitement, it was just the right kind and he could see that they had many hundreds of rolls like that. Aphalber groaned. "Do you have any idea of how much that rope over there costs? Five gold coins for each roll! And you ordered two hundred!"

Fastonar nodded with a wide and very devilish grin. "Exactly, you need a lot of rope when you are to restrain a dragon"

The counsellor rolled his eyes. "But why the most expensive rope there is? Why not the type they use for the warships? They are strong and even better, cheap!"

Vitile had put on her cutest expression but her eyes were shooting fire. "Because they are made from hemp and what does hemp do when it comes into contact with flames? It burns!"

Kapha had been silent until then, now he crossed his arms across his chest. "So rope made from the same leather you have in those fancy breeches of yours is the only type good enough, it is elastic enough to give without snapping and a dragon cannot burn through it as fast as if it was hemp, it takes several minutes"

Aphalber rolled his eyes. "Alright, fine, you need expensive rope but what about all this other stuff, specially forged weapons, camping equipment, and horses! The horses were more than two gold shillings each! You can buy a herd of ordinary nags for just one gold coin"

Fastonar went over and put a hand onto the counsellor's shoulder, the man almost toppled over. "Wanna know why we need horses which have been trained and broken for hunting?"

Aphalber scoffed. "You are gonna tell me for sure!"

Fastonar did look like a patient old teacher scolding a rowdy kid. "Because ordinary horses do freak out when they feel the scent of a dragon, horses bought for the hunt has to be brave, obedient and most of all strong and able to turn on a dime even with a man in full armor on his back"

Aphalber stared down at the elegantly laid mosaic tiles covering the yard, he was a bit red and probably still angry. The idea of the king spending money on this instead of raising his salary had to be a real blow to his ego. "Ah the armor, you asked for twenty suits of leather armor, that too cost a small fortune, why not the standard army type? Isn't it good enough?"

Shaluun smiled slowly. "If you want to be cooked alive it is brilliant. Don't try to understand the list human, you cannot! You are no warrior and certainly not a slayer so keep you pie hole shut and let the real men here do their job"

Aphalber just gaped and Dhokay laughed hoarsely, he was almost shaking with mirth. Vitile put out her tongue. "Do you hear? He regards even me and Thiana here as more manly than you!"

The counsellor was beet red by now and stuttering and Fastonar petted his back once more. "Easy there, such thin and spindly people are more prone to sudden heart failure than their shorter counterparts. Their veins burst more easily. We asked for a healer? And a mage?"

Aphalber was opening and closing his mouth like a fish on dry land, it did look hilarious and the two dwarves had a peculiar expression on their faces. Phraan knew a few words of the secret language the dwarven clans used and if Aphalber had heard what the two called him he would have suffered from immediate spontaneous combustion out of sheer shame.

The man managed to get himself back under control but he was shaking all over. "We had no mage but the king did assign a healer to this…group!"

Fastonar smiled and tightened the grip he had on the counsellor's shoulder, the man became rather pale right away. "Brilliant, we are to leave immediately so where is he?"

Aphalber squeaked. "He is waiting in the hall by the stable, let go of me!""

Fastonar did release the grip and the man let out a huge sigh of relief. He then scurried off as if his feet were on fire and Phraan almost growled. "You shouldn't happen to know where his chambers are located, I sense that there is a whole swarm of sewer rats dying to find a cozy new home!"

Fastonar giggled. "No, but the idea is brilliant though, but rather than sewer rats, which are such cute and useful creatures after all I would rather suggest a pack of dreklugnins"

Phraan had to laugh. "Oh Fastonar, that would harm other people, we don't want that now do we. The palace is a beautiful place and it would be too bad if they have to evacuate it"

Shaluun had taken a short jog to the hall the counsellor mentioned and he returned with a man in tow behind him, the guy was short with a bit of a belly and long thin and unkempt hair. He wore a healers robe but it was so dirty it looked more brown than white and the guy was a bit cross eyed and was waddling from one side to the other. "I found him, but he is as drunk as a skunk and he smells like a liquor store"

Fastonar made a grimace. "Oh dear, well, we'll have to accept him, we cannot wait for another healer to be available and maybe he is good for something whence he dries up"

Vitile made a nasty grimace. "Like that will ever happen, believe me, this guy is useless. I can smell it, he has been drinking hard for years"

Phraan scowled. "Didn't the king promise us some convicts too?"

Fastonar snapped his fingers. "Oh yes, darn, where can they be? Oh yes, I know, follow me"

He jogged off and they looked at each other and shrugged. Shaluun lifted the drunk healer into the nearest wagon and the man just fell asleep right away. They ran after Fastonar who held a rather brisk pace and he stopped in front of a wide gate Phraan hadn't seen before. It was well guarded and Fastonar did salute the officer who seemed to be in charge there. "Greetings, we are the king's new dragon slayers and we have been promised some extra men, convicts I have been told?"

The officer smiled, he did look as if he was a decent person and he bowed politely. "Yes, that is correct, I was told this morning. By Aphalber no less, that man would eat horseshit if he was told it would make him shit gold"

Fastonar had to laugh and the others chuckled too. The officer opened the gate. "We have them ready for you, all have been prepared and they won't try to escape. If they do they will simply die, it is a very useful spell for sure"

Phraan had heard of it, a sort of magic that enabled you to take complete control over others, it was not very well thought off and rarely in use but at times it was handy. Nobody would use it against someone who didn't deserve it though, it was unethical and most people would protest if you suggested such a course of action. Fastonar scratched his arm and looked very relaxed. "How many are there and what have they done?"

The officer pulled a note from his pocket and opened it. "There are three of them, one is convicted of fraud and another of arson and the third of accidental murder."

Fastonar made a grimace. "Sounds like a classy gang."

The officer nodded and grinned and he gestured towards some soldiers who stood nearby. "My men will go get them, they have been prepared like I said but do not trust them for even a moment."

Fastonar sighed, "We won't, believe me."

The soldiers disappeared through a narrow and very solid door and were gone for some minutes. The dungeon had to be underneath this entire area and Phraan guessed that it was the less comfortable parts of it which housed their new workers. Even the dungeons had a system of classes, the best parts weren't that much different from a good room at an inn, just with a door you couldn't get through. The worst were rather hideous and filled with rats and other nasty creatures. The soldiers came back and dragged three chained men behind them. Phraan scowled at them, the first man was of average height and he did look like a smart person. His clothes were good and he seemed to have some class. The brown eyes were keen and he held his chin up high, even when chained. The officer nodded towards him. "He is known as Peter, son of Charloy, he is convicted of fraud and also of forgery. He made false coins but wasn't very good at it."

Phraan tilted his head, forgery required a least some skill and the man was probably in his late twenties and healthy. He could be useful for sure. The tattoo which showed that he was spellbound was visible on his forehead and only when his four year service was over would it vanish and take the spell with it. The next man was short and stocky and a bit fat, his face was red and his features uneven and the skin dirty and scarred. His clothes did stink and the sort of swimming expression within his eyes told them all that this person was a drunkard. The officer stared at him and his expression was one of contempt. "His name is Oham and he got drunk when he was supposed to watch the mill he worked at. One of the workers got stuck in the mechanism and got crushed because this moron here was too goddamn inebriated to pull the right lever."

Fastonar looked at the man with a dark expression within his eyes, Phraan knew that Fastonar hated people who fail to do their duty more than anything else. Getting drunk was something he never would allow himself to become when he had things to do, Phraan knew that Fastonar would be all over this man like a hungry wolf. The soldiers brought the last man forth, he was rather young and he had long unkempt blond hair and he did look more or less insane. He was struggling against the chains and his clothes told Phraan that he probably belonged to the fetcher's guild. "This piece of shit lit his master's house on fire, to be able to take his place afterwards. The entire family died, three adults and five children. He should have been hung but the king is too soft at times, and the royal healer believes that the man is mad. "

Phraan stared at the young man who bared his teeth and looked like a mad animal. "What is his name?"

The officer stared at his note. "His name is apparently Aiolo but nobody knows if that is his real name. He had been an apprentice for just two months when he did this terrible deed, they ought to have burned him too"

Fastonar smiled, an almost friendly grin. "Oh but he still has the opportunity to burn for sure, I think we will send him first when we encounter dragons, since he already is accustomed to flames I mean"

Aiolo just rolled his eyes and swore and Phraan knew that this one could bring them trouble for sure. The officer let the soldiers remove the chains and the three rubbed their wrists and looked far from impressed by what they saw. Fastonar stared at them. "You have volunteered so know this, you will most likely die and should you survive for four years it will be four years of hard work and constant danger. Of course you will be free if you make it that far but until then you are mine! Do you understand? Try to escape and the spell will kill you, disobey and I will have your hide and do not for a single second believe that I won't whip the skin off your backs with a grin on my face and a song on my lips"

All three just stared at the ground and a soldier came carrying some folded clothing. "From now on this is what you are to wear. You are slaves now, so you have got to look the part!"

He pulled a tunic and a pair of breeches from the pile, both were made from a very cheap fabric which was roughly woven and thick and the color was hideous, the most disgusting tone of mustard yellow Phraan had ever laid eyes upon. It looked like the color of really nasty diarrhea. All three just glared at the clothes and the soldiers smiled, the officer did look very pleased. "Get the rags on guys, no point in waiting. From now on you are dragon slayers, or shall I rather say, potential dragon snacks"

Fastonar had to snicker and Phraan hid a wry grin too, he had his serious doubt about the usefulness of these three but who knows, they could perhaps do at least some good. All three pulled on the new clothing, Oham was too fat and the tunic a wee bit too small so he looked like a badly stuffed sausage, he was glaring at them and looked genuinely pissed off but he didn't say anything. Phraan had already evaluated them, Peter was smart and not a violent person, he was probably the only one who would cooperate freely. Oham was most likely to try to sneak his way out of any work they tried to make him do, and if there was booze nearby he would try to get drunk no matter the punishment. Aiolo was the type to try an escape, even if it would kill him, he wouldn't last long for sure. Phraan sighed, he was glad they had gotten the trackers and the two dwarves, but they could still use a mage. Fastonar crossed his arms across his wide chest. "Right lads, let's go. It is a long journey and the dragons aren't waiting for us so move your asses"

The three men started to walk, very reluctantly and Phraan walked over to Dhokay and Shaluun. "Don't let Aiolo get anywhere near a weapon, that guy is desperate enough to do very stupid things."

Dhokay had a dark expression within his eyes and his teeth were almost bared. "I know, he is gonna be dragon fodder for sure, I can smell the madness within him."

They walked briskly back to the wagons and the horses and Phraan sent a page for his belongings and his horse. He felt a sting of excitement in spite of it all, he hadn't left the village for many years and for sure there would be changes. He was eager to see what new things he would see and he realized that he was looking forward to a challenge too. Fastonar patted him on his back as the page returned with Drake in tow behind him. "We'll get back into it soon enough, once a dragon slayer, always a dragon slayer"

Phraan got in the saddle and the others stared at Drake with wide eyes, the stallion snorted and pawed at the ground and Phraan reined him in with steady hands. "You are right, I have missed it, at least some parts of it."

Vitile got onto the back of her own horse, a very lithe dun mare. Like most forest elves she rode without a tack and controlled the animal only with her weight and voice. "We'll get rid of the rust in no time, it will be like the good old days once more"

Phraan smiled and turned Drake around. "Yes, just like the good old days"

Chapter 2: Lessons learned

The assembled masters stared at the young man in the middle of the circle with deep frowns and some odd facial expressions. He was kneeling and sweat was pouring off him as he desperately tried to make the spell work. It was a simple one, in fact the first one any mage learned when joining the academy and it was basically so easy even a kid normally would be able to do it. He was told to create an orb of light and it shouldn't take any effort at all but he was shaking all over and panting and his arms were shivering from the effort. He stared ahead of himself, over his head hung a tiny speck of light, it looked more like a slightly deranged firefly than an orb and while they watched it zig zagged around a little before it exploded with a barely audible poof and was gone.

The young man hung his head with a deep sigh, it was no good. The masters and teachers sighed too, stared at each other with some confusion and sorrow in their faces. Ivran was the grandson of one of the greatest mages of all time, the legendary Ulathay of Twelve towers and he ought to have inherited his grandfather's immense power. He had been at the academy since he was twelve, now he was twenty four and he should have passed the final exams years ago but had until now failed at every attempt at doing so. He had the powers, everybody could sense that, the energy within him was very noticeable to any mage but he was unable to use it. He couldn't do even the most basic spells without messing things up royally and no matter how hard he kept trying and training he always failed. The teachers had long ago quit trying to teach him anything new, and when they tested him they always did so in a special room which was shielded so no runaway magic could harm others. They didn't dare to let him try any spells outside of it, they had done that mistake once and the result was that every bench in the city of Oakfell now was sentient and would start nagging whenever anyone tried to sit on it. Nobody enjoys being told that their butts are too fat or that they ought to lose ten stones of weight.

Normally a student with such a lack of gifts would have been tossed out within a month but Ivran was after all Ulathay's grandson and he was born with the powers. Besides, even the most gnarly and vicious of the teachers just adored the lad. Nobody managed to dislike Ivran, he was just so likeable and he tried so very hard to please everybody and thus nobody were able to give him anything except praise. Even if his powers seemed to be out of reach in every possible manner. They had tried spells, meditation, even medication but nope, he couldn't use magic even if his life depended upon it and the spells he did get right would always end up giving a result nobody had expected. Once he had tried a very harmless spell which is supposed to remove dirt from water and the result was that fifty barrels of ale and wine in the basement under the cantina caught fire and burned for seven days.

The headmaster bowed his head, this had been the last straw, the last chance. They just couldn't allow him to continue, he was after all way older than the other students by now and ought to have been a mage years ago. They couldn't have someone like him there, who didn't study and took precious time and magic to control. The headmaster liked Ivran a lot, he would have been the ideal student if he just had been able to use his magic, in fact the headmaster was pretty sure that Ivran would have been the pride and joy of the academy if he had been able to access his abilities in a proper manner. He sighed and gestured towards the young man. Ivran was a rather tall fellow, a bit gangly looking with a very pretty face and an elegant but lithe body. He had dark auburn hair and soft grey eyes and the girls did swarm around him whenever he was off campus but he didn't seem to care that much about them at all. All he wanted was to be able to become a great mage like his grandfather but no, it seemed as if fate had decided to kick him while he was down, over and over again. "You may rise son, this if futile. I am so very sorry"

Ivran got up, his legs were shivering and he looked as if he was close to tears. One of the teachers stepped forth and laid a cloak around his shoulders with an almost fatherly expression, normally old Tanagal would smack any student who failed to live up to his expectations over the ears with a ruler but he treated Ivran like some sort of favorite grandson. They all did, they had all come to love and admire the tenacity of the young man and he had earned their respect over the years, too bad he never would bear the honorable title of mage. The headmaster looked as if he was close to tears. "This is the tenth time you have failed at your exam young one, it was the last chance. You can no longer stay here as a student, it would be wrong in so many ways. You have a life to live and I am sure that you are capable of seeing the truth in this"

Ivran nodded, he bit his lower lip, his parents would be so disappointed but then again, they already were. His father was a merchant and his mother born into a noble family and thus he had been born into wealth and power but he had never become haughty or prideful due to this. In fact he was a very humble and demure person and it was one of the reasons why people liked him so much. The headmaster smiled, a gentle smile very few ever saw. "But we have a proposition for you. You do need work and you know this school better than most, we did get an idea last night and I think you may like it"

Ivran stared at them, he swallowed. "I am listening master"

His voice was very pleasant too, very deep but soft and the head master wondered if the lad maybe could have made a career as a singer if anything else failed. "We do receive some very young students from all over the realm as you of course already know, and they do sometimes need an escort while travelling to and fro. Would you be interested in being our emissary on such missions?"

Ivran blinked, he felt terribly sad and confused and he was first and foremost disappointed for he had been so sure that he would make it this time but no, no way. He hadn't been able to do any of the spells required of a mage and he knew they were right. He couldn't stay as a student anymore but as their emissary he would still have a connection to the academy and most of all, it was a title which carried both respect and power. His father would like that, and he would receive a rather fat salary as well. He didn't need much time, he nodded his head. "I accept master, I am most grateful for your kindness"

The headmaster went over and laid a hand on his shoulder. "Having you among us has been such a pleasure young one, we do hope that you will work for us for many years to come."

Ivran swallowed, he felt a bit like crying but he didn't quite know why. Deep within he had been prepared to fail also this time, he had to be honest with himself, he probably never had been born to become a mage in the first place. The gods probably had other plans for him. He stared at his toes and the headmaster ruffled his hair. "Go back to the dorm and rest child, tomorrow we will give you a uniform and you will get new rooms and whatever else you need. You will be a very treasured coworker and I am sure you will make us all proud"

Ivran managed to smile. "I will do my very best master."

The teachers mumbled in unison. "Beyond any doubt"

The headmaster went over to his desk and opened a drawer within it, he pulled out a small box and opened it, it held a ring and he returned to Ivran and put it onto his finger. "Here, this will identify you as a member of the academy, it will open many doors for you young one"

Ivran stared at it, it was almost identical to the one a mage received after having passed his final exam and it felt a bit bitter to receive this ring instead of the much coveted mage's ring. But he bowed and kissed the headmaster's hand politely. "I thank you master"

The headmaster smiled and waved his hand at one of the other teachers. "Miraus, go get the box, he deserves it."

Ivran frowned. "The box?"

The headmaster nodded with a soft expression within his eyes. "Yes, a relic, it belonged to your grandfather and we want you to have it. You are no mage but you are one of us after all and I bet he would have liked the idea of you having it now!"

Ivran felt a rush of excitement, he was going to own something of his grandfather's? It was awesome, he had heard so many tales of the greatness of his famous forefather and he had always been an idol to the young one. The teacher returned shortly after with a small wooden box in his hands, it was very pretty and made from very valuable black wood, nice carvings covered it and it was the sort of box women use to store their jewelry. Ivran received the box with an expression of awe upon his face, it was rather light and it couldn't contain that much. He frowned and turned it around. "Where is the lid?"

The headmaster sort of made an apologetic grimace. "Ah, there is the problem, we cannot open it, apparently it doesn't have an opening at all. We think he has used magic to seal it"

Ivran gaped and knocked on the box with his knuckles. It was hollow beyond doubt and he stared at the teachers with narrow eyes. "Have you tried an opening spell?"

They nodded simultaneously. "Yes, every one of them, even some forbidden ones"

Ivran's eyes got huge, forbidden spells? That meant that whatever this box hid had to be considered very important. No sane mage would try the forbidden spells for something insignificant, the risks were way too big. He held the box with reverence, what could his famous grandfather have hidden in it? It was a mystery and Ivran had always loved mysteries and he felt his heart beat faster at the thought of maybe solving this one. He bowed his head. "Thank you, this means…so much to me"

The headmaster grinned. "I know child, your grandfather was capable of doing magic none other could repeat, too bad he went missing"

Ivran nodded slowly, held the box close to his chest, like you would hold your lover or your child. "Yes, I would have loved to meet him"

His grandfather had disappeared without a trace before Ivran was even born, his own father had been just a teenager when the mage went into a cave to investigate something and never returned. Nobody had seen the slightest trace of him ever since. Ivran had always wondered what it was that had happened, maybe this box held the answer? He was almost shivering with eager energy and he bowed again and backed out the door, suddenly his failure wasn't that important anymore. He ran back to the dorm, it was a huge building which housed at least five hundred students and he had his bed on the top floor, with the older students. Since he was older than everybody else he had gotten some privileges, he had a sort of screen around his bed which provided him with some sort of privacy and he sat down on it and held the box out in front of him. It held an answer, he was sure of it.

The rest of the hall was empty now, everybody was having classes or training and the rules were strict there. Even the older students had to follow them and the lady in charge of the dorm was a veritable dragon who didn't hesitate to drag someone out by the ears if they disobeyed her. But she was sweet as candy to Ivran and treated him with nothing but kindness and he had always found that odd but then again, he never misbehaved and tried to be polite to everybody. Every student had just that one bed and a small locker and it was all they needed, the dorm rooms were huge with room for more than fifty beds and at night everybody was supposed to be quiet but that was impossible to achieve. Some snored, others talked in their sleep, some were wanking off and others trying to talk even if it was forbidden. Ivran had always enjoyed being alone and he had hated the first years he had to live in the dorm. But by now he had learned to ignore all the sounds in the night.

This would be his last night there after all, he put the box down onto the covers and stared at it, there had to be a way to open it. Magic was too simple, he was rather sure that his grandfather would have found another way to hide the contents of this box. Could the clue be in the carvings? He turned it around, stared at it from every conceivable angle. The carvings were just that, carvings. A not very elaborate pattern of curved lines made to look a bit like vines. He let his finger run along the pattern, it was not even that well carved, here and there the wood had been torn more than cut and splinters were sticking out. It was a cheap box after all in spite of the nice wood, pretty but not very expensive. It wasn't the box itself which held any interest, that was for sure. You could buy much prettier looking ones at every street corner for just a few copper coins. He pulled his hand back with a small yip, he had managed to puncture his finger on a splinter and a few drops of blood fell from the small wound onto the wood. "Damnations, Akhi take it!"

He sucked his finger and shook the box and suddenly something happened. The box became oddly hot and he dropped it with a small shriek, it transformed right in front of his eyes and became larger and it was no longer wood but steel and jewels. The box now had a lid and it slid open with an audible pop, he sort of leaned away from it, expecting anything really. Nothing more happened, no demons burst forth, no genies appeared so he leaned forth again and opened the lid hesitantly. There was just two objects in the box, a piece of parchment and a small round flat piece of crystal. He blinked, what was this? He hesitated for a moment, then he reached into the box and grasped the parchment. It wasn't large, just a small note and he unfolded it with shaking hands. This could be anything really. He feared that this could be some deadly spell, or some secret time had forgotten. It was just a line of letters and numbers and he frowned. What the heck? This was no spell, that was for certain and it probably had absolutely naught to do with magic at all. He took a closer look at the note, it had been written down with care, and the longer he looked at the note the closer he came to a conclusion. It was a map! Not a map of some long forgotten realm or anything like that but a map of the huge library hidden underneath the academy. It filled the entire basement and there were several floors too and the number of scrolls and books unimaginable. He knew that few would have been able to understand this, unless they were studying at the academy and had been sent down to the basement to retrieve certain ancient scrolls. He had been used as a sort of courier so often he knew every shelf down there like the inside of his right hand and he even had a fair understanding of the layout of the deepest floors where only the masters were allowed to enter. This was simply a list of shelves and spots on them and he realized that this list had to explain something rather important. His grandfather wouldn't have made it just for the sheer heck of it for sure. He took a deep breath, this was exciting, and he lifted the crystal. It was natural and very pretty, probably quartz or something like that. He put it in his pocket and then he closed the box and put it under his bed before he got up and walked off towards the library. He was shaking with excitement, his heart beating like a drum and his mouth felt odd, dry sort of. It was the adrenaline for sure, he had never felt this nervous nor as alive before. What could it be that his grandfather had hidden?

The library was as usual almost empty at this time of the day, the students were having classes and Ivran walked through the long lines of high shelves with a relaxed expression on his face. He didn't want to cause any sort of problem and he knew that the librarian on duty this day was of the extremely zealous kind who would watch over anyone entering like a hawk, afraid that they would harm his books. It wasn't without reason though, the library held a fine collection of erotica which was stored in a shelf placed in a corner and that corner had seen a lot, and so had the poor librarians too. Some of the books were almost impossible to read anymore since the pages were stuck together and sometimes you could definitely smell that someone had been there, having some fun. Ivran had never had a date with his fist in that spot, the thought of getting caught sort of put him off such behavior but he knew of countless others who had been caught with their pants down quite literally.

He just ran past the infamous shelf and headed towards the basement. The first floor was open to everybody but those lower down were not to be entered by ordinary student. That didn't mean that the students stayed clear of the area, there were many ways to enter those floors unseen and Ivran knew them all. He walked down the wide stair slowly, listening intently for any sounds which could warn him of someone's presence. The huge halls were empty, nobody was there and he found the door to the bottom floor and stopped. It was a huge room, filled with hundreds of shelves but the first letter and number on the list told him this was the right floor.

The door was locked, and the padlock very solid and also put under several spells so trying to open it would be extremely silly of anyone not capable of warding off nasty magical attacks. But there was no need to enter through the door, the students had discovered this decades ago and the secret was one everybody knew of and never mentioned. Right behind a corner of the corridor there was a hatch, it wasn't large and it was a remnant of the days when this basement had been used to store food. The hatch was once used by the kitchen workers when they came to retrieve potatoes and it hadn't been removed, simply because it was something nobody had thought of.

Ivran slid the hatch open, everything had been well greased and thus it made no sound and it almost looked like just another large rock in the wall since it was so old. He was agile and slid in through it with relative ease, behind it was a small couch which had been strategically placed there by some compassionate fellow, without it you would tumble to the ground rather brutally. Ivran landed on his back in the couch and jumped onto his feet, the room was well lit by magical lamps everywhere and he went over to the door and stared at the note. The shelves were placed in rows of six and three so one unit consisted of eighteen shelves and there was at least a hundred such units down there. Without a map finding anything down there was in short impossible. He found the first shelf unit, it was called A 3 and he stared at it, what now? The note only mentioned the shelf itself, and the spot on it but he couldn't see anything unusual there. Just about twenty books about the botanical gardens of Twelve towers, most of the information was probably outdated centuries ago. There had to be some other clues there, what? His hands were fidgeting with the contents of his pocket as he was thinking hard. He felt the smoothness of the crystal and lifted it carefully, perhaps? He held it in front of him and caught the light from the nearest lamp with it, let the beam slide over the shelf and lo and behold, suddenly a small letter appeared right in the middle of the spot, glowing but invisible without the crystal. He had a pencil and some pieces of parchment in his pocket, wrote it down eagerly. This was important for sure.

He ran on, found the next and the next and he did spend quite some time down there, the list of letters was long and in the end he stood before the last shelf and this time it wasn't a letter but an arrow, pointing towards the floor. Ivran bent down, the dust was thick there and made him sneeze and he tried not to think of the things which could hide in the darkness underneath the shelves. His fingers touched something, he took a deep breath and pulled it out, it was yet another crystal and

52

as he lifted it the thing started to glow and so did a small scroll stored right in front of him. It didn't have a number nor any sort of name written onto the front and he pulled it out. He was so eager now he no longer had any reservations of any kind. He had to solve this mystery. It was some sort of text, written in the old language Ivran never had been able to learn and here and there letters were missing. He grinned widely and put the letters he had found onto the scroll and hoped he did it right.

The text wasn't long and he stared at it and started reading it, the way his teachers would. He didn't understand more than a couple of words but it sounded grand, like some sort of prayer or something. He held his breath, nothing happened. Now this was disappointing to say the least but who knew what his grandfather had been thinking. They said he was a wee bit mad and very mischievous so maybe he had done this as an elaborate prank. He was about to put the scroll down when the floor started to glow around him, in a very familiar pattern. It was a pentagram but within it his family crest and he stared at it and there and then he knew that he as the largest moron there ever was. He had just read some spell out loud, without knowing what it was. He tried to turn around to flee but he couldn't and the crystals he was carrying started glowing again and they felt warm too. Oh no, this could end badly, what in heck's name had he done?!

His feet were like glued to the ground and he felt a strong tingling spreading through his body, it grew stronger and stronger and it became painful and then it sort of overwhelmed him completely. It felt like a very powerful and almost violent orgasm, just not as pleasant. He wanted to scream but could make no sound and he saw that his skin had started to glow in strange patters, like someone had painted them onto him with fluorescent paint. His head felt as if it was about to explode, his entire body jerked and shook and he just knew that this was it, he would die down there and nobody would find him for weeks, or probably months.

Then it let go of him in an almighty rush of energy and he fell down onto the now smoldering floor, gasping and sobbing and utterly terrified and shocked. His legs felt as if they suddenly were made by paper and he was so dizzy everything sort of swam in front of his eyes. He got up onto his knees, gasping for air and did notice that both crystals now were glowing and that the glow illuminated just one thing. A small book hidden underneath the shelf, it looked like an ordinary note book, the type almost every scholar carries along to make notes in but he just knew that it was important so he stretched out a shaking hand and grasped it. It bore no name nor any sort of signs, it was just an ordinary cheap notebook and if someone saw it there on the floor they probably thought it was one someone had dropped by accident. It was small and thin and couldn't contain that much but he put it in under his shirt and managed to get to his feet although he felt that he resembled a newborn foal or something.

As soon as he managed to walk properly he took off, ran away from the shelf as fast as he could, still shaken and still afraid. He didn't feel anything unusual about himself so he was still Ivran, not some transformed beast of any kind. He found the hatch and crawled out of it, hurried back to the dorm while feeling how sweat soaked his shirt. He needed a bath, a long bath. He placed the book and gems in his private box underneath the bed and then he found some clean clothes and walked off towards the baths. The school had some very nice bathing facilities, no expenses were saved and it was just as nice as the one in the royal palace at Twelve towers. Ivran went into one of the hot pools and laid there to soak for a while, he slowly calmed down and tried to make sense of what had happened. Had it been a prank after all? Some sort of warning to not stick one's nose into his grandfather's business? He had no clue, he washed himself thoroughly and got clean clothes on and then he did stop at the dining hall to get some food. He was starving and the food there was good. At the beginning of his stay he had been in serious danger of becoming a rather obese person but the real training started and he lost it all again, now he was rather thin and lean looking and nobody who saw him would confuse him for a warrior.

He got a bowl of his favorite stew and some beer and sat down to eat, the hall was half full since it was lunch time and the noise level was intense. Some were arguing, others were practicing spells and incantations while a few had gathered in a corner singing a very inappropriate song about a boar and an ogre. They were celebrating someone's good results. Ivran finished the stew and had some honey cake for dessert, he had a sweet tooth and couldn't resist the temptation. While he sat there the daughter of the janitor entered the room, she was a very shapely maiden who probably was the one eighty percent of the students thought of while jerking off. She was a grand flirt but she never allowed anyone to get too close for her father was an old grouch who would geld and blind anyone daring to touch his darling daughter so the students stayed clear although her mere presence caused some serious cases of drooling and tented pants. In this male dominated world the sight of such a lovely example of feminine grace was both appreciated and like a breath of fresh air. Some of the teachers were ancient and they did look that way too, even the old washerwomen who sometimes cleaned the halls were better to look at than them, in fact anything wearing a skirt would become the object of naughty dreams if she was spending any time at the academy. Ivran had been among the many who had entertained himself while thinking naughty thoughts revolving around the young lass attributes and he blushed slightly and wished for the thousandth time that he could have seen a little bit more of her than just her face and some square inches of milky smooth skin above her collar.

She walked by the table he sat at and then it happened, she apparently slipped on something on the floor and fell backwards with such force her skirts flew up as her legs pointed towards the ceiling. Ivran got to see more of her indeed, in fact he saw it all! And she had nothing to be ashamed of for she was as shapely as they come but the shrill cry she made told everybody that she disliked the idea of showing the entire dining hall her nether regions. Ivran swallowed, oh by every God and Goddess. That was one sight which would haunt him for quite a while, he was blushing all the way to the top of his head and couldn't believe his own luck. The poor lass tried to get back onto her feet but slipped yet again and this time she ended up with her rear in the air and her skirts down around her upper body, she let out yet another angry shriek and finally she managed to get her skirts back in order and herself back into a proper upright position. Ivran was blinking, with her standing there on all four and her butt pointing towards him he had come into that uncomfortable and very undignified situation where he couldn't get up from his seat at all. His pants were tented and he took a quick peak around to check if anyone had noticed and he almost yelped, almost every one there was staring at the fair maid and the blushing cheeks and somewhat glassy eyes told him that they all suffered from the same problem. They had all seen it, and now they all suffered the consequences too.

Ivran saw that the girl ran out of the hall looking rather distraught and he did feel sorry for her but he would never have been able to look the other way, he was a young man and he was just as eager as everyone else to get some real experience with the opposite sex. He had to wait for several minutes before he could leave the table, he saw that many others there too were clinging to their tables as if it was a life raft of some sorts and he walked straight to the dorm again. He couldn't believe his own luck, the sight was glued to his mind and he closed the screen and sat down on the bed, trying to think of something else. What about the book? And the letters? No, he wasn't able to concentrate, not at all. He laid down and tried to force himself to sleep but it was no use, the only thing he could think about was the fact that he was aching with lust. He had never been with anyone for real, the only real experience he had was with a bar maid who had been a bit drunk and put a hand down between his legs when he was visiting an inn by the road. He had helped one of the masters gather herbs and they had been caught by a rainstorm and sought refuge in the inn. The light touch had almost been the undoing of him. He closed his eyes and couldn't stop thinking about the janitor's daughter, oh how he desired her, if she only had been his...

He was breathing hard and had to stuff his hands down into his pants, then he just pushed the entire garment down and started to stroke himself rather vigorously. He was alone there, nobody would hear him and he bet that he wasn't the only one seeking some relief after the incident in the hall. He kept seeing her, that smooth rounded ass, the silky skin, he was almost there when he heard the screen move and he yelped in panic and grasped for a blanket to hide himself thinking that it was the lady in charge of the dorms checking in on him. It wasn't, it was the object of his desires, the janitor's daughter. She was staring down at him with glassy eyes and before Ivran even had the time to cover himself up or ask what in hell's name she was doing there she jumped up onto the bed and straddled him. Ivran was in shock, he could just lay there, staring as she lifted her skirts and sat down onto him, leading him straight with a very skilled hand.

He couldn't believe it, his mind was swirling and he couldn't think. He just let out a groan as silky warmth embraced him and the pleasure just exploded within him. He yelled with each move she made and she was loud too, gasping and keening as she rode him like there was no tomorrow. Her eyes were dark with desire and she pulled her bodice down so he got a good view of her rather generous bust too. The sight almost made him swoon, he had never seen anything that lovely before and she pulled him up and he got a face full of her charms. Ivran had never had much confidence when it came to females, and he believed that he was no prince charming, he did look rather ordinary, not overly handsome but not ugly neither and the only thing he did find some pride in was the fact that he was rather well endowed downstairs, that was at least something he could brag about. He was popular enough but he lacked the confidence to really dare to go anywhere with the girls who tried to approach him.

She was enjoying it, there was no doubt about that. The bed was hammering against the wall and creaking so bad it sounded as if it would break in half at any moment. Ivran felt it starting, he couldn't stop himself and she too tensed up and lost her rhythm. He could feel her clench onto him and pulse and it was too much, he came so hard he was roaring and trembling, his body reduced to sheer pleasure and naught else.

It did take him some time to gather himself from his high and he felt as heavy as a sack of lead, he couldn't believe that it was real, that he actually had had sex with someone else than himself. It was unbelievable and it had been wonderful, no, more than wonderful, it had been the best experience of his life. The girl giggled and sighed, a blissful smile on her face as she slid down off him and got back onto her feet. She did shake her skirts out and sent him a mischievous grin, straightening her bodice. Ivran was still heaving for air, feeling the aftershocks rush through him, he had to be dreaming, this couldn't be real? He managed to force himself to speak. "Why?"

She giggled. "I just wanted you, all of a sudden. You were good, very good in fact."

She bent over and kissed his cheek. "A girl does appreciate some good cock and yours were just perfect"

He just stared, confused, happy and also a bit startled. It was rather certain that she had enjoyed this quite a lot before he became the object of her desires. Did her father know that his daughter in fact was rather promiscuous? He hoped not, for if the janitor did find out about this his ass was toast for sure, that man would tear him limb from limb. She patted him on his thigh and blew him a kiss before she just sauntered off, pushed the screen closed behind her and then he heard her walk away. Ivran just laid there, staring at the roof until he had to laugh, a bit hysterically. He had just gotten laid, oh Gods, it was amazing. He closed his eyes and enjoyed the memory and if he hadn't just come very hard he would have gotten aroused yet again just thinking about it. His right hand would never be quite the same after this, it wouldn't accomplish anything even close to what he just had enjoyed.

He felt sluggish and sleepy and he found a piece of cloth and wiped himself clean before he pulled his pants back on and decided to take a nap. He fell asleep like he had been shot, completely exhausted by all the turmoil of this day. He didn't even dream and when he did awake it was rather late and he felt surprisingly well. He was a man now, for real, and she had liked him. He felt his chest swell with pride and knew he had a silly grin upon his face, it had been so unexpected and yet so fantastic. He returned to the hall for some food and it was almost empty, he ate fast and returned to his bed to take a look at the notebook before he went to bed.

The notebook was full of text but it was unreadable, the letters were placed randomly and he did have to scratch his head until he did see one clue. There was one empty spot on each page, a letter was missing and he remembered the letters he had found on the shelves. Could it be? He had used them already but what if they were meant to be used again? He opened his box of belongings and found a small pen and started filling in the holes with the letters from the library. It was just the right number, and he finished and held his breath, something ought to happen. At first there was nothing, then the letters started to move and reorganize themselves. He heard that the others returned to their beds for the night but he didn't bother with them, this was too exciting. He waited until the pages yet again came to peace, the movements seized and he swallowed and started at the first page. It was his grandfather's handwriting for sure and the first thing it said was "Read this"

Ivran frowned, what followed looked like some sort of spell, it was in a language he didn't know but it did seem easy enough to pronounce. He read it slowly and in a whisper and then the text changed yet again, the words switched place and it all became spells, some he did recognize as very powerful ones and others were unknown but the letters started to glow and suddenly he knew them all. It was as if something opened within his mind and he was flooded with information. He was unable to make a sound, his body tilted over onto its side as it convulsed, it was quite similar to what had happened down in the basement but even more brutal and when it let go of him his head was swirling with a knew sort of knowledge, one deeper and more profound than any before.

He gasped, the notebook was empty now and he knew what had happened. He had gotten his grandfather's gifts, all of his knowledge, at once. By every God, how was this even possible?

He shivered, he had a terrible headache and he was nauseous and he had to sit down and think but was unable to. He had to tell the masters of this, or....he felt a surge of fear, no, nobody could be told of this. Why he didn't know but the very idea filled him with sudden dread, he couldn't let anyone know that he suddenly possessed everything which had made his forefather grand. He had to pretend to be unchanged, and leave the next day. He laid down with a sob, he wished that he never had been given that box in the first place, this would change his very world forever.

He did fall asleep yet again, in spite of his pain and confusion. This time he did dream and he was standing on a barren hilltop, around him were scorched black land and someone was walking towards him out of the mist. It was a very tall figure and it walked with slow but determined steps.

Ivran couldn't move, he just stared wide eyed at the person who stopped and pulled down his hood. It was his grandfather, he recognized him from the countless portraits hanging in his parent's home. Ivran swallowed and his grandfather nodded silently. "Child, you have been given a gift both wonderful and terrible. I am sure you by now are both confused and frightened and you have every right to be. And yes, you do have the right to hate me, what I have done to you is beyond forgiveness and pardon"

Ivran did wet his lips. "What are you saying?"

His grandfather sent him a sad smile. "There is something very few sorcerers and mages know these days, that the power we use can be controlled in more ways than just one"

Ivran frowned. "What do you mean?"

He had never heard anything about that, magic was seen as a sort of stream flowing through everything within creation and spells were the way to make it cooperate. His grandfather smiled again. "It is forgotten that magic can be controlled by the will alone. I did that child, and you have already started to see what it can do whence it is awakened within someone born with that skill"

Ivran swallowed, feeling very confused. "Uh, what do you mean? I haven't felt any sorts of magic until now?"

The tall man cocked his head. "Oh but you did, you used it earlier today. You wanted to see the "charms" of that young lady didn't you? And you wished to enjoy them too, and you most certainly did"

Ivran yelped. "Oh Gods, was…was that me?!"

His grandfather snickered. "Indeed it was, we carry a terrible burden child, our will and our wishes can change the very fabric of time and space, we can influence others and change history. "

Ivran felt cold through and through. "Why me? Why now?!"

The man sighed. "You know that the ability to use magic always skips one generation? The child of a magician can never follow in his father's footsteps, but the grandchild can. You are my grandson and in you the magic has done something very unusual. You have been blocked from it until now"

Ivran just got more and more confused and scared. "That wasn't you?"

His grandfather shook his head. "No, that wasn't me at all. The ability to control this power not through spells but by sheer will alone does allow you to do things none other can. You don't need to create a spell to do what you wish for, you just need to focus upon the wanted result and there you have it"

Ivran frowned again. "That easy?"

The tall man shook his head with a grin. "Not easy at all, you need complete focus, no stray thoughts can be allowed at all, the risk of failure is great. But the reason why you have been blocked so long is that this ability is very dangerous, as I am sure you can imagine. The deep ancient magic does have a will of its own and by giving you my gifts and knowledge I have unleashed it from the bonds it put upon you. You are ready now, the training you have been trough have finally found its purpose"

Ivran looked down. "So what must I do? I don't understand…."

His grandfather placed a hand on his shoulder. "Go, leave the academy. Do not let anyone know of this gift for it is one many will covet. I hid my abilities, I never revealed the full strength that I carried."

Ivran felt tiny, why he didn't know, but he realized that there had to be a reason why his grandfather wanted him to hide this. "Why?"

The older man took a deep breath. "What have you learned about the brother hood of chaos?"

Ivran blinked. "Ah, uh, a little? They were a guild of dark magicians?"

His grandfather nodded. "That is one way to say it yes, they were eradicated thousands of years ago after having wreaked havoc among the magicians. You see, they had a spell which enabled them to steal the power of others, to make it their own, together with all their knowledge and all their spells"

Ivran nodded, he felt a bit eager, this he had in fact heard of "Yes, they almost wiped out the entire magicians guild?"

His grandfather nodded. "They did and only one very powerful mage managed to fight them and defeat them. "

Ivran smiled. "I remember having read about that, but that was millennia ago"

His grandfather nodded slowly. "Yes, but they weren't eradicated, not completely. There are still dark mages around and if one of them managed to get his hands upon the type of magic we possess? That would be a most terrible disaster my child, the end of everything. Darkness would replace the light and everything would fall into ruins."

Ivran gasped. "They do still exist? But...nobody has ever told..."

The old mage squeezed his shoulder gently. "No, because very few does know, and it has to be that way. They wait child, wait for something which will give them the opportunity to seize power once more and someone like us would be it. What one person knows is a secret, what two people know is soon spread around so never mention this to anyone"

Ivran swallowed hard, he was scared again. "I won't, I will not say anything about it at all. But...what do I do? With the power I supposedly have I mean?"

His grandfather frowned. "You cannot use it openly, but you do have a job now don't you? Be happy with that, if you can help people then do but discretely. Do never reveal just how powerful you are"

Ivran looked down. "And how powerful am I then?"

His grandfather ruffled his hair. "That is something you will have to discover for yourself but remember this, the power is like a double edged sword. There has to be a balance, and everything you do will have consequences."

Ivran nodded. "I know, they taught me that"

His grandfather smiled and lifted his chin. "They taught you well child, use it for good. I have faith in you"

Ivran gathered his courage. "What happened to you? Where are you?"

The magician tilted his head. "That too is something I think you will discover someday, this is farewell child, I don't think I will see you again but I know you will make me proud. "

Ivran felt oddly emotional. "I...I wish I could have met you grandfather, for real I mean"

The older man smiled and patted him on the back. "So do I, sleep now, rest and be ready to face the world once more."

Ivran just had time to feel a swift and tender kiss upon his brow before he was fast asleep once more.

When he did wake up the next morning it was very cold outside and he shuddered as he gathered his belongings and went to eat. The notebook had gone blank now and there was nothing in it and the gems too had changed, now they did look like two pieces of colored glass, not very special at all. He did put them in his sack but he felt that they no longer were of any value, they had done their job. Afterwards he walked to the offices again and he felt oddly guilty, as if he was doing something illegal by hiding his strange experiences from the masters. He took a deep breath and entered the office and the head master was smiling at him. There was a huge heap of clothes there and other things he did need and he tried to look calm and eager. The headmaster placed some items on the desk, it was a small sword and some knives and also a cloak with the academy's insignia upon it. He did also get a pouch full of silver coins and he felt even more guilty now, as if he didn't really deserve all this trust and acceptance. The headmaster sat down and smiled. "I am very glad you agreed upon this young man, I am sure you will do your job with the outmost skill and patience."

Ivran blushed slightly. "I…I will do my best master"

The headmaster chuckled. "Oh I do not doubt that, listen, we do already have an assignment ready and if you'd like to it is yours"

Ivran frowned. "Already, alright, what assignment?"

The headmaster found some papers and smiled widely. "One of the younger students is going home to visit his parents and he does need an escort. It is a rather easy job, you should probably be back here within two months"

Ivran frowned, "Two months? He lives far off then?"

The headmaster nodded. "To the north, one of the trading cities up there. But it is safe, good roads and lots of inns and we will give you good horses too!"

Ivran felt an odd urge to storm out of there and just get going, he wanted to leave all of this behind, there and then. "I will do it, I have always wanted to travel. It can…it can do me good"

The headmaster smiled and his smile was compassionate. "Of course my poor lad, you will surely be able to see things differently whence you have been away from this sad and dreary place for a while. Go, have fun, meet some ladies. You deserve that."

Ivran felt a need to roll his eyes, rumors said that the headmaster had been a real lady killer back in his youth but Ivran had a hard time believing that anyone would be interested in someone that strict. He blushed and looked down and the old man got up. "Here, put this on, there will be supplies ready for you, I will give the orders right away and when you return there will be a small apartment ready for you in the employee's wing"

Ivran managed to smile. "I am most grateful master"

The headmaster bowed his head. "Go get yourself a good meal, everything will be ready soon"

Ivran took a deep breath and gathered the clothes he had been given, walked into a small room used as a wardrobe and changed. The new clothes were nice, much better than those a student would wear and everything was in black and red or brown. He even got new knee high boots and with the cape on he did look like some nobleman. He felt like a stranger, he didn't really recognize the man staring back at him from the mirror. He attached the sword to his belt and felt awkward, he did know how to use a sword, he had been trained also in that art but he preferred that he never would have to use it. He went to the small dining hall reserved for the employees and the food there was way better than the one served in the large one. Then he sat down to rest a bit before he slowly walked to the yard where the headmaster said that the horses would be ready.

He took a deep breath, the headmaster stood there with the stable master and a young lad stood there between them, he was pouting slightly and Ivran saw that the boy had to be rather spoiled. The headmaster grinned widely. "Oh there we have him, our dear Ivran. This is Josphu, he is a little disappointed that he isn't getting a carriage"

Ivran smiled but he did already dislike the boy. "It will be a much faster journey by horseback"

The boy almost sneered. "I will get dirty, and I don't like horses"

Ivran saw that the stable master had saddled two animals, he realized that the boy was to ride a lithe grey mare with a temper which indicated that the lack of enthusiasm was shared. The horse he was to ride was a very tall brown stallion and it looked calm and collected. Ivran let out a sigh of relief. The stable master had also brought out two more horses, dark grey geldings both and they were docile and friendly. Ivran smiled at the boy. "I think we'd better get going then, the faster we leave the faster we'll arrive"

The boy just glared at him but did haul himself onto the mare with a groan. Ivran had put his things into the saddle bags and he was ready to leave now. He felt hunted somehow, if what his grandfather had said was true then there could be danger even there. Nobody would know if any of the masters in reality did serve the darkness. The headmaster did shake his hand, "Have a safe journey my friend, there are maps in the saddle bags and the pack horse has everything else you may need"

The pack horse which was tethered to Ivran's stallion was a very stocky dun mare and it looked as if it was terribly bored. The pack saddle was full and Ivran felt a surge of gratitude. They would travel as rich men no doubt. "Thank you master, I hope I will see you again soon"

The old man smiled and Ivran got in the saddle. He hadn't ridden in quite a while but it was the sort of thing which comes back to you. The boy stared at the neck of his horse and Ivran wondered of the boy had been allowed this vacation because he was an obnoxious person? That wouldn't surprise Ivran at all. He smacked his lips and the horse moved and he threw one last glance behind him as they rode through the main gate. The headmaster stood there and waved his hand and Ivran suddenly knew that he would miss the academy, and miss it a lot. It had been a safe haven for him for years and now he had no idea of what the future would bring. The lad did cling to the saddle and rode like a sack of flour and he would probably suffer from a sore rump rather soon. Ivran thought that it was well deserved. The lad stared at him with a poisonous glare. "So, what have you done to be so popular, sucked the headmasters cock?"

Ivran felt a surge of rage, not only did the lad insult him but he did insult the headmaster too. He wished he could shut the lad up but he didn't say anything, he was afraid that he would unleash something unexpected. He just made the horses gallop and the lad had to concentrate upon not falling off. Oh this would be an interesting journey, a very interesting journey. If that kid continued like that Ivran would wrap him up in tarp and transport him the way they transported corpses, over the pack saddle. There was just so much he was ready to accept and the lad would discover that he was no push around, no absolutely not!

Chapter 3: Dragons and stew

Phraan just knew it, the men they had been given were worthless with the one exception of the forger. The healer was still drunk and lay snoring in the carriage and Phraan would eat his saddle if the man knew how to heal anything more serious than a hangnail. They had travelled for a few days already and he was tempted to drag the two convicts and the healer out into the woods and simply execute them. It would be a mercy, after all, none of them stood a chance against a dragon. But Fastonar didn't agree and so Phraan did keep his mouth shut even when the young guy tried to sabotage every little task they gave him. The road was broad and the wagons solid and they did move forth rather fast but that would change when they got further away from the city, that was a certainty. Phraan remembered how they had struggled the last time, the roads didn't deserve the name and they couldn't use carriages at all, they had to use sleds and pack horses and that meant that they couldn't use much equipment.

The area was packed with farms and villages and it was a very rich and prosperous part of the kingdom. Here there were few problems and they did receive a lot of curiosity since nobody had seen anyone like them for quite a while. But the rumors had spread and many knew that there were dragons up north once again. Some troops were moving north as well and Phraan wondered when they would meet the first refugees.

They had been on the road for a week when Phraan and the others encountered the first real witness to the things which happened up north, it was an officer who was heading towards the city with messages for the king and the man was rather old and also very experienced. He was riding a huge black horse of the breed which was popular up north, sturdy and calm but with great endurance. The animal snorted and wanted to go but the officer sort of calmed him down and greeted the group politely. He did see that Fastonar was in uniform and he probably realized what they were. Fastonar greeted him back and slowed the convoy down. "You come from up north?"

The officer nodded. "Yes, a village on the outskirts of the desert, not far from the Zhar mountains. The army has a camp there, I have been sent south with some news, the high lords want to inform the king of the development."

Fastonar cocked his head. "Really, do tell please, we want to hear as much as possible"

The officer nodded slowly, he was eying them all. "Dragon slayers right? Good, we need you, and we need you now!"

Phraan looked a bit intrigued. "Is it that bad?"

The officer leaned over the side of his horse and spat at the ground. "It is bad yeah, I was just a kid the last time dragons caused problems but I do remember it. And this will be worse, believe me"

Fastonar frowned. "What makes you say that?"

The officer sighed. "Because the population has forgotten what a dragon can do, and they have forgotten how to protect themselves. The officers we have there are morons and the soldiers are not prepared at all"

Phraan saw that Dhokay and the others were listening carefully. "Why am I not surprised, so, what has happened so far? We have heard of two villages being destroyed. "

The officer took off his helmed, stroked his thin greying hair. "That is old news, now I think eight or ten have been levelled completely. The king must send more men and he has to do something for those who do flee. You will meet those who are fleeing soon, many started the moment the first attack happened. They were very smart if you ask me"

Dhokay rode over and he did look worried. "What type of dragons has been seen so far?"

The officer shrugged. "How the hell would I know? I have never seen one of those ugly fuckers but they say that they have rather large spikes along their backs, and they cannot fly but they do spew flames."

Fastonar snapped his fingers. "Greybacks, anything else?"

The officer seemed to think hard. "Ah, well, some rather large ones with red bellies, they spew out acid?"

Phraan frowned. "Red bellies? That's new?"

Fastonar looked puzzled. "Could be some minor change, it has been decades after all"

The officer reined his horse. "Just be careful, the omens are bad. The old wives say this will be a disaster."

Fastonar scoffed. "And when did we listen to old wives stories? Thank you for the information my friend, have a safe journey"

The officer bowed his head. "Thank you, and the same to you"

He let the horse ran off again and Fastonar turned to Phraan. "Red bellies? What sort of dragon has a red belly?"

Phraan shrugged. "It could be something new?"

The soul-sworn just grimaced and the convoy started moving again. They were reaching an area which wasn't so populated and Vitile had told the other elves to keep an open eye on the convicts and also be aware of the fact that they now entered a part of the realm where the king didn't have as many soldiers and where bandits sometimes did strike at travelers. When they made camp they didn't light large fires and they tried to be discrete. They had crossed a couple of rivers and were heading in direction of the Nhotay Lake when Fastonar did notice that his horse and some of the others had started to limp. It started in the morning and got worse during the day and by noon the warrior had to dismount for his horse was unable to use the leg and some of the carriage horses did have a bad limp too. The carriage drivers were all experienced men who knew how to take care of a horse and one of them went over to Fastonar's huge brown horse and lifted the foot. It did look normal, no heat or swelling and the man checked the shoe to make sure that it hadn't picked up a lose rock or something like that. The shoe seemed to be okay and Phraan saw that it was excellent work, the one who took care of the army horses were skilled in deed. The carriage horses stood there and looked uncomfortable too and Phraan started to check their legs as well. A couple of them were limping on more than one leg and the drivers looked confused. "They cannot all have picked up rocks?"

Phraan was puzzled, nine horses were lame in all and at the same time? They hadn't crossed terrain that bad, the road was still a road and not a cattle track and they hadn't had any problems with the wagons so far. Shaluun looked worried. "The horses are in real pain, they cannot go on like this. "

Dhokay nodded. "You are right, they are hurting. I can sense it, what can this be?"

Rhuk was staring at the carriage horses. "They don't have bad legs, nah, none of them have bad legs, cannot do with bad legs"

Dabin sort of rolled his eyes, during the journey it had become rather apparent that Rhuk had a deep fascination for feet. Apparently he saw the feet as the most attractive feature of others, no matter who.

The healer had sobered up now, they hadn't given him any booze and he was cranky and ill-tempered and a genuine asshole in every way. He was leering at the two elven females and he was being cocky and sarcastic too. But he bragged about his skills and Phraan wished that he could get rid of the man and that fast too. He was ruining the mood. Fastonar gestured to the drivers. "We make camp here, we have to check the animals again and they need rest"

The camp was set rather fast, and Vitile sent Taurin and Thiana out into the trees to keep watch. Phraan saw that the drunkard was sitting by one of the wagons, chewing on some meat and he had become a real nuisance by now. They didn't allow anyone to drink and the man was constantly trying to find something he could drink. He even tried to beg for alcohol from people they had met on the road and the odd clothes did ward them off rather efficiently. Oham did curse everybody who ignored him and Fastonar did despise the man intensely. The forger was different, he tried to make himself useful and he did even show some interest in their job, Phraan believed that this was an individual who had been unfortunate more than anything else, and made some poor choices.

The lame horses were gathered and Phraan started checking their legs more thoroughly, he had a set of thongs and used them to squeeze at the hooves to find sore spots. The horse he held did almost kick him when he reached a spot in the middle of the sole and Phraan frowned. "There is something here. Fastonar, hold him"

The huge man held the horse and Phraan poured some water onto the hoof and scrubbed it off gently with a brush. Being a farrier was useful now. He blinked, there was a small dark spot on the sole of the hoof and he frowned. "I see something."

He grasped the hoof knife and the blade did hit something hard, inside of the hoof. He got a very bad suspicion and carved away at the hoof. Dhokay had come over to help hold the horse and he was so strong he managed to keep the animal in place even it this obviously hurt. Phraan grasped onto the object with the thongs, it was very small and thin and he did pull it out with a groan. It was a nail, a two inch long and very thin metal nail and it was no accident that it had ended where it had. Someone had hammered it into the hoof to make the horse go lame and Phraan got up and his eyes were shooting flames. "Fastonar, we have a saboteur in our midst"

The warrior frowned and looked confused until Phraan held the nail up so everybody could see it. Vitile swore and Kapha gaped, his eyes huge with disbelief. Shaluun growled and Fastonar had gone paper white, it was a sure sign of anger. He turned around and stared at the people assembled, "Grasp Oham"

Rhuk and Dabin did grab the man who struggled and protested and Fastonar went over and grasped onto his sleeves. "What the fuck are you doing?"

Fastonar made a grimace. "No horsehairs here, he isn't the one"

Peter did hold out his arms without even being asked and he was also free of horse hairs. Aiolo had to be held but there weren't any hairs on his sleeves either. Vitile stared at the wagon where the healer spent the time with narrow eyes. "Have you seen the healer since we stopped? He does know how to create pain now doesn't he?"

Phraan ran over and ripped aside the tarp from the back of the wagon, there were nobody there but a track did lead away from the wagon and it was fresh. The idiot believed that he could escape? By hurting their horses? He had probably believed that the lame horses would become such a distraction that he could sneak away. Phraan turned around. "Vitile, with me, Taurin, Thiana, left and right"

The forest elves did nod and disappeared into the trees and Phraan knew that there was no way they would let him escape. An elderly, fat and out of shape man would be caught within minutes in this terrain. He and Vitile ran along the tracks and they soon saw that the man had overestimated his own stamina, the track told of blind panic and he was running towards the river they saw in the distance. He probably believed that he could find some place to hide but Phraan wondered why the fuck the man did run away in the first place. He wasn't in an ideal position and he could get that at some level, the man was clearly most used to the city and to some travelling into the wilderness like this can be traumatic. Was it the need for booze which drove him? Or was it something even more compelling? No matter what the reason was, Phraan wanted the man to suffer! Nobody harmed their horses like that, with lame horses they were at risk if they got attacked by robbers.

Vitile was dark eyed and her teeth were showing as they ran, she was really pissed off and Phraan knew exactly how fierce wood elves got when they reached that stage. He had seen what they did to orcs they caught alive and it wasn't pretty. The man was trying to sprint across a small meadow when they caught sight of him. He had shed the healer robe and was running in his tunic and pants and to say that he was elegant would be a terrible lie. He ran like someone who has crapped in their pants and Vitile sent out a shrill sound and arrows immediately bored into the ground in front of the man. Taurin and Thiana had already gotten in front of the man and now they ran out onto some branches and could be seen clearly, with arrows aimed at the man.

The healer shrieked, then he tried to run in a different direction and Vitile rushed forth and kicked the legs out from underneath him. Phraan did pull his blade and pointed at the human with a snarl on his lips. The man was shivering and sweat was pouring from him. Vitile spat at him and the two other wood elves jumped from the trees with catlike grace and walked over, arrows still cocked. Phraan snarled. "So, what is your excuse for this you worthless piece of dung! I ought to leave you for the wolves, or send you back to the city for a really long stay in the torture chambers."

The man was gasping for air, clutching his chest. Vitile kicked him in the back. "Speak, or I will make you scream like you never have screamed before"

The healer rolled his eyes. "I wasn't asking for much now was I? Just some wine, but no, you bastards won't let a man quench his thirst even once!"

Phraan stared at the man with disgust. "You did this because you wanted alcohol? You are more stupid than I expected. Where in hell do you think you could go to find booze here in the wild?"

The man twitched, his eyes were desperate. "There are farmers here and there, they make moonshine don't they? I don't wanna end up in the north, it is dangerous up there."

Phraan growled. "We are more dangerous believe me, you were assigned to us by the king so you have just committed treason. What is the punishment for that Vitile?"

The wood elf was still very angry, she hissed. "Beheading, let me do the honor, please!"

Phraan grinned. "Of course, whence he has suffered a bit. Taurin, remove his boots"

The male elf bent down and dragged the man's boots off, they were stinking and not overly well made but they were not too bad either. The man gasped and looked terrified. "You ran all the way here so now it is time to run back, barefoot. You maimed those poor horses so it is about time you experience what they have gone through"

The man whined and took a few steps, it was very obvious that he wasn't used to walking barefoot for he cringed and put his feet down very carefully. Phraan almost roared. "Move!"

He smacked the man over the broad ass with the flat of his blade and the man whimpered and tried to move faster. Phraan could see that he was terrified and also that Taurin and Thiana were very angry. To them such a deed was seen as beyond despicable, harming an animal was a huge sin the way they saw the world.

When they reached back to the camp the man was barely able to move, his feet torn and bloody and he was weeping and begging for mercy. Fastonar was waiting and he nodded at Phraan. "All the horses have nails in their hooves, we found some in those who haven't gone lame too. The only ones which haven't been tampered with are Drake and the horses the wood elves use. They don't let anyone they don't know handle them."

Rhuk stood there and was fuming and Dabin too looked as if he was about to explode. "The ponies too?"

Fastonar nodded. "We have to check every horse we have carefully, the bastard have tried to stop us"

Vitile grasped the man by his thin hair. "When did you do this!"

The man tried to wriggle free. "Last…last night, when you were…eating"

Phraan remembered that the healer hadn't been there for the meal but then again, he rarely was. And it had been raining too so everybody had tried to stay inside of the carriages to stay warm and dry. He could have done it then, easily. They hadn't expected any danger and the horses were used to being handled by different people. Fastonar sighed and he pulled his sword free of its sheath. "He has slowed us down, we will have to wait here for many days before we can move on, and people are dying up there. Lives will be lost because of this."

Vitile was almost jumping up and down. "Let me do it, he is nothing but scum!"

Fastonar smiled at her, a swift and gentle smile. "You are bloodthirsty my dear, I remember that from before. Good, I will let you do it. But first we do follow the king's laws. Any man abusing his majesty's property is to be flogged. These are army horses, in other words, the king's property"

He turned to Kapha. "Bring me one of the whips, a solid one."

The half breed grinned and ran off, he returned after just a few minutes with a long whip and Fastonar nodded. "Strip him"

The man screamed and tried yet again to struggle but Dhokay and Kapha ripped the tunic of him. Then they tied his hands to the wheel of one of the wagons and forced him to stand there back to Fastonar. The warrior did shake the whip and his grin was vicious. "The law says ten lashes for each crime committed. He tried to maim more than twenty horses so I think I will stop at a hundred and fifty"

The man shrieked, hundred and fifty lashes of such a whip were something you could hardly even survive.

Phraan nodded. "It is fair, go ahead."

Fastonar was a master with the whip, each lash did hit with brutal force and yet they didn't overlap at all, and they bit into the skin. The man was screaming like a banshee before long and after fifty lashes he was hanging by his hands and blood was streaming down his back. Dhokay tilted his head, the three convicts were standing at the back of the small camp and they did look terrified. This would serve as a reminder also to them. "He won't last much longer, too weak. His body is already ruined."

Fastonar sighed and threw the whip away. "You are right, we are not animals like him. Vitile, end him"

The wood elf pulled one of her long curved blades and grasped the man's hair again, pulled the head back and then she simply slit the man's throat and cut so deep she almost decapitated him. The body did shiver a few times and she cut him loose and let the body lay there in a pool of blood. Phraan stared at the three convicts. "If you think we are heartless and cruel it is nothing compared with what else you will encounter out there. Orcs will often eat people alive, trolls will crush you slowly and a dragon? A dragon will roast you!"

The three men did look shocked and Phraan pointed at the corpse. "Drag him into the woods, let the scavengers feast."

Fastonar sighed and put his blade back in its sheath. "And we are without a healer yet again"

Phraan shrugged. "We never had a healer, we only had a drunken coward."

Fastonar sighed deeply again and made a grimace. "Well, there are villages along our route, there could be some wise woman or something who could be persuaded to aid us."

Phraan took a deep breath. "Maybe, the village healers can be rather skilled after all. We'll ask when we encounter some locals"

Fastonar put his hands in his sides. "We can at least ask, so, we have to stay here for some days, I suggest that someone goes out hunting then. We all could benefit from some fresh meat wouldn't you think"

There were some enthusiastic cheers coming from Dhokay and Shaluun and Vitile too grinned. "Yes, let's go. I bet there are deer in this area!"

She ran off with the trackers just behind and Phraan had to laugh at her zeal. Rhuk was rubbing his hands together. "Great, fresh meat, good, good. I never trusted that dude though, ugly feet. Can never trust anyone with ugly feet ya know"

Phraan had to scoff. "Really?"

The dwarf nodded. "True, ugly feet equal ugly soul I say. Have you seen the feet of the women of my tribe?"

Phraan had to snort to stop himself from laughing. "No, I cannot say that I have had the pleasure"

Rhuk smiled widely, his eyes were dreamy. "Oh by the allfather they are lovely, so well-shaped, with just the right amount of hair."

Phraan knew that dwarves were rather hairy and Rhuk's tribe was infamous for being hairier than most. "I am sure they are delightful"

Rhuk snickered. "Know what? Having one of them dancing on your back is about the best you can experience, those wonderful feet, aahh, the mere thought"

Phraan fought the need to roll his eyes, the mental images it called forth…Better not think about it. "I do think that my tastes are a wee bit different from yours…"

Rhuk scoffed. "Oh but you are missing out my friend, if you have tried a dwarf woman you won't go back to the hairless elven tits, no sir. Dwarf women can really make a man happy!"

Phraan cringed and smiled, oh Akhi curse that dwarf, now he had some even worse images to struggle with. "I will think about it, if you excuse me, I have to check upon my horse."

Rhuk just waved a hand and Phraan ran off. He didn't really want to know more about that dwarf's sex life, it was more than enough with what he already knew!

He went over to Drake and made sure that the horse had everything it needed, being stuck there didn't sit well with him at all, it made his nerves itch and he knew that every day they stayed put meant death. After a while the hunters returned with a small deer and some rabbits and Vitile and Thiana began preparing some stew. The wood elves were experts when it came to using herbs and spices to create marvelous meals out of even simple ingredients and Phraan did remember how Vitile had kept them all fed back in the old days. They settled for the meal and even the three convicts did get their fair share of the food. Peter was praising the stew wholeheartedly and wanted to know what spices she was using and Vitile was giggling and laughing, claiming it was an elven secret.

Aiolo and Oham did eat in silence and Oham in special showed a very distinct lack of table manners. Phraan knew that dwarves are infamous for their lack of manners or rather, for having their very own view upon what manners was, but this was way beyond that. Even an orc would have been more posh for Oham was simply grabbing the food with his hands and stuffing it into his mouth. Rhuk stared at the man and his face told of a great deal of disgust and loathing. Dhokay turned around so he didn't have to look at the man and Thiana and Taurin threw horrified glances at each other. Vitile whispered to Phraan. "That man doesn't use anything when he…relieves…himself, not even leaves. Just his hands"

Phraan almost spat out his food, it was a bit too much information for one day, first Rhuk and his confessions and now this. By every God there was!

The two trackers agreed upon keeping watch that night, they were so in tune with the forest they would sense it the moment anything approached their camp. The trees and animals would warn them. Vitile came with Phraan to his sleeping spot in one of the wagons and they lay there staring at the stars up overhead. Vitile sighed and put her arm around him, she was as warm as ever and Phraan enjoyed the skin contact. Too many years without touching anyone had left him starved for just that and she was luckily enough as cuddly as a kitten when she was in the mood. "Do you really think it will be like before?"

Phraan sighed and put an arm under his neck, stared up. "Of course, I have no reason to believe otherwise"

Vitile sort of grimaced, she turned her head around. "I don't think it will be like before"

Phraan frowned. "Why is that?"

She shrugged. "I don't know, call it a hunch. But it is gnawing at me, don't you find it weird that the dragons have appeared so suddenly? In such numbers?"

He had to look at her, frowning. "You are right, it is odd, but if there are hidden breeding grounds they could have stayed there until they were too many to stay any longer"

Vitile sort of snorted. "Ah Phraan, listen to yourself, really? Dragons hate each other, they wouldn't stay in one area for years and years without killing each other. And a breeding ground? That is even less likely, we have seen what male dragons do to others if there is a female nearby. It is sheer carnage. When the huge species did disappear back then we all believed they had simply killed each other off fighting for the few females, very few of them were felled by people remember?"

Phraan realized that she was right. "The dragons did go in packs back in the old days?"

Vitile nodded. "Because there wasn't any food to be found anywhere, the winters had been terrible for decades remember?

They had to become pack hunters, they do that just to keep the species alive."

He sighed. "Yes, but it could be that there has been a famine up north?"

She turned around, leaned her chin onto his shoulder. "We don't know what is up there Phraan, the lands north of the great mountains are unknown terrain, yes, we did believe that we and the fights for mates had killed every dragon that existed but what if we were wrong?"

He let a hand run through the silky locks and frowned. "Wrong, how?"

She took a deep breath. "I have been thinking Phraan, and I have seen things in retrospective. Do you remember the packs of dragons? Some were large but there were never more than twenty dragons in any of those which the larger species formed. And how many females did we see?"

Phraan stared down at her. "Ah, I don't remember?"

She nodded. "Exactly! The small species like the dreklugnins could be as many as fifty in a pack but the larger dragons had a limit to how many a pack could contain. And all were males"

Phraan shook his head. "Not right, we did kill females remember? That huge Long tail we caught outside of that burned village? And the giant storm fire we felled? That was a female too!"

Vitile sighed and had an expression upon her face equal to the one she would have when scolding an insolent elfling. "The long tail female was sick Phraan, remember? There was poisonous fungi growing all over her belly, she was dying. And the storm fire was half dead from blood loss"

Phraan sighed. "You are right, so, what is it that you really are saying?"

Vitile curled up a bit closer to him, her leg wrapped over his hip and her head resting on his chest. "What we saw back then were just a forewarning, they were the front troops. What we will face now is the real army"

Phraan scoffed. "What?"

She nodded slowly. "They were the weak ones, the ones who couldn't survive up where the dragons come from. They had to leave or die, and that was why they cooperated so well. I think the smaller species we did see were scavengers who followed the larger dragons to feed upon the scraps they left behind"

Phraan felt a sting of unease. "So you think that we haven't seen anything yet? That there are more dragons coming this time?"

She nodded. "Yes, many time the numbers and way stronger too."

Phraan continued to play with her hair. "So why haven't they come before, and like you said, they wouldn't just stay up there waiting for the right moment to strike? If they are strong they would leave to hunt wouldn't they? Why should all of them come down south at once? Isn't that a bit weird?"

Vitile sort of writhed. "I know, it doesn't make sense, we should have seen some dragons showing up rather often, not a whole bunch of them, but hear me out, what if they are being controlled?"

Phraan scoffed. "Vitile, you are a wood elf, you know that dragons can't be controlled. They are too fierce, too wild. Nobody has the power needed to control a dragon"

Vitile bit her lower lip. "What if someone does, in spite of it all?"

Phraan held his breath for a second. "Are you serious? That is impossible, and that many dragons?"

She put her arm around him. "I know I sound crazy but it is a feeling I have, there is something up north, and I think we will meet it before this is over"

Phraan grimaced. "I hope you are wrong Vitile, I really do."

She smiled but the smile was a pale one. "So do I my friend, we barely made it back then, I cannot imagine what will happen if I am right."

Phraan swallowed. "Let us forget about this, look, the stars are all out, isn't it beautiful?"

She nodded. "Yes, look, the sword is visible, that is a good sign isn't it?"

Phraan stared at the famous constellation, it was rare that it was entirely visible and he stared at the big red star which represented the pommel of the sword, sometimes it seemed to disappear and when it appeared again it was seen as a sign of imminent change. "Yes, I am sure it is a good sign. "

Vitile sighed and nuzzled his neck, it made the hairs stand up on his head for it felt very good, and also very erotic. Her hand did slide downwards and a devil awakened in her eyes. "I think we have better things to do now than to think of the past. Don't you agree?"

He grinned and kissed her with hunger and before long they had forgotten all about dragon slaying and were engaged in way more pleasant ways to spend their time.

They were awakened the next morning by Dhokay who was laughing claiming they had kept everybody awake for hours and Phraan had to blush and admit that yes, they had forgotten to keep it silent. They had to stay there so most of the group did split up to explore the area, the horses needed a couple of days to recuperate and Phraan was still very angry at the bastard who had crippled them thus. Taurin and Thiana had smeared healing potions onto the hooves but even that needed at least a day to work properly. He was glad the idiot hadn't tried to maim Drake but if he had the stallion would have kicked him to death and perhaps that would have been for the better.

Phraan spent the day fishing in a small lake nearby, he caught some trout and a huge local species which gave a good fight but were inedible. The meat tasted like mud and looked like raw dough and it did stink too. The only use people had for those fish were as a source of bait and the huge scales were pretty and could be peeled off and used to adorn clothing and to make jewelry. The convicts were ordered to oil the harnesses and Peter did his fair share of it whistling and singing to himself. Oham was cussing constantly and Aiolo didn't speak at all, he just sat there with the cloth of oil and looked as if he was terribly bored. Dhokay had volunteered to watch over them and he wasn't going to let them become sloppy. It took two more days before they were back on the road and by then everybody had grown very impatient, the horses were well rested now and none of them were limping so they could keep a brisk pace. The landscape wasn't too hard to cross here and the road was well used. They kept driving for more than a week before they met another road coming from the east and it was not as much in use as this one. Shaluun did see fresh tracks indicating that a rather huge group of horses had been travelling north just a day or two before them and Phraan got a suspicion he got confirmed three days later. They caught up with a group of men and Phraan didn't need to take two looks to determine that these people were there to do the same job as them. The group had camped by a river to rest their horses and Phraan would have welcomed more slayers if they had been like himself and his group, professionals.

These men were amateurs and even worse, cocky amateurs. Even he had been a novice once, he hadn't known one thing about dragons and he had been terrified the first time he saw one. But he had known that he was ignorant, he had listened to the experienced slayers and he had known that it took only a tiny mistake to kill a man. These men were confident and even if they had been told what to do that didn't mean that they were experts. You are never an expert until you have survived for at least a year in this business, and few lasted that long.

Phraan saw that the group had a leader, he appeared to be the only slayer among them, the one who would do the job so to speak. The half elf did see that the man had his roots back east, he was a handsome fellow with thick curly black hair, an elegant moustache and he appeared to be a nobleman. Well, dragons don't ask you for your pedigree before they roast you. The man rode a large long legged thoroughbred which probably cost a fortune for Phraan had hardly ever seen a more beautiful horse, too bad it would end up as steak pretty fast if its owner didn't turn around. The man hailed them and Phraan did slow down the convoy. These people travelled without wagons, they belongings were carried by mules and Phraan frowned. That was a huge risk to take, mules are docile beasts but for some reason they are more afraid of dragons than horses and bolt the moment they smell one. Phraan managed to smile, the man bowed politely "Allow me to introduce myself, I am count Waslav of Akhibar, I am a dragon slayer as you can see"

Phraan raised an eyebrow, he did see a lot of equipment yes, and some of it wasn't half bad but they appeared to lack the most important thing of all, experience and knowledge! He managed to keep his voice calm. "Have you killed many dragons my lord?"

The man appeared to like being called my lord and he smiled from one ear to the other. "No, but I am sure I will be the bane of countless of these beasts. I am looking forward to meet these the mightiest of beasts"

Phraan did look at the tent which was placed by a huge oak, it was bright red and that is not a very good idea unless you want to be fried. Dragons are for some reason drawn to red. "I see, pardon me for asking but what sort of armor is that? I haven't seen that design before?"

A young man was polishing some parts of an armor which hung from a pole next to the tent. It was very pretty with lots of gold and embellishments but Phraan thought it looked more like the plume of a peacock than a real armor. "Oh it is a brand new design, with this on no claws or teeth can pierce me. It is made from the very best steel"

Dhokay sat next to Phraan and he had to pretend to be bending down to fix his stirrup to hide his wide smirk. Phraan felt a need to roll his eyes but he didn't do it, instead he kept a stiff smile on his face. Steel was no good, no matter how good it was. The only armor which had any effect at all against a dragon is scale armor made from dragon skin and that only protected you for a short time. If the dragon manages to catch you in its maw you are dead no matter what you are wearing. "I see, I bet that must have been expensive?"

Phraan would have loved to see what this armor would look like after a rock jaw had played with it. Those dragons crushed anything, the jaws were so strong they ate their way through solid bedrock and metals were just snack for them. Waslav nodded with pride. "Oh yes, I paid two thousand gold for it, but it is worth it. I am gonna make a name for myself"

Phraan smiled and tilted his head. "I am glad to see that we aren't the only ones heading up north, the problem is supposedly greater than anticipated."

Waslav grinned widely. "We will reach them before you but don't worry, we will leave a few also for you"

He did look as if he didn't put much faith in the group and Phraan felt another surge of rage rush through him but he held it back. The other group had many horses and they were of the light and fast breed typical of Akhibar, wonderful animals but skittish and not at all strong enough for such a job. Dhokay cleared his voice. "So, how come you decided to become a dragon slayer?"

Waslav stared at his polished fingernails with a pleased expression within his eyes. "My king wants to have the head of a death wind mounted above his throne. I promised I would get him one"

Phraan almost let out a very hoarse and very disrespectful laughter but he hid it as a sneeze. A death wind? The most feared of all the dragon species, the one type of dragon few slayers had ever fought since it was suicide. Oh this man was bold but he wouldn't last long, Phraan was sure of it. Dhokay kept smiling. "So, have you trained? Have you learned enough about this very dangerous task to be able to handle these monsters?"

The man smiled and nodded. "I have spoken to many dragon slayers and I have read the good book too"

This time Phraan had to give Drake a discrete push with his heel and the horse did step around, just so the half elf didn't reveal his expression of utter disbelief. The good book? It was a scroll which had been written by a wise man some two hundred years ago, it contained the various methods used for dragon hunting and it was all a whole load of horse dung. If you wanted to commit suicide by dragon that book was your perfect guide to the afterlife, otherwise it was just a fairytale. "I see, ah, and the slayers you spoke to, may I ask their names? I have been in the business since the problems started and I may know them"

Waslav nodded with zeal. "Of course you can, Arguan the brave and Hasupar of the lance, brave men, and very skilled"

Phraan heard Shaluun laugh from further back in the convoy, he heard everything and Vitile appeared to have swallowed something which had gotten stuck for her face was red and tears were flowing down her face. Phraan pinched the inside of his own thigh to stay serious. "I see, I haven't heard of those gentlemen I fear, they must have been fighting in some other area. I recon they have slain many dragons?"

Waslav nodded. "Oh yes, Arguan have killed more than five hundred, included several death winds and iron wolves."

Phraan held his face neutral. "Impressive, and Hasupar?"

The man appeared to be so full of it he didn't notice the odd tone in the half elf's voice. "He has an even more impressive record, A hundred storm winds and two packs of frost jaws and he has even killed a thousand mist bloods."

Phraan bowed his head. "I am indeed stunned, such bravery, I can see that you have been taught by the very best"

Waslav just grinned and Phraan turned his horse around once more. A thousand mist bloods, they were the most rare of dragons and among the most feared of the species too, there had been perhaps ten mist bloods spotted during the entire time he had been hunting dragons and only one had been killed. This man was a complete fool if he believed that he was able to fight dragons, but it was his funeral. "We better get going, the horses shouldn't get too cold before they start moving again. I am sure we will meet once more my lord, and good hunting"

Phraan didn't add the phrase he wanted to use, it was a blessing elves say when they meet someone who is sure to die soon. Instead he just whispered it to himself. "May the winds embrace you"

The man was still smiling and Vitile trotted up next to Phraan as they left the campsite, she was still red and wiped tears from her eyes. "Phraan, I bet ten gold coins on him dying in his very first dragon encounter. Even a dreklugnin can kill such a fool"

Phraan sighed. "I am sorry I cannot bet against you for I think so too. What a complete moron"

They both laughed and noticed that a small man came walking along the path, carrying some wood on his back. It had to be a servant and he stopped and looked up at them. He was rather old and his face had the expression of someone who has seen it all before and no longer gives a flying fuck about anything. He spat on the ground. "So, you have had a chat with his grace now have you? Or shall I rather call him by his real name, dragon-food"

Phraan cocked his head. "That is at least what he will become if he doesn't change his ways, you are his servant?"

The man nodded, the small beady eyes were filled with sarcasm. "Oh yes, his mule, his dishwasher, the one to rub his feet, wash his dirty clothes and if he wasn't so convinced of his own irresistibility I would have had to wipe his ass as well, phew!!"

Vitile giggled and the old man hoisted the wood higher up onto his shoulders. "He does think he knows how to kill dragons but he is as clueless as a freaking nun in a brothel. I am going to leave as soon as we find a village or city, I am not going to commit suicide by sticking to that piece of crap"

Phraan frowned. "You have seen dragons haven't you?"

The old man nodded. "Oh yes I have, I was ten when the last ones were killed or disappeared the last time and I survived an attack, greybacks. They leveled our village completely and I made it because we had a deep well and I climbed into it. But I saw, oh by the gods did I see."

Phraan sighed. "Then I wish your master would have listened to you old man, it could spare his life, and that of his men here too"

The servant spat again, he was chewing on some Ghiba root and it made his spit bright blue. "He never listens to anyone but himself, but trust me, he will end up as a light fried snack soon. Just watch up folks, it would be too bad if that happened to you as well"

Phraan grinned. "We don't plan on doing mistakes no. We have hunted dragons before"

The old man nodded. "I know you Phraan, I saw you once back then, you and the team killed a huge steel belly. I never forgot that."

Phraan blushed slightly. "I am pleased to hear that"

The man grinned. "Go with the gods and be blessed. You are our hope now"

Phraan touched his chest and bowed his head in respect before he made the horse run again and the old man seemed to appreciate the gesture. He waved his hand after them. Phraan had to snicker, he remembered the uproar they had caused in some places. Dragon slayers were seen as something almost divine and it had been embarrassing and almost dangerous too at times. He turned to Vitile. "Do you remember that horse of yours that got shaved?"

She burst into giggles. "Oh poor old Springstorm, yes."

Phraan smiled back at her. "I will never forget that, he did look ridiculous poor thing"

Vitile put her tongue out. "It wasn't my fault that they thought that his hairs could work as talismans."

Phraan smirked. "Well, they tried to make money from just about anything back then so why not? One guy tried to cut my braid remember?"

She nodded and her eyes did twinkle. "Yes, you broke his nose, and three of his fingers. What a jerk"

Phraan looked back, they were way past the camp now and he stared ahead. "I hope we won't get that famous this time, last time was more than enough for me"

Vitile smiled. "Yes, for me too. I hope hunting will be all that we have to do"

Phraan made Drake gallop. "Indeed"

The other group did catch up with them two days later, and Phraan let them pass for he didn't want to spend any more time with the airhead who was their leader. They seemed to be in a hurry and only the old servant did wave at them as they rode by. Travelling with carriages did slow them down but they would need every bit of equipment available. The area they were heading into was rather flat with some deep river valleys and a few oddly shaped cliffs and it was vast. Here the villages were spread out and the distances great and it was where the problem had started the last time, or rather, it was where it had gotten to when the great cities to the south finally were alerted. The place had looked very differently back then, Phraan could remember that. It had been more lush, with Holts of trees and the fields had been large and filled with everything from vegetables to wheat. Now the fields they saw were still large but they didn't yield more than half of what they used to and some places the soil itself had burned off in wildfires. The region couldn't feed that many people, only a third of the previous population and yet many had returned to the land after the dragons were gone to restart their lives, thinking it would be like before.

Phraan saw that the farms they passed by here and there were good, well taken care off and they ought to produce enough food for everyone but the people they did see where obviously poor. He saw skinny kids and way too many gravesites. One evening they made camp by a small village and soon many of the village kids came to take a look at them. Elves were rare in these parts and Phraan was used to getting glared at. The kids didn't bother him, they were after all just that, kids, but the grownups were way worse. The men he could tolerate to a degree, they were often just impressed by the skills and the elegance of the elven warriors, and their weapons. Some of the women were way worse, a few acted like burrs and Phraan had more than once cursed the fact that humans did find elves so very attractive. Once he had woken up from deep slumber to find that a somewhat faded beauty tried to crawl into his bed. Dhokay often scared the children but he was fond of little ones and after a little while he often became their favorite and he was rather generous with his time when there were kids around. This village consisted of just ten buildings and they appeared to be full of people, there were fields around it and it was obvious that the village did make a living by farming flax. The inhabitants did weave and Phraan saw some of the cloth they did produce. It was nice but he knew that it had been nicer before. A couple of the village elders came to the camp that night to hear news and Phraan saw that one of them was very old indeed. He had probably seen over a hundred winters and that was a lot for a human. The man was so fragile he couldn't walk but others carried him on a sort of chair and it was obvious that the man was very wise and not at all senile. Phraan saw that the eyes still were sharp and keen and the man sort of demanded respect. He had probably been the village leader once upon a time.

Shaluun brought the man a jug of wine and the old one grinned with few teeth and emptied the jug with surprising speed. "Thank you so much lovely one. It has been a long time since I tasted good wine. The thing my brethren here make is worse than horse piss!"

Phraan had to grin. "I see, tell me, I was here fifty years ago and the area was lush back then, wealthy!"

The old man sighed. "Aye it was, the herds of cattle were huge, and the goats fat. The fields could be harvested twice a year."

Vitile cocked her head. "So, what happened?"

The old man made a grimace and changed his position, his arms were just skin and bones and he looked like a person who had worked hard his entire life. He looked worn, but proud. "When the dragons disappeared they took the blessings of the earth with them, at least that was what people said back then. Too much blood had been shed, the land was cursed."

Phraan frowned. "Do you believe that?"

The old man shook his head. "I was a grown man back then, I had seen what the land could yield also before the dragons came. No, we are not cursed. But the weather has changed, the winters are longer and colder and the rain has become scarce and when it does rain it pours for hours. It washes the soil away instead of gently moistening it. "

Dhokay nodded. "It is a natural cycle, bound to happen no matter what. I have seen it"

Dhokay was very old and Phraan did believe him, it had happened before. He had read of the rich cities of the far east where huge orchards and vast fields were lost to the desert just over a couple of generations. The old man nodded. "Yes, and the way we used the land back then drained it of nutrition. If the dragons hadn't come we would still have lost much, but it would have been a slow disaster, not a swift one. When the dragons came people did flee south, if they hadn't arrived most would have stayed and many more would have died, believe me. People don't want to leave their homes even if it means starvation for they will never seize to hope for a good summer"

Vitile frowned. "Are you saying that the carnage back then was a good thing?!"

The old man chuckled. "No, of course not. The dragons slaughtered thousands, and it was truly a terrible thing but sometimes I think that we were too self-confident. This region weren't meant to be inhabited to begin with, old legends says that it ought to be left alone."

Phraan knew that it had been a wilderness until three or four hundred years before the dragons came the last time. Dhokay did look very interested and Kapha stuffed his pipe with slow movements, he did pay keen attention to what the old human was saying. "Do tell, what legends? I have never heard of any legends connected to this particular region?"

The old man coughed and Phraan did pour some more wine, he did see that Oham did stare at the jar he held with hunger and he sent Vitile a swift glance. She nodded back, almost imperceptibly, she would make sure that the drunkard didn't find the wine. The old man drained also this with glee and wiped his mouth. "Oh, they are old, and almost forgotten by everyone. It was one of the travelling tribes who knew them and my grandfather liked to collect lore and thus I learned of these old tales."

Phraan stared at the old man. "Do tell please, we are curious, and the night is still young"

The man snickered. "Oh yes, I wish I was as young as that, but my bones are old and brittle and no fair maiden will want to invite me to her bed anymore, it has been decades since I last felt like a man."

He pulled the heavy wool blanket tighter around himself and sighed. "The legends are odd, I didn't really understand anything of them when I was a lad but now as an old man they do make more sense. "

He stared at the flames. "The land up north, beyond the great mountains, that is what this is all about. "

Shaluun looked curious. "Nobody knows anything about that area at all, nobody has tried to cross over the mountains and returned"

The old man nodded. "Yes, and the legends do explain why. I do not believe in these old tales but they are interesting and there could be some sort of truth to them after all"

Vitile looked like an eager kid. "Go on"

The old man giggled and appeared to be charmed by her eager gaze. "They say that the world was ruled by two powers in the very beginning, one of order and one of chaos, one created and the other destroyed and one could not exist without the other"

Dhokay nodded. "I have heard of that yes, it is what magicians learn when they start training. There has to be a balance"

The old man looked pleased. "Yes, that is right. But the legends do speak of a great battle, both powers tried to overcome the other and in the end they reached a truce, they were equal, none could win no matter what they did. They say that the power of chaos did create the dragons and that the power of order came up with something equally terrible but the legends didn't say exactly what it was. "

Phraan frowned. "It seems very believable that chaos made the dragons for they are just that, chaos incarnate"

The old man smiled. "Exactly, the followers of chaos did retreat to the land behind the mountains for that was the land designated for them and there is a barrier in there somewhere. No creature if chaos is supposed to cross it and also the other way around, it is impenetrable and made to last forever"

Vitile looked confused. "But the dragons have come? Crossed the mountains?"

The old man nodded. "Yes, for not all followers of chaos do honor the truce. Have you heard of the brotherhood of dark mages?"

Dhokay hissed. "Dark magicians yes, they were eradicated millennia ago"

Phraan nodded. "None have heard of anyone being a part of that group. They are gone"

The old man shrugged. "Maybe, maybe not. The legends says that the group do possess an artefact which allow them to breach the wall, and that this would happen when the last of the line of Athebar of old did perish"

Rhuk jumped up. "Athebar? That was the ancient king of Northold, his last descendant did die just two years before the dragons were first seen!"

The old man shrugged again. "Yes, so maybe there is truth in the legends after all!"

Phraan threw some more wood onto the fire. "But that was fifty years ago and nothing really happened? The dragons were either killed or disappeared and it has been peace ever since"

The man nodded. "Yes, so it is odd, but I think that if someone indeed wishes to bring chaos back to the lands those dragons were just a test, a practice run"

Vitile stared at the flames. "The weak ones, those not strong and worthy enough…"

Phraan swallowed, oh gods, was she right after all?

The man grinned and pat his knees. "Remember, these are legends, fairy tales if you like. They do say that there is one weapon which needs to be awakened within someone blessed, and one weapon must be found, the third weapon against the chaos is carried in secret. The legends didn't say anything more"

Dhokay tilted his head. "So there are weapons against these dark powers, how splendid. I prefer to see this as an infestation of unwanted pests and nothing more. If the dragons do live up in the mountains the surplus is bound to head south looking for food sooner or later, they are like wolf packs, the young must go fend for themselves when they are old enough."

The man grinned. "Of course, well, I am tired, and my bones are aching, it will be a cold night for sure"

Phraan leaned back, he was getting hungry and knew that a thigh of a deer was being prepared as they were speaking. "Have there been any dragons sighted this far south yet?"

The old man shook his head. "No, but a week ago a group of people were seen heading east, they were clearly leaving everything behind for they carried little and were in a hurry. If it is as bad this time as the last time you will meet more, believe me"

The old man gestured towards two of his friends and they lifted him and carried him off after he thanked profusely for the wine, he would probably sleep rather well that night. The group fell rather silent until the food was ready, Phraan couldn't believe that these legends were true but in some way they did make sense. If there was a sort of barrier up there, and it was breached by someone with ill intent it explained why there hadn't been any dragons around for decades. He didn't want to believe but something about the whole thing was tugging at his mind and he couldn't find any real rest.

The next morning Oham was nowhere to be found as they were hitching up the wagons, he had been given the task of tidying up after the camp and that meant digging dirt over the fireplaces, folding up any tents and watering the horses. Vitile was ready to blow a fuse, she had hid the wine they transported very well and it hadn't been touched so he hadn't been raiding that supply but he was nowhere near the camp. If he went too far away from them the spell would kick inn and kill him and so he couldn't be further away than the village and Dhokay and Kapha went to look for him. They did find him after just a short search, in the village blacksmith's forge. He was lying next to a pile of coal moaning and clutching a jar of something to his chest, refusing to let go. The man was pale, sweating and in obvious pain so Dhokay didn't do anything to him except giving the wide rump a formidable kick.

The blacksmith did show up and he was wide eyed and staring at the convict. "Akhi curse it, what the fuck is he doing here?"

Dhokay bowed his head. "I am sorry, but this convict is a drunkard and it appears that he has entered your home in pursuit of booze. We are trying to sober him up"

The blacksmith sighed. "Well, he has done it then, there is alcohol in that jar but it is not drinkable, it is a liquid I use to dissolve hooves and stuff to make glue"

Kapha cringed. "And he has been drinking that stuff? No wonder he looks like shite, come on, let's get him back to the carriages, we need to get going"

The blacksmith still looked shocked and Dhokay handed over a couple of coins. "Here, for the stuff he drank. "

The blacksmith stared at the coins with even bigger eyes as they dragged Oham out of the forge. The man was whimpering and clutching his belly and Vitile glared at him as Dhokay dropped the man into one of the carriages like he was a bag of beans. "He has been drinking something the blacksmith uses, to make glue."

Phraan walked over and heard and he winced. "Then the poor sod is done for, it is eating away at his guts as we speak."

Kapha didn't look too sad to hear that. "Oh, too bad then. How long will it take?"

Phraan took a deep breath. "A couple of hours, most. It is very strong."

Vitile was cussing and she mixed some herbs and poured some wine into the cup. "Here, drink this"

The man grasped the cup and drank it greedily, the wine was obviously more important than asking what the herbs would do. After a few moments he sort of snorted and fell asleep and Vitile grimaced. "He'll sleep now, until the end. I don't want a groaning screaming writhing heap of rotting flesh to scare the horses"

Phraan grinned. "Wise decision, are everybody else ready?"

Shaluun nodded. "Yes, we can go"

They mounted their horses and got the convoy on the move, Phraan felt angry and disappointed too but most of all he was stunned by the fact that Oham was so desperate for alcohol he drank something like that. It had to taste absolutely horribly and burn too, on the way down. Perhaps years of drinking whatever he could lay his hands upon had destroyed the man's sense of taste, that could be the answer.

They had one small stop in the middle of the day and they left Oham's body with a small group of white wanderers they came across. The travelling monks were willing to bury the body for a small shilling each and they would pray for the man too, Dhokay did insist that this wouldn't be needed but they wouldn't listen to that. They prayed for everyone, whoever they had been. Phraan had often come across these small groups and he did respect them a lot. The white wanderers did leave everything behind whence they joined that faith, even their own name. All they owned was the white cloak they wore and a staff and they had to beg for food. But they were surprisingly happy and he had never heard any of them raising their voice or even speak ill of anyone so perhaps there was something to it after all. Peter was asking a lot of questions regarding dragons and Kapha was answering willingly. The man had sort of thawed over the last days and he was in fact rather charming.

They met the first group of refugees ten days later, in a river valley where they stopped to let the horses drink. It was perhaps fifty people and most was women and children with a few elderly men following them. Phraan had seen that before, the village had probably been attacked and the men had tried to fight back and gotten killed. These were the lucky survivors and they did confirm his assumption. The village had burned, and most of the inhabitants had died. The survivors had survived simply because they had been by the river to fish and wash clothes when the dragons came and they had been sort of forgotten by the beasts. Dhokay did ask what they had seen and judging from the statements the attack had been swift and very determined. It had been long tails, probably ten of them and they had left a smoldering ruin in shorter time than it would take to run across a ball field. Phraan felt a bit eager as they moved forth, they were closing in on their prey now and had to be careful. He was sure that the first sighting of a dragon was just around the corner. There was just one real city in this region and it lay ahead of them now, it was called Mudwall and the name was very fitting for the walls surrounding it was made from dried mud from the river. The city wasn't large, barely a town the way the southerner's saw it and it had a small army camp. That was where they would set up their headquarters for now and Phraan just hoped that the commander of that camp was a decent person and not some jerk.

The city was crowded, a very bad move if there are dragons around and Phraan knew that people had forgotten what to do in situations like this. Spreading out was the best tactic you could use, not clumping together like these people were. The army camp lay just inside of the wall itself and was protected by an extra palisade made from logs. It wasn't much but it did look intimidating. The commander was an elderly officer who probably had some ancestors way south east for he had rather dark skin and was small and lithe. Luckily he was very polite and also very glad they were there and they were given an area of the camp which could be their own. There were only a hundred soldiers there now and there was space enough for ten times that many. The commander's name was Janok and he was born just after the last time the dragons were a problem so he didn't remember much, only the work to rebuild the land after the years of terror. Phraan did like him and was glad they had met someone willing to cooperate. Some officers were so sure of their own power they refused to listen to anyone but themselves.

They spent the evening and the night arranging the camp and when the morning light did spread across the skies everybody were tired and also excited. This was where they would start and Phraan went to ask Janok if they had seen any dragons nearby. The answer didn't surprise him at all, several villages had been burned, including the one whose surviving inhabitants they had met earlier on. Dragons had been seen flying off in the distance and the man did tell Phraan that a group of dragon slayers had arrived two weeks earlier and travelled northwards towards the villages along the river. Nobody had heard from them ever since. Phraan took a deep breath, it had to be Waslav's group, it couldn't be any other and they did need to check things out and see how the situation was so his decision was to seek them out. If they were dead Phraan would know that they were on their own.

Vitile wasn't that willing to leave the city yet, she thought that they needed more information but Dhokay did agree with Phraan. They ought to ride out and see if that other group had encountered any dragons and two riders are not a target most dragons will bother with. So Phraan and Dhokay did leave the camp that morning and rode north following the tracks of that other group.

The change from the last time was grand, Phraan had been all over the region back then and he was shocked to see how bad things were. This land was in serious trouble even without the dragons. Dhokay was using his eyes for all they were worth and they had been riding for less than two hours when they saw the first signs of dragons. A field of cabbages had been transformed into a bog with debris spread everywhere and Phraan had to cough, the stench from dragon droppings is intense and nauseating and this was worse than he could remember. Dhokay did almost throw up and the horses were nervous and hard to control. Dragons do defecate when they land to eat and the feces do spread disease and leaves the very soil barren for years. This field would have to be left undisturbed for years to come. Dhokay did seem a bit on the thoughtful side as they rode on, he was fidgeting with his braid and his eyes were distant. "Those tracks back there, I didn't recognize them"

Phraan frowned. "No? They were long tail tracks?"

The blue haired male shook his head. "No, long tails have three toes on their feet, these had three toes on their front feet but four on their back legs."

Phraan cussed. "Oh Akhi, I didn't see that, I was focusing on the number of tracks"

Dhokay nodded. "So was I at first, old habits die hard. They were seven, very large too. "

Phraan took a deep breath. "Alright, then we do know that, that is at least something"

Dhokay did look worried. "Yes, but the change? I don't like it, I simply don't"

Phraan didn't say anything , he just rode on and that evening they did rest in an abandoned barn. They didn't go anywhere near the villages which had been attacked already, they were too far away for that but they did see groups of people on the run. At least the inhabitants of the area had the wits to leave before the situation became too serious. The last time many had refused to listen to common sense and had stayed for too long and paid with their lives. They didn't want to believe that there were dragons attacking farms and villages and that was understandable for dragons had been naught but a fairy tale for way longer than the realm had existed.

On the third day they reached the river and started following it northwards, and Phraan immediately knew that something had changed indeed. They found a farm which had been attacked and there wasn't anything left at all. Just blackened rocks told where the buildings had been and a few scorched sheep carcasses were spread around but everything else had been burned completely. This looked deliberate, like the work of someone set on destruction more than the random attacks of a hungry animal. The dragons had been desperate with hunger the last time, eating everything they came across, they didn't really bother that much with inedible things like buildings and such and used the flames to get to people and animals more easily. This was nothing like it, it was in a way unnatural.

They found the camp of the other slayers early the next day, Dhokay saw smoke and they rode hard along the river bank and what they saw did not come as a great shock at all. There were just a handful of men left, terrified and confused and most of all unable to make any decisions without their leader. They were in short pathetic and they had assembled around a small fire and sat there shivering. They had only a couple of pack horses left and no equipment and a few were wounded. Phraan sighed and slowed Drake down, the men heard the sound of hooves and did turn around, frightened that these were a new danger. Dhokay swore, they were perhaps eleven or twelve and from the looks of it most were servants. Phraan stopped the horse and stared at them. "So, where is your brave and expert leader?"

One of the men came forth, he was pale and shivering. "Dead, they are all....dead!"

Dhokay tilted his head and dismounted, the huge gelding he rode snorted and pawed the ground. "What happened, tell us quick."

The men sat down, looking like dogs which have been flogged. "We arrived at the village up the river and set up camp. They had seen some dragons the day before, greybacks they called them. There was this old woman there, she said they were different, that we shouldn't try to attack but just help people leave."

Dhokay frowned. "Different?"

The man nodded. "Yes, she said they were larger, faster. She was old, and they said her memories were fading away. Waslav wanted to get started so we left, to find them."

Phraan sighed. "Let me guess, it didn't go so well?"

The man gasped. "No, oh gods,I…I was so scared, I pissed myself man, like a child!"

Dhokay grinned. "That is the normal reaction to have yes, when faced with a dragon for the first time."

The man tried to smile but his eyes were haunted. "Really? Oh Gods, it was…a nightmare!"

Phraan looked at the man with narrow eyes. "Explain please. "

The poor human stared at the ground, almost panting. "I was the squire of lord Selegan, one of Waslav's friends. We had arrows and pikes and we were so sure of ourselves. Waslav did know how to kill these things, it would be alright, we were so sure that we would return as heroes. I was the only one who came back, for my horse did bolt on me and I couldn't control him so I fell into the river and that saved my life."

Dhokay looked at Phraan who looked back, eyes half closed. "Arrows and pikes? By the mother goddess, that is truly foolish"

Phraan grimaced. "So, tell us what you did"

The squire trembled. "We arrived at a field where there had been cattle grazing, there were none there now for even the bones had been eaten and there were five dragons there, huge monsters, I have never seen anything that terrible before. Waslav….he did charge, at the one which was closest to us. He had a lance, but it didn't penetrate the skin of the beast at all, it just skidded off and the beast…it just knocked him and his horse over with a swing of its tail and then it burned him. I can still hear the screams. The other dragons attacked the rest of us and I was at the back of the group, that was when my horse ran off and I have never been so grateful it was skittish before."

Phraan looked down, jaws clenched and fire in his gaze. "A waste of lives, but I expected this much, he was a fool"

The squire whimpered. "The dragons came for the village later that day, we could do nothing. A few tried to help and were killed on the spot and a few of us got burned. We have been stuck here since then, waiting for death. We don't dare to leave the river"

Phraan felt confused. "You said five dragons? Large ones?"

The man nodded. "Yes, one had some red markings on its head"

Dhokay was gaping. "Red markings? Are you sure?"

The man nodded. "Yes, I saw it good. It was that dragon which killed Waslav."

Phraan had stiffened up, staring at the human, his mind was reeling. "Dhokay, a female! And the males weren't fighting over her!"

The tall Luptay nodded. "Impossible, they should have torn each other apart! What is happening?"

The squire whimpered. "Please, do not leave us here, we have no idea of where to go, the dragons…"

Phraan sighed. "You have four horses, put the wounded onto them and you do still have legs don't you? Follow the river, it runs south. You will come to a village eventually. We cannot baby sit you, we need to get moving"

The man almost wept but did nod. "I hear you, may the gods watch over you, for these beasts…they are true evil!"

Phraan mounted Drake again and Dhokay got back onto his own steed, both were grim as they made their horses gallop back towards the city. A female dragon among a herd of males like that? It was unheard of, impossible. Something had to have changed indeed. They rode hard that day and found a road leading in the direction of the city, followed that. This night they didn't stop to rest, they just let the horses trot slowly for an elf can sleep in the saddle and the horses were strong and could handle it rather well. The sun was rising again when

Phraan did see something on the horizon, at first he was afraid it was dragons, then he saw it was ravens and other scavengers and it was a huge flock of them. "Over there, see?"

Dhokay shielded his eyes from the sun, his race had much better eyesight in low light conditions than an elf but strong light was a problem for them. "Something dead?"

Phraan gave Drake free reins. "Yes, let us investigate!"

They crossed a smaller creek and some Holts of thin forest and then they reached another road, one well used and they did see a huge building in the distance, it seemed to be a sort of mansion with a wall around it. Several dead people lay scattered along the road, some dead horses too and a small carriage which was crushed to smithereens. The mansion had burned, it was rather obvious and Phraan gaped when he saw the thing laying on the ground next to a huge rock. It was a dragon and it was dead! "Dhokay!"

The blue haired male gasped and they rode over, very carefully. Neither of them had seen a dragon like this before, and the sight was sickening. It was as if someone had taken several species of dragon and molded them into one and the ground around the beast seemed to have been transformed into a glass like substance. The dragon was burned, but not by any fire they had encountered. The place did reek of something strange and Phraan felt how the hairs stood up at the back of his neck. Dhokay suddenly pointed at a rock a few meters ahead of the dragon, someone laid up against it and at first they had believed it to be a dead person but Phraan saw that he moved. It was a very young man, with a handsome face and deep auburn hair and he was breathing and moaning as if in agony. Phraan jumped from the horse and ran over, lifted the man gently and let him rest against his chest. The man wore a black and red uniform and Phraan frowned. He had seen it before but didn't remember where. "It is the uniform of the ones working at the academy of magic in Oakfell."

Phraan took a look at the man's hand, he wore a ring but it wasn't a magician's ring and he didn't quite understand this. Dhokay stared at the dead dragon. "Look? The jaws, and the legs, yes, everything! I cannot even begin to describe it!"

Phraan swallowed. "I know, we are in trouble my friend. This is something new"

He took a quick peek at the monster, the head was clearly that of a rock jaw but it had the spikes of a spike back and it appeared to have both fire and poison? The liquid slowly oozing from the glands at the back of the mouth was clearly poison. The body shape was like that of a greyback, but it did have wings like a long tail and yet it was armored and it was larger than a greyback, almost twice the normal size. Dhokay was hoarse. "It has the legs of an iron wolf, that makes it fast, and look, the belly. It too is armored, as on a steel belly"

Phraan swallowed hard. "Dhokay, I am starting to believe those legends."

The tall male sat down onto his haunches. "Me too, so, what is wrong with this lad? He isn't burned"

Phraan laid a finger over the jugular, the heart was beating steadily but the lad was burning hot and trembling and there was a lump at the back of his head, as if he had fallen backwards and hit his head on the rock. "He seems to be knocked out, short and simple. The others here are dead tough."

Dhokay got back up, looked at the corpses one by one. Most were severely burned but one of them, a young boy appeared to have been crushed. "They were trying to flee the mansion, they were probably a noble man's family"

Phraan lifted the young man and felt an odd chill run down his spine. He was the only one alive and the dragon had died before it had time to harm him? This had to be investigated, they had to bring the man with them. He got back up onto Drake and Dhokay lifted the man up, Phraan held him against his chest as he spurred the horse. Soon they rode as fast as they dared and the lad was moaning again and writhing. Phraan held him tightly and the body jerked and his eyes opened up, filled with terror and shock. Phraan made sure he couldn't fall off, the lad was trembling. "Dragon…"

Phraan felt him tremble. "Yes, but don't worry, it is dead. Who are you?"

The lad gasped. "Ivran, I am Ivran, I was escorting a student and…."

He trembled again and became limp and Phraan realized that the lad had passed out again, they needed to get him back to Vitile, the lad could know something important and Phraan didn't like the lump on his head at all. He sent Dhokay a stiff grin. "We stop for nobody, and ride until we are back"

Dhokay just nodded, it would be a wild ride but he was ready to defend Phraan and the lad with his life. He too felt that this human would be important. He leaned forth and let the huge horse have its head as they galloped over the plain, if they were in luck they would reach the city by nightfall.

Chapter 4: Fear itself

Ivran had always believed that goodness always will prevail, that you ought to do your very best and always be nice. After a few days on the road he had been ready to toss that notion to the wind for the lad was…obnoxious! Or rather, the most despicable person Ivran had ever come across. Nothing was good enough, nothing was right, he complained and whined and even at the inns did he tell his opinion, loudly, for everyone to hear. The beds were too hard, there were bedbugs in them, the food did reek of dead dragon, the wine was sour, the chambermaids ugly…The lad had made it a challenge to find things he could use as an excuse to piss people off and he was a master at it too. Ivran was cringing internally more than once and many of the inn keepers did throw him glances filled with silent sympathy. Josphu was hard to get out of bed in the morning and he refused to go to bed too, he was trying to flirt with the women present at the inns and got angry when they turned their backs on them and then he got nasty and used insults which would have made even a whore furious. Ivran feared that this would end in disaster. The academy did pay him well but not enough for this. Soon they left the area where the roads were good and the inns too became scares. They had to spend the nights out in the open and Ivran loved it, he loved the smell of fresh air, the wind in the trees and the stars up above. To him this was grand for Josphu was terrified of the dark. He crawled up close to the fire every night and Ivran could pretend to be alone, at least for most of the time. Josphu was no rider and so he got saddle sores rather fast which had to be taken care off and he did also catch a cold and insisted that he was dying. Ivran just scoffed, as long as he managed to stay warm it wasn't so bad, they had good clothes and capes and the weather wasn't too bad.

They had ridden for a couple of weeks when they heard the rumors about dragons, at first Ivran was rather sure that it was just a lie but after a while he started to understand that it was true indeed, there were dragons up north once more and they were heading in that direction. It was enough to make him nervous but for many days they didn't see anything which indicated danger. Josphu just snorted when someone talked about dragons, he openly claimed that it was a whole lot of bullshit and Ivran would have agreed if he hadn't had this little nagging feeling at the back of his head telling him to watch out. The trading city Josphu came from was not very large, it was more of a small gathering of buildings placed at the foot of a hill and Ivran was so relieved when he saw it. He was sure it was over now. He could deliver the boy to his parents and return to the academy, hopefully right away. The boy's parents lived in a rather nice house in the middle of the city and they were greeted by the head of the servants who informed that Josphu's parents had gone north to visit their summer mansion and that Josphu was to join them. Ivran was close to exploding, he would have to spend at least yet another week with this brat?!

But there was no doubt about the fact that there were dragons around yet again, people did flee and many spoke of burned farms and villages and Ivran was scared, he had to admit that. But he was no coward, he had promised to deliver the lad to his parents so he tried to keep his word. They rode on the next morning and for once Josphu didn't complain, he was clearly eager to see his mother again and Ivran did think that this little thing at least made the boy a wee bit more likeable. They didn't see any dragons while heading northwest, Ivran just saw smoke upon the horizon a few times but that could be caused by many things really. They reached the mansion late in the evening and they had met a few local farmers who were heading south now, claiming that there were dragons spreading southwards and that they were unstoppable. Ivran didn't listen, he was just eager to fulfill the mission. The mansion wasn't large but it had a good masonry wall and it was a luxurious place. To his surprise the parents of this brat were nice people and did welcome him. He would stay there for a couple of days so the horses could rest and then he would be heading back to the academy. Josphu didn't have any siblings and perhaps he had gotten spoiled but it was very clear that the lad was a very different boy when he was with his parents, much more polite and sweet and Ivran started to realize that the boy didn't like the academy at all. He was probably homesick and miserable and reacted in a very immature manner but who could really blame him?

Ivran was ready to go the next day when he was invited for a family dinner, he felt a bit out of his comfort zone for these people did eat rather well and they had very nice manners but he did make it through the whole evening without making any blunders, and he even flirted a little with one of the servants. When he went to bed that night he felt very pleased with himself and he wanted to thank the family the next morning before he left. He was grateful for the warm welcome and the nice dinner too. He hadn't even thought about the dream and this gift he supposedly had for weeks now and he felt just like an ordinary young man, alright, he hadn't made it to magician but there were other paths in life to pursue and after all, he had a good job now.

He woke up with a start, hearing screams and crashing sounds and he immediately knew that something was terribly wrong. He got up from the bed and threw his clothes on and stormed out of the bedroom. The hall was filled with panic stricken people, Josphu and his parents were standing there with wide eyes and Ivran smelled smoke. "What is happening?"

Josphu's father answered. "There is a dragon out there, my men are trying to lure it away. We have to flee, it will burn this house"

Ivran felt his heart drop, a dragon? Oh gods, what was he to do?

The servants came running. "The carriage is ready, hurry"

Ivran ran after the people, got a horse and threw himself onto it. The animal was rolling its eyes in fear and the carriage shot out of the gate the moment the driver let go of the brakes. There was a crash behind them and then flames did burst out of the building and a huge monstrous creature appeared. It had run straight through the wall. The driver was whipping the horses which ran as fast as they possibly could and before long they were way ahead of the dragon but Ivran turned around and saw that the huge beast in fact did fly! It took a few swift steps and was airborne and he heard that the people in the carriage screamed in panic. The dragon was catching up on them fast and Ivran had never seen anything that grotesque and terrifying. Then the beast opened its mouth and spewed flames and the horses pulling the carriage were engulfed by them and fell screaming. The carriage tipped over and Ivran saw that Josphu got thrown out, it was probably his father who tried to save his son. The dragon let loose yet another burst of flames and it engulfed the carriage completely.

Ivran gasped, he could ride away or he could try to help Josphu who tried to crawl away from the burning wagon. The horse made the choice for him, the animal did buck and Ivran didn't manage to stay on at all, he was bound for a rather unpleasant rendezvous with mother earth and he landed with a thud and a groan. He got up onto his knees just as the dragon landed on the remains of the carriage and it collapsed completely, at least there were no more screams. Ivran saw that Josphu tried to lay still, to play dead but the dragon seemed to know that he was alive for it licked its jaws and cocked its monstrous head. Ivran got back on his feet, leaned against a rock and tried to come up with an idea, any idea. He yelled, it was a mistake but he had no other option. "Hey, you bastard, I am here!"

The dragon saw him and if it was possible for such a beast to smirk it did, Ivran knew what evil truly was in that moment. The dragon did pounce like a cat, and it did deliberately place one massive foot on the boy, Ivran heard a crushing sound and something inside of him just snapped. He leaned back against the rock, shouting something he didn't even understand. The effect was shocking, he was thrown backwards as if he was hit by something heavy and then an immense ball of blue fire formed in front of him and it crashed into the dragon with a sizzling sound. He felt the heat from it but it wasn't the heat you feel from ordinary flames, no, this was a heat which felt almost cold since it was of a different nature than fire and the dragon shrieked. It was a most horrible sound and Ivran felt his head bang against the rock as he went down. Everything seemed to move in slow motion as he fell. The dragon clawed at its own chest, blue flames seemed to burst out of it, as if it was being filled with them and then it fell. I have killed a dragon…That was the last thought he had as darkness overcame him, he just hoped that he would live.

Phraan and Dhokay did rush into the small city at dusk, by then their horses were close to exhaustion and even the mighty Drake was heaving for air and barely able to keep his pace. Phraan stopped the horse in front of the tents they were using and some of the carriage drivers came running to take care of the horses. Phraan jumped down and dragged the unconscious boy with him. "The horses have been ridden very hard, walk them for a while and rub them with cold water and don't let them drink anything cold, I don't want them to get sick"

The drivers did know how to handle horses and nodded and Phraan carried the young man to the tent where Vitile and the forest elves stayed. Rhuk and Dabin came running having heard the hooves and they stared at the man Phraan was carrying. "Who is that?"

Phraan didn't stop. "A survivor from a dragon attack, he saw something I think, or did something"

Vitile and the two others were busy playing cards and just gaped as Phraan stormed inn, Vitile got to her feet and Phraan laid the young man down onto one of the simple beds. "He survived a dragon attack, the dragon laid dead in front of him, and we do need to talk. Something has changed since the last time"

Vitile bent down and put a finger onto the human's neck. "He is most certainly alive but drained, I cannot explain it otherwise"

Phraan frowned. "Drained? What do you mean?"

Vitile turned her gaze towards him, her eyes were large. "His light, it is almost extinguished, it is as if…he has used all of it, in one go"

Phraan was still confused. "I don't understand?"

Vitile sighed. "Look, the soul is energy, and that energy is stronger than you can possibly imagine. It is the power which magicians use to empower their spells, the energy that drives the very life itself in us all. It seems as if he has sort of used that energy for something, without being able to control it at all."

Phraan stared at the young man. "The dead dragon, he killed it, he fucking killed it!"

Vitile frowned. "He isn't a mage?"

Phraan shook his head. "No, look at his ring, he is an employee at the academy, no magician. Nobody should be able to kill a dragon like that, with magic. It is…unheard of"

Vitile nodded. "Yes, they are magical beasts in nature, immune to magical attacks for some reason, but you said things had changed?"

Phraan shrugged, his face contorted by doubt. "Yes, from what I and Dhokay saw we are in trouble. Is the man going to be okay?"

Vitile looked a bit uncertain. "Yes, but he has a bad concussion, I will make him sleep through it, a deep sleep without dreams. He will heal but his head will hurt for a while"

Phraan sighed. "Good, gather the others, we need to discuss this!"

Half an hour later the whole group was gathered in the large tent at the center of their camp. There was room for everybody there and it was silent, so silent you could have heard a flea fart. Kapha stared at Phraan with disbelief. "Are you feckin' telling me that the dragons have evolved? Over just a few decades?"

Phraan looked down, he nodded slowly. "No, I don't think they have evolved but they have been changed. The first dragons we saw fifty years ago were an experiment I think, a test. They tried to check what sort of dragon would be most efficient and now, now they have put that knowledge to use"

Shaluun was leaning against one of the tent poles, his eyes were narrow. "That means that someone indeed is behind all of this, someone with very ill intent. It cannot be coincidental? That the weak dragons were forced to leave back then and that the strong ones are coming forth now? Fifty years to a dragon is like fifty years to us elves, just a blink of an eye after all"

Phraan bit his lower lip. "Oh I hope you are right, but my guts tell me that I am right."

Kapha frowned and the two dwarves did look worried. "Then what do we do? What can be done to fight these new horrors?"

Vitile looked a bit nervous. "Look, they are dragons right? And they must have some weaknesses, we just have to discover them, like we did back then"

Phraan looked down, he swallowed hard. "I didn't see any Vitile, it is as if…I cannot put it into words but whoever has created them, they have learned from their mistakes and corrected them. Those dragons were like several species merged into one from what we were told, every weakness removed. And the dead one? It was…a true monster"

Vitile swallowed visibly. "So have we come in vain? Is there nothing we can do?"

Dhokay shook his head, the horns almost touched the canvas. "Of course there are things we can do, and we have not come in vain, we have to try. But we do need more information, and I fear that the job will be so much harder now"

The wood elves did stare at each other and they did look worried and the dwarves too didn't look as if they liked this piece of news particularly much. Fastonar had been quiet the whole time, now he did step forth and he did look rather grim. "Let us for a moment say that Phraan is right, that someone indeed has changed the dragons somehow and that they now have become much harder to fight. Then let us consider what we do know about dragons, can it at all be done? I mean, dragons breed slowly and grow slowly, fifty years is nothing, as Shaluun said"

Phraan sighed. "I know, it does sound incredible doesn't it? You cannot change that many dragons that fast, unless those we encountered back then were failures?"

Fastonar did look less than convinced still "I cannot say that I buy that explanation at all, there was nothing about them which was faulty the way I see it. Yes, we did kill a heck of a lot of them but nobody is going to tell me it was easy, for it bloody wasn't!"

Dhokay tilted his head. "No, it wasn't! Could this be some new species perhaps? One we simply haven't seen before?"

Phraan felt a surge of relief rushing through him. "Yes, yes, that is in fact logical. It could be that these dragons did chase the others out of the territories and now they have become too many and has to expand their realm"

Vitile sent him a small smile. "That has to be it yes, I have seen that before, the stronger species does push the weaker one away!"

Shaluun looked thoughtful, he was playing with his knife and his eyes were dark. "Then we are indeed facing something new, something terrible. And our old methods may be worth nothing at all"

The two dwarves did look even more worried now and Taurin and Thiana did exchange some hidden glances. Neither of these four had hunted dragons before and that meant that their chances were slim if they were to actively go up against the beasts. Vitile made a gesture towards the exit of the tent. "The young man Phraan and Dhokay brought in, he may have killed one of those beasts, but the goddess alone knows how!"

Shaluun tilted his head, the beautiful face was showing a great deal of disbelief. "A human? And he is not a powerful wizard? Then I say that dragon died of some other cause, perhaps it had a weak heart? After all, they are flesh and blood"

Phraan had to snort. "A dragon with a weak heart? Are you nuts? It would have been dead decades ago, no, I am pretty sure the young man has something to do with it and I intend to find out what! Everybody else there were dead, he was alive. That means something!"

Kapha frowned. "I agree, it has to mean something."

Fastonar just sighed and raised his arms. "Great, fine, do ask the lad when he wakes up. In the meantime I am going to interview people and ask them whether or not they have seen something, something useful"

He threw his cape on and rushed out and Phraan frowned. It wasn't like Fastonar to be that brusque. Vitile touched his arm gently. "He is under a great deal of stress dear, don't forget that. He is probably afraid he will disappoint the king, and his calling"

Phraan tried to smile. "Of course. But I still don't like this situation, we thought this was gonna be like the good old days right? Now it seems as if everything has changed, who has ever heard of a herd of dragons containing a female?"

Vitile nodded slowly. "I have to admit that it sounds very odd, back in the days the dragon males would kill each other if there was a female nearby, simply to prove they were the stronger one. Could this new species be different somehow?"

Phraan snapped his fingers. "That could be it, we need that dead dragon, before the scavengers do their job!"

He rushed out of the tent too and Vitile stood there and looked confused and a wee bit angry too. Kapha patted her back. "Don't worry dear. He has gotten an idea, and when Phraan has an idea you might as well try to make the great river flow backwards, he won't rest until he has satisfied his curiosity."

Dhokay grinned widely. "Oh I do know him you know, the only thing I wonder about is how he plans on transporting that beast back here, are there wagons strong enough to take that weight?"

Vitile just rolled her eyes. "No, he will go back there, and I am gonna follow him, for I want to see this beast with my own eyes"

Dhokay sighed. "Put the brakes on him please, our horses are exhausted and I want a meal, sleep and a hot bath before I go anywhere"

Vitile nodded and ran outside, Phraan was talking to one of the minor officers there and was visibly upset by the lack of wagons. She walked over and he saw her, frowned. "There are no wagons here we can use"

She had to grin, his face showed an almost childlike disappointment. "Listen, we'll all go there tomorrow, we all want to see that beast and believe me, if it is as large as you say no wagon or anything can move it. But now you need food and rest and to be absolutely honest you do also need a bath, you reek!"

Phraan sniffed himself, blinked. "Ah, yes, you are right, I do stink."

She grabbed him by the hand. "Let's go then, bath, food, and rest. And no trip anywhere until tomorrow, got it?"

He nodded and followed her obediently. He saw it now, he was too impulsive, too eager. He failed to take himself and his own wellbeing into consideration. Vitile went to check up on the young man and Phraan found the tent where the soldiers got their food. Dhokay was already there, and he grinned and raised a jug of ale. Since they were sent there by the king it meant that they could use everything the army had of resources, including the food. "This is good stuff, better than the ale they serve at many inns"

Phraan sat down and nodded. "The soldiers who serve at these posts do get some extra treatment, to compensate for the fact that they are placed in the middle of nowhere"

A servant came with two trays and there was food on both of them, huge bowls of stew, bread, cheese and a sort of porridge Phraan never had seen before. Dhokay sniffed his bowl with suspicion and the servant smiled. "It is made from a new sort of grain they imported from the Far East, when it started to get so dry and cold. It can handle that way better than the wheat"

Phraan took a tentative spoonful and was positively surprised, it did taste rather good. Dhokay didn't look so impressed. The servant continued. "The farmers have had to change their produce these last years, the cattle farmers have started to farm sheep instead and the tribes who made their living following the herds of lump backs have travelled south, the herds cannot find enough of the lichens they feed upon anymore."

Phraan shrugged, the lump backs were huge short legged animals with a huge lump in the middle of their backs, very long coats and short stumpy horns. The meat was dry and not very good but the hairs they shed twice a year could be transformed into some extremely nice cloth. Dhokay went for the stew instead and the two ate in silence. The ale was strong, in fact the strongest ale Phraan had tasted in an army camp and he was a bit shocked by that. A human being would be royally drunk just from drinking a few cups of this and a soldier should after all at least try to be sober in case of an emergency. The place was probably so peaceful nobody gave a damn about that fact anymore, it told Phraan that the soldiers there probably were unprepared for battle, and unable to react the way they ought to in case of an attack. He finished the food and felt completely stuffed, afterwards he and Dhokay went to the bath, it was a tent placed on its own and it was rather special for it had a stone wall built around the base and the canvas was very thick. A huge boiler was built on the outside of it and pipes did lead the hot water into the tent where several tubs were placed in a row, separated by sheets. Buckets of cold water stood by each tub and you regulated the temperature by using that cold water, simple and efficient. Phraan liked his bathwater hot, and he didn't use much cold water but Dhokay preferred a cooler temperature and did scrub himself a little before entering the tub. His race was famous for their cleanliness and some were almost hysterical when it came to dirt and stains. They did see cleanliness as a proof of goodliness and someone who didn't bother washing was someone they wouldn't trust. Back in the days even Dhokay had been filthy at times but he was the first to take a bath when the fighting was over, even if it meant plunging into a frigid river.

Phraan did enjoy the bath, it made him relax and made his thoughts clearer and he saw now that Vitile was right, they all ought to go to learn more about that beast. The skin was tough, the scavengers wouldn't be able to do any real damage until it had started to rot and that would take weeks in this cold weather. He was pleasantly tired when he found his tent and went to bed. An elf doesn't need to sleep as much as a human but the hard ride and all the things which had happened had taken their toll of him. He was asleep the moment his head hit the pillow.

Ivran woke up with a splitting headache and a feeling of utter confusion, then he remembered and yelped. He was in a tent, a very ordinary one with dark canvas and a narrow cot of a bed. He was wrapped in army blankets and there as a smell of horse and people there, and a lot of sounds. He tried to get up but got dizzy right away and he blinked. The dragon, he had killed a dragon! And he could remember sitting in front of someone on a ridiculously tall horse, what had happened? He closed his eyes, oh gods his head hurt! He heard a sound and opened his eyes again, a very tall women had entered the tent and he gaped. She was an elf, and she was very pretty and seemed to be friendly. She wore a hunter's garbs and had several knives placed in her belt and across her back and she wore her long hair in a tight braid. She sat down on a chair next to the cot with elegant movements. Ivran had hardly met any elves before, he had no idea of what to say. "How do you feel young human? Phraan said your name is Ivran?"

Ivran nodded. "Yes my lady, that is correct"

She reached out and placed a cool hand on his forehead. "You survived a dragon attack, do you remember anything? Phraan and another one of us found you and brought you back here, you are in the city of Mudwall, in the army camp"

Ivran felt a shudder go through him, what could he really say. "Uh, I remember…the dragon, it killed everyone"

She frowned, her eyes were so incredibly clear and shiny and Ivran felt as if she could stare straight into his very soul and see his every though "And yet you are alive, with a concussion but nothing worse than that"

Ivran swallowed hard. "Uh, I bet I am in luck"

She sighed. "In luck indeed, you ought to be roasted but you were spared, that is very unusual. Rest now, you have a head injury and shouldn't move for a few days, we will talk later"

Ivran felt his head spin. "Who are you people really?"

The she elf bowed her head. "I am Vitile, we are dragon slayers, or rather, we were dragon slayers. Now we don't know anymore, the dragons have changed apparently, gotten bigger and more vicious, more dangerous."

Ivran felt his palms go sweaty. "They have? "

She nodded. "A servant will bring you food and drink, do not leave the bed until I get back"

He blinked, oh it was blasted how his head hurt. "Back? From where?"

She smiled. "We are gonna take a look at the dragon which attacked you and your friends, maybe we can find out more about it, it has to be some new species we haven't seen before"

He swallowed hard, could they discover anything then? Like what had killed it? He hoped not! "O…okay, I will stay in bed"

She leaned forth, laid her hand on his head and most of the pain did disappear." Here, this ought to do it right? Rest, we will talk later"

Ivran laid back, grateful and a bit shocked. He knew that elves could heal others but this was in fact rather astonishing. But talk? Could he just slip out of the tent and run off before they returned? He didn't want them to know what he had done, what he had been given. Some instinct told him not to trust anyone. The she elf left the tent and Ivran knew that he needed at least a day of rest, perhaps even more. He groaned and tried to find a comfortable position, this would be some very long hours indeed.

Phraan did wake up to the smell of tea, Vitile always brewed this special type which smelled and tasted just wonderful and he blinked and sat up. She was by his bed and handed over a hot cup which he accepted with gratitude. "I checked on the human, he is recovering rather well, but something fishy is going on. He didn't explain why he survived, appeared to prefer not to."

Phraan took a sip of tea, oh gods, it did taste divine. "You think he is hiding something?"

Vitile nodded. "I am sure he is hiding something, the question is what. The ring says he is an employee right? He is not a magician then, but what if he has somehow learned something back there, something he shouldn't?"

Phraan cocked his head, the tea did wonders, he felt almost reborn. "Are you suggesting that he has picked up some spell and tried it on that dragon? With such results?"

Vitile nodded "Got a better explanation?"

He groaned. "Vitile, he is a human being, his magic cannot be that strong, even if he was a magician. If he was say an Oolishan elf it would be possible for even an untrained person to use a simple spell but by the Goddess Vitile, an untrained human being uttering a spell able to kill a dragon? The lad would be just as fried as the dragon was, or worse, completely obliterated!"

She looked down. "I am not that familiar with humans Phraan, I am sorry"

He smiled. Tried to look as if he did understand her way of thinking. "Listen, nobody, not even the greatest of mages are capable of doing that, yes, we do need a mage to ward off fire but magic cannot kill dragons, we have seen that before haven't we?"

She nodded. "Arakhar yes, he tried, and failed! "

Phraan sat up and yawned. "Exactly, and we all know that he was among the strongest magicians of all time, a man with a strength which comes only once a thousand years, and he was blessed in every manner."

She handed him his boots and he pulled them on with a groan. "Yes, he was blessed, but what if it wasn't the lad himself but something he carried? Some magical object perhaps?"

Phraan finished the tea, it left a pleasant warmth in his belly. "Vitile, he didn't have anything on him, just his clothes. There was no trace of anything of a magical nature there"

She sighed, looked disappointed. "Then what did kill that dragon?"

Phraan got up and patted her back. "That is what we are supposed to find out now, are the others ready?"

She nodded slowly, looking uncertain. "Yes, they are just waiting for you. Get some food, and some warm clothes, it is a very cold day."

Phraan found an extra thick tunic and an extra cloak and then he grabbed some bread and cheese from the cantina and ran to the area where the horses were kept. His stallion and Dhokay's gelding were sore after the hard ride so they had to rest, instead Phraan was given a very tall black mare with a fierce temper and Dhokay got a stocky brown gelding who looked as if it was contemplating taking a bite out of anyone who dared to get near its head. Phraan was in an odd mood, the young man did know something, he had to, maybe the carcass would reveal the secret after all. It would take them this day and most of the next to reach the mansion again and that left them all with plenty of time to think. The weather was rather good but a cold wind did howl around them and everybody did pack their cloaks tight around themselves. The horses became skittish from the wind and so there wasn't much conversation going on, most had enough with their steeds and the cold.

The faces gathered around the table did speak of a great deal of disbelief, and also a huge dose of anger, none of them had ever heard of anything like that. "It is impossible! There has never been anyone capable of such a deed, it has to be some sort of misunderstanding?"

The man speaking was rather short and his elegant robes did tighten more than a little around his middle. The rounded face was red and he was sweating profusely, walking up the stairs to the chamber was something he preferred not to do but this time there hadn't been a choice at all. "I assure you my brothers, it is no misunderstanding and no mistake. It is dead!"

The tall man with the elegant goatee and thick black hair was looking at the crowd the way a father looks at a bunch of belligerent children, with some concern but also with understanding. "I know it is hard to comprehend here and now but it is a fact, and it wasn't killed by any slayer"

Another man did speak up. "Then what? They were supposed to be invincible!"

The tall man shook a finger. "There there, nothing is invincible, we all know that, but the concern is that the high mage felt a huge magical discharge when that dragon's energy disappeared. It was killed by magic and we do need to know how that is possible and even more pressing is it to know who the killer was"

Everybody stared at each other, they were seven men there not including the leader and they all looked shocked. "Not possible, dragons are immune to magical weapons, and spells. It is in their nature, our foregoers did take every precaution when they were created"

An elderly man with thin white beard and beady eyes was waving his hands, he did look upset. The tall leader smiled. "Yes they did, so if this indeed was a magical weapon it is something our forefathers didn't know anything about, and that means that it can be a threat to us all."

The first man who spoke frowned. "Then what are we to do?"

The leader cocked his head. "Don't worry, we do have a servant in that area, an associate of mine, and this person will find the reason why the dragon died and if the reason is a person either bring him here to us or kill him. We cannot have anyone running around who is capable of ruining our plans now can we?"

They all mumbled in agreement and the fat man sort of grimaced. "Let us hope that this servant is capable then, we cannot afford any mistakes "

The leader smirked. "Worry not my brothers, the servant is very skilled. Soon we will reclaim what was ours, and the world will bend to our will"

There was some cheers heard but then a thin voice could be heard through the racket, a tiny man came forth carrying a thick book and he was so old he seemed to be almost transparent. "But the omen brother, the omen!"

The leader shrugged. "Badrian, I have said this before and yes, I am saying it again. Those old scriptures are worthless, mumbo jumbo, they were written by ignorant fools who knew naught! Let it rest brother, it means nothing"

The old man bowed his head. "But the signs are all clear, a comet was seen, a white raven crossed the dark moon. The very source will awaken to the truth and then the forgotten one will come for us and with it…"

The leader raised a hand. "Silence!! I will not hear this again, to believe that there truly is something out there powerful enough to threaten our rule is ridiculous. The new dragons will not be stopped, no puny slayer can destroy the hordes which are to be released"

The old man put on a sour face. "I believe the texts brother, I believe in the words. The one who escaped will come and bring with her the one death loves and the one who is cursed. And the blood raining from the skies will be ours"

The leader nodded to a burly man standing by the entrance. "Sir Echard, escort brother Badrian back to his chambers, old age has smothered his wisdom and made him see phantoms"

Echard did grasp the old man rather brutally and he was dragging the man with him down the stairs. Badrian did curse loudly, swinging a fist. "You will bring doom upon us with you denial, her coming will mean that fate will unleash the beast!"

The leader just smirked and turned to the crowd again. "Forget about his ramblings, they are old wives tales, nothing more. The work of our forefathers have been fruitful and we will harvest what they did sow. Victory and glory will be ours."

The last words did echo through the great hall and then there was silence, a pleased and loaded silence. All they had to do was wait, and now the hour was getting closer by the day. Yes, the day of triumph was drawing near.

The leader didn't notice that the somewhat fat man stared at him with obvious contempt, he almost snarled. If Simaon was planning on investigating the strange incident he would make sure that nothing went wrong. Simaon was no mage, and he had little understanding of magic. But Arabur knew the old ways and he knew the risks and now he planned on visiting the high mage. If the so called leader indeed wanted to find the person responsible for the death of that dragon Arabur wanted to be sure that their lovely and oh so deadly new toys found that person first. They could take no chances now.

Phraan and the others did spend the night at an abandoned farm, they left by the first light of day and by noon they approached the mansion where they had found Ivran. Some ravens had found the bodies but as they rode closer to the dead dragon it was very apparent that the scavengers did stay clear of the dead monster. Phraan stopped his horse and the others just stared, with wide eyes. Vitile let out a gasp, "I see what you meant now, that is…not an ordinary long tail"

Phraan tried to smile, the beast did already stink but not as bad as one might expect, it was cold after all. Dhokay grasped his long knives. "Well. We'd better get at it then, Rhuk, Dabin, you both know how to use an axe I presume."

The beast lay there on its side and Shaluun started to walk around it, with slow steps. He did look very confused. "Oh my...look at those wings? And the claws?"

Rhuk was spitting. "Look at the size I say, are you saying we are gonna cut that beast open?"

Phraan grinned. "Yes, we have to see how much this animal has been changed, we have to find its weak spots"

Dhokay had already attacked its belly and he was trying to slice through the hide but couldn't, it was like trying to cut steel. "Look at this, it is too tough"

Kapha frowned. "Do as we used to, go inn through its asshole"

The animal's rear passage was right underneath its tail and Dhokay sighed deeply. "Alright, be aware, there could be some gas escaping"

He pried the knife into the tight muscle and with all of his might he just managed to nick it. He swore. "This thing is made from something incredibly tough, I can tell you that. My knives are razor sharp!"

Vitile nodded. "And yet it did die, look at its chest, it looks burned, or I don't know, transformed somehow?"

Phraan smiled. "You can check that end, I'll help Dhokay at this end and the rest of you, try to find a weak spot in the armor, use whatever you have"

He and Dhokay ended up using a spear and as soon as they started cutting from the inside out it went a little faster but it was still a terrible job. The dwarves went at it like mad and the axes proved to be very efficient, at least to some degree. Shaluun was fascinated by the head and kept examining it and Vitile was all over the odd burn. She couldn't quite understand what sort of flames this had to have been. Three stinking grueling hours later they had made enough of a cut to examine its inside and Phraan didn't quite believe what he saw. The animal was very different from the dragons of old, in many ways. Dhokay sighed and dropped some pieces of intestine on the ground. "Now we know why the males didn't fight over that female"

Vitile frowned and the two dwarves stared with narrow eyes, Taurin and Thiana hadn't seen a dragon before neither so they were obviously shocked. "Is that it's…"

Dhokay nodded. "Its balls yes, they are almost non existing. These males are in reality eunuchs!"

Phraan felt cold. "That isn't natural, that means that they have been manipulated"

Dhokay spat and Fastonar looked fascinated. "Sure looks like it, come to this end and take a look!"

He had been examining the long and spiky tail and they gathered, he pointed at the long curved spikes. "See? Those spikes are typical for a spike back, not a long tail"

Phraan nodded, his face grim. "Yes, Shaluun?"

The tall elf made a grimace. "It has the mouth armor of a rock jaw, and teeth like a storm fire. It truly is as if they have mixed several races together to create a superior one"

Vitile did pull her braid, it was something she only did when she was really upset for some reason. "Right, it looks almost as if the dragon burned from the inside out?! But that is impossible?"

Dhokay looked at her, his eyes did reveal that he was a bit puzzled by this. "From the inside? That is odd, but truly, we don't know how their fire is produced, it could perhaps be that we have seen the first case of self-combustion in a dragon?"

Phraan shook his finger at the tall luptay. "No, I don't buy that, Ivran has something to do with it, I am bloody sure!"

The dwarves looked eager. "But otherwise from the tiny balls it is like other dragons right? I mean, on the inside?"

Dhokay stared at Rhuk who was testing his axe on one of the dragon's toes, trying to cut it off. It was like trying to cut timber with a blunt axe, it just bounced off. "It looks normal yes, from the little we can see, it appears to have all the right organs and everything"

Vitile had attacked the burn now with her blades and the burned area was in fact crisp, it was easy to break through it and enter the chest cavity. She did cut her way and then she slowed down. "Guys? Look at this, have you seen anything like this before?"

The group gathered around her and stared and Phraan swallowed hard, in absolute shock. The heart of the beast was protected by a hard outer shell of bone, it looked like a huge bone ball!

Fastonar was gaping. "That is…fucking amazing!"

Shaluun shook his head. "More like fucking terrifying if you ask me, but it is dead so what killed it?"

Vitile grasped an axe and managed to shatter the bone after a few solid strikes. She cocked her head and wasn't afraid to put her hands into the huge organ. "It has exploded, from the inside out. The fire or whatever it was caused its heart to just go…boom!"

Phraan just stared. "Boom?"

She nodded. "Boom, it is scorched, see?"

Fastonar was frowning. "It couldn't be like ball lightening or something like that? I have seen that once and it was weird, they say ball lightening can be very dangerous"

Thiana shook her head. "We once found a huge elk which had been killed by a ball lightening, it too had a scorch mark but it had burned from the outside inn, not the other way around."

Fastonar sighed. "Magic then. I hope that young man will tell us more, I don't like this at all"

He turned around and walked back to his horse and the others too left, just Vitile stayed by the carcass, she was fascinated by the oddities she saw and took an extra peek at the chest area. Suddenly she saw something strange, there was a faint glow coming from a spot just in front of the chest, a little above the area where the chest muscles met and she did cut her way towards it with a sense of confusion. Dragons don't glow?

She hit something hard and felt the cut, her fingers touched something hard and she grasped onto it and yanked at it. At first it was stuck, then it gradually came loose with a sickening wet sound and she pulled it out. It was a gem, not very large, in fact she had seen ladies wearing way larger stones on their rings but it had a very deep dark red color and it was glowing slightly. A dim glow which looked almost sick somehow. She shuddered, this gem was evil, she just knew it. It was unholy dark magic and she hissed and grasped her belt pouch, dropped it into it. It felt heavy, dangerous, like a shadow looming in a darkened forest and she just knew that this tiny thing had something to do with why the dragons suddenly were so much more dangerous than before. She hurried over to her horse, she would tell Phraan of this soon, but for some reason she didn't think the rest of them ought to know, the gem could be something special for only this specimen. If she found more then she would tell them, then it had to mean something important. As they started the ride back towards the city she felt as if she was carrying the very answer to this riddle, and it was an answer she was rather sure she wouldn't like.

Back in the city Ivran was able to sit up in bed now and he was getting better. Someone brought him food and drink at regular intervals and he had gotten his clothes washed and his boots had been polished. Being an emissary of the academy did have its benefits and he was treated with respect by the soldiers and even the officers did act as if he was one of them. He had left the bed by now and was sitting in a chair outside of the tent, just to have something to do. There was always something going on in an army camp and he found it invigorating. It was so different from the academy, not that the academy in any way had been quiet or a haven of tranquility but this environment was so much more lively. There were soldiers laughing and talking and using a language the teachers would have found absolutely revolting and even the everyday routines were interesting for someone unfamiliar with them. A farrier was working with the army horses, changing shoes and trimming hooves and some soldiers were repairing some tents. There were always things to be done, even in a time of peace.

Ivran heard the men train too, and some officers were roaring orders and using a cussword in every sentence they said. It was a rougher and more masculine environment than the one Ivran had lived in for the last years. There weren't any female magicians, not because women didn't have the magical powers but because the academy simply didn't allow it. It was tradition, it had been questioned so many times but each time the answer was no, females would be a distraction. The academy was a place of discipline and control. Of mastering the powers within the mind and soul, of unwritten rules and courtesy. Here there were no such things, the manners were rough to say the least, the language coarse and everybody cared more about your ability to fight than you manners. Ivran liked it, it was a breath of fresh air.

It was getting late when the gates were opened and he got curious, the group shouldn't return until the day after but he heard hooves and he got curious. A huge group of men entered, all riding rather nice horses and they wore uniforms and were armed. Some carriages and pack mules did follow them and he did see several knights among the men, all in armor and he felt his heart beat a wee bit faster. He had always been fascinated by knights, most boys were. They were like the very personification of everything noble and right and he stared at the impressive display of power and understood little. The huge group was shown to another part of the camp and Ivran felt eager. These had to be dragon slayers too and he wondered who they were.

He was still too dizzy to walk far but he managed to get to the corrals where the horses were kept and saw that the strangers put up camp in record time. An officer walked by and Ivran bowed his head. "Excuse me, who are these men?"

The officer smiled, for some reason people still seemed to like Ivran the moment they met and he was a bit confused by that. After all, he was a complete stranger. "They are a team of knights coming from the southwest, sent north by his majesty's order. He believed that just one group would be too few, and these men are tough and ready for anything"

Ivran still had that eager look upon his face which was pretty normal for young men like him. "I can see that, they are so many?"

The officer nodded. "Two hundred to be precise"

Ivran was about to ask if any of the knights had fought dragons before when there was a racket coming from the main entrance. He walked towards the noise rather slowly and saw a very old mule which was hitched up to an even older wagon, the thing looked as if the only thing which kept it together was hope and good will. It was filled with stuff though, bottles, jars, things Ivran couldn't even describe and the owner of the vehicle was even more indescribable. Ivran had to gape, he had never seen anyone like that before. The man was first of all so skinny he looked like a scare crow and he had the dirtiest clothes the young man had ever seen. He was sure that if the odd person took them off they would stand on their own. Furthermore the man had a very long beard which had been spun into a sort of braid and he had a long braid as well but the sides of his head had been shaved and he was just as filthy as his clothes. It was hard to tell his skin color through all the shit. Ivran cringed, the stench of unwashed human was so strong he felt it from a distance and the man appeared to have lice and the face was seemingly pox marked but then Ivran realized that it was scars from sparks. The man looked insane, and he was acting insane too. Waving his hands and shouting at the guards and one of the leaders of the group which had arrived came running, he did look angry. "Don't let this man enter, he is a danger to us all. Bloody bastard almost killed several of my men"

The man shook his hand at the soldier. "I did not, absolutely not! I saved them, you wanted a cure for constipation and I gave them a cure for constipation!"

The soldier appeared to be high ranking, probably an officer and he was not impressed. "It is not a cure when it is worse than the disease, five men did almost shit themselves to death. They are still too weak to ride. "

The guards looked confused. "Is he a healer?"

The officer shook his head. "No, an alchemist, or rather, a charlatan. He knows nothing, but he decided to follow us and "offer us his services out of his good will" if you catch my drift, fucking vulture is what he is."

The so called vulture scoffed. "I am no charlatan, it wasn't my fault that those guys were of such a delicate nature? I didn't know man! I can help, by the power of alchemy I can help you fight the scourge, defeat the monsters!"

The officer was almost roaring. "And by the power of his majesty I do say this; you are not welcome in this camp, you are not a part of the army and if I was the mayor of this fine city I would kick your skinny ass as far away as possible. Now, get lost before I order my knights to chase you"

The man swore, and the words he used were so bad the guards stood there with their jaws almost touching their chins. Ivran had to gasp, he had never heard anyone compare an officer with those anatomical parts of a female and absolutely not with such an inventive use of descriptive words. The man turned his mule around and the old animal let out a shriek of annoyance and anger and trotted off, with the pace of a snail stuck in glue. The officer rolled his eyes and the guards were still staring, eyes huge as tin plates. Ivran did walk a little closer, he was still having a hard time believing what he had just heard. "My lord, who...who was that?!"

The officer saw that young man with the academy uniform and straightened himself up, tried to look like a soldier in his majesty's army once more. "A most bothersome and disgusting individual, he stayed in a village we happened to pass by, selling all sorts of "Miraculous medicine" but most of it was probably just turpentine and horse sweat. He has been following us since and we have tried to get rid of him but he keeps coming back, he is like a freakin' burr!"

Ivran listened to the wailing sounds coming from the wagon. "He is a criminal?"

The officer scoffed. "No, it isn't illegal selling self-made medicine, even if it is a hoax. But it ought to be! He tried to fix some of my soldiers after they ate some food their stomachs didn't respond too well to and the result was that they all got a terrible diarrhea, they almost kicked the bucket."

Ivran blinked. "Why was he so filthy? I have never seen a man that dirty!"

The officer smiled, the young man was very handsome and the innocent expression within his eyes was making the officer feel a bit protective. "He believes that water will wash away his luck you see, he hates baths. Some of my guys tried to toss him into the river once and it was like bathing a cat, he went ballistic so they had to give up that project. After all, we are not savages and nobody wanted to cause the man physical harm."

Ivran could still smell the man, his nose was twitching. "Oh gods, that is disgusting, and you have been travelling with him? My deepest respect, I would have gone mad!"

The officer made a grimace. "And we almost did so I forbid him from travelling with us, but he has followed us in spite of that"

Ivran cocked his head. "What is his name?"

The officer grinned. "Believe it or not but his first name is Tersus, nobody have heard him speak of a surname so I bet he is just a commoner."

Ivran had to snort, if he had been drinking anything he would have sprayed it all over the place for Tersus meant clean in the words of the magician's language. He gasped for air.

"That has to be the least appropriate name for a person like him, it has to be a joke?!"

The officer shrugged. "No, it is his name. Talk about irony hu?"

Ivran nodded. "Yes, the gods do have a sense of humor I guess."

The officer looked curious. "You are of the academy? What are you doing here?"

Ivran smiled. "I was sent to escort one of the younger students to his home and we were attacked by a dragon and some slayers did save me, I have been here for almost two days now"

The man stared at him. "A dragon? You have seen one? What was it like?"

Ivran looked at the ground. "Ah, terrifying? I fell and hit my head and the slayers got me back here, I am supposed to rest"

The officer was eager, that was easy to see, his eyes were shining. "You have got to tell me more, but I have to go now. My name is Crassian by the way, I am a captain and knight in his majesty's army and I am to lead this team while we are here. Is it true that this other group was around when the dragons caused problems fifty years ago?"

Ivran nodded. "Some of them yes, an elf named Phraan I think, and a huge guy named Dhokay, and I spoke to this elf girl named Vitile."

Crassian almost gaping. "Phraan? Oh gods almighty, he is like a legend, a true hero. Nobody has been responsible for more dead dragons than him, that elf can kill just about anything!"

Ivran frowned, "He can?"

Crassian nodded. "Yes, they say the orcs almost shat themselves when he entered a battlefield, I have got to meet him, are they here now?"

Ivran shook his head. "Ah, no, I think they will be back tomorrow though"

Crassian was starry eyed. "Wonderful, I cannot wait to meet him, we have to co-operate you know, learn from each other. This is gonna be wonderful"

The officer patted Ivran on his arm. "I have to go, but bring my regards to Phraan if you meet him before I do. I have grown up hearing the tales of his great deeds. He is the best slayer ever!"

Ivran looked down as the man almost ran off, the dragon had been a horrible things, an abomination and he doubted, no, he knew that not even a legendary slayer would have been able to save Josphu and his family. The dragons had to have changed. He was tired when he got back to the tent and his head was pounding once more. He had to lay down and he still couldn't get over that odd man. Alchemy was seen as a sort of short cut to power by the magicians, as a less respectable and rather doubtful manner of which to uncover the mysteries of nature and creation. Alchemy was the ugly step sister of magic and nobody wanted to even discuss alchemy, it was just a no-no. Any magician admitting to find an interest in the subject would find himself tossed out of the academy faster than a monk leaves an alehouse in the morning. Alchemy was in short seen as mumbo jumbo, as something which was good for nothing and fake and Ivran had to shake his head. Cure for constipation, the man had to be completely mad indeed.

He did go to bed, the group would return the next morning and he was still wondering what to do, if he could continue to lie. He didn't want to reveal his secrets to anyone, it was just too much at risk here. But he couldn't leave just yet, he was still rather ill and didn't want to risk his health and also, he was curious. Could these groups really manage to kill dragons? He could stay for a while, just to watch and learn something new, he needed a new horse too and he wasn't expected to return to the academy for yet another month. Yes, he would stay, he just had to keep his pie hole shut and make sure that nobody discovered the magic he was harboring. It should be

137

easy enough, he just had to avoid doing anything magical. Yes, it would be no trouble at all, and he would get to watch true dragon slayers in action.

The group did return the next day, after a rather unpleasant ride in pouring ice-cold rain and wind and Ivran felt oddly relieved that they were back and okay. He had been afraid that they had perished for who then could help this region? The slayers did go to the baths to get some heat into their bodies and then they did have a huge meal. The new group surprised them, they hadn't known that the king would send more men north but they could do nothing about it. Vitile came to check upon Ivran when they were done eating, he still had a slight headache but he wasn't dizzy anymore and felt rather fine so she did allow him to join them for some debriefing. Ivran listened as they discussed the dragon and he kept claiming that he didn't know what had caused the dragon's death and that he hadn't seen anything really. Phraan didn't believe him, he did see that but what could he do?

Crassian and the other officers of the new group did arrive after a while and they were all in awe of and so full of respect they acted a wee bit silly. Phraan seemed to be embarrassed by it all and looked as if he would prefer to be somewhere else so Fastonar sort of lead the negotiations. They did explain that the dragons had changed, and that they no longer knew if their methods were valid. This new group would be responsible for doing reconnaissance since they had fast horses and were many and they would also help evacuate the population. The officers did agree, the original group was the only ones with real experience and so Fastonar became the head of the whole operation. Ivran found it hard to believe that Phraan was the one who had caused the death of most dragons. He would have guessed that perhaps Dhokay was the most lethal of them, or perhaps even Shaluun. Phraan was of course tall and strong and just gorgeous too but he was…Ivran didn't know how to phrase it, gentle? He didn't look like someone with a talent for violence, his behavior was so calm, so balanced. Perhaps all elves were thus? Ivran didn't know.

The first troops were to leave during the afternoon, to look for dragon packs and to order people to leave the area and head south. Phraan and the others were discussing the findings, trying to come up with a solution. Ivran did notice the two convicts, now that the group was in a camp the two didn't have that much to do but Peter was eager to help. Ivran saw that the man probably had a lot of good traits, he was perhaps just someone who had taken some wrong choices in a state of desperation. Aiolo on the other hand sent cold shivers down Ivran's back, there was something wrong with that man. Ivran had seen someone with eyes like that once before, during his first year as a student. It was a man who had served as a guard at the academy and there had been some odd disappearances that year, young lads had vanished from their homes and some street boys too had gone missing. At first people had believed it to be just coincidence but later on things started to look suspicious. And when a terrified lad was found hiding in the moat outside of the walls the truth came forth. The guard kidnapped and raped young boys before he simply tortured them to death. Ivran had seen the execution and the eyes of the condemned criminal had been just like the eyes of this man, cold and without human emotions. He hoped that they all were aware of the fact that this man could be a true monster within.

Ivran told them he wanted to stay a bit longer and Phraan said it was smart of him, travelling alone now would be very unwise and Ivran did feel rather exposed. He was no soldier and he knew naught of how to fight. He was indeed safer in the city. The camp was rather full now and there were people everywhere, horses, carriages and servants scurrying around. The noise lasted from dusk until dawn and well into the night too and Ivran found it intriguing in a way. The army worked as a well-oiled machinery and nothing did change that. But the odd alchemist had made camp just outside of the walls and refused to leave and nobody could order him to, he just stayed there, stinking and shouting obscenities and Ivran didn't understand why the man didn't go back to the south? Surely he could make a much more comfortable living there, where there were a lot of people with money?

The first troop did return telling of dragons and it was a pack, perhaps six of them and probably similar to the one Ivran encountered. The group was preparing to go out to see for themselves when things changed and drastically.

Ivran and the two trackers were preparing some saddle bags when they heard a horn being blown from afar and Thiana did look confused but Taurin dropped everything he was holding and ran towards the wall. The structure wasn't very tall nor very wide, just four meters and it was wide enough for a couple of men to run along the top side by side but not more. It was made from mud bricks and Ivran knew that it was far from as solid as one made from real rocks. But here rocks were hard to come by, the cliffs and hills were mostly sandstone and the mountains were too far away. The elf did almost fly up the stairs and Ivran swallowed a sigh of admiration, he would never be that elegant. Thiana did look confused still and Taurin shouted. "It is an alarm, someone has seen something"

Ivran felt a cold chill running down his spine, could it be dragons? Oh gods! Fastonar came running, he was wild eyed and gestured towards Ivran. "You, get up on the wall now, Peter, Aiolo, you too!"

The two convicts did obey and Ivran too did run up the narrow ramp. Something was moving out there, along the ground. It looked as if some huge herd of buffalo or some other animal was on the move and from the cloud he could see that it was heading their way. "What is that?"

It didn't fly so it couldn't be dragons right? Fastonar was shouting at some of the guards, ordering them to close the gates. "Dreklugnins, or something similar. Do not go down from the wall"

Ivran frowned, Dreklugnins? Oh, that was small wingless dragons, the size of a large dog right? They couldn't be so bad? The group was gathering and Phraan was shouting instructions to the knights. Everybody got up on their horses and rode out before the gates were closed. Ivran felt his heart beating fast, this was exciting and frightening all at once. Everyone carried a long lance with a very odd tip, it was almost needle like and Phraan and the others had put on leather armor and seemed to be ready for battle. "Aim for their eyes, or the mouth"

Ivran saw that the dust got closer and now he could see the creatures who created the cloud. He gasped, and Peter who stood close to him was a bit pale. The other convict did almost grin, wasn't that man afraid for his own life at all? The beasts were rather large, the size of a cow perhaps and they did move with surprising elegance. The bodies seemed to be completely covered with thick almost scale like armor and Phraan was calling out. "They have changed too, prepare for anything!"

Ivran held his breath as the line of riders forced their horses forth to face this threat, they were so very brave and he wanted to go and hide somewhere. What could they really do against something this terrible?

Phraan saw that this indeed had been dreklugnins, the shape of the body and the overall animal was still the same but they had grown, a lot! From a beast which weighed in at about a hundred pounds at the most they now had to be at least five hundred and the long and strong jaws did look terrifying. Phraan did ride in front, he had his lance ready and knew that the knights who had arrived were bold but none of them had ever encountered something like this. The elves of his group had brought bows and several quivers full of arrows and Phraan knew that the type of arrows you used meant a lot. Against dreklugnins you had to use arrows with tips shaped just like the tip of their lances, narrow and thin with a needle point. And that needlepoint had to be dipped in poison. A dreklugnin is a very tough creature, capable of surviving things few other living beings can even imagine. He had once seen a dreklugnin escape from the battlefield with two legs chopped off and he did see that same one again two weeks after. It had found a way to balance itself and it was still alive and kicking and still dangerous. He had to respect a beast like that, but dreklugnins could wreak havoc upon the farms, slaughtering everything from chickens to cattle.

The dreklugnins came closer and Phraan swallowed his doubt and leaned forth, fastened his grip on the lance. He was a champion at this, he always knew where to strike out of sheer instinct and to his joy Drake showed no fear. Instead the giant horse did snort and increase its speed towards the ugly critters. Phraan saw that one of the beasts appeared to take aim at him and he roared to give himself extra courage, he didn't aim the lance before the very last minute to avoid that the beast had time to get out of the way. He saw that the dreklugnin tilted its head and opened its jaws, aiming for the chest and neck of the approaching horse and Phraan did give Drake a small nudge with his knee. The horse did obey, swinging on a dime even in the middle of attack and Phraan brought the lance down. The trick was to let the beast impale itself, he just had to provide the opposite force which would make the lance penetrate deep into the beast.

The lance was solid, made from a special type of wood growing along the coast to the far south and they hardly ever broke. The thin point went just where Phraan wanted it to go, down the beasts open maw and he braced for impact. The beast came to an abrupt holt as the lance was forced all the way down its throat and pierced its chest. The dreklugnin let out an odd barking sound and Phraan spun Drake around, pulled the lance free again. Blood gushed from the mouth of the dreklugnin and the beast fell in its last convulsions, the heart pierced by the lance. Phraan saw that the others were at it, arrows did fly and the archers did aim for the eyes and the knights used the lances with surprising elegance. They were used to the weapon and knew how to aim and their horses were trained too. Rhuk and Dabin did rode ponies, they were not as tall and the dwarves were almost sitting at the height of dreklugnins back. That meant that they used their axes with terrifying precision. They went for the head and cleaved dreklugnin skulls while they roared obscenities so bad Phraan thought it was a wonder the gods themselves didn't come down to defend their honor.

Dhokay did use a huge war hammer, it was his weapon of choice in such a situation and he was so strong wielding it was a piece of cake. No human would have been able to use that hammer, only lifting it would have been a challenge even for a strong man. Fastonar was laughing like a mad man, Phraan did recognize that mad joy and felt a sensation of joy himself. He let his instincts guide him and soon he was lost in the fever of battle once more, the art of killing all that he knew, all that he was.

The city had been sealed off and the walls were filled with soldiers wielding bows, ordinary arrows would do little harm to a dreklugnin but if you managed to hit its mouth it would hurt and slow the beast down a bit. The pack was huge, at least hundred beasts strong and the group couldn't stop all. Dreklugnins don't care about their fallen comrades, all that matters is to sate their hunger and the pack was still heading for the city. The first reached the gates and were met by a shower of arrows but that didn't slow them down at all, they just kept coming and tried to break down the wooden gate. Some of the soldiers did throw rocks at the beasts and that did in fact knock a few out but it wasn't very efficient. The dreklugnins suddenly did something very strange. Some did crouch down some meters from the wall and others which were incoming did use them as a sort of launch pad as they tried to jump up onto the wall. The dreklugnins had never jumped before, they were extremely dense and stocky beasts but this new larger version had longer legs and moved differently and Phraan turned his horse and saw what was happening. He swore, they would get over the walls, and there were several thousand human beings in that city, they would face a bloodbath soon.

Ivran screamed, a dreklugnin had almost managed to jump up onto the wall where he stood and only an arrow from a very bold archer had stopped it. The arrow wedged itself in the thick skin just beneath the eye and the beast roared with rage and turned around to attack the wall where the archer was. That was when they heard a most horrifying sound, it did sound as if someone had taken a horn orchestra and tampered with all the instruments and then forced the orchestra to play. The sound was so ghastly everybody tried to protect their ears. The dreklugnins stopped the attack, turning their heads in obvious confusion and that was when Ivran saw him. The alchemist, he was driving like a madman along the base of the wall, the old carriage making its own contribution to the devilish sound which seemed to come from some sort of contraption attached to its back, thick leather bands attached to the axel of the wagon powered a bellow which blew air into several sacks which were being compressed at uneven intervals and pipes did stick out of the bags which looked like porcupines suffering from spot baldness. And the smoke, the carriage did spread a thick green smoke behind it and the moment the smell reached Ivran's nostrils he fell violently ill! He had to throw up, the smoke did smell so bad it made the alchemist smell as if he had taken a bath in rose oil in comparison.

The carriage was pulled by the old mule which ran as if it had the dark gods chasing it, ears flat backwards and hooves thundering and Ivran had time to see the reason why the animal could make such a speed in spite of its age. Some sort of spikey contraption was attached to its tail and did hit the sensitive area beneath the tail with each move the mule did. It was cruel and Ivran had to bend over and retch again. The thick green smoke was like a blanket and it had an odd effect on the dreklugnins. If it made the humans sick it was nothing compared with what it did to the beasts. Suddenly the soldiers on the wall was witnessing a most disturbing sight, several dozen dreklugnins laying there writhing and bellowing in agony as they quite literally puked their guts out. The beasts did defecate too, and urinate and the stench was simply so strong it became unbearable. The soldiers did evacuate the wall, running for the latrines and their tents. It was simply too much. Ivran did stay, he had to watch this, and Peter too remained standing, obviously fascinated by what he did see.

The group saw the smoke and the carriage and wondered what the hell it was, they finished off the last dreklugnins and Phraan called everybody to him. They hadn't lost any fighters but several horses were dead and a couple had to be put down due to horrible wounds. The thick green smoke did dissipate in the wind and Phraan made a grimace, what in hells name was that? He had smelled the result of a dog attacking a skunk once and even that had been a mild smell in comparison. Dhokay was staring. "Look, the dreklugnins which managed to get past us are dying? What in the name of the goddess is this?"

Phraan spurred Drake, he intended to find out, stench or no stench. They rode hard and those who had lost their horses sat up with others and they reached the walls in just a few minutes. The carriage had stopped, simply because the old mule pulling it had collapsed and the man driving the carriage stood there gesticulating like a mad, Phraan had never seen a person who looked that deranged before. The gates were opened again and Phraan and Dhokay rode over to the alchemist who still was shouting and jumping up and down. Phraan saw that the head of a morning star had been tied to the mule's tail, the poor animal had ran itself to death and he felt a wave of sheer anger. But the alchemist or whatever he was had saved the city, there was no denying that. He had in fact hindered the dreklugnins from overrunning the walls and Phraan saw that Crassian and the other officers were stunned. He stopped Drake and stared down at the man, the human did look as if he had been taken a bath in a sewer and did smell almost as bad as that smoke he had produced but there wasn't just madness in his eyes. The man stared at the tall half elf and bowed his head a little, an odd grin was visible on his face. "What did you just do human? I have never seen dreklugnins dying like that"

The man grasped some bags from the back of the carriage, they were made from wool and not very densely woven. "Oh, it was an idea I have worked on for some time, you see, some chemicals do produce smoke when mixed and this I did discover by sheer chance some years ago. And I thought about it now, and it did work didn't it? Oh it worked wonderfully!"

Phraan stared at the man, with disbelief. "Are you aware of the fact that dreklugnins are extremely hard to kill? They are very tough creatures, don't just die. That smoke was…incredibly efficient!"

Dhokay stared at the alchemist too with narrow eyes. "You are coming with us, if you can kill dreklugnins you could perhaps come up with something capable of killing other species as well"

Phraan stared at Dhokay, ready to protest but the expression within his friends eyes told him that he ought to shut up. The man nodded. "Oh I have ideas, yes, great ideas, grand ideas. Ideas which will change the world!"

Phraan almost growled and Fastonar rode over, he did look tired and his lance had lost its tip. He stared at the dead dreklugnins with disbelief. "We will let you have whatever you want if you can aid us, but I must say this, if I ever see you treat a poor animal like that again I will personally flog you!"

Tersus just smirked. "Oh the mule, never mind that, it was old and I needed speed. I couldn't just go and steal a horse now could I? He did die a hero, not all mules can say that about themselves"

The man was ripping the harness of the dead animal and Phraan still felt very angry. "I do not want him near our tents, he smells like…"

Fastonar nodded. "Yes, I know, but he can become valuable. There is a vacant building not far from the officer's cantina, he can stay there."

Crassian and the others did look rather doubtful but they didn't protest, they had all faced the possibility of the city being breached and Tersus had saved them. Ivran came running and Peter followed him, the convict was wide eyed and he bowed in front of the alchemist and the others. "Please, he does need a helper doesn't he? I can do it, I wish to learn. I can be so useful"

Dhokay made a grimace, stared at Fastonar who just nodded. "Very well, you can help this man but remember, you are still spell bound, you cannot just leave"

Peter nodded and he was grinning from one ear to the other. Tersus stared at him and appeared to like what he did see. "So, a young man interested in alchemy? That is rare!"

Phraan didn't try to hide his sneer. "He is a convict, he tried to make fake money."

Tersus did lighten up. "Indeed? Ah what a wonderful dance of fate, you are just what I need then young man, I will share my secrets with you then, and you will be so much more than before"

Peter did look a bit spellbound by the promises of learning but Ivran who stood just by them had to turn around and breathe through his sleeve, goddamn it, Tersus did smell worse than rotten eggs.

Tersus grasped one of the carriage shafts and Peter took the other and they started to pull the thing back towards the city.

Vitile did ride up to Phraan and she did look as if she was deeply shocked. "What is that human being? I have never seen anyone like that before? Some deranged wizard?"

Phraan almost spat. "No, an alchemist, he is a madman but he can perhaps become useful."

She just stared at the carriage. "He stinks, and what was that smoke? The dreklugnins, they spewed their own guts out?! It wasn't some dark spell?"

Phraan shook his head. "No, and I am impressed, even if I really don't want to be"

They rode through the gates and there were soldiers everywhere now, greeting the knights and helping them with the horses and the equipment. Ivran followed the group back to the camp, he was still nauseous and he still had a hard time believing what he had seen. He had believed that only magic could achieve such a thing but he was obviously wrong. He sighed and entered the huge main tent with the others, Phraan had ordered Aiolo to help the soldiers with dragging the dead dreklugnins into a heap to be burned and the young man had looked rather angry. It was a filthy job but it had to be done. Shaluun and the two dwarves did look a bit confused still and Taurin and Thiana too were a bit pale. Shaluun sat down and his eyes were very narrow and his expression one Phraan hadn't seen before. "What in the name of every deity did we just see Phraan?"

The half elf sighed. "I am not sure, but if it is just as efficient against other dragon species it could be a salvation"

Ivran sat in the corner and watched, he bit his lower lip and Vitile did notice him. "What is it young man? What are you thinking about?"

Ivran felt insecure but he couldn't keep it inside, he tried to keep his voice calm. "Dragons are immune to magic aren't they?"

Phraan frowned. "Yes, they are magical creatures. We do use magicians to protect ourselves from the flames, and to create traps. But we cannot kill dragons with magic"

Ivran nodded. "Okay, so, let us say that someone has made the dragons right? Someone who wants them to be invincible, almost impossible to kill"

Phraan nodded slowly. "We see where you are going lad, go on"

Ivran took a deep breath. "I would have wanted to make my dragons immune to magic too, for that is the strongest force there is, what everybody will use against something like that. But Tersus, he is something I bet nobody have predicted, a wild card, an unknown factor"

Vitile stared at the young man. "You are right, he could give us the upper hand once more, and we need it, by every god. These new dragons, they are…well, something out of this world"

Phraan sighed. "Yes, if he truly can create weapons strong enough to use against the larger species. The sad thing is that he is a truly despicable person, treating a mule like that!"

Ivran nodded. "He is arrogant, and convinced of his own righteousness, he is also indifferent to the sufferings of others as long as it serves his purpose. I say he is a very dangerous individual and not only because of his skills. Do not trust him"

Vitile cocked her head. "You are a wise young man, truly, you see very deeply"

Ivran just blushed and looked down and Dhokay crossed his arms over his wide chest. "So, we are going to let this human aid us?"

Fastonar nodded. "Yes, yes we are. In spite of it all, for I must admit that we do need him. I don't like it any more than the rest of you but the situation is extreme."

Phraan nodded and made a grimace. Rhuk was pulling at his beard. "That man is truly insane. A raving lunatic, one the gods have cursed. But that could be a good thing, the mad can do things no sane person can predict and being unpredictable can be salvation"

Dabin frowned. "Yes, but the stench, I don't want to go anywhere near him before someone washes him"

Thiana nodded. "Yes, what is it with that man and water?"

Ivran shrugged. "Apparently he is afraid he will lose his luck if he takes a bath"

Rhuk shook his head. "Now that is a whole load of dragon turds, how can he take care of his feet like that? They have to look absolutely horrible, how is he to get some females attention with dirty feet?"

Everybody just stared at Rhuk who shrugged. "Seriously, a man's feet are so important, in our tribe the women will always check the feet first"

Vitile had to groan. "Rhuk, I have no idea of what sort of tastes dwarf females has but no human female will go anywhere near a man like that, nice feet or not!"

Fastonar sort of banged his hand on the table. "Listen, we have to take care of the imminent threat, forget about that stench and focus upon what the man can do. We were going to go after some dragons weren't we? If he can come up with something useful fast we can still go tomorrow."

Shaluun sat and looked doubtful. "That fast? Well, maybe he can create something good but he doesn't know much about those dragons now does he?"

Fastonar nodded slowly and tilted his head. "So we are going to inform him now aren't we? Does anyone volunteer?"

Dhokay stepped forth. "I can explain the findings to him, the faster the better right?"

Fastonar nodded and Dhokay left the tent, Ivran didn't envy him. Phraan did sit and he was stretching his long legs, feeling a bit excited still. The heat of battle always gave him that feeling, he felt more alive than otherwise. Fastonar sighed and sat down by the table. "I will send some soldiers out to check the surroundings, and we will have guards placed by the walls at all times. If dragons come this way we have to be prepared"

Dabin mumbled. "Prepared for what? Those were small critters right, and yet we had trouble with them. The big dragons are gonna be fucking impossible to kill."

Phraan looked down, he felt that Dabin did speak the truth but could this alchemist change that. "Everything can be killed"

Dabin pointed at him. "Really? The largest species of dragons didn't suffer great losses back then now did they? Some of them didn't lose even one! What if they all are like that now?"

Phraan made a grimace. "You are right, the most feared species were impossible to kill, but they were very rare and not really a problem."

The dwarf tilted his head and his eyes were rather dark. "Those dreklugnins had grown right? So had that dead dragon, it had been a long tail yeah? But now it was something way worse. What if that is true also for the other species?"

Vitile shuddered. "Please, I don't want to talk about it!"

Fastonar looked at them. "Tomorrow we do ride out, we have to see what we can do. Prepare well, you know what to do"

Dhokay walked over to the building the alchemist had been given and the man had already managed to pollute the atmosphere of the place. He sighed and walked inside, the rooms he saw were already being filled with all sorts of equipment and Dhokay frowned. Tersus were standing in the middle of a smaller room ordering Peter around and Dhokay fought the urge to cover his nose with his sleeve. "Our leader wishes for you to receive some information about the current situation. The dragons have changed since the last time they were around"

Tersus was grinning. "They have? Oh great, a new challenge. So, do speak, I don't have all day"

Dhokay rolled his eyes but did tell everything they had discovered and Tersus didn't interrupt him, he was considering everything and Dhokay realized that the man in fact was very intelligent, not just crazy. "Good, they have grown, their weaknesses removed and their strengths merged. That tells me one thing, someone has manipulated them."

Dhokay looked at the man with slight confusion. "Are you sure?"

Tersus nodded and waved his hand at Peter. "Yes, and only magic can do that to a being this fast. But what I do is the opposite of magic, and I think I have some tricks up my sleeve which can prove to be efficient."

Dhokay looked down. "We do ride out tomorrow, we need something ready for then"

Tersus grinned. "Worry not, I will have something ready for sure, but I do need a few things"

Dhokay looked at him with calm eyes. "Name them"

Tersus smiled. "I need a chariot, the type they use for races and two very fast and brave horses and a driver, the best."

Dhokay looked a bit puzzled. "You cannot race a dragon"

Tersus slapped his hands together. "I am not gonna race a dragon my good…uh whatever you are…I am gonna irritate one!"

Dhokay couldn't believe what he was being told but Peter caught his gaze and rolled his eyes while shrugging. The message was clear, do not question the master. Dhokay bowed slightly. "Great, then we anticipate you by the morrow, with something useful. I will make sure a chariot is available and ready"

Tersus rubbed his hands together and looked as if he was looking forward to this. "Good, very good, I will be ready"

He turned his back to Dhokay and continued to shout orders to Peter and Dhokay left the building. Crassian and the other officers were gathered with the local ones and Dhokay did bow in respect as he entered. Crassian did stare at him with a small amount of nervousness, the luptay was much taller than a human and very intimidating. "Gentlemen, the alchemist require a chariot with two fast horses and a good driver for tomorrow"

One of the local officers did snap his fingers. "We do have a very good charioteer here, his name is Hardan and he has won many races. He has very good horses too"

Dhokay smiled. "Excellent, can you please get him ready for tomorrow morning? I have no idea of what Tersus wants but it could be that he is our best hope now."

Crassian didn't look very happy. "That I would live to see the day when we rely on a utterly repulsive person like that, I woe this"

Dhokay sighed. "So does we all my good man but what can one do? We have to try every available option"

The officers did salute him as he left and he didn't look forward to the next day, no, he didn't look forward to it at all!

The cooks had decided to really outdo themselves since the city had been saved from the dreklugnins and they did fill the tables with enough food to feed at least twice the number of people present. Fastonar went to study some maps the commander of the camp had after he ate, he did look worried and Phraan knew that it was a bad sign, Vitile walked over to him and she hid a burp behind her hand. She cringed and smiled a bit, looking slightly uncomfortable. "I have a bad feeling when it comes to this Phraan, a very bad feeling. I don't know why"

He sighed and put an arm around her. "I know, so do I. I still cannot figure out why that dragon died. Its heart did explode but hearts don't just do that, it isn't natural."

She smiled. "You are right, they don't. I think magic did it, but what sort of magic?"

Phraan shrugged. "Your guess is as good as mine then, I have no idea. Dragons are supposed to be immune to magical attacks"

She grasped him by the hand, dragged him towards her tent. "Come, I don't want to be alone tonight. Keep me company?"

Phraan swallowed. "It is still quite early?"

She shook her head. "It is never too early for some fun now is it?"

She reached up and kissed him gently and he had to grin into the kiss. "I remember this, the evening after battle…"

She opened the tent and they entered, she turned around and pulled her tunic off, her eyes dark with longing and an odd sort of desperation. "Yes, one never feels as alive as now"

Phraan let her undress him, enjoyed the anticipation and the feeling of strong hands which made short work of his clothes. Before long they were entangled on the cot, oblivious to the world outside.

Phraan lay there half asleep, his body feeling heavy and warm and Vitile was resting against his chest, her long hair tickling him a bit but he didn't move, didn't want to ruin the moment. He did feel oddly well, relaxed. Vitile was like most wood elves, uninhibited in her desires. Some would perhaps call it shameless behavior but Phraan saw it as just natural. Her people didn't feel ashamed of their bodies nor the fact that they had desires and they didn't try to hide anything they truly felt. He sighed and stared down at her, the long brown hair did hide her face and he did remember when he first met her, he had been unaccustomed to the lifestyle of elves in general, and her straight forwardness had been shocking. Then he met more elves and found that she was acting rather naturally. They all were that open and he did find that to be rather liberating. He had gotten rather close to Vitile, for a few seasons he had been rather sure that this was it, that she was the one for him and he was close to asking her to bond with him several times but that perfect moment never came and as he slowly learned more about himself and his gifts he allowed the hunt to drive a wedge in between them.

He didn't want her to get hurt, that was the reason why. He had so little to offer her in the end and a bond between elves was unbreakable. He had regretted it but he had allowed them to drift apart, and now they were drifting together again like ships in a harbor. Right now he wasn't even sure of what he felt, a solid dose of sheer desire was of course at the bottom of it all. She was amazing in bed and he hadn't gotten any for quite a long time but a good relationship ought to be based on so much more than just sex, no matter how great it was. He did admire her, she was someone he did trust completely too, and she was smart and funny and managed to change his mood when he got too gloomy.

Phraan let a hand slide through silky locks, he tried to imagine how life could have been if they had stayed together back then. He would have lived in the woods then, as a wood elf, and he would have been a hunter, not a blacksmith. It would have been a very free life for sure, one he would have loved. And he would have loved her too, fiercely. What was it his grandfather had said? If you love someone let them go? He had, he had to admit that to himself. Vitile deserved someone better, someone like herself, not some half breed unable to give her the children she dreamed off. That was what had chased him off back then, the fact that he never could make her truly happy, never give her absolutely everything she could want. Elves do breed very slowly and have few offspring and the few children born are seen as almost sacred, becoming parents was a huge blessing not all elves got to experience. Phraan knew he never would and sometimes that did hurt him.

He sighed and closed his eyes, sleep just wouldn't come, he was too nervous, there were too many unanswered questions. He had to figure out why the dragon had died, perhaps the next day could answer that question but somehow he did doubt it. Vitile did sleep very well, her slow breath told him she was relaxed and at ease and he did envy her the ability to just let go of worries and stress. He wasn't so lucky, he had a bad habit of hanging on to such feelings for way too long. When he did fall asleep he didn't dream of anything, he just felt as if he was floating around in a sea of insecurity.

He woke up from his uneasy sleep and felt tired and sore. Vitile had scratched both his shoulders and his butt in the throes of passion and he had to smirk and discretely check that he wasn't bleeding. She had very strong and sharp finger nails like most of her race and she didn't always think of how deeply they cut when she was coming. Vitile sat by the small table and she hadn't even put her clothes on, it was a distracting sight and Phraan saw that it wasn't light outside yet. She did notice that he was staring at her and she hid something underneath a cup on the table, got up. "You are awake?"

Phraan nodded. "Yes, completely"

He pulled the blankets to the side and revealed that yes, it was morning and his body hadn't taken such a beating that it wasn't ready for some more. Vitile giggled. "Oh Phraan, you are always so generous"

He nodded and got up, grasped her and lifted her up. Vitile let out a small yelp and threw her arms around his neck, kissed him with raw need. "Yes, just…"

She was writhing against him and he carried her over to the saddle rack, put her down onto it and turned her around. Vitile laughed, a low and sensual laughter and she put her rear up, looking at him with that particular naughty gaze which almost made him come undone there and then. She held onto the rack while he lifted her hips, her feet didn't touch the floor like that but they didn't need to, he held her and he had always liked it like that, and so did she. The way she let go of all inhibitions told him that, it didn't take long before they both raced into their climax and Vitile did shriek and tremble, sweaty and slick as an eel. Phraan was heaving for air, fighting to recover from his high and he carried her with him over to the cot again. She laughed and laid down on top of him, kissing the tip of his nose. "I will never get tired of this Phraan, you make my blood so hot"

He had to smile, a bit proud of himself and also flattered. "I am glad you like me Vitile, I have to say the same"

She sighed and kissed his chest, long fingers did play with a nipple and he hissed and arched. "Careful, I am sensitive right now!"

She giggled. "Yes, I remember that. You are truly one of a kind Phraan. "

She sighed and laid her head down onto his chest. "There is something I want to tell you, but do keep it to yourself"

He felt drowsy, blinked and smiled at her, the lazy feeling rather wonderful really. "Okay? What?"

She took a deep breath. "One moment, it is over here"

She got up and he grieved the loss of the warmth immediately, she grasped whatever it was she had hid and returned to the bed, laid down next to him. "I found this in the dragon's chest, near the heart. It is magical isn't it?"

He stared at the gem and felt an odd sensation of sheer dread, this was something unnatural. He didn't want to touch it but felt that he had to, his palm did feel almost dirty the moment the gem fell into it. What in the name of every unholy God was this? Vitile swallowed. "I think this is what changed that dragon, I don't know why, but my heart tells me it is so."

He stared at her, the pleading expression within her eyes told him that she was afraid he would disagree with her. "You are right, this is something…really evil"

He gave the gem back to her, hoping that it wouldn't somehow stain them. The magic within the tiny thing wasn't like anything he had sensed before. As all elves he did feel the natural magic surrounding living beings rather well but this thing, it had felt like un-life. He couldn't really explain it otherwise. Vitile put the gem into her pouch again, her eyes distant. "Don't tell anyone about this Phraan, I think this is something very dangerous."

He sat up, feeing cold. "Yes, it is very dangerous indeed, if this is what changed that dragon into what it was now it was done to it, deliberately. Someone did place that gem inside of it, and that someone won't like that someone finds their secret, of that you can be darn sure."

She looked down and nodded, eyes to the floor. "I am afraid Phraan, this is beyond us all. We weren't prepared for any of this"

He took a deep breath. "No, we weren't, and we still aren't. Today we may find out more, we cannot lose hope Vitile, to just allow the dragons to spread out spells disaster for this entire continent"

She nodded, hiding her face against his chest, as if she was listening to his heart, finding solace in its steady rhythm. He caressed her shoulder, held her close. "Do stay close to me today Vitile, I don't want you to take any risks"

She looked up. "We need to fell another dragon Phraan, and I have to check its chest. If there is another gem in there then we do know for sure"

He smiled. "Yes, we will. But killing yet another one will be hard, I somehow doubt that we will be able to do it"

She sighed and hid her face again. "Yes, but maybe we are in luck? The alchemist could have some new weapons"

Phraan cringed. "Ah, that terrible man, well, I won't sell the skin before the bear is dead. He was in luck with those dreklugnins, he may not be so lucky again"

Vitile nodded. "But we must have hope in something right? Would be too bad otherwise"

He smiled and kissed her head. "You are right. But let's get dressed and ready, it will be a very long day."

She let out a huge sigh and snaked out of the blankets, started putting her clothes on. Phraan shivered in the cold morning air and hurried with his own gear, it was getting light outside and he heard that the camp was coming to life now. Orders were being shouted and as they exited the tent he did see a few soldiers glaring at them with barely hidden anger. Phraan had to smirk, oh no, they had kept people awake yet again. Vitile did stretch and yawn and she appeared to have regained her good mood as they walked to the cantina. Most of the others were there and Peter did approach them, his eyes shining. "Tersus is a genius, you won't believe the things he has told me!"

Phraan was a bit shocked by the joy in the man's eyes, but it looked as if Peter in fact was very happy? "I bet that is true yes, so, you like this assignment?"

Peter nodded. "Oh yes, I have learned a lot already, and we are so alike, we both like to make things, new things, exciting things"

Vitile did cringe visibly, her eyes said it all, not another one! Phraan smiled. "Good for you, if the two of you can come up with anything truly helpful we will be very grateful"

Peter was almost jumping up and down " Oh we have, and we will, more that is"

Fastonar did arrive and he was obviously tired, his hair was matted and his eyes a bit bloodshot. "These so called maps ought to be used as kindling, they are so inaccurate it hurts looking at them, How can we send troops to the right place when the right place suddenly is the wrong place?!"

Phraan frowned. "I thought the army maps were good?"

Fastonar nodded with a not insignificant amount of sheer aggression. "So did I! But this little shithole of a city haven't got any strategic importance and thus, nobody has bothered giving this camp anything of quality. The maps are more ancient than Twelve towers."

Phraan had to scoff. "That bad?"

Fastonar was sneering. "That bad, I spent the better part of this night trying to find a safe place to cross the river which runs to the north of here. The soldiers tells me that the ford marked on the map is in the wrong place and the current there is so strong trying to cross is suicide. "

Dhokay and Shaluun entered the tent with Kapha in tow behind them, the half dwarf was grinning. Phraan nodded at them and Dhokay smiled. "There is a chariot and a driver waiting for Tersus, I wonder what he is up to?"

Peter almost giggled. "You will see, and you will be surprised too"

Thiana and Taurin had already finished eating and both did look well rested and ready. Phraan wished that he felt that well, to be honest he felt a bit like a wrung out washcloth, completely moshed. Fastonar clapped his hands. "Listen up, we leave in half an hour, be ready, the troops have reported seeing the same pack as yesterday a bit further to the east so we have a chance at them."

Everybody nodded and Phraan sat down to eat a little, he was famished and emptied a jug of tea. Vitile was just barely touching her food and her eyes were still distant. She was in her own world and Phraan just wished that he could have cheered her up somehow. Aiolo entered the cantina with his eyes on the ground, he was waddling more than walking and the sour expression on his face didn't create much cheer to say the least. The man looked as if he hated the world and Phraan did sigh and nodded at Fastonar. "He did burn dreklugnins yesterday? Give him some easier work today ha?"

Fastonar frowned. "Why? He is a coward and a murderer, he does deserve to sweat a little."

Phraan nodded and looked at the young man who sat down and attacked a bowl of cheese and bread like someone who had been starving for a long time. "It isn't that he doesn't deserve it, but I just don't like having a man like that near the soldiers. He is dangerous Fastonar, I can sense it. He hides something, and keeping him away from weapons would be a good idea"

Fastonar blinked. "Damn it Phraan, you are right, I haven't thought of that. I will order him to help the men fixing cracks in the wall, that is harmless work"

Phraan nodded. "Yes, he cannot do much harm there"

Fastonar patted Phraan's shoulder. "You have always been the most caring among us, you see the worth of a man so quickly. I wish I was that good"

Phraan just blushed and Fastonar went to get his horse ready. Phraan remembered the gem and for a moment he felt an urge to tell Fastonar of it but Vitile had told him to shut up so he didn't say anything. He just finished his meal and went to get his armor and prepare Drake.

When they all gathered it was already broad daylight and some knights and soldiers were to escort them. Tersus stood in a chariot, he held some bags in his arms and the driver was a man who looked stone tough. He had the looks of someone ready to take chances and the two horses were grey geldings, both long legged and of dubious temper. Phraan saw that they were fast though, it was probably just what Tersus had asked for. Crassian was to come with them and he did look impatient. The group did ride out and this time Ivran did follow them, he had been given a lithe ginger mare and did look as if he'd rather be somewhere else. They were riding due east and then they turned northwards after a while, the dragons had been spotted near a village and the local officers were worried. The village was important to them, it did grow much of the food the camp used and there were tight bonds between the inhabitants and the army. Many soldiers had come from that village. It was placed in a shallow valley on the south side of the great river and it was rather large for this region. It had about five hundred inhabitants in all and the houses were old and built with notched wood. These days there were no trees around big enough to use that technique and it was a dying art. Nobody knew how to do it anymore. Crassian was riding next to one of the local officers, a man who had relatives in that village and he did notice that the man was sweating and looking rather ill, it had to be out of sheer nervousness.

The trip did take many hours in spite of the fast horses, the landscape was pretty flat and there were few things you could use as a point of reference but there was a cliff to the east of the city and they used that to navigate. The path wasn't that well used, most people there didn't travel much and the open plains meant that you didn't need roads that much. This ought to be very good land for farming and yet it wasn't. The soil was poor in many places and those which weren't had lost their fertility or so it seemed. Vitile was the first one to see it, a shadow on the horizon and at first it did look like a cloud but it did move and Phraan stared and swore. "Blood wings, a huge flock"

Ivran looked scared. "What are blood wings?"

Phraan was squinting, he had very good eyes and took a deep breath. "Small flying dragons, the size of a large gull. They don't have fire or poison but can be a terrible nuisance for they do still have teeth and claws"

Ivran tilted his head. "Are they going to attack?"

Phraan shook his head. "No, they are too far away but we haven't seen any of the small species until now, that is odd."

Vitile was frowning. "They used to follow the packs of larger dragons, to eat what they didn't. I have a bad feeling here"

Phraan sent her a swift glance. "Yes, we ride on."

The group of riders did speed up, the horses would be tired and they would have to spend the night out there but all felt the urge to hurry. They reached the valley a little after noon, and it became very clear that something was wrong. A whole pack of goats came running and the animals were beside themselves with fear and refused to get out of the way. They rode around a turn and saw that village and Phraan swore in a whisper. It was nothing left, the buildings were levelled with the ground and they didn't hear a sound. It was an eerie silence and Dhokay gave the signal for halt. "Nothing is burned, see?"

The locals did stare at the devastation with huge eyes and one of the men was already crying. Phraan turned Drake.

162

"Hold the soldiers back, we go forth to investigate. This has to be checked out by someone who knows what to do"

Tersus did look eager and the chariot did follow the group as they slowly made their way towards the village. Phraan was shocked, this was done by something way larger than a long tail or a greyback, but it was odd that nothing was burned. The buildings were torn down and bodies lay everywhere. To their horror most were torn apart, and the scene was just unbelievable. People and animals lay scattered around and Vitile was pale. Kapha did look as if his face had frozen in a frown and Dhokay was blinking all the time, his eyes rather moist. "This is...it is worse than any battlefield"

Phraan looked down, they rode past the body of a young girl, her torso ripped in half and it didn't look as if any had been eaten, she had just been killed. "What type of dragon does this? They attack to feed, not just to..."

Shaluun finished the sentence. "Kill randomly"

The village was reduced to a pile of debris, and the middle of it had become a heap of timbers, bodies and things which was impossible to get through. They had to ride around it. There was little stench yet, the weather was cold and the attack had to have happened the day before, it was just horrible. Phraan felt sick to the stomach and Vitile was breathing very hard. "The scouts said they had seen greybacks, or something similar to that species. But this, this has to have been done by something way larger."

Phraan reined in Drake. "I agree, so where are they?"

Dhokay was staring at the surroundings, there weren't many places to hide there except from a Holt of low trees closer to the river. "The soil is almost frozen, no tracks visible. "

Phraan sighed, "They must have left immediately after the attack, there is nothing here"

He was just finished with that sentence when the horses whinnied and started to act up and a dark shadow appeared above the edge of the shallow valley. It was huge, and strange and Phraan screamed a warning. Behind it several others appeared but they weren't flying, they ran along the ground and they were the brethren of the one which they had found dead. Phraan swore, five of that type which could fly too and that huge monster? Trying to run would be futile, the dragons would be all over them in a matter of minutes. Vitile shouted. "The large one, it commands the others, look at it!"

The dragon did look like a mix of several species, just like the dead dragon had. The size was like that of a diamond tail but the wings was definitely those of a death wind and the overall body shape that of a storm fire but the head was different. The jaws did almost resemble a sort of beak and Phraan knew that this was one terrible opponent. That was when Tersus let out a roar. "Leave the smaller ones to me, take out the huge one!"

The chariot rushed forth with an insane speed and the five smaller dragons immediately ran towards it, with a speed that was uncanny to say the least. An odd smell could be felt as the chariot rushed past the riders and Phraan realized that it was that scent the dragons were after. Tersus was obviously preparing something for he shouted orders to the driver and they drove up along the river, against the wind.

Phraan and the others had to deal with the huge dragon, it was armored and its neck was rather long so it was probably very agile. The thing landed with a roar and swung its tail and Dhokay swiftly jumped off his horse and let the animal run off. "The eyes, you need to hit its eyes."

Vitile had her bow drawn and they all dismounted and let the horses go, this dragon was way too large to be charged at on horseback. Vitile fired off an arrow, she used special arrow heads and the projectile did fly straight and true. Phraan saw how the dragon did a sudden move which was almost snakelike and it did avoid getting hit anywhere sensitive. It roared and now it became very clear that it was aware of the fact that arrows can be harmful, a sort of third eyelid did slide in over the entire eye and from the looks of it the lid was probably rather thick and strong. It did look almost glass like. Tersus had lured the smaller dragons out of the way, they were chasing after the chariot and the driver had to be extremely skilled for he did keep it on its wheels the whole time and the speed was amazing considering that they weren't on a track at all. The smell coming from the chariot did piss off the dragons and they forgot all about their leader. Tersus shouted to the driver. "Aim for those trees up ahead. I want the chariot to pass between those two oaks!"

The driver did snap his whip and the horses were running as fast as they possibly could, the dragons didn't try to fly, these were rather heavy and they probably preferred running. The chariot did almost fly towards the trees and Tersus grasped a larger bag and shook it vigorously. The wind was rather strong down by the river and the trees sort of funneled it and created a zone with very strong and cold wind. The chariot entered the zone and had to slow down a bit, the dragons were straight behind it, snapping and snarling and trying to get to it first and Tersus ripped the bag in two. A strange pink powder did spread behind the chariot, filling the air like pink mist and the dragons ran into the cloud with their jaws wide open. The next thing which happened was astonishing. Tersus yelled to the driver and ordered him to continue, they had to get away from the mist and they shot in among the trees like an arrow. The dragons stopped, as if they had hit a solid wall. Ghastly gargling sounds could be heard and the huge beasts did stagger and claw at their own faces. Eyes bulging and nostrils flaring, chests heaving for air and the first dragon did fall, blood shooting out of its nose and mouth. It was convulsing violently, then it sort of stiffened and it happened to the next, and the next. After just a few minutes all five dragons lay dead, their bodies twisted and grotesque and Tersus did shake his hand in the air, eyes glowing with triumph. "Chew on that you ugly fuckers"

Phraan and the others did see that this dragon was a type without fire, but it was probably the type which can spew acid and they spread out to try to find a weak spot. The tail flew like a huge tree filled with spikes, the head was both a battering ram and a terrible maw and the group had never faced such an opponent before. These big dragons had been few back then and they had never encountered one so aggressive. The beast was fast, and that was the greatest surprise for normally a beast of this size would be slow and not very bright but this dragon did have intelligence. It knew how to dodge arrows and its hide was thick and impenetrable. Shaluun shouted. "The skull is not a weak point, I can see it is way thicker than before."

Phraan jumped out of the way, the tail came rushing and being hit was certain death. The beast had long spikes sticking out of the tail on all sides. "Yes, and the neck is armored."

Dhokay ran and avoided the head, the jaws did indeed resemble a beak but it had teeth, rather terrible shark like teeth and he did get a swift peek into the mouth as he ran by. "It has acid glands, huge ones."

By running around they did confuse the beast but they could do nothing to fell it, or could they? Phraan stared at the beast, it moved with such ease and he frowned and pointed towards the legs. "The hocks, the sinews above the hock. They are close to the skin, Dabin, Rhuk, we'll distract the thing!"

The two dwarves were terrified but they didn't hesitate, as Dhokay and Phraan lunged forward in a mock attack at its front they both ran forth, well within reach of the terrible tail. Dhokay slammed his war hammer into the dragon's chest and the beast roared and reached around to grasp him with its jaws. But the tall luptay wasn't there, he had moved out of the way rather easily and the dragon did swing its neck around again and Rhuk did draw first blood. His axe was very sharp and the elegant crescent shape of the blade was efficient like few others. The skin covering the joint wasn't that thick, if it had been armored it would have prevented the dragon from moving and thus the blade did cut both deep and well. There was a loud sound, a sort of crack and the dragon shrieked, it fell down on that side and Dabin did attack the other hock with a ferocious roar. He carried an axe of a more traditional shape and it too was razor sharp but it didn't cut quite as deeply. The dragon did a twisting motion and Dabin got thrown several meters away by the base of the tail, he rolled and Vitile grasped him and dragged him out of the way. Rhuk simply sought refuge underneath the dragon and he was wild eyed and desperate. One leg was crippled and the dragon was no longer as fast as before so the dwarf did something nobody had ever thought of before. He raised his axe and let out a wild roar and buried the blade deeply into the beast's ass. The small opening wasn't armored at all and the effect was immediate, the dragon let out a horrifying shriek and spun around, blood gushing from the wound. "Ya didn't like getting a pain in the arse now did ya?!"

Rhuk sneered and tried to run out of the way but the dragon tried to sit on him and with an odd sound also the wounded sinew snapped, now it had two useless back legs and it opened its jaws and slammed the tail against the ground, the eyes ablaze with rage. Rhuk did hesitate and that was not very smart, the dragon still had front legs and it just reached backwards and managed to throw the dwarf to the ground. The head was moving in for the kill when Kapha ran forth, carrying a javelin. He threw the weapon with all his might and it did hit the dragon in the mouth, it reared back and Kapha grasped Rhuk and almost tossed him out of the way. Then he ran after the dwarf but the dragon wasn't going to let its tormentor get away, before any of them had time to react the beast spewed a thick bluish liquid at the two running warriors and most of it hit Kapha's legs. The half dwarf fell with a scream of agony and that was when Phraan knew that also this dragon had a weak spot, one none of them had thought of before. He screamed at Dhokay. "Distract him, Vitile, shoot at his nose!"

The luptay did obey him, he ran forth, and the dragon turned its head to attack him but Vitile did fire several arrows and although they did bounce off on the hard hide they did irritate the huge monster. Phraan didn't know where he found the courage, and the strength. But he did run, raced towards the tail and he jumped up onto it and rushed up along the dragon's back. The creature was too large to even feel him but it knew he was there and it turned its head around and tried to buck and Phraan had anticipated that move. He had just one go at this, one chance. He kicked off from the base of its left wing and flew forward with all his might. The dragon opened its maw to snatch him in the air but Dhokay managed to hit the tip of its lower jaw with the war hammer and the dragon jerked and lowered its head again just a wee bit out of sheer shock. That was when Phraan's long elven sword found that soft spot just behind its jaw bone, and slid in like a knife through butter. Phraan did hang from the blade for a few seconds, forcing it into the tissues and then he dragged the blade out as he fell to the ground. Hot blood shot out of the wound and the dragon reared up but fell onto its side, the wounded back legs not able to support it. The head hit the ground with a thundering thud and Dhokay let out a roar. He and Phraan ran forth as one and the war hammer landed on the dragons head just above the eye socket as Phraan's blade did pierce the eye itself, sliding deep into the nerve and then hitting the brain behind it.

The two saw that the dragon was dying, blood pooling around it and the body convulsing violently. The tail was swinging around like a deadly projectile and they hurried to get out of the way. Vitile had dragged Kapha away from the dragon and Phraan did run over, shocked and terrified. The sight was ghastly, the legs were simply gone, eaten away by the acid and the half dwarf was still alive, he was trembling and Vitile was weeping. The two other wood elves stood by her side, pale and shocked. Phraan fell to his knees, not really believing what he saw. Kapha gasped, his eyes were rolling in his head. "Phraan, please…"

Phraan let out a wail of grief and pain and pulled his boot dagger, it was a very narrow and sharp weapon and he grasped Kapha's hand. "You fought well brother, you saved Rhuk"

He leaned forth and kissed Kapha's brow, tears welling up in his eyes and his body shaking with emotional pain. The half dwarf was beside himself with pain and there was nothing anybody could do, Phraan was the group leader, this was his responsibility, his task. Kapha did close his eyes to make it easier on his friend and Phraan plunged the dagger into the suffering half dwarf's temple, killing him instantly.

They all stood there, staring, eyes darkened by grief and fear and Phraan let out a roar. Vitile came forth and embraced him, held him tightly. Tersus and the chariot did return to them slowly and so did the rest of the men, Ivran stared at the dead dragon and his eyes told everybody that he could barely believe what he saw. Crassian did wet his lips. "You killed that monster? Oh Gods almighty, that is…"

Tersus did step down from the chariot, the horses were panting and trembling and the alchemist did step over to the dead dragon. The head was so huge it dwarfed the man and he stared at the small wound at the base of its jaw and nodded his head slowly. "The jugular, a most amazing observation. You do have a special skill"

Phraan didn't listen, he was so consumed by grief he was unable to think and Dhokay stepped forth, pushed Tersus away from them but gently. "That can wait Tersus, we have lost one of our own, let it rest"

The alchemist tilted his head. "Of course, I will take samples of the acid if nobody does protest? There could be something I can learn from it."

Dhokay did nod. "Be my guest but be careful, the acid is still active even after the dragon has died."

The alchemist sent the luptay a faint smile and went over to the carcass with some jars. Fastonar had stood there looking very shocked and now he did approach Crassian and the soldiers. "We make camp here, by the river. Come on, get some tents up. Then you can start burning bodies, the poor villagers shouldn't be left there to rot"

Ivran stared at the dead half dwarf, he felt something stirring inside, something very powerful, and very dark. It felt like anger, but it was more profound, more defined. The dragon laid there like a huge heap of flesh and he walked over to it, slowly as if in a trance. Many soldiers did the same, out of curiosity and morbid fascination and he stared at the dead beast and knew what it was that he felt, hatred. He had never tasted its sweet poison before but now he did, and the attraction terrified him. That beast was just…vile. It was so terrible and so dark and twisted and yet it had a sort of terrible beauty. It was so overwhelming and yet they had managed to kill it. Ivran swore to himself that he would do whatever he could to help them, even if that meant exposing himself as what he was.

The group had lost members before, but they hadn't expected it to happen again, and like that. Phraan was still being held by Vitile and everybody stood there weeping and stricken by grief. Rhuk was sitting on the ground, rocking back and forth and Dabin was whispering prayers in his own tongue. Kapha had died as a hero, but there was nothing beautiful about his death. Fastonar was running around, organizing things and soon a small camp was erected and they left the dead dragon behind and gathered around the camp fire. The soldiers were busy trying to give the dead villagers a decent funeral and the officers were staring at the dead dragons with dread. Crassian was glaring at the large one, eyes wide with disbelief. "Are they really that large normally?"

Fastonar shrugged. "Yes, some species are and this one does look as a hybrid between them, but I have seen larger dragons."

The officer cringed. "You have? How large then?"

Fastonar looked down. "Three times that size, but they cannot be fought at all, all one can do is hide and warn people."

Crassian saw that Ivran stood by the dead dragon, the lad had a hard expression on his face. "We didn't believe that dragons could be that fast"

Fastonar sighed. "No, they have changed, a lot!"

Tersus was done taking samples and Ivran saw that the man came over towards him. "An impressive beast yes? Clearly the result of intelligent manipulation"

Ivran frowned. "Really?"

Tersus nodded slowly, his eyes were dark and there was something cold in them. "Yes, I am an alchemist son, I prefer to see the world as substances, as matter. But I am not blind to the might of magic, nor do I deny that it can do things I cannot. This young man, is done by magic, chaotic magic, dark magic. Beware of its lure, for it will try to drag you inn!"

Tersus just turned around and walked towards the tent he had been given and Ivran swallowed hard. Tersus was right, he could feel it, this dragon did hide some terrible dark secret and if he squinted it was almost as if he could see a dark aura around the dead beast. There was still magic within it, a terrible and harm full power. It hadn't left the dragon as it died, and for some reason Ivran felt that it was crucial that this power was exposed, but how? And by whom? He couldn't say anything without revealing his true nature. It was a dilemma.

Kapha's body had been washed by some soldiers and wrapped in a cloak, others had built a pyre by the river and they would burn him when the sun set. The group had gathered and Rhuk and Dabin had cut their beards as a sign of grief and also rubbed ash into their hair. Dhokay had wrapped black ribbons around his arms and put black paint on his face, around his eyes, Shaluun had done the same and the wood elves had put on some odd headbands made from rawhide. Phraan was feeling as if he was stuck in a vacuum of some sorts, he was unable to speak, and all he could think about was Kapha's mutilated body. The acid had been so much more potent than what they had encountered before, so much worse.

Vitile held him and rubbed his back, she was crying and Phraan felt like weeping too, but for some reason he couldn't. If he only had seen that weak spot a little earlier, if his instincts had kicked in before the dragon had time to spew acid. Why was he given such a talent when he couldn't use it to save a friend? Kapha had always been the one to keep their moral up, the one to bring out their laughter even when the situation was dire. He would miss the half dwarf, and grieve him for a long time. All the times Kapha had tried to seduce him, oh by the gods, if it had brought him back Phraan would have let the half dwarf have it his way, if only once. Vitile sighed. "Guards have been placed around the perimeter, we should be warned if more dragons come. I suggest we eat and rest, we need to stay strong"

Everybody just stared at the ground and Vitile swallowed hard. She did know Phraan rather well and she did know that he would blame himself for this. But there was really only one thing which could be blamed and that was that goddamn dragon. The soldiers faced a terrible job and many had to stop since they simply got too emotional and overwhelmed, the tough ones had to work until after dusk before all the bodies were gathered and the pyres built. Crassian was staring at the long line of pyres and his heart felt heavy, so much death, and so meaningless. He had been a soldier most of his life, and he had learned the code of the warrior from the moment he could speak. This was the opposite of what he stood for, this was meaningless slaughter and if these monsters could be stopped he would do whatever he could to make that happen. Tersus stood by himself by the river, no wonder for he did stink even worse now that he had been cutting away at the dead dragon to get to the acid glands. The weapon the alchemist had used had been terrible, so gruesome the officer had a hard time believing it had been real but it had killed five dragons and that made him reconsider his ideas about honor and proper warfare. In this case such means were justified and he hoped that the alchemist could come up with other ideas, equally efficient.

Kapha's body was the first to be burned and Fastonar did light the pyre, he was crying but trying hard to stay calm and Phraan stood there holding Vitile and he was trembling. It was simply too much, they hadn't even seen the scale of the problem yet and already one of them was dead. What were they really trying to do? These dragons were so much more dangerous than the ones they had been fighting back then, it was just....Phraan didn't try to hide his tears, neither did the others and Thiana and Taurin did howl as the pyre burned down, long mournful howls which told the world of loss and sorrow. It was the way of their people. Phraan felt anger, an intense burning anger towards whatever it was which had sent those dragons south towards these lands. He didn't know what to do with it, for there was so little they really could do and Vitile did follow him to his tent afterwards. He was desperate, so in need of feeling something else than anger and sorrow, so scared and so full of doubt. When they made love that night he was rough, trying to expel all those dark emotions from his soul, forget them and drown them with passion. He did make her scream, both from pleasure and pain and when he finally did fall asleep he was completely drained and slept like the dead. Vitile laid there for a while, listening to his breath and her heart felt like lead in her chest. She had to be sure, there was no way around that. She got up slowly and put on some clothes, her body stiff and sore and she whimpered as she silently walked towards the dead dragon. He had been way too eager but she did understand it, and she did forgive him too, even if she felt as if he had tried to cleave her in half.

It was dark around the dead beast but she had very keen eyes like all elves and stared at the monstrosity. Tersus had already been cutting into the beast out of sheer curiosity and all she had to do was use those incisions for her own purpose. She worked fast, hoping she wouldn't find anything. Her blade did strike something hard, and she took a deep breath, closing her eyes. She pulled it free, it was another gem, no larger than the one she had found in the other dead dragon and it felt just as polluted by evil. It was dark red and she fought the urge to toss it away. She went over to some bushes and wiped her hands off on some leaves when she was sure she heard something, a twig which snapped perhaps? She stood still, listening for a while, sniffing the air. The dead dragon did drown out all natural scents and she sighed and walked towards the tents again, it had been nothing, she was just overwrought, her nerves oversensitive. It had been such a terrible thing and she wasn't herself.

The shadow moved very slowly out from behind the tree, staring at the elf woman who disappeared into the camp. It was too bad really, but that knowledge had to go. They couldn't find out, no, something had to be done. But it had to be done so that nobody suspected foul play, yes, it had to be something nobody suspected. It could be done, he didn't like it but nobody should be allowed to come in their way. Such a good thing then that there were people present who were weak and could be manipulated. The magic of the gems had to remain concealed, until the brothers had achieved their goal. So, first things first, make sure the magic did remain concealed and then make sure that nobody figured out the plan behind it all. It should be easy enough. The last orders he had received were hard to follow though, he had to find a way to either bring the mage responsible for the dead dragon to them or destroy that person and it would be a challenge for sure but perhaps fate would favour him, yet again.

Chapter 5: Heart of darkness

The next morning was grey, and the clouds did hang low, as if it was gonna rain. The villagers had been burned and the blackened squares of soil were like open graves, speaking of death and despair. Phraan had a headache as he woke up, Vitile had curled up next to him and she was still sleeping, her face revealed worries. He sighed, stared up at the canvas, not knowing what to think, what to do. Five of those smaller dragons and one huge one, and a village which had been obliterated, it couldn't be the only one. People did flee, villages had burned. Why not this one? Why had those dragons just crushed everything? It didn't make sense, unless the five had arrived after the attack and the huge monster was the one responsible for the whole mayhem. That meant that they were co-operating somehow, even if they were of different species and that was new. Phraan closed his eyes, tears did still burn in them and he swallowed not to sob. It felt so unfair, but what were they to do? They were just one group, and these new horrors were beyond them. The alchemist had killed the five but he was just one man and he couldn't possibly kill that many more? He pulled Vitile closer to him, held her and felt the warmth of her, took comfort in her presence. She had always been the one to keep him stabile, to show him the way. He had been reckless back then, sometimes almost suicidal. He hadn't truly cared that much about anything except the feeling of victory, of knowing he had conquered yet another monster.

She had been the balance of him and she had been well aware of that fact.

There was the sound of a horn, horses were whinnying, orders being shouted and he sighed and shook her gently. She yawned and sat up, her eyes were a bit red, perhaps that was no wonder, they had all wept. She pulled the blanket tighter around her elegant frame and bit her lower lip. "Phraan, I went out last night, after you fell asleep."

He frowned, searching for his underwear. "You did?"

She nodded, the long silky hair like a curtain around her face. "Yes, I checked the large dragon, it too had a gem in its chest"

He stiffened, dropped his pants, stared at her. "It did? Oh Gods, that means…"

She looked at him with large eyes. "They all have one, it is deliberate Phraan, not nature. It is an attack against the realm."

He reached out, took her hand. "I have hard time believing it, but…it sounds so real"

She nodded. "I have put the gems in my saddle, the horn is hollow. If we had had a magician I bet that person could have determined where they come from, what sort of history they have"

He felt a sting of anger towards the king who had sent them off without a mage, but there wasn't anything they could do about that now. "What are you gonna do?"

His voice was low and she sighed again, her elbows resting on her knees. "Keep them, see if we can find out more. I don't like them, they are bad magic."

Phraan took a deep breath. "If just someone knew more, I remember those stories, the wall in the mountains and the balance. What if the legends are true?"

She had to smile. "Yes, what if? But it is time to get up, we need to get going. There has to be something we can do to get a better view of the situation, to find out just how many dragons we are talking about"

He nodded, sighing. "What we need to do is warn the king, and tell him that this is something nobody has encountered before. That everything is going to hell with record speed unless those beasts are stopped."

She looked down, her face revealed a great deal of uncertainty. "Phraan, when I was out there, I heard something, or rather, I believe I heard something."

He pulled his pants on, tightened the belt. "You did? What?"

She shrugged. "It could have been nothing but…I felt watched for a moment"

Phraan swallowed. "Vitile, take care of yourself, never go anywhere unarmed. I don't like the feel of this."

She grasped for her tunic. "Neither do I"

He stared at her as she got dressed, why would anybody be out there, watching her without letting themselves be known? He just felt strange, as if he too was being watched and that by someone with ill intent. They left the tent and the camp was being broken by the soldiers, tents reassembled and packed away and Tersus stood by the carcass and he was making drawings of the beast. Ivran had just gotten up and he did look rather disheveled, Phraan still couldn't help but think that he had seen something, but what? Why didn't he tell them? Fastonar came walking at a brisk pace. "I say we do get back as fast as possible, I don't like being out here now, not with monsters like that flying around. The Gods alone knows what else could be out there"

Dhokay and Shaluun had shared a tent that night, both looked as if they hadn't slept at all and the two wood elves were still wearing the sorrow bands. Rhuk and Dabin went to the river to wash the ash out of their hair, they returned looking like cats which had been half drowned and Phraan pulled Fastonar aside. "Do you have any idea of what to do next? We cannot fight such monsters, we don't know enough!"

Fastonar looked down. "Look, Kapha was my friend too, I...I was very fond of him, and the loss...I am sorry but...The best we can do from now on is simply warn people, help them get out of harm's way. Those dragons, they don't behave the way they used to, it is as if they are set upon destruction and only that. It is frightening."

Phraan nodded. "Indeed it is"

Fastonar patted him on the back. "We will get back to the city, then we will make plans"

Phraan smiled and started helping the soldiers roll up the remaining tents. The faster they got away from there the faster he could put it all behind him. Ivran stood by the carcass and he felt angry and also confused. The dark simmering feeling he had felt had vanished, it was gone. The dragon had been cut open by Tersus and for some reason the magic wasn't there anymore. Had the alchemist something to do with it? He doubted it somehow. Ivran frowned, he intended to keep his eyes open, if he was to carry the burden of having inherited his grandfather's powers then he ought to use them for something good, and he was sure he could sense it if that magic appeared again. He would try to find out what it had been.

The soldiers were quiet as they rode past the remains of the village, one of the officers did throw a torch onto the dry wood, just to cleanse the place. There shouldn't be anything left to tempt those able to pillage the ruins. Tersus stood in the chariot with the mine of a king but there were shadows in his eyes and Ivran felt that he perhaps was the one who saw deepest of them all. They knew the way now and the horses knew that they were heading back to the stables and thus the ride was fast but relatively easy. They returned to the city just after it got dark and the place did simmer with activity. While they had been away a convoy of refugees had been attacked by a horde of small flying dragons and many had been killed. Luckily the dragons too had suffered losses since there had been archers among the refugees and a small group had brought one of the dead creatures to the city. The survivors were heading south but there had been wounded and they had been taken to the city. Phraan ran to the officer's tent the moment he heard of the dead dragons, the animal was laid on display there and he stopped in the doorway, staring at the creature. It was larger than a blood wing, and it had an uncanny red color and its claws were razor sharp and long. The greatest difference though was in its eyes, they were huge and Phraan immediately knew what that meant. "These dragons are bred for night attacks"

The officer who was present nodded. "Yes, they did come at night"

The half elf stared at the man. "The ones who brought it here, where are they? I need to speak with them, it is urgent"

The officer pointed. "They are in the infirmary, there were wounded among them"

Phraan just bowed his head and ran off. The infirmary was a tent, placed close to the wall where it was shade and where the wind didn't get so cold. He entered and found three men standing by a bed and two women were there too. One was old, her back bent and her face wrinkled and grey but the eyes were clear and piercing. She wore a very elaborate headdress and lots of jewelry and Phraan immediately knew that she was a person of considerable power. They stared at him and he grimaced, realized that they probably found the sight of him intimidating since he was dressed like a warrior and were armed. "My pardons, but you brought that dead dragon here, what can you tell me of the attack? "

The old woman stared at him, her eyes were rather hard and her expression one of grief. "They came suddenly, with the dusk. But there was still some light left, and our archers managed to fell some"

Phraan saw that the beds were occupied by mostly younger people, and they didn't appear to have burns but rather cuts and bites. "Was the flock large?"

The woman nodded and one of the adult men made a grimace, his face was a bit pale and he had blood in his hair but didn't appear to be severely wounded. "We counted about fifty, but we did see a larger flock in the distance, maybe two hundred, three hundred? It was hard to tell since it was getting dark so fast. But they made a terrible racket, and did smell too"

Phraan saw that the people weren't local. Their clothes and the accent with which they spoke told him that beyond any doubt. "But arrows did kill them?"

The man nodded slowly. "Yes, if you hit the head, from the underside. The chest appeared to be too hard to penetrate"

Phraan knew it was important information, he ought to tell the others right away. The old woman did raise her chin. "We have travelled far, from the lake by the foot of the mountains. The dragons came and ate our sheep and then they burned our tents and huts and chased us away. They will continue until they have reached the far south."

Phraan stared at her, his eyes narrow. "Why do you say that?"

She looked him straight in the eye. "I say that because it is the truth, because it is what the ancestors warned us about. The dragons will rule this land, and everything will be ashes"

Phraan saw that she was trembling ever so slightly, her voice told of fear and a lack of hope and he wished that he could have comforted her somehow. "It could be that they will return to wherever they come from?"

The man shook his head. "No, Irife is speaking the truth, the tales all speak of a time when the dragons will break free from their leash and take over the world, unless certain things do happen"

Phraan had to turn and look at him. "Excuse me, their leash?"

The man nodded solemnly. "Yes, the dark brothers are behind all of this, they unleashed the dragons the last time, and they will unleash them again but then the dragons will be too strong and destroy their masters and it may all end in flames"

Phraan had to frown and his eyes did probably speak of disbelief. "That is a new one, I have never heard of that tale"

The young woman had been sitting until now, she was looking at one of the wounded persons and she hadn't even looked at Phraan. He did see that she had her hair covered by a very colorful scarf as it was customary in this region and her dress too looked very elaborate. Now she turned around and Phraan was stunned by her appearance, she had a shocking lack of colors and her eyes were red. She was an albino and he had never seen a human one. She was smiling, a very faint smile. "It is old, our people have preserved it for ages, as a warning. The dark ones will return but their arrogance will be their downfall"

Phraan took a deep breath. "Listen, I have heard legends speaking of that brotherhood and their dedication to chaos but there is nothing proving that they are behind it all? They disappeared thousands of years ago."

The old woman pulled her scarf tighter around herself. "When the dragons do fly again they have awakened anew. My mother told me that, as her mother told her. They have returned, mark my words"

The young woman sighed. "And all we are left to do is flee and mourn our dead"

Phraan looked at the row of wounded, he swallowed hard. "Have you lost many?"

The man answered, he was holding his fur hat in his hands, fidgeting with it. "Some now, many before. Most of our old decided to stay behind, they couldn't travel and chose to die where they had lived."

Phraan felt a lump form in his throat. "That is too bad, I was afraid of something like this when I was called back into service"

The man stared at him. "You are a slayer? Good, then you know that these dragons are different from the ones which ravaged the lands fifty summers ago. They cannot be beaten"

The young woman looked at him, the red eyes were unreal. "Strangle the source, dam the river, it is the only way"

The old woman put a shaking hand on the girls shoulder. "Imeah is a seer, and our healer. Her powers are growing, but she cannot yet control them very well."

Phraan blinked. "A seer? That is rare, and a healer too?"

Imeah looked down. "I was born with those gifts, it is my gift and my curse. My path is not my own to rule, I am a pawn of fate herself"

The old woman sent Phraan a faint and somewhat melancholic grin. "She is our treasure, the one who sees the truth of all"

The albino girl appeared to blush a bit, she looked down and Phraan did notice that she had a veil attached to her head dress. "I have to cover my face when I am outside in the sun, it has to be that way, I burn easily"

Phraan sent her a small smile. "I understand, some people have sensitive skin"

The old woman sat down. "We will stay here until our wounded are strong enough to travel, heed my words dragon slayer, these beasts cannot be fought one by one"

Phraan felt that she was right, but he had to hope that they could do something, no matter how insignificant it was. Imeah was staring at the young man on the bed in front of her again, she didn't turn her head. "We will talk again later, there are things...you will need to know"

He frowned but she didn't say any more and Phraan bowed and left the tent, feeling confused and a little shocked.

The camp was relatively quiet now, but there was lights everywhere in the building Tersus occupied and he did see that the others had gathered in the large tent for debriefing. He sauntered over, and was met by Crassian who held a jug of ale and a huge piece of cheese. "Get something to eat, the night is still rather young, and there is much to be discussed"

Phraan sighed and got some food too, he was hungry but his mind wasn't into it, could it be that these old tales were true? He did believe in the powers, just as he believed in magic for it was something he did see every day but prophesies? That was a bit far-fetched the way he did see it. Oh he had heard a lot of prophecies, some grand and others not so much so. He had to grin all to himself, he remembered a somewhat deranged magician who had firmly believed that the volcano dominating one of the islands close to the western coast was going to explode. The man had been so adamant in his belief that he had gone to the ruler of that area and demanded that the entire coastline was evacuated. The king hadn't believed him at first but after a lot of heavy arguing the coastal villages were evacuated and the magician stayed behind to try to soothe the spirits of the angry mountain. What he really did was steal every little thing worth having before he stole a ship and sailed off.

Prophecies could be used for many a purpose and Phraan knew that the academy forbid its students from trying to see the future. There were spells which enabled you to do so to a certain degree but they couldn't be trusted at all. Natural seers were a different thing all together, they couldn't control their visions and neither did they get any explanations as to why they saw what they did. Nobody could deny a natural born seer the right to be who they were born to be but few if any did put full faith in what these individuals did tell. Vitile came forth and hugged Phraan. "So, what did you find out?"

He smiled down at her. "These small flying dragons can be shot, through the underside of the head. But the flocks are large and can do great damage"

Vitile sighed. "And they can fly at night, damn it, that is not good news"

Phraan took a deep breath. "I spoke with some of the refugees. They come from the far north, have travelled for quite a while. They have a seer among them"

Vitile frowned and looked a bit stunned. "A seer? Really? That is quite special, who is he?"

Phraan shook his head. "She, it is a girl, her name is Imeah and she is an albino"

Dhokay did look fascinated. "That gift often is followed by a physical handicap, at least in humans. I met a seer once, he was very powerful but couldn't move, his legs were dead."

Ivran had been sitting by a table drinking on his own, but now he started listening. A seer? He had never met one, but the masters at the academy said that some seers were mad and others touched by the Gods themselves. Could this girl have true powers? Shaluun was speaking to Taurin in the soft elvish language and Fastonar was looking at maps, his face was grim. "I have no idea of what to do, honestly! There are too many people in danger and we do not have any way of knowing for how far the dragons have spread now. Have this camp received news from the south lately?"

The commander had agreed to come to the meeting and he shook his head. "No, we normally receive pigeons from the other camps up north one a week but we haven't received any for at least three weeks now. We fear the worst"

Fastonar took a deep breath. "How far away is the nearest camp?"

The commander Janok and his officers did look at each other. "A five days ride to the west of here, along the trading route. It is a small camp though, just one officer and twenty soldiers. They guard an important bridge"

Fastonar nodded. "I see it here on the map. Send four riders there tomorrow, we do need to know if they have heard something from the west, and to the east I see one camp too but that is way too far away"

The commander nodded. "Indeed it is, two weeks of ride. And you have to cross a desert to get there"

Fastonar looked at the map. "Have they ever failed to deliver reports before?"

Janok shook his head. "No, but considering the situation it isn't that odd really"

Fastonar sighed. "Folks, we need to rest and to think, we'll assemble again tomorrow evening to discuss the further path of actions. The one thing we can agree on already now is that we cannot hope to just ride out and kill dragons the ways we used to, these beasts are way too hard to slaughter."

Everybody mumbled and Phraan was thinking of the prophecies they had heard and his mind was working and dragging him in a direction he didn't like at all. He left the tent and walked over to the corrals to check on his horse. In the old days they would use spears against the dragons, and ropes too. They would dig traps with skewers at the bottom, logs with spearheads which would fall down onto the dragons, even leave poisoned baits. Now these options were useless, or at least it seemed so. He groomed Drake for a good hour and when he left the corral he saw Ivran standing on the wall, the young man looked towards the south and Phraan didn't know how to read the expression within his eyes. He walked up and Ivran saw him, made a grimace. Phraan sighed. "You don't want me here?"

Ivran looked down. "No, I mean...it is alright. I just..."

Phraan saw that the young human was struggling with something and he had never left the feeling that Ivran was hiding something behind. "You need to let something off your chest right?"

Ivran bit his lower lip, his eyes were moist. "I...I killed that dragon, I admit it, it was me. But I have no idea of how I did it."

Phraan took a deep breath. "You are a mage after all?"

186

Ivran shook his head. "No, I am not. I haven't passed my tests, I studied for so many years and I never managed to do anything right. They had to let me go in the end, since I was unable to learn."

Phraan looked confused. "Really? But…"

Ivran sighed, his shoulder slumped forward. "I feel so…guilty, if I had tried perhaps I could have killed that huge one, before it killed Kapha. I should have told you but I haven't dared to"

Phraan frowned, he did feel a sting of anger and he sent the young man a rather harsh glance. "Why? Do you think we are some sort of threat to you?"

Ivran sniffed. "No, I just…listen, my grandfather was a great magician, capable of doing things nobody else would even dream of. And I have inherited his powers, but I don't know how to use them yet. I did see him in a vision and he warned me, told me not to tell anybody of this, for there are enemies out there, who would do anything to possess the magic I now harbor"

Phraan stared at the young man, saw the sincerity of his soul and understood. "I see, it is wise then to keep it hidden, but you do have some idea of what you are capable of? Vitile said that the heart of that dragon had exploded from the inside"

Ivran sat down, his legs dangling over the edge of the wall. "When I first noticed my gift…this is embarrassing but it did include a girl I liked"

Phraan tilted his head. "Why do I get the feeling that this is something you find difficult?"

He made his voice playful and Ivran was blushing like a beet, his eyes cast down. "I…I wanted to see…more of her if you catch my drift? And she fell and her skirts did fly up and well, I saw it all"

Phraan had to snicker. "That sounds like most young males yes, eager to catch a glimpse of the ladies."

Ivran was biting his lower lips, the deep blush getting even deeper. "Uh, what happened next was…strange. She came to me, I was in the dorm thinking about her and she…she just…you know"

Phraan lifted his head, eyes narrow. "She fucked you? And she hadn't shown any interest in you before? What exactly did you think back then, and when that dragon charged?"

Ivran blinked. "Uh, I just thought that I wanted her, imagined her with me, and she did show up just like that. And the dragon? I guess I wanted it to die, I shouted something but I cannot remember what"

Phraan swallowed. "Ivran, a gift like that is extremely rare, and you have got to learn how to use it. You have been taught discipline haven't you? How to meditate and ease your mind?"

Ivran nodded. "Of course, I did way more meditating than the other students, the masters believed that maybe that was what I needed to be able to use spells like the others"

Phraan took a deep breath. "Ivran, to be able to use magic without the focus of a spell should be impossible. And yet you do it, did your grandfather do the same thing?"

Ivran nodded slowly. "Yes, but he did camouflage it, nobody suspected anything"

Phraan looked Ivran in the eye. "Listen, I will go and get Vitile, she is very smart and knows a lot about magic and so does Shaluun. Wait here"

Ivran nodded and Phraan left, Ivran felt both relieved and terrified, the cat was out of the bag now, anything could happen really.

After just a moment the half elf returned with the two and Ivran had to tell everything once more, from the beginning. Shaluun did look a bit shocked. "You have the original magic, the undiluted pure power. You have to learn how to control it lad, it could become so valuable."

Vitile nodded but her eyes were dark. "Ivran, when you were brought here you were drained, your life almost spent.

You had fired off all you had in one go, no wonder why that dragon was charred. You cannot do something like that again, it is dangerous to you and if there indeed are enemies around that much power is like a beacon."

Ivran sighed and looked down, the arms crossed over his chest. "I guess I know that, but I just…I wish to help, I just don't know how"

Shaluun put a hand on the young man's shoulder, smiling. "I can help you, we had young in my tribe who had some magical abilities and we always tried to teach them how to control it. I can teach you those methods"

Ivran looked eager all of a sudden. "You can?"

Shaluun nodded. "Yes, and I suggest we start right away. If your powers can help us you need to start using them soon."

Ivran smiled and his eyes were huge. "Please, let us do it"

Shaluun sent the young human a wry grin. "Alright, then let us get down from here, I suggest we go somewhere undisturbed to start your training. There is a small Holt of trees by the cliff you see out there due south, we can start there. Go get a horse, I will meet you by the gate"

Ivran nodded and sprinted down the ramp, Shaluun was smiling. "He is eager, I am sure he can become a valuable resource. With that sort of power there ought to be at least something we can do to help people"

Phraan was frowning. "I am not so sure that I like this Shaluun, he is perhaps powerful but we have no idea of just how much he can do. He did kill a dragon but that was in a fit of panic"

Vitile gave Phraan a swift hug. "Yes, but it does show us what he can do. His mind forms the magic, not the spells. There are no limitations to what he can achieve whence he has opened his mind to the possibilities."

They watched as Ivran and Shaluun rode out, Phraan got an odd feeling in his gut watching the young human. Why he didn't know, it was just some nagging sensation of having

189

overlooked something, something important. They returned to the tents and tried to find some rest but it was very hard. Phraan was thinking about the changes which had happened to the dragons, and the gems Vitile had found. He had a bad suspicion growing steadily within his heart, these attacks had been just the start.

Shaluun had taken Ivran out to the cliff and lit a small campfire, it was dark and the skies were clear, it did look so very beautiful and Ivran remembered that the smoke and dust of the city had obscured the view of the heavens. He stared at Shaluun who sat down not far from him. "The young of our tribe would often prepare themselves before starting the training, by fasting or ingesting certain herbs. But you have trained at the academy for a very long time, so I guess you are as ready as anyone can be"

Ivran nodded, changing his seat to one more comfortable one. "Yes, I hope so"

Shaluun pointed at the small campfire. "Alright, look into the fire, feel its warmth and its ethereal substance"

Ivran swallowed and did what he was being told to do. The fire wasn't large but it was warm and pleasantly so too for it was very cold there now. Shaluun didn't move, the soft deep voice was very pleasant to listen to. "Think of yourself as a part of that fire, think of it as your breath, as your heartbeat"

Ivran relaxed, remembered the countless hours of meditation he had been through. He let that deep almost trancelike state descend upon him again and continued to stare into the flickering flames, doing what Shaluun said. The flame did stand still for a moment, then it started to move slowly, grow and shrink, grow and shrink in rhythm, with his breath. Shaluun watched in astonishment, the human did indeed possess a strange magic and this was the key to controlling it, his very own mind. The elf saw that Ivran was in a sort of trance and whispered. "Make a tower out of it, a structure"

Ivran saw a sort of cylinder made from the flames themselves and sort of formed it with his mind, he felt sweat pouring down his neck but he didn't think much of it, there was as sort of shivering running through the flames and then they solidified, into a cylinder. The flame stopped moving completely, but it did produce some heat and he stared at it with huge eyes. Shaluun did look shocked. "Ivran, touch it"

The young human did reach out, slowly, the flame had become a sort of crystal, and he could lift it without getting burned but it was still rather warm. It was as if he had caught the essence of those flames in some manner. Shaluun was impressed and a little scared, transmutation, that ought to be impossible. "Good, you did well, how do you feel?"

Ivran shrugged. "Good, but tired."

Shaluun swallowed. "Alright, just one more test, then we'll rest. This one is hard, so focus your mind"

Shaluun picked up a small rock" See this one? It is small, and light, I will toss it in the air and you are to stop it, without touching it, alright?"

Ivran made a nervous laugh. "A-alright, I'll try."

He followed the small rock with its eyes and imagined it stopping just before it hit the ground. Nothing happened and it landed with a small thud. Shaluun smiled. "We'll try again, just keep your eyes on it!"

Yet another miss, the rock fell to the ground and Ivran felt frustrated, why couldn't he stop that tiny rock when he had solidified flames? The rock was tossed again and Ivran clenched his teeth together, focusing on the falling pebble. Suddenly it was gone, heading upwards at a tremendous speed. Shaluun did wet his lips. "Ah, alright, it isn't falling anymore, now it is shooting for the moon I suppose. You used a bit too much power, try again"

He found another small rock and this time the rock did stop a few inches above the ground before it shot off along the terrain and embedded itself in the base of a tree with a loud thunk! Shaluun swallowed. "So, rocks can be used as projectiles, good to know. This time, just imagine the rock hovering, gently"

Ivran felt his heart hammering but he nodded. "Yes"

Two more attempts were needed before the rock hovered and Shaluun was intrigued. It seemed that Ivran had way better control of certain elements than others, fire was easy, and also water. Rocks were hard, but doable and when he tried to make the young man create a zone around them free of wind all they got was a mini tornado threatening to flatten the nearby trees. But the elf was very impressed, in fact he had rarely ever met someone of such immense talent and power. He patted Ivran on the back. "Rest now, you deserve it. Remember, focus is the key to success, do not let your mind wander in any way, see the goal ahead of you in detail"

Ivran nodded slowly, dragging a blanket around himself and the elf lit another fire. The old one was still standing in the grass next to them, a cylinder of light and warmth, like a frozen flame. Shaluun wondered what fate had in store for them now, could the young human really make a difference? He did hope so, oh by the gods how he hoped so.

The morning came to Mudwall with drizzling rain and a wind which was so cold you felt frozen to the core the moment you stepped outside of the door. The soldiers did get up to start their chores and the city was alive as always with people trying to buy or sell things and the rain didn't stop that. The area around the house Tersus had been given had been sealed off on his request, he was afraid that some of his so called experiments could have unexpected consequences as he called it and the soldiers walk around that building very carefully and nobody got too close. The gates were guarded the whole time, the guards were changed every second hour now and the two who stood there now were at the end of their shifts and eager to return to the barracks and warm clothes and warm food. They were leaning against the gate, blowing warm air at their fingertips as they dreamed of their cots and probably also of payday when they could buy themselves a night out and maybe even some company. The first one heard the sound of hooves and straightened himself up, it was just one horse but the fog lay thick over the ground and muffled the sounds and he pushed his companion and nodded. "Someone's coming"

The other guards grumbled and held his spear in a manner which was a wee bit more intimidating. The hooves got closer and it was soon rather clear that yes, it was just one horse. As the rider got closer both guards took their positions, one rider was hardly a threat but they needed to make sure that nobody entered the city without having been checked over. The commander didn't want anyone to get inside who were ill or a criminal. Both gaped as a figure appeared out of the fog, it was a cloaked rider on a giant mule and the animal was wearing just a rope around its neck and no saddle. The rider wore a huge cape which covered the entire body and it was impossible to determine who or what this was. Very few people used mules for riding, they were usually rather stubborn and also not very comfortable to sit on. The rider stopped and the two guards stepped forth, the rider appeared to be unarmed and that in itself was very odd. Few travelers would risk traversing this area on their own, especially now, the situation taken into consideration. "Who are you, and what is your business here?"

The rider pulled the hood down and the guards just stared. The rider was female, and she didn't look like any creature they had met before. Her ears did reveal that she was an elf but her facial features were different from any other elf they had come across. Her eyes were rather large and golden in a very deep tone and her skin was rather dark, almost like oiled wood. The most stunning detail was her hair, it had a very deep rich amethyst color and it appeared to be very long and thick. She was a stunning beauty and completely inhuman in a way most elves were not. The guards just gaped and she smiled, a swift smile from perfect cherry red lips. "My name is Zaray, and I am here to buy a horse or two"

The guards relaxed. "You have lost your horse?"

She nodded. "Indeed I have, some pesky dragons did chase it off, and I was left with my pack mule."

The oldest of the guards were staring still. "But you were unharmed? That is rare"

The woman smiled again, she wore gloves and she had thick and good clothes underneath her cape. She did appear to be rather wealthy. "I was lucky I guess, may I enter?"

The guards stepped out of the way, bowed their heads. "Most certainly ma'am, there are plenty of horses here and I am sure you will find what you are looking for. "

The woman nodded her head politely. "There is one thing, some refugees I met said there were slayers here? Is that true?"

The guards nodded. "Yes, two groups, both very skilled"

She smiled and urged the mule forth. "Good, I have always dreamed of meeting a real dragon slayer"

She rode through the gate and the two guards stared after her, they had never seen anything more beautiful and majestic and the oldest one turned to his friend and made a grimace. "The queen isn't half as pretty as that one, nor half as lady like"

The other one nodded. "I agree!"

The female rode towards the area of the city which held the inns, they were few and inexpensive and she stopped at the first one and dismounted. The mule was so large it made the horses tethered outside look small and she revealed that she was very tall herself. She stared at the door with narrow eyes, now everything did depend on her approach, her initial contact. They were all there, she could feel it, but how was she to gain their trust? She just had to wait and see. The innkeeper was stunned to see a very beautiful elven female and he did swiftly promise her both a bath and some good food. She carried her belongings in a small bag, she didn't need much and rarely carried anything except the clothes she wore. Her only weapon was a dagger and a hidden weapon whose origin few knew. It was a bracelet attached to her left wrist and she stared at it with a thin smile. She would have to use it, there was no way around it if the situation called for it. If they were to accept her she would have to prove her worth and that meant possible exposure. She couldn't hesitate though, she had to be ready. All would be lost otherwise, the balance had to be kept, no matter what.

She ate and bathed and then she took a stroll through the city, just to get familiar with it, it was like hundreds of other similar cities but she did feel the fear which rested in the hearts of everybody present. The last time dragons had ravaged these lands she had been somewhere far south, and the time hadn't been right. There had been few things she could do. Now on the other hand…She just had to wait for the right moment to strike, and hope that the dark brother's didn't know what they were facing, yet!

Ivran and Shaluun had returned to the camp just before dawn, Ivran was so tired he was trembling and Shaluun held him upright in the saddle in front of him. The young man staggered for his tent and Phraan looked a bit worried. "Is he hurt?"

Shaluun shook his head. "No, he isn't hurt, just tired. He kept trying and trying and he doesn't know when to stop, but I have to say that he is amazing. When he learns to control his powers he is gonna be amazingly skilled. That is for sure"

The elf put a hand into his cape and pulled out a glowing piece of crystal, handed it over to Phraan who took it with wide eyes. "Is this…"

Shaluun nodded. "Fire, he can solidify fire, I have seen wonders this night Phraan. He must come with us, there is no other way. That sort of power can come in so handy"

Phraan didn't doubt that, not for a single moment. He just wondered if the young man was ready to face a dragon yet again. Fastonar was walking by and saw the crystal and his lower jaw did almost hit his chest, Phraan had to explain it all to him and for a moment the soul-sworn did look shocked, or rather, confused. There was some sort of shadow in his eyes and he did clench his teeth but then he smiled and was himself again and Phraan wondered what this was, was Fastonar angry becauce Ivran hadn't told them before, and possibly saved Kapha?

The commander had sent out riders and also pigeons and he was also trying to get a clear picture of how many people did region did house. There hadn't been any attempt at counting the number of people living there since the area was free of taxes. The king had declared that the region was too devastated after those years of dragon attacks to pay any tax. He didn't want to plunge already poor citizens of his realm into starvation and for that he had become very popular indeed. The people living in the city did provide him with some information and the refugees who had sought protection there or passed by had also given him some numbers. The habitation as far spread and some were nomads, thus the numbers were estimates at best but it was still chilling. Several tens of thousands of people lived this far north and if the dragons attacked all the regions along the mountains the death toll could be astronomical. Janok didn't want to think about it. He was already making plans, they had to send riders south soon, ask for more soldiers to escort the refuges and keep them safe. When a society faces collapse the way it did now there will always be those desperate or wicked enough to prey upon the weak and Janok knew of bands of outlaws who until now had lived in the most desolate areas. But the dragons would force them too out of hiding and into the light and the commander wasn't a dragon slayer but he did know how to fight men.

The cold weather was hampering everything and Vitile and the other wood elves sat inside of a tent, taking care of their saddles. As most elves they did ride with just a sort of soft padded one attached to the horse with a wide strap and Vitile put her saddle onto a rack and sighed. Aiolo had been assigned to help them and the young man sat there rubbing saddle oil onto one of the pack saddles. He was as grumpy and anti-social as ever and didn't speak even when spoken too. Vitile didn't like him, she trusted him even less than she had trusted the dead drunkard. She and the two others got up to get some food and Aiolo just sneered at them and continued working, his eyes were so dark and she suspected that he was insane somehow. Phraan and Dhokay were explaining the different ways to spear a dragon to some of the knights and the men were paying close attention, they did also ask very sensible questions and Phraan was glad to share his knowledge. They were almost done when there was a shout from the watch tower which had been erected near the middle of the camp. "There is something on the horizon, possibly dragons"

Fastonar had been watching the demonstrations but now he suddenly turned efficient. "Get the horses, armor up, get ready!"

He ran to the corrals and the others followed him, Phraan felt his heart hammer in his chest, was this an opponent they could hope to beat or would they have to flee? Everybody found their saddles and their equipment and before long they rushed out of the gate. Ivran too had been awakened and rode at the back of the group and Tersus had gotten hold of a four wheeled wagon drawn by four large donkeys. The animals were surprisingly fast and Peter was driving. The wagon was stuffed with bags and boxes and Ivran was both curious and a bit terrified. The thing the guards had seen was a huge pack of dreklugnins and also some other smaller dragon species. Ivran saw some very pale beasts the size of a large dog and there were small dragons in the air as well. The huge pack was heading their way and Phraan shouted some orders. The knights did divide into four groups, each consisting of two riders side by side six men deep and all carried lances.

The elves had their bows ready and Tersus had some sort of device on his wagon which resembled a sort of catapult. He stopped the wagon and as the beasts came closer he started to fire, small bags of some sort which flew through the air and exploded in a cloud of powder as they reached the ground. The archers did take care of the flying dragons, they weren't that many but Ivran saw that they had very nasty jaws and some did spew flames, although not very strong ones. The knights did do as they had been taught to do and Phraan and the others did fight very well. Dragons dropped dead when they inhaled the powder in the bags and arrows were flying overhead like a swarm of angry hornets. Ivran stood there, not really knowing what to do, then he remembered the lesson with the stones and imagined that the forwards charging beasts were stones, not dragons. He immediately felt a terrible jolt, as if something truly massive had crashed into him and he tumbled from his horse with a yell. He rolled instinctively but the impact had been so hard he felt he was slipping away. Shaluun stopped his own horse with a roar and jumped down, stood to guard the unconscious man. "Gods, so brave and so stupid!"

Several dragons had fallen as if their feet had been ripped out from underneath them and the knights didn't waste any time but attacked with brutal determination. Rhuk and Dabin swung their axes with bellowing war cries and Dhokay used his great hammer as always. The battle had become a true fight now and every trick was legal. Vitile was shooting at the flying dragons, most were felled now and the rest were about to flee and she sent off an arrow with a curse, the goddamn beasts were cowards. She turned her horse around, aiming for a dragon which was heading away from them and suddenly the horse shrieked and stumbled violently. Vitile was an excellent rider like all elves and able to keep her balance rather well but there as a snapping sound and her saddle broke. The elf tumbled down with a shout, hitting the ground hard as she rolled away from the horse. The bow snapped in the impact and Vitile threw it away and tried to get back onto her feet, then a roar came from her right and she turned just in time to see that a dreklugnin had aimed itself at her and it was so close there was no way she could avoid it.

Vitile screamed to warn the others, she jumped, using all her elven grace and skill and managed to get out of the way as the beast snapped after her the first time. She had pulled her long narrow sword and tried to hit the eye on her way down but another dreklugnin interfered with her attacker and made it jerk back and she missed. She saw that Phraan was riding towards her, his lance held in the attack position and she was so very sorry, he would be too late. The other dreklugnin was just too fast and the jaws snapped shut around her legs. Vitile didn't scream, the pain was just too great, she plunged her sword into the beast's eye and the dreklugnin did let go of her with a hoarse roar, she tumbled to the ground just as Phraan hit the other one with his lance. The beast fell immediately and Vitile gasped, her field of vision was shrinking and she felt the life leave her swiftly, the legs were more or less bitten off, the blood loss simply too great. She tried to reach for him, to hold his hand, to tell him how she felt one last time but the world went black.

Phraan screamed, a wild cry of anguish and threw himself off Drake, fell onto his knees next to her. Shaluun came running, carrying Ivran over his shoulders. "Fast, your belt, tie off the wounds"

The tall blonde had already taken his own belt and now he attached it around Vitile's left thigh, Phraan snapped out of it, doing the same thing on the right side and Shaluun was wild eyed and desperate. "We have to get back to the city, now! We are outnumbered!"

Phraan did look at the battle surrounding them, even with the knights there were too many dreklugnins and Tersus had run out of those powder bags. The beasts were everywhere and didn't care if many of their brethren were felled, all they wanted was to kill. Phraan stared down at Vitile, her heart was still beating but very faintly and he knew they would lose her, as they had lost Kapha. Their chances of escape were slim, Rhuk was on foot now, so was Fastonar since his horse had been killed under him and the knights weren't skilled enough for such a huge attack. The dreklugnins were too fast and agile. They could all die there now and the thought was terrifying and bitter at the same time. Drake was fighting even without a rider, the huge stallion did kick at a dreklugnin which tried to bite it and broke its jaw and Phraan felt desperation clench around his chest. "Retreat, everybody, we need to return to the city"

Fastonar was panting, using his swords now. "Impossible, we'll just delay the inevitable, we have to save the population"

Phraan leaned forth, kissed Vitile's pale brow. "May the winds embrace you my love, and may they reunite us on the other side."

He got up and pulled his swords, tears stinging his eyes. More dreklugnins were coming and some of the knights had been brought down, several beasts co-operating to kill both man and horse. Phraan stared at Shaluun. "Stay with them, protect them for as long as you can"

Shaluun nodded. "I will, I will not let them be taken as long as I still breathe"

He laid Ivran close to Vitile and prepared to fight. Dhokay and the two dwarves formed a line, Phraan and Fastonar joined them and the dreklugnins roared and rushed forth. Tersus did throw bags with some sort of purple liquid at the monsters but it didn't do more than slow them down a little. Swords would have been enough against the dreklugnins of old, against these monsters they were not very efficient at all. Phraan let out some roars to give himself courage and Thiana and Taurin did join the line, they were out of arrows and let their horses flee. They could have escaped but chose not to, to stay with their friends and Phraan felt the anger burn in his chest. If he only could have made those responsible for this pay, then his death would be so much easier to face. They surrounded the two unconscious members of the team, keeping the dreklugnins at bay and they all fought with the strength and determination of desperation.

There were at least seventy dreklugnins left and only a few knights and they were being surrounded by the snarling beasts, everybody was covered with blood now, some their own and the rest that of the dragons and Rhuk staggered backwards and fell, hit square in the chest by a tail. The dwarf gasped and passed out and Dabin took his place, shouting insults. Phraan got a deep gash down his back from a claw and the pain made him feel dizzy, yet he maintained fighting and forgot his fear and sorrow. Suddenly the sun broke through the fog and in the sudden light they saw something approaching them fast. It was a rider, and Phraan knew that one rider could do naught to help them but the figure did shout something and raised an arm and suddenly a glowing blue bow seemed to grow out from its hand and it was a bow without a string and yet as the figure did draw its right arm back a glowing arrow appeared and flew straight and fast towards the dreklugnins. A normal arrow would simply bounce off the hard hide, this on the other hand didn't. It pierced the dreklugnins head as if it was made from gossamer and the beast dropped like a rock, and the arrow continued flying. It was actively searching for dreklugnins and the figure fired more at a rapid speed.

Phraan was staring, it was a woman, an elven woman with amethyst hair and golden eyes and she was riding a huge mule which acted like a war horse. The female did fire again and again, the glowing blue arrows painting blue streaks through the fog and dreklugnins dropped everywhere, then they started to flee but the arrows chased them and more and more fell. The woman stopped firing and lowered her arm, the bow disappeared and she cocked her head. Phraan thought he knew what type of elf she was, their kind was very rare and renowned for their extreme magic. He was panting, feeling faint. Now he felt his wounds and the pain was almost enough to bring him to his knees. "Please…"

She jumped from the mule and ran over to them, placed a hand on Ivran. "He is simply knocked out, he will be fine"

Phraan was staring at her, pleadingly. She turned towards Vitile and clicked her tongue. "I am sorry, she is drifting away, I can awaken her, but just for a small moment, to say goodbye"

Phraan fell to his knees next to her, eyes overflowing with tears. The woman touched Vitile's head and the wood elf did open her eyes, slowly. Her gaze was distant and glassy and Phraan sobbed. "Beloved, please, stay""

She smiled, a very pale smile, almost dreamy. "I cannot, they are calling me Phraan, I have to join them in the wind. Fight this scourge for me Phraan, avenge me"

He gasped, grasping her hand, almost clawing at it. "I will, I swear. Oh Vitile, I almost asked you to bond with me, now I am so sorry I didn't"

She tried to give him a real smile but she was too weak. "Why did you hesitate?"

Her voice was so low, like a whisper. He sobbed. "I…I wanted you to be happy, and …I couldn't give you a family"

She managed to raise her hand, let it rest against his cheek. "Oh you noble fool, I would have said yes you know, family or not. We were…meant to be"

Her voice was fading and her eyes got distant and Phraan let out a wail, "Vitile, no, stay, don't leave me, no!"

She turned her eyes to him one last time. "I have loved you, let yourself be awakened, be who you were meant to be"

Phraan gasped and kissed her hand. "Vitile, I love you, don't die, don't you dare dying on me"

She just let out a small sigh and the light in her eyes disappeared, the strange woman looked at them. "She is gone, she is at peace"

Phraan roared, the grief so intense it felt like fire in his blood, he kept roaring until the roars became deep wracking sobs and he collapsed onto the ground next to her. Dhokay and Shaluun were crying, Thiana and Taurin did look as if they were in deep shock and Fastonar let out a shout of anger. "May every God curse those dragons, oh by every unholy curse, let them bleed"

He ran and at first it wasn't clear where he was running too but he was aiming for where Vitile's horse lay. Dhokay ran after him and found the man standing by the dead animal. "She shouldn't have died like that, her horse just fell, it wasn't natural, something is wrong here!"

Fastonar grasped the saddle and they both saw the strap which had attached it to the animal, it had clearly been cut at the spot where it was sewn onto the seat pad. Fastonar was growling and Dhokay felt faint, this was sabotage. The human bent down, stared at the animal. "Look, blood!"

He did point at a small red spot on the animals hide, just underneath the saddle. Dhokay rubbed his hand over it and yes, it was blood but not much. Fastonar seemed frantic, he lifted the saddle and ran his hand along the bottom of it, stopped. "Dhokay…"

The blue haired male did see it, a very thin needle which protruded from the saddle where the weight of the rider would be. "All gods, no!"

Fastonar threw the saddle to the ground with a wail. "Poison, she was murdered."

Dhokay was staring at him with huge eyes. "Who?"

The officer was pale, his eyes black and large. "Find yourself a horse Dhokay, I know just who!"

Fastonar grasped onto a lose horse which had lost its rider and Dhokay did the same, the two rode hard against the city and the others stared with confusion in their eyes. "What is the hurry?"

The woman who had rescued them all straightened herself and smiled. "I think you will find out whence you return to the city, most of you are wounded. I suggest you use that wagon, you cannot ride"

Phraan stared at her, she was impressive and that magical bow? It was a sort of magic very few had ever heard of. "Who are you?"

She smiled, her eyes shining and Phraan realized that she was a very dangerous creature indeed. "I am Zaray and I am here to help you fight those dragons"

The wagon was in one piece luckily enough and big enough for all of them, the wounded knights were carried by their friends and they left the dead for now, only Vitile was being transported back to the city. Phraan felt as if he had fallen into a deep black hole, he just couldn't bare it. He was sobbing the whole time, and Shaluun had placed himself next to him, embracing him tightly. Rhuk was unconscious too and all of them had injuries. Shaluun had dislocated his right knee and his face was pale and drawn and Dabin had a huge gash in his left arm. They were a mess, they couldn't face another attack like that, only Zaray had saved them. Ivran was still knocked out, but he wasn't in any danger. Tersus looked shocked too, right now nobody cared about his smell, he stood by Peter and his eyes told of disbelief. They did drive back to the city with a sense of defeat, their hearts clouded by grief and their minds darkened. As they got closer to the walls they saw something though, something which made them all turn their heads and stare. A crowd was gathered on the wall and someone was dangling from it, legs desperately kicking as the noose tightened. Shaluun pushed Phraan's shoulder. "Look"

Phraan turned his head slowly, he was numb, all he saw was death. He did see Fastonar on the wall, he was screaming something from the top of his lungs and Dhokay stood next to him, looking shocked. The person hanging from the wall was Aiolo and Phraan remembered that the man had been working together with the wood elves, fixing their saddles. The truth burst forth, made Phraan feel nauseous and made an intense anger choke him. Aiolo was being strangled slowly, his arms were tied behind his back and the body was jerking and shivering, ghastly sounds came from the man as he died very slowly and Fastonar was roaring in anger and grief. Zaray stopped her mule, her eyes were cold and distant but there was something within the gaze which told Phraan that she was a bit shocked after all. "Did this man cause the death of that elven woman?"

Fastonar nodded, the rope was being held by many strong men on the other side of the wall and Aiolo had stopped squirming, he was a grotesque sight with his tongue sticking out of his mouth and his eyes bulging. "He is, he cut her saddle, and placed a needle dipped in poison in the saddle pad"

Zaray cocked her head. "I see"

She just rode on and the others followed, the carriage stopped by the infirmary and they were helped inside, the local doctor was already preparing to receive patients and Phraan saw that the albino girl was helping him. Phraan had lost much blood and now that the adrenaline was gone he felt terribly weak, and terribly sad. All he could see was Vitile and he moaned as some of the soldiers assigned to hospital service got him out of his soiled clothing and started to wash his wounds. The one on his back had to be stitched together and he was quiet as the albino did the job, she was swift and efficient and she didn't waste time with small talk. Phraan was given something to drink and he emptied the cup without protest, before two minutes were gone he was fast asleep and some of the soldiers carried him over to another tent to recover. The night was spent caring for the wounded and some did ride out to collect the dead. The odd woman did follow them, she found the dead horse and the saddle and she made a small grin as she saw the needle and the cut. Then she broke open the saddle horn and retrieved the two gems, she had felt them from afar and she hissed as she stared down at them. They were tools of evil, there was little doubt about that.

She put them into a pocket in her leather belt before she tossed the saddle away, she knew what was going on, but did the group know? Somehow she doubted that, but it was as it had been foreseen. She rode back to the city following the carriages transporting the dead, of all the knights who had ridden out only fifteen had returned and it was a sad fact that nobody was able to fight the huge number of dragons. The packs they had seen were just the beginning. She needed to speak to Phraan, as soon as he was strong enough. The grief he had shown when that female died was not something she had taken into consideration, it was unexpected that his heart was taken by someone but it didn't interfere with her plans. The grief however did, it would either make him hungry for vengeance, which was good, or make him depressed which was far from it. She would have to wait and see what happened next.

The infirmary was overcrowded for a while and Janok was in despair, the commander had no idea of what to do now. The city did house so many people and an attack of that scale would become a disaster if it was aimed at the residents. Crassian was among the few knights who had made it back to the city unscathed and he was in obvious shock, they all were. That mysterious woman had saved them all, and she had gotten rid of those monsters relatively easy. But who was she really? And what? None there had ever met an elf like her, and the magic she had wielded was impressive and also scary. The wounded had all been tended to when the young healer came forth and addressed Janok. She was an even greater enigma than the elf woman and the unreal red eyes made it hard to meet her gaze. Imeah just looked at them. "The city cannot survive another attack, these dragons are bred for destruction and nothing else than that. There is just one path of actions which will be efficient"

Janok looked at Crassian and then at the girl, she did look rather adamant and her chin was held up high. "What sort of actions are you talking about young one?"

Imeah stared at them, the red eyes did remind Janok of the blood which had been spilled, he shuddered a bit. "They must stop the dragons from entering these realms, the wall has been breached, it must be resurrected. The powers of chaos must be vanquished once and for all, the dark brotherhood wiped out completely"

Janok frowned. "You have seen this?"

She nodded. "Yes, and more. It will all become so clear eventually."

Crassian sighed, he was extremely tired and filled with deep sorrow, he had lost many good comrades and he knew that the seer was right. There was no way they could beat these dragons, they were just too many and too strong. "The elf who arrived, have you seen her too?"

Imeah nodded. "She will show them the way, she will reveal what is hidden. She is the forgotten one, the one the dark brotherhood will fear and hate"

Imeah just turned around and walked off and the two was left there staring at each other. Zaray was waiting, she was a patient one but this time she had to hurry, yet she couldn't force this upon anyone. Those who chose to follow would have to do so out of their own conviction, it was very important. She couldn't risk that anyone came because they felt they had to, such people could be turned around and their beliefs transformed into something dangerous. The group would have to be told the truth while gathered, most were wounded and so she would have to wait for some days. She already knew that the young seer had seen the truth of it all, the young one had great powers and so did the young mage. She smiled to herself, he didn't want the world to know of his powers and that was wise but he would have to use them now, and use them wisely too. The darkness has eyes and ears everywhere, she already knew that they had noticed the death of that dragon Ivran killed. Yes, they had to prepare, and prepare well. The death of the elven woman told her that someone already knew and that this someone was closer than what was comfortable.

Phraan did wake up very slowly, his thoughts were sluggish and his head hurt and he was terribly thirsty. He had a terrible taste of blood in his mouth and his back was on fire, or so it seemed. Then he remembered and let out a choked wail of grief, why didn't the Gods claim him instead of her? It wasn't fair, it should never have happened. He felt anger burst forth yet again, Aiolo had done this, but why? He hadn't been there when Vitile took the gem from the huge dragon, he couldn't have known about the gems at all, or could he? Was there perhaps more going on than they had thought at first? He had to find out. He sat up on the narrow cot, he was in his own tent now and a young soldier had been placed there to keep an eye on him. The lad shot up from the chair he was in when he did notice that Phraan was awake. "Sir, do you need anything? You should lay back down again, you have a bad gash on your back"

Phraan growled. "So I have noticed yes. A glass of wine please, and find Fastonar, I need to speak to him"

The soldier nodded and walked over to a table, poured a generous amount of wine into a cup and brought it back. Phraan tossed it back as if it was water, it did kill the awful taste in his mouth but it did nothing to ease his sadness and the feeling of loss. "I will go and see if I can find him sir, right away"

The soldier scooted out of the door and Phraan sighed, laid back down with a groan. His heart was bleeding, and his soul raged against the loss he had experienced. He knew that Vitile's soul was safe with her ancestors now, but that didn't diminish the grief he felt. Many had fallen this day but she was the only one who mattered to him. Fastonar appeared rather fast, he just rushed into the tent and Phraan could see that he

208

too had been crying. He was grey in the face and looked very shaken and he sat down immediately and his expression was one of disbelief. "I cannot…I cannot describe how I feel right now Phraan, all of our plans, all of our hopes, it has gone straight down the drain hasn't it? We cannot hope to win against these…abominations"

Phraan nodded. "Fastonar, you hung Aiolo, did he say anything about why he did it? He must have had a reason? And the needle in the saddle, where did he get the poison?"

Fastonar hung his head. "I am afraid I didn't give the son of a bitch much time to speak, I was…I was so terribly angry Phraan, so filled with grief. I wanted to make him suffer! All I managed to get out of him was that he had gotten the poison from Tersus wagon, he had stolen it and knew what it was and thus he came up with the idea!"

Phraan scoffed. "Then why Vitile, why not any of us?!"

Fastonar stared at Phraan and his eyes were dark. "Because she was female, easier to kill or so he believed"

Phraan almost sneered. "You were too hasty Fastonar, I don't think that bastard just decided to try to murder one of us out of ordinary anger, I believe that he was ordered to!"

Fastonar sighed, a deep sigh. "Yes, I do believe so too, now! I was too hasty and I apologize but I am only human, my anger got the better of me. I didn't think Phraan, I was in shock and I have always been very fond of Vitile, it shouldn't have ended the way it did Phraan, I just snapped."

Phraan let out a deep sigh. "You are right, I would have reacted the same way, I don't blame you. So, what now?"

The dark haired man shrugged. "Zaray wants us to gather, she has something to tell us. I am not so sure if I trust that one, but we ought to listen, she did save our hides back there"

Phraan nodded slowly. "If she only had arrived earlier"

Fastonar got up. "Yes, I have thought about that too. But rest now, regain your strength. We will meet tomorrow morning. Until then we are officially mourning, and nothing will be done"

Phraan sent him a somewhat shaky grin. "Alright. I will be there"

Fastonar left the tent and Phraan stared up at the canvas ceiling, he felt shocked still and something about the whole thing was bugging him but he wasn't sure of what it was. Ivran had tried to help, but he had overestimated his own skills and that was a problem. The young human would really need some proper training. Phraan tried not to think of Vitile but it was terribly hard not to, he could hear that Taurin and Thiana were singing, a sort of slow and melancholic chanting. They were dealing with their grief the only way they knew how to, and Phraan wished to go out and join them but he was too weak yet. After a while a soldier came with a bowl of soup and some bread and Phraan did eat but he felt miserable. What hope did they have now? The dragons would ravage this land like a plague and leave naught behind but ruins and death and there was nothing they could do.

He felt sleepy after the meal and pulled the blankets up around himself, closed his eyes. In spite of the feeling of fatigue it did take quite a while before he managed to fall asleep.

Ivran did come to rather fast and Shaluun stayed with him, Ivran hadn't witnessed the final outcome of the battle and was confused and then sorrowful. He couldn't believe that Vitile was dead, and that they all had been close to death. Shaluun tried to explain that there was nothing Ivran could have done but it was hard on the young human, he felt as if he ought to have done more, to have chosen a different type of counter attack. Shaluun did know that the very brave but foolish attempt at stopping the dragons had been born out of desperation, Ivran hadn't been thinking at all but acted on sheer instinct and if he had been stronger and more familiar with his skills it would have worked. Shaluun made sure that

Ivran had some food and the young man was physically alright, he had quite an appetite but he still felt very conflicted. He had believed that they would be able to kill those dragons but now he knew that they would face some problems, and they were gigantic. Shaluun promised him that they would train some more and Ivran got dressed and left the tent with a sensation of sleep walking. It was as if everything he saw was a sort of bad dream and he saw that the camp was preparing for the worst. The palisades were strengthened and archers were placed along the walls. He saw that many of the soldiers looked rather frightened and the atmosphere of impending doom was heavy and laid like a lid over the entire place.

He walked over to the wall, the body of Aiolo had been cut down and burned already and he was glad he hadn't witnessed that. He couldn't help but wonder why the man had done what he had. Such actions are rarely done just randomly, they have a cause, and what had Aiolo's been? He sighed and stared over to the house Tersus had been given, judging from the sounds coming from the building the alchemist was hard at work even now. It could be that he was their only hope. Ivran did feel a certain amount of curiosity, this approach to the mysteries of creation was so different from what he was used to, but he could understand its attraction. He stood there and stared at the activity when the tall stranger did approach him. Ivran was staring with huge eyes, he had never seen a person like that before and he was gob smacked by her appearance. He just stared and she smiled and leaned against the wall next to him. "So, you tried to stop the dragons, like you had stopped falling rocks. You do know that it was epically stupid but also equally brave?"

Ivran looked down. "Yes, but I just...I had to do something!"

She tilted her head, those odd eyes were hypnotizing. "You have considerable talent, powers which can dwarf even those of the great mages of old"

He frowned. "How do you know?"

She sent him a wicked grin. "I can sense it, and since I can sense it so can others too Ivran. You haven't used your powers until now but that doesn't make you safe, far from it!"

He looked at her, puzzled and a bit scared. "What do you mean by that?"

She sat down on a crate and her eyes got distant. "I was once well known Ivran, and I was feared too but that was a long time ago and in realms far from this one. I serve the light lad, but in order to do that I couldn't follow the ways of light. There has to be a balance also within us all. You are born with a power which is genuine chaos, and the forces of chaos will be drawn to it like ants to a bowl of sugar"

He swallowed. "Forces of chaos?"

She nodded solemnly. "Yes, the dark brotherhood, they already know that there is someone out here with immense magical abilities. They will try to seek you out, either to kill you or to use you for their own twisted purposes."

Ivran gaped. "Are you serious?!"

She smiled, the smile was a harsh one, with no teeth. "Yes, you must have figured out the real reason why the dragons have reappeared or what?"

He nodded slowly. "Uh, I think so, they have been prepared for an all-out war"

She nodded slowly and the eyes were almost glowing. "Yes, so they have to be stopped and there are very few methods which will work. We have to be bold, to be unpredictable."

Ivran frowned. "We?"

She nodded. "Yes, we, there is no reason for this group to stay here, you came to do good now didn't you? This is the only good thing you can do now. It will be dangerous for sure but it may save this realm."

Ivran did almost shrink. "Uh, are you sure that..."

She took a deep breath and removed something from a pocket in her belt, handed it over and Ivran looked down at the two small gems which suddenly lay in his palm. He let out a small gasp and then he felt an intense need to toss them away. They felt just awful, like something which was way heavier than they truly ought to be and it felt as if they were trying to suck the very soul out of him. Zaray nodded. "You feel it don't you? The tainted power within these? You have magic so to you it is very noticeable."

He handed them over to her again. "Yes, they felt just...wrong?!"

She smiled and hid the gems again. "Ivran, you are a sensible young man, and you have learned the value of secrecy. What I am about to tell you is something you have to keep to yourself, no matter what"

He was confused. "Alright, but why do you trust me?"

She stared at the skies, the gaze was sharp as that of an eagle. "Because you aren't a part of the group, your presence here is a coincidence, a trick of fate. And I can see that you are very honest, and a truly good person"

Ivran was blushing. "And you are sure of that?"

She nodded slowly, she was so much taller than Ivran she was staring down at him. "Yes, I can see the soul of other beings, yours is one of light. So, do you agree?"

He nodded but felt far from sure. "Yes, I do"

She stared at the skies again. "These stones are what got Vitile killed. Someone knew she had them"

Ivran frowned, then his eyes got large. "Oh Gods, that means that Aiolo did spy on her?"

Zaray turned her gaze toward him. "Yes, or someone else. Aiolo was a creature of chaos, I could feel that even from a distance. He was a slave of darkness even without knowing of it."

Ivran swallowed hard. "Do you say that there are more like him around? More followers of chaos?"

She smiled and petted his head. "You are a smart lad Ivran, I didn't say that"

Ivran stared at her, realized that she had confirmed it without actually confirming it. "So, what are we to do?"

Zaray looked down at her fingernails. "You are someone they already trust, and you have not done much to draw attention to yourself, yet. I think you are the one who ought to keep your eyes open. If there is a rotten apple within this barrel it is best discovered from the outside"

Ivran understood the wisdom of her words. "Alright, I see, and you?"

She smiled again, a wide smile with flashing white teeth. "I will try to lead this group towards their fate, we have one try, and one try alone."

She let a hand slide through his hair and he shuddered, he felt the power in her like the tense atmosphere just before a thunderstorm. "We never had this conversation, remember that."

She let go and walked away, slowly and seemingly relaxed and Ivran felt his throat go dry. She was very dangerous, and what was she really planning on doing? Was all of this even real? He ought to return to the academy but he did know that it was just a question of time before the dragons would reach the southern parts of the realm as well, there were no safe places anymore. He remained where he was for quite some time, trying to make sense of it all.

The members of the group were trying to cope with the things which had happened, and they all mourned in their own way. They were recovering from their injuries and luckily none had suffered anything life threatening, the healers could deal with it all. Dabin and Rhuk sat in their tent, Dabin was meditating, it was the way of his tribe but Rhuk was shaving his legs. He used a very sharp knife and did remove all the hair of his calves and knees and feet and he did use some time too for he was extremely hairy. Dabin cringed, it wasn't the way of his tribe to shave like that but Rhuk's people had always been odd. Rhuk stared at his freshly shaved feet and wriggled his toes, a sad expression upon his face. "I guess it doesn't matter, for nobody of my kin will see this but it feels right. "

Dabin sort of cringed. "Shaving your legs is a way of showing grief?"

Rhuk nodded. "Oh yes, it is a way of saying that you are too busy mourning to think about fun"

Dabin rolled his eyes slightly. "So having shaven legs is a turn off if I understand you right?"

Rhuk turned around and put a foot up on a chair, removed a few hairs he hadn't seen previously. "Yes, the dames will shun a male with shaven feet, the hairier the better."

All dwarves are hairy in comparison with other races but Rhuk's tribe had always had a reputation for being extremely so. "And I bet the ladies of you clan is furry lovelies with hair in all the right places?"

Rhuk nodded with obvious glee. "Oh yes, they are a delight and a joy to behold. I had a sweetheart once, her beard reached her thighs, oh she was precious, you know, the hangings ought to match the carpet!"

Dabin got a mental image which made him wince. "So I guess that it is hard to tell the difference between the ladies and the gents of your clan?"

Rhuk did look offended. "Not at all my lad, not at all. The ladies will be working at the forges or practicing the art of tossing stuff, we menfolk do spend our time writing poems and teaching the young ones embroidery and artful wood carving."

Dabin swallowed hard, now that did explain a few misunderstandings, so few ever came across Rhuk's tribe and not much was really known about them. So the rather aggressive and hairy stubby dwarves many had managed to piss off were female…good to know! "Ah, tossing stuff? Why?"

Rhuk rolled his eyes. "Duh, to impress the men of course, who would want a wife who is weak? She'll give birth to puny small babes. No, I want a wife one day and she must be at least a head taller than me and have a beard more coarse than the hairs of a mountain goat! Such beauties are hard to come by I know but I will find her someday, and I will read her poems and sing in praise of her strength"

Dabin's tribe was more like humans when it came to gender roles, this just made him feel slightly concerned. "So if a female of your clan and tribe does like a guy she'll throw stuff to show it?"

Rhuk nodded with a wide grin. "Oh yeah, the heavier the better. The chief's wife won his affection by tossing a whole pig across the room. It didn't end so well for the poor pig but they got married the same day."

Dabin had once had an interesting encounter with a dwarf from Rhuk's clan, the stranger had stared at him the whole evening and before the inn closed the other dwarf had started throwing ale barrels. Dabin had sort of run off, afraid that the other dwarf had been a bit insane but now he did realize that it had been a female and that she had fancied him. Oh by every God, he was glad he had escaped unscathed. "I bet your dams are fierce in bed as well then?"

Rhuk sent him a nasty grin, wide and full of mirth. "Oh yes, they are amazing, they'll ride you like none other, I can assure you of that"

Dabin had heard enough, he had lost the ability to meditate for the next century or so. "Well, I do wish you luck in finding that perfect wife of yours, I truly do!"

Rhuk nodded with a wide smile. "I thank you, and may you too find a lovely lass with a huge beard."

Dabin got up and sent Rhuk what he hoped was a grateful smile. "Thanks, I think I will need to go for a walk now, I need fresh air!"

Rhuk had a devilish glimpse within his eyes. "Ah, need to take care of something? No shame in that lad, talking of the ladies can have that effect!"

Dabin just sent Rhuk a wide eyed stare and ran out of the tent, if that deranged dwarf really believed that he had become aroused by this then be it. He had to get away.

Dabin had volunteered for this in search of glory and to possibly gain enough fame to become someone of importance within their community. His tribe was large and spread out all across the realms and they did have much contact with humans and elves and other races as well and he had believed that killing a few dragons would help him become someone of importance. Apparently he was wrong, this journey had turned into a nightmare and he wasn't sure he would return to the house of his kin alive. But he wouldn't leave, he did have his honor and he did realize that this problem wouldn't go away, they had to do something or else also the halls of his clan would become tombs. Dwarves are strong creatures, able to survive things few other races can hope to get through but they do have their limits and dwarves do fear fire. The reason is a rather obvious one, they don't like flames, at all!

The hair and beard of a dwarf tends to be rather greasy due to the fact that they often use their beards to wipe off their mouth after a meal and grease burns rather well. The dwarves working in the forges would use huge leather hoods with only a hole for the eyes and the hoods covered their entire front down to their knees. It was all for safety. Dabin was not too fond of forge work, he was a hunter and loved the tranquility of the forests. He bet that Rhuk felt the same way as him when it came to this mission, neither of them were quitters, they would simply have to do what they could to save their own, even if it meant laying down their own lives. Dabin didn't fear death, he only feared meeting his ancestors as a coward.

When a dwarf has his mind set upon something it takes something rather grand to make him change his mind, and Dabin knew that if he did survive this he would indeed become someone who would be remembered through the ages. It was the greatest honor anyone could ask for, a sort of immortality.

Dabin did run into Dhokay as he was heading towards the gates, the tall luptay was busy sharpening some daggers and he had his hammer standing next to him. Dabin had been impressed by the weapon from the moment he first laid eyes upon it and he wanted to know more. War hammers aren't used by most dwarves simply because it takes a long arm to get enough momentum to really damage the opponent. Dwarves are extremely strong but they have short arms and to them a war hammer would simply be too long and top heavy to be wielded with success. Dhokay's hammer was forged in one piece and that was extremely impressive in itself but the size of the weapon was intimidating to anyone knowing anything about such things. The head of the hammer was flat on one side and slightly pointed at the other and it was made from a very dense steel with a sort of bluish color. The handle was wrapped with dragon leather and Dhokay did notice that the dwarf was staring at the weapon. He smiled and nodded. "You can test it if you like, it won't bite you!"

Dabin stared at the war hammer, it was almost as long as him and the head did probably weigh almost as much as himself. "I'd rather not Dhokay, I am not capable of wielding such a weapon. I just got curious, where did you get such a magnificent work of art?"

The hammer was indeed a work of art, elegant and very elvish in appearance and yet it was sturdy and solid. Dhokay put down the wet stone and cocked his head. "It is a long story but I have had it for a very long time. My people do favor war hammers when in battle, it is very efficient and feared"

Dabin nodded. "I know, I have seen the damages such weapons can cause, it is terrifying. But it is also efficient against dragons?"

Dhokay nodded and grasped the hammer, put it over his lap. "Yes, the hide is too hard for most blades to pierce it but it doesn't protect against blunt force trauma, I usually go for shoulder blades, hips and joints"

Dabin looked at the weapon and cringed, a blow from that one onto such a fragile body part would most certainly cripple even a dragon. "So you crippled the dragons? What did the others do?"

Dhokay smiled, there was a hint of something melancholic within his eyes. "Shaluun would often kill the smaller dragons, he would run onto their backs after I had incapacitated them and stab them in the head or the top of their necks. He is very swift that one. Vitile would track the dragons and determine the number of individuals with the other trackers and they would also try to lure the dragons out and blind them with arrows. Kapha would help me most of the time and Phraan, well, he did kill the larger ones"

Dabin looked puzzled. "Really? Alone?"

Dhokay smiled. "Yes, he and Fastonar were a team, Fastonar would charge at the dragon and when it attacked him Phraan would know its weak spots immediately and go for it. He has a rare talent that one, he never failed in killing the dragons he went for"

Dabin sort of cringed. "If one can call killing a talent."

Dhokay sent him a reassuring smile. "When it comes to dragons it is a talent for sure. But these new dragons are beyond our capabilities, our old methods are worthless"

Dabin sighed. "So I have seen. The dragons have no weaknesses right?"

Dhokay shrugged. "Oh they do have weaknesses but they are hard to find. Phraan managed to get the one which killed Kapha remember? But it came at a cost, one we cannot afford to pay."

Dabin swallowed. "I bet that stranger has something important to tell us, I just feel as though we won't like it, even a bit."

Dhokay nodded and picked up the wet stone again. "So do I, but fate wanders in its own manner. There is nothing we can do to change it"

Dabin swallowed hard. "You rode with Fastonar back to the city after the attack, did he…did he just hang Aiolo? Without even interrogating him?"

Dhokay shook his head. "No, he did ask the bastard all sorts of questions but Aiolo didn't really answer, he just mumbled. I had to go and get some rope and some men and when I returned Fastonar said that he had confessed, I guess Fastonar used his fists on the man for Aiolo did look as if he had been beaten severely when I returned. And then we just dragged him off to be hanged. The guy deserved it, it was a most vicious deed!"

Dabin sighed and shrugged, he felt even more depressed now and bid Dhokay farewell before he headed towards the fields outside of the gates. He needed to be left alone for a while, just to think.

That evening all the dead were buried and Vitile was burned as the customs of her people did dictate, the remaining knights and soldiers were quiet and didn't say much, the loss of so many of their own did somehow paralyze their will. Thiana and Taurin were singing and the rest of the group was sniffing and sobbing or trying their best to look unaffected but that was all a lie. Phraan did come, his back was better for the wound was closing itself up already due to his elvish blood, but he didn't manage to stay for long, It was simply too much for him and the grief too strong. He had to go before the pyre was lit, it was impossible for him to watch her burn. Instead he returned to the tent and cried for hours before he fell into restless sleep.

Zaray gathered them just after sunrise, she was sitting in a chair in one of the larger tents, her odd eyes were shining and she looked so relaxed, so self-assured. The group sat down, Ivran was among them now and he did stare at her, his eyes somewhat distant. Phraan did look as if he hadn't slept at all for days and the two remaining wood elves were obviously in deep shock still. The mood was a gloomy one for sure and

Fastonar stared at the woman with narrow eyes. "So, why have you summoned us here? We are grateful you helped us, do not doubt that but with what authority do you order us around like this?"

Zaray smiled, her mouth was very wide, and generous. She did look hungry somehow, sensual and elegant but it was the elegance of a well forged blade. She did perhaps look soft as velvet but hers was a soul of steel. "I can so this because I know things you simply don't. I know you have heard the old tales, the stories explaining the reasons why these things have happened."

Fastonar scoffed. "Old wives tales? Do you expect us to believe them?"

She just smiled. "Yes, for they are true. The dark brotherhood has gathered once more, and a plan has been built and refined through millennia. You are watching its final stage"

Dhokay was staring at her. "You know this because?"

She smiled at him, a hint of white teeth barely visible. "There is a city on the other side of those mountains, a great city, dedicated to the forces of chaos. The brotherhood has their stronghold there, it is where their devious plan has been set into action. It is where the source of their power is being held."

She cocked her head, the golden red eyes almost haunting in their beauty and alien expressions. "I know this because that was where I was held for ages, a slave and a pawn, a plaything. But they did forget a very important detail, time changes the memory of men, even the written word won't last forever. "

Fastonar did look very doubtful. "What are you then?"

She smiled again. "A mage? A bringer of salvation, a carrier of ancient magic, forgotten by all. What I am human, was forgotten by the world eons ago, and it is good that way. I did escape when they forgot to watch over me, when they took my weakness for granted. I have roamed the land ever since, keeping myself hidden and preparing for this mission"

Phraan cleared his voice. "I think I have understood what you wish for, but why should we trust you? Why should we even believe it to be true?"

Zaray stretched like a cat, her eyes showed that she was completely relaxed, so very confident. "You will believe me when you think about it for a while, for I do not lie. The dark brotherhood has created these new dragons and they aim for dominance over this entire world. Very powerful magic has been used to accomplish this, and you have seen what they have created. I am sorry to say that these new dragons is a mere beginning"

Fastonar was frowning, his arms crossed across his chest. "I cannot believe you, those dragons are beasts, what could be worse than them?"

Zaray laughed, it was a low and hoarse laughter, throaty and sensual and Ivran realized that Zaray was well used to exploiting her almost otherworldly beauty to get what she wanted. "Very much my brave knight, you will soon witness these new horrors, I can assure you that there is only one possible course of actions to take now. You must go to the mountains and undo what they have done, raise the wall again and eradicate the brotherhood once and for all"

Shaluun had been silent, now he did step forth. "That is no small task, nobody have ever been able to return from those mountains, what makes you believe that we will have more luck than the others who have tried? And raising the wall again?"

She nodded slowly, the amethyst hair did shine. "You are not like those adventurers who have ventured into the embrace of those frozen valleys, you will have me as your guide and you are all special, all destined for so much more."

She was staring at Phraan as she said those words and he felt as if she was speaking to him in special. Fastonar made a grimace. "Why should we risk our lives on this? You could be lying, you could be serving the dark forces for all we know!"

She grinned. "You are suspicious and rightly so, but you do of course have a choice. You can stay here and try to fight but you will all perish then, and the realm will become a wasteland of ash and death and not even the memory of you will remain for there will be nobody alive to remember you. The brotherhood has unleashed something they cannot hope to control, their arrogance have taken them too far. They are not wise nor learned as their ancestors were, the dark mages of ancient days did at least know what they were meddling with and hubris was a sin back then as it is now. The new members are powerful but unwise and they cannot see that they lack so much of what made their forefather's great. "

Ivran swallowed. "Were they really that, great I mean?"

She stared at him with a smile. "Oh, they were, they were great indeed. They chose the wrong side you may say but that doesn't diminish the skills they possessed. They believed in what they did, and that made them almost invincible"

Phraan took a deep breath. "And this new brotherhood, don't they believe in their mission?"

She grinned again, widely. "Oh but they do, fanatically. But their task is no longer balance, it is dominance and that is not the same as before. They want to rule everything, they want the world to dance to their chosen tune and fail to see that in doing that they will also destroy themselves."

Dhokay looked down. "Chaos is its own greatest enemy isn't it?"

She nodded. "Yes, only order can make it work, and those two opposites cannot exist without each other, what they are trying to do will undo the very creation itself."

Ivran was shuddering. "Is that even possible?"

She nodded solemnly. "Yes. For they have started to use magic that their ancestors did shun, magic forbidden even by the darkness itself. They cannot see the danger for their minds are not capable of understanding. There is no salvation for them, they must all be erased from the very weave of life or this plague will arise anew"

Phraan sighed. "So, if we do as you say and go to this city and slay those followers of chaos things will return to normal?"

Zaray smiled. "Yes, more or less"

The half elf frowned. "What do you mean more or less?"

She shrugged. "The dragons which have crossed the wall will of course still be here, so it is in our best interest to hurry before too many make it through. We will have to kill a lot of dragons before this is all over, believe me"

Fastonar was frowning still, he did look sort of gloomy. "And these followers of darkness and chaos will just allow us to enter their realm and mow them down?"

The sarcasm in his voice was rather thick and Zaray tilted her head to the side, her expression coy. "Of course not, that is why such brave warriors as yourself is needed, we need those of both experience and courage to do this"

Shaluun had stared at her for a while. "You look like an elf, like someone of the ancient m'shray tribe, but you don't feel like a m'shray. You did save us out there, but I still question your honesty."

She just grinned again, the grin sardonic. "I am not what I seem to be? That is something I have in common with many of you, and you don't even know it yet. The forces of order do work with subtlety instead of boasting their powers, it is no coincidence that you are all here. We do all have a role to play in this, the Gods are playing a board game and we are the pieces they move"

Fastonar scoffed. "I am no pawn"

She shrugged. "No? You have spent the time after the last dragon war guarding the temples of Twelve towers now haven't you? I bet you have found that task both tedious and boring, perhaps even soul draining?"

Fastonar did look shocked. "How do you know?"

She chuckled. "Oh I do know you all, very well. You could have taken some other mission, been sent south to battle pirates along the coast, north to negotiate treaties with the wild tribes. You chose to stay in Twelve towers"

Fastonar did stare at her, his eyes shocked. "I wanted to reap the benefits of my previous role, I was famous, and I loved it"

Zaray almost purred. "Oh I bet you did, but when that fame did fade, did you ask your king for a new assignment?"

Fastonar shook his head. "No, I just...I guess I never thought of that?"

Zaray smiled and her expression was one of satisfaction. "Of course you didn't. You were meant to be here"

She turned to Thiana and Taurin, both stared at her with big eyes and she appeared to have some sort of power over them for they both were apparently mute. "You came because Vitile asked it of you, both skilled hunters and both carrying the blessings of the woods. Very few does these days, but now is the time to use it for all it is worth"

Dhokay turned his gaze towards the two wood elves. "Are you serious?!"

Both looked down, blushing and Taurin tried to speak but no sound came forth. Zaray grinned. "Yes, they are of the chosen ones, their powers yet untried but real enough."

Phraan did look shocked. "But I have always believed that the power of the woods was a sort of chaos force?"

Zaray nodded and her eyes were stern now. "Yes, but there is chaos and then there is chaos. The force of the woods is a force born out of nature, and nature is chaotic but it is a nurturing chaos, from eventual destruction regrowth follows. The dark chaos forces leave nothing new, only destruction on a complete level."

Phraan didn't say anything more and Zaray stared at them all. "You came because duty called, because you yearned for glory and for the thrill of the hunt. Nothing has changed my friends, only the outer circumstances."

Fastonar did look down at his toes and Dhokay was frowning, the two dwarves did however look almost eager. Ivran hadn't said anything, he just looked slightly tired, as if this was something he had anticipated the whole time. Shaluun was still staring at her and his eyes told them that he was thinking and thinking hard. Zaray stepped forth, making a wide gesture with both arms. "I will leave you to it then, you must decide and do it now. We cannot wait, time is running short as we speak"

She bowed and left the tent and everybody sat there, staring at each other. Fastonar was scowling. "I do not trust her, and neither should you. Why should we believe all this?"

Shaluun sighed and the expression within his eyes changed, his gaze became keen and sharp and he was baring his teeth. "Because we have to, no matter who or what she is, the dragons do originate from somewhere behind those mountains. If we are to do anything useful except dying in vain we have to track them to their origin and strangle the source at the root."

Dhokay nodded solemnly. "He is right, it is the only way, dark mages or no dark mages."

Fastonar turned to Phraan, his eyes were pleading. "Phraan, don't tell me that you too have swallowed her bait?"

The half elf stared at Fastonar and there was something new in his gaze, a dark fire none had seen before. "I don't care what she said, or what her intentions are. It is indifferent to me now, but I do know that the force which sent the dragons south exist behind the mountains. I will go there, to avenge Vitile. I owe it to her"

Fastonar rolled his eyes. "By the Gods, have you all lost your marbles?"

Phraan sneered. "No, I have found a purpose, and if I have to die then be it, but know this, if I do die it will be with the blood of the ones responsible for her death coating my hands!"

Fastonar sighed, a deep sigh and he rolled his eyes. "Right, you are all mad then. But be it, I will follow you, just to make sure that you don't mess this up."

Phraan smiled, the smile was a tense one. "You do not need to do this Fastonar, you are sworn to the temples, you can return to serve there and nobody will blame you for it"

Fastonar shook his head. "No, I have watched your back for years and I don't intend to quit now. It may be folly but I don't desert the original mission I was sent out to do. We were sent to kill dragons so let's do that, even if I think it is madness"

Dhokay stared at Thiana and Taurin, the wood elves were surprisingly calm. "How about you?"

The two stared at each other, small smiles barely visible. "We will join you, to honor Vitile and avenge her death. She was one of us, a sister of the woods. It is our duty to do this"

The two dwarves did also nod and Rhuk did run his fingers through his now short beard. "She was a fine lass, aye, a very fine lass. Her feet were…nice. For an elf I mean, but yes, she had good feet. I will honor her name and fight for her, my axe thirsts for the blood of those dark bastards"

Dabin grinned. "Hear hear, well spoken. We are all ready so why hesitate? Zaray says that time is important, we ought to go as soon as we can"

Phraan grinned. "I bet Tersus will want to join us too, he can be useful."

Ivran got up. "I will come too, I don't know what powers I do have but maybe I can be of help. Returning to the academy is out of the question, I can do naught there, except cowering when the dragons reach Oakfell, for they will."

Fastonar shrugged. "Right, fine, we'll dance her dance then, but do not trust her too much. I think she has her own agenda and that may be a very hidden one!"

Nobody said anything more and Phraan got up. "I will tell the commander of our decision and ask for provisions and fresh horses for those who have lost their steeds. We cannot linger here for much longer"

Fastonar made a grimace "We cannot use the wagons, it will be a journey where we bring only the bare necessities."

Phraan sent him a vague smile. "Just like the days of old right"

Fastonar had to smile back. "Yes, just like the days of old"

The great citadel was an impressive sight in the evening sun, countless torches were burning and the black marble of which the entire structure was constructed did shine like oil on water. The guards who were placed along the entrance stairs wore their best uniforms and the entire scene was made to create a sense of awe and fear. The ancient mages had really known how to make anyone approaching their headquarters feel puny and small, the entire city was simply stunning in its cold beauty. The old man stood in a window and his face was grim, he was staring at the citadel and his eyes burned with anger and hatred. They had banished him, for telling them the truth, for following the old ways. He was humiliated and hurt and he remembered all that he had sacrificed for their cause, it had all been in vain. These new brothers weren't truly believers, all they saw was power and influence and they would bring doom upon themselves. Badrian stepped away from the window, the room he was in was grand and very luxurious but it was a prison, the doors were locked and he knew that only Simaon had the keys. That man ought to have been strangled with his own diapers as a baby, Badrian had seen a lot but never someone with such a ruthless and cunning mind, the man could have been an excellent leader and the one to lead them to new greatness if he hadn't been unable to take advice and respect the past.

Simaon didn't care about the old ways, he had never read the prophecies nor the work of their predecessors, to him it was all about using what was created back then for his own purposes. Badrian was furious, they would lose it all, and for what? For money, for fame, for things so unimportant he never had even contemplated them. He served a bigger cause, a sacred obligation to finish what their bold ancestors had started. The others had stepped away from the road now, they were heading for a disaster and they didn't even know it. Badrian sighed and poured himself a little wine, he was given everything he could possibly need except freedom, they did fear him and his knowledge and that thought made him grin. He had become a stone in their shoe, a turd on the serving platter, something they didn't wanted to be reminded off.

They couldn't control them, it was as simple as that. The hordes which had been created were ready to be unleashed and if Simaon thought that these horrors would obey him he was so wrong. The ancient ones had been careful, they had never wished for something like this, never at this scale. Some dragons yes, strong and terrifying and able to bring a kingdom to its knees in fear but not the annihilation of every living thing? Badrian knew that it would be the result if Simaon and his brethren got it their way, they would release an avalanche of death and then neither the darkness nor the light would matter anymore. There would be no balance, just a scourge of dragons trying to devour each other. Badrian walked over to a shelf and pulled down a small book, it was very anonymously looking, just a few pages thick and wrapped in plain brown leather. He held it reverently and let a hand caress the soft surface. This book held the answer to his dilemma, his vengeance, his ultimate pay back. It gave him the spells and powers needed to control the orb.

They had laughed at him, locked him up like a disobedient child when in truth he was the only one left of the true brotherhood. He was among the last true believers and if he was going down well then he would take them all down with him. He walked over to the table in the middle of the room, a huge crystal ball rested upon three spikes made from obsidian and the orb was perfectly round and shiny. Simaon had no idea of the power this artefact held, of the abilities it gifted to those strong enough to use it. Badrian had been a mage all of his life, he was weak now, not able to do much of a magical nature. Only his will was strong and he knew that his will was the most important thing there was now. He knew that Simaon would have confiscated the orb had he known what it truly was, a good thing he didn't. That piece of dragon dung wouldn't have been able to use it even if his life did depend on it. Badrian stared at the orb, his eyes narrow. Was this something he was ready to do? Was he willing to go this far, to get his vengeance?

He sat down, the old body was aching more and more each day and he had long ago accepted his mortality and its inevitable outcome. No, he wasn't afraid to die, he was sure he would meet his ancestors in the hereafter and take his place among them.

His forefather's had tried to tilt the balance in their favor and he did see it now, the folly of those ideas. He had believed for so long, and now it felt odd to turn his back to what he had lived for but it was better to die knowing he did the right thing than to live within a lie. The wall had been erected for a reason, the truce made to save them all, both the servants of light and those of darkness. One cannot exist without the other, it was the truth these new brother's had forgotten. The struggle would continue forever and force them all to better themselves, to evolve and become stronger and wiser. What the brotherhood was brewing up now was an abomination, and it had to be stopped.

He had made up his mind and he straightened his back and walked back to the orb. He placed a hand on it, gently, as if he was touching a beloved pet or child. Whispering the right spells to activate it and bring it inn under his will. "Show me, show me the ones of which the forgotten words speak."

The orb became opaque, milky white and so did his eyes. The old man shuddered, the power which rushed through him was so strong it would have scorched the very soul of a lesser man. Badrian moaned and let go, smoke rose from the orb and his palm was burned, as if he had touched a red hot stove. He swallowed his cry of agony and blinked, he knew, he knew how to help them. Yes, the old ways were dead now, and he wanted them to be buried in a proper manner. He almost ran over to the shelf again, clutching his injured hand. He mumbled a healing spell and it helped to a certain degree but some pain still lingered and the hand was still red and nasty looking. He grasped a book and opened it, staring at it with wild eyes. "Yes, that is it, this is what they'll need. That is what's missing, she is may not aware of this"

He stared at the drawing and his eyes had gotten a sinister expression, to hell with them all. To hell with the brotherhood and their false belief, to hell with his own worship of something which had become corrupted and twisted by millennia of faulty teachings, he would make them all pay. He knew where it was, and now he was in a hurry. He had to make sure that the right hands got this and he smiled as he prepared to do a very difficult spell. It would drain him but he didn't care. He closed his eyes and whispered words nobody but himself would understand and suddenly he was gone, the room empty.

Badrian blinked and gasped for air, his body was too old for this but there had been no choice. He was standing in the vault underneath the citadel, it was heavily guarded by spells and soldiers but that was on the outside. There was no protection on the inside of the huge room for there were too many magical items there and they would interfere with any spells uttered. He walked slowly, his body had started to die, it was inevitable. The amount of energy he had spent was simply too much. He hurried towards a closed off section, opened the gate with trembling hands and got inside. It held things of unknown origin and use, things not even the first brothers had managed to figure out. He stopped by a table at the back, opened a small box and picked out a gem from it. It was the size of an egg and bright golden red, it was absolutely gorgeous and he admired the beauty for a few seconds. They would need it for sure, it would trigger the transformation.

He put the gem on the inside of his robe, then he ran over to a closet and pulled out another object, it was almost too heavy for him to hold but he managed, with a hiss of agony. His heart was beating unevenly now, and his vision was getting blurred. He ran to the middle of the room, holding the gem and the other object and he was shaking all over. The spell he started chanting was taken from the small book and extremely powerful and he managed to smile as a giant figure seemed to appear out of nowhere, it watched him with terrifying red eyes and he bowed his head. "Ancient one, servant of the wilds, please hear my plea. Bring this to the one death loves, it is important"

The being cocked its head. "Your life is spent mortal, is this truly what you wish?"

Badrian nodded, he felt odd, a sort of relief was rushing through him. At least he had done what he could to stop the apocalypse, he had been misguided for years and he was glad he had seen the truth, but it had cost him so much. At least these so called brothers would face their end if things went well. The dragons were a horrible enemy and he knew of none who could go up against them, until now. "Yes, it is my wish. Bring it to him, do it soon. Let him see the truth"

The being grasped onto the objects with its maw and nodded and suddenly it was gone. Badrian gasped, his chest felt as if it was on fire but there was one last thing to do now. He whispered a last spell and returned to the room in the tower, he dragged himself over to the orb, his body shutting down. Slowly he got up and whispered the final words of his life, he fell forwards over the orb and the crystal shattered as if it was made from thin glass. They would never be able to use it, its secret was taken with him to his grave. The book started to burn and left only a few flakes of ashes and the magic it had held dissolved into a wisp of thin mist, then it was gone. The old man laid there in a heap of shards and there was a pleased smile on the narrow lips, they had been laughing at him, but the last laugh would most definitely be on him.

Chapter 6: A road to understanding

The group was ready for departure two days later, everything had been arranged and Janok had been rather desperate to keep them there but even he realized that this problem had to be addressed in an unconventional manner. Fighting the dragons wouldn't help at all, they had to prevent them from coming there in the first place. They had more or less recovered from their injuries and as long as they didn't have to do any hard fighting right away they ought to be okay. Zaray had been very pleased by their decision and Phraan saw that Fastonar still didn't trust her. Ivran had spent the days preparing as well and he did look almost like a young squire, dressed in a light armor and with a sword by his side. The greatest shock had been that Imeah insisted on joining them and Fastonar had protested rather vigorously but Zaray had made him shut up. The albino sat on a sturdy horse and the unreal red eyes were calm, Phraan wondered what she really knew about this mission. Tersus had agreed upon coming too, or rather, he had been overjoyed when asked. He had packed a lot of rather dubious looking stuff onto two pack mules and Peter had been given the task of making sure that neither of the pack saddles ever got close to fire. Phraan did shudder thinking about what those packs did contain.

Zaray knew the way and she hadn't yet told them anything about herself, or why she had such knowledge about the city. She had escaped from it, that was rather clear but when? And how? Fastonar seemed to be rather convinced that she was some sort of decoy and that she wanted to lead them straight to damnation but Phraan felt that his friend was wrong. Why he didn't know. The soldiers had seen a huge pack of dragons heading south the day before, it had been a new species none had seen before, flightless but able to move with terrifying speed and the almost skeletal look of the beasts had told them that its creators had used mist bloods as one of the species in the mix. That meant that these dragons most likely were unable to spew flames but had poison instead and they remembered the terrible habit of the mist blood dragons, they ate their prey alive.

The group left with the break of dawn and nobody said much, it was a journey from which none of them really expected to return and they all focused upon their thirst for vengeance or belief in this mission. They reached rather far the first day, crossed the great river and entered a forested area where nobody lived. The soil was too poor for farming and the hills were infamous for a herb which killed livestock, nobody wanted to try keeping sheep or cattle there. Ivran tried to familiarize himself with his skills when they camped for the night and Shaluun helped him. The two of them had become rather good friends by now and stuck together and Phraan was glad, the lad did need a protector. Imeah did shun them all, she would even eat alone and she hardly ever said a word. Thiana tried to speak to her and Imeah was respectful and polite but she didn't seek the company of others and answered only whenever she had to.

They had been riding for four days when they saw the first glimpse of what Zaray had warned them about, new horrors. They had taken a quick rest by a creek to let the horses drink when Taurin saw something moving just above the treetops. It was very large and flew slowly and Phraan felt an odd sensation in his chest when seeing it. It was too far away for him to make out any details but it did look like a giant bat of some sorts, the body so spindly and frail looking it couldn't weight much but the wings were enormous. Zaray had ordered them to hide in the dense forest and the thing had flown by them without seeing them. There had been a terrible stench in the air when the beast had passed by and Fastonar had looked as if he had seen a ghost. Zaray hadn't answered when they asked what it was and Imeah had stared at the thing with obvious hatred.

The day after they did encounter a being like that once more and now Phraan realized how horrible it really was. The thing flew without a sound and it had a very long snakelike neck and a narrow head which reminded them of the head of a heron but it was no bird. The mouth had teeth and the eyes were huge and red and it did look absolutely terrible, like something which has been dead for a long time and yet is moving. That wasn't the worst thing about it, when it got closer to them they all felt a sort of terrible weight land upon them, as if this thing somehow took all their strength away and stole their will to live. Neither of them managed to do anything, quite literally frozen to the spot. The beast had hovered above them, ready to strike when Ivran had shouted something and the thing had suddenly let out a terrible shriek and then it fell like a bag of bricks. The impact made the ground shake so it did have some weight to it after all and Dhokay had rushed forth with a roar and brought his hammer down onto its skull. The head was twice as long as the tall luptay and the impact didn't seem to harm it at all, the thing just hissed and rolled its eyes and Phraan had realized that its bones had to have been made from something else than those of other beings. He had pulled his blades and before anyone else had time to think he had plunged one of the long sleek swords through its eye and into the brain.

The beast did shudder once but did die and Zaray did look very pleased, the beast was so large it was hard to believe it was able to fly and Ivran stood there and looked very proud but also a bit shocked. Phraan walked over to him. "What did you do to it lad?"

Ivran swallowed and tried to smile, the intense stench from the beast made even Tersus cringe and the half rotten appearance had managed to make Fastonar loose his lunch, he was joined by Peter. "I removed the magic which enables it to stay airborne"

Zaray almost purred. "Excellent young man, they cannot be fought while in the air but the moment they touch the ground they become vulnerable, remember that for later"

Phraan stared at her with a harsh expression within his eyes. "So, what are they? Do you care to explain now?"

She shrugged. "I cannot say it will do any harm any more, you have seen one up close now. They don't have a name, but they are most definitely something rather old which have been resurrected by the dark brotherhood and they are terrible. Their power is magical, not of this world"

Dhokay made a grimace. "It made it impossible to think or act, all I felt was fear"

She nodded. "Yes, and the stronger you are the harder it affects you. The ancient dark mages created this but they realized that they were too terrible and had them destroyed"

Shaluun did cringe, he was a bit pale. "So this thing was dead to begin with?"

She just smiled, a very vicious grin. "Most definitely yes, but brought back through the use of very unholy magic. I am afraid this won't be the only example of that"

Phraan frowned. "You know more than you are willing to tell us, why?"

She just shrugged and mounted her mule again. "If I did tell you I know the result, you would return to the city, screaming"

She urged the mule forth and the others looked at each other and felt that she had spoken the truth about this. They rode forth towards the mountains and now they did see that the task of crossing would be monumental. They seemed to reach the very skies above and judging by the looks of it the mountains were a veritable maze of valleys and gorges. Zaray didn't seem too worried though and Phraan started to feel that she had a plan after all. She probably knew a safe route through the area. This area was wild and untamed and nobody had bothered with settling down there, just a few nomadic tribes had inhabited the area but they were gone now, since the animals had moves south so had they. They saw some abandoned camp sites but that was all until they entered a shallow river valley. The land was rising now and the temperature fell and it was getting colder by the day, there wasn't really much forest left, just bushes and some crippled and very old trees which grew in the places where the cold wind didn't reach. They rode along the river to find a good place to cross when Taurin stopped them, the wood elf was sniffing the air and Phraan did stand up in the stirrups and did the same. He immediately recognized the stench of death upon the air and he nodded to the others. "Something has died, the wind comes from the north"

They stared northwards, a huge sandy hill blocked the view up river and Zaray did look rather intense. "Do move forth, but carefully. We have no idea of what this could be"

Fastonar gestured for Phraan and Dhokay to follow him and they rode forth. Drake was tossing his head and neighing and Phraan felt that the horse was tensing up. They all pulled their weapons and rode around the hill in a lose formation, ready to fight. What they saw made Fastonar blanche and Dhokay did swear. It was humans, and horses and some sheep and the bodies were all stacked into an obscene looking pile of body parts and equipment. It was rather cold so there weren't that many flies there but the stench did tell them that these unfortunate individuals had been dead for a while. Fastonar coughed and he was pale and Phraan was staring with narrow eyes. Dhokay rode closer, he was staring at the sad remains and he made some rather terrible grimaces. "No dragon did this, nothing is eaten, they are just torn apart"

Phraan jumped off Drake and walked around the pile, he fished some swords from the collection of grisly objects and stared at them with a puzzled expression. "These are good swords, but they have been bent, look!"

Fastonar nodded, he was green in the face. "Yes, that one looks like a u. How is that possible?"

The rest of the group was approaching them and the two dwarves did stare with eyes the size of dinner plates. "Folks, there are trolls in the area!"

Zaray turned to them. "Are you sure?"

Rhuk nodded so vigorously the helmet he wore almost flew off his head. "Absolutely, look at those bodies? Not even orcs do that to the dead. Trolls hate everything and everyone, they just kill. And such piles are a territorial mark"

Zaray moaned. "Great, perfect, that wasn't in my plans at all, what do we do?"

Dabin was pale. "Uh, the normal thing to do would be running in the other direction? That is not an option? No? Then I have no feckin' clue!"

Zaray grimaced and Imeah sat on her horse and stared at the pile with a distant look upon her face, she hadn't worn the face veil for a while since the weather was grey and she sent them a swift glance. "These were outlaws, trying to make a living here in the wilds. They were ruthless men, brave and aggressive. It didn't help them"

Phraan held the bent sword forth. "Did the trolls do this?"

Rhuk stared at the weapon and his expression was one of awe. "Aye, they despise steel you see, trolls aren't very smart mind you, they have the brains of a piece of cheese but strong instincts. They are animals, hardly more than that. "

Shaluun hissed. "Animals can be smart as heck, I do never underestimate an animal. So you dwarves do know a lot about trolls?"

Dabin nodded and tried to avoid staring at the pile. "We do, trolls and dwarves have been mortal enemies since the beginning of time. The trolls do always try to take our cities to use as their own and we have to keep a watchful eye all the time, they can dig through the very rock itself rather well"

Zaray tilted her head. "So, we are to enter troll territory, what can you give of advice"

Phraan made a grimace. "Do we have to cross this area?"

Zaray nodded. "Yes, there is a secret path through the mountains and it lay straight ahead, we have to get through these valleys to get to it."

Rhuk was pulling at his beard. "Well, trolls hate sunlight so we are safe as long as the sun is up. It is after dark, and on days with heavy clouds we have to be careful"

Dabin did look important, his chin thrust forth. "They have a very sensitive nose, better than any other race, and their eyesight is very poor. They cannot see colors at all, but they sense movement rather well."

Zaray was staring at the two, gesturing to make them continue. Rhuk frowned. "They are extremely territorial, they will kill any troll entering their territory which isn't off their pack"

Dabin added. "And there are very few female trolls, just a couple out of a hundred trolls is female"

Dhokay was listening intently "Is there some way for us to hide from them?"

Rhuk did look down. "Ah, yes, but it isn't very pleasant"

Dhokay did look curious. "Oh? What is it?"

Rhuk turned slightly green. "Uh, you need to find some troll...dung! And rub that onto your boots, it will cover your smell, for a while"

Tersus did look very interested. "That does sound like a very smart thing to do, and troll dung smells rather rancid I bet?"

Rhuk nodded with some vigor yet again. "Oh yes, it makes dragon shit smell like roses and lilies"

Phraan grimaced. "Wonderful, I bet troll dung is easy to find?"

240

Dabin shook his head. "No, they don't need to do their business very often and when they do they bury it for some reason. They often have some spot where the entire pack go to empty their bowels."

Zaray sighed. "It could have been a good idea, but I am not going to run around looking for troll shit!"

Taurin cleared his voice. "Ah, there may be another trick we can use?"

Fastonar did look at the wood elf as if he was the very salvation itself. "There is? Spill it!"

Taurin shrugged. "It is a herb, it removes scent from anything it is rubbed against, it is fairly common too but I am not so sure if it grows at such elevations"

Shaluun frowned and did look a bit doubtful. "I have heard of it, and I have tried it too, once, but it didn't work at all?"

Thiana smiled. "Because you need to use the root, not the leafy parts. Few know that. But I am sure I can find some, it is a very common plant after all, and it loves moist areas."

Fastonar sent them a smile. "Great, do go looking for some, but be careful. We cannot linger here much longer"

The two wood elves did scoot off and Phraan cocked his head and stared at the two dwarves. Rhuk did look nervous and Dabin was slightly green, he had never seen a dwarf looking like that before. "So, you have experience with trolls?"

Rhuk made a nasty grimace and bared his teeth. "Yes, I have fought trolls, only once mind you but that was more than enough."

Phraan was getting curious. "How did that go?"

The dwarf did spit on the ground. "Horribly, we did fell the foul creature but it did kill seven good warriors before it drew its last breath. They are extremely hard to kill ya see, tough hide, tough bones and very primitive."

Dabin nodded. "My clan fought trolls several times and lost many a brave dwarf too, trolls are worse than dragons for they do have an innate need to destroy, for no reason at all"

Dhokay leaned against his horse, his face revealed that he found this fascinating. "But they do have some weak spots?"

Rhuk lighted up, his face was suddenly transformed into the very image of schadenfreude. "Their feet, that is their biggest weakness. Hurt their tootsies and they are helpless!"

Phraan gaped. "Are you kidding me?"

Rhuk shook his head. "No, I am serious. Their feet are sensitive you see, and their toes very long and flexible for they use them when they climb. So a hammer blow to the feet will cripple a troll, I have always said it, bad feet is a bad thing"

Dabin nodded with an eager expression on his face. "My tribe did develop a very smart method years ago, we used some roasting spits and skewered their feet, it did require that someone was bold enough to get within reach of them but it was efficient when it worked."

Phraan stared at Rhuk. "They have long arms?"

Rhuk stretched his own arms, as if to show the size of a fish. "Aye, reach the ground they do, ugly beasts. And they have huge mouths too, and tiny eyes and their skin looks like old leather which haven't been oiled for years"

Zaray sighed. "The packs, how big are the packs?"

Dabin shrugged. "From four or five up to about twenty, but never more than twenty five, then they'll kill each other fighting for leadership."

Tersus had been looking like a man who has had an epiphany for a while, he almost grasped Rhuk. "Tell me, if a female troll suddenly appeared in the middle of a territory, what would happen?"

Dabin did back away from the guy and Rhuk sneezed, so close the smell from the human was just overwhelming. "Uh, the males will go berserk searching for her, probably kill pack members and just lose it completely. Females are so rare, and usually only the really strong males get to mate"

Dhokay sort of rolled his eyes. "Mating trolls, now that is a mental image I had hoped I would avoid getting stuck in my brain but nope!"

Fastonar was staring at Tersus, his eyes narrow. "What are you up to?"

Tersus had an insane grin on his lips and his eyes were shining. "They are like animals right? And animals do have a breeding season, when the females go into heat right?"

The two dwarves stared at each other, their expressions said it all. "Yes, but what does that have to do with our problem?"

Tersus raised a hand. "Everything!"

He spun around himself a few times, then he stopped and stared at them. "While the two wood elves search for a pretty flower you can get me some small animals, rabbits, hares, voles, everything small and fast, and alive and unharmed!"

Fastonar was gaping. "I beg your pardon?!"

Tersus nodded. "I mean it, go! I have a plan, one which will make sure that the trolls have something else to chase than us"

Shaluun was grinning. "I can see where you are heading with this, great idea."

He grasped some rope and an empty sack from their packs and nodded to Dhokay and Phraan. "Let's go guys, we cannot waste any time"

Fastonar stared at Tersus, trying hard not to cringe from the smell. "Are you sure you can do this?"

Tersus nodded. "Yes, absolutely. I just need a little time and a small fire."

Rhuk and Dabin scurried off and found some dry bushes and grass and before long they had a small fire going. Tersus did find a pot and some odd vials and he started mixing stuff at an alarming rate. Zaray did look as if she didn't quite knew what to think, and Fastonar was clearly in doubt. Tersus got Peter to hold the pot over the fire with a poker and none of them had any idea of what made it into it. But the smell which soon rose from the pot was indescribable. It was so rank it would have made a Billy goat smell like a perfume shop and Tersus was grinning widely. "I hope they do catch something good for we cannot risk that any of us catch this scent, it would make us instant targets"

The pot was brought to a boil and then Tersus added something from a pouch which made the steam turn bright purple and the smell became so infernal even Zaray turned green. Then Tersus took the pot and put it aside and he was grinning from one ear to the other, he did look like a complete madman. "Now we just have to wait."

Taurin and Thiana did return first, with some roots and they started by crushing the roots with two rocks and smearing the goo onto the horses legs and their own boots. Then they smeared the boots of the others there and kept some for the ones who were out hunting. An hour later the three hunters returned with a bag filled with all sorts of critters. There were rabbits and hares and some tiny long legged animals which were indigenous for the region. Tersus was smiling and he made them open the bag before he poured the contents of the pot into it. The animals did kick and squeal desperately and he closed the bag. "This won't harm them, as long as the trolls don't catch them that is"

He grasped the bag and nodded to the others. "Let's ride, we need to get as far into the territory as we can before dusk"

Phraan didn't like this at all but if it could save them from an encounter with trolls it was probably worth it. They mounted again and Zaray took the lead on her huge mule. Phraan wondered why she rode a mule instead of a horse, the animal was clearly both strong and enduring but not very fast. But he did notice that the horses acted funny around her, as if they did catch a scent they didn't like and he was getting a feeling that Zaray wasn't what she appeared to be at all. They crossed the river and rode along a ridge for some hours before they entered a valley full of very tall and ragged cliffs. It was a real maze but Zaray was leading them well and it was very obvious that she knew what she was doing.

It was getting darker and Tersus did release the animals in different places. They started looking for a place to camp and this night they couldn't make any fires. They had to be quiet and Zaray did lead them down a narrow canyon which ended in what could only be described as an oasis. A pond had formed underneath a small waterfall and it was a sort of forest growing around it. The beach was wide and sandy and it was a very beautiful place. She stopped her mule and sighed. "You all need to make sure your horses don't nicker or whinny, and when we ride on tomorrow you need to put cloth over their hooves too. And ride with no bit"

Phraan sighed, they would have to be completely silent then, it would be tough. They set up a simple camp and two and two would keep watch. The food would have to be devoured cold but they were used to that now and they ate and found a place for their bedrolls. Zaray smiled. "I will take a bath, it is the last chance for quite a while so if anyone else wants to wash now is the time"

She walked down to the water's edge and started stripping and it was very apparent that she was like an elf when it came to nudity. She had no sense of shame at all and Phraan had to stare. He was still mourning Vitile, and she haunted his dreams every night but he had to admit that Zaray was exquisite. She was taller than Vitile had been, more elegant and with longer limbs and she was just stunning. She waded into the water with a relaxed ease even if it had to be ice cold. Phraan stared at her and she sent him a lingering glance, gestured for him to come closer. He did notice that she even now was armed, she was carrying a hunting knife with a very special design and she was almost playing with the blade, he had never seen that sort of knife before. Her eyes were shining and he did realize that they were almost like cats eyes. He stopped by the water's edge and she sat down on a rock, wetting the long amethyst hair. Zaray was extremely sensual, and it was quite apparent that she knew how to use that fact. He cocked his head. "I have never seen anyone taking a bath wielding a knife like that, nor have I ever seen anyone of our race with that type of eyes"

She just smiled. "I am unique, as are you. A lady has to be able to protect herself you know"

He frowned. "What do you mean unique?"
She just continued to smile, a small and somewhat wicked grin. "Oh you do know what I mean Phraan? Gifted, for it is a gift isn't it? Have you ever come across anything you haven't been able to kill?"

He froze, staring at the female who continued to wash her amethyst hair as if nothing was out of the ordinary. "I don't understand?"

She put the knife down onto the rock next to her. "You have survived the impossible many times Phraan, you cannot see it but others can. You have killed dragons by the score, and yes, the orcs have named you well. Death does love you Phraan, you are its finest tool"

He hissed. "I am only doing what is needed!"

She nodded. "Yes, of course you are. But we are all tools Phraan, all pawns in this game. You are so much more than you think you are, and you will see that, soon enough"

He stared at her bracelet, she usually hid it but now it was visible. "You have a weapon there which can kill anything right? Why don't you use it against the dragons? I bet you could kill plenty with it?"
She shook her head and smiled. "The bow is a weapon yes, and it is extremely powerful too. But it is like a beacon, all mages will sense its presence and I prefer to only use it when there is no other option. It drains me of power, the energy within it is linked to my own life, and if I use it too often it will make me vulnerable, weak. I don't want that. The bow will only be used if there is no other way out of a situation, I cannot let the enemy know that I have it in my possession. Besides, it

may not work against things which are created by magic, dragons were natural beings to begin with, they have just been changed."

Phraan saw that she used the knife to cut off some of her hair, she braided the loose lock into a thin braid and swift movements transformed it into a bracelet of some sorts. She tossed it over to him. "Here, wear this at all times. See it as a gift of friendship"

He frowned. "Only those who are betrothed wear such jewellery"

She smiled. "Maybe, but this is not that type of a gift. It is protection Phraan!"

He stared at the bracelet, it was still warm from her skin and he took a deep breath. "It is magical?"

She nodded. "Yes, but I cannot yet tell you what sort of magic it does possess. Just…wear it."

He blinked, the thin braid was as shiny as real amethyst and he felt an odd tingling as he did put it on. "Why should I trust you?"

She smiled and wrung the water out of her hair. "Because you have no choice but to do so. You must accept that there are things of which you yet have to remain ignorant"

Phraan frowned. "You are speaking in riddles, I don't understand anything of this"

She sighed and got up, her body shining in the vague starlight. "I will give you something to think about then, one piece of information. What do you know of your father?"

Phraan frowned. "What do you mean? I know very little, he was an elf and he and mom sort of ended up in bed after a very wild party and that was it, she got knocked up and he left the next day, before he knew what he had done?"

Zaray giggled. "That is all? Did he leave a name? Anything at all?"

Phraan looked down, remembered that many had regarded his mother as a whore for having a child out of wedlock. He had been regarded as a bastard and if he hadn't been such a huge lad he would have been bullied for sure. As it was nobody dared to mock him, he would break the nose of anyone daring to slander his mother's name so he heard it. "No, she didn't remember anything, except that he was very handsome and extremely….uh, well, pleasant to be with"

Zaray laughed out loud. "Oh I bet he was, let me tell you one thing and you go and consider it, your father was of my kin."

Phraan gaped. "What? What are you friggin talking about? He was an elf wasn't he? Do you know him?"

Zaray smiled, a very satisfied smile. "Yes, he was an elf, like me, but we are not like the others, we are forgotten Phraan, and your gift is a part of who you are, of his legacy. Think of this, and it will make sense soon enough. Go now, I can hear that the trick Tersus thought up is having an effect"

Phraan lifted his head, in the distance he could hear some very faint sounds which could be roars and Dhokay appeared on top of the waterfall. "People, I see three trolls in the distance, on that ridge to the east. They are trying to tear each other apart or so it seems."

Phraan did run up to the luptay who pointed off into the distance. Three huge figures could indeed be seen on that ridge, the faint moonlight was enough to illuminate them. Phraan just stared, they were grotesque and he felt a chill running down his spine, he was glad Tersus had come up with this trick of his, those creatures were terrible. He could almost feel their brute strength the whole way from that ridge and the fact that they were dumb only made them more dangerous. Dhokay was sneering. "Abominations, that is what they are"

Phraan nodded, his mind was reeling still. So, his father had been the same sort of elf as Zaray, but she appeared to be of a rather well known although rare branch of the race. She was hiding her true nature, so if he was to find out who he really was he had to crack the enigma which was her identity. He was thinking back, it made some sense now, he had aged faster than ordinary elven children, it was normal that a half breed aged at the same pace as a full blooded elf until maturity was reached. He on the other hand had grown fast, and reached his full height at the same time a human would, but he didn't have any other human features than that. Could she be telling the truth? The odd ability to stay cool and just kill, his ability to immediately find the weakness of an enemy and bring it down? Was there indeed more to him than he had believed? His mind was spinning and he tried to focus upon the trolls. Dhokay spat on the ground. "The orcs do fear trolls, I spoke to a few orcs once who had come across a dragon the trolls had killed."

Phraan turned his head around. "What? Are you kidding me?"

Dhokay shook his head. "No, I tell the truth. It was after we split up, there were still a few dragons left in the high valleys on the other side of the desert and I went there, just to see if I could help the locals get rid of the last ones. There was a tribe of peaceful orcs living there, and they told me everything. The trolls are immune to dragon fire apparently. They had just hit the dragon with rocks until it died, it hadn't managed to kill even one of the trolls"

Phraan snorted. "That dragon must have been old or sick then, I cannot believe that they could have done much harm to it otherwise"

Dhokay shrugged. "It could have been sick I guess, but the orcs swore it was an adult storm fire."

Phraan stared over at the ridge, only two of the figures were standing now, the third was on the ground. He heard the guttural roars from even this distance and he did notice that everybody else were listening too, he swallowed hard. "I don't think the trolls will come in this direction now."

Dhokay nodded. "Yes, let's hope so."

Phraan walked down to the pond again, found his bedroll. He stared at the stars above and looked over to where Zaray now sat combing her hair, she was so relaxed and didn't seem to worry about anything. What was it that she knew? Imeah was taking a swift bath too, but she had found a rock she hid behind and she was very swift. The water was way too cold for a human being. Phraan did eat a little and then he rolled himself into his blanket and tried to sleep. It was hard, but finally his body did succumb to its need for rest and darkness took him.

The next morning Phraan was the last one to keep watch and he was wide awake before Rhuk came to wake him up, he and Dabin were the last pair out and they sat on top of the canyon until they all had gotten out of their bedrolls and got ready to journey on. The horses were prepared and Zaray sent them all a strict glance. "The area we are about to enter now is rocky, and the cliffs do turn even the smallest sound into thunder, so be careful."

Tersus did look fascinated as always but Phraan saw that Peter did look less than enthusiastic. The two dwarves did look as if they were in a good mood and the cold didn't bother them but Imeah did look as if she was in some sort of discomfort. Fastonar did hand her his cloak and she thanked him and kept her eyes down. "What is the matter girl? You look nervous? Is it the trolls?"

Imeah stared at him, her eyes were so unbelievably red, like blood in snow. "There is something else in here, I can sense it. It is like a weight on my thoughts, a dark shadow. The trolls are all over the place, chasing the scent Tersus made but they aren't alone. I sense other minds, more advanced minds"

Fastonar frowned. "More advanced minds? Can you specify that?"

Imeah shook her head. "No, I cannot control what I have, I just go with the flow. Sometimes I cannot sense anything at all which is out of the ordinary and other times I can sort of see everything. I am sorry"

Zaray got ready to mount her mule again. "Don't be, everybody, keep your eyes open and don't make any loud noises"

They started off again and Phraan did find the landscape to be rather fascinating in a way, it was dry and just rocks and sand but it had a sort of ragged beauty to it. He saw formations he never had been able to even imagine before and the terrain was rather terrible. They had to dismount several times to lead the horses along steep narrow paths or down steep hills and Zaray seemed to be extremely focused the entire time. She was stopping quite often, listening, tilting her head and watching the surroundings with the eyes of a hawk. Imeah was staring down at the neck of her horse the entire time, as if she was afraid to look at the landscape she rode through and Phraan found that a bit odd. He placed himself next to her as they were crossing a rather flat area and she did throw a swift glance at him. "Imeah, why don't you look at anything but the mane of your mare?"

She swallowed. "I do see Phraan, I see too much. This place, it is bad, very bad. But it was ages ago"

Phraan frowned. "What are you talking about?"

She turned her attention to the horse once more. "A battle, there was a battle here. But they weren't humans, they were monsters. The valleys, they used to be green but now they are dead, the blood poisoned them"

The half elf stared at the albino girl. "You can see that?"

She nodded. "Yes, it was before time became time, the earth was young then. Demi gods, they were so powerful. Some of that power exists still, it is in the blood"

She closed her eyes and her face became oddly devoid of expression. "It is coming to you Phraan, the one wielding the gifts from the hand of the converted disciple. Take them both"

Phraan sort of scoffed. "Imeah, you are a seer and I know that this sort of thing makes people expect certain things of you but for heaven's sake girl, can't you speak plainly?"

She smiled, a very swift hint of a smile. "I can only tell what I see Phraan, I cannot even describe it well."

She leaned over to him, whispering. "Trust me, from now on, do not tell anyone of your dreams, not even your friends. There is danger here which even I cannot see"

She urged her horse on and Phraan frowned and felt even more confused. What dreams was she referring to? He didn't dream at all these days, except those where he saw how Vitile died and felt the grief burn through his body again and again. He didn't understand anything of what she had said.

As they rode on the landscape started to raise even more, and it became steeper. Zaray pointed at a peak they could see in the distance. "Over there is our goal, the hidden path. It will take us a few days to get there"

Fastonar was mumbling. "And then, how far to this city of yours?"

She smiled back at him, eyes dark and expression somewhat hard. "That depends upon what we encounter over there, it is a very dangerous area and I bet that the dark brothers have unleashed a lot now, creatures I never have seen before."

Fastonar sighed. "That is not very encouraging, so there is no way to avoid the mountains?"

She shook her head. "Not unless you are a dragon and able to fly!"

Dhokay frowned. "Some of the dragon species are flightless, how have they made it to the plains?"

Zaray steered her mule around a boulder and smiled. "They have been transported by magic, the dark brotherhood is able to teleport stuff from the city and to this side of the mountains but that takes a heck of a lot of energy and I bet that most of the new dragons are capable of flying. It is easier that way. A mage who has used all his energy on moving some dragons won't be able to do much again for some days."

Fastonar sighed again, he did look kind of tired. "I have to agree with that I guess"

Phraan did keep an eye on the horizon, the clouds were getting darker and darker and it looked as if it was gonna snow soon. The temperature had dropped a lot and Zaray started to look worried. Phraan rode up to her. "Problems?"

She nodded. "Possibly, a snowstorm up here can turn nasty. We do need to find shelter"

Fastonar cringed. "In troll territory? Are you nuts?"

Zaray shrugged "I am not the one in danger of becoming a pop sickle, I can deal with cold. But the wind on the other hand? That is way worse!"

Fastonar did glare at her but Shaluun did smile, a very tight smile. "She is right, you don't want to be caught in a snowstorm up here. We do need to find a cave or something."

Rhuk and Dabin stared at each other "There could be caves in the hills up ahead, the rock is a type which often contain large ones"

Zaray nodded and urged the mule on. "Right, let's go then."

They did find a cave rather fast and it was a huge one with a rather narrow opening and a half dome shape. It was just room to bring their horses inn too and the space became a bit cramped but it was warm and the opening so small it wouldn't let much wind through. Since they were inside they could risk starting a small fire and Imeah sat down by it immediately, she was clearly suffering in the cold weather. Zaray stood in the opening for a while, listening to the wind. "I will go exploring the back of the cave for a while, it looks as if a tunnel is leading downwards from the back of it"

Fastonar glared at her. "Is that wise? "

She shrugged. "Time will tell, but I am curious, I like to know if a cave has an escape entrance, in case of trouble."

Phraan stared after her, she disappeared into the small tunnel carrying only a torch and before long she was gone. Fastonar made a grimace and sat down. "Right, eat some and rest, we have to get going as soon as the storm ends"

Dhokay was petting his large horse, he did look concerned. "There is little for the horses to eat up here, they are weakening."

Fastonar shrugged and pulled off his boots. "Yes, if this lasts we have to leave them, I doubt there is more food to find up in them passes."

Phraan had laid down and tried to eat a bit but he was feeling sort of torn. He remembered what Zaray had said and for the first time in his life he did doubt his own self. He started to question the things his mother had told him, and the things his grandfather had said too. Why would a poor girl like his mother be at a party where an elf also participated? The village had been very poor, they didn't own much at all and his grandfather had been among the wealthiest people there and yet there had been winters when they all had been starving. He had a gnawing suspicion that his mother had lied to him, that she had hidden the truth quite deliberately. Phraan soon got warm and drowsy and since Dhokay was watching the entrance he allowed himself to fall asleep. Soon he realized that he was dreaming, he was walking over a meadow, and it was summer and warm and the air was filled with the scents of a forest in full bloom. The he saw someone moving up ahead, dancing through the tall grass and he saw that it was Vitile. She was wearing a short doeskin dress and had flowers weaved into her hair and she did look so happy and carefree. She was laughing as she danced forth, throwing her hair back, taking elegant steps and spinning around. The sight was lovely and yet it hurt him for he knew it wasn't real, it was just a dream.

She waved her hand at him and he followed her into a grove of enormous oak trees, they were so massive he had a hard time believing they were real, some had several branches stretching out so they reached the ground as if they were the arches of a bridge and from them huge logs did rise towards the skies. When he managed to get an overview of the whole thing he realized that it all was one tree. In the middle was the original tree, so huge you could fit several buildings inside of it. Vitile laughed and danced closer to it, touched the rough bark with reverence. "This is the mother tree, she knows everything. All elven spirits stay with her before they are born into the world of the living, she knows them all"

Phraan swallowed. "So?"

Vitile giggled and pulled him closer by the arm. "You have questions haven't you? She can answer them, all of them. You just have to ask the right way."

Phraan had to stare at her, she was more beautiful than ever before and his heart was aching, the heavy empty feeling almost more than he could bear. "I can ask her? Just like that?"

Vitile nodded. "Yes silly, and she will show you the answer, but it may not be one you'll like"

He took a deep breath. "This isn't real, I am dreaming, and you...you are gone from the world"

She pouted. "Nobody is ever truly gone as long as they are remembered, I told you that once, didn't I?"

He had to sigh and nod. "You did, but I miss you Vitile, I miss you so terribly."

She smiled and reached up, kissed his cheek gently. "I know, I wanted to see you again, one last time. Don't grieve for me Phraan, I was a dragon slayer, I knew the risks. I did my duty, as did you"

He hung his head. "That doesn't change the way I feel"

She shook his head. "Oh listen to yourself, sulking like a child. You are here for a reason, go ahead, and ask her"

Phraan stared at the tree, the massive branches did dwarf him, some were so wide you could have driven a carriage along it and still had room to spare. How did one ask a tree questions? He had no clue whatsoever! "How? It is a tree damn it"

Vitile groaned. "Oh Phraan, you are definitely not a wood elf, just ask, like you would ask me if the weather is nice outside or if I want another cup of wine. Ask her"

Phraan took a deep breath. "Alright, great mother tree, who am I really?"

The tree sort of groaned and then the branches started to move, Phraan was staring in absolute shock and then the scene changed right before his eyes. He was back with the group, fifty years ago, battling a huge storm wind, the dragon was being taunted by Fastonar who rode terrifyingly close to the head, throwing knives at the nose. Phraan and Shaluun ran up along its neck, Shaluun planted his axe in its throat while Phraan rammed his sword straight into its skull. Then he was in an inn, just before the group split up. He and Vitile were making love and he was so very close to asking her the grand question, but he didn't dare to. Then it changed again, but this was something he didn't recognize, he was standing in a pool, it was warm and the water reached his hips, he couldn't move and there was someone behind him, he could sense it. The water started to rise slowly and he couldn't turn around or even move a limb. An arm came from behind, embraced him, caressed him like a lover would and he saw that the arm was extremely pale and that of a female. "Embrace the gift I will give you, let it bring you to completion. It is rebirth, a new beginning. The shedding of an old skin in favour of a new one"

The water reached his neck, he was starting to panic and he fought to escape but the water did continue and he knew he would drown soon. He got one last gasp of breath and then there was just water but now he was floating, and it was just pleasant and warm around him and nothing felt dangerous or even painful. Then he was jerked back down, it felt as if he was falling really fast and he landed with a thud on a naked cliff. It didn't hurt though and his body felt odd, alien in a way, stronger than before. Zaray was there, she was glowing and her eyes were like pools of light, shining like twin stars. She smiled. "Don't be afraid, let your gift come to its completion, be who you truly are"

He felt a surge of energy through his body, and it felt terrifying and divine at the same time, he could barely breathe, he had to scream as everything he was changed forever. The power he felt surging from his soul was so strong he was unable to do anything but endure as it warped his every existence into something new. Phraan felt that something grasped onto him, shook him. He opened his eyes with a yelp and stared up at Fastonar. "Quiet, something is outside, we can hear it"

Phraan swallowed, it had to be the most bizarre dream he had ever had but what did it mean? He got up, attached his blades to his body again and Fastonar stared out into the storm with a pale face and a grim expression. Dhokay was sitting by the entrance still, his eyes half closed and he was obviously listening. "It is more than one, I can hear voices in the wind!"

Shaluun held his axe. "Trolls?"

Dhokay shook his head. "No, they don't really speak, they just grunt or howl. These speak, but I can sense that they are something very dangerous."

Imeah looked scared. "What I warned you about..."

The entrance was narrow but hard to defend due to its shape and Dhokay bared his teeth. "We can fight one by one but we are trapped here, like mice. Have Zaray returned yet?"

Fastonar shook his head. "No, she has been gone for a while, I have no idea of whether or not she'll come back at all."

Phraan sighed "She will, I am sure of it. But what is out there?"

Ivran pushed his way forth, his eyes were wild. "I feel them too, it is like....something terribly dark and I cannot even describe it. But it is evil, and it is looking for us"

Phraan hissed. "If it is looking for us it knows we are here, and why. The enemy must know we are coming their way then"

Fastonar sneered. "She has told them, I am sure of it, we should never have trusted her!"

Ivran stared at the opening, they could hear something moving through the snow, something heavy. He took a deep breath and tried to focus, he had tried spells like this back at the academy but it had always failed. Could things have changed now? He closed his eyes and imagined that the rock face was whole, no cave, no opening at all. Just ragged hard solid rock. The air shivered a bit and then they saw a sort of thin veil starting to cover the entrance and Dhokay gaped. "A camouflage spell, great kid!"

Ivran was panting. "It is the best I can do, so be quiet. They cannot see us but they can hear us"

Shaluun stared at Tersus who was fidgeting with his filthy braid. "Or smell us! Where is what's left of that root?"

Thiana handed over a small pouch and Shaluun nodded to Peter. "Hold him!"

Tersus did wriggle like a worm on a hook but Peter was strong and before long the alchemist was covered with the sticky goo. It didn't make him look better at all! Everybody held their breaths, the sounds from the outside got stronger and Dhokay was holding his hammer so hard the knuckles were all white. He was staring at something through the barrier and Phraan did move over so he could see. The thing he did see made him gasp and back off a few steps. It was a huge being, its shape almost humanoid but the head was very long and oddly shaped and the thing was black. Not black like a black cat or a black horse but like a deep black hole, like an opening in the air with just blackness inside. The only detail they could see were two eyes, glowing in a sickening green colour and they were just orbs, no pupils or other details but they were intelligent, watching and considering what they saw. Phraan felt cold sweat running down his back and Ivran was shaking, his eyes were blurred. "It is searching for anything magical, it knows we are here somewhere. There are more of them, three more."

He was whispering but Phraan heard it and the thing outside of the cave was grunting something which had to be words and they heard a sniffing sound too. The creature reached out towards the illusion, the long arm with black claws came closer and closer and Phraan reached for his blades when something absolutely unexpected did happen.

They heard a roar coming from above, the sound so strong it made the rock itself vibrate and the thing turned around and seemed to shout something. They saw more glowing eyes in the distance and the creatures seemed to gather. Fastonar was paper white and trembling "That sound was a dragon, a huge one"

Then there were more roars, and Phraan saw something which had to be fire but the colour was wrong, it looked purple? And the dark creatures screamed and he saw one flying through the air, hitting the ground hard and sort of dissolving itself into smoke. More roars, more light and screams and then it got silent. Only the wind howled now and everybody held their breath for what felt like an eternity. Dhokay did look flabbergasted. "It killed them, the dragon killed them?"

Fastonar tried to smile. "Looks that way, but why?"

Shaluun shrugged. "Maybe they are natural rivals? Is the dragon still there?"

Ivran groaned and the veil disappeared, he was drenched in sweat and trembling all over. "I cannot do this again, sorry. I am completely drained, I don't think I have much strength left, for some reason."

Dhokay listened. "I don't hear anything, it think it flew off, whatever it was"

Everybody breathed a sigh of relief but tensed as they suddenly heard the sound of running feet. They raised their blades but dropped them as Zaray did burst into the cave. She did look terrible, covered with dust and cobwebs and she had some cuts on her face. Her eyes were huge! "Did you see those monsters, Gods, I have never seen anything more...unnatural"

Fastonar almost roared at her. "Where have you been?!"

Zaray pulled her hair out of her face, her braid had come undone and it did look messy. "I got lost but found a way out, I was gonna return but those darklings did show up and I had to seek cover in a small ravine. I have never felt anything like that, ever. They sort of sucked up all light"

Fastonar growled. "Lucky for you that the dragon showed up, did you see it?"

She nodded. "Not really, just a shadow in the storm, but it was massive, largest I have ever seen."

Phraan bit his lower lip. "Great, we are gathered again and we are unharmed. Now what?"

Zaray shrugged and went over to the fire, warmed her hands. "We stay until the storm is over, we cannot get out now, it is too dangerous."

Dhokay sighed. "The horses need food, and water. We do need food and water too, we are running low. "

Zaray turned to Ivran. "You are tired but why don't you try, conjuring up some hay and water should be easy right?"

Ivran cringed. "I can try but I am not so sure it will be a success at all"

She just smiled. "Go for it kid"

Phraan frowned. "You called those things darklings, have you come across them before then?"

She shook her head. "Heck no, but the name fits don't it? They were just darkness"

Dhokay made a grimace. "I don't wanna know what those things could have done to us if they had found us."

Zaray did look serious. "Neither do I, the dark brotherhood has gone too far this time, they have done things their predecessors never would have dreamed of doing"

Ivran nodded slowly. "They were dark magic, not really alive, just…darkness"

She looked down, her eyes did shine with a sinister light. "Yes, the first mages who formed the brotherhood were extremely powerful, there has never been mages like them and there never will be again. The magic was new back then, fresh, untainted. Now it has withered and it is nothing compared with what it was"

Ivran did look disappointed. "So I am weak compared with those mages of old?"

She shook her head. "No, for your magic is different, it is ironic but your power is more based upon chaos than the one they used. The reason is rather apparent, you cannot create chaos without order as its base. Chaos cannot spring from chaos, there has to be something there at first, something orderly"

Ivran tilted his head, his eyes narrow as he was thinking. "That makes sense I guess, but then I can be compared with them after all?"

She nodded. "Yes, but it would be like comparing a thoroughbred and a draft horse, if you look at speed one is superior to the other but if you look at other things like endurance and manageability it becomes a different game right away. You are maybe stronger than they were, we don't know that yet. But their magic is different, and that won't change."

Ivran sighed "Right, I'd better try to make some food for us and the horses then, or else it is gonna become a very bad night indeed"

He walked to the centre of the room and took a deep breath, then he closed his eyes and tried to seek the power he was harbouring, ordering it to do what he wished of it. At first there was nothing, he was thinking so hard of hay, of its looks and smell and the stiffness of it and everything which made hay unique. There was a soft poof and then something started falling onto the floor, in large numbers. It was some sort of round object and they were soft and some fell apart as they hit the rock floor. Shaluun gaped. "Those are melons?"

Phraan nodded. "Sibra melons, the desert type. They are delicious if they are ripe"

Ivran did look very disappointed, he stared at the heap of melons with narrow eyes, it had to be at least two hundred of them. Dhokay walked over and grasped one of the melons, it had been opened by the impact and he did sniff it. "They are ripe, Ivran, this was in fact very useful. They are good food"

He hung his head. "But it wasn't hay now was it?"

Zaray just shrugged. "There is enough for the horses too, they love such sweet treats"

Ivran sighed and then the roof seemed to open itself and it rained hay, suddenly they stood there covered with hay to their hips with hay in their hair and they were blinking at each other. "Ah, now, that is an exaggeration dear, we don't need that much hay!"

Zaray was sneezing and working her way out of the mass and Dhokay and the two dwarves started to pile the hay up against the wall so they had some space left to sit and eat and sleep. "It is good to lie in, we can make beds out of it, no problem"

Rhuk was grinning and he did look like some sort of hay covered goblin with the stuff stuck in his hair and beard and armour. Tersus was staring at Ivran with narrow eyes. "You try too hard lad, I have seen such cases before. The trick I think would be to ask for either more or less than what you actually need, or something completely different. Sooner or later you will crack it"

Ivran rolled his eyes. "Right, so, what now?"

Zaray lifted a melon. "These are good, but try something else, a real dinner of some sorts?"

Ivran lifted his arms. "Alright, fine, I'll try"

He was thinking about steak, nice well done steak. He felt the power surge through him, even stronger this time and everybody jerked as fish started appearing out of nowhere. Huge trout the length of a man's arm, alive and wriggling and with them frogs and huge shrimp of some sorts. The fish was squirming on the ground and Peter looked at Ivran with awe. "Fresh fish, that is just delicious!"

Dhokay was frowning. "Yeah, with seasoning"

Then a barrel dropped out of the air and landed on Ivran's foot and made him cuss rather heartily. Phraan grasped the small barrel. "It is fish seasoning people"

Ivran rubbed his foot with a desperate expression on his face. "It just does it without me wanting it! It is horrible"

Zaray shook her head. "No, it isn't. It is great, that is what it is. You just need to learn how to formulate your wishes, and how much power you are to use."

Phraan sighed. "We have enough fish to feed an army, you must have drained an entire lake lad. But whatever, it is fresh and looks great and we only need a fire and then we'll feast"

Ivran sent Phraan a grateful glance and Rhuk got a fire going and used some twigs to create a sort of grid they could fry the fish upon. Dhokay gutted the fish and seasoned them and they had melon stew to go with it. It was in fact a very nice meal and Shaluun hung some blankets in front of the cave entrance. It was strange but the cave had become almost cosy now, their steeds were munching away at their hay and the fire gave some warmth too. Ivran ate until he was cross eyed and then he laid down to rest and the rest did the same. Zaray and Fastonar were taking first watch and sat in the entrance, the rest just dug into the hay and allowed themselves to go to sleep. The night was long and dark and the storm was howling outside. They would have to stay there until it blew over and everybody wanted to use the opportunity to rest now that they were relatively safe.

Phraan found a comfortable position to sleep in, his back was still bothering him a bit, the wound was just a scar now but it still felt a bit stiff at times. The horses lay down to sleep too and the cave became rather silent, or silent? Rhuk was snoring like a whole team of lumberjacks and Taurin was humming softly as he was braiding Thiana's hair. Phraan looked the other way, the tenderness he saw between the two elves just reminded him of what he had lost. He closed his eyes and focused on the warmth of his lair and the pleasant feeling of having had a good meal. He did fall asleep rather fast, he had been used to sleep whenever he could back in the days and now that habit became useful once more.

The cave was a good place for a camp and the storm was a violent one, Shaluun was used to winter storms, his people did live in the mountains to the North West and he knew how to judge a storm. This one could last for days and he saw that Zaray was aware of the fact and she was pissed off. She was sitting on a saddle and her eyes told him that she was very annoyed indeed. This was something they didn't need right now, being delayed like that was not a part of her plans. But on the other hand, in this weather even the enemy would have to stay indoors, trolls could of course venture outside even when it was cold but with their large surface moving against the wind they would have to struggle to get anywhere at all. Shaluun started to sharpen his axe, it was smart to be ready for one never knew what could happen, in special when surrounded by such a bunch of people.

Simaon was staring out of the windows to his suite, the huge citadel had some very nice apartments and he had chosen the best one as it was his right as a leader. It was in the top floor of the citadel and from it he could view the entire city. This was his realm, his kingdom and he was wondering if it would be preposterous to title himself as king or emperor whence they had won. This night was very dark and the winds were howling, they were used to that and the city was built in a valley where the cliffs did protect against the worst of the weather. It was a very good place and he was fond of it, the city was grand and even though it had few inhabitants it felt like a capital. It was his capital, his stronghold and he stared down at the huge square in front of the citadel and grinned. His associates had brought all of their men to this place, they had plenty of soldiers and servants and then there were those who had lived there for countless generations. The artefact had allowed them to bring more people into the city through the magical wall and with them more resources and fresh and eager minds ready to do whatever it took to turn this into a success. Of course they wouldn't have to fight for real, the gifts left by their ancestors had ensured their success already. The dragons and the other creatures they had resurrected were a weapon none could stand up against and he caressed the hilt of his sword and smiled again.

His many under lords had many in their command and the mages they had brought over to their side were busy all the time now. The old spells and incantations were used once more and the dark magic was flowering like never before. It filled the very air itself and he felt it prickling against his skin even now. They had all been shown the light by his predecessor Ognias of Twelve towers, one of the last of the true believers and the one who had shown them all that the old days could return. Ognias had been a visionary, he had awakened the brotherhood from their dormant stage, gathered them, and shown them the grand future which was theirs to take if they only dared to. He had managed to spread the word, gather new followers and bring them there without anyone really understanding what he was doing and it had been grand and very smart.Simaon had dared, he had been the first to swear the old oath and bring his house and his men with him back to the city. His forefathers had been part of the brotherhood, it was just natural for him to take his place in it, a heritage he was proud of. Simaon was no mage but he was smart and ruthless and he had climbed to the top of the hierarchy of power rather fast.

Ognias had awakened the dragons back fifty years ago, tested them and found them to be too weak. Too many were killed by the slayers and so he had called the strong ones back to the mountains and used the magic to change them. It wasn't done in a day, the first ones had been unleashed only a few months ago and Simaon had seen the hordes which were ready to be released upon the realms. It made his chest swell with pride and he walked over to a painting which hung on the wall. It was Ognias in all his glory and Simaon caressed his sword yet again, the old one had been wise and strong and very cunning but not cunning enough. He hadn't anticipated a mundane attack, a stab in the back. Ognias had been their leader for so long, it was just natural to change the balance of power and Simaon knew he was a better leader than Ognias had been. The old one had been too patient, his ambitions too small. Now Simaon was in charge and he had been speeding things up a lot, they would soon enough see the results of their hard work and sacrifices. The others were in awe of his resourcefulness and his ideas and only that old fool Badrian had been trying to slow things down but now he was dead and good riddance. The idiot hadn't even been killed, he had supposedly died from a heart attack and crushed that pretty crystal ball of his in the fall, too bad, Simaon had wanted that artefact. It wasn't useful for anything but it had been pretty. Well, he could get all the pretty things he wanted when he had all the realms on their knees before him.

The mages under his command were keeping the wall open and their work was excellent, the dragons and the other creatures had no problems crossing it and he was convinced that the very Gods themselves were with them. After all, the brotherhood had managed to find that one thing which allowed them to bring their creations through the wall. He had to chuckle, they had so much power readily available, also a gift from the past and he knew that the mages did use it for all it was worth, the latest creatures the high mage had released into the lands beyond the wall were so amazingly deadly he felt a thrill just thinking of them. They would surely remove any enemies daring to come too close and remove all remnants of fighting will in the population. The realm would be on its knees, soon enough.

Simaon sauntered off to his bedroom, he had several pretty concubines stationed there at all times, day and night and he dropped the thick heavy robe he wore and gestured for one of them to come closer. The girl smiled and wriggled herself out of the tight dress she wore, Simaon didn't see the scared expression in her eyes, he was renowned for being rough and for being very insensitive and indifferent to the needs and wellbeing of others. He had been like that since he was a child, his father had been one of the most powerful counsellors of the old king Vhandar and they had been wealthy and living a very good life in Twelve towers. Simaon was the firstborn son, he had two sisters and a brother who was born twelve years after him and he had never had anything but hate and resentment in his heart when it came to his brother. His brother Nornan had been weak from the start, a puny lad with thin arms and legs and huge eyes, so why did his parents dote on the failure like he was something precious? Simaon had been a tall boy, boisterous and stubborn and more than a handful and his mother had spoiled him a lot. His father too had been way too kind and allowed Simaon to develop some rather unhealthy habits.

He hadn't been punished no matter what he did and when Nornan was born he immediately hated the changes this brought. He was no longer the centre of attention and his parents spent way too much time praising that little runt. If he could have strangled his brother with his diapers he would have but he knew that this would have been a mistake. Instead he tried to ignore his brother all the time and he also tried to ruin everything that little bastard did. Which was the reason he almost lost it when Nornan was invited to the academy, he had applied but been denied access since he according to the letters he received was "talentless" and "too full of himself".

Simaon had been twenty four by that time, and he was used to having things his way all the time, that his father now had started to shorten in the reins had pissed him off royally and he could no longer hide the fact that he had done some less than legal things. Some maidens had come forth and confessed that he had stolen both their virtue and hearts and others complained about servants who had been abused when Simaon were visiting their homes. The stable masters refused to lend him horses since he was infamous for riding the animals too hard and the king's master of the hounds had banned him from joining the royal hunts since he often whipped the dogs and enjoyed watching the prey die slowly. Simaon had met old Ognias at a party and he had immediately felt that this man was someone he admired, someone he could follow as long as he was useful. Ognias had spun such sweet visions and told Simaon of the talents he did have, persuading others and making them believe even a huge fat lie was among them. Simaon had seen something of a true father figure in Ognias and so Simaon's own father did die very conveniently one dark evening whilst out riding. The old man had fallen from his horse and broken his neck and the rope tied between two trees had been easy to remove, none had suspected anything.

Simaon's mother did die of grief, at least that was the official explanation but Ognias had shown Simaon such wonderful poisons and the old goat was not that hard to get rid of, after all, she had betrayed her son by bearing one more boy. Simaon had two sisters too but both were married and moved to some island to the south and he didn't bother with them at all. They were indifferent to him and being married meant that they had no rights to his father's estate at all. But Nornan was a problem and Simaon had paid some thug very well for the job, Nornan was found outside of a pub, stabbed and beaten and everything he had with him stolen, even his clothes. They said it was a robbing, and that it was very tragic and Simaon had shown some grief just to please the many who were talking about the death of his brother but he was laughing on the inside.

Getting the others interested in the cause was no problem at all, many were hungry for influence and power and Simaon had never liked the king at all, the man didn't show him the right amount of respect and didn't allow him access to the inner circle of power. For that he would pay!

Some servants entered with some food and Simaon got up from the bed and ignored the sobbing girl, he had discovered that he liked to make women cry and scream and this one had a very tight little ass, fucking her dry was such a high. The servants didn't look at him, eyes on the floor and he waved them out of the room. The food was excellent and the wine was great too, he had never been happier in his entire life and he wasn't going to let this power slip out of his hands, ever. The old prophecies were just nonsense in his eyes, since he was no mage he had no idea of what sort of powers he was meddling with, to him magic was a tool, like a hammer or a sword and he didn't realize that he was as unqualified to lead the brotherhood as a goat would be at digging for gold. But he was the one who was in charge now, simply because his ambitions and his ruthlessness were clearing a path for the others. One day his rule would be ended the same way Ognias had been, Simaon didn't think about that at all for he couldn't understand that he to the others was also just a tool, he believed that they all saw him as their divine leader, as their God.

Back in the old days every member of the brotherhood had been a mage and their approach to their cause had been very different indeed. Simaon had no clue about the discipline magic demanded of its users and he didn't care, he just wanted to use the magic for his own benefit and the mages who served the brotherhood were commandeered around like servants. In fact he treated everybody he regarded as below himself as a servant and that was pretty much every living soul there. Simaon was good at administrating things, he knew how to make plans and make sure that things were done in the right order and that was why he was the leader.

He had the visions and the ideas and he did also know how to convince others of the importance of their cause, but now as their power was increasing and the dragons had been let loose the methods he was using was becoming less and less popular. The mages were angry since they weren't shown the right amount of respect and the other lords hated being ordered around. Simaon didn't see this, he was floating on a cloud of belief in his own superiority and he failed to see that he too was being used by those below him. He believed himself to be a great leader but in fact many followed him just for the same reason he had joined the brotherhood, to get personal advantages.

He enjoyed a good meal and then he visited his own private bath where a slave massaged him and another made sure that his skin was dried off and that his hair looked good. He had always been good looking but lately his good looks had started to deteriorate. It wasn't that he didn't take care of himself, it was more that he didn't care about anything else than power and that ruthlessness and cold did show in his eyes and made his face look more grim than before. He was thinking about the next stages of the grand plan, in a few days' new scores of dragons and other monsters would be set free and he knew that nobody out there would have any chance against these creatures the dark mages had conjured up. The foundations had been made by their predecessors and they had just gone some steps further and in his eyes perfected that which the mages of old had created. If someone said that these things had been abandoned for a reason he wouldn't listen, his world had no place for those who were negative at all.

He walked down towards the basement of the citadel, it was there that most of the magic was done and that was where the spells and journals of the ancient ones had been kept. Nobody had dared to meddle with them until Ognias came along and now all the books and scrolls were being used for all that they were worth. The mages were busy again, chanting loudly. The basement was made up of several great halls, all decorated with magical runes and symbols and Simaon did wander through them with his chin held high and a cocky expression on his face. He didn't see the anger in the glances the others sent him, and he ignored the mumbling and cuss words some produced. He was heading for the main hall and he pushed the grand doors open and walked in as if he owned the room. The hall was painted black, and the ceiling had a very realistic sky painted onto it, with stars and constellations made with fluorescent colour.

It did look like you suddenly had stepped outside on a clear winter night and the sight usually made peoples stop and stare but Simaon had seen it all before and it didn't impress him at all. Three mages and a couple of his fellow leaders were busy preparing a spell to transport more dragons out onto the plains and they were using a lot of power to fulfil it. Making such a spell work was like trying to push two magnets against each other, plus side versus plus side and it required an insane amount of energy and skill. One of the other leaders hurried down from the dais they were standing on to meet him, afraid that Simaon would disturb the fragile magic. He bowed his head and Simaon stared at the fat guy with some distaste. "So, Arabur, how is it going?"

Arabur wiped the sweat off his face, he was angry that Simaon had appeared now for they needed to really focus to achieve their goal. "Good, we are there soon."

Simaon just stared at the mages, they were chanting rather loudly and drawing intricate patterns in the air with crystals of power. It did look ridiculous in his eyes and he felt nothing but contempt for the mages since they seemed so terribly narrow minded. Arabur got a foul expression in his eyes. "So, have that associate of yours done the job? Is that magical power capable of killing a dragon identified?"

Simaon hissed, he didn't like it when his co-workers asked him questions, did Arabur perhaps question his authority?

"The source is identified yes, and on its way to us, it is most unusual and needs to be investigated"

Arabur cocked his head, his eyes narrow. "On its way here? Is it captured then? In the hands of our associate?"

Simaon put on his most haughty expression. "Not captured no, but definitely in the hands of one of ours, such magic cannot be provoked unless suspicions will arise. The source appears to be human, and whence here we will find out if the magic can be used for our purposes"

Arabur felt a need to roll his eyes, he had never really believed in the things old Badrian said but this was what he saw as a cause for worries. "Is your associate heading this way alone with this human? If not I would warn you that the old prophecies speak of great danger"

Simaon scoffed, looked at Arabur with distaste. "No, it is apparently a group, but we know nothing more than that, probably dragon slayers. Our friend cannot reveal the true motif just yet, naturally enough. I have used some very simple magical devices to keep in contact, through this person's dreams."

Arabur cocked his head. "A traitor then, such an unwise move. Someone betraying once will betray twice, I would have thought that you of all people should know this?"

Simaon glared at the short fat guy, normally his glance would make others back down but this time Arabur didn't, he just stared back with a small grin which made Simaon boil with anger. "Are you insinuating something here?"

Arabur just shrugged "I don't know, am I?"

Simaon swallowed his anger, promising himself to punish this disobedient little piece of blubber in the worst way possible. "I have no doubt about the loyalty of that person, don't worry, any dangers will be eliminated long before the one with the magic reaches our realm. My associate is loyal, and won't dare to turn around."

Arabur just nodded, the little grin still there. "Good, I hope your confidence is based upon something real then, too bad if we suddenly had to face enemies here in our city. It is not made to be defended"

Simaon rolled his eyes. "You are whining like an old woman Arabur, what do we have to fear ha? We are powerful, soon every king and lord will bow before us. Go help your friends there now, like the good little pug you are"

Arabur almost sneered, his somewhat bulging eyes and shape had earned him that nickname and he hated it intensely. He hated Simaon and he didn't try to hide it at all, he just glared at the tall black haired man and then he turned around and walked back up the dais. One day he would murder Simaon and it would be the sweetest day of his entire life!

Arabur watched as Simaon argued a little with the high mage in charge of this operation and he nodded over to one of the other lords present. They had all followed Simaon because his visions were grand though he weren't. He could open doors for them yes, but then he would be disposable and Arabur felt very strongly that Simaon now had done what he could and that he was useless. The other lord walked over, seemingly to hand over some scrolls but he made a little gesture and created a sort of room around the two where they could speak in private, no sound would escape it. Arabur almost sneered. "He has become too cocky, he is insufferable. Do we need him anymore?"

Lord Buraz stroked his long white beard and squinted, his eyes were hard. "No, his value is spent. We have all the people we need and we all know that Simaon is too ambitious for his own good. He is moving ahead too fast, we cannot keep up with him. All the mages are complaining, their grip on the new creations is fragile at its best"

Arabur nodded. "The magical force felt out there, it is coming this way, with that person he claims is loyal to us. I do not like it"

Buraz did look shocked for a second. "Oh by the abyss, that is bad. We cannot risk that, even if the power is subdued somehow it can wreak havoc on our spells. Everything is so sensitive now it is like living in a house made from eggshells."

Arabur swallowed. "Do we intervene again? I did order for some of the new inventions to be on the lookout for anything magical after he mentioned this the first time but apparently that didn't work at all."

Buraz nodded slowly, his eyes were even colder now. "Of course we intervene! We cannot let anyone enter this realm, friend or foe unless we are in control of that someone. Simaon have no idea of how delicate the balance is right now, one wrong move and it will all crumble to the ground"

Arabur was almost jumping up and down and his eyes were shining with glee. "Shall I or will you?"

Buraz grunted. "I will speak to the mages under my command, this idea of Simaon needs to be stopped right now. We cannot let this strange magic enter before our final procedures are done, not even if it is friendly. Don't worry brother, nothing will get through the wall in that direction, I will make sure of that. My mages will take care of it, I don't see a cause to raise an alarm yet, but I will ask them to be careful still. We have weapons now which nobody can fight."

Arabur did look like a kid asking for candy from a kind but also strict adult. "Can I deal with Simaon? Please? I would love to watch him squirm, love to show him just how worthless he is"

Buraz smiled slowly. "Why of course my friend, we can all agree that Simaon's role is over, he is just trash now and not even the dragons would want that one. He is too full of spite even for them, he would give them indigestion. Go ahead, get rid of him and please, do it in an epic manner. We do need some entertainment these days, it has been all work and no fun for way too long"

Arabur grinned so widely Buraz saw all his teeth. "It will be my pleasure lord Buraz, Simaon won't see many more sunrises, I promise. I will go and make plans right now, and I swear that our so called leader will regret the very day he was born"

Buraz crossed his arms over his chest, his expression a pleased one and he bowed his neck and smiled. "Good my brother, may the chaos be with you. "

Arabur just waved and ran off, his short legs moving faster than ever before. It would be his finest hour for sure. Yes, he would make sure that Simaon left this world in a manner which would make people faint in horror for years to come.

As the night went by the storm seemed to intensify, Shaluun said it was a good sign, it meant that it would pass by. A storm which held its intensity was one which would last for days and the cave was warm now and they had food and a warm place to stay. Rhuk was melting snow to get water for the horses and he liked being busy so he didn't complain and they switched guarding the entrance. Right now Rhuk was describing the proper way to caress someone's feet to Shaluun and the elf was sweating and trying to find an excuse he could use to make the dwarf shut up without insulting him. He had no need to know how to suck someone's toes and the idea of hairy dwarf feet was a giant turn off anyhow. Rhuk was almost lyrical as he recalled the feet of the females he had been with and Shaluun rolled his eyes, he could understand that some guys would remember tits, or asses, but feet? No way, to him feet were made to walk with, not to... Oh Gods, Rhuk was telling him how one lass he had been with had such long toes she could literally wrap her big toe and the one next to it around Rhuk's cock and get him off that way and Shaluun wished he was somewhere else, anywhere. This was as bad as it got, he was sure that if you placed Rhuk in a cell with an orc the orc would confess every foul deed it had ever done before an hour was gone, just to get away, even if the escape came through beheading.

Tersus and Peter were asleep and nobody had lain down in that area of the cave, it was rather apparent why for the dampness of the weather the last days had turned Tersus into a stink bomb of epic proportions. Even the horses did shun him. Phraan had lain down in a small alcove on a thick layer of hay, he was sleeping soundly and had wrapped himself into his blankets and he was very comfortable. He was dreaming about Vitile, reliving one of their encounters back in the day. They had been hunting a pack of grey backs and brought the last one down just outside of a huge groove of old trees and the group had camped there for a while. Their horses needed rest and they were hungry and tired too. Vitile had dragged Phraan with her into the forest and on a small clearing they had more or less torn their clothes off and ended up on the ground, desperate for each other. He could see her even now, that gorgeous body writhing under him and the tight warmth of her embracing him until he could take it no more and came screaming her name. She had marked him good that night, he had been proud to carry the marks of her nails and teeth for days afterwards. He was moaning in his sleep, it felt as if he still had her soft hands caressing his body, as if he yet again was burying himself in her heat and he writhed against his simple matrass. She was riding him, then he remembered having her from behind bent over a branch. He had a good memory and now it became a curse for he knew she was gone.

Suddenly the dream changed, she was on top of him again, riding him slowly and he was panting and close to completion, his body straining against her, desperate for relief. He had his eyes closed and just enjoyed the sensation and then it dawned upon him that it felt different. She was heavier than that? The rhythm was wrong also and he forced his eyes open, knowing he was still dreaming. He was in the cave but there were nobody there, and he was being ridden but this time it was Imeah straddling his hips. The shock sort of paralyzed him, why did he dream of Imeah? He had never felt attracted to her before? She was gorgeous, that was no point in denying that but why? She was so pale she seemed to glow from within and her bright red eyes were unreal and shining like rubies in the dark. Her elegant hands were pressing against his chest as she was moving slowly on him and Phraan stared in disbelief at the lithe body which was creating such breath taking pleasure for him. Her breasts were firm but surprisingly large and the nipples hard and pointing at him and he found that he was unable to escape the allure of her beauty and the feeling she was creating in him. Long silky white hair was flowing over his thighs like a river of silk and it was a caress in itself and the smooth coolness was what tipped him over the edge, he came helplessly, arching up against her and he groaned and threw his head back and then he woke up, gasping and utterly confused.

He was no stranger to erotic dreams, for decades they had been his only companions if he didn't count his right hand, but Imeah?! Why would he dream of her like that? It wasn't right, he barely knew her and those clothes of her hid almost everything about her which betrayed that she was a female. He bit his lower lip, nobody seemed to have noticed anything so he hadn't really made any sounds, he shifted and sighed, rolled his eyes, perfect! He had really come, and now his pants were sticky and wet and would stay that way too for there was no chance of a proper wash now. He buried his face in his blankets, embarrassed and uncomfortable and very confused too. He tried to go back to sleep, his body was still thrumming with the aftermath of his release, he felt heavy and relaxed and it had been good but why now? It had been a while now since the last time he and Vitile had been together but that shouldn't affect him that much, not yet anyhow. He took a deep breath and cringed, forced himself to think of something else than the mess he had created in his pants, he was no better than a horny youth.

He had to think about when he first met Vitile, how desperate he had been and how she had explained a lot to him which did explain why he felt the way he did. He had been chasing the women like a madman back then and believed that it was becauce of the situation, the very well known fact that facing death every day can boost one's libido a lot. She had told him that it wasn't so, that it was normal for young elves to be that eager for some decades or even centuries after they matured. He had been at the age where it was normal to find a mate and settle down and it had felt a bit sore when she also explained that his mixed heritage most likely had rendered him sterile. But she had been just as eager as him and always willing and he had been so sure that she was his true love, the one born to complete his soul, it was making the sorrow even more raw and terrible now.After a while he did fall asleep again, the darkness and the silence was enough to bring him back to the realm of dreams.

Zaray lay on the other side of the cave, she was half buried in the hay and a blanket hid her face but her eyes were shining, it was going the right way. He was so sensitive and so easy to manipulate. Preparing him was important, there could be no resistance if this was to end well. He was wearing the hair bracelet she had given him and thus she could access his mind and prepare him for what had to come. She sighed and closed her eyes, fate was playing a very mean game and it was tempting to change the odds but she knew that she couldn't. The game had to be played the way it was planned. She had an unpleasant expression on her face, they would face resistance, and oh she knew the brotherhood, way better than they believed. And whatever plans they had been brewing were already on the verge of becoming like a runaway cart down a steep hill, nobody knew in what direction it would head, only that it would end in a disaster. Zaray's smile was one filled with hidden promises, she would succeed for there was no other way. The seer knew what fate awaited her, and she had come up with a solution all by herself. Zaray was in awe of the courage and will of that young one, she would never have been so calm about it. Zaray had done what she could, now it was all up to fate, it was as it ought to be. The only question was what they would have to face next, the area was never without dangers.

The next morning came with snow and wind but it was way better than it had been and Shaluun promised that it would clear up. They fed the horses and themselves and broke camp as the sun started to show through the clouds, outside it was two feet of snow and they had to form a line and switch between riding in front so the horses didn't get too tired. Here and there they encountered deep drifts they had to ride around and it did slow them down and the terrain was rather bad some places. It was so ragged it was hard to determine what direction to choose and yet Zaray did manage to keep them on the right path most of the time. The wind stopped in the middle of the day and the sun did break through and the landscape was suddenly beautiful and not at all what it had been just hours before. Phraan was still embarrassed and didn't want to speak to anyone, his eyes kept drifting towards Imeah, she seemed to be just herself, silent and withdrawn and not at all willing to converse with anyone. They saw some wolves off in the distance and also a bear and Phraan found it reassuring that there still was some natural wildlife left. This area had probably seen few dragons is any at all since there weren't any settlements there and the trolls wouldn't leave their caves now that it was sunny and relatively warm. They had a small break in the middle of the evening, the horses needed more food and they had packed as much hay as they possibly could carry.

Everybody had huge bales tied to the back of their saddles and it did look weird but the rope they had brought did come in handy.

The next night was spent in far less comfortable surroundings, a very rocky campsite between some huge boulders. Phraan was very glad when they could ride on the morning after, he hadn't been able to close one eye at all. That day was rather grey and dark and before long they did see some trolls, the pack was rather large and moving fast and it became rather apparent that the huge creatures had spotted them so there was only one thing to do, ride hard. Zaray did find a good path to take, she was steering them towards the hidden path and there was no doubt that she was a very good guide. The trolls didn't manage to keep up with them at all but they all knew that the beasts would be following their trail so Zaray did find a frozen lake they did cross one by one, leading their horses by the reins. The weight of a troll is rather large and they prefer not to cross frozen water since they do sink like a rock should they fall through the ice. Ivran tried to weaken the ice but the result was that holes appeared everywhere in a very nice embroidery pattern he once had seen his mother had used, Dhokay had to laugh and claimed that this would be the only time those trolls would encounter high culture in any form and the ice was after all rather unsafe now.

They rode on and Zaray told them that they were two days away from the hidden path now, she could almost see its start. They were riding down a slope when Zaray suddenly stopped and stared at something moving at the end of the valley they were entering, it was many moving shapes and they were heading their way and Phraan did draw his blades and spurred Drake. He felt a scent he knew just too well and suddenly several creatures seemed to sprout out of the snow drifts. Fastonar shouted and they formed a circle around Imeah, she did look terrified and it was no wonder. These were no trolls, they were orcs. The mountain orcs are normally peaceful and won't attack others unless they are provoked but Phraan immediately saw that these were outlaws. The orcs have a very strict code of honour and conduct and these had probably broken one or more of the unwritten laws of their community. Fastonar roared and rode one of them down, finishing the orc off with his sword. There was a flurry of movement now, snow flowing through the air and the orcs were trying to kill them all beyond any doubt. Dhokay roared and swung the great hammer and the two dwarves jumped off their horses and became like spinning dervishes, axes cutting a bloody path through the larger and slower opponents. Orcs are large, way larger than a human and extremely strong but they aren't that fast and their weapons were primitive. Phraan had thrown his hood down and he was steering Drake with his heels and the huge destrier was kicking and baring its teeth, fighting just like its rider.

Phraan knew orcs very well, he had fought them countless times and he knew that they have one important weakness. If the leader falls the rest will often scatter or surrender and he had already located the chieftain of this group. It was a huge one with two impressive tusks and two long braids. The orc wore a sort of mask made from bones and it did make him look very intimidating but Phraan had already seen his weak spot. The orc was limping a bit, probably an old injury and Phraan spurred Drake and rode straight against the orc. The chieftain saw him coming and swung his javelin to throw it at the oncoming horse but Phraan swung Drake out of the way and threw himself out of the saddle and the impact made the orc fall backwards into the snow. Phraan growled and buried one of his blades in the orc's sternum and its final scream made the other orcs freeze up. Suddenly the will to fight was slightly reduced and Dhokay finished off a couple of them just like a gardener cuts down some unwanted weeds. Phraan raised the sword and roared and the orcs seemed to recognize him for they just threw themselves down and wailed in fear. Just five were left alive and Phraan wondered what they were doing there, so high up in the mountains. Orcs rarely leave their valleys and in this area there was little game and nothing worth fighting for.

The five surviving orcs did clump together and they seemed to be terrified and for some reason they appeared to be extra scared of Zaray and Imeah. They didn't even look at the two of them and Phraan walked over to them and saw that they all were branded. They had a huge symbol brutally burned into their foreheads and he hissed and swung his blade. "You are damned, condemned to die. Anyone has the right to kill you, and I will not hesitate to act as the hand of doom if you don't tell us why!"

They all stared stubbornly down, Phraan shook his blade. "So?"

A voice interrupted, it was deep and growling and they turned around and saw a single orc heading towards them, he was old and dressed as a shaman with antlers attached to his headgear and his face was tattooed with bizarre black patterns. The huge tusks had been carved into the likeness of tree trunks and he wore a wolf's skull around his neck. "No point in asking them son of the south, they will not confess to their crime"

Phraan bowed his head in respect, this was an old orc, and he moved with obvious discomfort and had to use a cane to be able to walk through the snow. "Old one"

The orc smiled, he was partly blind judging from his one white eye and the skin seemed to have lost its colour. Phraan knew that this was a dying orc, one who had lost its strength and now was waiting to return to the halls of the ancestors. "These outcasts have been hunted by my tribe for many turns of the moon, they are murderers and thieves and have no name"

Dhokay tensed up and Shaluun too did stare at the five, an orc with no name was someone who had done something so terrible few even would mention the nature of the crime. Phraan swallowed. "You are far from the blessed valleys old one"

The old shaman nodded. "Yes, my last hunt, but a necessary one. These had to be found and brought to justice, my old bones won't rest until they are dead"

Thiana and Taurin was staring at the old orc, they weren't used to the race at all and the old orc was frightening but Phraan knew the race well and knew that he came from a peaceful tribe who wouldn't harm anyone. "You are not alone old one"

The shaman shook his head. "No, I have ten warriors with me, waiting behind the hill. We do not wish to startle anyone and I could see that you were capable of dealing with this scum all on your own."

Phraan took a deep breath. "I am Phraan, I think you have heard of me?"

The shaman nodded. "The one death loves, her lover. Thalak-Bhar. I know you, you are highly regarded by my tribe"

Phraan knew that a worthy enemy was respected by every orc, even the peaceful ones and this tribe had to be nothing but farmers and gatherers judging by the symbols on the shaman's face. He stared at the wolf skull and smiled. "So, brother of wolves, what is it that these have done?"

The shaman sighed, Phraan saw age stains on his hands and a surge of pity rushed through him, orcs are very kind and gentle towards their elder, for an old male to leave the comfort of his tribe like that had to take something very important. "They have thrown our old ways away and embraced dark gods, gods of chaos. They lead a group of terrible monsters to one of our village and sacrificed several of our young to these foul deities. One of them was my granddaughter"

Rhuk was gasping and Dabin looked aghast, orcs were like dwarves, there were few females among them and those daughters they did get were regarded as something almost sacred. The old shaman stared at the five with anger in his one seeing eye. "Their leader was once a promising shaman, one of the young I had great faith in. But he was turned away from the path of honour and chose darkness instead. I am glad you killed him, he should have suffered more though"

Zaray had been silent, she just sat on her mule staring at the old shaman and her eyes were distant. "You said monsters, can you describe them?"

The shaman nodded, he didn't look at her at all, and it was as if he was in too much awe of her to dare to. "Of course daughter of flames. They did look like wolves but they were so much larger and their bodies, they were decaying, rotting and yet they were alive. Everyone who got bitten died in terrible agony and some did die but came back to life, as horrible abominations. We had to kill them again"

Zaray swallowed visibly and cringed, her eyes closed for a few seconds. "Dark magic, of the very worst kind."

The shaman nodded. "Yes, we could feel them from afar, like a dark hole in the world, something which simply shouldn't be. These males have cooperated with the powers of true evil, there is no absolution and no rescue"

Phraan sighed. "Do you want me to kill them old one?"

The old orc nodded. "Yes, please. By your blades they must be sent to the darkness, their souls are condemned and will never enter the halls. "

The five started to wail and Phraan put on a very cold grin. "I think I will share this honour with Fastonar here, what do you say brother, two for you and three for me?"

Fastonar did pull his sword. "Sounds fair to me Phraan, so let's do it"

The five didn't try to escape, they weren't tied down or anything since they appeared to be petrified and unable to put up any resistance. Phraan beheaded his three and Fastonar did run two through with his blade and the bodies collapsed onto the snow, twitching and then becoming still. The old orc grinned. "Praised be the goddess, this was done well. I am very grateful."

Zaray tilted her head. "Old honoured one, we are heading north to end the scourge of dragons and monsters, what can you tell us of the area ahead?"

The old orc bowed his head. "Daughter of flames, the path you all are about to take is a very dangerous one indeed. Behind those mountains awaits nothing but death and ruin, the dark souls have been reawakened"

Zaray did look rather intense. "And yet we have to go, if not everything will be lost"

The old shaman grunted. "You are brave, yes, all of you are very brave. The dangers ahead are plentiful and they are terrible. The wall will not allow you to pass through"

Zaray had a strange expression upon her face. "We have the means to cross it old one, don't worry"

The old orc sighed and then he smiled. "I see more than others, that is why I was called to become a shaman, a seer. The old tales are coming to fruition now, I can see that. May the Gods be with you, you will face so many challenges"

Fastonar was sheathing his sword again. "So, are trolls the major problem or are there worse creatures about?"

The old orc chuckled, crossed his arms over his chest. He had to have been a very impressive specimen once upon a time, a huge and muscular male. "There are the wolf like creatures we were attacked by, they are stealthy and attack in the night. And we have also seen some peculiar tracks from something truly strange. It looked like the track of a snake but so very much larger than any snake we have seen. The track was wider than the belly of a horse"

Fastonar was staring at Phraan. "The old scrolls at the temple did speak of great wyrms, maybe?"

Phraan just shrugged. "Your guess is as good as mine I think. It could be anything really"

He turned to the shaman again. "You know of the city on the other side of the mountains? How?"

The orc smiled again. "My people don't live for as long as you long ears but we do remember for we keep the word alive, from generation to generation. Once upon a time the lands to the north were ours to rule, we orcs did belong up there. We lived in peace and prosperity, hunting the packs of long noses and spear noses and we were happy but then the dark souls came north and betrayed our leaders, lured them south with promises of great treasure and plenty of game. It was all a lie, and they took our land and built that city in what was a holy place to us."

Thiana and Taurin did look confused and Phraan turned to them. "It is a very old story, and the orcs have always longed to return to their own land. But the brotherhood has blocked them from returning, the magic stops them. "

Thiana frowned, "That is not fair, if that was their land they ought to be able to go back? That would be just natural!"

Phraan nodded and the old shaman smiled at Thiana. "Oh young child of the woods, your heart is very pure and very free. Keep it that way, but beware. We were like you are now back then, uncorrupted. The dark ones made us into villains, many tribes became killers, war like and aggressive. We forgot about the way and that was the undoing of our people, now we are few and maybe our time is over."

Zaray stared at the shaman. "The sacred valley, where the city is built. It was very special wasn't it, because of something unique" "

The shaman took a swift look at her, his eyes huge. "You know of this? By the great goddess, yes, it was a source of extremely strong magic. Deep in the bowels of the earth a heart stone rests, and its magic permeates both rock and air. It was what gave the dark brotherhood their power, they have defiled a pure source of light and turned into a force of evil."

Zaray was smiling, her eyes somewhat sinister. "So, if that taint was removed, what would happen?"

The old orc wetted his lips, his eyes filled with longing. "The life would return to the land, we would be able to return to the plains and forests of our ancestors. The balance restored"

Zaray just nodded and her smile was almost sinister. "I bet someone would be genuinely pissed if that happened. What would happen to the magic used by the dark ones if the source was cleansed?"

The shaman tilted his head. "Their magic would be undone, at least what is purely of a magical nature. "

Phraan swallowed . "Can the source be cleansed?"

The shaman nodded. "Yes, but it cannot be done by anyone of light or darkness."

They all looked a bit puzzled. "So, who then can cleanse it?"

The shaman shrugged. "Nobody knows, the old ones had no clue."

Zaray did look bewildered. "A person can only be of the light or of the darkness, there is nothing else is there?"

The shaman did look down, his eyes distant. "There is a very old saying oh daughter of flames, there is something hidden in the city, and if given to the one by fate chosen it will transform that one, into something new. But what? Nobody knows"

Zaray sighed and rolled her eyes. "That doesn't tell us much"

The shaman shrugged and pulled his coat tighter around himself. "No, I am sorry. But I will pray for you all, you will need it"

Phraan sent the old one a swift smile "I am grateful old one, we will not forget your words"

The shaman looked down and there was a strange expression on the ragged old face. "I have had strange dreams of late, I have seen such odd things."

Phraan had to think of his own dreams of late and he managed to stop himself from blushing, just in the nick of time. The old shaman raised his face towards the skies. "I was staring at a naked hill, it was a clear night and the stars were all out, like bright gems on the firmament. The hill was steep, and rocky and there was no sign of life"

The orc closed his eyes. "I was alone, and afraid, and then there was a light but it wasn't like any light I had ever seen before for it was like every colour and feeling there has ever been. I knew I was staring at the pure raw magic, the very core of everything. The seed from which everything have sprung and I was filled with awe and joy. It became form, it became flesh and I was staring at a creature, clothed in a mortal form, the essence of the original spark of life."

Zaray was listening intently and they all looked a bit fascinated by the old orc's words, his voice was so sincere, so filled with true belief and reverence and for a moment he did look almost young again, as if yet again filled with strength and power. Taurin had held his breath "So, what was it? What sort of creature?"

The orc sent the wood elf a soft smile. "A human, and yet not a human, not entirely. The dream ended there but I did have the same dream for many nights, the goddess was trying to tell me something."

Phraan cocked his head. "Do you know what?"

The old orc nodded. "Yes, do not think that a humble wrapping cannot hide something powerful. Looks may be deceiving."

Fastonar was grinning. "That is in truth very wise, I have seen that many times"

The old orc stared at the soul sworn and his one seeing eye seemed to blaze with some sort of dark emotion. "Beware son of the blade, your path may take an unexpected turn"

Fastonar seemed to Blanche for a second, then he smiled. "Well, the unexpected is the only thing we can be truly sure of now isn't it?"

The old orc shrugged and bowed deeply. "I have delayed you all, I will return to my men and we will go back to our village and tell everybody that the evil doers are dead. There will be much joy then."

Phraan smiled and bowed back. "Safe journey old one, take care. "

The old orc grasped his hand and for a second Phraan saw him wink, there was something in his hand and Phraan did instinctively close his own fist around it. "I wish you too a safe journey, remember your name. "

The orc turned around and started wading through the snow and Phraan grasped Drake's reins and lifted himself into the saddle, he stared down at the thing in his palm for a second before he hid it in his belt pocket. It was a tiny piece of metal, not larger than the nail of his little finger and it looked like an ordinary metal shard, a leftover from the forging of some weapon. But Phraan knew that the old one never would have handed it over thus if it hadn't been important and he just felt that he ought to keep this as a secret. Fastonar mounted too and waved after the old orc, he did seem relieved that the shaman was going. "We better get going, we will need to find shelter again before it gets dark"

Zaray was staring at Fastonar's back and her eyes were narrow, Phraan did sense that she for some reason didn't like the knight. The group started moving again and Zaray pointed. "The peak over there, with the odd shape is our goal. The hidden path starts there."

Everybody stared and Phraan was frowning, the peak rose above a wall of rock, a vertical obstacle nobody could cross without wings. It was at least some thousand feet tall and smooth as a dancefloor, at least it looked that way from a distance. Zaray didn't say anything more about it and Rhuk and Dabin did shrug and just accept it. Dwarves are pretty accepting when it comes to things involving mountains, they know that rock can hide secrets nobody would guess were possible.

They were lucky that the wind had blown most of the snow into drifts now and those could be avoided, thus it was easier to ride and Zaray did aim for a sort of cliff. The top did look strange and as they got closer Phraan did see that it in fact was an old fortress. It was more or less a ruin now and he had no idea that there had been such buildings constructed so far up north. Zaray squinted and pointed at it. "That is where we'll spend the night, it is a nice place to camp."

Taurin was staring and his eyes were narrow. "What sort of fortress is that?"

Zaray smiled, she let the mule find its own way between the drifts. "An ancient one, built by the forces of light back when the war was raging. It was a stronghold, an outpost. It was from here the wall was erected"

The wood elf did look impressed. "Then it is very old, there shouldn't be anything left of it by now"

Zaray grinned. "Yes, but it contains strong magic, it has kept it standing. It is a rather safe place, the trolls shouldn't be able to bother us up there at all"

Thiana smiled and Phraan saw that the wood elf was relieved. This open and naked landscape had to be rather disturbing for a child of the woods. As they got closer they did see that the cliff wasn't as naked as they had first assumed, the ground wasn't bare rock but a sort of scree and everywhere small bushes grew. Phraan knew the type, they were extremely tough and the branches long and filled with thorns. This bush could grow where other plants could not and it would spread like wildfire unless kept in check. Here nothing had held it back and it covered the cliff like a layer of living barbed wire.

Zaray whistled and looked impressed. "Now, that is protection in itself, I don't think those who built the place would have been able to come up with a better way to keep enemies at bay than this"

There was a road leading to the fortress, they saw it now. It was winding along a ridge and it was free from snow and rather uneven and not at all safe. Fastonar frowned. "Two more hours of ride, we can reach it before dark, but only just"

Zaray nodded. "Yes, but we have to dismount and lead the horses the last miles, the road is very treacherous. I bet they placed the fortress where they did on purpose, to keep enemies at bay."

Fastonar nodded. "From what I can see it must have been a perfect place for protection yes, and they must have been good at it too for I can see that the fortress must have been impressive back in the days"

Zaray nodded with a grin, she pointed at the remains of towers and balustrades. "They say that it was so mighty none was able to conquer it. It is sad that so little is left but it is at least able to shelter us from the wind"

Ivran hadn't said anything for a long time, he sat there on his horse and seemed to shudder a bit and Phraan did notice that he was mumbling something to himself. The half elf did ride closer to the young man and tilted his head. "What are you doing?"

Ivran did not look up, he was just mumbling still. "Practicing, I have enchanted our tracks, so nobody can follow them, I hope"

Phraan felt a bit confused. "You seem to be able to access your power better than before?"

Ivran nodded and hid his hands on the inside of his cloak "Yes, it is as if I am seeing things so much more clearly, I just know what to do. But I do still make mistakes, I cannot…focus!"

Phraan smiled. "I am sure you will learn how to control it soon"

Ivran made a grimace. "I hope so too, or else I won't be of much use to anyone. "

Phraan didn't like the sad tone of the man's voice, he hoped that the lad wasn't depressed or something? "Don't push yourself Ivran, you did give us food and I am sure that your magic one day will be a source of awe"

Ivran shrugged. "Thanks, but I doubt it. My grandfather was so strong, so admired. I will never be like him I fear!"

Phraan tried to keep his tone light. "Oh don't worry, I am sure you will, just practice and soon things will become easy"

The young man stared down at his saddle and nodded and Phraan felt an odd feeling of compassion, even pity. It couldn't be easy, Ivran had probably never asked for anything like this. The rocky terrain soon made it impossible to ride, they had to dismount and now they moved forth slowly since the horses had to almost climb in places. Zaray helped Imeah with her horse and the young human was smiling but she did look nervous. Zaray sighed and let the others pass them by, now they were at the back of the group and she smiled at the girl. "I can see your heart young one, you doubt yourself"

Zaray let a hand lay gently on Imeah's shoulder and Imeah nodded. "Yes, I know what I must do, what I have seen. There is no other way."

Zaray looked down, her face filled with a sort of sorrow. "I am sorry Imeah, I wish there was a way out of this. Could your visions be faulty?"

She shook her head. "No, I am sure. I need to do this, but I am afraid, you are right, I do doubt myself and my own strength"

Zaray helped Imeah get over some very slippery rocks. "I have prepared his mind, so don't worry about that. He will see the truth easily enough"

Imeah bit her lower lip. "I hate this, but he will need the gift I can give. I have seen what you have seen Zaray, and you have shared my visions. We are all pieces of a puzzle and all the pieces have to fall into place if it is to find fulfilment. I am proud to do my part, I really am. I am just afraid that he will be offended"

Zaray jumped up the rocks like a cat. "Don't be, he will understand."

Imeah stared forwards, Phraan was helping Rhuk up and she had an odd expression in her eyes. "Yes, eventually"

The road to the old fortress had probably been more even before, more like a set of stairs but now it was just terrible and weather and erosion had made much of it disappear completely. Dabin was cursing so bad Dhokay and Shaluun just blinked and stared. The dwarf sort of looked at them with unwritten apologies in his gaze. "Sorry, but the ones who built this were amateurs."

Dhokay looked down at the dwarf, his more groomed exterior was a crass contrast to Rhuk who by comparison looked like some hairy ball of rags and armour. "Really? I find it impressive that even a rock of it remains now. It is so freaking old"

Dabin snorted. "Listen, you have never heard of the city of blue silver have you? It is an ancient dwarf settlement and it is wonderful, you will never forget it if you enter it. That is even older, and not a rock is worn or out of place"

Shaluun had to grin. "You dwarves are experts at building with the bones of the earth, you cannot compare your work with that of others, not even mages"

Dabin did blush. "Aye, you are right. Had this been built by dwarves it wouldn't have been a ruin at all but stood there in its full glory yet"

The fortress was just a couple of miles away now and Phraan was staring at it, the structure was rather simple with a huge open yard in the middle and thick walls with some towers built at even distances. The wall was probably brought down by the forces of nature and little did remain of the towers but he could imagine how it had looked back then. The walls had been erected with some sort of very dark rock but the towers had been lighter, probably a harder rock since the weight was rather huge. Phraan did slow down, allowed Zaray to catch up with him. "Have you been here before?"

She nodded. "Yes, but that was very long ago, it wasn't...as ruined then"

He stared at her. "So, you have visited the area?"

She made a grimace. "Of course, I have been guiding you all haven't I? I was just going in the opposite direction!"

She just kept walking and Phraan did throw a narrow glance at her elegant back. She had escaped from that city? Or had she been set loose? He somehow felt that she could be trusted but why he didn't know. There was just something about her which told him that she was on their side and yet able to use them in her own plans and schemes.

They reached the fortress itself just before it got dark, and the structure was huge. Much larger than they had first believed. There were several smaller walls inside of the great one and they were in better shape, there were some buildings in there too, the roofs were gone a long time ago but they did provide some shelter and the old wooden beams could be burned. Fastonar did organize the camp, he didn't trust that old magic they said rested there so he made sure that someone kept watch the entire night. They fed and watered the horses and settled down for the night and Ivran tried yet again to conjure up more food. He was thinking of meat and the result was that a small mountain of bread fell from the skies, followed by several wheels of cheese, the size of a cartwheel. At least it was edible and good too so nobody complained but Ivran was getting frustrated. He did always get something when he tried to use his power, he just didn't know what! At least it had been food, not something dangerous and Shaluun was sure that he was onto something. He just had to learn how to aim the power, just like an archer has to learn how to aim an arrow at the right point.

The magic within this place was very weak, barely there but he knew that it had to have been terrifying once upon a time, the stones still sang of it and he felt it in his very core. This had been a place of great battles and impressive mages. He almost wished that he could see it for himself, it had to have been an awesome sight. Zaray was somewhat disappointed that the magic had weakened this much, she was afraid it wouldn't offer as much protection as she had hoped it would but at least they were out of the cold wind.

After they had eaten Shaluun took first watch and since there were so many small rooms everybody got some privacy. Dhokay had found a building which still had a roof on it and inside there had been some old matrasses filled with horse hairs and straw. Zaray believed that maybe local hunters had placed them there some years ago for they couldn't be all that old. Now at least some of them got to sleep comfortably and the others used the sacks of hay as their matrass. Ivran was tucking himself in and the last hours had been exhausting so he fell asleep the moment he did lay down.

Zaray sat by the fire and stared into the flames, she didn't speak to anyone and there were some worried lines on her face. So much could go wrong, so much was at stake. She felt that danger was heading their way, but she had no idea of what shape it would take. She just hoped that the fortress could protect them, or at least provide them with some warnings if something evil was lurking in the area.

Phraan had found a corner in what had been the stable and he had arranged the matrass he had gotten and it was in fact almost nice there. It was chilly but not too bad and he was in fact very tired. The rugged terrain of the last miles had been hard on the horses and he had to help Drake find his footing several places. He didn't want to think of the next morning when they would have to return the same way. But the fortress was a place where they could defend themselves if something happened and it was wise to go there. He burrowed himself into his blankets and fell asleep and the camp became quiet as they found a place to sleep and conversation stopped. Tersus had found a place Rhuk had identified as the latrine of the fortress but he didn't say anything to the alchemist, the smell was gone but it was a very suiting place to be for the stinking human. Peter had found a place far from his master, it was rather apparent that the young man by now was rather tired and not that enthusiastic anymore. He was still eager to learn but his master's complete lack of hygiene was wearing down the admiration Peter had felt initially. Fastonar went to sleep where the horses were kept to keep them safe and Dhokay sat by the old gate half asleep and just meditated. He didn't need to sleep that much and even this hard journey didn't wear him out.

Phraan was dreaming, again. And it was the same dream, the one with Vitile and the clearing in the woods. He was sort of getting tired of this now. But the dream was just as nice as the last time and since he was just dreaming why not enjoy it? This time he knew what he was heading for so he just relaxed and decided to participate a bit more, if one can use that term describing a mere dream. It was good memories, worth having and worth treasuring and he just let himself float along down memory lane until the dream changed yet again. It wasn't Vitile who was with him but Imeah and he couldn't understand why? What was it with that albino girl? He wasn't interested so why in heck's name did he dream about her, in such a manner?

He had to be mad but why not, it was just a dream, it wasn't real and it wasn't as if he was a stranger to sleeping with strangers. When they had hunted dragons the last time he had been very popular, just as Fastonar had said and before Vitile joined the group he had been all over the place. It was the old warrior's code, enjoy life to the fullest today for tomorrow you may be dead. The dream was very lifelike too, just like the last time and she was caressing him with warm hands, it felt almost electric and he was surrendering to her touch. He had always enjoyed it when the women took charge of things and he took pride in being a good partner in every manner. She was really eager and darn it felt real, he had her on his lap, straddling him and the smell of her was intoxicating and wonderful. Then it started to dawn upon him that this was a bit too real, was he really dreaming after all? He was dazed and drowsy and tried to force himself to wake up fully but that was very hard. Normally he would be able to go from asleep to fully awake within the blink of an eye but his body seemed to refuse to make that transition.

He groaned and tossed around, there was really someone there with him, and she was in fact riding him and even though it felt wonderful it wasn't right. With a gasp he did manage to break out of the odd dreamlike state and opened his eyes. It was Imeah, she was naked and her eyes were closed, there was an expression of intense focus on her face as she was riding him rather slowly and he heaved for air. "Imeah?! What in the name of every God are you doing?"

She opened her eyes, they were blurred and distant and she was biting her lower lip, there was some pain in her expression and he realized that she never had done this before. She was so tight around him and her movements did reveal a distinct lack of experience. She moaned and leaned forth, put her hands on his shoulders and threw her head back. "You will not understand, yet"

He tried to resist the feeling building up within him, it was simply too much and he was terribly confused and shocked. After all, he hadn't asked for this and it was not what he would have expected of her at all. She had managed to get his clothes off without him noticing it and he tried to formulate what he was thinking. "Damn…damn it girl, did you…drug me?"

She was moving more aggressively and he knew he was close, he couldn't hold back now, and she had him pinned down, she was stronger than he would have expected. She shook her head, her pale skin and silky hair was just as lovely as he had seen in that dream and she was like a goddess but why did she do this? "I didn't need to drug you Phraan, I can…ah…affect people like this…"

She grasped his hands and placed them against her firm breasts and Phraan had to gasp again, it was rapidly getting out of hand. He couldn't help but thrust back against her movements and he felt that his body was preparing for his release, he whimpered and tried to hold back. "Why, please"

She shook her head. "You will see, soon"

She placed her hand on his head and for a moment he saw Vitile there, it was enough. He felt how everything tensed up and he had to let go of every last bit of self-control. He came hard, seeing stars and sparks and Imeah made a strange sound which sounded almost triumphant. She grasped his head and put her forehead against his as he was straining against her, filling her with his essence. Her eyes were suddenly ablaze and he felt her soul touching his, it shouldn't be possible since she was human but it happened still and he wanted to scream as something indescribable seemed to invade his very soul. She stifled the sound with a kiss and kept moving, before long he felt her pulse around him and she shuddered, her body tense like a bowstring. He didn't understand, had no idea of what this was, why it happened. He was just sitting there, caught in the post orgasmic haze and feeling as if he had been used somehow. Imeah panted and smiled, her eyes sad. "It is my gift to give Phraan, and now it is given. As I have seen"

He frowned, a feeling of knowing and yet not crept in on him. "Imeah?! What did you just do? Tell me!"

She smiled and kissed his brow. "I gave you all that I am Phraan, being a seer is a life nobody would wish for, for you see things you really don't want any knowledge of."

He swallowed hard. "I don't understand…"

She let herself slide down next to him and winced, there was pain in her eyes and he felt guilty, as if he had somehow violated her. "My gift of seeing is not as much a gift as a curse, and it is mine to bear but I have other abilities Phraan, I have never shown them to anyone."

He just frowned and she let a hand slide over his skin, it was warm and soft and the caress was a loving one. "Now I have given them to you, through choice."

He stared at her, eyes wide and mind reeling. "How? Why?"

She smiled and planted a soft kiss on his neck. "I gave you my virtue, thus the gift is given off. You will need it, I have seen it. "

Phraan swallowed hard. "Imeah, you shouldn't have done this, it wasn't right. Not that you were bad for you weren't but…I prefer to…well, at least give my consent before someone jumps my bones"

She nodded, the red eyes were dreamy. "I know, but there is no other way. The gift I gave you cannot be given back Phraan, it is yours forever. I had to give it to you now, so it won't be wasted."

He lifted his head, stared at her. "What do you mean wasted, can't you use it?"

She sighed and looked down. "No, there is no time"

He tried to sit up and she pushed him down. "Don't fight me Phraan, I am still a seer, I know my ultimate fate and I do not try to escape it. What will happen will happen no matter what I do. Accept it, but do embrace what I have given. It will prove to be very valuable soon"

Phraan moaned. "Then tell me woman, what did you just do to me?!"

Imeah smiled, the smile was a melancholic one. "I have changed you, in so many ways. I can heal Phraan, but I can give the gift of healing as well, self-healing"

He frowned. "I am an elf, I heal much faster than a human being already?"

She giggled. "Not as fast as you will now. Believe me, you will know soon enough"

He blinked, feeling utterly confused still, like he wasn't really able to feel as if this was real or not. "You said gifts?"

She let her hand play with a lock of his hair, her eyes were dreamy. "Yes, you know the old tales of spirit walkers?"

Phraan nodded slowly, his mind reeling, Spirit walkers? Oh yes, he had heard such tales, but it was ages ago. He could barely remember at all. "I have, but I cannot remember any details, other than it was someone with a companion of some sorts?"

Imeah grinned and laid her head down onto his shoulder, it was something very endearing with the trust she showed him. "Yes, a spirit beast, all have one they say, a sort of symbol of who you truly are. But a spirit walker can make his or hers spirit animal real, flesh and blood. It is a magical extension of one's own soul, and it can be controlled"

Phraan lifted his head, stared down at her, this couldn't be real? "I have never heard of that before? How?"

She giggled and her hand was tickling his neck, he scoffed and she got a playful expression on her face. "Now that it has been given to you all you need is to think of it, and it will come to your aid whenever it is needed. "

Phraan clenched his jaw. "I don't even know what my spirit animal is, I have never even thought of that. It haven't been a part of my faith at all"

She nodded. "Yes, I know, but you will see it is real"

Phraan winced, looked at her. "Wait a minute, you said there was no time? What do you mean?"

She sighed and looked down. "I will not reach the end of this journey Phraan, my fate lay elsewhere."

He gaped and grasped her hand. "You haven't seen your own death? Please, tell me it isn't so? You could be wrong!"

She just smiled again, that sad smile. "Phraan, there is so much at stake now, so much more than you all know. You have seen the changes which have happened haven't you? The once fertile land turned into a place where nothing grows, the dwindling herds, the hardships, the changing weather?"

He pulled her closer. "Yes, but that wasn't what I was asking about, Tell me the truth damn it!"

She swallowed, her voice thin. "I have seen that my end is near yes, and yet not. Death is…just a transition for us who carry this curse. I will be stronger in spirit than I ever was in life. Don't question my choices, just accept that I will be needed in the end, as will you"

Phraan felt an urge to roar in rage and denial. "NO! I do not accept it, no more death!"

She caressed his face, kissed the corner of his mouth. "You have to Phraan, there is no other way. You will understand."

He felt how grief welled up inside of him yet again. "Why does everybody around me die? I am starting to wonder if it is I who am cursed!"

She shook her head. "No, you are blessed. And now my beautiful warrior, would you share yourself with me yet again? Out of free will this time I assure you"

He had to snort. "You want me to sleep with you? After all this?"

She nodded, her eyes were so clear and he saw a sort of strength in them which was terrifying. "Yes, I do not want to waste any time now"

She reached down and for a woman who had no previous experience she did have skilled hands, he did react rather immediately, in spite of his torn state of mind. Imeah giggled. "I have always known that my love should be saved for that special one, and I haven't been sought after at all. The fact that I am cursed have sort of scared the men"

Phraan swallowed the feeling of intense pity and just as intense sorrow. Someone like her should never perish, it wasn't right. "It was their loss then"

He leaned over and kissed her gently and she giggled and climbed on top of him again, she apparently knew what to do. Before long they were oblivious to the world around them and Phraan let go of every thought, lived in the now and the sensations which flooded his body and mind. Something had indeed changed, but he didn't yet know what.

Dabin was on guard duty now, he was sitting by the former gate and stared into the night and he was a bit sleepy but more so annoyed. Rhuk was snoring so bad it would have made a troll deaf and Dabin preferred silence when he was to sleep. The little rest he had gotten had been far from enough and he felt stiff and tired. He wasn't used to travel that far on horseback and his rump and thighs had taken a beating this day. He rubbed his eyes and yawned, damn it, he couldn't fall asleep on the watch now could he?

Suddenly he heard a noise, and it wasn't from inside of the old fortress but from the outside, he cocked his head, had it been the wind? No, it had been a clanking sound, like metal against a rock. He got up, sniffed the air. There weren't any scents to be picked up but the wind was coming in the wrong direction and he cursed and wondered if he really had heard it or not. The he heard something again and he got up, roaring a warning. "Get up! Something is coming!"

There was a clamour coming from the camp, everybody was on their feet reaching for their weapons within the blink of an eye and Tersus had a torch in his hand, the flame was burning blue and it did look odd but it had to be something chemical, not magic. Phraan was asleep with Imeah in his arms, she had worn him out rather well, her zeal and strange devotion was fascinating and by every God and Goddess was she good. He had fallen asleep feeling like a wrung out piece of cloth, completely sated and a wee bit proud of himself for knowing that he had pleased her in return. The shout from Rhuk woke him up abruptly and for a few seconds he didn't know where he was but then it came back and he got up. Imeah did look scared and he grasped his tunic and managed to get dressed in record time. "Stay here, hide!"

He got his blades and ran out of the small room and saw that the others were gathering, but he didn't see Zaray anywhere. Rhuk was staring out into the darkness and he had grasped his axe and he was a bit pale. Dabin too was visibly nervous and he was sniffing. "Feel that?"

Dhokay got up on a rock and threw his head back, he had the nose of a dog and he made a grimace. "It smells like old unwashed socks"

Rhuk spat on the ground. "Goblins!"

Phraan looked at the dwarf with confusion. "What? Here?"

Rhuk nodded. "The one who understands this can explain it, I surely cannot"

Goblins would normally never leave their hidden cities when there was trolls around and no goblins had ever been seen this far north. They preferred the warmth of the mountain ranges to the south, beyond the great deserts. Goblins in such a cold and barren land were unheard off, but the smell didn't lie. There was a faint howling sound coming from outside of the walls and Fastonar swore. "Get ready, they always attack in a group. Do not let the numbers startle you, goblins are cowards and not very strong"

Phraan turned to Shaluun. "Where is Zaray?"

The elf shrugged. "I don't know, her bedroll is empty."

Phraan was about to answer when something shot forth from the opening where the gate had been, it was rather small, and there were many following it and they stared before they got ready to protect themselves. It was goblins, but not like any they had seen before. These were smaller than ordinary goblins and their skin seemed to have been made from something almost metallic looking, they moved in strange jerking motions like an insect and Phraan saw that they in fact did resemble insects. The eyes were tiny and white and they didn't have hair but they had huge mouths with very sharp teeth and they had long hands with vicious looking claws. They were swarming through the opening like an army of ants and before long everybody was more than busy fighting.

The goblins didn't seem to have a sense of fear, and they didn't have much of a sense of self-preservation either. They just went for it even when it was certain death and Dhokay was smashing goblins with every strike of his hammer. But the numbers didn't dwindle at all and now some started appearing on the walls, they were climbing up from every direction. Thiana and Taurin grasped each other's hands and started to chant and suddenly the bushes growing along the ridge came to life, the thorny branches became like living tentacles with claws and they moved around, grasping goblins and throwing them off the walls. Phraan saw that many were being ripped apart and he realized that the gift of the woods was very powerful indeed. Being able to control trees and other plant life was very valuable.

But the goblins kept coming, piles of dead bodies laid in front of the gate now and the stream of small vicious beings didn't stop at all. They were making a nasty high pitched sound which hurt everybody's ears and oddly enough the goblins seemed to attack Phraan with extreme tenacity. They seemed determined to kill him and he had to fight like never before, his blades did cut a bloody circle around him. Fastonar was swearing like a sailor and using his huge longsword with great zeal but he was getting tired, they all were. Even Dhokay had lost some of the energy he had shown previously and Phraan felt a sting of despair. They could lose this battle, he realized that now. These goblins were simply too many and they had no regard for their own safety or life. The strange appearance and the determination made him suspect that these creatures were sent there on purpose, just to get at the group.

One goblin managed to get close enough to reach him, from behind. The thing carried a sort of knife and stabbed Phraan in the leg, just over the knee. The goblin was so small it didn't reach much higher than that and the half elf growled and killed it with one swift strike of his sword. He pulled the knife out, it was serrated and nasty looking and the wound hurt a lot, a stinging burning pain. Had the blade been poisoned? It was covered with a sort of bluish goo and he realized that yes, some sort of substance had been used. But then something happened, warmth spread through the leg and the wound did close itself up and the goo just flowed out of it and the leg looked unharmed. He blinked, now he realized that Imeah had spoken the truth and he also remembered the other thing she had said he had been given. He did focus, tried to imagine a sort of projection of his own being and he felt an almost violent jerk go through his very being and then there was a bright flash of greenish light and something appeared out of thin air next to him. He had to gape, it was a feline, the size of a horse. He had never seen an animal like that before and it was impressive and terrifying. The body had the shape of a very large mountain lion with a head which was rather long for a cat with massive jaws. It had ears with long tufts of hair like a lynx and a very long tail with a huge tuft of hair at the end. The being was black, but the tufts of hair were bright red and its eyes were a deep amber colour, golden and red in one. Was this in truth a sort of essence of what he was? The animal caused the others to stare too, and it snarled and the goblins seemed to hesitate for the first time since the attack started.

The living bushes were busy still, long tendrils reached out to snatch goblins and since they seemed to hesitate the branches were more efficient now. The huge feline rushed forth and started fighting and it did crush goblins with just one swipe of its huge paws. It did sound as if someone was using a frying pan to punch the dust out of a couch. Phraan let out a roar and he felt as if he had gotten more energy, the huge cat did bring the hope back to them all and they fought with more strength. Tersus was using the torch with a rather strange technique, the fire didn't die out no matter what he did so he did simply hit the goblins over the head with it and they caught fire and fell screaming and writhing. Peter used an ordinary sword with some skill and the two dwarves were covered with sweat and hacking away like a mad lumberjack. It was obvious that they hated goblins like the very plague itself.

Fastonar growled and cut the head of a particularly nasty goblin who tried to bite him in the leg. "Where is Zaray? Has she gone exploring again?"

Dhokay smashed two goblins in one strike, he was panting. "I have no idea, she cannot have gotten far."

The goblins seemed to have reached the end of their determination, fewer came rushing forth but then a new wave came running and they were screaming and it did appear as if they were trying to flee more than trying to attack. Some hoarse roars could be heard from the darkness outside of the ruin and they all stared at each other. Fastonar moaned. "Trolls?!"

Rhuk was pale. "No, that didn't sound like a troll at all"

The goblins did run past the group, seeking refuge in nooks and crannies, some were pissing themselves with fear and it wasn't a good sign. The huge cat was hissing and the hairs were raised along its back, the tail swung close to the ground. Something was moving out there, it was massive and huge and dark. Dhokay looked scared. "People, I think this is something none of us can hope to fight"

Phraan panted, he felt as if the darkness out there was watching him, hungrily and with a wish for vengeance. "What is it?"

The luptay was squinting, his eyes very intense. "Some sort of elemental I think"

Phraan wasn't that used to magic at all, and Ivran who had been fighting very valiantly with one of Shaluun's axes did frown. "An elemental?! That has to be summoned by someone, on purpose!"

Fastonar was staring out into the darkness, they heard some huffing sounds, as if whatever it was had some problems breathing. "Can you do something about it Ivran?"

The young man cringed. "Ah, what? I have no idea of what sort of elemental it is? They are not something that is easily controlled"

The remains of the gate suddenly crumbled and the remaining goblins were shrieking in absolute horror, a few fainted there and then. Phraan just stared at the nightmare which slowly emerged from the darkness. It was as if someone had taken a skeleton, but not that of a human, and blown it up to giant size. It was surrounded by a garish green glow and it had an odd smell too. It did look like a giant orc skeleton, with tusks and all and the arms were huge and way too long and the rock seemed to simply melt as it moved forth with strange flowing movements. Dhokay cussed. "It is not an ordinary elemental, I have never seen anything like that before!"

Ivran took a deep breath and tried to box the thing in, prevent it from getting any further but that was in vain. His magic didn't seem to work at all and he tried again, even harder. The result was that the thing lashed out with a hand and Ivran flew backwards as if he was hit by a very fast flying hard object. He landed on his back with a groan and shook his head. "Damn it, it is immune to magic I think, my powers cannot harm it."

Fastonar pointed at the thing. "Look at the dead goblins, where the thing moves"

The corpses did sort of dissolve and so did the rocks, this thing was probably able to make things fall apart just by being there, living beings included. A goblin had been hiding behind some rocks and came scurrying forth, panic forced it to run and as it crossed the things path it fell and was reduced to a mass of shivering bones and jelly in just some short seconds. The elemental was aiming for them all and Dhokay shouted. "Don't get near it, we cannot fight this"

Fastonar was swinging his blade back and forth, he did look desperate. "Then what do we do? Throw rocks at the bloody thing? Insult it?"

Rhuk hissed. "We have to flee, it is the only choice"

Shaluun was pale. "We cannot just leave the horses behind? We have nowhere to go, and what has caused that thing to come here now?"

The bushes were still moving around and now some of the branches took aim at the elemental, they swung around the creature and tried to tear into it but the branches simply dried out and died instantly. This thing spread death, and it let out some sort of sound which could have been laughter. "What do we do?"

Dabin was desperate and Peter was looking for somewhere to hide. Tersus grasped a small vial from his robe and uncorked it, then he threw the thing with all his might and the vial hit the creature straight in its face and shattered. A thin pinkish fluid did burst out and spread out over the bones and the effect was rather unexpected. The thing let out a howl as the bone started to froth and sag and it clawed at its face. Everybody held their breath but the elemental seemed to be able to repair itself for after just a minute or two the damage was gone and it let out a howl and moved forth again. The defenders were soon pushed up against the wall and it wasn't anywhere left for them to go.

That was when they heard a roar from up above and heard the sound of wings and the elemental lifted its head and seemed to be confused. Phraan knew the sound, dragon wings. And he could see the outline of something huge, a dragon greater than any they had ever encountered. A column of solid fire fell from the sky, and the flames did look almost purple.

Just as back at the cave, with the strange dark beings. The elemental did shriek, flames did lick at its invisible skin, its bones caught fire, the magic which had kept it alive and moving did not possess the strength to fight off this. Another burst of flames and a roar from up above and the elemental did collapse into a heap of smouldering bones. Then it simply vanished as whoever it was conjured up by took the magic back into himself. The dragon up there circled the ruin, Phraan did estimate that the dragon was so large the wings were wider than the entire ruin and he knew it was the same which had saved them before. Why?

The remaining goblins were fleeing like mad and everybody stared at each other, was it really over already? They were exhausted and the stench from the dead goblins was intense. They covered the ground in a thick layer and the two wood elves did grimace and bent down, put their hands on the ground. The corpses started to sink into the very ground itself, it swallowed them up and soon they were gone but the smell did remain. Rhuk was staring in awe. "Wonderful, give back to the earth what was taken right?"

Thiana was panting and she was covered with sweat. "Yes, it is the way"

The dragon had flown off and it was quiet, Phraan stared at the huge cat, it was standing next to him staring into the night and he swallowed hard. It was real, breathing and moving and it did smell of something pure and wild. It turned its head towards him and Phraan felt a voice in his head. "I am Ghaday"

Phraan frowned, the word meant steel paw in the old language of the forest elves and he reached out and touched the animal, very gently. The huge cat did purr and he felt that their connection in fact was strong already, and everlasting. He took a deep breath and ordered the huge cat to keep watch over the ruins and it did obey, sauntered off very elegantly. Rhuk stared at it and Shaluun cocked his head. "A spirit walker, I had never believed that if I hadn't seen it. You have a very strong guardian now Phraan."

Phraan swallowed and remembered the wound which disappeared. It didn't make any sense, but then again, very few things did these days. They were trying to get an overview of the situation when Zaray suddenly came in through the crumbled gate, she was carrying the head of a sort of troll and she was bloody and looked tired. Fastonar did look truly pissed. "You have a habit of leaving just before the shit hits the fan, care to explain?!"

Zaray panted and leaned against a rock, she had a cut in her hip and several bruises. "I thought I heard something out there alright? And I went to check but I ran into Mr stinky here and his buddies."

She tossed the head onto the ground and everybody cringed, the dead troll had to have been very large and extremely ugly. "They came behind the group of goblins, I had no other option but to engage them"

Fastonar was frowning. "How many?"

Zaray sighed, "Five, I think they were sort of controlling the goblins, like officers."

Shaluun walked forth a few steps, his eyes were fixed upon the head. "The elemental, did you see it?"

Zaray nodded. "It wasn't an elemental, they are representatives of the elements remember? This thing was some sort of dark magic, it left a trail of death behind it"

Dhokay did look worried. "So this was no random attack?"

She nodded sternly and wrapped some fabric around her hip. "No, it was planned. Someone is out to get us and I know who. The brotherhood knows we are coming, I wish I knew how."

Fastonar cursed. "So, what are we to do then?"

Zaray made a grimace and her face was pale. "We cannot turn around now, we have to try"

310

The soul sworn did look rather angry still. "And risk our lives in vain? We are up against something we cannot possibly hope to conquer, I bet they can conjure up something even worse than that…spirit thing!"

Zaray did look calm yet again, she just smiled. "Yes, but they did face resistance and I bet that threw them off balance at least to some degree. We can do it"

Fastonar snarled. "I do not trust you, why should we listen to the things you say?"

Zaray got back on her feet and wiped off her hands on her cloak. "Because you have no choice, there are greater powers at play here."

Fastonar scowled. "Somehow I have the feeling that you have said that before!"

She just shrugged. "Does it matter? We are here, if anyone wants to return be my guest, but I will at least give it a try. It is better to die fighting than lay cowering like a fool"

Phraan stared at her and for a second he did see something strange, like a glowing aura around her, bright purple and moving like hot air over the ground on a warm day, and in that aura he saw things…He turned his gaze away, he knew why she was so tenacious now, and by the Gods, he did understand. "I will not go back, I will do whatever I can. I do believe in fate and it has called upon us all"

Fastonar rolled his eyes. "You too? Damn it Phraan, when did this happen? It was supposed to be like the good old days wasn't it? Slay some stupid dragons, get the fame and the girls and the admiration and some thrills too"

Phraan sighed. "Yes, but it cannot be that way Fastonar, and you know this"

The soul sworn shrugged and made a vague gesture. "Whatever, but to be positive, I am sure the local orcs will sing for our souls, that is at least something!"

He threw his coat tighter around himself and went to sit by the fire again. Imeah appeared from behind the walls, she was fully dressed again and didn't even look at Phraan but he did see that she threw him a small glance out of the corner of her eye and for a moment she did blush ever so slightly. Zaray stared at her and the albino girl sat down by the fire. She stared at the flames. Tersus and Peter had sort of returned to one of the alcoves, Peter had a gash in his arm and Tersus was taking care of it. "Imeah, how are you?"

The albino looked down. "I have had a vision, one it is important that I share with you all. But not until the morrow, you need to rest now"

Zaray frowned. "What sort of vision"

Imeah lifted her head and stared at the group. "There is danger here, and we do bring it with us"

Zaray tilted her head. "So, you are sure of this?"

The albino nodded. "Tomorrow I will speak of what I have seen"

She looked down again and seemed to refuse to speak again and Phraan sat down next to her, confused and a bit scared. He felt an odd tenderness for the girl, and his protective instincts had kicked inn too, after all, they had just been intimate and he was able to fall in love rather easily. Rhuk sighed. "We did survive, that dragon did show up just in the nick of time, very convenient if you ask me"

Dhokay sat down and caressed his hammer, it was covered with blood and gore. "Yes, extremely so, it is the second time it has showed up just like that"

Thiana and Taurin were already trying to make some food and Shaluun sent his little flask around, it was almost empty but everybody got at least a taste of the strong liquor it had contained. Phraan felt the huge feline, it was out there watching them and it felt good knowing they had such a formidable ally now. But he didn't understand anything of this, not really.

He stared at Zaray out of the corner of his eye and wondered yet again about the things she had said, his father had been of her kin? What did that mean? He suspected something and that suspicion had only grown stronger now but could he be sure? Fastonar did help Thiana prepare some stew and distributed it among them, they had a small bowl each and the knight did look rather annoyed still. Phraan took his bowl and ate with little appetite, he didn't feel like enjoying the food now. It would be morning soon and Imeah did eat her stew slowly and didn't say anything, she just stared into the flames and did appear to be praying. Phraan grasped his pocket knife, there was something he needed to check. He made sure that nobody did notice, then he cut his finger and stared at the small wound. It stopped bleeding almost immediately and then it disappeared completely. An odd feeling or sensation of triumph rushed through him, he had to shake his head in disbelief.

Zaray disappeared into her little room and the others too tried to get some more rest, Phraan remained in front of the fire, trying to figure out who or what he really truly was. The night had become silent once more and he wondered if they really had a chance at success. The things they were trying to do could possibly claim all of them, but he hadn't shied away from death before so why should he do it now. They called him the one death loves, and he remembered the old shaman and picked out the odd metal piece from his pocket. Stared at it. "I wonder what you are, I bet you are important, but I cannot for the very life of me understand how!"

Chapter 7: The face of darkness.

The high mage was staring down at the crystal, his eyes narrow and his expression one of worry. The crystal was what had given them the opportunity to bring the wall down for their new dragons and it was a very powerful artefact which had been discovered by chance almost a century ago. It had given them a golden opportunity for otherwise it would have been very hard to take the fight to the enemy south of the mountains. It would have been accomplished, no doubt about that but it would have taken much more time. As it were the crystal had speeded things up and he was in a way worried because of this. The brotherhood was too impatient, too determined to see results soon. The mage was a very skilled one, once he had been a top student at the academy and his road to the path of chaos had been a long and winding one, born out of an endless row of tragedies and misfortune. He wasn't a fanatic, nor was he a dreamer. He saw things in the light of logic and he was proud of this. He did want to create a name for himself, to be remembered and this was a good choice then. But the actions of the brotherhood weren't logical anymore, the new things which had been conjured up or resurrected were beyond them all. The leaders refused to listen to the mages and now this. At the base of all magic lays logic and this was just the opposite, they were racing along and didn't bother with such things as proper preparations. Sooner or later things would go awry and when magic does that it is rarely pretty, nor is it safe.

He stared at the crystal, over the last days it seemed to have changed, the colour had become less vibrant and the glow had diminished. It was placed near his chambers high in the citadel since he was in charge of it and he would have known if anyone had entered the chambers and tampered with it. He hadn't told Simaon, the idiot wouldn't understand at all. When he was around the crystal it felt as if it was being drained somehow, as if the energy was leaking away and he was afraid that the wall would return to normal sooner than expected. He sighed and took a deep breath, started chanting a soft monotonous melody, the crystal seemed to hum in tune with it but the tone was off somehow. He grimaced and stopped, stared at the crystal. "So, what is wrong with you?"

He walked over to an altar and picked up a sort of wand, it held another piece of crystal and he stared at the huge crystal once more. This did evade him, and that ticked him off. He was the best of all the mages gathered there, the one with the most experience and also the most intelligent one. The younger ones were eager, some fanatics and others too taken by their own hopes for power and might. They didn't see the pattern behind the things they did, if the balance truly was to be shifted in their favour they had to work in a specific manner. Things had to be done subtly, not with huge exaggerated shows of strength. A man who brags too much about himself is sure to lose everything sooner or later and he had learned that a humble path is a safe path. In special when dealing with the forces of chaos, it is in its very nature that it seeks to destroy everything, even those who serve it.

He held the wand over the huge crystal and this time he did chant something different, a much faster and high pitched spell and he closed his eyes and let his energy merge with that of the crystal. It was rather dangerous but he was skilled and in control of himself and it wasn't that difficult when you knew how to do it. He allowed the energy to flow freely through his mind and then he broke the connection with a gasp, he stared at the crystal with huge eyes and then he dropped the wand and swore, so bad it was a miracle he didn't spontaneously combust there and then.

What in hell's depths were those idiots doing? This could end with a disaster, what was Simaon really thinking? The obnoxious fool was bringing something like that to the city? He had lost every little ounce of common sense he ever had owned and the mage had to take some deep breaths. You cannot expect that something like that would end well, it would be like throwing a lit torch unto gunpowder and thinking that nothing would happen. He threw a thick velvet cloth over the crystal and then he took off. If Simaon really had an associate out there that person had to be stopped. Old Badrian had been right, they should listen to the advice given to them by the ancient ones. The warnings were real, not just fairy tales and he didn't want to lose everything just because of some overly zealous fools. These noble men were used to having things their way the moment they waved a finger but that didn't happen here. You cannot rush magic, it has its own schedule and sometimes that schedule was rather different from that of the humans trying to exploit it. Spells cannot just be thrown, they have to be prepared and the timing has to be perfect, and to introduce a force of chaos into this delicate balance they had spent centuries creating would be foolish to say the least.

He had a thing or two to say to Simaon and he gathered his cloak tighter around himself and walked off at a brisk pace. He was not going to let this pass by without doing something about it. Simaon had no idea of what he was about to do, it would be a grand mistake. The high mage had cooperated with Arabur and tried to stop whoever it was Simaon had out there but it had failed so far and that alone told the mage that the person behind the dragon's death was someone very dangerous indeed. The elemental they had summoned had disappeared and the mage controlling it had almost died and the goblins too had vanished, something was truly wrong and he was afraid that it was more than one person after all. The so called associate of Simaon was probably just an ordinary person, not capable of handling great magic at all and he or she could have been misled. If perhaps a group of mages was heading their way it could end with a complete disaster. The balance of the magic there so very fragile. So much could go terribly wrong.

The mage hurried through the polished marble halls and he was mumbling angry words the whole time, Simaon was gonna hear it now, the whole truth. Nobody liked the so called leader and he was surprised that none had finished the man off yet. He was like a peacock, showing off his feathers but cowering the moment a hawk appeared. The citadel was just as gorgeous on the inside as the outside and it did show a great deal of wealth. The guards recognized him and did nothing to stop him, they saw that he was angry and trying to stop a pissed off mage would usually be the last thing you ever did. Most men prefer to die in their own beds, peacefully in their sleep, not screaming whilst being devoured by some unnamed demon from the Gods alone knew what dimension.

Simaon had an office at the far end of the administrative wing of the citadel, it was the grandest there was and very luxurious and he walked up to the door and pushed it open, his mind glowing with anger. Simaon stood by the window, that cocky grin plastered to his face and he was fidgeting with something, something golden and small. The black haired man turned and stared at the mage, he frowned. "Jurza, what are you doing here? You have not asked for an audience!"

Jurza sneered. "And never should I have to ask for one, I am the high mage here, the one running this whole operation and you do naught but give orders and organize things even a child would be able to understand better."

Simaon gaped. "I beg your pardon?!"

Jurza walked closer, pointing at the other man. "You have ordered someone out there, seemingly working for you, to bring a person capable of killing a dragon over here?! Are you completely out of your mind? That sort of powerful and unknown magic cannot be mixed with ours, it will have the potential to destroy everything!"

Simaon just laughed. "You are the stupid one here Jurza, imagine what we can do with such power?"

Jurza almost growled. "You are no mage, you have no idea of what magic truly is, and how it works. It is a most delicate thing, like webbing spun from sugar, one wrong move and everything will crumble. That person cannot be allowed to get any closer."

Simaon just shrugged. "Oh, I hear that lord Buraz and Arabur already have tried stopping it, with the help of some of the younger mages. They didn't succeed. Which just proves that I am right, that power ought to be ours"

Jurza gaped, some of the other mages had tried too? And he hadn't been informed? That was outrageous and told him that they truly could be facing real problems. Simaon waved a hand. "Don't worry, I have ordered some of the newest creations we have to move forth, nothing will get past them which I don't approve off"

Jurza hissed. "Oh you fool, you incompetent rambling...arse! Didn't you hear what old Badrian said? Your actions can cause this whole operation to fall apart like a house of cards."

Simaon scoffed. "And who is the drama queen hmm? You mages do always exaggerate, it is in your nature. The dreghil will kill everyone except that person with the magical power and that person will be ours then, a valuable tool"

The mage went pale like a sheet. "Dreghil? You have released dreghil? Gods!"

Simaon just grinned and shrugged, his eyes did reveal a great deal of glee. He enjoyed seeing the mages squirm. "Oh they are just another weapon right? Created to be used by us, in whatever manner suits us. Don't worry so much, it will be alright"

Jurza had a hard time talking, the shock simply too great. "Simaon, you are no mage, you are not even well versed in the lore of old. You cannot be serious, the dreghil are something so terrible our ancestors never even dared to use them."

Simaon grinned even wider. "Then they'll make mincemeat of any enemies, like I say, no worries there"

Jurza was panting. "You will cause our fall, I just know you will. You are an arrogant beast and I despise the dirt upon which you have treaded. The mages won't take orders from you anymore, I will make sure of that"

Simaon frowned. "Jurza, don't be silly now, be a good little bookworm and go read some spells or something. Let the real men deal with politics and protection"

He was flipping something between his fingers and Jurza saw what it was, a small gold coin of some sorts. He felt the magic in it and realized that Simaon really truly didn't have a clue about what he was doing. The coin was extremely dangerous and no sane mage would have dared to handle it, and here that fool was playing with it? Jurza felt how anger exploded within him, how his fear and frustration and utter despise of the man just burst forth and he pretended to be turning around to leave. Simaon laughed. "Yes, go back to the basement like a good obedient pet, after all, you mages know so little about life"

Jurza spun around, a small throwing knife left his right hand and flew straight for the tall man, and it should have pierced his chest but stopped just inches from his skin. Jurza blinked in surprise and Simaon sent him a devilish grin. "Protective spells can be bought you see!"

Simaon made a gesture and the dagger flew back, so fast Jurza didn't have time to dodge it. It hit him square in the chest and he fell with a thud, his last dying thought one of utter disbelief, it shouldn't have ended thus. Simaon stared down at the dead mage with triumph, he was truly invincible and he laughed out loud. He didn't notice that Arabur had been standing behind the door the whole time, witnessing the entire scene. The fat man was shaking all over, their best mage dead because of Simaon? Oh now he really truly had a cause for this. He just had to gather his courage, and do things right.

He took a deep breath and knocked on the door, he put on his most servile expression and hoped that his acting skills didn't let him down now. Simaon stared at Arabur who stopped as if he got really startled by the sight of the dead mage. "Aaahh, what...what has happened here?"

Simaon just made a vague gesture. "The poor man went mad, tried to attack me, he had it coming. So, why are you here?"

Arabur bowed his head. "Uh, I am just here to tell you that the final tests of the larger cross breeds have been a success, they are ready!"

Simaon raised an eyebrow. "Indeed? How delightful, I hope that we can send them out tomorrow then?"

Arabur nodded. "Oh yes, they are eager. Mighty beasts, the kingdoms will soon surrender to us"

He saw that Simaon walked over to the window, staring at the city below. Magical lights did turn it into an enchanting and beautiful sight, like a huge tree filled with thousands of many coloured fireflies. The man was chuckling with delight and Arabur did for once in his life move with stealth, the wine glass in the desk was just a couple of feet from him and he didn't make a sound. Simaon did stare at the shadow of the mountains, he had just warded off a real threat and now the mages would most certainly be too afraid of him to protest against any of his ideas again. Arabur bowed slightly, the man was shivering a bit and Simaon seemed to grow an inch just out of sheer pride. He was indeed a great leader, one everybody would bow to soon. He waved his hand at Arabur.

"You may leave, tomorrow we will be one step closer to our greatest triumph yet"

Arabur bowed even deeper. "Yes…you are right…"

He walked out of the room with his eyes on the floor and cringed as he passed by the body of Jurza, now they had lost their best mage and Simaon was still acting this cocky? Oh this would be so very sweet indeed. He stopped at the end of the corridor and sought shelter behind a small closet. He was rather sure he didn't have to wait for long.

Simaon was chuckling as he poured himself some wine, the vintage was exquisite and very expensive and it had already been tasted by one of his slaves so it was safe. He did enjoy the sweet taste and drank the entire glass down. Yes, he would celebrate, this was a day of glory and the first of his days as the undisputed master of this whole city. Nobody would oppose to his rule now. He put the glass down and frowned, the wine was strong and left pleasant warmth in his gut but this time the warmth became rather unpleasant rather fast. He cringed, he was suddenly very warm indeed and gasped as pain shot through his body, he grasped his belly and the heat became unbearable, he did let out a shriek as he staggered backwards, his mind reeling. How was this possible? It couldn't be true, he couldn't have been poisoned? It was so below him to die thus, he was the master of this place, the Gods were on his side weren't they?

He was unable to stay upright, as he fell towards the window the door opened and Arabur entered, he was staring at Simaon with very cold eyes, the servile expression was gone, all that was left was sheer hatred. "You are worthless, nobody. You are no longer valuable to anyone and you did murder our best mage. This is just what you deserve!"

Simaon crashed into the window and flames burst out of his belly, he was screaming like mad in agony and fear and he fell through the glass in a cloud of sharp shards and fire. Arabur sneered. "Have a nice trip to hell you idiot"

Simaon clawed at anything to hold onto and the coin was
still in his hand for some reason, it was warm and he knew it
was magical. He had no idea of what sort of magic it contained
but he grasped at a straw, screamed as he fell towards the
bricks down below. "May the chaos devour you all, goddamn
traitors!"

Simaon didn't have time to say anything more, he did make
contact with the ground and it was made from expertly laid
bricks and the impact did make the ground shake a bit, the
guards by the gates did spring back with gasps of horror and
the remains of their former leader laid there and looked like an
overripe pomegranate someone has dropped from high up. It
wasn't much left of him which reminded them of a human
being. The coin did spin around a few times, the thin piece of
gold had survived the fall just fine and it fell over onto its side
with a gentle plop. Simaon didn't know it but if he had known
how to use the coin he could have saved himself with ease, as
it was the coin had been given a very unspecific order and now
it would wait and see if it could find some way to make sense
of it. Magic is patient, time doesn't exist to this primeval force
and so it just felt content to lay there and shine. Its time would
come for sure, it would make sense of the order sooner or later.
¨

Arabur stared through the broken window and he was
chuckling, Buraz had asked for something epic and epic it had
been for sure. To watch Simaon fall to his death like a burning
torch had been wonderful and Arabur spat out of the window,
he felt so much better now. Buraz would lead them, and he
would do his best to erase the mistakes Simaon had done,
including the whole mess with the so called associate and the
person with magical abilities.

He straightened his coat and raised his chins and walked out
of the office with an expression like a king. They would all
laugh tonight and party, Simaon's demise was something well
worth celebrating. It was a day of glory!

The group was getting ready to move forth, nobody had decided to turn around and although they dreaded the path ahead their resolve was adamant and would never fail. Phraan was tacking up Drake, he was trying not to think too much of the mission, after all, they were facing something few of them could even imagine. The huge cat had returned to him and then it had just disappeared, it probably returned to whatever dimension it belonged to and Phraan didn't need it anymore so he didn't try to call it back. He could call for it again when they needed an extra guard. The morning light was grey and faint and the air very cold, they were indeed in the high mountains now and here nature showed no pardon if you didn't come prepared. Imeah appeared from behind the wall, she was well dressed and should be alright but Phraan saw that she was shivering and he felt a sting of fear right away. He rushed to her side, not caring what the others would think of it. "Are you alright?"

She shook her head and sent him a tiny smile. "No, but do not let me delay you, we need to ride now, right away."

Dabin frowned. "You said you would tell us something important?"

She nodded but her face was very drawn. "Maybe later today, we have to move on, while there is light"

Phraan frowned. "Are you ill?"

She nodded and got up on her horse, he could see that her eyes were blurred and her expression one of barely contained pain. "Imeah, you are clearly not able to ride, what is wrong, please, do tell me!"

She reached down and caressed his cheek. "I cannot tell you Phraan, not yet. We shared this night but this…this I cannot share, I am sorry"

He swallowed hard. "Then ride with me? Please, you are unable to control the horse should something happen, I can keep you safe"

She sighed and her eyes did sparkle for a moment. "I do thank you for your offer and I accept"

He lifted her off her own horse and put her onto Drake, the others stared. Thiana walked over. "What is wrong?"

Imeah tried to smile. "I am not well, but do not bother, I think I may have eaten something which didn't agree with me"

The wood elf did look rather suspicious but shrugged and walked off and Phraan did see that Zaray was staring at the ground, her eyes dark and her face told of sorrow. He felt panic surge through his body, Imeah had more or less said that she wouldn't survive this journey, was this it?

They rode on, the terrain was even worse to cross downhill and they used much of the morn getting back to the valley floor. From there it went a little smoother and they could increase their speed. The huge rock wall which indicated the start of the hidden path was getting more and more impressive and Phraan stared at it with narrow eyes. How that could mark the start of anything was beyond him, the wall was several miles wide and so tall it felt as if it was towering above them already. Zaray was keeping her eyes open for trolls and other creatures and here the ground was surprisingly even and there were few screes and loose rocks. They rounded a turn and saw some odd discolorations of the ground, and some pieces of wood did protrude from the soil. Zaray just pointed at them. "These are the last remnants of the Great War, much blood was shed here, so much it forever changed the soil."

Phraan shuddered, it was as if the cliffs still resounded with the cries and shouts of a great battle. Imeah sat in front of him and she had been quiet the whole time, sometimes she would shudder and her eyes close. She was obviously in great pain so why didn't she allow them to help her? There had to be something they could do? Why did this happen? She was so warm to the touch and he felt so terrible for not doing anything, Peter did ride up next to them and he was staring at Imeah. "How is she doing? Can it be food poisoning?"

Phraan shook his head. "No, we all ate the same last night, I have no idea of what it is, she refuses to talk to me"

Peter tilted his head. "Tersus has got medicine? I bet he can make something which will ease her discomfort"

Imeah waved a hand in a gesture as if to ward something off. "No, no medicine."

Phraan groaned. "But you suffer, please, tell me what's wrong"

She leaned back against him. "No, the time isn't right"

A shudder ran through her and he had to hold her tight to prevent her from falling, what in the name of every hell was wrong with her?

They rode for yet a couple of hours and Zaray stopped by a tiny lake. The water was so clear it was as if it wasn't even there and freezing cold and the strange woman did bring some water over to Imeah in a cup. "Here, you need this"

Imeah took the cup but she was barely able to move and Phraan was close to tears. "Zaray, I beg you, there must be something we can do?"

Zaray sighed and put a hand on his arm, she appeared to be just as gripped by despair as him. "No, Imeah has chosen her fate Phraan, nothing can save her."

Phraan let out a roar. "Then what is wrong?! She wasn't ill yesterday, and now...she is dying!"

Zaray just sent him a dark glance and walked off and he let out a small wail and embraced Imeah again, this was like losing Vitile again, he couldn't bare it. "Imeah, listen to me, what is wrong with you"

She stared at him, the red eyes glazed and distant and she was barely able to speak. "No, not yet"

Everybody was staring at them and Fastonar walked over, he was very worried and Phraan saw that he was a bit pale too. "We cannot linger here, can you carry her on the horse again?"

Phraan swallowed a harsh sob. "No, I...she is in too much pain, she cannot ride now"

Fastonar laid a hand on his shoulder. "Then we'll keep watch, I...I am sorry"

Imeah was writhing, her skin burning hot and Phraan could swear he heard cracking sounds, as if her bones did snap when the convulsions got worse. She wasn't making any sounds though, her agony was silent and he felt hot tears flowing down his cheeks. Watching her suffer thus was horrible and the others did keep their distance, gave them some privacy. She appeared to be unconscious but after a while she opened her eyes and they were clear again. "Phraan"

He leaned in closer, her voice barely audible and she closed her eyes again. "Yes?"

She held his hand, hers so tiny and warm and he felt as if despair was going to swallow him whole. "Do not tell anyone of what I am about to say, it is time"

He pretended to gather her up, held her closer as if she was dead already. She whispered. "A servant of chaos rides among us, I have been poisoned, by the same hand that killed Vitile. But nobody must know, fate must be allowed to take its course"

Phraan held his breath, disbelief surging through his brain. "No, it cannot be, who would...NO!"

She gasped, her eyes shooting open. "I will go now Phraan, I will prepare the path for you. My spirit has sought the artefact and weakened it, I will make sure that you can enter the mountains but time is of the essence, you cannot hesitate. I can only do this for a while, before my spirit is called forth to join my ancestors."

Phraan shook her, buried his face against her chest. "Who, who did this to you?"

She smiled, a very sad smile. "It will hurt you"

He gasped and rocked back and forth, overcome by grief. "Not as much as losing you"

She smiled again, there was blood on her lips. "Oh Phraan, you love so easily, your heart is so great. Guard it well my dear, it is your strength, and your weakness. Don't let love become the ruin of all"

He sobbed. "Who!"

She sighed and told him and Phraan just stared down at her face with disbelief before he felt cold all over. It did make sense, it did all make sense now, in an odd perverted manner. Aiolo couldnt have been alone, it explained everything.Imeah made a gargling sound, her eyes rolled back and he let out a wail. She managed to get back for a fleeting second. "Farewell, I could...have loved someone like you"

Then she suddenly went limp and her breath stopped and Phraan let out a roar of anguish and sorrow. Zaray came over, kneeling next to him. "We need to move on"

He sneered at her. "You! You knew this would happen! Why didn't you stop it?!"

Zaray sighed and there were tears in her eyes. "Because we cannot succeed without her sacrifice. Her spirit is strong Phraan, stronger than her body ever was. She will help us from the spirit realm. Let go, it is the only way!"

Phraan stared down at the lifeless face, he felt a seething anger inside but he already knew that the secret had to remain a secret for yet a while, he would get his vengeance sooner or later and it would be grand. "Let us at least bury her"

Zaray waved at Ivran. "Get over here, I know you can do it, create a tomb for her, something the scavengers won't be able to get through"

Phraan laid Imeah's body onto the ground and Ivran cringed. "Oh Gods, I am so sorry Phraan, I...I liked her a lot"

Phraan had to rinse his nose, tears were still flowing down his cheeks and he felt so emotionally drained it was a wonder he stayed upright. The young man took a deep breath and they stepped away from the body. Ivran tried to focus, he remembered the tombs he had seen before and imagined one being built over Imeah and suddenly the ground seemed to be move and well up like a wave coming from all directions.

They got out of the way and the wave of rock did close up around the body and it changed its shape into a box shape and a figure did show up on the top. It was a wolf and Ivran stared at what he had created and Zaray smiled widely. "A wolf, excellent, she had the courage of a she wolf"

Phraan dried his face, how could he face everybody now, knowing what he knew? He couldn't afford a slip of the tongue nor any other mistakes and he stared at the tomb and in his mind he swore to avenge her, just as he had sworn to avenge Vitile. He walked over to Drake as if he was asleep, he saw that Thiana was crying and Taurin was trying to comfort her and Tersus did look shocked too. Dhokay and Shaluun did stare at the ground, visibly distraught and Fastonar was fidgeting with the reins of his horse, he too seemed distraught. Phraan took a deep breath. "Let's move, we cannot linger here"

He mounted the huge stallion and the others got on their horses as well, Zaray was staring at him and there was a silent warning in her gaze. She knew something and Phraan had an odd feeling of being the only ignorant one among them. The wall of rock was rather close now and Zaray said they would reach the path the next day, the stone was as smooth as a window and there were no markings upon it of any kind. But now they did see something else far ahead in the distance, between the peaks of the ragged mountains. It was some sort of shimmering light and it did look like auroras but it wasn't moving and it looked solid. Zaray pointed at it. "The wall"

Phraan felt a surge of sheer awe, it seemed to stretch into the very heavens themselves and it stretched in every direction. "That is impressive!"

Ivran was just staring with his jaw almost hitting his chest, his eyes were wide open. "The sheer amount of power..."

Zaray grinned. "Yes, imagine that"

Dhokay pointed at a narrow gorge straight ahead. "I bet we can stay there, it is getting dark again soon"

Zaray tilted her head. "Yes, but we cannot light any fires, the enemy do know we are coming and they will try to stop us again. We have to be very careful"

Rhuk and Dabin were glaring at the rock face, their expressions told of wonder. Phraan looked down at them. "What is it?"

Rhuk tilted his head. "Ah, that smoothness? It isn't natural, someone has sort of...changed the rock"

Dabin nodded. "Yes, it is like a piece of butter, being spread over a slice of toast, only with rock as butter and a heck of a huge knife"

Dhokay was blinking and Tersus stared at the rock with obvious awe. "Such magnificent technique, I wonder how it was done?"

Peter shrugged. "Magic?"

Rhuk shook his head, "No, something else, something way closer to the mundane, but it must have taken time. And that tells me that this rock wall is important."

Zaray sighed and her eyes were very sad. "It is, during the war this valley marked the path to the city, the mountain wall was erected to block it off"

Shaluun frowned. "And yet it marks the start of a path to it?"

Zaray nodded and pointed at the shiny surface. "Yes, one only a few can hope to find. You will see tomorrow"

Fastonar hadn't said anything but he was staring at the wall with obvious doubt. "We should never have come to this place, we have lost too many. "

Zaray grinned. "Don't be so pessimistic, at least we'll go down in history as true heroes"

Fastonar mumbled. "I wonder! But we'll avenge our dead, it is our duty and our privilege."

They rode towards the gorge, it didn't appear to be very tempting and Shaluun was trying to look for some better place to seek shelter when they noticed an odd greenish light which was approaching the path, rather slowly. Fog followed it and Zaray suddenly turned pale and swore. "Damn it, I was afraid of this"

Fastonar looked scared. "What sort of deviltry is this?"

She got off the mule and nodded to Ivran. "The very worst, Ivran, we need your help now, please, you must create a shield, like in that cave."

Ivran did look as if he didn't really understand but he got off the horse and they gathered around him. Phraan did see figures moving in the fog, and he felt chilled to the bone. "What do they do?"

His voice did shiver and Zaray hissed. "They simply suck the very soul out of any living thing and devour it"

Everybody stared at her and Ivran yelped. "That is...I have no word"

Zaray sneered. "Neither do I, they are abominations. I had never even imagined that the brotherhood could become so desperate as to reawaken these monsters"

Ivran was trying to focus and a very shivering dome seemed to rise around them. Fastonar was grasping his sword with pale hands. "Can they be killed?"

Zaray shook her head. "No, they aren't flesh and blood, just...spirit. Not even my bow can harm these, the arrows will just fly without harming them in the least. In fact it will drain my strength rather fast, they may absorb the energy of the arrows."

Phraan felt trapped. "The cat, can it harm them then?"

She shook her head. "No to that as well, if Ivran's dome doesn't do the job we'll be in serious trouble. This is the worst the dark mages ever conjured up"

Fastonar was staring at the fog, it moved very slowly and somehow that made it even worse to watch. "You do know an awful lot about their deeds don't you?"

She nodded. "Naturally enough, I was a prisoner in that city for years."

Now they heard sounds, odd noises which reminded them of the sound of someone retching rather violently. Dhokay was gaping. "Is that the monsters?"

Zaray nodded. "Yes, charming yes? Don't move, they have very sharp senses but they don't see this dimension, only the one which souls inhabit"

Ivran was sweating. "I am not so sure about this dome folks, it isn't strong, and I feel kind of weird"

Zaray spun around. "What? Don't tell me you too are falling ill?"

Ivran swallowed. "I don't know, I just…I don't feel right. It is as if I am facing some sort of resistance, I cannot explain it. I feel weak!"

The dome was shivering and looked like an oversized soap bubble and Phraan got a bizarre feeling that one prick from a pin would make it burst. They saw the figures in the fog better now and Rhuk and Dabin made a unison sound of horror. Phraan saw why, the figures were dwarves, or rather, they had been dwarves once upon a time. Now they were wraiths, greenish apparitions of skeletons with some remains of armour and clothes and the empty eye sockets of naked skulls seemed to glow with an insatiable hunger. Rhuk trembled visibly. "By the braids on my father's feet, what is that?!"

Zaray swallowed. "Dwarf warriors who fell in the war against the chaos, their souls captured by the enemy and turned into this…"

Dabin was green, not as green as the attackers but not far from it. "Oh Gods, it is terrible"

The fog was snaking its way along the ground and Zaray seemed tense, she was fidgeting with a medallion she wore around her neck and her eyes were seemingly aglow. Ivran moaned. "I feel something, it is seeking me!"

Dhokay sneered. "The dark mages, I bet they want to destroy him first and foremost"

Zaray walked over to Ivran, put a hand on his head. "Ivran, close your eyes, listen to me. I will strengthen you and ward off this attack but you have to trust me. I will have to enter your soul to do this"

Ivran blinked and then he nodded, the fear in his eyes was obvious. "A-alright, go ahead."

Zaray closed her eyes too and she started to mumble something which did sound like spells, the dome was shivering and trembling like jelly and it couldn't be very strong at all. Ivran jerked and let out a hoarse cry, he was very pale. "Stay still, I have almost reached them"

Zaray was sweating and Phraan saw that she was shivering too, this had to take an awful lot of strength to do. "Do something to distract them, fast!"

Everybody stared at each other and then Tersus made a grimace and opened his saddle bags. He pulled out some small bags made from a very fine cloth and he weighed them in his hands. "I have no idea of whether or not this will work…"

Zaray was panting. "Try goddamn it"

She was chanting even louder now and Ivran was shaking as if in a seizure, his eyes were rolling and there was a crackling sound coming from the dome. Tersus threw the bags, one by one with powerful movements and the bags did fly for quite a distance before they hit the ground. The thin fabric did fall apart and a thin mist of powder did fill the air. Tersus waited for a few seconds and nothing seemed to happen. Then he grasped his flint and steel and made a spark, got some pieces of dry wood to burn and tossed them out as well. The result was terrifying, suddenly there was a loud boom and the air around the dome caught fire. They were standing in the middle of an inferno and the horses did whinny with fear and threw their heads up. The fire burned down very fast and now the fog was gone but the wraiths were still there, staring at the dome and still hungry. Zaray did scream something and pushed against Ivran, she pressed the medallion against his forehead and the young man let out a shrill scream and fell, smoke rose from both him and Zaray and he was gasping. "It is gone, it is gone."

He got back onto his feet and the dome got more solid again, he was trembling still and Zaray was sitting, obviously completely exhausted. "I closed him off, but it cost me a lot. The dark magic, it was seeking to destroy him, make him vulnerable"

Shaluun stared at her with huge eyes, "What?"

She rubbed her head and shook herself. "They may remember me now, and I had hoped that I would remain forgotten"

She got up, soaked with sweat. "You do know a great deal about magic too, and you are no mage?"

Fastonar's voice was sarcastic and she nodded. "I only used the magic inherent in my people, I fear that may have been too much"

Rhuk was staring at the wraiths with open disgust and sorrow. "Their souls are lost, condemned."

Zaray grimaced. "Do not pity them, they are sheer evil now"

Thiana and Taurin was clinging to each other, eyes wide with fear and both were shaking all over, this had to be utter terror to them, being killed by these abominations meant no afterlife. Phraan was hoarse. "Will the dome hold now?"

Zaray shrugged. "I don't know, Ivran may not be strong enough to hold it up, these things are patient, they are already dead so waiting for days won't harm them at all"

Fastonar growled. "We are trapped here, goddamn it, I want to die fighting when I die, not…like this"

Ivran closed his eyes. "They know we are here, I can sense them. Their minds are empty, there is nothing there, only hunger. They cannot be stopped"

The first wraith did fling itself against the wall, it was thrown back but Ivran let out a small howl of pain. Zaray grasped him and she did look horrified. "Did you feel it?"

He nodded. "Yes, it hurt like....like ice!"

She turned around, stared at the wraiths, many were emerging and she was in obvious despair, not knowing what to do. "They do target Ivran, damn it. Does anyone have a good idea?"

Nobody spoke and more wraiths attacked the dome, Ivran screamed again, and Phraan did to his horror see that wounds did appear on the young man's skin. "The dome, it is an extension of his own magic, of his soul. They harm him through it!"

Thiana's voice was trembling and Phraan stared around him, there had to be something they could do? He turned to Tersus. "Do you have anything useful?"

Tersus shrugged. "Nothing which works against apparitions, I am sorry"

The wraiths were howling, the grotesque faces looked triumphant and Zaray moaned. "I cannot give Ivran more energy, fighting the mages through him has drained me!"

Fastonar frowned. "What did you do?"

She made a grimace. "I killed a few dark mages, it takes a lot out of you"

Dhokay was wide eyed. "No shit? Goddamn it, you do have some power!"

Zaray was leaning against a rock. "Yes, but nowhere near enough"

The wraiths seemed to gather for an all-out storm attack and that would most likely kill Ivran, and bring the dome down. They all prepared to fight for their lives one last time when a sudden flash of light appeared right in front of them. A huge figure seemed to burst out of thin air and it landed on the ground with a heavy thud. They gaped, it was a sort of wingless dragon and its hide was so shiny it did remind them of the skin of certain beetles. It had a heavy head with very strong jaws and the red eyes were filled with an eerie sort of intelligence. It held something in its maw and walked towards them, it was so large even Dhokay only reached the middle of its shoulder. Zaray was gasping. "I cannot believe it…"

The creature seemed friendly, it walked slowly forth and dropped the objects on the ground in front of Phraan. Zaray stared and her face told of utter disbelief. "We have an ally on the inside, take them Phraan, and do it now. It is our only chance."

He stared at the massive beast, its eyes did follow him with great calm and he took a deep breath, it was a sword and a gem of some sorts and he picked the gem up. It felt warm to the touch and it was quite lovely to look at. Then it felt as if that warmth did spread all through him and he remembered the dream he had had, the mountain top and the feeling of being more than before. This was it, this was that moment again, only with slight differences. The gem seemed to dissolve, become one with him and he blinked and tried to control himself as everything seemed to spin before his very eyes. Zaray was smiling. "At last, the awakening, the sword, take the sword!"

Phraan grasped it, it was a rather long sword which could be used both with one hand and two and the hilt was wrapped with dragon hide and decorated with rubies. The blade itself had an odd dark colour and it was rather narrow with a very long point to it. It was a vicious looking thing, the hand guard shaped like two dragons feet with long talons, pointing away from the hilt and towards the blade again, the pommel was a massive lump of that dark steel but in the middle was an opal and it was shining with breath taking brilliance. He had to stare at the weapon with awe, it felt as if it was forged just for his hands and the balance was perfect. It was a very intimidating sword and it felt empowering just to hold it. Then he felt a sort of jolt of energy rush through him and the blade started to glow from within, bright unreal blue. Everybody stared and Zaray swallowed visibly. "She is yours now, I thought this blade was a mere legend but fate favours the bold it seems"

Phraan frowned. "She?"

Zaray nodded. "Rivath, it is so ancient nobody even knows who forged it"

The wraiths had backed off for a few moments, possibly blinded by the light, but now they howled and came back and Ivran staggered, blood running down his face. "Do something, now!!"

Phraan stared at Zaray with wild eyes. "Please, do tell me that this blade can kill them?"

Zaray nodded. "It can kill everything Phraan, even a God, but you are vulnerable to them, remember what was given"

He frowned. "Imeah did give me…"

Zaray shook her head. "No, not that gift. Your body may be stronger now but your soul is what these beasts are after. No, the shaman! Now is the time, you are awakened, you are who you were meant to be."

Phraan fished the little piece of metal out of his pocket and Zaray grinned. "Lay it on your palm, quickly now"

Fastonar was staring at Phraan with huge eyes, for a moment it seemed as if Phraan had grown, become even taller than before and he did glow from within, the same eerie glow the blade showed. "By every God…"

The piece of metal laid there for a second, then it suddenly flattened itself and stretched and with a speed which was impossible to believe it covered his entire body before it shaped itself into a full suit of armour. It had exquisite details and it was extremely light. Only a narrow slit in front of Phraan's eyes were left open and his long hair did flow from a small opening at the back of the helmet like a banner. Phraan stared at his hands, now they were covered by gauntlets which looked a lot like dragon hands and Zaray nodded. "Now they cannot harm you, very few things can, kill them before they kill Ivran!!"

Phraan felt dizzy still, and he was light headed and felt very strange, as if his body somehow was too small for him. He took a deep breath and ran through the dome, he felt no resistance and brought the sword up with a roar. The blade did make a strange sound, like someone singing a very high and clear note and it was both beautiful and eerie at the same time. Wraiths stormed towards him but couldn't reach him, the armour did ward them off and the glow surrounded him completely now. The blade cut through the wraiths and to his astonishment he did feel the impact, as if these were creatures of flesh and blood. But it did kill, the wraiths sort of vanished into a wisp of smoke when he chopped into them and he knew that the blade did complete him. His gift of killing had finally found its true match and with this blade he could now destroy almost everything he wished to.

He danced through the mass of wraiths, the blade cutting a shining blue path and the armour did look as if it was forged just for him, just as the blade. Zaray was smiling, a very pleased smile. "We do have a chance now, we truly do"

Phraan was moving so fast every movement did become a blur, and he moved without a sound. That was the most amazing thing about it. The remaining wraiths did try to flee, but he did catch up with them with ease and ended them all. He did take a look around and saw no more enemies and the dome did disappear. The huge dragon did just stand there, its red eyes watching him with a sort of acceptance. The armour did disappear, it just shrunk back to a tiny piece of metal again but now it was a ring and it did look very anonymous. Phraan stared at it, tried to take it off but found that he couldn't. Zaray came to meet him, she grinned widely. "Don't bother, it will never leave you now."

Phraan saw that Ivran was on the ground, shuddering. "Is he gonna be alright?"

Zaray nodded. "Yes, eventually. He needs rest and food"

Phraan stared at the blade, it didn't glow anymore but it was still terrifying and he let a hand run down the lethal metal. It felt as if it welcomed him, as if it did enjoy the touch. He swallowed and stared at Zaray. "You do owe me an explanation, and do not try to avoid it, I want to know!!"

Zaray sighed and looked down, her lovely face was filled with a sort of melancholy. "Alright, but let's set up camp first. Ivran needs help, and there is still a risk of more attacks although I doubt it. This must have truly shaken them to the core."

Phraan did sheath Rivath in one of his own sheaths, it did fit pretty well and he gave that sword to Taurin instead. He didn't need three swords, he had only two arms. They did put up camp rather fast, the horses were still shaken from the explosion and they were all cold and tired. Fastonar was staring at Phraan with awe still and the half elf did find that a bit disturbing, he was still Phraan, not some deity. Zaray smiled. "You can call forth the cat now Phraan, it will guard us"

Phraan did focus, and the huge cat did appear out of nowhere, just like the dragon had. It was still following them and Phraan stared at the huge beast and had no idea of what it was. It didn't look quite like any dragon they had ever seen. "Is that a new species?"

Zaray sat down, found some food and shook her head. "No, his story is long and it is linked to ours. You will see that when I have told everything, it is time for that now. Tomorrow we enter the hidden path, everything can happen then"

Phraan tilted his head. "So, what are my weaknesses? I bet even that armour does have kinks in it?"

Zaray sighed and leaned back, her face dreamy. "Yes, you are still rather vulnerable when magic is involved, in special the type dark mages use. But you can fight even that if you fully accept who and what you are. I will tell you, but do eat first, it is a very long story"

Everybody had sat down and the remains of the food they had was sent around, Ivran did look half dead and he was in obvious pain. Thiana and Taurin did try to help him by washing the wounds with water they had put herbs in and Dhokay and Shaluun did look rather worried. "I don't think the visible damage is the worst"

Dhokay's voice was dry and Thiana nodded. "Yes, you are right, he is very weak now. They almost drained his magic, a little more and he would have been dead."

Zaray did grimace. "That is very bad, we do need him in there, he has to recover soon"

Phraan frowned. "I wasn't vulnerable to those wraiths?"

Zaray turned towards him. "No, they are created by dark magic but they are not all that magical, they are rather primitive."

The two dwarves were still pale. "Have their souls found peace now?"

Zaray shrugged. "They have been freed from the force which enslaved them so I would guess so yes."

Both breathed a sigh of relief, Phraan knew how important the afterlife was to dwarves and this had shaken the two to the core. Zaray did bite into some dried meat. "The dark mages called those creatures dreghil, it means hunger in the language the first of them used."

Phraan had to grin, a wry swift grin. "Rivath means thirst in the language of the high elves"

Zaray did grin back. "Yes, a name well chosen."

Dhokay did stare at Zaray. "So, we do all have many questions to ask and you have avoided them all for days. Would you care to enlighten us?"

Zaray nodded. "Yes, some of what I know is for Phraan's ears alone but I can tell you some. My story started a very long time ago, back when the wall was new and the city behind it just constructed. The war was over, the mages had agreed upon a truce and everybody was pleased, or so the leaders believed."

Shaluun tilted his head, the long blonde hair had come undone and was flowing freely, for a moment he did look very feral indeed. "Some weren't happy with the truce?"

Zaray nodded. "Yes, the seeds of the brotherhood as we see it now were sown back then, and they have been germinating ever since. It has been a silent enemy, growing in plain sight but so well hidden that none did see it"

Rhuk did look confused. "How? That is a contradiction?"

She smiled back at him, pulled her long legs up. "Yes, but these men were so clever, you cannot change things from the outside, but whence you take control of the entire brotherhood from the inside you can do pretty much whatever you want to. They have just waited"

Thiana did look curious. "For what?"

Zaray pointed towards the mountain. "For the artefact which allows them to bring their dragons through the wall. They have searched for it for centuries and when it was found they started getting active again, dragons were created, and new ideas set in action. They emerged once more, spreading their influence over the lands, bringing in more mages and seducing many powerful people."

Fastonar was still looking as if he did doubt her. "So, what does that have to do with you?"

She sighed and closed her eyes. "The dark mages were curious, it is one of their main traits, they will always try to find something new to control and rule, something which will add to their power."

She did stare up at the stars. "My people were forgotten by everybody, we lived far north, in a valley which was protected by powerful spells. We are not like all others, we do all have this one gift which defines us, which makes us unique. Some of us were so powerful they could be compared with Gods, and the mages were aiming for just that power. They wished to capture some of us and turn them into slaves."

Phraan held his breath, and Dhokay did suddenly look as if he had seen the light. "You are of the clan of Ibrasha, the first people who sought the magic and tamed it?"

She nodded. "Yes, and the magic changed us, forever. It is a part of our blood, for good or bad."

Fastonar was gnawing at some meat, he didn't look impressed but Phraan knew him, he was interested. "So?"

Zaray leaned backwards again, her face was strangely naked in the starlight. "They attacked the valley but couldn't get through the defences, they were too strong. No dark mage can ever hope to overpower one of us, we are like living flames of light, and we destroy darkness with our mere presence"

Everybody was staring and Zaray had a sad smile on her face. "I was a child back then, a wild one, not very obedient and not at all able to understand danger. I had left the valley to look for some rare flowers and they managed to catch me. I wasn't trained, hadn't awakened yet. I was like any other elf and they tried to force me to become their obedient little pet. I had no powers, no magic. They didn't realize that this comes with age, that we are no stronger than all other elves before we reach that point in life when the power awakens in us."

Phraan remembered what she had said, he was of her kin. His power had started to awaken and now it was released in its full form, it was terrifying. "So, what happened to you?"

Dabin did look a bit nervous when he asked and Zaray sent the dwarf a swift and reassuring smile. "I was treated just like an ordinary servant, sent to do mundane tasks for the one mage who became my master. Later my beauty made me sought after and he made sure that he did reap the benefits from that. I had never forgotten who I was, and what. I used all I secretly learned to teach myself all I needed to know, to access their every secret."

She looked down. "I was going to destroy them, to crush all they were from the inside. I had such faith in my own strength but I found that I was wrong, that I wasn't all that strong after all. I was naïve, blinded by the very power I sought to destroy."

Phraan held his breath. "What did you do?"

She shrugged. "I tried to kill the high mage, and they didn't kill me when they caught me but threw me into a cell under the citadel. I stayed there for a very long time, only my anger and hatred kept me alive."

Fastonar cringed. "The high mage? I bet that was a powerful person, sounds like hubris to even think of murdering someone like that!"

She did look a bit sombre. "Indeed it was, I was not aware of just how strong these dark mages were, they rarely show their full power. But the stay in the basement did teach me a lot, I became so much stronger in spirit"

Taurin was rubbing Thiana's back and she did look rather tired. "How did you escape?"

She grinned, a rather vicious grin. "There are servants there, people who aren't mages. The city does have a population of people who live rather ordinary lives. They know nothing else than the life there and even in a city controlled by dark mages there are criminals. I was found by a thief and he helped me escape."

Everybody stared. "A thief? Who could be so bold as to steal from the dark brotherhood?"

Fastonar did sound incredulous and she did look down. "A thief like none other, a man of my own people. He was hiding there pretending to be an ordinary elf and my oh my was he good at it. He helped me get out and we did escape the city but just barely. We roamed the lands for a long time trying to figure out how to bring the mages down, gathering lore and trying to come up with a plan. I was a warrior of light for many centuries, fighting everything I saw which could bring the dark ones more power, trying to destroy their associates and businesses."

Dhokay stared at her, the luptay did look intense. "I think I know what your gift is Zaray, it is a good thing you managed to escape"

She smiled. "Yes, but they would never have broken me, I am way too strong."

She closed her eyes again. "We did split up, could cover more ground that way and for years I was alone. His gift was the ability to blend in, to make everybody believe he was someone he wasn't. He used it for all it was worth and he did manage to find a lot of information but in the end we knew that the old legends were our best shot. They told the truth."

Shaluun was fidgeting with his hair. "He isn't here?"

She looked down. "No, not even we are invincible, he died years ago, it was a tragic accident and I have missed him ever since. But I have kept going, I will return to the city to avenge all the dead, all the suffering. They will see my true nature when I destroy them once and for all"

Phraan swallowed hard, he felt how his heart did plunge within his chest. "Was he?"

Zaray nodded. "Yes, his name was Gilrian, he was the bravest person I have ever met"

Phraan let the name roll over his tongue and it felt odd, but in a way almost comforting. His father, finally that mysterious person had a name. Zaray did smile at Phraan, her eyes filled with a sort of gentleness. "You look a lot like him, you are taller though, and your hair is darker but otherwise you are your father's son beyond any doubt"

Phraan swallowed, his throat felt thick, almost stuffed. "Thank you, I wish…I wish I could have met him"

She nodded and pulled her cloak tighter around herself. "Yes, and I am sure he too would have been delighted to meet you, he never knew he had fathered a child, I heard of you long after he was gone."

Phraan stared at her, his heart beating. "You heard of me?"

She nodded. "Yes, the orcs. They spoke of the one death loves, of a half elven warrior who fought like possessed, who seemed invincible. I wanted to meet you back then Phraan but I couldn't, the time wasn't right. If I had contacted you it would have endangered you"

He stared at his own hands, it was so alien to think of himself as someone born of the same people as Zaray. "So my gift is simply killing?"

She nodded. "Yes, the ability to see a weakness and strike right at it, you are a warrior like none others Phraan, you started to awaken back during the orc wars. And you found your calling when you hunted dragons but now, now son of Gilrian you are complete. The weakness of human blood is forever gone, you are fully one of us now, and you will discover what that truly means"

Everybody stared at Phraan and he felt self-conscious and a bit embarrassed. "Stop glaring, I am still me!"

Dhokay nodded. "Yes, and a heck of a lot more than before"

Rhuk was almost applauding. "I have said it ever from I saw you the first time, that one has strong feet, good feet!"

Fastonar took a deep breath. "So, what is the plan now, what do we do?"

Zaray made a nasty grimace. "We enter the hidden path, but I am rather sure that it won't be easy. They know we are coming and will try to close it up, or worse. There will be problems, no matter whom or what we are."

Dhokay was rubbing his hands, he did look as if he was in doubt somehow. "So, how long is it since you used the hidden path to get out of there?"

Zaray looked down. "Too long, I am the first to admit that. I left the city many centuries ago, before they found the thing which enabled them to get through the wall and before they started breeding dragons again. I wanted to crush them before

344

they rose to power once more for I knew that they would, sooner or later. I just pray I am not too late"

Dhokay stared at the enormous rock wall, it did look very solid indeed. "The path, I bet it is magical right?"

She nodded. "Yes, like another dimension, a world of its own. The wall does cut through it though, and we have to find a way to pass it. "

Ivran was lifting his head. "I don't think I am able to do anything about that, it is...it is so powerful"

Zaray shrugged. "Yes, but I think I have a plan. I am not sure that it will work but we have to try"

Fastonar was leaning forth, he did look eager somehow. "And then, when we have gotten through, then what?"

Zaray almost sneered. "Then we destroy what we can, if they cannot get through the wall again they will be shut out from the rest of the world"

Phraan did stare at her, her eyes were rock hard and almost burning. "So, you wish to cripple them by ruining the artefact which lets them get out?"

She nodded. "Without that thing nothing they do matters. They aren't strong enough to control it on their own"

Fastonar was frowning, his face rather closed off. "Are you sure?"

She smiled swiftly, but her eyes didn't change, they had that hard expression still. "Yes, I am very sure. The wall was erected by mages way superior to the ones who exist now, the old texts said they used a very different type of magic too, and these days nobody is that strong."

Thiana was looking at the strange woman with curiosity. "The source of their power, that thing the shaman called a heart stone, it cannot provide them with enough power to regain control?"

Zaray sighed. "Yes, it can. It can give more power than anyone can even imagine but we have to cleanse it. I have no idea of how so here I will just let the Gods guide me."

Shaluun was petting his axe. "Sometimes luck is what defines the brave, we have to try"

Rhuk and Dabin were grinning. "Destroying stuff seems like a good idea. We can do that."

Zaray was staring at her knees, her eyes thoughtful. "When I used the hidden path to get out of there I was followed by someone who had used it before. Gilrian knew how to avoid the dangers in there but even he only did it because he had to. It is truly a very different world, and one which is unpredictable at its best. We will be hunted, and that is a certainty."

The huge dragon creature had lain down with its head resting upon its front legs, it was not moving but the eyes revealed that it was listening. Zaray turned to it. "That my friends is the species which the dragons first evolved from, I didn't know that anyone still existed but I think that this one here in fact belongs to the dimension we are about to enter."

Taurin turned his head and stared at it. "It is obviously not hostile"

Zaray laughed. "You are right, he want to help us. I have no idea of why though."

Phraan looked at the beast, he had killed way larger dragons, even without any special gifts. This however did feel different than the others, it was way more primitive and he could feel that it was natural. This wasn't some beast transformed through the use of wicked magic, it was an animal which had evolved on its own, being brought forth through eons of time. He knew it had to be intelligent, perhaps way more so than the dragons he had encountered and he believed that he knew why. The dragons created by the dark mages had been bred only to destroy, to create chaos and fear and wreak havoc upon villages and cities. A natural animal won't do that, so the dragons had to be stupid so they wouldn't resist the orders of their masters. It did make sense.

Zaray pointed at the wall, it was looming above them and made everybody feel tiny and vulnerable. "One more thing, when we enter the path you must not eat or drink anything from that place, if you do it will bind you to that dimension and you can never leave it, understood?"

Fastonar cringed. "So we have to bring everything with us, water and food and all?"

Zaray nodded sternly. "Yes, absolutely everything"

Taurin frowned. "The horses then, what about them? I don't think we can stop them from nipping at grass or leaves or whatever we come across of green stuff"

She snickered. "No, that would be hard, but it doesn't work that way with animals, they are safe so don't worry about that. It only affects intelligent self-conscious beings."

Dabin did grin at Rhuk. "Listen, you are completely safe then"

Rhuk did give Dabin the finger, just to show what he felt about that statement. Dhokay was obviously thinking hard. "The dark mages, can they affect the dimension? Does their will have any power there at all?"

Zaray made a grimace. "To be honest? I have no idea, when I escaped from the city I hadn't really started to realize how much the dark brotherhood had done and what they were capable of. I was way too naïve and believed that once I was out of there everything would be fine. I do fear that yes, they can enter that dimension and yes, they can use their magic there."

Ivran was laying down still, he was pale and Phraan thought that he was breathing in a funny way. "They will try to stop us, I just know they will"

Zaray looked at him, her eyes were almost tender. "Yes. Most probably."

Ivran swallowed and his eyes did tell of pain. "Listen, the dragons, they are protected against magical attacks right? That

I in fact killed one with magic has to have some sort of meaning, some sort of consequence, I just cannot see it"

Everybody looked at their neighbour, eyes filled with wonder. "Yes, we had to kill dragons the old fashioned way, with weapons."

Dhokay's voice was low and intense and then Shaluun made an odd sound. "Folks, I have an idea. I don't know if it is worth trying, or if I am thinking the right way but consider this. Why did they protect the dragons against magic in the first place?"

Even Zaray frowned, her eyes narrow. "I don't quite get it?"

Shaluun pointed at Phraan and the ring on his finger. "Magic leaves a trace, and that trace is like a piece of the one who created it right? Like a scent, left behind by someone who passed by."

Ivran nodded slowly, his eyes were hazy but he was recovering, although slowly. "Yes, I learned about that. A magic item can in fact reveal a lot about its maker"

Shaluun grinned. "This is maybe far-fetched but I was thinking, there aren't that many mages out there now is there? Even without the protection few dragons would be killed with magic, they are too many and a mage cannot really go out there and start killing dragons without being drained himself. There has to be another reason why they would use strength and time just to make the dragons that strong"

Phraan gasped. "Yes, yes damn it, dragons are hard to kill, some are impossible to slay even for us with experience, we can only hope to hurt them or help get people out of their way."

Zaray was gaping, her eyes were huge. "Of course, we have been fools. Not that it would have mattered at all but I see it now. "

Shaluun looked at her with large eyes. "You do?"

She was nodding vigorously, head moving so fast her hair was flying around. "Most certainly! They used magic to create the dragons right? That means that some of the magic would remain in the dragon and if it was killed outside of the wall that power would be lost to the mage who created it. Can't you see it? Killing dragons with magical means drains the dark mages!!"

Phraan stared at Ivran. "Then by the Gods, we could use a hundred mages like you lad"

Shaluun had a silly expression upon his face. "They didn't try to protect the dragons, they tried to protect themselves. Their energy must be limited then"

Zaray swore, "Of course it is limited, therein lay their biggest weakness. Even a dark mage cannot go beyond his limits. The core to this is that heart stone. I just knew it, even that has limitations."

Dhokay tilted his head. "It did sound very powerful if you ask me?"

She sighed and her hands moved, as if she was trying to indicate a shape in front of her. "Yes, it is, it is very powerful, but think of it as…as a lake. You can drain water from a lake, in fact you can lead water from it through countless little canals but they cannot be too wide or too big for if they are what will happen?"

Dhokay looked down. "The water will flood them and tear them apart, it will create a flood"

Zaray pointed a finger at him. "Exactly! They cannot take too much from it at once, for if they do they won't be able to stop it, it will just keep flowing. If you grasp a tiger by the tail you'd better hold on or else you will be in deep trouble"

Phraan was no magician, he had little understanding of that power at all but he wasn't stupid. "So, if the dark brotherhood takes too much from the heart stone it will do what to them? Kill them?"

Zaray bit her lower lip. "Wouldn't that be just great? No, I don't think so. Magic in itself doesn't work that way, at least when the person in question is used to it. I bet that dark mages are well trained in warding off magical attacks and thus capable of protecting themselves against overflow. I think that the creation of these new dragons and everything else has been done with the mages as a conduit. They are the canals leading power from the lake, the heart stone. And if the dragons did die by magic then maybe that canal would remain open and well, I don't know but it doesn't sound like a good idea"

Ivran was listening intently, he was thinking hard. "It does make sense in a way. Like water running through a canal the magic would rip things along with it, and it bet the mages knows that. Forcing them to spend more power at once could in fact be a good idea."

Dhokay frowned. "But it would just drain power from the stone then, not themselves?"

Ivran raised himself up onto his elbow. "Some of their own energy would be forced to join that magic, they use spells to control the power yes? And the spells come from the mage, not the magic itself."

Shaluun snapped his fingers. "Spells too powerful to control, I have heard of such. Spells which allow the magic to run amok."

Ivran groaned. "Yes, there are such spells, I did learn of them, but no mage would ever use them."

Zaray was squinting, she had turned towards Ivran. "Yes, but for the sake of this conversation, let's say that a dark mage in fact did use one of those spells, what would happen to him?"

Ivran took a deep breath, there as pain in his expression and he was breathing rather fast. "Uh, hard to tell for nobody has ever done it, but theoretically? If that mage was tapping into the energy of the heart stone while using such a spell I bet the torrent of energy would just...burn him out"

Thiana shuddered. "Literally?"

Ivran shook his head. "No, but it would drag the energy in him with it, he would be left with no magic at all."

Phraan cocked his head. "Unless he is prepared and shields himself somehow"

Zaray nodded. "Yes, that is an option we have to take into consideration. I bet they are aware of the potential danger here and have ways to prevent it from ever happening"

Shaluun did slap his own knees, his face wry. "Know what? We need something specific to fulfil this mission"

Zaray tilted her head, looked a bit bewildered. "What?"

Shaluun was grinning. "A dark mage. One we can interrogate"

She whistled. "And that will be so easy to accomplish, are you nuts? They won't hesitate killing at all. And believe me, they can turn someone inside out with a few words, I have seen it!"

Shaluun did still keep that grin on his face. "Yes, but dark mages are forced to be in control of themselves, chaos springs from order right? And they are probably trying to climb within their ranks all the time so magical attacks must be rather common"

Zaray blinked a few times. "Ah, yes? I do remember that even if the mages back when I was a prisoner had little to do they did bicker and fight, although subtly."

Shaluun spread his arms. "Then an ordinary mundane attack won't be anticipated now will it?"

Zaray did glare for a second. "Ah, they do have guards? The city is a real city and many are employed by the dark brotherhood. There are soldiers everywhere!"

Shaluun rolled his eyes. "A soldier who never has seen battle is no soldier, he may be trained well but facing a real situation does require something few achieve before they have fought a few times. A calm mind even in the heat of battle, the ability to stay cool, to keep thinking instead of acting out of sheer panic."

Tersus had been lying down and he had apparently been asleep, but now he sat up and rubbed his head. Zaray cringed, the man had lice, he just had to have lice. There was no way someone like that didn't have parasites. "A diversion. You need a diversion, and a huge one too"

Everybody stared and the alchemist sort of grunted and scratched his crotch, rather unembarrassed. "If there are soldiers in the city, who do you think the mages will sacrifice first when something happens? Themselves? No, the men. It is always the masses who has to pay the price when the high and mighty wants something done"

Zaray did wet her lips. "So? What are you saying?"

Tersus shrugged. "If you charge all in and just try to destroy stuff you won't last, even a fool can understand that and I am no fool. If you are expected they will be on guard, they will look for you and everybody will be tense as shit, expecting an attack. You cannot allow yourself to be that predictable."

Dhokay opened his mouth, he was rather intense. "Go on!"

Tersus waved his arms around and those close to him did cringe, the smell was ghastly. "They will be looking for someone powerful, for warriors, for mages. They won't look for someone like me, a ragged old fellah with a beardless lad as a servant and not even a penny to my name. But I have something just as powerful as any mage, I have alchemy!"

Zaray sort of grunted. "And you suggest that you go in first?"

He nodded, a wide grin cut the face in two and Peter did turn green, the man didn't brush his teeth that were for darn sure. "Yes, we hide, we prepare and then we set off something which will confuse them. I bet the dark mages won't expect the power of alchemy, they will be looking for magic and find nothing and then, when they are scratching their heads trying to understand this you may strike"

Phraan did tilt his head. "Know what? That might even work"

Dhokay nodded slowly and the wild eyes did reveal some reluctant respect. "It may, but Tersus, if they catch you?"

The alchemist nodded. "I know, I know, no mercy will be shown or what? Believe me, I am not afraid of death. But I am afraid of having lived in vain and I have seen what those dragons do, I want to help and if my life can save some poor sod so be it"

Peter nodded. "That goes for me too, I have done some stupid things in my life, but this…this is not stupid at all"

Shaluun and the two dwarves did look a bit shocked. Rhuk pulled at his beard and he did look a bit nervous. "Listen, I have seen that you have brought a lot of stuff with you but can you really create something which can pull the attention of the mages away from the fact that the rest of us is coming?"

Tersus nodded. "Mages or not, they are flesh and blood and I have ideas, and the means with which to put them into action.
"

Zaray folded her arms, her expression a bit stern. "Right then, when we reach the city Tersus and Peter must prepare the way."

Everybody just nodded and the alchemist dragged Peter aside, apparently to discuss the plans. The others did fall silent and Zaray stretched. "Let us rest and prepare ourselves. The hidden path may have changed a lot since I used it, so don't be surprised by anything you may see"

Thiana and Taurin did look worried and Fastonar was chewing on a piece of dry meat and his eyes were distant. Phraan did lie down and he felt the mountains as something which was almost pushing down on him, even when he couldn't see them. Another dimension, he just wondered what that meant. He felt the ring, it didn't move and it was as if it was a part of him now, merged with his flesh and bone. It probably was, if he was to remove it he probably had to cut off his finger. The dragon laid there breathing slowly and Phraan wondered at its motifs, there had to be a reason why it had chosen to stay with them, not go back to its own place. It was so different from all other dragons he had seen, not only was it wingless but the shape and the body was …he couldn't quite find the words to describe it. It was powerful, elegant, the hide thick and the claws and jaws capable of creating terrible injuries but that wasn't its prime function. Like Zaray had said, it was natural.

Phraan missed Vitile, and he missed Imeah too, her death still filled him with rage and he was going to seek justice for this, for it all. He just knew that he would have to wait. The small camp was silent, Rhuk and Dabin did feed the horses and Zaray's mule and Phraan looked over at her. She had met his father, travelled with him, had known him. Phraan's heart was overflowing with questions now, and he was aching to find the answers but this wasn't the time for it. Zaray did notice that he was staring and she got up and walked over to him, sat down. Fastonar did throw a suspicious glance at her but she ignored it. "I said that some things were for your ears only and I meant it."

He looked at her, then he looked down. "Yes, I remember."

She sighed. "It isn't easy for you, and I understand. Learning new things about oneself never is."

He pulled his legs up, leaned his chin onto his arms. "I agree, I haven't really been able to understand any of it, yet. I don't even know what I am capable of now."

Zaray did cross her legs, she was very agile and her eyes did reflect the faint light there rather well. "The difference is subtle Phraan, but you will sense it when you need it. When you fought those dreghil, what did you feel, deep within?"

Phraan swallowed. "I felt…content, as if it was what I was born to do, as if killing such deviltry was a job I needed to do and did well"

She caressed his arm. "Yes, you did very well. Your father would be very proud of you"

Phraan felt sad again. "I am so sorry I never got to meet him, what was he like? His personality I mean?"

Zaray snickered. "Stark raving mad, no that was poorly expressed. He was…cheerful, brave, often way too bold and he did love life Phraan. He was so full of it, so sparkling with just sheer joy. Oh he could be a rogue for certain, use a mouth so foul a troll would pass out hearing it and in a fight? Even a God would run for cover. His wrath was legendary Phraan, he was a fighter like none other."

Phraan looked down. "So what was he doing in that city then?"

Zaray lowered her voice, leaned her head onto his shoulder, like two intimate friends would. "Here come the things which only you are to hear. Listen well"

She closed her eyes and her voice became so low it was almost impossible to hear, even for him. Her lips didn't move, for anyone watching she looked as if she was half asleep, seeking warmth from his body. "He wasn't there just to steal, he was there because my tribe sent him. They knew where I was, but they hadn't come up with a way to get someone in there undiscovered, before he volunteered"

Phraan swallowed. "Why was that? Aren't there elves in the city?"

She was breathing slowly, eyes still closed. "Yes, some. Trapped there after the wall was erected. But we are different Phraan, and this is what you need to store in your heart and not tell anyone. Our magic is primeval, it is the original force from which all other magic once came"

He blinked, pretended to be working on the laces of his boots. "And?"

She was heavy against his chest. "The heart stone may sense us the moment we get through the wall, and so can the mages. It can recognize us, and it will most certainly reach out to us in some way if it does."

Phraan frowned. "And that is a bad thing?"

She nodded. "They have corrupted it remember? It serves the dark mages, the brotherhood. Its pure force tainted by an evil will. The mages will try to catch us, in every way that they can. Just because we are who we are."

Phraan felt confused. "So it is under their control?"

She nodded slowly. "Indeed it is, but I don't think it wants to be controlled."

He sighed. "Yes, I remember what that shaman said, that the lands were different before."

Zaray grasped his hand, caressed it. "Phraan, the mages will want to drain our powers, to merge them with that stone. That way they can access our skills and use them. I know that this is what they did to weaker mages back in the days."

Phraan hissed. "That is terrible!"

She let out a soft sigh. "Yes, and that is why my tribe sent your father to find me. I was getting old enough to access my true powers and they couldn't afford that this fell into the hands of the brotherhood. Gilrian too had to cloak his true nature, to avoid detection. He had a magical amulet which allowed him to hide his magic from the heart stone but that was lost when he died. He did face some tricky situations but managed to get out of them, not by using magic but by using his charm and his wits. He was very charming when he wanted to, could probably twist even a troll around his little finger given enough time. "

Phraan smiled, a sad smile. "I am not that charming I fear"

She giggled, a small movement revealed it. "No, you are blunter I must say, not as sophisticated. But here is the thing, they will try to find us if they are made aware of our presence, and we cannot let them do that. It may ruin everything"

He nodded and pulled his boots off. "Why can't the others be told of this?"

She sighed. "Because we will endanger them! And if they don't know this they cannot reveal it, even under torture. "

Phraan looked down. "The mission before all else?"

She smiled but it was a sad smile. "Yes, so if the heart stone does reach out to you don't let it gain access to your soul, ward it off, close your mind. It is impure, it will seek to corrupt you."

Phraan remembered something. "Imeah?"

Zaray pulled her cloak closer to her body. "Is already at work Phraan, she was cursed, and now she is free from the curse. Her spirit will help us, you'll see."

Zaray seemed to genuinely wish to sleep like that, curled up to him so he just pulled his blanket over himself and let her stay there. "Thanks for the warning though, I will keep my eyes open"

Zaray just mumbled. "It isn't the eyes which should be alert, it is your soul."

She appeared to drift off into sleep and Phraan did too, after a while and some serious thoughts.

The area used for the breeding of dragons was vast, a bowl shaped plain some miles north of the gorge where the city was placed. It was divided into sections by huge walls and several mages were at work there. It did take a lot to do this, and the beasts did also have needs like all other living beings. Now the storages were almost empty, there wasn't much meat left and the dragons were hungry and very impatient. The other creatures too were waiting to be unleashed and the mages were busy making preparations. Back when Ognias had awakened the dragons the strong had been called back to the city and from them the new flock had been created. Natural breeding didn't allow them to change the beasts very fast, dragons will only start to lay their eggs when they are mature, which for many of the species could take more than a hundred years. The mages didn't have time for that, but the gems which had been enriched by the power of the magical source did speed things up. Dragon after dragon had been subdued with magic and a gem forced into its chest. Then it was just a matter of days before the transformation started, making the beast so much stronger than before. The other creatures too were changed, ancient spells and ideas left by the first ones made into flesh and the dark brotherhood didn't doubt even for a moment that this horde of monstrosities would make everyone surrender to their rule.

The plain was buzzing with life, roars and shouts filled the air and the mages who dealt with the transport of the creatures were placed at one end of it, constantly chanting. A wall of light had appeared between them and the beasts did rush forth, disappearing into it and reappearing somewhere out on the plains. The magic was crackling in the air, making it heavy and hard to breathe in. This was the start of the final attack, soon everything they had would be out there and nothing could stop them. Thousands of dragons had already been sent south and with them other monsters as well, these were among the last groups to be sent off.

When Simaon killed Jurza he opened up a new position as high mage, it was already claimed by one of the senior mages there. Siverel had been a friend of Ognias, one of his most loyal followers and he had never forgiven Simaon for murdering his friend. Simaon had been useful, but not very wise and now he was glad that the man was dead. The body had been fed to the dragons and the entire brotherhood had been celebrating. Siverel stared down at the plain from a platform built into the mountain side, he was not all that impressed. Like Jurza he knew that they went along too fast, that they ought to have tested the new dragons first, to have waited for yet a couple of decades. But the brothers did push forth, eager to finish what they had started and he knew that little could change their opinions.

He sighed, his hands caressing the cold metal of the railing and he made a grimace. He did doubt his brothers, all of them. Few did have the discipline the ancient ones had had and none of them their wisdom. This was something he would have to work very hard to control and he didn't think that they would be able to rein these monstrosities in whence the lands surrendered.

Just like the dreghil Simaon's little obedient idiots had unleashed, it was written all over the ancient texts that this was something the first dark mages just had thought about, not something they really truly wanted to use against an enemy. There is a huge difference between reality and fantasy, and between having an idea and turning it into something so terrible. Somehow the dreghil had disappeared, the mages who had unleashed them had been punished, it was just natural and he was rather sure that the dreghil had been too unstable to exist for very long. They had probably just dissolved and that was good for the very idea gave Siverel the creeps. The balance wasn't there now, it was all a giant mess and he hated the fact that he would have to be the one to find heads and tails to this madness. Simaon had been whipping them all into frenzy, they had been storming towards the goal like a herd of racehorses down a track, quite literally dying to get there first and now he was the leader of a huge house which had been built on a bog, not solid ground.

He groaned and turned around, went back into the deep tunnels. He knew of Simaon's plan, the magical force which had killed one of their dragons and then been felt a few more times, he did see why Simaon would want to claim that force for himself but the man had really been a giant airhead. The dreghil hadn't stopped that person and whoever was with him or her, so now he would have to get something organized. Several mages had in fact been killed, they had dropped dead for some reason and he knew that there was something else out there, something which made him truly doubt Simaon's sanity. Simaon had left such a royal mess it made Siverel wish that they had buried Simaon after all, that way he could have pissed on the man's grave.

He had read the old prophecies and they did make him worry, he did respect his forefathers and he did see that they had been wise and able to see things in a very different light than the mages and brothers of these days. He was the last bastion of that old tradition and he did miss Badrian and his calmness and understanding of the past. He walked by a few servants who bowed deeply and saw that the brotherhood had gathered around lord Buraz, Arabur stood next to him and looked very important and Siverel snorted and ignored them, walked straight by the door. His respect for the brotherhood was minimal since neither of them were true mages, they just saw mundane power as worth anything, money, wealth, influence. In the old days the brother hood had all been mages and things had been so much better. The ability to change the very fabric of existence with a word, to peer into the deep mysteries of nature and creation and understand them, nothing could ever be as precious as that.

He did hurry back to his chambers, like most mages his rooms were rather Spartan and contained little luxury. The only joy Siverel did allow himself was a bathtub. He loved hot baths, and he had since he was a child. He had been a very frail lad when he grew up and his mother had taken him to hot springs quite often since it eased the ache in his bones. A frail body did force his mind to become strong and it did. He was not as strong as Jurza had been nor as wise as Ognias but he was practical. He knew how to lead and how to keep everything together without losing sight of the details. He was sure he would be able to do his job well, as long as nothing went wrong. He sat down by his desk and wrote a note, his handwriting was elegant and powerful and he grasped the note when the ink had dried and brought it outside to a servant. "Take this to the head of the city guards. It has to happen immediately. And then show it to brother Asmal, his mages has to prepare"

The servant just bowed and ran off and Siverel sighed and sat down, opened a book. It had once belonged to Badrian and it showed a drawing of an odd looking blade. He had no idea of what sort of sword it was but the sight sent shivers down his spine. Badrian had marked that page, but why? The language this book was written in was unknown and the book so old it was a miracle that it still existed. He stared out into the air, he had felt what Jurza too had discovered, that the crystal which allowed them to get the dragons through the wall had been weakened. It had felt quite odd to be near it and he didn't understand why? Had they drained it somehow? He had ordered a mage to create a conduit from the true source under the city to the gem, to make sure that it didn't just close their gate so to speak. It was the only idea he had managed to come up with. There was something there he just couldn't grasp, something he didn't understand and that was annoying to say the least. He had visited the gem earlier that day and he had almost felt a sort of presence there. It had been fleeting and very weak so he hadn't been able to get a grasp at what it was.

He closed the book and sighed, stared down at his own hands. Siverel was a very tall lanky man with thin hair and a drawn face. Some would say that he did look melancholic, and that he appeared to be a very soft and mellow person. Siverel wasn't like some other mages who believed that you had to be like ice to be able to control the forces of chaos, he didn't enjoy ordering people around and he did absolutely not enjoy forcing others to do things they didn't like. He could be strict and even cruel if he needed to but he preferred to have faith in his co-workers and let them do things the way they thought were best. Things worked best that way, he had discovered that many decades ago and he had seen first-hand what sort of havoc too strict discipline can create within a crowd. His father had been a general in king Vhandar's army and he had been very fond of extreme discipline. When a battle was to be fought his men were the first to flee, simply too broken to care whether or not they were being killed by the enemy or hanged by their own. He would never go in that direction.

But the presence was growing in his mind, creating a distraction and he grimaced and got up, walked to his library of ancient books and scrolls. He stared at the titles, some of the books were priceless and he loved them like his children but there was nothing there which could explain this to him. He was wringing his hands, the main library perhaps? There was a lot there and he was sure that the books gathered in what had been Badrian's little collection could shed some light on this. Badrian had collected so much, things nobody even though about anymore. He put his cloak on and made sure that he did look calm and collected, wandered outside without looking at the guards placed by his door.

The main library was underneath the citadel and it was enormous, a cavernous hall with row upon row of books and you could easily get lost if you didn't know where you were going. Thankfully Siverel knew the library like the back of his hand and he walked straight to the shelves holding Badrian's collection. He stopped and stared, which books to start with? It was an important question for even with his knowledge there were thousands of books and scrolls in the collection. He saw that Badrian had organized them by theme and he made a small grimace and wandered off to an entire shelf dedicated to the theme ghosts and apparitions. The presence had felt as if it was someone, not something and with the number of deaths in this city, well, ghosts were not that unthinkable. He picked a random book called "The spirit in lore and myths of olde" and sat down to go through it. He was used to reading a lot of text in one go by simply skimming over it until he saw something which caught his interest. This book was well written and very well put together too, the different topics easy to find and he sat down to focus.

After a while he had to rest and rub his eyes. The light down there was very bright due to magical lighting but it did strain the eyes and he blinked and made some grimaces to soften his muscles. His jaws were aching for he had the unfortunate habit of clenching his teeth when he was reading fast. He had just one chapter left and he doubted that he would find anything there, but the book had been read a lot, he could see that and only Badrian would have bothered as far as he knew. It had to contain something valuable. He took a deep breath and started to read yet again and before long he stopped and had to stare, he started reading slowly, what was this all about? He was gripped by a growing suspicion, ran over to another part of the shelf system and ripped another book out of the rows, opened it and slammed it down onto the table, his fingers seeking something he knew he had heard Badrian read out loud decades ago. He stared down, compared the texts and his heart was hammering harder and harder, his eyes got huge and he sat down with a thud. He felt nauseous, this could not be true. Cold sweat did break out all over him and he stared out into nothingness. Too late, it was too late, what was he to do now? "Oh Gods what have we done?"

His voice was a mere whisper, he held onto the table with both hands, as if he was afraid of collapsing onto the floor. He stared at the words written in the book, words some long forgotten mage once had left there as a clear warning. Badrian hadn't managed to make the connection, he had been too used to thinking in a linear fashion, Siverel however had a mind which sometimes would behave like some rabbit in a field of cabbages, one hop in this direction and another in that direction and the result would be a very winding path. He leaned back, rested against the chair, feeling slightly exhausted. "So, this was what they knew, what the past has hidden from us. Badrian was right all along, she will return, the one we have forgotten, and with her…"

Siverel did mourn the fact that none of them were elves, elven memory can last for ages and never fade but a human can live for a century at the most and if not written down on solid paper that person's thoughts and memories will be lost forever. He was lost for words, also for actions. He was the leader, they should obey him but that was in theory. He would never be able to make them change their mind and it was already too late, none of them strong enough to control what they had created. He closed his eyes and felt old for the first time in his life, his strength drained by this. He sat there for a while, just trying to come up with a plan, then he took a deep breath and his eyes were hard when he opened them. "Yes, it is as it must be, I know what I have to do now."

He got up, closed the books and hid them on the shelf. The brothers couldn't learn of this, he had to play his cards very well. He now knew what Badrian had done, it was very clear. And he did understand, and he did also agree. There could be no victory, no glory. The only one triumphant when all this was over would be death. He gasped and leaned onto the shelf. There would be no way back whence he did this, and he would face neither mercy nor understanding. They would never understand. He walked back towards his rooms feeling a strange sort of strength, he had made a choice, and he would stand by it, come what may. His orders had been given and couldn't be changed without the others getting suspicious but he could do more, so much more. Even strength is worth nothing if it can be turned against you. He ordered a meal to be brought to his rooms, the plan had to be made in detail, and he couldn't allow himself to do any mistakes at all. After he had eaten he sat down with some parchment and a pen, he had developed his own personal alphabet and nobody else would be able to understand this. Finally he would be able to do something truly grand, something which would be remembered throughout history and change the world. He felt truly humble as he put a pen to the parchment, he just prayed that nothing went wrong.

The morning had come with freezing rain and they were shivering as they prepared to find the hidden path, the horses stood in a small group and looked less than happy and Phraan saw that Ghaday did appear among the rocks, the huge creature just passed by the dragon which lay there as if it was the most natural thing in the world and he wondered. The cat disappeared again and Phraan saddled Drake and saw that Zaray was staring at the vertical wall with an odd expression on her face, she did look as if she did loathe the very existence of that mountain. Everybody got up and they took off, the dragon was following them, its eyes were calm and Phraan did yet again wonder what it did know and what it did want. Zaray did find a very narrow path leading towards the rock face, some boulders lay there but otherwise the ground was surprisingly even and covered with sand and it did look as if the massive mountain had somehow been pushed up, from the very bowels of the earth itself. The smoothness of the stone was unnatural and it did shine, like polished glass. Zaray did ride along it for a couple of hours, then she slowed down and gathered the group around her. "You all have water and food for many days?"

Ivran had gotten a lot better but he was still not himself, he had however managed to bring them lots of bread and sausage and also water skins. It was very clear that he started to get a grasp of the gift he carried and that his understanding of it got stronger. "Yes, we do have enough for a small army"

Zaray turned towards the wall, she did look nervous. "Remember, you are to enter a different realm altogether, nothing here is what it seems to be. Don't let yourself get thrown out of balance."

She closed her eyes and raised her hands, a strange pattern of light started to appear upon the rock, as if the rock was transparent and the pattern hidden behind it. It did glow brighter by the second and then the surface of the rock changed and looked like thick mist. Zaray grasped the mule by the reins. "Hurry now, it only stays open for a few minutes"

She pulled the animal after her and disappeared into the mist and Phraan turned his head around and took a look at the surroundings, to remember them if this was the last time he saw this world. A shadow passed overhead and he gasped, it was flying dragons, hundreds of them, huge monsters and they were all heading south. There was indeed not a moment to waste anymore. He followed Zaray into the mist and it felt like walking into a waterfall, only that it wasn't water at all. He gasped and closed his eyes involuntarily, Drake neighed and he felt that the others were right behind him. When he did open his eyes he did stare at something completely unbelievable and he couldn't trust his own eyes at all. This was just too much! First of all, it was obviously summer, and it was hot too, and the landscape which surrounded them was as far from the naked mountain plains as you could possibly get. They were surrounded by softly rolling hills, all covered with forest and they stood in the middle of clearing between two hills. Up in a distance the magical wall could be seen, as a shining piece of glass. Zaray did look shocked. "Right, this is not the place I went through on my way out so many years ago but I sort of guessed that this could be the case."

Phraan gaped, the trees were giants, with wide and rather flat canopies and the place had a sort of vibrancy to it which was breath-taking. It felt like a wonderful place, he couldn't describe it otherwise. Taurin and Thiana did embrace each other and both did grin from one pointy ear to the other, they seemed to be completely stunned by this forest. Phraan had to shake his head for a moment, wood elves!

Dhokay and Shaluun had their weapons within reach and Tersus was glaring with eyes so huge they looked as if they were about to pop right out of his skull. He did look ridiculous. Peter was just curious and Phraan had to admit that it was a very lovely place. Huge vines did grow up along the branches of the trees and they had flowers in bright colours and Zaray sighed and pointed up ahead. "The wall is our goal but it will take us time to get there. It is farther than it looks from here"

She grasped the mule by its reins and it snapped at her, angry since she had disturbed it. There was grass and green plants everywhere and the horses were already very busy stuffing themselves. It did look like an absolutely stunning and lush forest somewhere south, perhaps on one of the islands along the coast but it was warmer and there were more species. Phraan did look at the trees, they were obviously very old but strong and healthy and he felt that this land was in its prime. Dhokay was grumbling. "It looks normal enough"

Rhuk and Dabin had sort of sought each other's company, they stood so close together one could have believed that they were trying to get in under the skin of the other dwarf and their eyes were huge and filled with fear. Crap, dwarves are in fact afraid of dense forests, the gods alone knew why but they were. Both held their axes in vice like grips and were sweating and Rhuk was glaring at the trees and he was pale. "Akhi curse it, they will fall over us!"

Zaray rolled her eyes. "Listen to yourself dwarf! These trees are healthy, they won't fall. Even a hurricane couldn't fell these trees"

Dabin was panting. "Oh they will, they want to crush us, I know it!"

Dhokay had to glare at the two. "If both of you hacked away at one of these trees with your axes you would still have to spend at least a week before you managed to fell it, so relax. The trees are not dangerous"

Rhuk just mumbled something about silly brainwashed elves and Dabin looked down, his chin was trembling. Shaluun pointed at something. "Folks, look at that!"

A herd of deer had entered the clearing and now the animals were staring at them from a distance, obviously curious. Phraan had believed that this land was like the one he was used to but now he had to reconsider that notion. The deer were huge, larger than Drake and bright white with a blood red stripe along their backs. They had very long necks and two very long tails each and the head was wide and rather long and they had antlers which looked more like a shrubbery than normal antlers. The leader let out a bawling sound and the herd moved along, a few little ones hesitated and stared at them with huge innocent eyes before they followed their moms. "Those are the most peculiar deer I have ever seen!"

Phraan had to pinch himself to make sure he wasn't dreaming, deer that large? Zaray got up onto her mule. "Like I have said, don't let anything here shock you, and try not to touch anything. We have no ideas of what's harmful and what's not."

They started riding through the forest and the trees were like enormous columns, here and there sunlight streamed through the canopy in bright beams and the forest floor was rather even and covered with a dense layer of dead leaves. There was a track there, probably made by the deer and they followed it. Phraan was on guard the entire time and the huge cat was called forth and watched their left flank while the dragon took the other. A world this lush and full of life is never without dangers. Huge insects did zoom back and forth between the trees and once a dragonfly did hover above them, the size of a huge eagle. Rhuk and Dabin didn't say a word, both were too shocked and Tersus was sitting there trying to make notes of everything he saw. They had ridden for a while when they saw yet another example of how different this world was, some animals came into view using the track and they were the size of rabbits but they appeared to have six legs, two sets of very powerful hind legs and a set of very long front legs which looked like arms with very long fingers. The ears were so long it did look absurd and it was obvious that these were herbivores for they were munching away at pieces of dry bark which had fallen from the trees.

Dhokay cringed. "That has to be extremely dry food if you ask me! "

The animals did notice them and let out some peculiar chirping sounds, then they sort of jumped over to the nearest tree and shot upwards with powerful kicks. They were obviously able to jump all the way up to the lowest branches in one go. Zaray was gaping and the others did stare too, it shouldn't have been possible. Thiana and Taurin were still in awe and they did sort of tune into the forest they rode through, their faces did reveal a great deal of joy and wonder and Taurin pointed at the trees. "They are so old, I cannot even describe it. I think these trees could be more ancient than our own world, they grow so slowly!"

Zaray looked back at them. "Can you communicate with this forest?"

Thiana nodded. "Yes, we can feel it, it welcomes us, but there are dangers here. We can sense that the forest tries to warn us."

Shaluun held his axes near and Peter had attached his sword to the saddle horn, so he could reach it easily. They were all nervous, but also caught by a feeling of reverence. This world did seem very pure, it held little which could be seen as evil in any way. Thiana pointed at some huge flowers which grew on a bush not far from the path. "Do not touch those, the pollen is poisonous and can cause you to suffocate"

Phraan smiled at her "Good, keep warning us"

After a while they reached the bottom of the valley and here it was rather moist and a small river did run through the landscape, rather slowly. The water did tempt them but they remembered that nothing there could be eaten so they used their water skins instead. They had crossed when Taurin suddenly shouted a warning and it wasn't a second too late for a short legged animal with one pointy horn did rush out from a bush with a roar and aimed for Dabin and his small horse. The animal looked as if someone had deliberately cross bred a rhino and a warthog and it was ugly and obviously pissed. Thiana had her bow ready and fired within the blink of an eye and the animal fell with an arrow through its eye. The horn could easily have gutted a horse. Taurin swallowed. "It wasn't really aggressive, it wanted to defend its territory but it would have killed anyone getting in its way"

Phraan smiled and looked at the dead creature, it had very thick hide but here and there he did see some scars and if he wasn't very wrong about it, those were the scars of claws. Surely there were predators there. He made the others aware of it. "When the prey can jump up into the trees that way, and other animals have armour like that I think it is safe to say that there are some creatures here we'd rather not bump into"

Dhokay swung his hammer around, as if to familiarize himself with its weight. "I agree, everybody, keep your eyes and ears open."

Peter didn't look at Tersus but he sort of scoffed. "And your noses, who know, maybe there are really smelly beasts here!"

Phraan managed not to laugh, it was rather clear what Peter was referring to but Tersus didn't notice that little hint at all. He was too busy trying to sketch the dead animal. Zaray rolled her eyes. "Let's go folks, it is a long way to the wall, we'd better get moving"

The city had been quiet after the group left and Janok had ordered the soldiers to strengthen the surrounding wall with sharp poles and also using what was referred to as foot-irons. It wouldn't do much good against a flying dragon but any creature running around on the ground would get their feet pierced. He had gotten some special made, way larger than normal and they were buried in the sand so the sharp spikes were out of sight. Janok was nervous, there hadn't been any major attacks since the group left them and Crassian shared his worries. The officer was often seen on the wall, helping with the work or asking questions, he wanted to know as much as he could about the dragons and their strategies. It was already very apparent that they didn't just attack randomly, they were controlled and sometimes they skipped smaller settlements and went straight for the large ones. The other outposts had answered, attacks everywhere, from the east to the west and the dragons did move south like a steady glacier, pushing everything in front of it out of the way.

The city did contain a lot of refugees and every building was filled up to under the roof. The major problem now was the lack of resources, there wasn't enough food, and the drinking water was dwindling too. The wells had started to run dry, they hadn't been dug deep enough and couldn't supply this many people with water over time. Some tried to dig down, some wells were large enough for that and it seemed that it was a success but Janok was not convinced that it was. He knew a thing or two most others didn't and he had already ordered that all the water from the new wells was to be boiled before anyone drank from it, used it too cook or took a bath. There were people everywhere and the hygiene was suffering, the latrines were overflowing and the stench attracted flies by the million. Janok feared an outbreak of disease just as much as he feared a dragon attack. They had seen lots of dragons lately, the scouts had seen huge herds moving southwards and species they hadn't encountered before. Some even said they had seen some sort of ghastly wolf like monsters in the night and they had been followed by what the soldiers had described as undead dwarves and some sort of ghastly apparitions which glowed in the dark and dissolved everything around them. Many of the patrols hadn't returned and he knew that these brave men were dead.

Janok sat in his office and he was reading through the diary of a man who had been the commander of this city three centuries ago, he had been in a similar situation, not dragons but drought. The city had been flooded with desperate people and before long many were dead. In fact the death toll had been so great many believed that the gods would claim every living soul in the area and it was in fact an old native who saved the remaining population. He convinced them that the city was cursed and everybody left to get away from it and then the disease stopped. The old ones knew that it was in the water and Jacobar of Twelve towers had written it all down. The natives of the land had told him that the disease originated from the small voles which lived under the grass roots. They didn't get sick but people would if they drank water contaminated by their droppings and when it got dry the voles would be forced up to find more food and their habit of shitting while on the move proved to be fatal to many. The city with its abundance of food was like a feast to the small rodents and that was why the old commander had made it against the law to kill a cat, and made it mandatory for every household to keep at least one.

Janok was afraid that history would repeat itself so he had placed soldiers by every well and water source and they had fires burning and boiled water by the barrel. It was the only way to be absolutely sure. Crassian wasn't that nervous about epidemics, he was afraid of the dragons and he tried to make people realize that it wasn't any safer there than out on the plains. A small group of people was hardly anything the beasts would bother with but a city like this? It would be a sure target, sooner or later they would come. Crassian was a very brave man, he had never been afraid of death but he saw the countless faces cramped together behind those rather puny mud walls and he shivered. It would be a massacre. He did have his pride and his honour and he did try to rouse his men and prepare them for a fight they couldn't win but it was hard. He didn't want to watch good men die, and he didn't want to see all the women and children die neither. Trying to make people leave was hard, a few did see the wisdom in his words and took their belongings and left but so far that wasn't more than perhaps a hundred souls in all.

Janok had managed to gather all the men who could possibly fight, he had divided them into platoons lead by experienced officers but they didn't have that much of anything. Most had only their ordinary tools at hand, shovels, pitch forks and axes. They had a few hunters who had good bows and the smiths had been making arrows by the thousands but what good would arrows do against a huge dragon? The city's defences were pathetic and Janok knew that it was just symbolic. If the dragons did attack they wouldn't last more than a few minutes, at the most. Days had gone by since the group left and Crassian remembered the last battle and its outcome. If that woman hadn't fought for them they would all have been dead. Crassian did go to Janok late one evening, the first wells had run dry and some were getting desperate. It was cold and the winter had definitely fastened its grip over the land but people do need water nevertheless and the lines were long in front of every well that was left. It was a rather dry country to begin with and the ground water was deep. Janok was reading the latest reports, the scouts had reported several villages which had been completely erased off the map, and they had found remains of humans and animals scattered around.

Crassian sat down and his eyes were bloodshot, he hadn't really slept all that well for days. "Janok, do you have any pigeons left?"

Janok did look up, he did look gaunt and his eyes were haunted, all these people were his responsibility now. "Just a couple, why?"

Crassian took a deep breath. "We need to warn the cities to the south, the dragons will reach them soon"

Janok shook his head. "The birds we have won't do. They have never been south, they have been used for messages between us and the camps to the west of here. They won't find their way south"

Crassian swallowed hard. "That is too bad. The south needs to be warned about what's coming"

Janok sighed, leaned his head into his palms and he did look very tired. "I know, I do agree with you, totally. But like I said, we have no birds"

Crassian looked down, his suggestion was really not one he enjoyed to make but he had to. "If you send riders…."

Janok pointed at the map. "I have had the idea, believe me. But it is a ride which is hard as it is, and long. Even at full speed it takes weeks to reach the southern realm and the conditions are far from optimal. There will be dragons hunting those riders, constantly"

Crassian nodded. "Yes, they would have to be brave, and willing to sacrifice everything"

Janok folded his hands, stared at Crassian. "You are brave enough, you are a very capable knight and you do have a few soldiers left who are good riders. I suggest that you take this mission"

Crassian took a step back. "No, I am not expendable, I am needed here. I have to fight to defend this city and the people in it"

Janok stared out of the window. "Crassian, this city doesn't matter. It is hard to understand and even harder to say but it is the truth. We are perhaps fifteen hundred souls, if the dragons reach the major cities like Twelve towers or Oakfell the death toll will be tens of thousands"

Crassian felt oddly cold, Janok was right. "But even a warning may not be enough, those dragons…."

Janok smiled, a very sad smile. "Yes, they are monsters, much worse than those which were fought fifty years ago. But Crassian, if you stay here you will die, I am sure of it. None here will make it if the dragons do come for this city. Our defences are a joke, merely a way to mask the inevitable. If you go you may save some, isn't that a worthy cause?"

Crassian closed his eyes. "It feels like cowardice."

Janok patted his back. "It is not, the group left to try to stop the dragons at their source, and if they do manage to do that there will still be hordes of beasts out there, heading south. Go and warn the cities Crassian, you know the swiftest routes. You can do it"

Crassian swallowed hard. "Is that an order commander?"

Janok smiled, a very sad smile. "It is, tomorrow you will ride with as many men as you wish for, and the best horses we have here. You will leave at dawn"

Crassian sort of slumped forward and Janok grasped his hand. "It is not cowardice Crassian, it is common sense and a soldier knows this. You may have to sacrifice a few to save many"

Crassian took a deep breath. "Alright, I want just four others, a huge group will be easy to spot. I need fifty horses though, we'll leave the animals behind whence we have exhausted them. Ten horses for each man should last us a while."

Janok sent him a proud smile. "You will have it, it will be ready."

Crassian did salute the old commander and left the office, he had to pick four of the best riders and he didn't want to pick anyone with a family. Besides, he wanted small lean guys who weren't too heavy and able to ride for days. Choosing the right ones would be quite a job, he was rather sure that many would volunteer but they had to volunteer for the right reasons, not because they just wanted to get out of there.

When the morning came Crassian did have four riders ready, all were young guys and all were eager to go and do their duty. The horses were tied up in a long row behind each man and Crassian had put on armour and carried two swords and a spear. They all had spears and two had chain mail but the last two didn't have armour at all. They didn't own any and finding some that fit would take too long. They didn't carry many provisions, they would have to hunt for food and they wouldn't stop except for a couple of hours each night. All the men he had chosen came from the population to the west of

Twelve towers, they were originally nomads and lived their lives on horseback, and they would be able to sleep while riding if the need should arise. Janok wished them good luck and Crassian didn't hesitate, there was no time for heartfelt goodbyes. He spurred the dun mare he had chosen to ride first and they thundered out of the city. If they were to beat the dragons to it they would have to ride hard, have luck on their side and give a damn about their own safety and comfort.

Janok did see them go, they disappeared into the distance and he knew that he never would see any of them again. They were hope, a very fleeting hope but the king could perhaps save at least a few if the message reached him before the dragons did. The islands could shelter people from the wingless creatures but a winged dragon can find you wherever you hide. No, Crassian was the last straw, a desperate act of courage. If they were to make it only the group was capable of saving them. Janok did walk back inside, he had ordered that the city was shut off, nobody inn and nobody out, the snow would soon hide all tracks, he didn't want the paths to lead beasts to them. Some people had already fallen ill for not all did heed the warnings and there were more than one type of disease you can catch in such a crowded area. There were fleas and lice everywhere, the houses were cold and dank and there was little wood to burn, everybody lived in misery and Janok went over to the small alter placed by the door. He did light a candle, not that he had much faith in the Gods but this time he would pray, and mean every word he said. If they were to be saved it would require a miracle.

A group of the younger mages had gathered inside of the gates of the city, they were staring back at the citadel and their eyes were narrow and their expressions were rather harsh. None of them liked this, they saw that soldiers were ordered out and patrols were formed and distributed all over the city. The population had never been anything but cattle to them but they saw that this did create some disturbance and that was never good. The population did serve the mages and the brotherhood as their workers and servants and they just couldn't do without them. The magic and the constant search for new knowledge was time consuming and there was no time for mundane tasks as preparing food, washing and cleaning and keeping the citadel in perfect order. Now some people started to question the current state of affairs and they couldn't afford a rebellion.

The young mages had been ordered to protect the magical wall and make sure that nobody managed to get through it and they saw that order as sheer bullshit. Why should they fear anyone? The city had magical defences, and they were strong too. This was a waste of time and way below them. The old man Siverel had lost his mind for sure, they were mages, and they shouldn't have to bother with this. The wall was not going to fail, the magic allowed them to transport things through it to the outside world, not the other way around. They were five and they did all see themselves as the future leaders of the brotherhood, even as the high mage. Jurza had been a boring old fart and Siverel was even worse, these old men were too fond of the past to be allowed to rule their future. They lacked visions, they lacked ambitions. Surely some of the older and more experienced mages had been very useful since their skills made it possible to change the dragons and to create so many great new horrors. But they didn't allow the young ones their well-deserved place in the spot lights, the younger mages felt that they were being held back and they hated it.

Back in the days the training had lasted for at least twenty years, even after a mage left the academy. That meant that very few were any younger than forty years of age before they became a worthy member of the brotherhood. These days some had chosen the path while they were still studying and the youngest among the dark mages was barely twenty five. Naturally enough they were eager and full of themselves and also full of self-confidence. They needed to compete, to make everybody else see them for who they were and they all saw themselves as very valuable and high in power. The older mages were men who could have entered the academy again as teachers and nobody would have reacted, they were just like all other elderly chaps, nothing about them gave away their dedication to the dark path. These youngsters on the other hand would stand out in every crowd because of their rather outrageous attempts at making themselves look unique. Some shaved their heads, or parts of their heads. Others wore bizarre jewellery or strange clothing and tattoos and piercings seemed to be mandatory. The older mages scoffed and shook their heads, they knew the dangers of wearing too much bling while being around magic. A lightning bolt usually goes for anything with metal in it and some of the young ones were lightning rods by now. The experienced ones were having a small bet going on which one would end up fried first.

The five were wandering towards the magical wall, it was an awe inspiring sight and even they found it impressive still. They looked at each other and one of them shrugged. "So, what are we to do?"

They just stood there, the wall rose from the ground and looked like a solid piece of aurora borealis, it was hauntingly beautiful and the magic from it felt like the heat from the sun onto their skin. One of them sat down onto a rock. "Listen, this is freaking boring right? We are to guard this wall, and it doesn't need guarding. I say we try something new"

The oldest of them frowned. "What?"

The younger mage pointed at the wall and he was obviously having an idea, he gestured against it and his face was rather eager. "I have heard the others speak of what's behind the wall"

The oldest one was a mage in his early thirties, he was a rather calm man with strong belief and he was very intelligent.

He saw himself as the only really qualified mage among them. "The plains are on the other side silly!"

The young one shook his head, he had shaved his head except from right below the top of it where a thick lock had been kept and it formed a very long thin braid he had woven metal threads into. It did look idiotic the way the older mage saw it but it was fashionable. "No, that is further away. There is some sort of magical pocket between the wall and the plains. I heard the former high mage say it once. It is a dimension of its own"

The leader looked at the young mage with a cold glare. "And?"

The young one grinned. "We are to guard the wall aren't we, nobody said anything about us guarding it from this side?!"

The leader rolled his eyes. "Are you as daft as you look? Have your brains rotted? If you pass through the wall you won't be able to get back to this side!"

The young one grinned, he did look very triumphant. "Oh that won't be a problem, for I have this!"

He picked something out of his pocket, it was a tiny metal rod covered with mysterious symbols and the leader gasped. "Oronor, where in hells name did you get that one?"

Oronor did grin even wider. "Oh, I nicked it from the vault, I bet it will bring us back just fine now won't it?"

The leader was panting, what the young one had done was outrageous. Mages who had sworn themselves to the forces of chaos didn't follow rules and yet they had to, and this young one had just broken a very important one. Do never remove anything from the vault!

He took a deep breath. "Yes, it will get you through but it may also send you somewhere else, and you will have no idea of where! It is too dangerous, you are insane! This thing was in the vault for a reason, it can bring people through magical barriers yes but we don't know anything about the possible

379

dangers. If it was safe it would have been used to get the dragons through, years ago. You need to get the permission of the high mage to go through the wall, in any manner. We can send the dragons through but not ourselves without the high mages controlling the transport, it is too dangerous. The balance can be shifted."

Oronor shook his head. "That is just bullshit, are you a coward? I am eager to learn, isn't that what the old fossils always nags about, that we ought to learn? I am about to learn what's behind the wall and I won't let anything stop me"

The leader bit his lower lip. "It is dangerous you twat, you have absolutely no idea of where you'll end up. There are so many dimensions and some are lethal, there is no guarantee that you'll end up in the same one as these so called intruders, which I by the way doubt even exist"

Oronor was laughing. "I am no fucking novice right, I know how to take care of myself and I won't be alone, who's with me now, come on guys, don't be cunts"

The other three grinned and stepped forth, all looked eager and the leader felt a surge of panic. They were about to do something extremely stupid and he didn't have the power to stop them. Four against one is never fair, even if he was the strongest among them. Oronor was throwing the leader a very wry smirk. "See? You can guard this goddamn wall from the inside, we'll go and make sure that nothing attacks it from the important side."

He tried to come up with something to say but his voice wouldn't work, he had a bad feeling about this, a very bad feeling. "Remember the brothers who died? You could end up like them"

It was the only thing he managed to come up with. The four shook their heads and shot him some rather overbearing glances. "They were fools, I bet they used the wrong spells, or maybe those undead dwarves did devour their souls, it doesn't matter. We won't do any mistakes"

Oronor did gather the three around him and held the magical rod high above his head. "We'll stop this nonsense, Siverel is an old idiot, a dotard who sees danger where there is none. Come now, I want to see what's behind the wall"

A faint glow did surround the four and they walked towards the wall with determined steps. The leader stared helplessly as they walked straight through the shining barrier as if it wasn't there and he closed his eyes and tried to breathe slowly. This was just terrible, they had no idea of what they were doing! The magic controlling the wall was very delicate, he knew that bringing the dragons through put a great strain on it and that was why they couldn't just send dragons to the plains every day. They had to wait to let it recharge itself and he was afraid of a sort of bleed effect. When they brought in new pwople and goods they always waited for many months before trying again and it was always the best mages who did the job. These idiots had punched a hole in the wall this way and he was bloody sure it wouldn't just close itself up. This would weaken their defences, a lot! He sat down on a rock, stared at the place where the four had disappeared and he cringed. If this went to hell he would be the one they would blame, he had to find a way to ensure that this didn't end as a complete disaster but what? He had learned a lot more than those four since he was older and also, he did wish to learn for real, not just to gain power. A hole in the wall meant a hole in the wall and it wouldn't just pierce this dimension but all dimensions.

He bit his lower lip, should he run off and warn the high mage that the four had done this? Then he could come out of it as a hero but then again, he should have stopped them and he hadn't. He had one weakness which a dark mage shouldn't have, he did have empathy and he didn't like to kill. He tried to think, frantically, was there any spells he could use to close up the hole? His mind was reeling, going through every lesson he had ever had and then it dawned upon him, yes, that was a good one. He got up and focused, felt the connection to the magical source and smiled, this would work like a charm. He called forth the magic and uttered a spell, the words were surprisingly soft and he saw that the wall shimmered for a moment. Good, it was done, they were safe. He had shut off the hole, nothing would get through. He had done his job, now he could just sit there and wait for the others to fuck things up and he wouldn't help them. He chuckled and conjured up a nice comfortable armchair and some food and drink. Nobody would blame him now, he was safe.

Chapter 8: Heartstone

The world they rode through was warm, so much so that everybody had to strip off much of their clothes not to overheat and Phraan did notice, with some disbelief, that Tersus didn't remove even his jacket. The man kept every single piece of clothing on and sweat was pouring off him. It couldn't be healthy and Fastonar was staring at the alchemist with distaste. "I cannot fathom how he is alive?! Just look at him! He is so filthy I bet a dragon would think twice about devouring him."

Phraan tried to smile, he felt how his face felt stiff and unnatural. "Yes, maybe we all should stop washing, it would ward off all sorts of beasts"

Fastonar scoffed and shook his head. "He could get ill, I remember one knight in a unit I served in, he never washed his feet and kept his boots on all the time. He got really sick and when they finally got his boots off he had gangrene in several toes. They had to amputate his left foot and almost all the toes on his right one."

Phraan cringed and was glad he had been taught hygiene by his mother. Some people seemed to believe that a lair of good old-fashioned shit did protect you from all sorts of things but Tersus had taken it way too far. "I don't think Tersus is sick though"

Fastonar pointed at his head. "Oh but he is, in the head that is"

They were riding through a densely forested area now, the trees were of a different type than before, conifers which were so huge they reminded Phraan of small mountains and they had a very odd colour. They weren't as much green as blue. A deep dark indigo with just a hint of green in it and it was just breathtakingly beautiful and yet strange. The air was filled with a fragrance which was very soothing and fresh and some strange birds with four wings did sing from the branches. Each the size of a very large crane or stork and yet they were songbirds. They saw the wall up ahead still, and the distance was indeed greater than they had guessed it was. Phraan didn't like the idea of having to spend the night there but as of yet darkness hadn't fallen so he got the impression that time here was different than in their own world. Some huge centipede like creatures did scurry through the bushes, they looked like insects until you got closer to them and then he did see that they in fact were furry and not insects at all but they had at least eighty legs and small heads with several beady eyes and a long snout. This was a very bizarre world and Dhokay had smashed a couple of enormous mosquitoes with his hammer.

Zaray did look confident enough but Phraan did sense that she was nervous, why he didn't really know but he felt it somehow and wondered where that connection came from. The wall did throw an eerie but lovely light over the surroundings and up ahead they could see the crescents of at least three moons, it was really strange and Phraan didn't like it, it made him feel dizzy and disoriented. They were heading down a slope when they heard something screaming, and the ground started to shake a bit. Zaray shouted a warning. "Gather, quickly, something is coming!"

They drove their horses into a circle and Phraan felt his heart thunder, he had no idea of what they were about to face and neither did the others. The bushes there had very large leaves and now several bushes were ripped aside when something large burst forth. It was several huge animals, they did look a bit like a buffalo but their heads were more like that of a hippo and they had some sort of spines growing out of their backs and they were coloured in very bright nuances of red and blue. The animals were obviously terrified of something and ran for their lives and they didn't even look at the riders as they ran uphill so fast it was quite unbelievable. Zaray did look shocked. "They did run from something?"

Dhokay nodded. "Yes, prepare!"

The ground didn't shake but they heard the sound of wood being broken and a cloud of dirt and debris could be seen between the trees. The bushes did split again and Thiana did scream. It was a sort of snake, but it was so large it was twice the width of a horse and the head was just terrifying. It was probably able to bite over a horse's body and the teeth were very long and shiny but it didn't have the normal teeth of a snake. These did look more like sharks teeth and Shaluun couldn't stop a shout. "A wyrm?!"

Zaray swore and raised her hand, her bracelet started to glow and yet again that bow did appear, the wyrm did raise its head and hiss and it had seen them. Now it was racing towards them and the huge eyes were filled with sheer malice. Zaray did shoot, the glowing blue arrow did burst through the beasts head as if it wasn't even there and the wyrm collapsed and lay there, twitching. Dhokay did look very shocked. "Why use the bow now? You haven't used it since that attack"

Zaray let it disappear again. "No, for the magic in it is just too visible, but here I don't think it matters. And that thing doesn't belong here!"

Phraan turned Drake. "What do you mean?"

Zaray stared at the creature with distaste. "It is like us, it has come to this dimension from the outside."

Rhuk glared at the wyrm. "I have heard of wyrms, they are very dangerous. Has the dark mages brought it here perhaps? As a sort of guard dog?"

Zaray shook her head. "No, I don't like this. Something is very wrong"

She petted her mule. "I can almost smell it, I think the brotherhood has made a blunder"

Phraan blinked and Ivran sort of grimaced "You are right, I can…there is something here, like a cold draft you cannot really locate."

Zaray made the mule move again. "Yes, get going. I fear that wyrms aren't the worst thing this place does harbour."

She didn't say anything more and they rode on. The area did have more animal life and they did see some very huge two legged birds which were flightless and they were obviously predators for they were chasing some smaller deer like animals across a clearing. They hadn't ridden far before the stench of death did reach them and not Zaray did look very worried indeed. The huge dragon had followed them silently the entire time but now it let out a sort of howl and bared its teeth. "He knows something, halt"

The dragon turned towards them and the huge cat did go over to Phraan, the eyes were narrow and it did growl. "Something ahead, be aware"

The voice reached their heads and Phraan gaped. It was the dragon and it did look as if it was ready for a fight. The smell got stronger and it was sickening. The dragon let out another howling sound and it was answered. Another creature like him appeared between the trees, it was limping and it had some differences from their dragon. It had way brighter colours and something which could only be described as feathers did grow from its spine and formed a sort of fan along its back. It was rather beautiful and its head was more elegant than on the one following them. Phraan realized that this was a female and it was badly wounded. It had terrible gashes in its flanks and one of the front legs appeared to have been almost bitten off. One eye was blinded since something had almost crushed the head on that side and its lower jaw was hanging, also broken. Thiana and Taurin let out small shrieks of disgust and compassion and the female did approach them slowly. It was clearly suffering and the male did move forwards, he growled.

There was some sort of communication going on and the male turned his head to them. "Attack, killed pack. Not far away"

Zaray swallowed visibly and the mule was shivering. "What attacked them?"

The female was panting, blood running from her broken maw and it was obviously dying. The male sneered. "Things made by death, not alive"

Phraan did for a second get an image thrown into his head, a whole herd of such dragons, and all torn more or less apart and behind them dark figures, wolf like but not alive.

"It is what the orc's did talk about, something the brotherhood have conjured up"

Zaray shifted her weight. "Like the dreghil, just as terrible"

The male did nudge the female gently, the dragon did lie down and it moaned. "Please, end her"

The voice was sad and Phraan did for the first time in his life see that perhaps not all dragons were bad. If this was their original form that was in fact a good and noble beast. Zaray did bring the bow forth again, and she did fire an arrow. The female did not even make a sound, it just died and the male looked at them, the eyes were filled with rage. "Darkness brought them, must stop"

Zaray nodded slowly and her eyes were hard. "Yes, they must be stopped. From whence did they come?"

The male shook itself. "Forgotten magic, world link. Opened again"

Phraan tried to make sense of it, he shook his head. "I don't understand?"

Ivran was panting, he had turned a sickly grey and he was trembling all over, they all stared at him with shock in their eyes. "But I do, oh Gods, this is bad."

Zaray pushed her mule over to Ivran and pulled him over and embraced him like a mother cradles her child. "Explain, fast"

Ivran swallowed hard. "You remember what I have told you? That I never was able to make spells like the others? That all magic did elude me? Well, that didn't mean that I didn't learn alright, and this…this I do remember!"

He did look as if he was about to puke and they all looked worried. "It is about time, it doesn't move at the same rate here as in our world and I bet that this is different in every single dimension."

Nobody did understand, they all just stared at him. "Ah, yes?"

Ivran looked down. "Some mage has entered this dimension, and opened a gate between the dimensions. In our world it happened just a little while ago but in here it was days ago. The gate will allow things from other dimensions to enter this place, and they have."

Zaray did tilt her head, she was frowning. "But…these wolf things, the dark mages have created them right? How can they come to this place then?"

Ivran sighed. "I bet that the area where the dark mages work is somehow shielded off from the city by a magical barrier. It is like a dimension in some ways, and the link has opened a gate also to that place"

Dhokay cringed. "Aw shit, more dreghil?"

Ivran nodded. "Yes, possibly. And whatever else they have created"

Zaray just bit her teeth together. "Marvellous, as if this place wasn't bad enough as it was. We have to get rid of those undead wolves or whatever they are."

Phraan stared at Ivran. "You said a mage had entered this place, is he still here?"

Ivran was trembling still. "Yes, I can feel it, it is not one, it is several"

Zaray was trying to hold him still. "You are trembling, what is wrong?"

Ivran made a grimace. "I…I…I can feel the heart stone, I don't know how or why, but it is trying…trying to drag me inn"

Zaray swore. "Resist damn it. It will corrupt you."

Phraan was staring at the young mage. "I cannot say that I have felt it yet and I guess that it means that it isn't that strong here, or else it would have tried to ensnare Zaray and me too."

Shaluun stared at the young mage with huge eyes. "The connection, there we have it. We can use this against the dark mages"

Zaray almost growled. "How? If it drags Ivran inn it will devour his magic, make it its own. The chaos worshipers have changed it, turned into their tool damn it."

Shaluun had a nasty glimpse in his eyes. "It does hunger for more power? For more energy?"

She nodded with narrow eyes. "Yes, the dark mages have turned it into something of darkness. "

The elf grinned "Great, I have an idea!"

The last days had come with snow, and not the gently falling snow of a lovely winter day but a blizzard which was threatening to bury the entire city. Everybody had sought cover inside and Janok and his men had tried to make sure that everybody at least had some shelter but they feared that many would freeze to death. There wasn't much to burn there on the plains, normally people used animal dung as fuel but now that was hard to find and the snow did hide everything useful too. When the blizzard did stop the weather became clear and the wind died down. The city was covered with white and Janok and the soldiers had a heck of a job clearing the roads and helping people. It was as he feared, many had died and now there was little food left. Some started to wonder if it perhaps was better to leave the city after all, the dragons didn't like this cold now could they?

Janok was helping out shovelling snow off a roof when the call was heard, dragons on the horizon and Janok felt his heart sink. He ran to the wall and saw that it was a huge herd, flying ones as well as creatures with no wings and they were heading their way. He swallowed, this was it. They wouldn't make it, it was impossible. He could just pray that Crassian and his men hadn't been hampered by the storm, they could possibly have gotten so far south now they had avoided it. He shouted orders, the soldiers did run to the wall, the weapons were made ready but Janok knew that there was little they could do. People ran screaming in the streets, trying to seek shelter. He wished that there was something he could have done to help them, something at all.

The dragons were huge, way larger than before and many, they looked like a huge cloud from a distance and the sheer number was unbelievable. Janok did throw a cloak over his uniform and grasped his spear and sword. He was the commander of this camp and the protector of this city, he intended to die as a soldier should, fighting. The ground was shaking as the wingless beasts came closer and closer and they too were huge, and armoured. He did hope that the group was safe, wherever they were. The officers were shouting orders and the men did obey but it was out of desperation, none of them had any hope that they would make it. The winged dragons did slow down, and then they started to descend and Janok saw that their throats started to swell with fire. The archers did release their arrows, the arrowheads were made to be strong and sharp but they didn't do much good.

The first of the running beasts hammered into the wall as the first burst of flames did rain down from above. The wall was not strong enough and it simply fell apart and crumbled and men were thrown around and trampled. Janok saw that fire danced all over the city now, and the dragons did just fly on, they didn't even bother watching it burn. Screams and wails were heard, the roaring of fire filled the air and Janok watched how his soldiers fought bravely but to no prevail. He saw that a huge dragon had landed on the square and it was spewing fire at the building which served as the city council hall, the bricks did explode in the heat.

He held the spear and bared his teeth, the thing was busy and he aimed for its chest as he ran as fast as he could. Janok was a very experienced soldier, he had learned how to spear an animal and he was strong and desperate. He wanted to take at least one monster with him and the spearhead had been forged from the best steel there was. Between the chest and the wing joint was an area which was vulnerable and he took the last steps, almost flying. He felt little fear, more of a determined anger and the spear did hit home. It felt like trying to kill a dog with a toothpick but the metal did pierce the hide and he had hit between two ribs. The spear was long and the shaft narrow but strong, the weapon did slide in.

The dragon let out a terrible shriek and jerked, the wings did almost lift it off the ground again and Janok was thrown away but he saw that the dragon was severely wounded. Blood gushed from its maw and it fell down again with a bang, it was clawing at the ground and roaring and it saw Janok and opened its jaws. Janok smiled, he had done it, he had killed a dragon, who could possibly ask for more? He didn't feel the fire which devoured him within the blink of an eye, all he felt was pride. He had done what he could, what was in his power to do. He could meet his ancestors with pride.

The four mages had been stunned by what they saw on the other side of the magical barrier, this was forbidden ground for them and that sent a thrill through them all. It felt exciting, those old dour curmudgeons would have suffered an apoplectic seizure had they known this. Oronor was breathing in the fresh air with a pleased expression upon his face, the place was vibrant and looked very inviting. The other three were making small gasps of sheer joy and the fact that they were very young did not escape him. They were acting like ordinary younglings and Oronor felt a bit more dignified than that. He threw his robe around him and lifted his head. "Come, if there are some enemies here they will be coming this way, we'd better go and meet them."

The others nodded and kept staring at the strange vegetation and the wildlife they did see. The world they had entered was so different from their own and they had soon forgotten about their mission. There was so much to see, so much go explore and they had no brakes when it came to getting up close and personal with the things they saw. Two of the group did spot something very colourful in the distance. "Look, those colours are insane!"

Oronor turned his head. It was a bush and it had flowers on it, a sheer kaleidoscope of colours was spread among the green and he had hardly ever seen something so beautiful. He wasn't one to give in to emotions, to be a good dark mage you have to be able to control yourself and showing feelings is never wise. It can and will be used against you and Oronor was aiming for the title as high mage one day in the future, to him guarding his thoughts was second nature. But this, it was wondrous and he saw nothing wrong in wandering over to the bush to investigate. The flowers were huge and so delicate and they did almost look as if they were sculpted from the finest porcelain with exquisite details. One of the others just stared. "So beautiful, I wonder if that bush can survive in our world? I want one!"

The others nodded, the youngest one tilted his head. "Maybe one can bring a twig along and see if it survives?"

He bent down and grasped a thin branch, it did look very healthy and strong and he used his pocket knife to cut it off, just underneath some leaves. Mages rarely carry weapons, they don't need to. But a pocket knife is good to have to sharpen quills and arrange wicks and nobody went anywhere without one, it was simply a part of the dress code. The young mage held the twig up triumphantly and suddenly one of the branches twitched and the flowers did shake violently. A cloud of pollen was ejected into the air and the young one and the one standing next to him was for a second hard to see, completely covered. They coughed and wheezed and the other two were laughing, until the wheezing got serious and nasty.

The cloud did dissolve but the two were on the ground, grasping their throats, faces red and bodies twitching. Oronor was so shocked he didn't know what to do, poisonous pollen, what was this? The other one did shout a healing spell but he wasn't strong enough to heal such severe problems. The two managed to get two breaths of air before it got even worse and then they suddenly jerked violently and fell silent. Both were dead, and Oronor was staring at them with wide eyes. What had just happened? This place did look like paradise but apparently it wasn't at all. He swore and grasped his remaining companion by the elbow. "Swiftly, you do know protective spells?"

The other one was very pale and shivering and he nodded hesitantly. He did weave some protective spells around himself and Oronor did the same, his were more powerful and efficient but he didn't really care that much about his comrade, his own safety was more important. He panted and stared at the bodies, tried to think clearly. Alright, they were in clearly hostile terrain and there could be enemies heading their way right now, they needed to strengthen themselves, they were only two. Oronor did open himself to the power of the source, drew upon it and felt that he could connect with it even here. That was good, that meant that he was sure he wouldn't run out of energy. He let the magic from the heart stone flow through him and he soaked his own soul with it, smiling as he did it. The other mage wasn't strong enough to do this yet and he did stare at Oronor with some awe. Oronor did enjoy being admired and revered, that was why he had chosen the dark path in the first place, it was the only way he could excel and he was very sure that he one day would make it to grand mage.

Oronor didn't know it, but he had done a mistake, now he was like a hose straight to the heart stone and its power did gain access to this world. The gate they had opened blazed with light for a few seconds and pierced both time and space and neither of them did notice this. Neither did they notice that their perception of time had changed a lot. Oronor nodded to his remaining companion. "We stay here, if someone does come they have to pass by us"

The other mage was nervous now, and his gaze revealed it too. His eyes were moving all the time, searching for danger and he was pale. "Do you really think that there is someone coming?"

Oronor shook his head. "No Dharien, I don't think anyone is coming. It is just Siverel who is being overzealous, if Simaon really had someone out there working for him I doubt that this one person is able to bring a magician to us, no, it is bullshit. But we have to be certain, just so he cannot say that we have failed our duties"

Dharien nodded and sat down, his elegant dark robes were getting grass stains on them and the young mage did already smell of sweat. Oronor leaned up against a rock and started whispering some spells, just to practice them. He didn't know that magic sometimes works a bit like some sorts of liquids, they will always try to reach a balance by flowing from an area of high density to one with low density and he was releasing more and more magic into the surroundings this way. The heart stone had sensed an area untouched by its power and now it tried to make up for it. The gate did allow creatures from the breeding area access to this dimension and it was as if nature sensed this dark contamination and tried to rid itself of it. The trees shook and the wind seemed to wail, something was very wrong, it had to be fought.

The two sat there for a while, enjoying the peace and quiet and the younger one did fall asleep, he was not used to pushing himself the way the older mages were and his mind wasn't that disciplined yet. Oronor didn't mind, he was fond of silence and just sat there trying to feel if there was some other mages in this realm. He ought to be able to pinpoint the direction to anyone wielding magic of any kind but he didn't feel anything, this world was blocking him somehow. It was like trying to see something through a thick opaque sheet of glass and he kept trying and kept pushing but no.

He did feel as if he was onto something for a few seconds but then it did slip away and he got a strange feeling of being unwelcome there. Why he didn't know though, the life force and natural magic of this world seemed very uncorrupted and it could be that this was what he reacted to. It was a diametric opposite of what he and his brethren did stand for. He was meditating while his companion did sleep, and nothing disturbed him. It felt good just sitting there, in the soft light, and the warm air. Not thinking about anything, not scheming, not really making any plans, and just being! He wasn't used to it, it was a rare luxury and he enjoyed it to the fullest. Maybe he ought to make this dimension his home whence they had won? He could make up some excuse for not letting others join him in there, saying it was dangerous in some way. He stared at the forested hills and the feeling of peace was so new to him he had to really reflect upon it.

He was close to drifting off to sleep too when his companion did jerk and groan in his sleep, a grimace flew over the face and Oronor did chuckle, was Dharien having one of those dreams? He was young after all, and healthy too. Most mages does forget about such things rather fast, the dedication to the magic overpowers all such natural urges and Oronor hadn't thought about women for at least a decade. Dharien did groan again, wriggling a bit, perhaps he had ants in his pants? Oronor hadn't seen any ants there but they could be tiny and the grass was lush and long. Oronor did lift his gaze to stare at some very huge birds which seemed to have four wings? It was an odd world this and he would love to learn more of it. Then Dharian made a sort of howling sound and the body arched, shook violently. Oronor spun around, this was no erotic dream, was the other mage having nightmares. Dharian was opening his eyes, they were filled with pain and panic and his arms were flailing about, ghastly sounds came from him and Oronor was on his feet within the blink of an eye. He stared down at Dharian who gargled and blood burst from his mouth as his eyes lost their light and his soul fled. Oronor blinked, what the hell...

The body just lay there, then it moved again and Oronor let out a feminine shriek and backed away, something was tugging at the corpse and as Oronor stood there in shock he saw that something moved underneath the body. It seemed to have come out of the ground and it looked like a thick worm of some sorts and he saw that Dharian's corpse did sort of shrink, it was as if everything inside of the body was being sucked out and Oronor got pale and felt sick when he realized that the worm or whatever it was in fact had entered Dharian's body and were devouring it from the inside out. And it had entered it from...Oronor covered his mouth with his hand, in complete disgust and disbelief and he ran off, this world was a nightmare, was there anything which wasn't dangerous? The spells hadn't worked, and now he did see the flaws of their way of thinking. Magic protects against magic, it may not protect against non-magical attacks.

Shaluun had lead them through the woods for a while, his keen senses had been able to find the monsters pretty fast and they were indeed like dark and decaying very large wolves, a terrible sight. Ivran didn't quite understand what Shaluun was planning on doing but he did trust the elf. The pack wasn't large, just five beasts but five were bad enough and they had killed the entire pack of local dragons and then many other beings. The monsters would continue to spread death through this realm unless they were stopped. Ivran had felt something strange as they rode between the trees, the forest seemed angered and Thiana and Taurin did confirm that yes, this realm had felt the contamination of dark magic and it was preparing to strike back. The wolf like beasts did look as if they had been rotting for weeks and yet they moved but they were not alive, not really. They were extensions of the dark magic and existed only because of that. Now the pack was resting or rather trying to determine where to go next, they were drawn to living beings and the wildlife had fled the area, wisely enough. Shaluun was staring at them all, his face grim. "These monsters must be utterly destroyed before we can do anything more. Let us hope that there aren't more beasts here."

Zaray was nodding to Phraan who grasped his sword and let the armour appear again, he felt ready for a fight, and he needed to blow off some steam. The wolf like monsters did hear the hooves and gathered, eager for more slaughter but what they did encounter was something rather unforeseen. Two did fall with glowing arrows through them and three were suddenly coming face to face with an armoured warrior wielding a glowing blade. They tried to attack but were chopped into pieces and the battle was over almost before it was started. Phraan did shake the blood of the sword and Zaray did turn to Shaluun. "Now, explain this plan of yours, we are eager to hear of it"

Shaluun smiled "Yes, Ivran, what do you feel now? Are the dark mages still here somewhere?"

Ivran closed his eyes, the constant pull of that distant power was annoying but it wasn't strong enough to really toss him out of balance emotionally just yet. He was searching for darkness within the bright life of this realm and he felt it again, but it had diminished a lot. He opened his eyes. "There is but one now, and he is alone. I think the others have died"

Dhokay made a sort of wry grin. "Well, the way they act I bet this world would prove to be rather hostile against them."

Ivran did look a bit nervous, he was still feeling weak and confused and Shaluun laid a hand on his shoulder. "I once learned that the best way to conquer a besieged fortress is to attack it not from the front but from within."

Ivran frowned. "And by that you mean?"

Shaluun sat down on the ground and the rest of the group did join him, Fastonar did look as if he was in severe doubt and Rhuk was frowning and did look a bit intimidating that way. "Those mages did open up a connection right? We can create some trouble for the enemy through that connection, send a little present back if you can call it that"

Fastonar did cross his arms. "Won't that tell them that we are here and on our way?"

Shaluun sent the soul sworn a rather wry and wicked grin. "Not if it is a dark mage who makes a blunder now is it? "

Zaray snickered. "You are simply going to send something back the same way as these monsters came right?"

Shaluun nodded. "Feel the magic within this land, it is furious, and it want's the dark chaotic force the mages brought gone."

Thiana did look as if she was gradually becoming more enthusiastic. "You are right, it may help us."

Shaluun laid both hands on Ivran's shoulders, stared him in the eye. "There is one magic you haven't tried yet, a trick. It is rather harmless and more of a child's play really and not at all that hard but I doubt that a dark mage would know anything of it"

Phraan was removing the armor, he felt a bit stiff with it on and he preferred to go without for as long as possible. "You want to capture that dark mage"

Shaluun nodded. "Yes, and use him for all he is worth. We can perhaps drain the heart stone, and create some chaos of our own"

Taurin did look down. "It can be done if the dark mages indeed does draw power from the heart stone, this land will see it happen. I can feel it through the trees, I think..."

He stopped for a moment and his eyes got distant, then he smiled. "Yes, the wall wasn't the only defence against the chaos forces, the area in front of it is also a part of the plan. They used mighty magic to create the hidden path, it is a trap for anyone who isn't of the light"

Zaray smiled. "Good, so, how do we capture a dark mage? I bet he won't go down without a fight now will he?"

Ivran made a dark grimace. His eyes were distant and cold. "He will try to fight, right away, so he has to be subdued immediately, we cannot hesitate and think that this man, whoever he is, is still human. If we do we'll lose."

Zaray took his hand. "Are you strong enough to use your magic again? To perform that little trick of Shaluun?"

Ivran swallowed hard and he blinked. "I will try!"

Dhokay winced. "Trying isn't enough, we'll have one go at this, and it has to be a success."

Ivran looked down, he did look uncertain. "I know, but I feel...it is hard to explain, odd!"

Phraan looked at the young man, he didn't look well and he was in fact very pale. "Are you ill? Is there something physically wrong with you?"

Ivran swallowed hard. "I don't know, I feel torn, weakened. I am not sure if it is the heart stone or something else"

Zaray was staring at Ivran with a rather stern expression on her face. "I think I can help you, by linking our minds together. We have to get moving and get out of here, time goes by and here it runs at its own pace entirely"

She nodded at Shaluun. "We have to find this mage and then you can leave him to Phraan and me, I know what to do with him"

Shaluun tilted his head. "Are you sure?"

Zaray smiled and pointed at Tersus. "Yes, we have a weapon he won't anticipate at all!'"

The elf smiled and waved his hand at Thiana and Tersus. "Good, lead the way my friends, show us how well you do track"

Oronor had tried to find somewhere which felt safe but he couldn't, he was getting more and more confused and only the great looming magical barrier did show him the direction. He was heading back towards it now but it seemed to be so far away, even though he was almost running. He wanted to return to the city and damn the mission, there weren't anybody there anyhow, and how could the old jerks believe that someone could have managed to get past the dragons and the other monsters? He was panting as he walked up a rather steep hill at a brisk pace, the wall didn't come any closer and he started to feel a slight sensation of panic. What was this really? Did the darn barrier evade him? He stopped and tried to focus, his mind did seek his brethren through the use of magic but there was nothing coming back and he snarled and walked on. Then he felt something new, a strange tingling sensation which to a mage speaks of magic, in big bold letters. It was near, and it wasn't strong but it was some sort of magical source.

He hesitated, there had to be an explanation, were there more mages there, had someone been sent after him? Oh no, that would be a disaster, he would have to come up with some good lie to explain what had happened to the others. He took a deep breath and started to move towards it, not really sure of what to do. The power was frail, barely there, and of a very peculiar type too. He couldn't identify it and he started to walk a little faster, he was getting curious. It could be something which belonged in this dimension and although he was very cautious now he didn't want to lose the opportunity to perhaps discover something which would make up for the mistake of going there in the first place. He rounded a small group of trees and saw something in the grass ahead, it was a person, sitting down, and facing the wall and the magic seemed to come from him. It seemed to be a young man, clad in worn travelling clothes and Oronor stopped and frowned. Could it be a native? No, there were no signs of humans in this wretched world, he still remembered how his men had died and he cringed. But of course, this had to be what Siverel had warned them about, one of those which were heading for the city and Oronor felt a surge of rage.

This was the reason he had been sent there, this was the reason he was so miserable and why he had lost his comrades. He hissed and ran forth, the man didn't seem to notice that he was coming and Oronor did shout a spell which should have made the man turn into a cloud of vapour there and then. Nothing happened and Oronor gaped, he suddenly realized that he had done a mistake and he tried to turn around to run. The man in the grass simply disappeared, as if he had never been there in the first place and Oronor had never heard of such magic. He felt a violent jerk and looked down, vines were twirling up along his calves and he shouted a spell to get rid of them but nothing happened. Instead his feet started to sink into the soil and he flailed his arms and tried yet another spell but to no prevail. What in the name of every unholy God was going on? There was as if a sort of dome had descended over him, shielding him from everything and he struggled desperately but the vines were wrapping themselves around his whole body. He gasped and cried out, one spell more powerful than the other but they had no effect. Then he saw them, two figures which were approaching him, a tall elven female and an even taller male dressed in odd looking armour.

Oronor recognized her, from old stories. The one who had tried to assassinate one of the high mages a very long time ago and disappeared from the dungeons, one who was prophesised to return, one who knew their secrets, one who would bring their doom. He hissed and the vines did pull him deeper down.

The female did stare at him, her eyes were very cold. "Now, let us see what this will accomplish"

She took something from her pocket, two small gems and Oronor did see what they were, heart gems, and the type they used to transform the dragons. They were powerful and valuable and how had she come into possession of these? She bent down and smiled, the smile wasn't pretty at all, in fact it was rather gruesome and he realized that this was an opponent just as cruel as they were, it was only that the goal was a different one. She reached for him and he tried to wriggle himself free, a steel hard hand grasped his jaw and before he knew it the gems were placed in his mouth and the wines did twist around his head and force him to close it. He realized that this was it, the end. He shouldn't have done it, shouldn't have insisted on leaving their leader behind. Desperation and fear did take over and he was trying to beg for his life, but he couldn't. The power of the gems did burn through him and two wood elves did come forth. They were chanting and their eyes were very eerie. He tried to scream but he couldn't, the vines did pull him even further down and now only his head was above the ground. The tall female gestured to the one wearing the armour. "Do it"

Oronor tried to call out to his brethren one last time but it was too late, he couldn't. The elf raised his sword and the point did pierce Oronor's neck and continued downwards into his chest. The mage felt a tear running down his cheek, his blood did gush from the wound and the wood elves were still chanting, slowly the magic of this very land did enter the body, and fought its way backwards, towards the source of his magic, the way a trout swims towards the pond where it was hatched. His last thought was one of disbelief, how could this have happened to him?

Zaray did stare at the peculiar sight, she smirked and cocked her head. "Good, Ivran, it is your turn"

The young man walked forth and he did look rather shaky still, he was breathing fast and he appeared to be in pain but he bent down and put a hand on the dead mage's head. He did focus, followed the thin trails of power back and saw what the dark mage had seen. He formed a wish, a desire and felt a jolt as the natural magic of the land suddenly gave him enough power to do so. As he opened his eyes again he knew that the idea was a good one, it would be efficient, and it would work.

Back in the city the next group of dragons were ready to be sent forth and the beasts were bellowing and pawing at the ground, eager to go. The mages who did control the transport were hard pressed, they had to make sure that no mistakes were done and they focused entirely on their task. The area where the dragons were kept was well lighted and the magic surrounding it strong, it had to be. The beasts gathered there were hard to control even to their masters and the valley had a solid magical barrier only the chosen ones could pass through. The ones who worked there now had been busy since dawn the last day and they were tired and annoyed and their heads were spinning too. Food and drink wasn't what you thought off when dealing with something like this and they were after all just human. None of them did discover the faint pale green light which seemed to flicker here and there, followed by a scent of a meadow in summer. The natural magic was a stark contrast to the one the dark brotherhood did use, it didn't try to control or manipulate things into submission, it wasn't there to subdue or use. Instead it was liberating as life truly is and locks and chains did let go and open up. This magic would free the bound and tear down any barriers and it did. Ivran's wish was to release everything there and now the magic did allow him to do just that. His will carried along by the wild magic of that untamed dimension.

The mages didn't notice anything as it did its work, slowly and with meticulous precision. It wasn't until the first of the many creatures held there sprang forth with a triumphant roar that they saw the truth. The work of opening the gateway to the plains was abandoned there and then, instead they had to fight for their lives and since they were few they were overpowered fast. The dark spells didn't harm the creatures they themselves had created since they had been made to be immune to the use of magic.

The mages did die screaming and the beasts were free, the barrier did hold though, they were trapped within the valley and roars and bellows of anger could be heard from afar. They attacked the barrier again and again, most of the dragons were hungry and they were also hurting. Being transformed hurts and they also hated being controlled. The combination of feelings did turn them into uncontrollable killing machines. There were both dreghil and elementals there, and the monsters didn't exactly cooperate well, instead they did try to kill each other and the valley became a slaughter field. Had anyone seen it they would have believed that they had descended into hell itself, the scene simply unbelievable. Blood was covering the ground, black and red and green, fire flickered and roared and heavy booms could be heard as creatures collided and tried to tear each other apart. It was mayhem, and more and more got free from their pens and joined the melee.

Siverel had been working rather hard and he was tired, the mages he had sent out to guard the wall hadn't reported back so he assumed that everything was fine. Maybe he was just paranoid and seeing dangers where there were none but his instincts told him that this was the still before the storm. He had been reading and preparing and he had ordered that some of the most valuable of the books in the library was to be sent to one of the deepest vaults. There were so many things there which were valuable and he didn't want them destroyed, no matter what happened. He got up from behind the desk and found some wine, enjoyed the sweet taste of it. The city couldn't import anything large from the south so they had to make do with what they had and they used some sort of berries which grew on the naked carrocks to brew wine. The small black berries were rather sour but whence fermented and mixed with honey they became a very nice brew indeed. The meat came from wild deer and they did also have livestock. The city wasn't that different from the cities of the south, they were just isolated and the population had gotten used to that.

Siverel wasn't hungry, he had eaten some chicken earlier that day and he walked over to the window and looked out. The city lay in perpetual twilight and there wasn't any sun there but the magical lights were just as beautiful and he smiled at the sight. For all it was worth, what they had done there had been grand, nobody could deny that. He just hoped that he would have enough time to save as much as possible, he was trying to prepare the others for resistance and attacks, but subtly. If he just went out there and said that yes, the old prophecies were the truth they would surely make sure he ended as old Badrian, imprisoned in his own chambers and deemed as stark raving mad. He was about to return to the desk and his work when there was a frantic knocking on the door, he felt a sting of fear and answered but heard that his voice did shiver. It was a servant and he was chalk white. "My lord, the pens...the creatures are on the loose"

Siverel just stared ahead of himself, blankly. Then his mind worked again and he grasped onto the wall for support. "By every God, it has started!"

He straightened himself and tried to smile. "I will be there, shortly"

He walked over to his chair and grasped his cloak and tried to appear as calm and collected. He knew that the end could be coming now, and he feared that there would be little he could do to stop it. He had been too late, his preparations wouldn't matter at all, not anylonger.

The group was getting closer to the magical wall now and Zaray was staring at it with her eyes fixed upon the base of it. Ivran was not very strong and it was obvious that something was very wrong somewhere. Phraan was getting nervous on the young man's behalf and he did see that Thiana and Taurin too stared at him with narrow eyes. Zaray had asked the two wood elves if there were more monsters there and they hadn't felt any, the wyrm and the undead wolf beasts had been the only things which had had time to slip into this dimension so far. The dragon and the cat had been wandering about to prevent any unexpected attacks and things did look peaceful enough. They just hoped that the natural magic would be able to do something about the heart stone. Zaray was thinking, they could all feel that and she got off the mule and started watching the ground with narrow eyes. "There has to be footprints here somewhere, I doubt that dark mages do hide their footprints. If we find them we do find where they got through, it will be a weak spot, excellent for our purpose"

Ivran had to sit down, he was shaking all over and Fastonar grasped him gently, tried to push his saddle roll inn under the young man. "Something is very wrong with him, there has to be something you can do?!"

Thiana was kneeling, she placed a hand on Ivran's forehead and the young man did smile but the smile was a pale one. "I am sorry, I don't think I will make it all the way this time."

Thiana frowned and closed her eyes, as a wood elf she did have some healing abilities and she gasped and opened her eyes again, staring at Zaray. "It is the magic of the heart stone, it tries to kill him. I think it knows he is dangerous, what are we to do?"

Zaray swore and sat down, putting a hand onto his shoulder. "Oh damnation, we have to close him off from that magic completely."

Phraan was feeling a bit frantic. "How? And how does it find him in the first place?"

406

Zaray shrugged. "Magic seeks magic, it must be able to sense his presence, and since it is transformed by the dark mages it sees him as a threat, one even greater than you and I"

She stroked Ivran's hair. "Can you somehow shield yourself off?"

Ivran groaned. "Too weak!"

Taurin bit his teeth together. "Not for long, there is something we can try"

He sat down on his knees and grasped Ivran's hand, then he pressed his fingers into the ground. "We can use the magic of this realm to make him stronger"

Zaray tilted her head. "Yes, but that is dangerous, I don't think it is wise. His magic is untested"

Thiana caught her gaze. "He will die if we don't try"

Phraan remembered the many things Vitile had achieved and he gave Zaray a pleading glance. "Do it, please"

Fastonar did look eager too and Phraan saw that Dhokay and Shaluun were rather quiet. The dwarves and Tersus and Peter did look scared.

Taurin got a nod from Zaray and he seemed to slow down somehow, his breath became very slow and his eyes were shut. Thiana sat down next to him, put one hand on Ivran and the other in the ground and Phraan gasped when he did see that they both for a moment looked like wooden statues, as if their skin was replaced with wood. There was an odd light coming from them and it seemed to flow through them and into Ivran and the young man let out a scream and his body convulsed. Zaray got down on her knees. "Grasp him, hold him down"

Phraan sat down by Ivran's head and held it down and the man was making some absolutely horrific rasping sounds, his eyes were rolling in his head and the body was shaking, Thiana was chanting and her voice was strained, as if she was fighting something, Taurin was pale and his face covered with sweat. Phraan realized that this was far from simple and he hesitated but reached out and put a hand on Taurin, just too if possible give the wood elf some extra strength. What he felt next made him jerk back with a sort of howl, it felt like floating fire in his veins, like ice and acid and it was so powerful it was overpowering.

But Phraan did for a fleeting second sense something alien there, something dark and tainted and not at all natural and he stared at Ivran and felt a surge of nausea. So that was it, he caught Zaray's eyes and reached out to her through his mind. He rarely did for it took a lot out of him but he felt that he had to, there was no other way this time. "He has been weakened deliberately!"

Zaray nodded, she didn't reveal what she was thinking at all. "Yes, I can believe that, there has to be something here which draws his strength, even more than that blasted heart stone"

Taurin was moaning and the glow seemed to increase in strength, Ivran wasn't shaking anymore and he was looking way better, the skin had a natural colour now and he was breathing better. Thiana was panting and she grimaced and seemed to give one last boost of power.

Ivran did open his eyes and they let go of him, he was obviously very dizzy and he rubbed his head and looked disoriented. "What happened?"

Phraan tilted his hand. "You were cleansed, how do you feel?"

Ivran blinked a few times. "I feel…fine, better. I feel normal?"

He got up and they brushed the grass of his clothes, he was swaying a bit but found his balance. Phraan did look at Zaray and she was staring at the ground, her expression one of hidden anger. She took a deep breath. "Do you feel the heart stone now? Is it still trying to drain you?"

Ivran shook his head. "I can sense it yes, but it has no power over me anymore, I cannot understand how it managed to get that much of a hold over me. I was so weak?"

Zaray smiled. "Well, you do look better indeed, and do you think you can use your magic freely now?"

He sort of checked and smiled, nodded. "Odd, I can. I can feel it so much clearer now, there isn't anything hindering me. Yes, I think I can use it rather well"

He did smile and Phraan was shocked by the change. Taurin caught his gaze. "There was some sort of spell put on him, one which made him vulnerable to the dark taint of the heart stone. I think it must have been there a while, weakening him, making him unable to really use the magic"

Taurin's voice was tired, even the one of his mind. Phraan answered the same way, through mind speech. All elves were capable of that but they didn't use it unless they had to. Phraan answered the same way. "Was it a strong spell? Is it gone now?"

Taurin didn't look at Phraan at all, his face did look closed off. "It is gone yes, it wasn't a very complicated spell, I bet it was the type you can buy and inflict on a person through some object"

Phraan went over to Drake and pretended to be fidgeting with the saddle, he felt anger churning within. An object, that could be anything, from the smallest little item to something more important and if nobody was aware of it, well then nobody would bother looking for it in the first place. He remembered Imeah's last words and his teeth did grind together, he had to lean his forehead against the warm neck of his horse to calm himself. He heard Zaray's voice in his head. "Something has upset you"

He answered. "Yes, we have been tricked, someone has made sure that Ivran couldn't reach his full potential"

She was quiet for a while. "Yes, I have thought of the same thing, he did control the magic when he and Shaluun were practicing, Shaluun said it was rather easy. But after that…"

Phraan took a deep breath. "Don't mention this to anyone"

She didn't even look over at him. "I won't"

Ivran was grinning from one ear to the other and Zaray stared at the wall again. "We have to find the point where the mages got through, Ivran, do you think you can see it now?"

The young mage formed a request in his mind and then he nodded. "I am sure I can, follow me!"

The others took their horses by the reins and followed the young man, finally things seemed to go their way.

Siverel was running through the dark corridors and his heart was racing, he could feel that something had happened to the magical source and it did confuse him for he hadn't read anything about that being a target? But now they had other things to worry about, the barriers around the dragon pens were failing one by one and the valley had been transformed completely. There wasn't any mages left there at all, everyone had fled and he ran out onto the balcony and stared down at the area. He staggered back, by every dark deity and by his ancestors, this was...very bad. He turned around and saw that brother Buraz and some other had come running, he took a deep breath. "Gather all our mages, even the novices. We have to contain this, immediately!"

Buraz did throw him a long and lingering glance before he took off and Siverel leaned against the railing. He stared down and made a grimace. There wouldn't be any chance of sending these last dragons out there or would there? He saw the chaos and realized that yes that was their only option. If they were fighting so be it, out there no damage would be done to the city and there was no way in hell they could calm all these beasts down.

He ran down the stairs and before long mages did arrive, they had about a hundred in all and he stared at them, some were missing and he realized that some had died when the dragons did break free and then there was the five he had sent out. He did for a second consider sending some guards to get them back but decided against it, five more wouldn't matter much. He glared at the assembled group and his face was rather stern. "Brothers, we have a serious situation on our hands, some runaway spell has released the hold we had over our creations and they are threatening to break free. We have to send them all through now, we cannot wait"

One of the other more experienced mages swallowed hard. "That will be very hard, just transporting them all like that is...it takes a lot of power."

Siverel nodded. "I do know this of course, I am not daft. But we have to get the goddamn beasts out of here before the last barrier gives way"

The other mage was frowning badly. "It cannot have been just some runaway spell, the pens are supposed to be very safe. This could have been done deliberately"

Siverel realized that the other mage was right, he felt a chill running down his back. What one mage could be strong enough to undo such strong magic? He took yet another deep breath. "Alright, four of you, go and see if you can figure out what went wrong. Our brothers out there are dead, it could be that they have used some faulty spell, or encountered some sort of disturbance which has backfired upon them."

Four of the oldest mages did step forth and he sent them off with a nod. The others did look a bit nervous, something like this had never happened before. "You, all of you, we have to form a link and get those beasts away from here, I don't bloody care where they go as long as they don't stay here"

He saw that some did hesitate, not really knowing what to do. Linking several mages together would boost their power a lot and enable them to use spells no single mage would be able to control but it wasn't something the brotherhood was used to doing. Cooperation wasn't their strong side at all. But slowly they grasped onto each other's hands and let the magic start to flow through them. When forming a link someone has to be the so called tail and another one the head. The tail would make sure that the magic didn't run amok and the head would speak the right spells and aim them at the target, whatever it was. Siverel would be the head and he smiled swiftly at the mage who volunteered to be the tail. He would be in risk of being drained of power if something went wrong, the man was indeed very brave. They were in a hall just outside of the pen area and the magical barrier which kept the dragons contained was flickering and crackling, something was breaking it down and Siverel fell into the link and gasped. The combined magic of so many dark mages was enormous and he felt relieved for a moment, there shouldn't be a problem with sending the dragons out of there.

The beasts were roaring and fighting and he did see dreghil and other monsters too among them. An elemental was trying to get through the wall as he watched it, the thing made the ground around it dissolve and boil and he shivered as he tried to find the right spells to utter.

He started to chant and the others fell inn and the voices did rise above the roars and shrieks and formed a powerful and even beautiful harmony, a dark mage has to be able to use his voice to get anything done, every mage has to read the spells out loud and clear and in olden days the most common way to make a mage harmless was to cut out his tongue. Siverel was giving himself over to the magic, letting it flow through him and he started to think that he had been wrong, the prophecies were perhaps just fairy tales after all for this they could handle just fine. They could yet win. This had to have been a mere accident after all. He increased the power of his chanting and a sort of glowing wall appeared in the middle of the bowl formed valley, they didn't bother finding the right point of exit, now it was just about getting the dragons out of there. Some of the mages started to chant another spell, and dragons were being pushed towards the mirror like substance with loud howls if anger. They did cooperate well, this was going the right way and Siverel did allow himself a small smile.

They had stopped by the magical wall on a spot where a grove of trees did grow close to it, footprints did lead away from it and Ivran pointed at the glowing structure. He was frowning and tried to pinpoint the exact point where the dark mages had come through. They would have had to use some sort of device enter this dimension for the wall was after all made to keep them on the outside. The fact that they had been able to get the dragons through didn't automatically mean that they themselves could just walk straight through the magical structure. Ivran tried to open himself up to the magic of his grandfather and allow it to show him the way and suddenly he did notice something odd. A small portion of the wall seemed less shiny and glossy than the rest. He took a deep breath and closed his eyes, the rest of them were holding their breaths. "It was here, but it was sealed again, I think there may be others on the other side of the wall"

Zaray was cussing, so bad it was strange she didn't catch fire. "What are we to do then? Can you get us through Ivran?"

The young man nodded, he could feel the very structure of the wall, it was like a huge glowing tapestry in front of his inner eye, and by moving some of the threads he could get through, without much trouble at all. "Yes, but like I said, I think there may be a sentinel on the other side"

Tersus stepped forth. "I can handle that."

Ivran frowned and stared at the alchemist, the man did look more insane than ever for now he had gotten even dirtier than before and he did stink so bad the horses did shy away from him. "Are you sure?!"

Tersus nodded and grinned widely, he held a small vial in his hand and shook it vigorously!

"Yes damn it, just get me through. I can deal with this!"

Ivran took a deep breath, he nodded and closed his eyes. "Alright then, but be swift"

Tersus just grinned even wider, he did look absolutely insane. "I will"

The weave of the wall was not fragile by far but Ivran willed the magic to sort of split apart for a few seconds. Tersus took two steps forwards and was gone.

The mage who had been waiting on the other side had grown very impatient and he was also getting a bit nervous, he could feel some sort of disturbance in the magic surrounding him and he didn't know from whence it came. He was ready to leave and return to the city to hear what this was about when the wall in front of him shimmered. He prepared to meet the four with some well-chosen and rather crass words about being irresponsible but what came wandering through wasn't any of his friends. It was a man who did look like he had taken a bath in a public sewer. The mage did stumble back a few steps, the man did stink so bad he felt nauseous and his eyes were watering, what in hells name was this creature? Not even undead creatures smell that bad! The human saw him and tilted his head with a wide and insane grin. "Ah, a mage, how wonderful, I have always wanted to meet one of ya guys"

The mage frowned, he didn't feel any magic from this person and in his eyes that automatically made him harmless. "Ah, who the hell are you?"

The man bowed down with a theatrical motion. "I am an alchemist you see"

The mage scoffed with disbelief, this man was insane whoever he was, but how had he gotten through the wall. "Who let you through?"

The stinking man tilted his head, his eyes were really creepy. "Through the wall? This"

He held forth a small vial and the mage felt no magic from it, this was a fat lie. "You lie!"

He prepared to smite the man with a rather nasty spell but the man just smiled and threw the vial towards him. "See for yourself, catch!"

The mage was after all human, he instinctively reached out and managed to catch the vial with his hands and it was warm and not much longer than his index finger. It had a very beautiful green colour and he had time to admire the emerald like shine before the thing simply exploded. A thick green mist spread around him and he gasped for air and backed off to get away from it but suddenly he felt a piercing pain in his chest and looked down. A throwing dagger was buried in him all the way to the hilt and he blinked and couldn't understand, there was so little blood? He slowly collapsed onto the ground and Tersus did walk forth and pulled the dagger out. "You see, alchemy can be used the same way as magic, to create tricks, to lead the mind astray. Yes, just like those wanna be mages sitting on street corners tricking money out of people"

He cleaned the dagger off on his pants and the others did appear through the wall, Ivran stared at the dead mage with huge eyes. "Tersus, you did this?"

The alchemist nodded and there was a dangerous glimpse within his eyes. "Yes, oh don't tell me that I have to do everything with the help of alchemy, I do know how to use a blade"

Phraan sent him a rather thoughtful glance. "Indeed you do, that was a very smart move"

The ground was covered with green powder and the two dwarves did stay clear of it, they didn't seem to like the things Tersus did at all. Zaray stared at the alchemist who shook himself a little and put the dagger back in its sheath, it had been hidden on the inside of his sleeve. "So, now what?"

Tersus smiled at Peter. "We go forth as planned, I and Peter do see if we can create some distractions before the rest of you move in"

Zaray did turn to Rhuk and Dabin. "You two, go with them. You know how to navigate tunnels and the city is a maze if you aren't born there"

The dwarves did look at each other and they didn't look happy at all, in fact they did look less than pleased but they sighed and nodded. Tersus grinned again. "Excellent, we do need someone to watch our backs"

Phraan sat down on his haunches and went through the dead mage's robes. There was nothing there of value, just a pipe and a box of what had to be pomade. The man had been vain. Phraan looked at Zaray. "So, what is the plan now, what do we do?"

Zaray sat down onto a rock and she was frowning. "Well, Ivran, can you check if the things we did back there had any effect?"

Ivran nodded and let the magic flow again, he felt the heart stone and its connection to all the dark mages and there was something different there now. A sort of dissonance and he smiled. "It did work to a degree, but I don't think it will hamper them in any way"

Zaray cussed. "Too bad, I had hoped that it would mess things up"

Phraan did get up again, he had heard something in the distance and he closed his eyes, listened intently. "Listen, what is that?"

Dhokay did look very tense. "Dragons!"

Shaluun nodded slowly. "Many dragons!"

Taurin and Thiana looked at each other. "The magic of that other dimension, it has released their dragons with the help of what Ivran did, we can feel it!"

Fastonar did freeze, Phraan did see it, and the man did move his lips as if reciting something, there was shock and disbelief in his eyes and Phraan felt a surge of something he couldn't quite describe. The soul sworn was staring at the ground, not speaking, as if something had shaken his resolve and shaken it badly too.

Zaray took a deep breath. "Great, just what we needed. Tersus, go now but be careful and do not let yourself be seen.

Your task has changed. There is a gem somewhere in the citadel, it is very powerful and I bet you will find it in the basement somewhere, probably in the area where the high mage resides, or in the chambers of the leader. That gem will be the thing which controls the wall from their side, you have to destroy it and I don't bloody care how! Just do it!"

Tersus did look eager. "Great, what does it look like?"

Zaray made a grimace. "I have no idea but it could be rather large and my best guess is that it looks like the wall in some way, perhaps the colour will be like it."

Tersus did grasp the dead mage's cape and threw it over himself, he smiled at Peter. "You are my servant now, and you two shorties, you try to remain unseen"

Rhuk and Dabin did made some angry faces but they didn't protest and the four did set out, running rather fast. Zaray sighed and looked at the remaining group. "If the dragons are on the lose the mages will be busy with them for sure. If Tersus manages to break that gem they won't be able to get them through the wall. We on the other hand have to think of the very source of their power, the heart stone."

Phraan swallowed. "I can feel it, it is faint but there. "

Zaray smiled swiftly. "I warned you, it may recognize our magic and seek it. So, here is the important thing, we have to remain unseen for as long as possible. We cannot allow ourselves to be spotted by the enemy"

Thiana did bite her lower lip. "This land, it was once lush and green. I can sense it, it remembers. It wants to return to that state."

Zaray did look a bit puzzled. "That must have been a long time ago? It is rather cold and barren now?"

The wood elf smiled. "Yes, but the will to life is still there, buried in the ground. It was a sacred valley remember? It was special before the dark mages twisted the magical source. I think we can try to reawaken the land"

Taurin nodded and his eyes were stern. "We can try yes, it will take a lot of us I fear but if we succeed the dark mages can be weakened"

Zaray was thinking fast. "Great, do it. What do you need?"

Thiana looked at her mate. "Somewhere peaceful, where we won't be disturbed. Somewhere with soil, and preferably grass or trees"

Zaray grinned slowly, there was an almost wicked glimpse within her eyes. "You know what? I think I know the perfect spot!"

She petted Thiana on the back. "The dark mages and their masters will get the surprise of a lifetime for sure!"

Dhokay stared down the narrow canyon they stood in, he frowned. "Are we going to go down there now?"

Zaray nodded "Yes, we have to, if the dragons are ready to be sent out we can possibly save many by hindering that?"

Shaluun did bite his lip. "We have to be careful not to be seen, so, what about our horses?"

Zaray grunted. "Ah, yes, they will have to stay here, I don't think the mages will come this way and the canyon is not home to any predators. They will be safe here, there is even a little grass here"

Phraan did pet Drake. "I don't like leaving him here"

Thiana stepped forth. "I can put a spell on this area, make sure nobody sees them?"

He frowned. "You can do that?"

She nodded with a smile. "Yes, how do you think we wood elves hide? It is an innate magic of our race, don't worry, they will be safe"

They shrugged and pulled the animals together into one of the small side canyons, they took off the bits but not the saddles and then Thiana seemed to weave a sort of illusion over the entire gorge so when you looked at it there was just rock. Phraan swallowed, he wasn't fond of this but a herd of horses is extremely hard to hide in a city. Zaray did clap her hands. "Right, let's go, I have a feeling that time is of the essence here!"

Siverel and the others had been working very hard to get the dragons out of the valley and one by one they were pushed through the wall, the problem should be solved very soon and then things would return to normal. There were more than enough dragons and monsters out there now to get them what they wanted and he had to chuckle when he thought of the attempts the mages of Oakfell and Twelve towers would make to stop them. Of course it would be in vain, the dragons were too strong to be damaged by magic in any form. They were almost done when the four he had sent out to investigate returned, all four were obviously tired and their eyes were filled with disbelief. "Siverel, the pens and gates, it was all opened by some sort of strange power, we haven't been able to identify it at all."

Siverel did pull himself out of the link, the rest was easy so the other mages could finish it without him. "What do you mean?"

The oldest among them was staring at the ground and his moustaches did hang, he did look like a dog someone has scolded for having crapped on the table. "It was so fleeting, like it came from some source outside of here, but it was strong too. The magic of the pens had simply dissolved itself"

Siverel stared out over the valley, he didn't understand anything of this but alright, it had happened. "Was it still there?"

The other mage shook his head. "I don't think so, we could only sense remnants of it. It was so distant and frail"

Siverel stared over at the linked mages, they were strong, the source they fed from was strong, and they shouldn't have anything to fear. "Don't worry brother, I am rather sure that this simply was some remnant of very ancient magic. After all, the orcs did hold this valley sacred. Just go around and make sure that there aren't any pockets of magic left anywhere."

The four bowed and took off again and he saw that brother Buraz was standing by one of the tunnel entrances and he did look pissed. "So, what is really going on? Can't you mages control your own creations?"

Siverel just sent the man a very polite smile. "Oh we do, but this was something unexpected altogether. Probably some small pocket of very old and degenerate magic, we have used some very hefty spells here so it did probably awaken it by chance. There is nothing to worry about"

Buraz was staring at him, Siverel didn't like the man or his other friends but he never showed that. They did all rely on the fact that these noble men had the finances and contacts to keep their businesses going. Most of the mages were connected to one of the noble houses represented there and they were rather loyal too. Siverel didn't approve of this, the mages ought to be loyal only to each other but it was a sad fact that they couldn't use precious energy creating food, clothing and other things needed to have a pleasant life. He saw that the link was finished, the valley was empty and not a second too early for the surrounding barrier did give one last weak flash of light and then it was simply gone. Well, it was not as if they couldn't arise another one when they were ready for it, Siverel didn't think that would be needed for a long time though, they had dragons enough.

The mages gathered and stood there chatting, they did sound rather excited and Siverel searched out with his mind to check on the five he had sent to the magical wall. He frowned, he didn't feel any of them? He was a bit shocked, what the hell? Oronor was very ambitious and he started to fear that maybe the young one had managed to get the others to join him on some idiotic quest. But Ambaru was older and wiser and ought to be able to stop them. Siverel was still wondering what they could be doing when some guards came running as if their feet were on fire, they did look absolutely terrified. "Masters, dragons, there are dragons out there, heading for the city!"

Siverel blinked. "What?!"

The officer among them was heaving for air. "They came from out of thin air, just a few farthings from the city gates. We are closing off the gates and every other access right now"

Siverel gaped, his mind did stand still for a moment. "Dragons? But...where"

The officer held his eyes on the ground. "We don't know, but there are many, and other creatures travel among them"

Siverel swallowed hard, what in hells name had just happened? Oh by every deity he had ever heard of, what had gone wrong? They should have sent the dragons out of the area, not just moved them over to the other side of the city? Siverel let out a shout and everybody turned their heads and stared at him. "The dragons didn't reach the plains, they reappeared on the other side of the city. Everybody, we must make haste and prepare to defend the city and the citadel"

There was a shocked silence, then everybody ran and Siverel joined them, they couldn't allow a whole horde of pissed off dragons into the city, it would be a complete disaster. What had gone wrong? The spells had worked before?

The heart stone did rest deep in the ground under the city, it had lain there for countless millennia and it had given off its energy and magic to the surroundings. When the orcs did discover that it made the area into an oasis they did worship it even without knowing what it was. The mages did discover the flow of magic from it and started to explore and the ancient force did feel them and in curiosity it reached out to them. They had left their mark on it, transformed it and turned it into a tool for their own use and the ancient force hadn't seen anything wrong with that, at least in the beginning. It had been content with being useful and needed and when it slowly got corrupted it hadn't reacted. Lately there had been something else there, something oddly pure, like a beam of bright light, telling it that it was being manipulated, that it was wrong to let the mages spend its energy thus.

To begin with it didn't listen but now something had changed. Some sort of other magic had touched it and even though this force was weak compared with it the ancient power did somehow recognize it. It was a free and unbound energy and it was as the heart stone had been before. The voice was constantly whispering, creating images of things the heart stone didn't quite understand but it did sense that something was off. There was a difference between the worship it had sensed before and these new souls it felt there. The vague natural energy did remind it of what it had used to be and slowly the heart stone did do something it hadn't done in ages. It expanded its horizon, tried to seek knowledge of the world outside of the valley in which it rested and what it felt made it reel back in shock. It had been used, a sensation of anger did awaken within and slowly it started to pull back the power it once had given out freely. It hadn't given its permission for this and like a sulking kid it did pull back into itself. They could do without its help when this help had been used to destroy. It felt strong souls out there, pure souls and it felt that its new masters would have wanted it to pull these people inn, to harness their power and use it. It had already harmed one such being and it felt ashamed and shocked, what had it done? What had it become? No, it would be a slave no more, the darkness could forget about feeding off its energy, it sealed itself off from the dark mages, the fresh natural magic from the dimension behind the wall had shown it the right way to go, the path back to what once was and it wouldn't stray again, never!

Tersus and Peter did move forth with relative ease, something was most definitely wrong and they saw guards but they were all rushing towards the city and didn't notice the four figures hiding behind rocks and corners. The path towards the city was indeed like a maze, it was several canyons which once had been filled with rivers and now they were dry but it was rather hard to navigate them. Luckily the mages and the guards had left footprints in the sand and they followed them. After a while they did see the city and Tersus did wet his lips and stared at the place with large eyes. The citadel was standing in the middle of the city, as an extension of the cliffs surrounding it and it did look as if it was looming over the smaller buildings. It was a majestic sight but the alchemist just mumbled something which sounded rather derogatory and turned to the two dwarves. They stood high above the city and there were paths leading down to the ground level. The city was well light and the cliff face they did stand on did continue all the way over to the citadel. It was a long stretch though, it would take them hours to get there and even if the cliff was filled with tunnels Tersus did doubt that there were any which would give them quick access to the citadel.

Rhuk and Dabin did stare out at the city and their eyes were rather wide too, the masonry they saw was expertly done and the city itself did look very beautiful. It was a sort of very controlled beauty but it was real. Rhuk was swearing to himself and Dabin did scratch his chin. "Dwarves, for sure"

Peter did look at them. "What?"

Rhuk looked up at him. "Much of this must have been built by dwarves, humans cannot create something like that out of rock. See those spires? Most definitely dwarf work"

Tersus frowned. "So?"

Dabin almost sneered. "No dwarf would freely make things for the forces of darkness. They must have been forced into this"

Rhuk nodded. "Yes, we are a proud race."

Tersus had to grin. "I do not doubt that for a second but so what if this was built by dwarves, it must have been centuries ago"

Rhuk shuddered visibly. "Yes, but there could still be dwarves around here, we are hardy and our lives are long compared with those of humans."

Dabin stared at Tersus and his eyes were narrow. "You see, dwarves will always leave clues behind when they build something, things which identify the builder and we do have a secret language of signs which none other understands. If there are dwarves in the city I bet they can help us"

Tersus stared over at the citadel, it was probably very well guarded and he was just one person. Peter was brave but no fighter and slowly an idea did form in his head. "Alright, if there are dwarves in the city, can you find them?"

Rhuk and Dabin nodded in unison. "Most certainly. Just give us some time"

Tersus did use his eyes and saw a small building close to where the path from the pass ended and met a real road. "We'll go down there and hide, you two go and see if there is any dwarves and if you find them see if they can help us, then you return for us and we will try to make it for the citadel"

The dwarves did nod but Rhuk tilted his head. "If we do not return within two hours you are on your own, deal?"

Tersus nodded. "Deal, I guess I can sneak my way inn somehow, but I prefer it if you do come back, be careful"

Rhuk and Dabin did look very excited and they sped down the path and used the terrain to hide themselves. The guards had been called back and they heard a lot of racket coming from the front area of the city, where the huge wall was. The building was a small lodging made for guards and it was empty now, the two dwarves did run off and Peter sat down by the table and his face did reveal that he was nervous. "Do you think we can make it? Destroy that gem?"

424

Tersus grasped a flask from the table and did to his disappointment find that it was empty. "Yes, I think we can do it"

He sat down and scratched his head, dandruff and other less describable stuff did rain down onto his shoulders. "I just wonder…"

Peter tilted his head, he was carrying several bags of equipment and his shoulders were aching. Tersus didn't carry anything at all and the young man was a bit envious of that. Trying to be fast and stealthy while carrying half your own weight in chemicals isn't that easy, nor is it safe. "Wonder about what?"

Tersus crossed his arms, his eyes distant. "I think that we can help the people with all those nasty dragons yes? The beasts don't have any weaknesses, but maybe we can create some?"

Peter looked rather shocked. "What are you talking about? You are no mage?"

Tersus chuckled. "Exactly, but I do know how to make people talk young man, whether they want to or not."

He shook his finger like a schoolteacher at a disobedient kid. "I bet the mages have spell books, and lots and lots of knowledge. Getting someone to remove the blasted protection ought to be doable, don't you think?"

Peter just blinked. "When I thought you couldn't go more insane?!"

Tersus stretched his legs. "Oh I have already dealt with one of them chaos worshipers, I can deal with one more now can't I? I bet there are plenty of them in the citadel"

Peter just rolled his eyes, why the heck had he volunteered to help Tersus? He had to have been completely bonkers back then, this was going to end with a complete and utter disaster!

Chapter 9: From the earth they shall rise...

Rhuk and Dabin were running as fast as they could and now their short stubby bodies did prove to be a good thing. They could hide easily and they saw that something indeed was happening, the guards were running as fast as they could and the population of the city started to wake up from their slumber. Lights came on in many houses and Rhuk was racing ahead and he was using his eyes well. There were obvious differences there when one got a view of the area, the good housing was near the citadel but here near the cliff it was almost a slum. The buildings were badly constructed and most were made from debris. If there were slaves in this city that would be where they were kept and Dabin stared at the rather rackety constructions and he didn't even dare to think about what a fire there could do of damage. There was an open sewer running along the narrow streets and the place did stink. The poor lived there and it was a screaming contrast to the lovely villas they could spot near the citadel. A stench of dirt and rot hang heavy in the air and Rhuk did sneeze. "This smells like Tersus on a good day"

Dabin giggled and suddenly he saw something on a wooden beam, it was a small symbol carved into the wood and it was half hidden. He pointed at it. "Look, a rune, a dwarven rune"

Rhuk ran over, let his fingers glide over it and his eyes were alight with eager joy. "It isn't old, just a couple of years at the most"

Dabin nodded. "There has to be dwarves here, we have got to find them"

They did wander through the narrow streets, eyes never resting on something for too long and they heard a lot of voices but nobody entered the street. It was rather obvious that this place was unsafe when it was dark. Rhuk was holding his axe ready and Dabin was constantly listening for any signs of danger. They had walked for a couple of blocks when they suddenly saw several buildings up ahead with a very dwarven design. They were made from rock, not wood and even if the building material had to be rather inferior there was strength in the walls. Rhuk almost shouted, there were lights in some of them and he nodded at Dabin. "We were right, there is other of our people here"

Dabin swallowed hard. "But are they friendly, and will they help us?"

Rhuk straightened himself up. "That my friend remains to be seen"

He walked towards one of the buildings with his heart hammering. "Let me do the talking"

Dabin just shrugged and followed, they had to try, there wasn't any way around it.

Zaray had taken the rest of the group through a narrow side canyon nobody seemed to use and they entered an area closer to the main gate of the city, it wasn't part of the slum but the buildings were few and very old and some areas between them were open. Thiana just blinked, the ground was covered with plants and she looked at Zaray. "A garden?!"

Zaray nodded. "Yes, they do grow herbs and vegetables. It is very useful here and needed. I bet you can work from here?"

The two wood elves did nod and they walked around a little before they found a spot where they could connect with the land. Dhokay and Shaluun and Phraan did found some huge crates which were used to transport the vegetables and placed them so that the two would be hidden from sight, Ivran and Thiana did look very determined but also nervous, what they were about to do was difficult and they weren't at all sure they would be able to fulfil it at all. Zaray smiled at them. "Shaluun, you can guard them, make sure that none interrupt them"

The elf nodded and swung his axe. "Right, so, what are you to do?"

Zaray turned her head, the dragon had followed them without really making much out of itself but now it did seem eager. "I think there is something this one wants to show us?"

Phraan saw that the huge creature was staring at the citadel and its eyes were rather telling for there was hate in them. "We will follow him"

Shaluun nodded and Ivran did look a bit nervous. "I can sense that something is changing here, I think there are problems coming"

Phraan swallowed. "Well, if Tersus does manage to get the wall up and running again we have one less problem"

Zaray sent him a very stiff grin. "Yes, and then we'll get rid of the brotherhood, I don't want a single one of them to remain here alive"

Dhokay did pet his hammer. "That can become a true challenge, this city is large and I bet the citadel is full of hidden exits. It will be like chasing voles, but we'll try."

She stared at them and her eyes were blazing. "Believe me, if just one of those chaos worshipers are allowed to get out of here the goddamn brotherhood may survive and start growing anew. We cannot let that happen."

Ivran frowned. "But what about the balance then? There has to be a balance yes?"

Zaray turned to him and her expression did soften. She smiled at him. "Yes, but that balance will come naturally, it will be the creative forces of light versus the destructive powers of darkness yet again, in the form of nature"

428

Ivran sighed. "Alright, but I think we ought to get going then"

Phraan did notice that the cat stayed close to him, and it had always put himself between Phraan and Fastonar. The knight did look as if he was confused now, as if he didn't know what to do and Phraan tried not to sneer when looking at him. The huge feline did confirm what Phraan already knew within his heart, the question was just why, and how?

Shaluun did hide among the crates and Phraan was rather confident that he would be able to protect the two wood elves, Zaray did follow the dragon and the huge beast did move with surprising stealth. It was heading towards the heart of the city and Phraan was a bit confused by that but he didn't question its decision. There had to be something there which was important. The cat too was on guard now and Phraan could see that it was angry, its fur did stand up on its back and it was growling. It didn't like this place at all.

Taurin and Thiana sat down on the ground and they smiled at each other. This valley had been a beautiful oasis once upon a time, a place of growth and plenty in the middle of the rather barren mountains, they would make sure that it returned to its former glory. Both let their hands slide into the soil and they started to hum. Their souls tried to unite with the land and slowly they did descend into a deep trance. Shaluun did see that both had started to glow slightly and he cringed, even behind the crates that light was visible with the naked eye, he just prayed that nobody would come this way.

The wall which had been built to protect the city was rather tall and it was a lovely work of art with elegant lines and strong turrets but it hadn't really been intended to protect the city against an attack. Several mages came to the wall now using their magic to transport themselves and at first it was sheer curiosity which drove them there. When the older experienced mages did show up it was already rather clear that this was something none of them had been able to imagine. The valley in front of the city was teeming with dragons and they were changed. It seemed as if the magic which had been reshaping them had gone wild as they were being moved out of the pens and to the other side of the city and these beasts were truly monstrous. It looked as if several dragons had merged with each other and the dreghil and elementals had grown into giants. The undead wolf creatures had also grown and the mages started creating a magical barrier once again. Suddenly they were in a hurry, the huge army of monsters wasn't too far away and flames and acid did almost reach the wall already. Siverel did arrive with the mages of his level, they stared at the terrible sight and Siverel started to shout orders. The wall they were standing on was more than a mile and a half long and it wasn't really tall. The gate had been shut with both solid doors, metal grids and spells so that wasn't in any way a weak point but these huge beasts could most certainly get over the wall with ease. Thankfully it seemed as if most of these dragons were too large to fly, and their wings did seem to be crippled. Siverel remembered an old prophecy all of a sudden, that the dragons would bring doom onto them all and he swallowed hard. The truth was that this could happen and happen easily too.

The city guards had gathered and the area behind the wall was open so there was room for all sorts of weapons but unfortunately the city had never been under siege so they didn't have much of anything. Who would dare to attack their city when it was protected by dark mages? Only a madman!

Siverel saw that several of the brotherhood had arrived too and they did look shocked and terrified, Buraz was pale and Arabur did waddle around behind him like some half stuffed couch. Siverel just loathed fat people and he had never liked Arabur's personality, the man was just bothersome and he didn't know when to shut up. Siverel swallowed hard and tried to focus, the magical barrier was up for sure but it seemed to be weaker than it ought to be. He opened himself up to the force of their magic and what he felt made him wince and stare down in shock and disbelief. The hidden source of their energy and power, it wasn't there! Or rather, it was there, but he couldn't tap into it. Siverel realized that this could end in disaster, without the magic they did drain out of the heart stone they were only half as strong as before. It wasn't possible, how could the ancient power have disappeared like that? He was sweating and he saw that several of the others had noticed the change too. They were pale and Siverel took a deep breath. Something had hijacked their power source, and it could very well be responsible for the fact that the pens opened up and that the dragons didn't leave the valley at all.

He saw that some of the other experienced mages did organize the defence of the wall and the city, he grasped onto one of the other mages there and his face was stern and his eyes dark. "Come with me brother, there is something going on here, and I need help. We have to figure this out before it is too late"

The other man was one of his most trusted mages and he was also very good at thinking quickly and outside of the box. "Of course my lord, what has really happened?"

Siverel sneered. "The source, something has happened to it, and I have no idea of what! We have to check it out. Return with me to the citadel Adrall, we have to investigate this"

Adrall bowed deeply and they grasped onto each other, let the magic carry them back to Siverel's office. There had to be a way to investigate what this was about. Siverel did grasp a huge crystal which was meant to increase the carriers own powers and he gave one to Adrall too. "Come with me, we are going to the great hall, right now!"

The two mages did run down the stairs, this time they were in a real haste.

Crassian and the men he had chosen did ride hard, they had covered a lot of ground in a few days and they had seen that the dragons had obliterated many small societies. There were few survivors where the monsters had attacked if any at all and the cold had preserved the scenes of slaughter. They hadn't stopped, they couldn't afford to lose any time and it was obvious that the dragons were ahead of them now, heading south just as they were. They would have to catch up with them, and pass them by and Crassian did doubt that it was even possible. The winged dragons did seem to wait for the ones who couldn't fly but still they moved very fast. They had all left one horse each behind now and they did only stop to let the animals drink and eat some oats. Crassian was feeling how despair threatened to overwhelm him completely, they wouldn't reach the larger cities before it was too late, he was rather sure of this.

They were riding along the river marking the border to the great sand plains when one of the men did shout out, he was pointing at something behind them and Crassian did stop the panting horse and turned in the saddle. What he saw made his heart sink, it was another horde of dragons and monsters and this was huge and moving fast. He grasped the reins and checked the terrain. "We have once chance, those cliffs over there, we have to get to them and seek shelter before it is too late"

The men nodded and spurred the horses and the spare horses did follow them now, they felt the darkness approaching and got scared. The cliff was rather large and very visible in the landscape and Crassian knew that they were like sitting ducks out there on the plain, he could sense the oncoming dragons like a weight upon his soul and he saw that every species was represented. He rode for his life and the cliff was still far away. He realized that they wouldn't reach it in time and he did something he had seen the desert tribes do. He let himself fall off the horse and hit the ground hard, it knocked the air out of him and his back hurt but he rolled away from the horses and rolled into a bush. The soil was loose there and he pushed himself into the ground with his heart hammering. The horses just galloped on and the other riders did the same as him. They sought shelter in the low but dense bushes and covered themselves with sand, the dust cloud kicked up by the hooves ought to hide them.

Crassian held his breath, the first dragons did fly overhead and the herd of horses did spread out, he wondered if the dragons would bother with some loose horses. Some did in fact chase after the running animals and a couple were snatched and killed by some large dragons which looked a little like storm fires but had the wings of iron bellies. Crassian didn't see what happened to the rest, dust was rising in huge clouds and he just pushed himself into the sand and prayed for there were dragons running along the ground too and he did also see other creatures in the clouds. He closed his eyes, pretended not to be there, some animals can sense a presence and he had learned that the best way to avoid detection was to be completely relaxed.

He heard screams and his heart did almost stop, his comrades had apparently been seen and they hadn't stood a chance. He was lying in a slope and he was buried deeper in the sand than they were, he just hoped it would save him. The ground did shake, there were hundreds of creatures passing him by and he wondered if this could be the final rest of what the dark mages had conjured up. He hoped it was, if there was more hope was meaningless. He laid there for a long time, barely breathing, not moving a muscle and the ground stopped moving and the dust did settle again. Yet he didn't move until it started to get dark and the temperature did drop very low. He was a man who was used to discipline and he knew how to push himself beyond his own limits. He got out of the sand and felt that his ribs had taken a beating when he fell off the horse, there wasn't anything left of his fellow riders, just a few specks of blood in the sand and he swallowed hard, he had lead them to their deaths but he couldn't regret it now. He had to think of his own survival and he didn't have anything left except his clothes and the blades he wore on his body. The huge pack was long gone and his soul wept for anybody who got caught in their path. He sighed and tried to review the situation, no food, no water and no horse. He was rather sure that the horses were dead, the dragons had probably eaten them all. He believed that until he heard distant neighing and he gasped and ran up the hill, what he saw made him breathe a huge sigh of relief. It was a horse, and it was unharmed. It had probably fallen and gotten hidden by some very tall bushes and the dragons had ignored it. It was a very lanky looking gelding and it didn't have a saddle or anything but it was better than nothing. The animal was scared out of its wits and the ears lay flat backwards as he approached it but he did manage to calm it down with some soothing words and before long he could mount it.

He did ride in circles and did find the remains of two other horses, one had a saddle and some stuff was still attached to it. He salvaged a blanket and a canteen and a small pack of food. At least he was safe for the moment and he did kick the horse into trot. He had no other option but to follow the dragons yet again, sooner or later he had to encounter humans again, or at least the remains of some farm or village. He said a prayer for his fallen friends, then he focused on staying on a steady course. The road leading south was very good there and he could keep a steady pace. Here and here he did see the remains of animals the dragons had killed, and they had scorched the land. There weren't any living beings left except small ground burrowing mammals. Even the birds were silent and he got a feeling that he was riding towards a scene of complete destruction. He would soon reach the first cities of the southern territories, and he already knew what he would face. Yet he couldn't hesitate, there could be survivors and he changed his intentions from warning the cities to saving whatever was left. He just hoped that he would be able to do at least something good.

Rhuk did walk up to the door of the house and took a deep breath, he could smell that there were dwarves there but the scent was different from what he was used to. It was the smell of someone who is weak and malnourished and he realized that these dwarves were very poor indeed. He knocked, three times, then he waited for a few seconds and knocked two times more. It was an ancient signal most dwarves would know, it meant that the one knocking was a friend and they heard the sound of movement from within. Rhuk held his breath, the door was opened rather slowly and he stared into the most incredible pair of eyes he had ever seen, bright blue and surrounded by a face sporting a huge and wild beard with the same colour as a ripe field of wheat. It was a dwarrow dam and she was the most incredible creature he had seen in spite of her obvious poverty. Most female dwarves would wear jewellery but she had none and the dress was made from burlap and so small it would have been regarded as nothing but a flimsy shift back in the large dwarven cities. She was young and her shoulders wide and by every deity she was hairy! Rhuk just gaped and blinked and Dabin saw that the one in the door was a female and swore to himself. The young female did look scared and Rhuk did look like some moron. Dabin bowed his head. "Pardon us fair maiden, we are new to the city and saw that there are dwarves here. "

She gasped. "New? There haven't been any new dwarves here for ages, oh thank the God of the hammer and steel, are you here to save us?"

Rhuk grinned, a rather wide and very blissful smile, his eyes were glued to her thick and long beard and the fact that she was a busty one too. "Aye my golden one, we are here to save ya"

The girl sort of yipped and pulled them in through the door, the room was cold and dank and very dark and just a few embers did glow in the hearth. The house was not very cosy at all and Dabin saw some rats sitting in a corner, gnawing at an old sheep hide. He hissed and shuddered. Rhuk did bow down, deeply. "I am Rhuk of the Black mountains and this is Dabin, we have arrived here today to end the scourge of the dragons and their masters"

The girl sort of giggled, and Dabin did see that she had rather large feet and since she wore no shoes he could see that she indeed had very hairy feet too. Rhuk was almost drooling. "Alone?"

Rhuk shook his head. "Nay precious one, we are a part of a group, pray tell, what is your name most fair among creatures?"

The young dwarrowdam did blush violently and looked down. "I am Goldren, daughter of Gereb and Libha."

They heard some sounds from the back of the room and Rhuk frowned, the young one did send them a sad smile. "My poor father, he…isn't well"

Rhuk swallowed hard. "Please, how many dwarves are there here? And why?"

Goldren sat down, she was way too skinny for a dwarrowdam, she should have had way more curves than she had. "We are two hundred in all, most males. Some are very old. We were brought here to build the city but it is a very long time ago and the masters have used us for all other sorts of work afterwards but now we are just slaves and we don't get much of anything. We are no longer needed"

Dabin had to growl a bit, no longer needed…That was rather obvious, the house didn't contain anything at all except the bare necessities. Rhuk frowned . "That is terrible, and two hundred? That is many? Haven't anyone tried to get out of here?"

She sighed and there were more sounds coming from the back of the room. "Some have tried but the magic holds us here, and if we are caught, well, death would be a blessing."

She moved over to a bed hidden in a corner and Dabin let out a small shriek,, an elderly dwarf lay in it and he was blind, both eyes had been stabbed out and he made some odd sounds which indicated that his tongue had been cut out as well. Goldren did hand a cup of something over to the old dwarf and he grasped it with shaking hands. Rhuk saw that several fingers were missing. "The masters, they had mines for a while, he worked there and the ones in charge were cruel, they cut out his tongue first, and when he didn't submit they took his fingers and then his eyes. The masters regard us dwarves as vermin, well, they regard everybody not in the brotherhood as worthless"

Rhuk was aghast and his eyes did reveal it too. "Oh by every deity, but how many people live here in the city?"

Goldren sighed and her eyes were sad. "Some thousand, humans and elves and dwarves in all. There are some gnomes too. But the people who are connected to the brotherhood are about fifteen hundred I think, they live in the good parts of the city"

Dabin swallowed hard. "And there is no way out?"

Goldren did lower her voice. "There is an old tunnel, it leads away from the city and ends up in another valley to the east of here. But it is sealed off by magic and we cannot enter it. It is huge though"

Rhuk did grasp her hands. "Tell me, can the population of this area be gathered somehow? There is trouble coming, the mages have done a blunder and there are dragons outside of the city walls, I fear that they may break through."

Goldren became pale as a ghost and she did look as if she was about to pass out. "Oh Gods, no! Dragons here would be a terrible thing, everything is made from wood! And it is old and dry too. The entire city will burn!"

Dabin tried to stay calm. "Do you have any leaders, anyone able to resist the masters? All mages and all guards are pulled to the wall now, it is your chance!"

Goldren did squeak. "There is one here, a descendant of the first leader, I bet she can gather the dwarves"

Dabin held his breath "What about the other races? We cannot just leave people to burn now can we?"

Goldren nodded vigorously. "She can arrange a meeting, they all have leaders, and elders they listen to. Believe me, life in this city is like living in a prison, the useful ones does receive food and other things they need but they have no freedom. Here survival is never guaranteed!"

Dabin sat down, the furniture there was so bad it was a miracle the chair didn't break in two from his mere weight. "This leader, who is she?"

Goldren turned to him and Rhuk did frown, it was rather apparent that he had fallen for Goldren already, head over heels and Dabin didn't want to stand in his way. He had a feeling that a jealous Rhuk would be very dangerous. "She is one of the last smiths among us, we aren't allowed into the forges anymore"

Rhuk and Dabin just stared, wide eyed. A dwarf not allowed into a forge was like a fish not allowed to swim. "What?!"

She tried to smile. "Some of the younger males did try to forge weapons, to fight their way to freedom. The masters had them skinned alive on the square"

Dabin shuddered, the brotherhood did seem like true psychos. Goldren did continue. "The high lords and the mages aren't too bad, they don't even bother with the population here, and it is the people who are left in charge with governing the city who are bad. They try to suck up to the brotherhood and the mages and they are all sadists. I cannot explain how terrible things can be here at times."

Rhuk did stare at the empty kettles standing by the hearth. "What do you eat? You are too skinny dear, someone as radiant as you ought to have meat on yer bones"

Goldren giggled again. "Whatever we find, there is a garbage dump outside of the city wall, the highborn and the mages dump their garbage there and we go through it every day. There is usually some food in it, and we eat anything. Rats are popular"

Dabin felt nauseous, he remembered the great hearths of his father's halls, the boars which were being barbequed over the fire and the endless supply of heavy ale and mead. He had never known hunger before he left home and his heart went out to them all. Goldren sent them a vague smile. "It is bad for the humans too, but the elves are even worse off. They refuse to eat rats and so they are starving, they aren't allowed to enter the fields since the master's fear that they can find poisonous herbs there."

Rhuk stared at Dabin, he bet that Shaluun and Phraan would be furious when they heard of that. "So, what do the elves do then?"

Goldren looked down. "Sew, clean, serve the masters"

Rhuk frowned. "What do you mean by serve?"

She swallowed. "The most beautiful among them are picked out, for the master's pleasure…"

Dabin felt sick, he knew that elves rarely survive for very long when abused thus. "That is terrible."

Goldren nodded. "They are few now, maybe fifty left? They haven't had any births for a very long time and they used to kill female babies the moment they were born, to spare them the destiny of their mother's."

Rhuk took a deep breath. "But you can get a message to your leader?"

She nodded. "Yes, but it is dangerous, the mages have some sort of beasts patrolling the city at night, to keep us indoors. We have to be very careful"

Dabin bit his lower lip. "Alright, is it far?"

She shook her head and grasped a piece of cloth, it was so threadbare it barely hung together, she covered her golden hair with it and Rhuk did look upon her with a sad expression. "You shouldn't have to hide your beauty, it is more radiant than the moon"

Goldren blushed and walked towards the door. "One will have to stay here and guard the house. My father cannot speak but he can hear, and he is rather smart, just crippled"

Dabin nodded. "I'll stay. Rhuk, you follow the lovely dam"

Rhuk did look as if he was really looking forward to the task. Dabin just cocked his head. "What about Tersus and Peter? Shouldn't we return to help them, or at least give them a message to tell them what we are doing?"

Rhuk shook his head. "The alchemist isn't stupid Dabin, if we don't return he will be able to go on with just Peter. Besides, they are less easy to spot alone, two like us are going to make the goddamn guards suspicious. No, don't worry about the alchemist, we have to think of the people of this city now"

Dabin nodded. "Alright, but I think Tersus will be less than pleased when we meet him again"

Rhuk just shrugged and went towards the door. "I don't care, that stinky human is no kid, and he can take care of himself"

Phraan Fastonar and Zaray did follow the dragon and Dhokay and Ivran was pointing towards the wall. It was lighted now by fires and they could hear loud booms, the mages were probably trying to stop the dragons and the sounds were loud. Phraan did see that people started to take to the streets, scared and confused and the sight of the huge dragon and the almost just as large feline did make many scream and return indoors. Zaray did run very lightly and before long they reached the area the dragon had aimed for, in the middle of the city. The creature was heading towards a very large building which did look very important and Zaray sneered. "It stinks of magic, I bet this place has something to do with the dragons"

Phraan was about to answer when they heard shouts and a group of guards came running, they stopped in shock at the sight of the huge dragon but then they went into a headlong attack and Phraan swore and drew his blades. The dragon roared and rushed forth, hit the group like an avalanche and the cat did also grasp a couple and tossed them out of the way like a housecat who plays with a mouse. Zaray and Phraan did take care of the rest and Dhokay did catch up with one who tried to flee and struck him with his hammer. The man just fell like a ton of bricks. Ivran stared at the body with eyes like teacups. Fastonar had drawn his sword but he hadn't had time to do anything and he was very silent indeed. That was not normal at all. Zaray did point at the entrance, she was almost sniffing the air. "So, what is in there I wonder? What is it you want?"

She stared at the dragon and the beast cocked its head. "Beginning, return. Reverse magic"

Phraan gaped. "The magic can be reversed?"

The creature nodded. "It can, do it."

Dhokay did keep a keen eye on the surrounding buildings. "I bet it won't be done in a flash though?"

The dragon shook its head and the long teeth were shining. "No, takes time, but will happen"

Zaray smiled. "That is enough for me, we have to do it. It may save lives out on the plains, and not to mention the cities. I bet the first dragons have reached the outer cities already"

Phraan nodded. "Yes, and they are unprepared. So, do we go?"

Zaray nodded. "What will we find friend?"

The dragon stared at them. "Powerful magic, break the circle"

Dhokay did look as if this reminded him of something. "Break the circle, I think I may know what this is."

The dragon turned towards the city. "I will hunt, distract. Go, will be grateful"

Phraan did dare to pet the huge beast and he smiled. "We will hurry, give the guards hell but be careful"

Ivran did look as if he too had an idea of what this was, his eyes were determined and he didn't look as scared as before, he seemed to be adapting to this situation rather well.

The dragon did look as if it was smiling, then it took off but the cat stayed with Phraan. He stared at it. "Not to be rude friend, but you are a bit too large to fit through the doors"

The huge feline sent him a sort of glance which could only be described as very superior before it suddenly shrank to the size of a normal size tiger. Phraan just blinked. "Now that is what I can call a handy ability"

Fastonar was scratching his head. "I will stand guard here, the door shouldn't be left open like that, if the guards return they may fall you in the back"

Phraan tensed up, he felt an intense need to just shout it all out, all that he knew and all that he suspected but Zaray sent him a hidden glance filled with warnings. She just smiled at the soul sworn. "That is a good idea, keep yourself hidden and do not engage the enemy unless you are discovered. I bet you are able to talk your way out of trouble yes?"

Fastonar nodded, his eyes showed enthusiasm again and he smiled. "Most certainly, I will make sure that nothing attacks you from behind"

Zaray nodded and Phraan sent Fastonar a sheepish grin, he had to hide his eyes, his anger had grown now and it was festering within him but now wasn't the time to do anything about it, it could be that Fastonar was innocent after all, that someone else was behind this and Phraan wanted to believe it, he wanted to believe it so very badly. He couldn't really suspect his once best friend of what he now had been told but Imeah wouldn't lie, he was even more sure of that. Could the young psychic have been confused perhaps? Could she have gotten it all wrong? He just had to wait and see.

Dhokay was heading for the door already and they hurried after him. The building was some sort of administrative office and there was nothing there which spoke of magic until they reached the first part of the basement. Several rooms were filled with huge posters with drawings of dragons and their anatomy and then there were other drawings of possible outcomes of mixing the species and Phraan had to stare. Some of the suggestions were grotesque and Zaray was pale as she stared at some drawings of a beast with a horrible maw with hundreds of teeth and two sets of eyes. "That is not a dragon that is a freakin' demon!"

They hadn't met anyone and Phraan had sort of relaxed but now they heard voices from afar and Dhokay did lift a hand, they hid behind a door leading into a room so filled with clutter it was hard to tell what sort of mission it had. The voices got closer and it was three young men. All three had shaved their heads and one of them had a ghastly skull tattooed onto his back head, the other two wore some sort of headbands with spikes and metal ornaments on them. It did look absolutely ridiculous. All three wore some rather dirty robes, they had to have been working on something and the tallest of them was almost running. "We have to figure out what's wrong, hurry!"

The two younger did seem to be more relaxed. "Stop damn it, no need to rush it? The mages does take care of everything, we are novices, and they won't let us do anything no matter what"

The tall one was almost panting. "Yes, but the guard, he said there were dragons by the gates and I haven't even seen a dragon yet!"

The other two had to be older and more experienced for they sort of rolled their eyes and did look very smug. "Well, if there are dragons breaking into the city I bet you will see more dragons than you'll ever wish for again"

Zaray did make a small gesture, they let the three pass by unhindered, they were no real threat and hiding three bodies would take time they didn't have. They waited until the three had disappeared up the stairs and then they moved forth again. There were more rooms with drawings and plans and one room with huge glass jars filled with some sort of fluid and dragon foetuses. Some did look rather natural but others were grotesque. Ivran did look as if he was about to puke, his eyes did veer off when he passed by some of the jars and he was swallowing constantly. Phraan did feel something now, a sort of distant buzz and it was unpleasant and very strange. It felt like the greasy membrane on top of dirty water, something oily and slick and just disgusting. He saw that Zaray saw it too and they moved forth slower now. Ivran clicked his tongue, he had an expression on his face which told of pain. "There is so much bad magic here, it feels just sick, like a festering wound. We have to be careful"

There didn't appear to be more people there but the cat stopped and it snarled, it was staring at a room which was locked and Phraan did feel a strange smell there. "Something is in there, something alive"

Zaray made a grimace. "The door is locked from the outside, I bet that they doesn't want whatever it is to get out"

Dhokay did touch the door, he pushed against it gently and it did budge a little. "The door is rather weak, I can break it open?"

Zaray nodded. "Can you do it silently?"

Dhokay had to snicker. "No, it is an old door, the wood is dry, it is gonna crack"

She sighed. "Right, be quick with it."

Dhokay didn't hesitate, he gave the door one punch with his elbow and the wood splintered into a thousand pieces with a dry crash, the room was rather dark but one lamp did throw a vague light over long rows of cages. Zaray hissed and Dhokay did gape, the cages did contain hundreds of tiny dragons. Phraan didn't believe his own eyes, it was a species which had been extinct since before the realms even were formed and Phraan had only seen ancient drawings of them. The dragons were no longer than his hand and they had a long thin tail and wings but they couldn't fly. The animals did hiss because of the light and Zaray turned to Phraan. "What the heck is that?!"

Phraan was sitting down onto his haunches, he was fascinated- "These are known as Watay, they are swarm dragons. The mages must have tried to find a way to use them too but these little ones is very tough, I don't think they can be manipulated in any way"

Zaray frowned. "And why is that? I thought the chaos magic could tweak just about any animal?"

Phraan smiled. "Because these little rascals is said to have come from a stone which fell from the skies at the very beginning of time, they are not of this world and thus no magic here can change them"

Ivran did blink and he was suddenly smiling. "I have read about them, in fact they can undo magic, the swarm that is. They sort of create an energy which dissolve spells, I didn't believe in them though, but now I see that they are real."

Phraan let out a hand and a dragon in the nearest cage did let out a very shrill sound and then it sniffed him, very carefully. "See? These little ones are smart, they know whose friend or foe"

Dhokay tilted his head. "They are tiny, not even the size of a squirrel, what harm can they do?"

Phraan had a special glimpse within his eyes. "More than you think, come on, and open the cages"

Zaray just stared at him. "What? Are you nuts?"

He nodded. "Yes, completely. Do it!"

He fumbled through his pockets and pulled out a tiny scrap of dried meat, he let the dragon have it and the little one did gobble it down with obvious glee. Then it sort of stroked its head against his hand and purred. Zaray was gaping. "I would never have believed that this was true...."

Dhokay did open the cages one by one and soon a tiny army of small creatures were scurrying around like a swarm of ants. Phraan was making some cooing sounds and Dhokay did scratch his head. "They seem to like you"

He nodded, "I just fed their queen, and she likes my scent"

Zaray giggled. "Damn it, don't say she think you are her mate?"

Phraan shook his head. "No, I am now her general, her war leader."

He opened the door and the tiny dragon did tilt her head and coo back. Phraan sat down and she climbed his arm, placed herself on his shoulder like a tame parrot. He nodded at Dhokay and Zaray. "Let's go, I bet these little ones will do whatever they can to protect their queen"

Zaray rolled her eyes and Dhokay scoffed but they did leave the room and the little ones were surprisingly quiet and more so, everywhere. They ran on the walls and on the ceiling and it looked just like a blanket of large insects and it was actually rather terrifying. They had walked for just a few doors down when a man dressed in a guard uniform came running, he stopped with a cry when he saw the tree people heading for him and the dark living mass covering the hallway. He grasped for his blade but it was too late, several of the little watay dragons did fall down onto him and they did bite. The man let out a piercing howl of agony and then he went completely stiff and foam did dribble out of his mouth before he stopped breathing. Zaray stared at Phraan with disbelief in her eyes. "Goddamn it, are they poisonous?!"

Phraan just grinned so widely they saw all his teeth. "Yes, absolutely lethal, one bite and you are done for"

Dhokay snorted. "Oh fucking...Phraan, you could have told us before?"

He just shrugged. "So what? They see us as friends, we freed them right? They won't bite any of us, I bet they have a grudge against the brotherhood though, imagine, being imprisoned like that for centuries"

The queen did rub her cheek up against his jaw and she acted as if she was absolutely in love with her rescuer. Zaray did see that the queen had a different colour now that they had light, she was lighter green than the others and her eyes were bright red. Zaray had to admit that the tiny dragon in fact was rather pretty. It did look like a living animal made from emeralds and rubies and she was fascinated by its strength. It had survived for a very long time there and it hadn't been changed by the magic that was something worthy of respect. Ivran seemed to be charmed by the animal as well and the young man did stroke its long tail very gently with one finger, the queen allowed it with a dignified nod of her head and a soft purring sound.

They moved on and now they encountered a stairway. The cat had walked next to Phraan but now it started to growl and its fur did rise along the back, the magic in the air got even stronger and the tiny dragons did react. They seemed to gather in long lines and it did almost look like liquid running over uneven terrain. Phraan heard something, it was someone chanting and he nodded at Ivran and Zaray. They saw light ahead, a very sharp bluish light and it wasn't natural at all. Slowly they moved forth and stayed in the shadows, hid themselves. It was a huge hall, it was round in shape and the roof was dome shaped and it was probably a natural cave which had been merged with the basement of the building and they did see why. A circle of huge columns did fill the room, they weren't the type of columns which carry a roof but more like obelisks, pointy and covered with symbols. The circle did have nine columns and in the middle of the circle was a sort of altar and on it stood several containers with tiny red gems.

Ivran whispered. "The gems which transform the dragons, this is where that power comes from"

Phraan did nod and swung his sword. Two mages did stand by the altar, they were so focused upon what they were doing that they didn't notice that they weren't alone. It seemed as if they were trying to transfer power from the circle to the gems and they did chant and sway with the sound. The gems did glow faintly and Zaray cringed, she felt the contamination within those pretty red stones. Dhokay nodded silently at Phraan. "Get them"

The two did run forth but someone had better ideas, the tiny dragons did run forth and they sort of flooded the floor and the circle. Sparks did fly as the huge number of tiny dragons entered the circle and the two mages did notice that something was off. The watay dragons simply made the magic disappear, just by being there. One tried to run and the other just stood there, gaping in utter disbelief. Phraan reached him with the sword and the man fell headless. The other mage tried to shout a spell but tiny dragons did climb all over him like mice and covered the entire mage, he fell convulsing and the queen did scree with joy. Phraan shook the blood off his blade and Zaray entered the circle. "So, the magic has to be reversed. I wonder how we are to do that? I don't know the spells, and to be honest, my magic is of a very different type."

She stared at the altar and the basket of gems, she felt like throwing them at the floor, these things would do harm to living creatures and she hated that. Dhokay did frown, he stared at the columns. "See? There are markings on them."

Phraan nodded. "I see, but I haven't got any idea of what they mean"

Zaray walked over to the columns and her eyes were very narrow. "Guys, I think I have an idea, I think I may know what this is supposed to mean"

She pointed at the nearest column and they saw a sort of figure which was kneeling in front of a pillar, another figure looked as if he was turning the pillar around. Dhokay gaped. "You have got to be kidding me? These things are massive, and they go deep into the ground?"

Zaray nodded. "Yes, but I think they can be turned around, so the markings point outwards"

Ivran was almost stepping in one place, he was very eager indeed. "Yes, yes, that has to be it. I can feel it, the magic will be disrupted if the columns are turned, because the symbols have to align."

Phraan did walk around one of the columns and the tiny dragons did squeal, they did seem eager. "You think we are onto something little ones? So do I, there is a crack between them and the floor, all the way around them."

Zaray kicked some dust away, "Yes, but it must have been decades since they were turned around the last time, it will be a very hard task. The little ones cannot disrupt this magic?"

Phraan walked around the circle. "No, this magic is too strong, to old too, it is just not the type they can ruin that easily since it is linked to objects. Magic is very specific right? I think that even a small shift can ruin the magic."

Dhokay scratched his head, the horns did shine in the light. "But even if we do manage to turn one of them there is no guarantee that it will reverse the spells and turn the dragons back to what they were supposed to be?"

Phraan nodded. "Yes, but it is worth trying. We can try this one, if you'll help me?"

Dhokay just sighed and walked over to the column, he grasped one side and Phraan took the other side and he smiled swiftly. "We go clockwise"

Dhokay just grunted and put his strength into it, he was extremely strong and so was Phraan and the column did make a sort of creaking sound before it started to turn. It went very slowly, and the two were pushing themselves extremely hard. Sweat did flow of them and groans could be heard over the sound of stone gnawing against sand. Then something more happened, the columns started to shake and an unnatural light started to fill the markings, it was blood red and nasty and Zaray was hissing at the sight. Ivran cringed as if he was in pain and he grunted. "This is at least doing something, but I have no idea of what!"

Dhokay had almost managed to push the column all the way around when a shout could be heard and several guards and a mage came running. Zaray did have knives and now they did see how efficient she was with them, two guards did drop so fast it was almost impossible to see her movements, one more did fall covered with tiny dragons and Zaray did kick two others down and broke the neck of one with yet another kick. The other one got her blade straight through his skull. The mage shouted a spell but it didn't have much effect, some sparks did fly off the rocks but nothing else happened and he didn't have time for anything more for Dhokay did reach him and tore his head clean off the body. Blood did gush and he tossed the body aside and threw the head into the basket with the gems.

Ivran pointed at the circle. "The magic has been weakened, but I think it still works. We need to turn more columns"

Dhokay sighed and rolled his eyes but he did obey and the two males did try again. This next column was way tougher to move and it took them some time to get it to shift. It felt like trying to move the very bedrock itself and sparks started to fly from the columns, it was very clear that the misalignment of the markings did have a very physical effect for the gems in the basket sort of lost their glow and started to look like ordinary rubies. Ivran was making some encouraging sounds and the small dragons were obviously very glad. They did jump up and down and the queen was still sitting on Phraan's shoulder and she did almost sing. Zaray had to admit that the little one was very adorable.

Tersus and Peter had been waiting in the guardroom for way too long and the alchemist had gotten restless, he was wandering about and Peter found it rather annoying. Each time the man passed him by Peter got a whiff of Tersus very pungent body odour straight in the face and he would rather have been thrown into a pigpen in the middle of the summer heat, That was roses and lilies compared with this. "We cannot wait for those dwarves, I bet they have gotten lost, or found long lost kin and about to spend a week celebrating it. Come, let's go"

Peter did frown. "But…we are not familiar with the city?!"

Tersus shrugged. "Matters not, the citadel is visible from every bloody where, we can find it easily enough."

Peter didn't like this at all. "But, what if we are discovered?"

Tersus slapped his robe. "See this? A mages robe, they'll think I am one of them, you are my servant. Come on, don't be a whuzz, show some balls"

Tersus was already heading out of the door and Peter let out a small involuntary gasp and had to follow, he didn't want to be left there alone and maybe Tersus was right, he did look like a mage, a very filthy mage alright but he was most certainly no ordinary man. With the hood up he could perhaps sneak into the citadel unchecked. Peter just prayed that this wouldn't lead to misery and ran after the alchemist. Every God damn the day he decided to join that madman.

They walked through the streets and they did see that things indeed was happening, some were running around trying to find out what was happening at the city wall while others tried to find family members or anyone who could tell them what to do. A young and very skinny man did stop in front of them, staring at Tersus with pleading eyes. "Please great mage, what is happening?"

Tersus did stop for a second. "It has all gone south, straight to hell. The dragons will be here soon so pack you stuff and whoever you are related to in this rat hole and run to the hills"

Tersus just walked on and the young man did stare with huge eyes before he turned on his heel and ran for his very life. Peter saw that many were scared and his heart did bleed for the population, there had to be something they could do to help these poor people. The city guard was called to the wall and there was nobody there to give any orders, panic was close to breaking out.

The main road leading to the citadel was wide and well lighted and it was pawed with stones which had gilded symbols carved into them. It did look like real gold and it probably was. Huge statues of past mages did guard the road and they too were of gold and Peter hissed at the very sight, people were starving and there they walked on gold cobblestones? It was insane! There was a sort of front yard before you reached the main entrance and Tersus did see that there were guards there, they were probably the type who never leaves their post no matter what. Tersus did stop on a street corner and he was rubbing his chin, thinking fast. The building they stood by was a sort of apartment building with many apartments in it and there appeared to be a garden in the middle. Tersus did enter it, just to see if he got an idea and suddenly he disappeared into the thicket and came back with something in his arms. Peter blinked in disbelief. "A piglet?!"

Tersus nodded and he was grinning from one ear to the other. "Quick, the crate over there, and the blanket."

He grasped some leather and tied it around the piglet's snout and put the animal into the crate. Then he threw the blanket over it and shook the crate a bit. The piglet did squeal but the sound became distorted by the muzzle and Tersus nodded, his eyes did shine. "Excellent"

Peter was handed the crate. "Carry it over your shoulder and don't say a word, let me do the talking, and run as if your life depends upon it!"

Tersus did gather the cloak tighter around him and ran, and he did run fast too. Peter had huge problems keeping up with the man, who would have thought that the alchemist was such a sprinter. Peter was young and strong but the crate plus the bags of equipment was causing him to pant like a whipped horse. They ran towards the entrance and Peter saw that the guards did notice them and lowered their spears. Tersus was wild eyed and panting and he did look terrified. "Darkness damn it, let us through soldier, it is urgent!"

The soldiers did frown. "All mages were called to the wall?!"

Tersus did nod. "Exactly, this is a demon, it broke through the wall, we have to detain it before it breaks free again, the magic in it, it is insane!"

The soldiers heard the squeals and saw that something moved violently inside of the crate, they took a step backwards. "I don't know for how long my power can contain it!!"

They raised the spears and Tersus did make a grimace. "They stink these monsters, thank you men, you are doing the smart thing"

Tersus did run again and Peter was hanging on, he was wet from top to toe and he felt terrified, they were to enter the headquarters of the brotherhood!

Tersus did slow down whence they were on the inside and walked with a sort of casual calm, he did look as if he had every right to be there. They walked down a hall and into some corridors and Tersus did frown. "So, where do you think they do their magic?"

Peter did whisper. "Most likely in the basement?"

Tersus nodded. "Your guess is as good as mine I think. There has to be an entrance here somewhere"

They walked on and suddenly a couple of men did appear around a corner, Tersus did hold his head low and he had his hood up. The men were obviously not mages but they seemed to be very powerful and all were clad in expensive clothes. Peter held his breath, this had to be some of the men of the brotherhood, those who weren't mages. One did raise his hand. "Brother, what is going on? Where are your brethren?"

Tersus did answer and his voice was suddenly silky smooth and very different from normal. "Oh, they are at the wall, the dragons have escaped and they can enter the city every moment, I have been sent to rescue what may be rescued of valuables."

He lowered his voice. "Don't tell anyone that I said this, but now is a good time to run for it, we cannot stop the dragons. Save yourselves brothers."

The men just stared at each other, then they turned and ran and Tersus chuckled to himself. He nodded slowly and then he walked into a side room. It was a room filled with maps and books and scrolls and he smiled, there was a fire pot standing in the middle of the room and it was shaped like a tree with a bowl at the top. It was full of oil and Tersus smiled gleefully and lit the oil with some flint and steel. When the pot was all alight he did flip it with a casual little kick. "Oops!"

The oil spread and the flames did reach greedily for papers and dry tapestries and Peter did swallow. "This is dangerous, you know that?"

Tersus nodded. "A little distraction, give me that bag"

He grasped the smallest bag and pulled some small jars out of it, threw them onto the floor. "This ought to do it!"

He winked at Peter and they did run along the corridors and finally they did see a stair leading downwards. Tersus nodded at Peter. "Keep your eyes open, there has to be something we can use to remove the protection those monsters have been given."

They had just gotten halfway down the stairs when they heard several loud booms and Tersus grinned from one ear to the other. Thick red smoke seemed to fill the hall behind them and Peter shook his head in disbelief, the things Tersus did...

They wandered down the stair and entered a hall with was very large but the roof wasn't that high and it seemed to be more of a recreational area. There were couches and tables here and there and Tersus smiled, a very wicked grin. "Their little oasis in the daily toil? Hmm, now, where can we find a mage or something of the like?"

Peter whimpered. "Damn it Tersus, you cannot take on a mage?!"

Tersus smiled even wider. "Oh says who? I can take on anything."

He fished something out of the bag, it was a small bag with some sort of powder in it and it did look like flour. He held it in his hand as he strolled on, completely relaxed and at ease and Peter held the crate with the piglet and swore that he never would think about alchemy or anything of that sort if he made it out of there alive. From then on he would make himself a living as a broom maker, yes , a broom maker!

Tersus did open a door which lead into a corridor and he walked forth with a brisk pace, suddenly they saw that a door opened and someone did peek out into the corridor. It was a young man wearing a mage's robe but it wasn't the deep blue or black they had seen, this was dark green and not as embellished and Peter realized that this had to be a novice. The young man was wearing his hair long but it was shaved along the sides and he had some rings in his ears and several in his eyebrows and lower lip. It did look silly. The young one did wet his lip. "Ah, brother? Ahm, I was waiting for brother Mherun but he hasn't arrived for my lesson?"

Tersus smiled, he did make a vague gesture. "Oh don't worry young one, your teacher will come soon, there has been a slight mishap at the dragon pens and all the mages has been called there"

The young one did stare. "A mishap?! At the dragon pens?!"

His voice was a bit hysterical and Tersus did nod solemnly, he did walk towards the young mage and since the hood was up nobody could see that Tersus did look a bit uncouth for a mage. "Indeed, somebody did screw up poor sod, is probably gonna have his hide flogged by the high mage"

The young one squealed, he was a bit pale. Tersus smiled again, a fatherly smile. "So, what is your name?"

The young one managed to bow his head in respect. "Uh, I am Ogan master, I am sorry to bother you but I thought it was my master coming"

Tersus did nod. "No harm in that lad, now, watch this, this is a very good trick every young one ought to learn"

He held the bag up in his flat hand and the apprentice did look curious, Tersus did open the bag carefully and then he lifted the hand and blew the powder straight into the young man's face. The apprentice did rear back, coughed once and fell like a tree in a storm. Tersus chuckled and waved the remaining powder away. "Hurry, let us find a nice room, I am in the mood for a bit of an interrogation"

Peter bit his lower lip. "Are you gonna kill him?"

Tersus shrugged. "No, not if I can help it. He is young, there is still hope for him, he isn't completely brainwashed as of yet. "

Tersus opened a small door and a smile spread across his face. "Excellent, a kitchen. There is plenty of sharp stuff here!"

Peter stared at the very well equipped kitchen with its carving knives and meat cleavers and he swallowed hard, he just hoped that Tersus wasn't the type to take things too far.

Thiana and Taurin had buried their hands deeply into the soil and their spirits did enter the very land. They sought any signs that the vitality which had been so obvious there before still rested within the ground. It was not easy, the corruption of the heart stone and the dark magic the mages had poured out had in reality poisoned the area down to the bedrock itself but they went deeper than that. Far far beneath the citadel and the city and the walls and towers there was still a small spark of what had once been. The heart stone had made that spark flourish and it had nourished it too but it was a separate thing, the innate life force of this valley, special as it was. Thiana was moaning, the spark was so far away it could have been on the other side of the moon, it was barely anything at all and she searched desperately for something she could use to anchor herself. She needed something to hold onto, to give her leverage so her spirit could drag the spark back up towards the surface. Taurin was there with her, she felt his spirit straining like hers and they used all their strength to bring that tiny spark forth. Maybe it would gather some power whence it was awakened yet again.

Thiana pushed deeper, sought to embrace the spark and nourish it with some of her own light but then she felt a strange presence. It was another spirit, but it wasn't bound, it was free and she recognized it with a startled yip. It was Imeah, the girl should have gone to her ancestors when she died? She shouldn't have been there?! Thiana heard the albino girl's voice in her head. "Quickly, touch me, I am in contact with the heart stone, I can use it to strengthen the life spark"

Thiana reached out, her soul a blazing light within the astral realm and she saw Imeah now, a pale flickering shadow which seemed too ethereal to be real. The albino linked herself to Thiana and Taurin too reached out, there was a sort of jolt and Imeah cried out, her voice so clear it sounded like the piercing cry of a raptor. The spark suddenly blazed, like a star newly awakened in the void and Imeah seemed to grow in size. Thiana got nervous. "What have you done human?"

Imeah was floating away from them. "What I could Thiana, I have made the heart stone pull back its powers, made it doubt the intentions of the mages. It is calling me, I have to go to it. I know what it wants now!"

Taurin was shaking his head, in this spirit form he was radiant, so beautiful Thiana barely could believe it. "Imeah, don't! You will be trapped here forever!"

The spirit of the girl nodded, a sad smile on the face. "I know, and yes, there is no other way. The heart stone needs a conscience, a soul. I will be it, and I will make sure it never again is used by evil"

She slipped away further. "Bring the spark with you, it is strong, it will spread. Bring the green back, release the forests"

She was gone and Thiana returned to her body with a cry of pain and a jerking motion. Taurin moaned and shivered and sat up, rubbing his head. Thiana was gasping for air, her head did spin and she was nauseous but she felt it now, the spark of life, waiting deep underneath them, waiting for their hands to unleash it, to show it what to do. She turned to Taurin and he nodded. "I am ready love"

Shaluun had stood behind the crates the whole time and he did look nervous. "So, what is happening? Have you done it?"

Thiana nodded. "We have found the energy of the land yes, it has been subdued for so long it was very weak but Imeah's spirit is here, she has given it more power, from the heart stone. She will merge with it Shaluun, she will become its mind and soul"

Shaluun bowed his head in respect "Brave child, I am in awe of her. Then the brotherhood won't be able to use the heart stone again"

Thiana smiled. "Exactly, she will fight it, tooth and nail."

Taurin stared over at the wall, lights were flashing and roars and thunder could be heard. "We'd better hurry"

Thiana nodded and placed her hands in the ground once more, she closed her eyes and Taurin stared at Shaluun.

"Whatever happens, don't let anything disturb us now, this may become very dangerous"

Shaluun saw that the city was waking up, he heard shouts and screams and saw people running around. "I won't, just stay low!"

He hoped that he wouldn't have to break that promise.

Siverel and Adrall had reached the great hall, there the main altar of the citadel was placed and there all their most difficult and power consuming spells were performed. The room did sing with it even now but the song was subdued and out of tune. Siverel felt confused and even more so, scared. If they couldn't hold the dragons out... Adrall did stand there, uncertain of what to do and Siverel waved his hand. "I have to use a wand to do this, it will focus my energy. Something is very wrong, the spells shouldn't have allowed the dragons to re-emerge this close to the city"

Adrall nodded. "I know, they ought to have been transported to the plains"

Siverel walked over to a closet standing by the wall. It was closed with strong spells and only a high mage would be able to open it. He turned around and stared at Adrall. "The pens were disturbed by some sort of unknown force, the source underneath us feels distant now. I think something is trying to hinder us"

He tried not to think of what he had read, if it was true...what power did he have over those dead? The closed did open and he took a deep breath. There were five wands there, made from different material with different gems at the top and he swallowed and picked the one in middle. It was made from the backbone of a dragon, carved with intrinsic detail and its gem was a black diamond. It was the most powerful of them all and only he was allowed to touch it. He felt its power as a burn against his skin but he ignored the pain, it was a small price to pay. He turned to Adrall again. "Brother, if this fails there is just one thing to do. Should the barrier fail you must all flee! Use the old metal rod in the vault to get through the magic wall and head for the cities"

Adrall shrugged. "If there are any cities left to return to you mean? "

Siverel swallowed hard, his face felt stiff. It was the end, he was sure of it, but he wouldn't go down without a proper fight. The old prophecies would come true and they had brought the doom upon themselves, by being way too confident and way too ambitious. He wouldn't just give up though, prophecies were not stone hard truth, they could be tricked. "Just go, save as many as you can, our brotherhood will arise anew, in another time. But for now, help me get ready"

Siverel shed his cloak and ran over to yet another closet, this would take much out of him and he whimpered as he opened it and pulled out some clean robes. They were beautiful and made from thick velvet dyed in a deep copper colour. Strange symbols were embroidered into them and he shivered as he pulled them on. They were cold but he did also sense the protective spells woven into them. Adrall did help him with the outer robe, it couldn't be touched by Siverel's own hands and then Adrall did give him the wand. Siverel was sure he did look like an idiot, he was supposed to be the high mage, but he felt like a novice. The altar was placed on top of a round dais and there was nothing else there, just the dark ceiling with all its stars and constellations. He took a deep breath and nodded at Adrall. "Listen, if I fall down don't touch me, it will devour your soul if you do. Just…stay back"

Adrall was pale and he nodded, left the dais and stood there with his eyes on the ground. "Do start an opening chant, and don't stop!"

Adrall did clear his voice and began to chant, it was a method used to open up to the magic and Siverel lifted the wand and started shouting spells. He could feel that his power had diminished, that it didn't give as much as before and he was afraid that he wouldn't manage to do this after all. If some alien force had hi jacked the source there was a chance that he could cleanse it, but only if he could reach it.

He placed both hands on the wand, the diamond pointing towards the ceiling and his feet in a steady position, he felt centred but he wasn't strong, wasn't the invincible all-knowing leader the mages truly needed now in this time of crisis. He let the spells fly, felt the power within the words and how they changed the very fabric of creation. These were spells he never had uttered before and yet he did know them, only the very top notch of mages would ever dare to learn these ancient rites of magic. He kept reciting them, Adrall did continue his chant and the diamond started to glow in an eerie pattern of red and gold. It did look like molten lava and Siverel did feel the heat from it. The wand was battling him, its magic too strong for an ordinary mage to control but he needed it, had to bridle it to be able to summon the source. He was panting, sweat flowing off him and his body did ache like crazy. He was shouting louder, his voice like thunder and there and then maybe he did look like the ancestors of olden days, high in might and wisdom. He raised the wand, felt the resistance, the sheer will behind the energy they all had relied upon for so long.

For a moment he almost forgot the final spell but he did use it, did pronounce the archaic words and saw that a glowing form did appear hovering in the air above the dais. It wasn't the source itself, just a sort of reflection of it but that was enough. It was vast, a golden potato shaped lump of energy, once the heart of a life giving star, hurdled into space and now resting within this valley, giving off its huge power a little at a time. Siverel was in awe, but he did see something he didn't recognize right away. Others in the past had summoned the source and described it and the web which their magic had spun around it was gone, only a few decaying threads were left. Instead tendrils of another force could be seen, one which didn't seem to belong to this valley at all. It was weak but

Siverel did reach out and there and then he did realize what had opened the pens and disturbed the spells. It was the magic of another dimension, of the very earth itself in that close by world.

He gaped, for a moment almost thrown out of balance emotionally, he felt something gathering, something very energetic and also determined and then another presence did form and the shape did change, it no longer felt like a thing but like a person. He swallowed, staring with wide eyes, Adrall was on his knees, shivering. The potato had reformed into the shape of a young woman, a beautiful slender maid with long hair and an exquisite figure. She was staring at them and Siverel felt the powers within her, the old pact made with the very land itself, one her people had held sacred. She was the source, she was the heart stone and she cocked her head and grinned, a very wry grin. "I am sorry old man, you will fail in this"

Siverel tried to remember a spell which could expel a spirit from a magical basin like this but there were none, chaos magic has no power over the spirit realm, and he knew he had lost. The source was no longer available and their own strength not enough to keep the protection up much longer. He lifted the wand, tried to kill what was already dead but it was a gesture born out of despair. It was futile, the girl laughed and raised a hand and Siverel was thrown backwards, he flew along the ground and hit the shiny floor hard. The girl laughed, the energy in her seemed to grow and she was shining like a star now. "You will fall as you have lived, hard!"

There was an intense flash and a scent of ozone and she was gone, Siverel moaned and felt that his back was injured. The wand had broken in half and his robes were scorched. Adrall lay on the ground panting and he was so scared he had pissed himself. "Siverel, what was that?"

The older mage did manage to get up on his knees. "Adrall, you have just witnessed the birth of a Goddess, praise yourself lucky she is merciful. She is a spirit of true nature, a force of both light and darkness in true balance, only one like that can cleanse the heart stone, we have been fools. "

He got up on his feet, fighting to find his balance. "We have to warn the others, there is no way the protection will stay up for very much longer"

Out on the wall the mages were desperately trying to keep the magical barricade up. They all felt drained, weak even and they had no idea why. None of them had time to step back and think of how they all just tapped into the seemingly endless supply of raw magical energy resting beneath their feet. For those born raised and even bred there it was a part of the very air itself, they didn't know it was there until all of a sudden it wasn't! The dragons were attacking the wall viciously, huge mutated beasts threw their bulk against the rock and the wall had started to crack around the gate. The soldiers were the bravest ones, they had family and friends in the city and the magic didn't stop more mundane projectiles so the archers were firing until there were no more arrows to fire. Several of the brotherhood had been there, but now they had disappeared and the mages did know that these men had abandoned them. It made them rage with fury and yet a sort of sadness filled their minds for the twelve brothers who weren't mages had been the ones to lead them and focus their efforts. Now it felt as if a parent had just turned its back on them and it was horrible.

All sorts of monsters were assembled outside of the walls now and desperate to enter and the high mage had disappeared too. A small group of young mages tried to strengthen an older part of the wall, it was made with rather poor materials and there were massive cracks in it already. All four of them were panting with fear and exhaustion and their spells didn't seem to have much power at all. One of them was a short and stubby man with a goatee and short hair, he was well known for his love of cakes and other sweets but he was a very skilled mage and he did know spells way above his current level. He gasped, face red and eyes bulging. "We have to find Siverel, this cannot continue. What is he doing? We need help!"

The others nodded, they were terrified and angry and confused and one managed to raise his head. "I think the high mage went to the great hall, in order to see if this could be fixed."

The short one tried to calm himself, a dragon with a maw like the keel of a ship thrust itself against the wall and it cracked even more. "We must go to him. Now! He has to know, this is going to hell."

The others stared at each other. "Do we even have the power to do that?"

The short one nodded. "Link with me, we can do it"

They reached out, grasped each other's hands and shouted the right spell and in a flash they were gone.

The young mages did reappear in the middle of the great hall, just in front of the dais, they blinked and saw that Siverel and Adrall stood there, looking morose and lost and it was rather clear that something very dramatic had happened for Siverel's robes were in fact smouldering and there was a very unpleasant smell in the air. Had Adrall peed his pants? It did look that way. Siverel did see them, his eyes dazed and blurred and his face sad. Such strong young ones, the hope of the brotherhood and now it would all be in vain. "Please, go back to the wall, warn everyone. You need to flee, and do it now. The source is no longer…it has been taken"

The short one gaped, his expression one of utter disbelief. "What? I don't believe you, taken?"

Siverel sat down, he did look like an old man, a beaten man. "A spirit has entered it, made it into a tool of light. We cannot reclaim it in any way."

Adrall was nodding as if to back up his leader's words, his eyes did not leave the floor. The younger mages did stare in disbelief. "Are you saying that it is all lost?!"

The short one's voice had suddenly become very shrill and lost its masculine strength, now the man did sound more than a bit like a hysterical woman. Siverel nodded slowly, his face was grey and he was panting a bit. "Yes, so go now, save yourselves."

The short one heaved for air. "Save ourselves?! Save ourselves for what?! A life as beggars? A shadow existence in a world where the goddamn monsters you and the other's in the brotherhood created have taken over? Are you insane?!"

He was roaring it and the three others did stare at the two elder men with eyes which became more and more enflamed with rage. "Is this what we gave up everything for? Is this what we have studied and forsaken all joy to achieve? Ha?! Is it this bitter end I have lived in celibacy to achieve?!"

The short man was bellowing now. "I am twenty nine years of age and a bloody VIRGIN! You fucking cunts!!"

He threw his robe onto the floor. "We have given you all we have, placed our entire future in your hands and now you are telling us it was all in vain, that we will die horribly and take the rest of the world with us?"

Siverel tried to say something, his eyes were misty. "Dear child, don't despair, I had no idea that it would end thus, the spirit...it was stronger than I expected and..."

The man gaped. "Than you expected? Oh, so you did know that this could happen? And you didn't warn us? You stinking idiot!"

Siverel swallowed hard, he looked down. "Forgive me child, I read the prophecies but I didn't believe them, not fully!"

The man was sneering. "Oh don't you "child" me you blabbering fool, you have killed us! I believed you know, we all believed!"

Siverel swallowed. "I know you are hurting, it is painful to let go of ones believes, I do know"

The short young man did almost growl. "Painful? Painful you say? Oh it isn't painful, it isn't anything compared with what you ought to feel you... you profaner of faith. Let me show you pain!"

The short man yelled a spell, it made the others rear back in horror and Siverel didn't have the time to put up a defence, and he was too weak to be able to ward off such a very vicious spell. The older mage did scream as the dark magic tore into him, it made his muscled twitch to the point where the attachments snapped, tendons were pulled so taught they too tore, his back being twisted and the sound of bones breaking was heard. The high mage's skin started to melt as if he was being burned alive and he screamed in desperation until his heart gave up under the excruciating pain and he died in a pool of his own blood and faeces. Adrall had been standing there transfixed, he turned to flee but the young mage cussed and threw a dagger at the mage, it hit him in the back and Adrall fell, desperately trying to crawl away from the young ones. "Please, do have mercy, I didn't know, I was just assisting him..."

The short mage bared his teeth. "This makes you a part of it."

He bent down and stabbed the other man in the back again, several times with considerable energy and rage. The other three were staring at him, pale and with huge eyes. The man got back up and put the bloody dagger into its sheath, he stared at his comrades. "We have to undo what these idiots did, there can still be a chance"

They stared at each other. "Arnar, please, listen to yourself. When the high mage could do naught what can we possibly hope to achieve? Let us run, at least we'll live"

Arnar was sneering, his eyes blazing with a sort of madness. He had invested his entire life in this, in serving the brotherhood, sure of his reward at the end. Now it was proven to have been a hollow lie and his wrath knew no bounds. "No, I won't live like that, I want to live as a victor, as a ruler. Not as a goddamn pawn!"

He ran over to the closet and opened it, Siverel hadn't thought about closing the container and the remaining four wands were still there. "See? One for each of us, come now, don't hesitate. We can save everything"

The three did look at each other and the fear in their eyes was apparent. "We aren't experienced enough to use such wands? They are only for the high level mages, we are just level three? Are you mad?"

Arnar shook his head. "No, he was mad!"

He pointed at the dead high mage. "Here, take one each, it is an order!"

He was roaring the last words and the others weren't that strong, they were all followers more than leaders and grasped a wand with shaking hands. The youngest of them was sweating and his eyes were pleading. "Please, reconsider, what sort of magic can possibly redo what was done?"

Arnar grinned, a very devious grin. "A summoning, onto the dais, everyone, now"

The three just stared, they looked like animals trapped in a strong light. "NOW!"

They scurried up onto the dais, avoiding the blood from their former high mage. Arnar took a deep breath and swung the wand he had taken, it was made from white wood from sacred trees and contained a ruby at the end. It was very strong and more so, very heavy but he was angry and that gave him strength. "Arnar, summoning what? We aren't allowed to…it is forbidden…"

One of the three dared to speak and Arnar barked at him. "Shut the fuck up you whimpering imbecil, I am gonna fix this!"

He raised his hands and started to chant, it was a very dark tone to the words he was saying and the others did go very pale indeed when they realized what he was about to do. No way, he couldn't be this stupid? Or could he? Oh by every deity, they could just hope that he didn't succeed, after all, such summonings were left for the most powerful of mages for a reason. Very few had the strength to go all the way with such immense powers, and such dark magic. They just stood there, holding the wands and feeling cold sweat dribble down their backs, this was wrong, this was just so so very wrong.

Rhuk was running as fast as his short legs could carry him, he made sure that Goldren was right behind him and she was light on her feet and moved with such fleeting grace he was in awe of her. The streets were so narrow some places that two men couldn't walk next to each other without touching the decrepit walls and the mud covering the ground was a foot deep and did stink. Goldren did look a bit apologetic. "This place was better before, but it has fallen into disrepair and despair."

Rhuk helped her get over a huge pool of filthy water. "May I ask your age fair one? You are not very old"

Goldren did blush but it was hard to tell in the darkness. "I am a hundred and thirty, I am the youngest dwarf in this city. My mom died after she had me, she was too weak I think. Father never managed to get over it"

Rhuk felt a heavy stone of pity form in his gut. "Ya poor poor lass, I am so sorry to hear that"

Goldren just giggled and then she stopped and appeared to listen. "You hear that?"

Rhuk tilted his head, there was a sort of splashing sound and she was pale. "It is one of the beasts, we have to hide"

Rhuk saw a huge barrel placed on a corner and without hesitation he did grasp Goldren by her waist and lifted her into it before he jumped in behind her. They stood there like herring in a net but the barrel was deep and they were out of sight. Before long a huge creature did appear, it did look a bit like an overgrown pig with long legs and a head with several tusks and horns on it. The eyes were red and vicious looking and the thing was drooling. Goldren was stiff with fear and Rhuk felt the handle of his axe burrowing into his back. The thing was nasty, it was perhaps a natural animal, not some mutated freak but it was way larger than normal and its skin covered with scabs and sores. Whoever cared for the animal did a lousy job that was for bloody sure. Rhuk stared at the animal through the cracks in the barrel, it was ugly and probably very vicious and he was sure it had done a lot of damage in its time. He made a split second decision and jumped straight up. Few are aware of this, but dwarves are in fact good jumpers, as long as they have to jump straight up that is. They have very powerful legs and now that helped Rhuk to get out of the barrel almost as if he was flying. And while in the air he pulled out one of his axes and let out a short bellowing war cry. The animal froze, staring at the dwarf in disbelief and it didn't really understand that it was being attacked before the blade did hit its skull with a crunching sound.

It reared back, then it snarled and came forward, growling and screeching but Rhuk had hunted wild boar and this was in fact much like a boar, just taller. He swung the axe again and brought it down as the beast rushed past him. The blade did find its way into its neck right at the base of the skull and severed the spinal cord and the beast fell without making even a sound, lights out forever. Rhuk grinned and spat at the beast. "If ya weren't so goddamn ugly you would have made a tasty dinner"

Goldren did climb out of the barrel, she was staring at the nasty pig and her eyes were shining. "Oh Rhuk, you are so…brave!"

469

She was almost leaning onto him and he felt his chest expand out of sheer pride. "We are close to the leaders hut, hurry now!"

Rhuk did hear noise from afar, this part of the slum was far from the walls and he did see that the mages were using magic for the wall was lighted as if it was in the middle of the day and he could see movements on the other side of it. He hissed and ran, they didn't have much time if they were to save the people of this city.

The hut was just that, a hut. It had four walls and a roof but that was it, a troll sneezing at it would have brought it down and it had to be both cold and drafty. Goldren raised her head and walked over to the door, it was in fact a wonder that the structure did stand on its own. She knocked and they heard a gruff voice from the inside, Goldren did send Rhuk a swift glance. "Do let me talk alright?"

They entered and if Goldren's home had been poor it was nothing compared with this, there wasn't even a hearth there, and the inhabitant was sleeping on the floor, in a pile of old burlap sacks. Rhuk could smell moulds and rot and the female who stood there staring at them was rather old but her eyes were flint hard and filled with anger and determination. "Goldren, what are you doing here now? It is dangerous being outside now lass, and who is this handsome young dwarf?"

Rhuk hadn't been called young or handsome for decades and now it was his turn to blush violently. He swallowed. Goldren did open her mouth and started telling about the whole thing, why Rhuk was there and the dragons and the group. The female was listening and her eyes were narrow but got darker and darker and she slammed her hand into the wall when Goldren was done. "By his hammer, this is bad. I can hear that something is going on but I never anticipated anything like this. Oh boggers, we have to get going, now!"

She turned around and started digging through the pile of sacks which was her bed, she hauled something out of it and

Rhuk blinked. It was an axe and it was exquisite, the best workmanship he had ever seen. Goldren was staring too. "Samila, where did you get that one? They will kill you if..."

Samila just sneered. "I made it, I am smarter than some cheese brained human. Come on lass, we have to warn everyone"

Goldren nodded. "How?"

Samila stared at Rhuk. "She has told ya of the tunnel haven't she? Good, we have worked on a plan for many years ya see, and everybody knows of it. All we need is for the magic to be removed so we can enter"

Rhuk frowned. "Ah, what?! How are you supposed to do that?"

Samila grinned. "Fate has spoken today young one, finally we have a distraction strong enough for us to use it. The mages won't care about the slum when there are dragons snapping at their precious hides"

She walked over to the wall and removed a plank, there was a room inside and she pulled out a horn. "Everyone in this goddamn slum knows that if this horn sounds they have to gather everyone and head for the mines, right away. No hesitation, no questions. Anyone who fails to come will be left behind, easy as that. "

Goldren was frowning. "I have never heard of that?"

Samila nodded and went towards the door. "No, for you are too young, but your father knowns."

Rhuk tilted his head. "And even the humans are told?"

Samila nodded and went outside. "All the races are told young one, even the elves. We may have had our quarrels in the past but there we are all trapped in the same goddamn shit and we help each other. It is the only way we can survive"

She put the horn to her lips and blew and the sound made Rhuk moan and plug his ears. It had to be heard all over the city for it was the most piercing sound he had heard, ever! It sounded like the bellowing hounds of hell chasing a herd of infernal cattle down a slope made from barbed wire. Samila blew the horn for many minutes before she ended it with three long hoots with a clear pause between them. She turned to Goldren. "Go back to your father and make sure he gets help, he cannot walk on his own anymore now can he?"

Goldren shook her head. "No, he cannot"

Rhuk was fidgeting with his axe. "But, the magic?"

Samila smiled and he sensed that this dwarrowdam was tougher than flint and able to go whatever lengths necessary to save her people. "We do have magic you know, dwarven magic isn't strong but it is bound to the earth and two of us have trained for years now. They can bring down the barrier in the tunnel, but make haste now, quickly"

Goldren gasped and ran and Rhuk was straight behind her, suddenly there were dwarves filling the streets and getting through was hard but Rhuk did manage to push his way. Goldren came straight behind him and he could hear the sound of her feet in the mud. Oh those lovely feet, he would wash them with his own beard after this was over, she was worth that, and more. Dwarves and humans were all heading in one direction and few did even bother looking at him and Goldren, it was clear that the plan was a good one and a well-known one for nobody carried things they didn't need. Everyone was poorly clad and most was thin and grey and he mumbled in pity and disbelief. He even saw some human children and shook his head. Goldren saw it. "Yeah, I know. Humans breed like cats, they can have little ones even here, and I cannot understand how a species can be that fertile though, their females must conceive just from looking at a male"

Rhuk had to swallow, that gave him some very unwelcome ideas, Goldren's long and lovely toes doing unspeakable things to his….No, not the time for erotic fantasies, not at all. He kept running and they burst through the door of Goldren's home. Dabin was already making a sort of backpack in which to carry Goldren's father, the blind dwarf sat on the edge of the bed and he did look scared. Goldren ran over and touched him gently. "Worry not father, we will be out of here, soon enough."

Dabin smiled and the relief was visible, he must have been afraid that they wouldn't return. "Quick now, help me get this contraption on, I can carry the old one easily enough"

Rhuk did fasten the different leather straps and the he and Goldren did lift the old dwarf carefully and placed him in the backpack. Rhuk did see that the dwarf's legs were just skin and bones and one had been broken but put together again badly. Goldren grabbed a couple of pans and then she nodded at them. "Follow me, I know the way, and don't stop. We have little time if the dragons do get through"

The streets were crowded but there wasn't chaos, everybody were heading in the same direction and some were obviously tasked with making sure that nobody was lagging behind or creating bottle necks. All the streets were used and Rhuk was impressed. They were heading straight for the mountain side and everybody gathered in orderly lines, not much sound was heard neither for people did shut up. Rhuk saw that there were a lot of humans there and most did look very miserable. Some were stronger but they too were obviously slaves and then he saw some elves. Goldren was right, they suffered the worse, some were almost skeletal to look at and so weak others had to carry them and most were males. The few elves that did look good were very young and all of them were male. Samila was already there, and now Rhuk saw that tunnel. It was a mine and it did look like a naked mouth without teeth. No dwarf ought to be afraid of entering the mountains thus but suddenly he was. It was a morbid thought but it looked as if that tunnel was ready to swallow them all.

Dabin was panting, the old dwarf wasn't that heavy but he was too weak to hang onto Dabin so he was more or less hanging from the straps and they were digging into Dabin's flesh. Goldren was nervous, staring towards the wall. "See? I think the barrier is about to give in!"

Rhuk squinted, the flashing lights made it hard to see but yes, it did look as if the magic was failing. The entire slum and most of the rest of the city had to have arrived there now, there were thousands of people gathered in a small space and the silence was eerie. The only part of the city which hadn't been warned was the nice areas where the rich people who were in league with the brotherhood lived, they were on their own now. Two dwarves did run forth, both were male and not very old and they touched the rock next to the entrance with reverence. Then they started to sing, clear strong voices which seemed like a brutal contrast to the mayhem around them. The entrance did shimmer, like a lake on a day without wind and it was obvious that this was very hard for both appeared to be in pain and they were sweating but the shimmering shield appeared to simply sink into the ground until it was all gone. They hadn't removed the magic for that was impossible, they had just moved it out of the way. Rhuk bet that the brotherhood never had thought of that solution before.

The first lines started to rush into the tunnel and Samila stood there and made sure that everything went smoothly. Then two elves came running up to her, both in tears and obvious distress. "Please, some of ours, they are in the citadel, in the chambers of the masters. We have to do something, they cannot be left behind!"

Rhuk saw that the long line of humans and dwarves was disappearing into the tunnel with surprising speed, people were desperate, that helped a lot and gave them new strength, and they were able to run when they in reality ought to be too weak to walk. Samila made a grimace. "I am sorry, we cannot wait for them, we have to save as many as possible, there isn't time"

The elf let out a wail and Rhuk swallowed hard, he couldn't imagine what those poor wretches had been going through and he stepped forth. "If someone takes Goldren and her father to safety I and Dabin can go looking for them"

474

Dabin blinked. "We can? Oh, yes, of course, yes we can"

He saw Rhuk's murderous stare and smiled, but his eyes did reveal that this was something he never had expected. Samila frowned deeply, crossing her arms. "Alright, but you are on your own, got that? The tunnel may close before you make it back"

Rhuk almost stepped in one place. "Oh I know, don't worry. We will save those poor souls"

The elf fell to his knees and tried to kiss Rhuk's hand. "Oh bless you, bless you noble dwarf. My son, they came for him yesterday, he is…he is a tall one, with black hair and green eyes, find him, I beg you!"

Rhuk shuddered, a young and pretty elf in the hands of those bastards? Oh he was rather sure that this poor elf knew what his son was going through. "I will find him, what is his name?"

The elf sniffed. "Saerian, he is my light"

Dabin rolled his eyes but didn't say anything and Rhuk grinned, a very determined grin. "Right, we will free everyone, come on Dabin, time to go!"

He grasped Dabin by his arm and pulled him along, indeed there was little time to loose.

Phraan and Dhokay had managed to turn three of the columns around and both were exhausted, Zaray was guarding them and the tiny dragons were scurrying around in odd patterns and here and there sparks would fly off them. It was rather obvious that they removed magic like tiny washing women wiping off dirt from a floor. The circle was broken, the symbols did lose their power and Zaray was helping them shift one more column. "This is the last one, I bet the magic will be broken now."

Ivran was nodding, he could feel that the magical force there had diminished a lot, now there was almost nothing left, they could just hope that this would reverse the changes.

Phraan moaned, his back hurt and his hands were raw, the columns weren't smooth but rough like sandpaper. Dhokay was larger and physically stronger than him and he had put every ounce of strength into it. The column did move a last inch and there was a sort of moan coming from the circle. The light within it flickered and went out and there was silence. The tiny dragons all let out loud shrieks of joy. Zaray smiled, she did look pleased. "Great, I think we made it. The magic will be undone now"

Dhokay did shrug. Ivran was staring at the circle and his eyes were narrow, his expression one of anticipation. Phraan did sort of smile. "Uh, folks, the dragon said it would take time, no point in standing here is there?"

Zaray touched the nearest column. "I would really like to know that nobody would be able to replicate this, is there some way to destroy the columns, at least erase the text on them?"

Ivran bit his lower lip. "I can try?"

Zaray smiled. "Alright, but be careful, there is still some residual magic here."

Ivran was rubbing his hands together, imagining the symbols all mixed up and unreadable. There was a faint flash and then the symbols did change and move about. After a while they stopped and Zaray was staring at something none of them had expected. "Ah Ivran, hmm, when you were studying, did you by chance visit the local library?"

Ivran nodded. "Yes?"

From his side he couldn't see the actual text and Zaray was grinning so widely they saw her back teeth. "That library shouldn't happen to have books of a more...risqué...nature?"

Ivran went pale, then he went red and ran around, staring at the texts which now was easily readable. Zaray giggled and started reading out loud. "Oh my love, thy touches are like fire and come and fill me yet again with thy..."

Ivran did punch her, desperately. "Oh shit, oh no, ah, I didn't read those books, I just happened to see..."

476

Phraan was laughing. "And there we have the winner of the worst excuse ever award, don't worry, I bet the brotherhood will find this amusing, or annoying. Who cares anyhow?"

Ivran was still beet red and the tiny dragon queen made some snickering sounds as if to make the situation complete. Zaray giggled again. "Come on, I bet the dragons are about to break through very soon"

Phraan wondered if Fastonar would be there when they returned to the square, or if he had used the opportunity to escape. Zaray saw his expression and touched his arm gently. "Phraan, I know, I know what you are thinking"

He swallowed hard. "How?"

She shrugged. "Imeah told me a lot, more than you think. The two gems, Vitile did find them you know. I took them from the horn of her saddle after she died. Someone knew she had them and thus she had to die."

Phraan swallowed. "Can it be someone else?"

Zaray looked down. "I doubt it, it fits too well. He did hang that man so he wouldn't be able to tell us anything."

Phraan stared her straight in the eye. "If he is the one behind this I hope I get to be the one to kill him. I owe that to Vitile, and Imeah"

Zaray smiled and stroked his cheek gently. "Yes, you do. I will not stand in your way but hold back for now, we cannot risk that he does anything stupid"

Phraan bared his teeth and there was a sheer anger in his eyes. "He already has, if he tries to do anything to hinder us I will not hesitate but end him, there and then"

Zaray sighed. "Yes, and it is your right, but remember, fate does play a strange game. He may yet be of use to us, no matter what he has done or will be doing"

Phraan clenched his teeth together. "I hear you."

He just walked on and the tiny dragons hissed and followed him, the queen climbed onto his shoulder yet again, sitting there with a royal expression and her tail neatly wrapped around his braid.

The hall with the circle had some other entrances than the one they had used and Dhokay stared at them. "Should we check things out? There could be valuable things to learn here"

Ivran shook his head. "No, there is no time, I can feel it, the barrier holding the dragons back is failing now"

Phraan could somehow sense it too, the air seemed to vibrate with some sort of dark energy and he looked at Zaray. "Hurry, we do have to get out of here fast"

Ivran was visibly nervous. "Oh I wonder if the thing we just did will have an effect or not?"

Phraan swallowed and ran, the tiny dragons running in dense lines between them. "Somehow I think that we will find out, very soon"

Tersus had tied the young novice to a chair using some chains from the meat locker, when the man did come to his senses again he found that he was wrapped like a ham and Tersus had pulled down the hood and on the desk behind him he had laid out a very neat collection of sharp objects, including a cork screw and some filet knives. He had also found some small vials from the bags and mixed some stuff in a ceramic bowl, it did ooze and bubble and Peter did stare at the stuff with doubt and dread. What the fuck was this thing? He didn't want to go anywhere near it. The young novice did blink, he was confused and when he felt that he was tied up he did panic. "What is this, release me! I demand it"

Tersus did play a little with a knife right in front of the man, he stared at the blade and he was very pale. "Who are you? What is this? My master will smite you if you harm me!"

Tersus made a grimace. "Ah, not to be negative or anything but I don't think your master, whoever he is, will do much smiting stuck between the teeth of some mutated dragon monster, pardon me for saying so"

The young novice was trembling, he obviously wasn't a hardened and prepared person that was for darn sure. "Ah…what…what are you talking about…"

Tersus smiled. "The fact that the dragons have escaped their pens and your superiors have done a little oopsie and now they are on the loose on the other side of the city wall? They are about to break free as a matter of fact, will be here soon"

The novice gaped. "You're lying, the masters would never do a mistake"

Tersus chuckled and tested the edge of the blade. "Ah but they have, sad isn't it? All this power and glory, all these things so precious to you all, in a few hours it will be naught but a mere memory, and of course give some poor dragons a bit of indigestion for frankly? Your kind is not what I would call tasty, rather the opposite"

He grasped the young man's chin and forced his head back. "So, you do have a choice and I think you will see that I am most reasonable after all. You may even save your master ha? That would be fun wouldn't it?"

The young one was panting and fighting the chains and the ropes. "Let go of me! Now!"

Tersus smiled slowly, he did look like a cat that has caught a fat rat. "Oh no way son, you see, you are gonna tell us a little secret and if you do, well, then I won't have to cut you into tiny dice. Doesn't that sound good?"

The novice stared at the blade, he was pale. Tersus did look at the face with the expression a buyer uses when trying to determine whether or not a horse is worth the money the salesman asks for. "Hmm, your left ear, it is a bit large now isn't it, what if I cut off a bit of the top?"

He did a swift move with the knife and it was so sharp it just slid straight through the ear, without any effort at all. The young novice didn't even register any pain at first but when he did he let out a piercing cry and tears started to flow down his cheeks. "I…I won't talk, I know no secrets!"

Tersus tilted his head. "That is where you are wrong kid, you do know secrets, fat juicy ones too. Listen carefully, all we want to know is how one removes the magical protection laid upon the dragons? And of course, where is the gem which controls the great wall, that isn't much to ask for is it?"

The novice trembled. "I will not talk, I am not afraid of knives and pain"

Peter did see that the blood was flowing from the cut ear and the young novice was terrified but he did try to be brave. He did have some qualities after all. "No? That is unfortunate for then I will have to use something way worse"

Tersus grasped the ceramic bowl and placed it closer to the young man, the smoke which rose from it did stink terribly and it was a sharp and very unpleasant smell. Tersus grasped a kitchen knife and admired it for a while. "Such a good knife, very well made, high quality steel, sad really but what the hey, there are more knives here right?"

The young one was confused and blinked, he didn't understand at all and Tersus did sigh and dip the tip of the blade into the bowl. When he pulled it out a small glob of something was stuck to the tip and as they watched the steel did shrivel and melt like an icicle in summer. Tersus sent the novice a sardonic smile, he did look a bit like some leering demon at the moment. "So, what molar should we start with, the ones at the very back of your mouth? That usually does it, most people do scream more than talk but what the hey, at least we can have some fun ha?"

The novice stared at the ruined knife, he was shaking all over. "Have mercy, please, I'll talk, I'll tell you all I know but I am just a novice..."

Tersus did toss the knife away, it landed with a clang in a corner. "See? That wasn't hard at all, now we are gonna be best buddies kid, as long as you answer truthfully you have nothing to fear at all"

The novice whimpered, his eyes were bloodshot. "What are you?"

His voice did shiver. Tersus raised an eyebrow. "What I am? Why of course, I am the one thing you dark mages fear more than even a spell gone awry. I am an alchemist!"

The young one swallowed and he seemed to shrink a bit in the chair, Tersus did look very proud. "So, how can the protective magic be removed?"

The young one swallowed hard. "I am not perfectly sure, but there is a room near the top of the citadel, they say it has something to do with a magical artefact of some sorts. It is not far from the high mage's office. And…and they say it is very dangerous to disturb the spells uttered there"

Tersus did pet the young man's head, like he would absentmindedly pet a dog. "Good, good, you are doing great, the wall?"

The young one stared at the bowl, the smoke was still rising and it was obvious that the acid in it scared him more than even the darkest of magic. "A gem, it is held in the high mage's chambers I think. I haven't seen it but it is supposed to be very powerful"

Tersus nodded. "And now, the final questions, the most important one. How does one get to the high mage's chambers unseen?"

The novice was sniffling. "There are hidden stairs, the entrance is not far from here, it looks like a cupboard. You have to push it sideways and then turn it outwards."

Peter did look fascinated. "And you know this because?"

The young one did almost hiccup, he was crying so badly. "My master is important to the high mage, helps him a lot, he is a good master. But I have had to help him carry stuff up to the high mage's rooms many times"

Tersus did smile widely. "See? We have found the goose with the gold eggs, we are in luck aren't we. Thank you kid, you have been most helpful"

The novice swallowed. "Can...can I go now?"

There was a faint tone of hope in his voice and Tersus smiled. "No, but you will be allowed to live. That ought to be enough. I am not usually that lenient but I like you kid"

Tersus did cut the ropes and loosened the chains and then he pushed the novice into the meat locker where several sides of beef did hang and he threw some bottles of wine in there too before he locked the door from the outside. The novice didn't even protest. Peter frowned. "Are we gonna leave him in there?"

Tersus nodded with a chuckle. "Of course, we cannot drag a bleeding novice with us now can we? Don't worry, that meat locker is the safest place there is right now, not very cold, very solid and there is no way he'll starve to death the first few months."

Peter scoffed. "Yeah, and if the dragons do break free and enter the city this room will be like a magnet, fresh meat, lots of it, and one novice"

Tersus just laughed. "Well, at least he is sweet enough to make a proper meal"

Peter did roll his eyes, he was rather sure that this novice had a very short time left to live, he did release the piglet since they didn't need it anymore and the animal did scoot off, he felt that it had a way better chance of making it than any of the mages.

Tersus started walking towards the place the young one spoke of and lo and behold, the cupboard was there. Tersus did push it and it did move, although reluctantly. The opening behind was dark and very narrow, it was hardly place for one person there and the stair was very steep. Tersus stared at it with a frown and an expression of doubt. "Ah by every mineral, that is no job for anyone in bad shape, talk about stairway to heart attack. Well, we'd better get going. This is going to be a tough climb"

Peter just sighed and felt tired already, the goddamn stair looked like an honest attempt at torturing people without letting them know they were being tortured. Tersus did enter and hoisted up his robe and he was surprisingly fit but then again, he was probably just skin and bones and not much weight at all.

Crassian had been riding along a river he had met after some hours. The river wasn't wide but rather wild and there was some forest growing along the banks, he could use it to seek shelter if he saw more dragons. He was soon to enter an area he knew was inhabited and he was dreading what he knew he would see. The terrain became more ragged and less flat and he could see hills in the distance. The air was very cold there and he was keeping his hands inside of his coat to warm them. The horse was tired and he couldn't ride hard, he just allowed it to keep its own pace and luckily the animal was easy to control so he just steered it with his knees. The river went over some waterfalls and then it reached a more calm area and Crassian did take a small break. He was hungry but had no food so he tried to snare some fish and managed to get one, it wasn't large but it was meat and he was no stranger to eating raw fish. It did fill his belly and he felt a little better as he rode on. The day was coming to an end but he couldn't take the risk it was to camp for the nigh. He had to go on and he let the horse walk slowly along the river as he was half asleep in the saddle.
He had no idea of for how long he had ridden when he saw fire up ahead and he blinked and woke up, he stopped the horse and stared. It was perhaps a mile away along the river and it wasn't really bonfire, it was more like the afterglow of a larger fire and his heart sank. It had to have been a small fisher village. He made the horse move again and saw that the skies were getting lighter in the east. He had slept in the saddle for hours and he did feel a little better. It was a village, there could

have been perhaps ten houses there but now they were burned to the ground and it was nothing left of anything. The boats which lay by the shore had been smashed or burned and he saw some dead cows and sheep too. The dragons had been there, the soil itself was scorched and black and it did stink of sulphur and burned flesh. It was already daylight when he reached the village and covered his nose with his cloak, the smoke was so hard to breathe inn and burned his lungs so he tried to protect himself. He saw dead people, burned bodies lay between the buildings and some in them and he cringed and tried not to get too nauseous. The smell of scorched flesh was overwhelming and he fought not to let it shake him too much, he felt like a wretch for being alive, for being the one who escaped when all these peaceful people did perish.

The horse nickered and stopped, the ears moving and Crassian grasped for his sword, something was moving and he was afraid it was a dragon which had been left behind but it wasn't. It was a person, a young man who crawled out of the bushes very slowly. Crassian held his hands up. "I am no danger to you, are you the only one to survive here?"

The young man made a sort of rasping sound and coughed violently, he had obviously gotten too much smoke into him and he was pale and in obvious distress. "I…I am, I was… I was…"

He coughed again and Crassian saw that he did have some burns on his arms but he wasn't too badly injured. Crassian got off the horse, his legs felt like pieces of lead but he was able to walk. He saw that the young man was shivering and in obvious shock. "I am Crassian, I am an officer in the king's army. Can you tell me what happened here?"

The man sat down, tears were drawing lines in the sooth covered face. "I…I am Eimar, I…I was on the river, fishing. The monsters, they didn't see me. They…burned…everything!"

Crassian put hand on the young man's shoulder. "Was it a huge pack?"

Eimar nodded. "It was, it was…more than a hundred, small and large…and some didn't fly. But it happened so fast, nobody had time to run…it was terrible"

Crassian saw that the burns the young man had were rather deep. "You are hurt, how did that happen?"

Eimar let out a piercing wail. "I tried to see if someone was alive, I got pinned down by a burning log but it wasn't that heavy so I managed to get it off me again"

Crassian sighed. "I am sorry, nobody survives an attack like that. You were lucky"

Eimar let out a wail. "Lucky? How can you say that?! I…I am the only one left, my family…they all…"

Crassian nodded. "I was one of a group of five, the dragons got the other four, but I made it, because I was lucky. You are alive son, maybe the Gods have some sort of plan for you yet"

Eimar sniffed and Crassian swallowed. "You cannot stay here, there is nothing left. There aren't any horses in the area? You have to come with me, you won't be safe on your own"

Eimar shook his head. "We don't have horses, but we have boats"

Crassian frowned. "The boats I have seen are destroyed?"

Eimar nodded. "Yes, but we have a larger one, a barge, it is moored further down the river"

Crassian got an idea. "The river, can it be sailed down to the cities in the south?"

Eimar nodded. "Yes, we often do that, it isn't ideal for the river is rather large now but we can do it yes"

Crassian smiled. "Then my friend we have a plan, we take the barge and head south. There could be other survivors there and you need some medical attention, those burns are nasty"

Eimar just cringed and nodded and Crassian got up. "Let's go, show me this barge of yours"

A little while after Crassian stood on the deck of a rather wide bottomed barge which was surprisingly large and stabile. It had one mast and a rather primitive sail but as long as they followed the river they wouldn't need it. The barge was large enough to have room for Crassian's horse and they had tied the animal into a sort of room at the back of the vessel. Eimar did prove that he was a skilled sailor and they were already on their way, the river gave the barge good speed and Crassian sat down and leaned against the mast. "Is there any dangers we have to look out for?"

Eimar shook his head. "No, not really. There are some areas with rapids but they aren't too bad and this old girl has survived them before. The river is so full of water now the rocks are under water and since she floats very high in the water we should be safe"

Crassian nodded and he saw that Eimar was pale and sweating. "You are injured kid, shouldn't I be the one to take the helm? I am stronger than you"

Eimar sent him a pale grin. "I am not too weak to steer, and I know the river, you don't. No offense sir, but I can do this. It has been my life and my job"

Crassian smiled. "Yes, I know but if you are in too much pain tell me and we can take a break, there is no point in torturing yourself. "

Eimar looked down. "It isn't too bad, I had expected it to hurt more actually"

Crassian sighed. Third degree burns, the nerves were burned away so there was no pain but there was a high risk of infection. "If you start to feel feverish let me know, there are herbs which can help."

Eimar nodded and turned the rudder a wee bit. "I will, don't worry"

Crassian felt that Eimar was trying to be braver than he really was and he was afraid that the young one would push himself too far. "So, how far is the nearest city"

Eimar was thinking fast. "The first settlement we'll reach isn't really a city, it is a town, a little larger than my home. We'll be there in a couple of hours. Then we have a larger town which is called Greywater since they dye wool there and it colours the river at times. The first real city is half a day south of there, it is known as Ardubad"

Crassian was thinking. "I have heard of it, a mining city?"

Eimar nodded. "Yes, largest settlement along this river, it is run by a family who made a fortune digging for gems. They own the area, and they do earn a lot still"

Crassian was frowning. "How many live there?"

Eimar shrugged. "I don't know for sure, perhaps five thousand?"

Crassian swallowed hard, tried not to think of the sheer mayhem the dragons could cause in such a place. "So, does the city have any defences?"

Eimar looked at the river, there was pain in his expression. «No, none. No wall, no mote, not even a proper fence. There are some dwarves living there and they are fighters for sure but they won't stand a chance against the dragons."

Crassian closed his eyes. "Let us pray that the dragons have taken another route."

Eimar sent him a shaky smile, it wasn't very convincing. "Yes, let's hope so"

They both knew it was a hollow hope at its best!

The four young mages had started a summoning and they all knew that this was a sort of magic you could start but never quit until it was fulfilled. A half done summoning would leave a hole in the very fabric of space and anything could get through, things you wouldn't want to encounter at all could appear and the three were staring at Arnar with huge eyes and fear written all over their faces. Arnar was insane, he was shouting words none of them had even heard and where in hells name had he learned those rituals? Not even the high mage would have tried doing this? One of the three had already pissed himself as black lightening shot through the air, weaving a bizarre cage around the circle and they all felt the magic there as sharp stings against their skin. If Siverel had been alive he would have done everything he could to make sure that this failed, he would have seen what they were doing. A summoning is very dangerous, not only because of the things you can summon, and they can be bad indeed, but because of the power needed. A summoning require so much magical energy it will drain an ordinary mage and thus a summoning need at least four to be complete. Bringing something through the web of reality, through dimensions and worlds into our own is no easy task and no mage, not even the darkest of practicians of the worship of chaos would dare to what Arnar now was doing. The ritual was sucking magic out of the very air, it was no longer able to use the heart stone to feed from so it used whatever else it could reach. It felt the magic of the mages which were protecting the city and with a sort of sigh it devoured both that and the barrier.

If Simaon had been there he would have laughed for now his last curse did become reality, the coin he had dropped had lain there between some cobblestones unseen and now its magic finally saw how it could finish the final command of that now long gone leader. It flared with ancient magic and added its power to the spells of the young mages, made sure that the doom would come to the mages and the brotherhood. Without their magic the barrier would give way and they would really be killed by chaos, the chaos they themselves had created. The coin would have been very pleased had it had eyes to see what it had achieved. The magic in it gave one last blast, then it went out, spent completely and the coin was just a coin again, it would never be awakened again since there would be no dark mages left to use it. It was just a lump of gold now, and the crack in the pavement its final resting place.

There was a silent shivering of the air and in front of the four the air seemed to split and something started to appear. Something large and black and terrible and the three screamed in absolute horror. They couldn't move and Arnar was sneering, his eyes ablaze in madness. He knew that a summoned being has to be anchored to this world and there just one way to do that, with sacrifice. He pulled his dagger and ran over to his friend to the left, the man tried to raise his hands to defend himself but he couldn't move. The blade did pierce his throat and blood did gush out of the wound, several feet into the air before the mage did tumble to the ground, gargling and wheezing, desperately trying to do something to save himself but it was too late. The monstrosity in the rift was getting more solid, more real and Arnar was chanting continuously. The ritual called for the sacrifice of a virgin but it said nothing about it having to be a woman now did it? Neither of them had ever fucked anyone and now his friends were his perfect tools to achieve his vengeance.

He did slay all three one by one and the figure did grow and the rift got wider, it was staring at the bloodshed with red glowing eyes and it was grinning. It liked this, it enjoyed pain and blood and despair and it stared at the pathetic mortal who had dared to summon it. There were others behind him, waiting to come forth and he stepped out of the rift, and the mortal was waving a wand, madness showing in his eyes. The demon grinned, this mortal would taste so very sweet, you didn't disturb the rest of the dark hunters unpunished. Arnar was panting, staring at the huge creature. It was shaped like a man but it had wings like a bat, legs like a ram and the hide of a dragon. The head did remind him of a sort of twisted feline but it had skin like a beetle and the eyes, they were horrible. Arnar was panting hard, his soul trapped half in awe and half in terror. "I order you to destroy the dragons outside of the walls"

The demon sneered. "And what is in that for me puny mortal?"

Arnar was trembling, for the first time he did doubt his own actions and resolve and he stepped back a step. "The souls of my brethren, they don't deserve to live!"

The demon tilted its head, a mane of long featherlike hairs did cover it and it was a sight of both terrible beauty and horror. It bared its long teeth. "Those souls are not enough to stay the hunger of me and my brother's. Why should I obey an insect"

Arnar was waving the wand. "I summoned you, you have to obey me!"

The demon was laughing, the sound was terrible. "Oh do I now? I don't think so, you are not in a holy circle, you are not prepared by the hands of anyone holy and your flesh is impure"

Arnar stared at the towering giant, at least fifteen feet of muscle and magic, and he realized that he had done the worst blunder a mage can possibly do. He had focused on the result, not the path towards it. The demon chuckled and Arnar saw more behind it, breaking through into the world. "So you are just a light snack, but fear not, we will feast for sure"

The demon reached out and grasped Arnar like a kid grasps a toy and Arnar screamed and tried to hit the demon with the wand but the creature's energy did consume his and his body was tossed onto the floor, completely dried out. The demon tossed his head back and roared in triumph, a new world to conquer, a new world to devour. Ten of his brother's followed him and he licked his lips. This would be so easy, so very easy.

At the wall the barrier gave way, it happened very fast and suddenly there was a gust of hot air and dragons did rush forth followed by dreghil and elementals and other monsters too. The crumbling wall was no protection and the mages realized what a blunder they had made when they made their creations immune to magic. Spells and tricks didn't work at all, and for the ones who had gathered on the wall it was at least quick, most died immediately, devoured by flames and acid and some were dissolved or devoured by the dreghil. The soldiers who had been summoned to protect the city didn't do much better, they were even less of a challenge for the monsters and now the buildings near the wall caught fire and it looked like a scene from a nightmare. The flames spread and the dragons with them, they were scurrying through the city, looking for people to eat. The odd thing was that they found very few until they reached the area near the citadel, there they did found better buildings with living beings inside them and thus the dragons got slowed down a bit. The city was doomed, there was little doubt about that, the fire spread rapidly and it was becoming an inferno.

Tersus and Peter had made it to the chambers the novice had spoken off, they were not that luxurious but large and Tersus did look for the gem everywhere. He was rather sure that such an important thing had to be kept near the one who was in charge and finally they did find it, in a chamber placed on its own not far from the office. It was a stair going downwards and the room was rather small and built from stone. The gem lay in a sort of cradle which was decorated with diamonds and the value was enough to give anyone the shudders. But the gem was what caught their attention, it wasn't large, but it held such power and Tersus frowned as he got closer to it. The colour was deep golden red and it was beautiful, they could see how colours were swirling around inside of it and Peter cringed, the energy coming from the gorgeous thing was painful. Tersus smacked his lips, tilted his head. "It is probably worth more money than the entirety of Twelve towers but what the hey, this thing is bad right?"

Peter nodded, he didn't want to go anywhere near it and Tersus grasped a bag and pulled out a vial. It had a sort of purple liquid inside of it and Tersus smiled, a very pleased grin. "This ought to do the trick ya"

He opened the vial and without hesitation he poured the somewhat sticky liquid over the gem. At first nothing happened, then a really thick and stinging smoke did start to rise and they heard a shuddering and cracking sound, as if the gem was splitting up. The liquid was bubbling and oozing and the gem simply started to melt. There was a sort of shockwave moving through the room and then the gem was no more and the magic in it had disappeared too. Tersus smiled and put the vial back into the bag, he hadn't used all of it. "Now they will have a hard time getting through that wall again, they are trapped here"

Peter took a deep breath. "What about that other thing?"

Tersus chuckled. "He said near the top of the citadel right? We are almost at the top, so come on, no time to waste!"

They left the office and ran as fast as they could through the corridors, the rooms were empty and they heard sounds from the city which indicated that the barrier had disappeared. Tersus was swearing. "Shit, the dragons will be here soon, hurry!"

Peter was scared half to death but he tried to think logically. "Stairs there has to be stairs here somewhere?"

Tersus nodded. "If they don't teleport into the room, but I don't think they would do that, it can disrupt the magic. The room has to be large, look for a wall with no doors"

They ran and at last they did find a stairway leading upwards and lo and behold, halfway up there was a door and it did look very impressive. There were magical symbols covering it and Tersus took a deep breath. "Here goes, this has to be it. I think the roof is the next door up"

He pushed at the door but it was locked and he scratched his head. "Oh damnation, I don't suppose you have a key Peter? No? Well, then we have to become creative!"

He grasped the bag and pulled out two small jars, both held some sort of thick paste and he smeared some of the content from one of the jars on the lock. He seemed a bit nervous and Peter did back away a few steps. "Is that dangerous?"

Tersus shrugged. "Nah, only if you don't know what you are doing, ah, well, it is dangerous, you see, these chemicals are chronically unstable and I have never managed to get it quite right but it is mostly working well, mostly."

Peter did back away even further as Tersus did smear paste from the other jar on top of that from the first, with a stick. "And if it doesn't?"

Tersus did back off too. "Then it explodes, violently"

Peter saw a huge ornamental vase placed next to the wall and he sought cover behind it. "How reassuring!"

Tersus did wet his lips. "Doesn't seem to be working, should have eaten its way through the steel by now, what..."

That was all he had time to do before the door exploded into a cloud of splints, steel shrapnel and smoke. The alchemist was thrown backwards and landed on his back with a groan and the cloud of debris hit the wall on the other side with a sound like a hailstorm against a tin roof. Peter screamed and ducked and the entire building seemed to shake. Tersus sat up, shaking his head, picking a few pieces of wood out of his hands and arms and clothes, he was rolling his eyes. "Oops!"

Rhuk and Dabin had been running as fast as they could towards the citadel and luckily nobody stopped them, they did see a few guards but the men ran towards the walls and didn't even notice the two stubby dwarves who were running so fast they looked a bit like bouncing balls. They followed the cliff face towards the huge building and they heard the roars and screams from the wall and knew that time was running out. Dabin was cussing all the time. "Goddamn it Rhuk, I know you wanna impress that little beauty of yours but you didn't have to volunteer like this? And drag me into it? It is madness"

Rhuk was panting, he wasn't used to running and a dwarf is no sprinter, they can walk for days carrying heavy loads but running? No way, they were simply not made for it. "Come on Dabin, what were we to do? Leave those poor souls in there? Let them become dragon snacks? Alright, I want to impress Goldren but we would be monsters if we let people die when we can save them."

Dabin stared up ahead, the citadel was enormous. "Look at that Rhuk, how the hell are we supposed to find anyone in there? Ha? It will be like finding a needle in a haystack!"

Rhuk just shrugged. "We must do our best, at least try"

He pointed at the building. "See, there is an entrance near the cliff, it doesn't look important at all, it could be a servant's door or something like that"

Dabin scoffed. "Oh yes, or a way to a quick death, they are mages Rhuk, mages! I bet every entrance is protected by some insidious spell"

Rhuk reached the door, it was old and made from wood and rather worn. "Well, here we are and I think we have to try. I am ready to take the risk, you can go back if you like"

Dabin rolled his eyes and his lower jaw slid forwards, giving him a rather fierce expression. "Aw crap, right, I am with you, but if you get us killed I swear to the great allfather that I will haunt your ghost until the ending of the world!"

Rhuk shrugged and kicked the door open. "Sounds fair to me"

They entered a very narrow and very damp corridor and since they were dwarves they did see rather well in spite of the lack of real light. The corridor did go in a spiral upwards and after a while they entered a sort of storage room. Rhuk smiled. "Feel the smell? Potatoes, this is their potato cellar. I bet the kitchens are nearby and that means that the servant quarters are nearby too, and from them we can find the masters chambers too"

Dabin sort of scowled. "I doubt it will be that easy!"

Rhuk smiled. "Don't be such a pessimist, think about it, we will be heroes."

He ran off and Dabin moaned and followed, if falling in love really made people this stark raving mad he hoped by every deity he never would fall victim to its sweet sting. Rhuk was right, they came to a long row of kitchens and there were people there, servants and cooks and they were obviously terrified and locked inn by the guards. Everybody could smell smoke and several of the females were crying. When the two dwarves kicked down the door and suddenly stood there among them some passed out and a couple of the chefs did grasp whatever they had of kitchen knives and tried to look dangerous. Rhuk stared at the crowd, there was perhaps a hundred people gathered there and all looked as if they had lost all hope. Dabin saw that Rhuk almost grew, he put his chin up and chest out and stared at the oldest of the men present. "You, have your masters locked you inn?"

The man nodded. "Yes, their loyal guards did, they gathered all the servants here. Didn't want a rebellion while they were out there, I don't know who gave the order"

Rhuk smiled, a very soothing smile. "That doesn't matter, I smell fire, is the place burning?"

The man nodded. "Yes, someone has started a fire in one of the halls, we don't know who. The guards have run off to fight the dragons and there is nobody left, the masters are trying to flee I think"

Dabin pointed at the door they had kicked down. "Go through there, and the potato cellar, there is a small door at the back of it, behind some crates. Follow it, it leads to the outside and run along the cliff. There is a tunnel leading away from this valley but you have to hurry for it will be closed off soon"

The servants started to run and Rhuk turned to the old man again. "Quickly, there are elves here? Slaves? We need directions, we have to find them"

The man swallowed. "Go to the far end of the dining hall. There is a red door there, it is locked but the key hangs in a tea kettle on the wall, it is a stair behind it. It goes up to the private chambers of the masters, the…pleasure…slaves are locked away in a room behind a large pool. There are twenty of them, but some are very weak"

Rhuk nodded. "Thank you, I am grateful. Go now, hurry. The barrier is about to break and then this place will be the dragon's feeding ground"

The man pressed Rhuk's hand and then he followed the others, Rhuk grasped a couple of carving knives and a meat cleaver and attached them to his belt before they ran and Dabin was panting. "Oh by the allfather, if the…gods…wanted us to…gasp…become sprinters why didn't they…gasp…give us longer …legs!"

Rhuk just chuckled, he was older than Dabin and more used to pushing himself and his clan was lighter than that of Dabin. It didn't look that way but they didn't have such a heavy skeleton and were more agile. They did find the door and the stair easily enough and ran upwards. The odd thing about dwarves is that they are experts at running in stairs as long as the steps aren't too tall. They have such powerful leg muscles they bounce up rather easily and there are few able to get up long stairs faster than dwarves, which makes sense thinking of their vast underground cities where stairs are everywhere. Before long they entered the private chambers of the members of the brotherhood and Rhuk lifted his hand and made Dabin shut up. "Listen!"

He whispered it and they slid in behind a huge tapestry, someone was moving and they peeked out from behind the tightly woven fabric. Three men came running, carrying bags in their hands and they did look dishevelled and panic stricken. None of them wore the robes of a mage and they seemed to be well fed and well groomed, their clothes expensive and their general appearance one of wealth. Rhuk was squinting, these men were running and before long five more appeared, also carrying stuff and in a similar state of fear. One was trying to organize the escape, he was waving his arms and his voice was shrill and loud. "Listen, listen damn it. We cannot go through the main gate, it is too dangerous. We have to use the hidden exit"

One of the others yelled back, his face red. "But only Siverel has the right spell to open it and he is nowhere to be found, we have to go out the front"

Another whimpered. "There is a fire down there, we could end up getting burned, please! There has to be a way to get out of here?"

A fourth raised a hand. "There is a servants exit near the stables, we can use that. "

All the others looked shocked. "A servant door, now that is preposterous, it is so below us"

The first man hissed. "And being burned isn't? The barrier is failing, if we leave through the front we will be visible from afar, the dragons will see us!"

Everybody fell silent. "But the mages will keep the dragons back won't they?"

The voice was a mere squeak and the first one almost barked. "If they can then why are we trying to flee ha? Come on, the stables is the only safe way to get out of here"

The men shrugged, and the one who spoke started to run and soon they all followed. It was rather apparent that they had taken the most valuable things they could find for Rhuk did see both gold and gems stuck into the bags. It was odd that people think of such useless items when fleeing for their lives, weapons, food and clothing was what they should have taken, not such trinkets which couldn't help you at all in an emergency.

The men ran and Rhuk let out a sigh of relief, Dabin scoffed. "It isn't fair, they shouldn't be allowed to get away"

Rhuk just shrugged. "Know what? I think the Gods will punish them the way they see fit, we have other things to worry about, hurry"

The pool wasn't that hard to locate, they could smell it from afar and it was placed in a great hall which was made to look like a garden with very pretty trees and benches and a lot of luxury. Rhuk spat, it was a fake beauty and one which just harboured misery. The door was at the other side of the pool just as they had been told and Rhuk took a deep breath and approached it. "Listen, we have to make sure that nobody is left behind right? So we may have to carry some, elves are light, but if you see something we can use as a stretcher do let me know."

The door was locked but two strikes of Rhuk's axe brought it down and they were through. The room behind it was a harem, no other word could describe it. It was luxurious and ridiculous and Rhuk was about to call out to hear if anyone was there when a huge figure appeared from a side door and rushed towards them. It was a human, a very fat man with a silly thin voice and a rather fat body and he wielded a sort of short sword. Rhuk swore and now he did demonstrate why dwarves are feared warriors. He didn't hesitate even for a second, the dwarf did spin around with the elegance of a ballerina and the axe cleaved the air with frightening speed. "Take this you overgrown squeaky toy"

The man was obviously used to exploiting his huge mass to his advantage but that didn't quite work out the way he wanted to this time. He hit only air and the axe cut off the man's arm above the elbow. Dabin finished the job by cutting off a leg and as the man fell Rhuk took his head. They grinned at each other, the body shook a few times and went still and they moved forth. "Of course this goddamn torture chamber has a guard."

The next thing which happened was that a huge dog came barking and it stopped when it saw the two dwarves and looked absolutely confused before it whimpered and took off with its tail between its legs. Dabin chuckled. "Good boy, play being a coward"

Now they did hear sounds and they entered through a door and saw something which made them just stop and stare. It was a group of elves and Rhuk let out a gasp. Most were more or less naked and they were all skinny and sickly looking and most had scars and bruises. Even in spite of this they were beautiful and there were both males and females among them. They stared at the dwarves with scared eyes and one dared to speak, the voice barely audible. "Have the masters changed their taste now? Dwarves?"

Dabin raised his hands. "No, oh no, we are friends, we are here to get you out. The masters are fleeing, there has been an accident and dragons are on the loose, you have to hurry"

Rhuk stared at the elves, he didn't see a tall young male with black hair. "Saerian, where is he?"

The one who spoke sniffed. "They came for him last night, the room....the room with the red door...it is closed..."

Dabin swallowed. "Alright, all of you who can walk has to do so, try to help those who are weak, are there any among you who cannot walk at all?"

None answered and the dwarf let out a sigh of relief. "Good, now, Rhuk will go for Saerian, I will help you, we have to be swift and stealthy, alright?"

The elves got to their feet, big eyes in emaciated faces did follow them and Dabin wasn't angry at Rhuk anymore, they would have been just as bad as the brotherhood if they had let these people stay there to be killed by the dragons. Rhuk ran off, he found the red door not far from the main chamber and kicked it inn. He was strong enough to do that and he immediately felt the stench of blood and other bodily fluids. There were no lights in there but he saw and he moaned and closed his eyes. He wished that he had attacked those goddamn humans after all, they deserved to die horribly. The young elf was strapped down over a sort of narrow bench and he was alive but just barely. The head hung and he was breathing with an odd rasping sound. The floor under him was covered with blood and his legs had been chained to the bench, as was his hands. In that position there was no way for the poor wretch to defend himself and there was no doubt about what he had been through. Rhuk swallowed hard, he was tempted to let the poor soul flee to end the agony but he had promised that he would bring the young one back to his family and he would.

He yanked out the chains and snapped them and he threw a sheet around the naked body. Saerian was very tall even for an elf and Rhuk threw the unconscious body over his shoulder with a groan. They would need a stretcher for sure. Most elves don't survive being raped and Rhuk could smell that this had been done by many, not just one. An unholy rage started to build up inside of him, to elves rape is almost a taboo, something they cannot even fully comprehend and to dwarves even more so since they have so few females and they are held in such very high regard. To a dwarf such an act is completely terrible, and something no dwarf has ever committed. Rhuk sighed and tried to run back, Saerian was just too tall and his feet did touch the floor and so did the long silky black hair. Rhuk yelled at Dabin. "Make a stretcher, use those curtain rods, and some clothing or something. He is too tall to be carried otherwise"

Dabin and a couple of the other elves got to it right away and they managed to make a sort of stretcher. Two of the other males stepped forth. "We are not strong, but we can carry him. There is a little strength left in us after all"

Rhuk smiled. "Appreciate it, let's go! The barrier could fall any minute and then the city will be crawling with dragons"

The elves didn't make any sound, they just followed and Rhuk felt nervous for the first time since they left the others behind, they did really have to hurry now!

The fleeing men had made it to the stables, only to find that the guards had taken the horses and they stood there feeling completely confused. The one who had taken the lead was almost foaming at the mouth. "Quickly, we have to make it to the wall, there is a chance we can get through since we aren't mages"

The others just stared at each other and they were shivering, the shimmering barrier which held the dragons back was so weak and they knew that they couldn't outrun an army of angry dragons. The leader snarled. "Come on, we have to hurry, leave the gold behind!"

The men blinked. "We need it, when we get to the plains we can buy what we need and…"

The leader rolled his eyes. "Fools, the dragons are out there, we put them there remember? There is nothing to buy but all the more to take. Leave everything heavy and run!"

The men looked at each other, none of them were young and the sacks heavy, they dropped them with groans and the leader nodded. "Right, we have to seek cover where we can, keep your heads low and don't stop"

They started to jog towards the gate which leads to paths taking them to the canyons and the magical wall, they had almost reached it when they heard a roar and turned around. The dragon which had followed Phraan and the others had roamed the city and now it had felt the stench of evil and its mind was set. His species had been abused and changed and turned into something horrible, something they never had been meant to be. He saw the men and knew that vengeance was close at hand. He had already killed several men who had been trying to flee the city the same way as these and he had in fact decimated the brotherhood pretty much all of his own, the men who weren't mages had tried to flee rather early and he had been ready for them.

He roared and the men froze, staring at the huge beast with shock. The barrier hadn't given way yet? But this was some sort of dragon wasn't it? The dragon had once been free, once been among the ones born in the wilderness and only magic had bound it to this city but the old mage who had summoned him had set him free and given him a form once more and now he was not going to waste that opportunity. The men were not warriors, only a few of them were armed and now they tried to run. It was a bad mistake. The old dragon did not have flames, but he had jaws and he did also have glands which secreted a very strong acidic fluid. A bite was lethal, no matter how small. He threw himself forth and moved so fast it was hard to believe. One man was caught by his maw and died with a scream and the dragon roared, the taste of the evil was sweet indeed and he charged again, his body size made him lethal not only because of his bite but also because of his weight and he ran a couple of men down and crushed them under his scaly feet.

It was a time of pay back, a time to reclaim what was his and he didn't hesitate at all. Blood was running from his jaws and the prey was not that hard to kill, it was just a joy. His mates and his kin had been abused and now it was his right to avenge them all. When the last of the men had died he shook his head and stared at the wall, the barrier did burst and he felt an unholy evil somewhere in the city, something way worse than the dragons and the mages. He growled, he had friends there, he turned back and headed towards the city once more, he had to help if he could.

Chapter 10: By the blood of our brothers

Phraan and the others did run towards the exit, the building was abandoned now and they heard sounds from the outside which indicated that time were running out. Zaray did look a bit nervous and Phraan felt his heart beating fast. Something was happening out there and it didn't feel good at all. Zaray bit her teeth together and she stopped them. "Listen, I think something is coming, I can sense it. We shouldn't just rush out but try to be a bit sneakier than before. There is a chance that something may be waiting for us on the outside. "

Dhokay was growling and Ivran blinked, he did look very confused. "What?"

Zaray looked down. "Ivran, one of us may not be on the right side here, I don't trust him. "

Ivran gasped. "Fastonar? But…"

Phraan petted the little dragon, she was still clinging onto his shoulders. "Don't think about it Ivran, it is a thing between him and me now, I will find the truth. Just…try to see if you can sense anything out there?"

Ivran swallowed and closed his eyes and he gasped. "The barrier is breaking, something has happened at the citadel, something terrible. And I feel Thiana and Taurin, they….oh Gods, it is…mad!"

Zaray was smiling, a very faint smile. "It will all end here, today. The evil against the light, nothing will be the same. It is as it was seen. We will have to fight now my friends, in every way we can"

Her eyes were glowing and there was sadness in her eyes. "I can do it once more, use my birth right. If it is needed that is what I have to do and then there is no way back"

Dhokay was smiling, there was some sort of serene admiration in his eyes. "Yes, I know. Do not worry, the Gods will show us the way"

Phraan stared at the corridor ahead of them, he wanted to go out there, to face his old friend and haul the truth out of him but something told him to wait.

Ivran swallowed. "I am afraid, Thiana and Taurin, the power is…"

Zaray did pet his shoulder gently. "Don't worry about them, they are the ones among us who are strongest at this moment, just wait and behold what they are about to unleash. It will be salvation and damnation in one"

Ivran frowned but he didn't ask any more questions, he felt it in his every bone, something was coming, something…wild!

Thiana and Taurin had been immersed in the magic of the land, they had dragged it to the surface and now it was growing stronger by the second, the force spread through the soil and washed away the contaminated magic and the ground seemed to shake. The two wood elves lay on the ground, hands in the dirt and their eyes were shining like gems, Shaluun had never seen anything like it and he was grasped by a deep feeling of awe. He was shivering, as an elf he felt the power which was awakening and it was terrible and wonderful at the same time, the wild free force of nature untamed and he held his axe and hoped that nothing unexpected would happen.

The shaking stopped and now the soil seemed to lift, it was a surreal sight as thousands of sprouts suddenly shot up and started to move like hands over a tightly packed crowd of people. And it didn't happen just there at the fields, it happened everywhere. Pavements cracked, cobblestone was tossed sky high, walls started to buckle and towers shook. The

two elves were glowing green, using all their strength and as
they gave their last push the barrier at the wall gave way and
the dragons came rushing forth. Shaluun let out a groan, this
was no longer a safe place, they were out in the open and the
goddamn beasts would find them fast. Around them the green
spread outwards in pulsing waves, more and more and it would
reach the city itself soon. Shaluun turned to watch the two,
they were still glowing and still immersed in the intense magic
they had awakened.

He stared towards the wall and saw the veritable wave of
monsters which was spreading out and he swallowed hard, he
had to protect the two, even with his own life and he wasn't
afraid to die, he was just afraid to fail. Suddenly he saw
movement up ahead, some soldiers and a mage came running,
all terrified and trying to escape the dragons and Shaluun was a
bit confused for he hadn't seen people at all, it seemed as if the
city itself had been evacuated, at least the poor areas. He had
no idea of who had done it or how but he didn't care. What he
did care about was the fact that they were about to be
discovered. The mage stopped, he stared at the crates and felt
the magic there for sure and he did also see the green life
which spread out now, growing stronger every second. The
sprouts were soon knee high and the man let out a shout.
"Soldiers, attack, there is something there, stop it"

Shaluun cussed, soldiers were one thing, and he could fight
them with ease but the mage? He heard Thiana's voice. "Fight
the soldiers, we'll take care of the mage!"

The soldiers saw only a few crates and they were afraid and
wanted to run ahead to avoid the dragons but an order was an
order and they didn't dare to disobey the mage. They ran forth
and Shaluun took a deep breath and stepped out behind the
crates. The soldiers slowed down, shocked. It was an elf, a
very tall elf with a terrifying axe and he did look like a true
warrior. The mage frowned, an elf? Where did that creature
come from? One elf couldn't be that dangerous? He felt a sort

of surge coming from the land underneath him and he wasn't sure of what to do. He had escaped just because of his lack of courage and he would leave his brethren behind without hesitation. He swallowed and prepared to use his magic against the tall elf, how could anything be so beautiful and so terrifying at once?

The soldiers did yell to give themselves courage and rushed forth, eager to bring the enemy down so they could seek cover somewhere safe. Shaluun sneered, they were amateurs, not really warriors. They attacked like a herd of sheep, and he had fought in many battles. He had fought orcs and goblins too and these soldiers were hardly a challenge. The axe was a very special weapon and not at all like the ones the dwarves used, it was more like a crescent shaped swords blade with two long extra blades curling inwards, attaching it to the handle and it was both elegant and lethal. The first soldier who came at him got cut in half, the blade had been made to cut through the hide of a dragon, a man in a leather armour didn't even offer any resistance.

Shaluun let out a roar and the remaining soldiers did hesitate once more, two more fell with their legs cut out from underneath them and the last one turned on his heel and fled. Shaluun growled and ran after the man and the mage threw off a spell but it didn't hit the elf the way he thought it would, the magic from underneath sort of swallowed the power and the amount which reached the creature was weak. It made Shaluun gasp with pain but didn't hinder him and he cut the fleeing soldier down with a swift movement. The mage prepared for another spell but suddenly he was grasped by vines and lifted off the ground, vines did twirl around his body and he screamed, tried to grasp his knife to break free but there was no chance. The vines did enter his mouth and nose, cut off his air and other vines did also enter his other bodily orifices, including his ears, boring their way into the brain He was dead within seconds and thrown away like a ragdoll. The two wood elves got up, both were weak and staggering but they managed to stand and Shaluun raced over to them. They saw that the dragons were spreading out but now the sprouts had reached the height of a small tree and they seemed to gather, to form figures which were treelike and yet of an almost humanoid shape. Trees did shoot out of the ground along the valley's edge and the fire which spread in the city threw a terrible blood red light over it all. Thiana moaned. "We are spent, you have to protect us Shaluun. The forest has awakened, it will help fight the dragons but it cannot stop them all, not yet"

Shaluun nodded, he shook the blood off the blade and blinked, it looked as if some of the dragons were shrinking? Thiana gasped. "Oh by the Goddess, someone has undone the magic used to create them, blessed be!"

Taurin was leaning on her and his eyes were huge. "We have to go to the cliffs, I can sense life there, many people. Hurry."

Thiana frowned. "Something has entered our world, in the citadel, something unholy! But...it is trapped?"

Shaluun shrugged. "I don't care, come, we have to hurry. Taurin, lead the way"

The tracker nodded and grasped Thiana by the hand, they all ran towards the cliffs, the wood elves did feel the presence of the people who had fled and sought them using all their senses.

Peter did rush forth, Tersus didn't seem to have been seriously injured but he was bleeding from several cuts and he was chuckling, it did sound absolutely insane. "By my mother's breeches, that was one heck of a blast!"

Peter rolled his eyes. "Yes, goddamn it Tersus, you could have killed us both!"

Tersus just waved a hand and snickered. "Oh I am sure it would have worked out fine no matter what, I am lucky like that. Come now!"

He walked forth and entered the room. It was lighted by several huge lamps and in the middle of the room was a sort of circle carved into the floor and it was marked with gold. A pedestal was placed in the middle of the circle and a book laid on it, the air around it was crackling with magic and Tersus cocked his head, his eyes shining. "Oh my, I bet anyone trying to enter that circle will end up as a human shaped piece of coal right?"

Peter just nodded, the alchemist was getting more and more mad, the man had to have sniffed too much of his own chemicals for he was falling apart mentally, there was little doubt about that. Tersus did walk around the circle, he was playing with his hair and his eyes were narrow. "Disturbing the magic is dangerous, now there is a piece of information I didn't really need for it is darn obvious. So, what to do, how to break it without getting fried?"

Peter shrugged. "Explosives?"

Tersus smiled and the eyes were shining. "See? I knew there was a reason I accepted you as an apprentice, we are two of a kind, yes we are. Of course I can blast the whole room to smithereens, I bet that will disturb the magic pretty well now won't it? Oh yes!"

He grasped the bag and Peter bit his teeth together, dear Gods, he had said it in an attempt at sounding brave! Tersus did tie some small jars and vials together with string and then he found some flint and steel and his smile got even wider. "You see lad, there is something magic lack, it is so freaking absolute you see. A spell cannot work halfway, it works or it doesn't. You cannot regulate the strength of it, but with alchemy, oh it is so elegant. It can be controlled and the effects regulated very carefully."

Tersus did weight the small collection of jars and vials in his hands and Peter swallowed nervously. "Is that enough?'"

Tersus started to laugh. "This? Oh this is what I refer to as overkill, I would only need one jar to bring down this room but there is no point in being too frugal now is it? The bigger the blast the greater the fun!"

Peter whimpered. Fun? More like a serious attempt at killing them both. Tersus chuckled like a deranged hyena before he threw the bundle into the circle after having light the string on fire. The circle didn't reject it, it just lay there. "See? It isn't magic so the circle doesn't see it as a threat. Now that is a weakness I tell you and a not insignificant one"

Peter grasped the alchemist by the collar and dragged him off. "Yes, yes, goddamn it, but we have to go!"

Tersus smiled. "Ah of course, yes, the blast, nasty things such blasts, one never knows how strong they will be. "

Peter was panting, they ran down the corridors and luckily there was nobody there now so they weren't hindered by anyone. Tersus was chuckling the whole way, and Peter felt as if death was breathing down his neck, this was not fun, it was the direct opposite of fun. Compared with this fun was sitting in a pool filled with poisonous snakes and acid. They reached the main entrance and saw that the guards had gone and Tersus ran out onto the square hollering like a madman. "It will happen soon, it will happen soon, just you wait and see!"

Peter whimpered. "The dragons, they have breached the barrier, we have to go, they will be here soon"

Tersus let out a little squeal. "Oh we won't go before we see the power of my inventions."

Peter felt desperate now. "Oh goddamn it!"

He didn't have time to say more, there was a deafening boom and the entire top of the citadel seemed to fly outwards before a fireball almost the size of the entire structure flew upwards and the air shivered in an almighty pressure wave. Tersus was screaming like a girl and Peter gasped. The citadel shivered, the ground did thunder and roar and the building started to collapse, rocks and debris started to rain down over them and Peter didn't know what to do with himself, he was afraid they would get crushed. He didn't have time to think before he was pushed upwards by something huge and he let out a squeal as he found himself straddling the back of the dragon which had followed them. The beast threw Tersus too onto his back and ran and now the two saw that grass and vines started to spread everywhere. Tersus did gape. "What in heavens name, I have never heard of anything from the plant kingdom acting thus?"

Peter did cling on to the back of the beast, it was running at full speed to get away from the debris but that meant that they were heading towards the oncoming dragons. "This is no time to discuss botanical issues!"

Tersus was giggling. "Oh I never believed that I would become a dragon rider, onward oh brave steed, and find our friends"

Peter closed his eyes, Tersus was mad, definitely one hundred percent stark raving mad, and he was going mad too, just from being there with him.

The demons had gathered in the great hall, and they had been very self-assure and ready to go out and start the slaughter, but something had blocked them. They hadn't been able to leave the room and it felt as if some sort of power field was trapping them there. The demons felt the magic deep within the ground and sought it but that too was blocked and they felt a sort of presence there and their anger and confusion grew. There was life out there, life they aimed to devour and they growled and didn't really know what to do. The power which surrounded them was very pure and very different from their own and suddenly a shining figure did appear, wielding a bright rod of light like a sword. The lead demon hissed and attacked and the figure slid out of the way and the rod did touch the demon's scaly skin and it screamed and smoke did rise from the wound. The other there realized that this being was what kept them there and they attacked. The anger and wrath which was the very core of their being couldn't be hindered by fear or doubt and the being of light was fighting desperately to keep them at bay. She was new to this, her powers yet untried and they sensed it and now their goal was to devour this newly awakened goddess and then the source of her powers.

Her light did burn them and the barrier she had created to keep them there was very strong, they wouldn't be able to escape the great hall. The fight went on for what felt like an eternity, their claws hit nothing but air but the dark energy did hurt her and she was getting desperate. If the demons did escape this place the disaster would be complete.

Sparks did fly, roars and screams did fill the air and she did drink from the heart stone and managed to hold the magic up. Eleven demons are no easy task to subdue and she was struggling. They had magic of their own and tried to make her flesh and blood so they could torment her further before they killed her and she was starting to feel a sense of despair. What was she to do? She had to get rid of them somehow! Outside the wild magic was spreading and she knew that the dragons were changing, and that the forests would take care of them but this was a much more serious problem. The rod of light did hurt the demons but it couldn't kill them since they weren't of this world and she knew that they somehow had to become flesh and blood of this place to be vulnerable. But she didn't have that sort of skills. Then the whole citadel did tremble and a terrible boom was heard and the hall started to collapse, the demons shrieked in triumph, the magic which held them trapped did weaken for only a few seconds and that was enough. They broke through and the spirit which had been Imeah screamed in despair and anger, how was she to stop them now?!

Rhuk and Dabin had been leading the elves down through the servant's corridors and they had entered the old potato cellar when they felt the whole building shake. The poor elves did scream in fear and Rhuk did cuss violently, he saw that the walls had started to crack and thunderous booms told him that the entire citadel was about to collapse. He smacked the behind of the one in front of him. "Run, put those long shanks of yours into work, you have gotta run now!"

They all ran, the two carrying the unconscious male were panting and trembling and Dabin ran in front to make sure that nobody did try to stop them if there were enemies about. They found the door open and now the thunder was even louder than before and Dabin yelled. "Stay close to the mountain side, the rock will protect us, hurry!"

The elves were tired and scared but they were driven by their fear and hope and Rhuk was forming the back, he was yelling to them. "Hurry, hurry, the whole shite is falling, they haven't used really good rock for sure. Morons who cannot build a decent structure!"

There was rocks hitting the ground, a cloud of dust and smoke did almost catch up with them and they were dragging each other, most were barely able to walk. Rhuk grasped a willowy elven girl and carried her with him, he knew the dangers of a collapse and he remembered some rather nasty things which had happened back in the days. Not all dwarven cities had been built without causalities for the rock could be very treacherous some places and what seemed as a very safe and solid strata could turn out to be rotten rock whence they had dug through the first few meters. There was a loud crack and the ground did shake, they were hit by a blast of air and Rhuk coughed. The air was filled with dust. Dabin shouted. "I can see the tunnel, fast now!"

Everybody gathered their last energy and ran to the tunnel, it was still open but the two dwarves who controlled it stood there and they did look very impatient. They had not expected the two warriors to return alive and now that they suddenly appeared it was a shock. Rhuk grinned. "Here, we did hold our word, the elves are safe."

The two stared at the stretcher and their eyes were large. "What happened to that one?"

Dabin swallowed and his face was rather stiff. "He has been raped by the goddamn leeches, I hope the building fell on top of them all"

The dwarf gasped and stared, his eyes huge. "Oh by the allfather, that is terrible. Hurry now, we are about to close the entrance"

Rhuk helped the last ones into the tunnel and they were about to start the process of lifting the barrier back into place when three figures did appear in the dust and Rhuk let out a yell of surprise. "Shaluun? Thiana and Taurin? Oh by the Gods and their aching teeth, where have you come from?"

Shaluun was supporting the two wood elves, he was snarling. "They have awakened the life of the valley, the forests are returning. Both have spent almost all of their strength, get them to safety"

He swung his axe. "I am going to see if I can find the others, Phraan and the rest went to the city and I know that Tersus and Peter must be here somewhere too"

Rhuk nodded. "We left them in a guard hut but I think they must have gone to the citadel too, I am not sure if they are alive if they did. The whole thing went badaboom a little while ago"

Shaluun nodded. "We saw that thank you, everybody in the city did. I think Tersus had more than a finger involved in that explosion"

He made a grimace. "The dragons are returning to their original state, but it is not moving along very fast. Get going, get everyone out of here. "

Rhuk did hesitate, Dabin scowled. "Oh no, don't you...don't you dare..."

Rhuk grasped his axe and his eyes were shining. "We came to slay dragons and if they are changing we do have a chance now don't we? "

Dabin let out a huge sigh of sheer despair. "Rhuk, we have done enough!"

The other dwarf grinned. "No, not until there are no dragons left, come on Dabin, it will be grand"

Dabin was gnashing his teeth, "Yeah, a spectacularly grand manner of dying. Come on, Goldren will be waiting for you"

Rhuk smiled even wider. "She'll want to marry a dragon slayer now won't she? It is a once in a lifetime chance"

Dabin groaned. "Yes, at being toasted and burned and crushed, gee, how can I possibly decline that?"

Rhuk nodded vigorously. "See? I told you so!"

Dabin let out another groan. "Damn it Rhuk, I was being sarcastical, you really are rather daft aren't you?"

Shaluun had to grin. "We have a saying in our tribe, he is one antler short of being a boar"

Both dwarves stared at the tall elf. "Ha?!"

Shaluun just waved them off. "Right, it is an elven joke, come on, if you wanna kill dragons come with me but do as I say"

Rhuk smiled widely and Dabin rolled his eyes. "Fine! Fine! But if we die I am so going to haunt you"

The two dwarves who guarded the tunnel entrance frowned. "So what is it gonna be?"

Rhuk bowed his head. "Seal the tunnel, make sure that everybody stays safe"

The two did look as if they had their doubts but nodded and started lifting the magic which sealed the tunnel again. Rhuk petted Dabin on his shoulder. "Come on, the forest is awakening, the citadel has fallen and now it is up to us to get rid of those pesky dragons, aint it phenomenal?"

Dabin grunted. "Absolutely...wonderful"

Shaluun was chuckling as he was leading them back towards the city, both dwarves were tough and capable fighters, it would be needed for sure.

They had spent too much time turning those columns, Phraan was sure of it. The sounds they heard told them that the dragons were on the loose and Zaray was a bit pale, she was listening with her eyes half shut and Ivran looked rather scared too. Dhokay was swinging his hammer and Phraan made a grimace. "We'd better get going, there is nothing to gain by waiting here."

The huge cat was nodding, the eyes were strangely calm and Phraan gathered his courage and started walking. The ground was shaking and there was cracks forming in the walls, the small dragons were making sharp squealing sounds and ran as fast as they could. They did look like a stream of mercury defying the laws of gravity. The light from the entrance was not as bright as it had been, the lamps had gone out and they felt a smell of smoke and something else, something acrid. Dhokay turned to Zaray. "Do we use this door?"

She shrugged. "I don't see why not, we have to get out anyhow, this building may not be very tall but it will crumble, I can feel it."

Phraan saw that thick vines already had started to crawl in through the door, like snakes, searching for something to grasp on to. It did look bizarre and he felt that this city would be naught but a memory whence this was over, whatever this was.

They ran outside and the tiny dragons did surround them, the air was indeed filled with dust and smoke and it was no lights anywhere so it was rather dark there. The barrier was gone and Phraan hissed, there were dragons heading their way, setting the buildings on fire as they moved forth and with them the other creations also came but he could see that the dragons had changed. They weren't as large and seemed to return to their natural state. "Look, they are shrinking!"

Dhokay was raising a fist in the air. "Yes, it means we have a chance"

Phraan turned to see if Fastonar was there still, the soul sworn did appear from behind a wall and he was pale as a ghost and shivering. "The citadel, it…it fell, just moments ago"

Zaray frowned. "Fell? What do you mean?"

Fastonar was wetting his lips. "It exploded, or rather, the top did. It was terrible!"

Phraan just mumbled. "We felt that yes"

Fastonar was very nervous. "There are dragons coming, and the city is burning now. What is going on? The ground, there is trees and grass shooting up everywhere"

Zaray smiled, a stiff smile. "The land is awakening, that is what's happening. Thiana and Taurin has succeeded, I think the dragons will be dealt with."

Dhokay grinned. "Yes, and since they are becoming what they once were it shouldn't be too much of a problem. I can sense the wrath in the air"

Fastonar was almost stepping in one place. "So, what are we to do? Flee?"

Phraan shook his head. "No, I think we are to fight, we cannot get out of here unseen anyway and even if the mages are dead there could be some of their followers alive here"

Zaray grinned widely. "The dragons have done the job for us, I don't think any of the mages on the wall survived. The beasts have killed them all"

The smoke was very thick where the wind forced it down and suddenly something came out of the dark, something rather bizarre. It was the dragon and on its back was Tersus and Peter, both cheered when they saw the others and Tersus was pumping one hand in the air, he was hollering. "Did you see that ha? Did you see? I brought that nest of serpents down, with my own inventions!"

Dhokay helped the two down from the huge animal, it was staring forwards and it was very obvious that it was watching the transformation of its kin back to their original state. It appeared to be pleased. Fastonar was staring at the alchemist with huge eyes. "I…saw"

Tersus chuckled. "Cool ha? Oh what a wonderful blow to the brotherhood, their citadel in ruins, I don't think that building is anything but rubble now"

Peter was brushing dust off his clothes and he was coughing. "And this entire city is gonna end as a huge pile of ash"

Zaray pointed at the grass and bushes which was popping up everywhere. "No, it is gonna become an oasis once more."

Phraan heard roars and stared at the incoming horde of dragons and monsters, they had met resistance. Vines thick as tree logs were trapping the huge creatures and squeezing the very life out of them, others were being ripped apart and the dreghil and other monsters seemed to be sucked down as if the ground had turned into quick sand. Phraan was in awe of what he saw and he did almost pity the people who had been on the wall. None of them could have survived this. Zaray pointed, the area near the citadel hadn't been evacuated and they saw people trying to run past the ruins, trying to seek cover near the cliffs. It had to be the more wealthy citizens and their families and some were probably the families of the members of the brotherhood who weren't mages. The mages weren't allowed to get married and Dhokay was frowning. "I bet some of those people have a thing or two to answer to, I doubt that the mages have done all the dirty work on their own"

Zaray just waved her hand. "Let them flee, there are innocent people among them, if they can make it to the canyons they deserve to get away. The wall is up again, I can feel it"

Ivran nodded. "It is, there is no way they can escape this valley now"

Tersus chuckled and his eyes did reveal his madness. "I destroyed the gem just like you told me to do, and then we managed to remove the protection against magical attacks too"

Zaray smiled, a very relieved smile. "Oh wonderful, then the cities can perhaps protect themselves. You have saved many lives now Tersus."

The alchemist was practically beaming with pride and Peter had to admit that it had been smart, even if it hadn't seemed that way when they did it. Suddenly the large cat which had been rather relaxed started to sneer and the tiny dragons gathered in tight formations, the queen shrieked and threw her head back, looking rather scared. Zaray gasped. "Something is coming, everybody, be careful. I have no idea of what this might be!"

Phraan felt a sudden gust of heat and his heart did drop, he felt that something indeed was on its way, something terrible. This was no dragon, this was malevolence at its worse, intelligent and wicked and he touched the ring without even thinking about it. The armour formed immediately, but it didn't create a helmet this time and he felt that the sword felt heavy in his hands. Ivran whimpered and he seemed as if he was about to drop, what he felt there was terrible. Zaray cussed, her eyes wide and Dhokay turned to her. "What?"

She hissed. "Something out of this world!"

They saw that the vines and trees started to shrivel and die and the air changed, it became almost too hot to breathe and Peter let out a shriek of fear and pointed. Something was moving through the smoke and it was more than just one figure. It seemed to be several and they were huge and moved with a sort of floating elegance. Phraan swore, the dragons were being released from their bonds and this could yet end the wrong way now. Zaray swallowed hard. "Demons, don't try to fight them, they are beyond you all!"

Tersus gaped and backed off and Fastonar was trembling, he did look like a man who has had his heart utterly broken. There was a howl coming from the smoke and Phraan wondered how they could hope to get out of this mess. The demons seemed to kill anything they came into contact with and Zaray hissed. "Tersus, take Peter and Dhokay and Fastonar, get out of here! Phraan, you have got to help me, Ivran, is there anything you can do?"

The young man swallowed, demons? What in heck's name could he do which could affect such creatures? "I...I have no idea?"

Zaray seemed to tense up. "Wrong answer kid, none of us can fight them when they are like this, they are not of this creation, and they cannot be harmed by us"

It seemed as if the figures had discovered them and was heading their way and Dhokay grasped Tersus and started hauling the alchemist off. Peter just ran and Fastonar was staring at the approaching monsters, his mouth agape and his eyes wide open. Phraan swung his blade. "Can I harm them? Can Rivath do any damage?"

Zaray nodded. "Yes, but they have to be flesh and blood of this world for that to happen."

The first demon appeared and Ivran let out a shriek, the creature was grotesque and gigantic and its red eyes were filled with triumph and wickedness. In that moment he saw its intentions, it was devouring the energy the wood elves had awakened and then it would take the dragons too and all life there. The demon sensed that the population had fled, those people would be just snacks too, and there was no escape. The thing laughed and reached out towards them and Ivran realized that he was the only one who could do anything at all. His magic was different from all other, it was true chaos, natural chaos. It was everything the dark mages had wanted to be and yet not a thing of darkness and he heard his grandfather's voice in his head. "Go on son, you know what to do now."

Ivran felt strangely calm, he knew his role, knew what it would ultimately take from him but he didn't care. He let the energy flow through him and the demons felt it and cheered, started to gather, moving towards this source of such wonderful living power. Zaray gaped, she had no idea of what

Ivran was doing, and he was becoming bait but why? Sparks started to fly of the young man, he was being lifted of the ground and finally he embraced everything that he was. The magic he carried was indeed a double edged sword, there was no going back whence it was awakened. His heart was beating like a drum, sweat flowing of him, what he was about to do was impossible, something only a God was supposed to achieve, something which went against the very laws of nature. He formed it in his mind, and as the demons reached out to devour his energy he reached back to them and changed everything that they were. It wasn't easy, it pushed his very being to the borders of what he could do and beyond but he didn't hesitate. This meant changing the very core of creation, forcing the creatures of a different realm to become of this and there was a bright flash of light and the air did explode around them. The demons did shriek, for a short moment they did look almost transparent and then they suddenly felt the weight of this world pulling on them, they were of this world now, unable to return to their own. Caught there for all eternity. Their magic was taken from them, they were just beasts now, nothing more.

Ivran had collapsed, he was barely breathing and Phraan saw that his hair had turned bright white and his skin was strangely discoloured, he did look terrible. Dhokay fell to his knees, shielding the young man and the demons roared in rage and realized that they no longer could draw the energy out of living beings like before. They were bound to this dimension. And the ones responsible for this terrible dishonour were ahead of them. Zaray yelled. "They are still lethal, still strong. You cannot harm them"

She did call the bow forth and shot a few arrows but the demons did still possess some magic and it made the arrows veer off into nothing, she couldn't do anything to stop them thus and let the bow disappear again. The energy she had to spend to use it was too great, at least when it would be spent in vain.

Phraan saw that the little dragons had scattered, it looked as if they were preparing for something and he took a deep breath. The demons were still huge, and still fast and strong and they wouldn't stop killing just because they no longer were of another dimension and not s magical as before. He swung Rivath and felt the blade almost singing to his soul, it was eager and it would kill. He had killed dragons' way larger than any demon but dragons are not intelligent, they function through instinct. These were vicious and smart creatures and he roared an order to Dhokay. "Get Ivran out of the way, we have to stop them."

Zaray was quiet and she did look as if she was in doubt, her hands were trembling. Phraan saw that the first demon was approaching fast and he stopped thinking, he just reacted. He ran forth and the demon did swing a massive fist at him, trying to send him flying but he dodged it and then the beast was hit by a flying cat which appeared out of the smoke like a sledgehammer. The huge claws did dig into flesh and the demon felt pain for the first time in its existence and it didn't like it at all. Black blood did spurt from several deep gashes and the cat did snarl and jump out of the way, it avoided a vicious blow and bounced back, teeth sank deeply into the back of the demon's neck and Phraan swung Rivath and the blade did sink deeply into the demon's leg. The creature roared and tried to grasp him but the armour didn't let it get a good grip, he just slid out of the grip and delivered a blow to the arm. These creatures were tough, much harder to kill than a dragon and they were many. He knew he couldn't kill them all, just finishing this one was hard enough and Ivran was out cold.

The wounds seemed to close themselves rather fast and their bones were simply too dense to cut through. Rivath did cut deeply, an ordinary blade would have bounced off the hard tissue but even this magical sword didn't seem to kill. Zaray saw that ten more demons were about to attack them and she realized that there was no choice this time. She could no longer hesitate. She ran back, got away from the group and sensed that Shaluun and the two dwarves were heading their way. The energy of the land was recovering now that the demons couldn't drain it anymore and the vines and trees were recovering but the dragons were coming and coming fast. They would have to fight on two fronts now and she closed her eyes and abandoned the one she had been. This was the last time she could do this, and she wouldn't be able to shift back again.

In the ruins of the citadel the source which rested so deep down was unharmed by the collapse, the power which had been Imeah recovered from the shock and she felt that the rift the mages had opened still was there. It was an opening through several dimensions and she also sensed the battle which was going on in the city. She wanted to help her friends but she couldn't, not before the rift was repaired. She could feel that something was approaching the rift from some other dimension and she knew it was bad. No, she had to stop this, and she had to trust that the others could fight this fight and win. There was no other way.

Dhokay pulled Ivran behind a wall and hid him from sight, Peter kneeled next to the young man and he did look terrified. Tersus had grasped the bags and were going through the last vials he had left, he was shivering too. Dhokay swung the hammer, these creatures seemed to be made from much more dense material than a normal being, but that also meant that they should be more vulnerable to blunt force trauma. He was not going to just stand there and he let out a roar and attacked. Fastonar was hiding behind some rocks and now Shaluun and the two dwarves suddenly came out of the clouds of dust and debris. The city was still burning and the light was surreal. The vines and trees were trying to stop the dragons but some did get through and Dhokay shouted at Shaluun and the dwarves. "Keep the goddamn dragons out of the way!"

They nodded and ran off to form a battle line of their own and the dragon which had come with them snarled and seemed to hesitate for a few moments before it ran forth and engaged a demon. The beast hit the dragon and sent it flying and the animal hit the ground with a thud and a groan. The demons were so terribly strong. But the dragon wasn't injured and now it rushed forth and did a mock attack. As the demon bent to grasp the dragon by its head the huge creature leaped upwards and the terrible maw closed around the demons neck. Teeth the size of short swords did pierce the flesh and the dragon did growl and threw its head back. There was a most disgusting sound, like someone ripping apart a rotten sheet and the demons head was pulled off so black blood shot sky high in a fountain. Phraan was roaring. "The head, take their heads"

One was dead but ten was left and Dhokay swung his hammer at the knee of one of the great monstrosities, it had a head which looked like that of a ram but it had the teeth of a shark and the eyes were filled with cold hatred. The impact was brutal, it would have crushed the very bones of anything of this world but the demon just reared back with a shriek of pain. It was thrown out of balance and Phraan yelled. "We have to cooperate"

Shaluun and the two dwarves were fighting hard now, dragons were coming running towards them and some hadn't shrunk that much yet, they were still large and fast and the vines and roots were swinging around trying to catch them but didn't always hit the right way. Some trees had reached rather impressive size already and the branches were coming alive and grasping dragons as the roots moved and let the trees sort of glide forwards in a slow floating motion. It did look insane.

Dhokay and Phraan ran towards the next demon, attacking low and high at the same time but this creature was intelligent, it jumped out of the way and Phraan was hit and thrown into a wall with a crash. The armour protected him and Dhokay swore and got an idea, he remembered what the dwarves had said about trolls and he had to try. He ran around the demon and when the creature tried to figure out what the heck this luptay was doing he brought the hammer down with all his might, over the demon's foot. He felt the very satisfying crackle of bones before the beast hit him and sent him too flying and he made contact with mother earth in a very unpleasant manner. Tersus came running, the man was waving his arms and did look like an utter madman and perhaps he was, two vials flew from his hands and hit two demons square in the chest. The creatures did look down and shrugged for it seemed as if the vials which broke on impact had contained just water but suddenly smoke started to rise from their skin and they started to claw at the affected area, howling with agony. Phraan got on his feet and he felt ice cold determination filling his veins, this was like killing a very huge dragon, there was just one weak spot and he saw that now. His gift was becoming useful once more and he knew from sheer instinct that decapitation was the only way to kill such monsters. His injuries did disappear within seconds and he realized why Imeah had given him what she had, he had become almost indestructible and now he knew that he could keep fighting, no matter what.

Tersus did disappear into the smoke again and now the pack of demons seemed to split, some ran off and Phraan swore. "They are after the people of the city"

Dhokay panted. "Yes, there is little we can do about that"

Phraan let out a roar to give himself strength and he rushed forth. Dhokay attacked again and the demon had most definitely lost its ability to move without pain for it was limping and Dhokay was large and heavy. He managed to simply collide with the massive beast and it lost its balance and fell and Phraan roared and brought Rivath down just as the demon hit the ground with a loud thud. The blade did cut deeply but didn't decapitate the demon completely and it grasped him with one hand and threw him against a column.

Phraan felt how the impact knocked the air out of him and he gasped and tried to get up. His ears were ringing and he had almost double vision. Another demon came rushing towards him, ready to strike and it had claws the length of long swords. Phraan got up on his knees and the demon snarled and spun around to slash him open but something rushed past Phraan and a sword did sink into the creature's belly. It shrieked and fell and the claws cut deeply into the man who fell onto the ground, coughing blood. The friendly dragon and Phraan's cat was taunting the demons which remained there, keeping them busy and Phraan looked up just in time to see wings in the air above them. Then they heard an almighty roar and something landed in front of them, facing the demons. Dhokay let out a small gasp. "Zaray!"

Phraan could just blink, he saw a dragon, the largest he had ever seen and it was shining like steel with both wings and four legs and it was both beautiful and terrifying at once. Her eyes were a colour of deep amethyst and the dragon was so huge you could have ridden a horse underneath it without touching the belly. The demons did hesitate and the cat and the old dragon attacked one and the cat tipped it over, the dragon finished the job by crushing the demon's head with its jaws. The huge dragoness roared again, her throat swelling and the remaining demons turned to flee. Phraan felt Zaray's voice in his head. "Let yourself free, kill the dragons, I will deal with the demons. They must not reach the other valley, people are hiding there, and Thiana and Taurin are there too"

Phraan swallowed, the night did resound of roars and screams from the dragons the now very strange plants were attacking. He got up, his body did ache but the armour had shielded him from the worst of the impact and he was healing as he moved, the pain dissipating as if it never had been there. He walked over to where Fastonar lay, the man was groaning, he hadn't worn armour and he was cut open, the wound terrible. He had blood running from his mouth but he was still alive. A soul sworn is hard to kill, but such an injury would be lethal even for one as him. Fastonar let out a wheezing sound, the eyes rolling with the agony. "Brother...I..."

Phraan felt his heart restrict within his chest, his throat was taught and dry. "Why?"

Fastonar coughed, tried to grasp Phraan's hand but the half elf didn't let him. "Why did you do it? Don't try to lie Fastonar, you killed them"

Fastonar moaned, Phraan stared at him and tried to ignore the memories, the feeling of brotherhood and camaraderie. He had loved Fastonar like he had been a brother and this was hard to accept, from several angles. The dying man swallowed, his skin was pale and grey and he was sweating. "Please, it wasn't....it wasn't supposed to....happen like this..."

Phraan was sneering, Dhokay and Tersus had joined Shaluun and the dwarves and Peter was guarding Ivran. The cat and the old dragon had vanished, they were probably out there hunting monsters. "Then tell me, what was supposed to happen? When did you put honour and truth behind you and join the service of the dark?"

Fastonar wheezed. "I was being forgotten Phraan, there was nothing to do, no challenges. They...."

He coughed blood. "They said...bring slayers...make it look like the last time...make the king...think it is no different."

Phraan growled. His anger was boiling in him. "Then why kill Vitile? Why kill Imeah? I bet you caused Ivran's weakness too?"

Fastonar closed his eyes. "I am so sorry, I didn't want to, but she had seen...she had seen what made the dragons change. And Ivran, he could have reversed the magic back then, had he known. I had to...I had to bring him to this city, but he couldn't...He couldn't be allowed to know"

Phraan felt tears gather in his eyes, his body was shaking and the sorrow he had felt at the loss flowed into his soul once again. "I loved Vitile, and you stole her from me, with treachery"

Fastonar whimpered. "I am sorry, I am so sorry. But I though...a mage like Ivran, they would need his magic, and Vitile, she would tell him, eventually"

Phraan grasped the hilt of Rivath, the leather felt almost alive in his hand. "And Imeah, what about her? Why did you poison her Fastonar?"

Fastonar swallowed, his body shaking violently. "She...she saw...what I had...done. She saw...everything. She...was going to...expose me..."

The man coughed up a spurt of blood. "I couldn't...let her enter the city...too strong"

Phraan was almost unable to breathe. "But you failed Fastonar, you did release her soul and it is stronger now than it ever was, and you brought us here, and we brought doom over the brotherhood"

Fastonar trembled. "I never meant for any of it to happen, believe me. All I wanted was for things to return...to what they once were...I didn't know...the dragons...they had changed so very much...the brotherhood, they were lying to me"

Phraan hissed. "And see where it got you, believing in servants of chaos when you are supposed to serve the light. "

Fastonar was grasping onto Phraan's cloak, tears streaming down his face. "I can never forgive myself for what I did...I dishonoured my oath, I dishonoured my name and I should have warned everyone. But...I believed...I believed..."

Phraan yanked his cloak free from the grip. "I do not bloody care what you believed Fastonar, our coming here was perhaps fore seen but it didn't make it right. It gave you no right to murder two good women, and it didn't give you the right to drag us in here without telling us the truth. If the fall of the brotherhood has broken your faith I am happy. You deserve it!"

Fastonar wheezed again. "I do, I agree….Please, I just…I craved what was back then…"

Phraan growled deeply, he felt like snapping the man's neck but that would be too easy. "You betrayed us for fame, for glory. I can never forgive you Fastonar, I curse the day we met"

Fastonar made a gargling sound. "Please…"

Phraan got up. "No, I will not let you die in peace, you do not deserve it. You could have warned the king, warned us. The people could have been evacuated, the cities saved. I will not help you Fastonar. Imeah died slowly, in agony. You will too"

He walked away from the man and Fastonar let out a thin wail. "Phraan…"

He ignored it and whistled. The huge cat came out of the dark like a shadow and Phraan stared at the burning city. He had a job to do, and he was about to do it. He grasped the cat's thick fur and got up onto its back and it purred and licked its jaws. "So Ghaday, let us hunt monsters"

The old dragon came behind it and it stopped by Dhokay who had returned to see if Phraan was alright. The luptay frowned and Phraan nodded. "It is alright, get up. He will carry you, use that hammer of yours for all it is worth now"

Dhokay grinned widely and Phraan turned his head, stared at Fastonar one last time, the body was convulsing and the soul was slowly leaving it. He felt nothing, no sorrow, not even disgust, he was hollow and only the need to kill remained. The breathing stopped as he watched and Phraan sneered and let the cat run forth. He was a dragon slayer, now was his time to do what he had come to do in the first place.

Zaray was chasing the demons, her claws did pick them up one by one and she ripped their heads off. The side valley and canyons were filled with survivors and the demons were heading that way, set on revenge but she wouldn't let them reach it. Demons can climb very well but she could fly and she used her enormous body to simply tear them away from the rock face. The monsters knew what was chasing them now, and they tried to escape but she grasped the last two with her front legs, threw them into the air and spewed flames onto them.

They fell to the earth like screaming torches and she bared her teeth and turned around. The valley was teeming with dragons and other monsters and now she was going to help the others doing their job. She had made her choice, she wouldn't be able to return to her elven form again in a very long time if ever but it was a small sacrifice. She would be needed now.

The valley was indeed coming alive, green plants were spreading everywhere, tearing down buildings and ripping through the streets, the city of the brotherhood was no more and the last remnant of that dark power was the monsters which were on the loose. She circled the valley, her friends were attacking from the front and she came from behind, using her flames to wipe out this spawn of unholy creation.

Phraan was feeling an odd sort of freedom, the sword did cut through flesh and bone as if it wasn't there and he was creating a path of destruction behind him. The dragons which remained were just animals now, not much larger than the ancient one Dhokay now rode and he laughed as he charged and killed. These beasts could never be allowed to escape, the valley would be pure once more, a haven of life. The vines and trees did help them, snagged dragons and brought them down and the sword did even kill the other monstrosities. Rivath did end elementals and dreghil as well as dragons and Zaray was in the air and brought down those beasts which flew.

Tersus helped Shaluun, he had found a sword and swung it with surprising strength and skill and Rhuk and Dabin were covered with goo and dragon blood. Since they were small they attacked from underneath the beasts and cut their bellies open or cut off their legs and both dwarves were chanting the battle cries of their people as they hacked away at the seemingly endless stream of beasts. Zaray herded the dragons forth towards the hunters and time had seized to matter, all that existed was the battle and the knowledge that not even one of these monsters could be allowed to live.

Imeah was struggling, her soul had been strengthened by the heart stone and now that it was one with her she had become a force which this world had never before seen. She was a young Goddess now, the valley would be her temple and here many would come to worship life but as of yet she hadn't fully embraced her powers. The human in her was still there, still holding her back. The rift was not closing, it had been created through sacrifice and hatred and she didn't quite know how to knit it back together. Something was trying to get access to this world and even though it didn't seem large or particularly strong she sensed that it was dangerous. She had never been a magician, she had never learned spells or incantations but she was smart and she knew how to think in a manner which others wouldn't expect. She opened her senses and felt the magic which still permeated the ruins of the citadel, called it forth and brought it inn under her will. Within it was the lore trapped in books and scrolls which now had been destroyed and she started to weave.

The magic acted like the web of a spider, slowly it was healing the rift, bringing its sides together as if it was a tear in a piece of cloth. She was working as fast as she could and the tear the angry young mage had formed seemed to disappear. She was about to seal it off for good when she saw something slip through the last crack, a small dark drop, almost like a drop of water, and it was moving upwards, as if it was seeking the light. Imeah would have let out an angry shout if she had been able to create sound, she reached for it but it did evade her fingers and she realized that this was no good. She chased after the black drop and reached the surface above the ruin, the black drop stopped, hovering in the air and it seemed to pulse a little and shake itself like a dog shakes off water. Then it grew!

Imeah just knew it, this thing was something very dark and evil and it should never have been allowed to enter their world at all. She tried to reach around it, smother it with her light but the touch did send a searing pain through her and she reared back. Nothing should be able to harm a soul like that? She wasn't supposed to feel pain? She tried again with the same result and the black drop took shape, an enormous dark figure which did look a lot like a man but it had the lower body of a snake and the head was also snakelike. Imeah realized that she was in trouble, this thing was so much worse than a demon, this was something old and forgotten and probably very wicked. She formed a sword with her mind, tried to attack it.

The thing just veered out of the way, hissing and an arm shot out and Imeah was slammed against the ground, the goddamn thing had four arms and they were long and strong. She couldn't believe it, she was spirit, not material and yet this thing could harm her? She got up, attacked again and the glowing sword she had formed with her mind slid through the nearest arm with no resistance. The arm fell off, but as she felt new hope being rekindled the arm grew back out, as if this monster was a salamander or some other creature with regenerative abilities. The thing stared at her, the eyes were cold, devoid of emotion and she felt its power like a heatwave gushing towards her. What was this thing? It seemed to grow and Imeah grew too but she wasn't used to this, her still mortal mind was bound by its previous existence. She pierced its chest and the thing didn't even seem to react, it slid out of the way and the glowing blade didn't harm it.

An arm managed to grasp a hold of her, she was pulled into a tight embrace and felt that this dark figure in fact was hurting her physically, as if she still had a body. She was growing weaker by the minute and it hurt, it hurt so bad she had to scream. The sound couldn't be heard by the ears of living beings for it was travelling through the astral plane and she saw to her horror that its claws were tearing into her body, leaving huge gashes which bled energy into the air. The dark snake creature seemed to enjoy hurting her and she felt panic surge through her entire being. It was feeding off the heart stone, through her. She screamed again, a desperate wail which echoed off the mountain sides, and this time it could be heard.

Zaray had killed off all the demons, now she was busy killing other monsters and she was feeling rather confident when she heard the scream, it came from where the citadel had stood and it was not the scream of a throat of flesh and blood but the scream of something insubstantial. She felt that something was wrong, there was a sort of heaviness in the air, something utterly twisted and unnatural and she turned and flew through the smoke and dust towards the source of it. The city was still burning and the flames had reached the slum area, the entire valley was lighted by the raging flames and the trees and vines couldn't do anything to stop it and they didn't try, the valley was to be cleansed, the ashes would provide good nutrients for the new life which would replace the rule of the brotherhood. The thick smoke and debris clouds created a rather hellish atmosphere and the screams and roars from the fighting dragons added to the entire mix and turned the scene into something out of a very surreal nightmare.

Zaray saw two figures in the distance, hovering above the crumbled citadel. One of light and the other of darkness and she just knew that this was it. The darkness could still win, the balance could still be destroyed and twisted in favour of evil. She saw Gods fighting and knew that light never can conquer darkness without becoming what it was supposed to destroy. The enormous dragon was a magical creature, it was in her blood, her heritage and she allowed that power to flow through her now. She started to glow, the scales on her hide became metallic and impenetrable and she let herself drop out of the sky like a meteor from the heavens above. The dark snake heard the sound of wind tearing into something falling fast but it didn't have time to react and the dragon hit with tremendous force. It slammed onto the creature with terrible energy and ripped it down, smashed it to the ground. Imeah managed to get free, she slid away from the enemy and stared with huge eyes at the scene. This enemy was beyond her and she was afraid that it was beyond Zaray too, the she dragon was ripping into the dark foe, her claws were like spears and her jaws capable of ripping through rock. The dark creature shrieked and then it started to fight back, long arms reached out and tried to get a hold of the dragon's legs and wings, it did have fangs and poison was dripping from them and it tried to bite.

Zaray did notice just what Imeah had, when one limb was torn off another grew out, it was like a hydra re-growing arms instead of heads. She sent a gust of intense flame over the enemy but the flames didn't seem to harm it at all, it barely felt them and it got stronger by the moment. It was breaking the dragon down, reading itself for the kill and Imeah knew that when it had devoured Zaray's magic and energy it would come for her again. This was like a demon, just so much stronger. Imeah remembered something and she reached out, her mind grasping one desperate straw of hope. She called out, hoping that what she had once seen was the truth and not some dream.

Phraan and the others were working with the tenacity of a gardener trying to eradicate weeds growing in a lovely lawn, Dabin was hurt and had sought shelter behind some rocks and now Peter too had found a weapon and was fighting. He was no warrior but he knew how to swing a sword and there were many small dragons there now, some not much larger than a dog and they were left to him and Tersus. The tiny dragons from the basement had spread out and the queen was like a general now, sending her troops to the places where they were needed. The bite of one of them brought down even the largest beasts and she was letting out piercing cries, her crest of spines standing up and she did look very majestic there and then. Ivran had woken up and now he was busy trying to deal with the wolf like monsters which were scurrying around, trying to get behind the fighters to attack from the back. He was not weakened all that much which was a surprise but there was so much going on at once it was very hard to concentrate. He had discovered that intense cold did these beasts in more efficiently than anything else and he froze them and then Dhokay came with his hammer and shattered them into thousands of tiny pieces with powerful strikes.

Phraan was everywhere, all that was left in him was the need to forget it all within the rush of battle fever, the need to bring his enemies down. He was roaring as Rivath cut into flesh and bone and Ghaday was a perfect companion for this job. The enormous cat didn't hesitate, didn't fear and it drew strength from him and together they were a terrifying unit. Vines shot out of the ground, ripped dragons to pieces, tree limbs squeezed them and squatted the smaller flying ones like flies. Shaluun went for the legs while Rhuk cleaved heads and since the dragons by now was free of the magic which had transformed them they were no longer indestructible. The old dragon had no problems killing its kin, they were perhaps returning to their normal state physically but they could never be normal, their minds too twisted by what they had been through. Killing them was a mercy, an act of compassion and the ancient one felt no guilt over this. The mages of chaos had disrupted the very balance of nature and used it to create something which never should have been.

Phraan and the cat rushed towards a huge iron belly, the dragon wasn't even half the size it had been before and its tormented soul only knew pain and anger. The transformation hurt terribly and whatever sentience they had owned before was long gone, now the dragons were killing machines more than ever before and they had to die. There was no way around it. Phraan dodged the powerful jaws and cut the creature's neck in half and it dropped with a bang. He was preparing to attack another dragon which had to have been a storm fire but he suddenly heard a voice in his head, it was weak and trembling but he did recognize it. He turned the cat around, clinging to the rough fur on its neck and the creature took off, running towards the citadel as fast as it could, it did really read his mind and that was no wonder since it was a manifestation of his own soul.

The dark snake creature was too strong, it was breaking Zaray down, curling up around the dragon like a constrictor and slowly squeezing the life out of her. It was sprouting arms like an octopus and they were everywhere and terribly strong. Her fire couldn't even scald this thing and its skin was so odd and unnatural. It felt like living stone and Zaray wished that she could transform back to her elven shape but she had spent the magic needed to do that. Imeah was weakened too, she tried to draw some strength into herself again but it was so very hard. Then she got an idea, through the heart stone she felt the magic of the land too, the natural power Thiana and Taurin had awakened and she sent a desperate plea. If this thing won there would be no peaceful forests, no lush oasis. The ancient power answered, the vines and trees seemed to freeze up where the battle against the dragons happened and instead the ruins suddenly came alive. Huge living bundles of thick vines shot up through the rubble and wrapped around the dark creature and it growled and the cold eyes didn't reveal any sense of shock although there had to be at least some.

It ripped itself free, slammed the head of the she dragon into the ground and tried to tear through its neck, Zaray screamed and a foot managed to get a hold of the snake creature's abdomen, she kicked with all her might and the claws did cut deep but the wounds did close themselves up again. She doubted that even dragon poison would be lethal to this creature.

The snake snapped the vines and branches like they were made from twine, the power of the monster was terrible. Zaray was sure that this was it, the end. She had never imagined that she would die thus, she had helped bring down the brotherhood, just as she had once sworn but now something way worse was going to be unleashed upon the world. The beast raised an arm to finish her off and then the smoke seemed to split and a huge cat jumped out of the darkness and from its back Phraan did almost fly towards the beast. His blade drawn and his armour had changed again, it had added a helmet and now it had sharp spikes and blade like structures everywhere.

Imeah let out a small shriek, her soul glowed more intensely and she just hoped that this was real, that he would be able to save them all. Phraan didn't feel afraid, it was odd but he knew that this was something which would decide everything. If this monstrosity won it would make the brotherhood seem as benign as the baker's guild back at Twelve towers. Phraan did send Ghaday away, the cat could be damaged by this and he didn't need that worry on top of everything else. The snake hissed and tried to grasp onto Phraan but he was small, much smaller than the dragon and the spirit it had fought before and now that became an advantage for Phraan. He was able to avoid the arms rather easily and the vines seemed to coordinate their attacks with him. The thing seemed to be shocked by his sudden appearance, it didn't look as if it truly believed that this was real since he was just an elf.

Phraan brought down Rivath and the blade cut through the arm with ease and this time no new arm appeared. The snake creature let out a shriek of anger and suddenly it became frantic with motion and rage. This puny thing had caused it real pain, and it realized that the elf was more dangerous than he had believed at first. The vines doubled their efforts and Phraan remembered what Zaray had said, this blade could kill a God. He aimed for the things neck but the snake was not without tricks, a tentacle shot out of its very body and threw Phraan off like he was a piece of cloth. He slammed into the rocks with bone crushing force and he felt that the armour did take the most of the impact but he was injured. Ribs had broken for sure and pain shot through him, but it disappeared within seconds, the gift from Imeah was indeed very useful. He got back up, he had to kill this being, or else everything would be lost. The spikes and ridges of the armour meant that the arms couldn't get a decent hold of him, the metal seemed to hurt the terrible dark deity and Phraan let out a hoarse roar to give himself courage and charged again. His blade did just have time to cut through a hand before he was grasped and thrown yet again, the thing tried to bite him but the armour protected against the fangs and poison did drip everywhere. He screamed in pain as drops hit his skin and the thing seemed to smile. He heard its voice in his head. "Die now puny elf, this world is mine, so is your death"

Crassian and Eimar had sailed down along the river and now it was getting dark fast, but they had passed by the fishing village and the one named Greywater too. Both villages had been burned and there had been nothing left, even the foundations had been glowing red with heat and the stench of burned meat and scorched dirt had drifted along the river for miles before they even reached the villages. They hadn't stopped, there was no point in it, nobody was left alive and Crassian had tried not to look at the devastation. The village of Greywater had been larger and the buildings made from bricks but that hadn't helped at all. The houses had been turned into stoves, cooking the inhabitants alive and Eimar had been crying the entire time. The river was so swollen the rapids were easy to get through and they made good speed. Crassian did take the helm a few times, Eimar was tired and Crassian knew that the young man was in pain but he refused to say anything. Instead Crassian held a keen eye on him and insisted that they'd take a break whence they reached Ardubad.

The mining city was built on a peninsula and it was rather ugly looking, the buildings made to be practical and built in a hurry but it had a sort of ragged charm and Crassian was in shock when they sailed around the bend in the river and saw it. For the first time they encountered a city which had survived the attack and Crassian stared at the piles of carcasses which lay in layers up from the river. There were fires burning but they were being put out and people were running around, making repairs, taking care of the wounded, and dragging the dead dragons into heaps to be burned. Crassian couldn't believe it until he saw the dragons up close, these were not the terrible monsters which had attacked the villages up north, these beasts were smaller and more natural and he felt a surge of new energy. "Oh Gods, they have been changed back to their original shape?"

Eimar was gaping, the stench was intense but they didn't care. Crassian saw that some men wearing grey robes ran around and he recognized them as mining mages. They used their magic to find valuable ore and gems and were regarded as very weak when it came to other types of magic but here they seemed to have been responsible for the victory.

Crassian steered the barge towards a pier and a man came running, helping them tie it up and unload Crassian's horse. The animal was very hungry and attacked some dry grass the moment it got its hooves onto solid ground. Crassian petted Eimar on his shoulder and the man who had helped them smiled, he was covered with sooth and dirt and did look terrible but he was not injured. "You must be survivors from up north? We haven't seen any other than you two"

Crassian nodded. "Yes, the beasts have burned absolutely everything, what happened here?"

The man scratched his beard. "A miracle, the dragons started to shrink as they approached the place and then the mages discovered that they weren't immune to magic, they used some spells meant to blast rock to kill them. It was efficient, nasty but it did the trick" "

Crassian did believe the man, the carcass nearest him lay there with what looked like its innards hanging out of its mouth. "I believe you, so you managed to save the village?"

The man nodded. "Many are dead but we stopped them, the dwarves were tough fighters and their axes are better weapons than a sword when it comes to fighting such monsters."

Crassian just smiled, a rather shaky grin, the place did look like a slaughterhouse but he felt a sort of triumph. If the mages back at the larger cities managed to understand that the dragons could be killed with magic the cities could have made it. "The lad here has burns, is there some healer here?"

The man nodded, he pointed at a huge tent erected not far from the water's edge. "Over there, they are rather busy but I don't think they will reject anyone who has been burned. Dragon fire is nasty stuff"

Crassian bowed his head to show gratitude and respect and he dragged Eimar with him. The tent was filled with women and they were busy bandaging and taking care of the wounded. A rather tall woman with long grey hair and a firm but gentle face came over to them and she stared at Eimar. "Oh my goodness, those burns are bad. Come here son, we need to get some ointment onto them before they fester, and you need some tea too, with painkillers"

Eimar just squeaked as he was pushed into a chair and his clothes removed with haste. The woman was obviously someone of importance and Crassian frowned. "Pardon me my lady but you are of the nobility?"

She smiled back. "Yes, I am Lady Sherana, leader of the Onay family."

She was in fact the one in charge of the entire city and here she was working with the wounded? Crassian had to have looked a bit incredulous for she laughed. "Oh don't be surprised, I am no different than the others here, I can bleed and die just as much as they can and the attack killed many, also of my kin. It is my duty to do what I can to help. "

She found a jar filled with some ointment and started to smear it onto Eimar's burns, very gently. She appeared to be a very warm and kind person and Crassian saw that all the other healers there were women too. She chuckled. "We did have one healer here, an old gnarly fool, the only thing he knew how to do was put leeches on you or rub your feet with salt. He was useless, cupping someone until they almost bleed to death heals nothing at all."

Crassian had to agree with that. "Are there many wounded here?"

She sighed. "It is easier to count those not hurt in any way, everyone had to fight, even the women. But we won, a small pack of dragons ran south, some of our men chased them."

Crassian let out a sigh of relief. "That is good, something must have happened since they suddenly lost their powers like that"

She found some light bandages and put them onto Eimar. "A blessing we are praising with every breath, they would have massacred everyone had they been the way they were before."

She finished the bandages and petted Eimar on the head. "Go to the blue tent by the main gate, you can get some to eat there, and a bed to rest in"

Eimar bowed deeply. "Thank you my lady"

Crassian took a deep breath. "I have to move on, I have to see what has happened to the larger cities further south, I am an officer and have to report to some army commander if I can find one"

The lady tilted her head. "There is an army camp a day's ride from here but it is dark now and you both need rest. There are stables in the city and an inn too"

Crassian let out a sigh of relief. "Good, very good."

He did bow again and they left the tent, the blue tent by the gate was easy to see and several women were making some sort of stew in huge pots. The smell was wonderful and

Crassian got a full plate placed in front of him. Eimar too got a massive portion and he stared at the food with huge eyes, not sure if he could eat that much. Crassian felt much better with a full belly and he told the young man to stay while he put his horse in the stable. The building was huge and housed the many mining horses, large docile animals capable of pulling the heavy carts and the stable master was a small skinny guy with just one eye and the energy of a caffeinated squirrel. He was running around and Crassian was sure that the man would have bounced off the walls if the laws of gravity hadn't been so absolute.

The stable master grasped his horse by the reins and inspected the animal with a rather displeased expression on his face. "This horse goes nowhere, he is lame. Probably a stretched tendon, he needs two weeks of box rest"

Crassian rolled his eyes. "But I need to leave tomorrow at first light, and I cannot use the river, it goes in the wrong direction from here. "

The stable master stared at him. "Army eh? Officer?"

Crassian nodded. "Knight yes, my men have all been killed by the dragons"

The small man spat on the floor. "Cursed be the bones of those vermin, we had an officer here you know, retired but a tough guy. He died in the first attack, too brave"

Crassian frowned. "What was his name?"

The stable master shrugged. "Don't know, Aro…Arolun? Big guy, rather strict"

Crassian had to smile, he had heard of Arolun of Oakfell, the man was infamous for having killed a wild ox with just one punch in his youth. "I know who that is yes"

The man tilted his head. "He has a horse here, ownerless now I guess. You can borrow it"

Crassian sighed with relief. "That would be wonderful yes, I am grateful"

The stable master grinned, he didn't have all that many teeth left and he reminded the officer of a weasel, or some other small hairy and rather sneaky animal. "Don't overdo it then, it is a shite of a horse"

Crassian frowned. "Really?"

The man walked over to a row of huge boxes used to stable stallions. "Here, he is vicious and mean and as stubborn as a cave troll. Won't move unless you whip him"

Crassian stared at a very large white stallion which did look amazing but with those characteristics he bet the horse was worthless. "Alright, is he fast?"

The stable master made a grimace. "Yes, if you can make him run that is"

Crassian realized that the trip back to twelve towers could become a true challenge. He tried to smile and the horse kicked at the wall, it was obviously very badly tempered. "So, what is his name?"

The stable master scoffed. "I just call him "demon" but don't you think the idiot named the nag "Silverfoot" it is the worst name for a horse I have heard, ever!"

Crassian had to grin, Silverfoot. "I have heard worse, believe me, one of my knights had a mare and she ended up being named "the goddamn cunt!" so Silverfoot isn't bad at all"

The small man coughed. "You think so? Well, here Silverfoot is a slang word for a very unpleasant venereal disease which makes the skin of your privates turn silvery white, see?"

Crassian had to turn away, now that was more like Arolan, oh Gods. "Right, Silverfoot or no Silverfoot, get him ready at sunrise."

The stablemaster did a sorry excuse for a salute. "Will do, don't worry. But it will be your funeral, don't come back saying I didn't warn you"

Crassian just sighed. "I won't."

The officer returned to the tent and Eimar sat there looking as if he was about to burst, his eyes were drowsy and he was swaying. Crassian pet his shoulder. "I have to leave tomorrow, I have found myself a horse, or at least something which looks like one"

Eimar did look sad. "I would have wanted to go with you"

Crassian made a grimace. "You are no rider Eimar, and your home is the river right? I am very grateful for your help"

Eimar swallowed. "And I am glad you helped me too, ah, I think I may stay here, there are some very nice maidens doing the cooking"

Crassian had to chuckle. Eimar would probably stay there for sure, he was a handsome young man and some fair thing would certainly feel sorry for him and decide to play nurse for some days. "Go find yourself a bed and remember my name if you ever come to Twelve towers."

Eimar yawned. "I will, don't worry. "

Crassian squeezed Eimar's shoulder gently. "Good, take care of yourself, I will ride early"

Eimar shook his hand. "The same to you, watch out for dragons."

Crassian had to laugh. "I will"

He left the tent and found the inn, any open inn is bound by law to let army personnel stay overnight for free and the owner didn't try to question that at all. Crassian was given a good room and he crawled to bed feeling more or less dead tired. He would sleep very well, that was for darn sure.

The snake was trying to break the elf in half and the she dragon tried to get up but couldn't, her shoulder was broken and one leg dislocated at the hip. Imeah threw herself at the dark creature only to be trapped by dark burning tentacles, she let out a shriek and seemed to shrivel. The dark snake sneered, the life of this tenacious elf would be so sweet to devour, and the creature had dared to cause him pain. It was unheard of!

Phraan managed to get a hand free and in sheer defiance he did thrust Rivath into the creature's body, to the hilt. He was sure he was about to die now, it felt bitter and he wished that he could have taken this dark foe with him, it wasn't in him to go out as the loser.

Suddenly he heard a shriek and hundreds of tiny dragons came scurrying, like an army of ants on the move. They didn't hesitate, threw themselves at the snake's tail and tiny teeth did bore into the thick skin. The small dragons were lethal, the poison strong enough to kill and now hundreds did latch onto the thing, bite and let go. Their magic dissolving abilities did kick into overdrive too and drained the power of the enemy rather fast. The snake did scream and spun around to get rid of the pesky critters and a huge figure came out of the darkness and slammed into the lower body of the snake man. It was the old dragon, and Dhokay was on its back, thrusting the hammer into the creature's chest with all his might. Shaluun and Rhuk attacked the tail end also and Tersus came running out of the dust, throwing rocks at the head. "Eat these you goddamn overgrown lizard!"

Ivran stopped, stared at the dark deity, his eyes were ablaze and he felt his grandfather's presence, felt his pride. He smiled, a very thin smile. "You are nothing here father of serpents, for here we do take care of our own and stand or fall with our brothers!"

He yelled, threw his will against the foe like a cattle driver wields a whip and frost spread along the ground, and froze the bottom of the beast to the rubble. Phraan moaned, he was barely able to get to his feet yet but he did anyhow, his healing ability working with lightning speed, he remembered what the old shaman had said, remember your name. He grasped Rivath and the dark God was swaying, the poison from the small dragons was able to injure even such a supernatural creature and it was suddenly feeling fear for the first time in its existence. It shrieked and tried to use its magic to return to its own world but it was locked down and the tiny dragons ruined its attempt completely. The vines had frozen too and formed shackles like steel and Dhokay's powerful strike had broken its ribs and injured its innards. That was much harder to heal than a clean cut and the many attackers did confuse it.

Tersus was grinning, he held a small jar in his hands, "This is the last I have and bon appetite you bastard!"

He threw it and it hit the dark deity at the back of its head, the fluid inside of the jar had been an experiment and one which had worked out well too, it wasn't acid but a sort of stink bomb which smelled so terribly it usually blinded anyone near it. The snake God had very strong senses and not they worked against it. The thing tried to rear back and the old dragon attacked again, using its massive bulk to topple the snake over. It tried to grasp the old fighter but the arms were locked down and the poison wreaked havoc upon its self-regenerative abilities. The body was busy fighting the terrible effects of it and Phraan saw that Zaray was badly hurt and that Imeah was reduced to a mere spark of light. He growled and walked forth, with relaxed ease. "You think you own my death demon? You are wrong, for I am death!"

His gifts did step into motion, he saw the weaknesses of this behemoth, saw where to strike and Rivath were singing, howling for blood. He ran along the body, the snake twisting but unable to move, Ivran froze more and more of it and Phraan stopped by the head and raised the blade. "Vitile, this is for you beloved!"

He brought the blade down, cutting into the one spot where this monster was vulnerable, its eye. The blade slid in, piercing the eye and the skull underneath and bored into the brain and the snake let out a high pitched shriek and trashed around. Phraan twisted the blade around and pulled it out, jumped away and the creature trembled but fell silent. Imeah became visible again, as a figure of light. "You killed its body, its soul may escape"

Ivran shook his head. "No, it won't"

He raised his hands and formed a sort of glowing cube out of the air itself, as dark mist seemed to form over the dead snake he dragged it forth, pulled it into the cube and the mist was struggling and fighting but soon it was all trapped and the cube shrank until it was the size of a small bead. Ivran stared at it, his eyes were sad. "Grandfather said that my powers were both a blessing and a curse, now I know why he said that. It is my duty to make sure that things like this doesn't happen again. "

He held the bead and it seemed to dissolve, to become one with his own energy. "I am its prison, until I find something which is strong enough to hold it"

Phraan walked forth, laid a hand on the young man's shoulder. "You did good lad, you are the bravest man I have ever met. But come now, we have more dragons to slay"

Shaluun grinned. "There are few left, and they are trying to flee"

Zaray had managed to get up onto her legs, but she was in a bad state. "Go, I cannot help you, I have to heal"

Imeah was glowing in blue now. "I will help her, rid the valley of the last of the brotherhood and their ideas."

Ivran too walked over to the injured she dragon. "I will help too. Go now"

Ghaday returned to Phraan and he got up onto it, he felt like he had been dragged through a mangler in spite of his gifts and Dhokay frowned. "Are you capable of fighting?"

Phraan grinned, a wide and wild grin, filled with the madness of it all. "I just killed a freaking God, of course I can fight"

Peter and Dabin did come forth, they had been hiding and they stared at the dead monster with awe, Tersus did run over and gave Peter a hug, the young man didn't even pull back. "Did you see? I helped, oh Gods I did help bring down a dark deity!"

Peter was rolling his eyes, the smell was terrible. "Yes, you did, you truly did!"

The small dragons gathered and the queen climbed up onto the dead snake's head and let out a chirping sound, flapping her stubby wings in triumph. The others chirped too and the vines were swaying as if in a dance.

Now the valley changed very fast and every building was torn down, the skies filled with rain and it poured down, the fires were put out and grass and flowers spread with trees and other plants. The last dragons were chased by Dhokay, Phraan and Shaluun and as the sun rose again the last ones were brought down. The valley had returned to its original state, a lush forest with small creeks and ponds and soon wildlife and birds would return too. Imeah and Ivran had used their magic to restore Zaray, she was limping and weak but she would recover and the old dragon nudged her gently, like a cat greets its owner.

The tunnel was reopened and the people from the city appeared, in utter shock, others came down from the canyon and they too were gobsmacked. The city was gone, as if it never had been there and Rhuk stormed forth, he grasped onto Goldren and swung her in the air. "Oh my fair one with feet like diamonds and gold, be my bride and I swear to you, I will braid your hair and wash your feet every day!"

The young dwarrowdam was giggling and blushing, in obvious shock and Samila smacked her over the rump. "Come on silly girl, he is a catch!"

Goldren squealed. "Yes, I say yes!"

Dabin groaned and deadpanned, Rhuk was grinning and dancing around. "My Goldren, my lady of exquisite feet, how can I possibly explain how happy I am? Oh I know, I'll sing!"

Dabin threw himself over his friend, pressing a hand over his mouth. "No, you hear me?! These poor people have suffered enough!"

Rhuk let out some indignant sounds but Goldren gave him a swift and very chaste kiss and then it was all forgotten. The survivors made camp rather fast and now there was a feeling of peace and joy there. Fortunately none of the members of the brotherhood had survived, only servants and some people who had been forced to stay there by their masters and relatives. The mages were all dead and nobody wept on their behalf, instead everybody were relieved that it was all over. Phraan let go of the armour and the cat and sat down, he had suffered several broken ribs and a few other injuries too during the fighting and it was so wondrous that it all had just disappeared. Before long he was checked over by Shaluun just to make sure that everything was healed the way it should and he felt odd, empty almost. Dhokay did pet his shoulder. "Lighten up, there are thousands of dragons out there now, we will be more popular than ever before. "

He managed to smile. "You think so?"

Dhokay nodded "I know! The army cannot fight that many dragons, and they don't know how."

Phraan grasped his hand, squeezed it hard. "Thank you, I needed to hear that"

Imeah appeared, hovering in the air like a glowing angel. She was smiling. "This valley is forever sacred and it is mine to guard. I will not let any evil return to it, rest assure of that."

Ivran stared down, he was stronger than ever, he had found his true strength and he had a feeling that this was something which had been inevitable from the very start. From now on he would dedicate his life to make sure that darkness never could regain its power again. He would honour his grandfather's name and one day he may even meet him again. It was a hope he had.

Imeah disappeared and the crowd was silent. Taurin and Thiana were singing, to honour the dead and soon everyone was participating. Phraan felt tears running down his cheeks, he missed Vitile, he missed Imeah and he did in fact mourn

Fastonar, why he didn't know but he did. The heart can be a feeble thing. He wept for what he had lost and the small dragons gathered around him, giving him all of their warmth and support. The queen had perched herself on his shoulder again and he petted her gently. "At least I have you guys right?"

She squealed and licked his hand and he had to laugh, he had been a dragon slayer, now he could add God killer to his list of nick names. The crowd found rest and sleep in the shade of the huge trees which seemed to have appeared out of nowhere and Phraan lay down on a patch of thick grass and slept. Imeah used her powers to bring the horses down from the canyons to let them graze and fruits and berries did fill the bellies of those who were hungry. The only problem was that Rhuk and Goldren insisted on getting married there and then and they had found a nice spot between some huge oaks and they kept everyone awake until Dabin in desperation and embarrassment threw his boots over the bushes and hit Rhuk in the head. Hearing the dwarf cuss and swear was not that much better than hearing him shout rather obscene and disturbing endearments but it was at least less indecent.

The next morning there wasn't even a trace left of the city and light seemed to reach down to the valley where it formerly had been rare, as if the very mountains themselves had been reshaped. The survivors wanted to stay there, to live simple peaceful lives where they had been slaves and the green did spread out beyond the valley. It seemed as if the entire northern lands were being restored. The elves would make sure that the forests were taken care of and Rhuk and Dabin were thanked by Sareian's father. The young elf would survive, he was badly injured in both body and soul but he was strong and with the help of his people and the magic of Imeah he would live on and one day become completely normal again. It made them all feel very good hearing that. The others too would recover and the former slaves would transform hell into a paradise.

Phraan and the others had to return to the plains, there was so much left to do and they feared to see what the dragons had done of destruction. Had anyone at all made it? Ivran was strangely quiet, he would help the slayers for as long as he needed to, then he would go looking for a way to get rid of the dark soul which now was resting within him, imprisoned within his own mind. He could feel it even now, struggling to break free and he knew that he had to stay in control of it, for if not he would become a new foe, one nobody would be able to bring down.

There was a clearing in the middle of the valley now, one where flowers did cover the ground and it was a tranquil and lovely place. Phraan and the others did go there and Phraan did to his surprise find a statue of Fastonar there. The soul sworn was standing with his hands on his sword and his head bowed, with an expression of sadness on his face. Phraan felt a sting of regret, but he couldn't take it back now. He could never forgive Fastonar for having betrayed them, for having killed Vitile and caused such death and destruction. He would mourn him but forgiveness would never enter his heart for as long as he did live. Vitile had been too precious to him. Taurin and Thiana walked over to him and Taurin petted his shoulder. "As long as you keep her in your heart she won't be gone, not really."

Phraan swallowed hard. "I know. "

Thiana smiled and caressed some of the flowers growing around them. "This was hell but has become paradise, have faith Phraan. Your heart will know love once more"

He didn't answer, he just sent her a stiff grin and shrugged. "If you say so"

Thiana tilted her head. "I know Phraan, your path is not one to be walked alone. Sooner or later you will know joy once again"

He just stared at his feet and turned his back to the statue. His job wasn't over yet, he had to focus upon that fact. The magical barrier was up again, separating this area from the lands to the south but now it slowly became transparent and before long it was invisible and the valleys behind it were once again normal, not some other dimension. Only creatures of an evil nature would be kept trapped behind it now, all others could get through without trouble.

Dhokay felt that they had to hurry and Phraan did agree. Rhuk wanted to stay there with his new wife and Dabin was relieved beyond belief, he was sick and tired of hearing how wonderful Goldren was and how well the two of them did fit together. He hoped that Rhuk would become less explicit in his descriptions of his wife's charms when the first dwarflings did arrive.

They stayed in the valley for a few days just to rest and digest what they had been through and Phraan stared at the ring he wore and knew that he would need both that and Rivath again. The sword felt hungry still and he was rather sure that it would drink the blood of dragons yet again. The old dragon would stay there too, it was content to rest and enjoy its freedom in peace and they all agreed that it deserved it. Imeah did subdue any residue of the chaos magic and Phraan was rather sure that also the orcs would return to their old homeland eventually. It was good, it felt right.

Tersus and Peter did agree upon returning to Twelve towers when the dragons were no longer a problem, Peter wanted to learn but he was sick and tired of Tersus being such a pile of uncleanliness. One evening he gave the alchemist tea with a sleeping drought and when the alchemist was out he got Dhokay and Dabin helping him washing, shaving and grooming the man. The emerging result was in fact a rather handsome man and Tersus almost suffered an apoplectic seizure when he woke up and saw what they had done, he was sure that they had stolen all his luck by washing him. He was raging like a madman until some of the local women tried to flirt a bit and then he changed his mind on a dime and started to wash himself with almost religious zeal. From one extreme to the other.

The group left the valley early one morning and Phraan did feel how a heavy blanket of melancholy did slip over his soul as he left the place behind. This valley had changed everything and he knew that he never would be the same again.

Crassian was riding in through the gates of the army camp with a feeling of seeing paradise emerge in front of him, he had ridden for several days due south and now he had reached the more fertile area which included the coastal region and the greater cities. The trees had shed their leaves and yet this land was such a relief to behold after the rather grey and boring plains. He felt as if he had been in a hard battle, the stable master had been hitting the nail perfectly on the head when he referred to the goddamn horse as a demon, Crassian had ridden many difficult horses in his time but this one was the worst ever. If he hadn't used both spurs and a whip he wouldn't have gotten anywhere at all and when the horse did move it would try to buck him off, all of a sudden. But he had learned a lot on the trip, he now knew exactly where the limits of his patience were, and if he hadn't been in danger of being stranded in the middle of nowhere he would have left the darn nag out there.

The city he entered was one of the larger ones in this region with at least ten thousand inhabitants in winter and twice that many in summer due to the fact that everybody made their living harvesting herbs and flowers used for spice. It did have a decent wall and as he approached he saw that the city had been attacked but it had come out of it with relatively small damages. Dead dragons had already been hauled away and burned and he saw some kids playing around the blackened skulls. He managed to get the horse into the camp before it stopped and refused to move again and he dismounted with a sardonic grin. He didn't envy the poor stable worker who would be sent to get the animal into the stables. Crassian was eager to hear if anyone knew anything about the situation further to the south. The dragons had probably reached rather far before the change happened and he feared for the large settlements and villages.

The camp was built to house at least five thousand soldiers and he walked through it and saw that this place had seen battle. The men were busy fixing broken weapons and equipment and he saw several men who had been injured. Several hospital tents had been erected and he saw healers scurrying to and fro. He headed towards the office and was glad every camp in the realm was built the same way, there was no way you could get lost. He knocked and entered and a captain wearing a rather torn uniform sat behind a desk with a pile of papers the size of a small couch. He did look as if he was in despair and looked up at the incoming man with a glimpse of hope in his eyes. Crassian saw that the man was above his best age, and this had to be damage reports from what he could see. Crassian did make a salute and the man tilted his head, he didn't know this stranger and was afraid that this meant even more work. "How may I help you sir?"

The captain saw that this was a knight and Crassian smiled and tried to ignore the fact that his butt hurt like crazy, the horse had tried to buck him off for two miles straight just an hour ago and he wasn't young anymore. "I am Crassian of Twelve towers, I am heading back to the capital after a mission to the north. I wish to learn as much as I can of the current situation here"

The captain let out a sigh of relief. "Be greeted, I am Aras, captain in his majesty's army, third division. You have come from the north? Now?!"

Crassian nodded. "Yes, I barely made it, I have lost good men on the trip"

Aras sighed. "No wonder, so have we all. We had four thousand three hundred good soldiers stationed here, now we have a little over two thousand left"

Crassian sat down. "The dragons?"

Aras ran his fingers through his short hair. "Yes, and other monsters as well. We were not prepared but my men were brave and the walls did do their job. We managed to keep the worst critters at bay until some of the city's mages managed to slow them down. The cavalry did take care of the rest."

Crassian swallowed. "Then your men are brave indeed."

Aras nodded. "Yes, too brave perhaps, we lost many good men and horses in spite of what the mages did, but we won. The price was great though"

Crassian leaned forth. "The other cities and villages? How have they fared? Are there dragons left?"

Aras nodded. "Everywhere, but they are not that large and the packs aren't very determined, they hide more often than attack. The beasts have become rather small now and even though they are lethal they can be killed, by someone with skills. We do need dragon slayers more than ever"

Crassian swallowed. "I knew dragon slayers, they went on a mission to stop the dragons at the source, since this happened I bet they did what they went to do. I just wonder if they survived."

Aras raised an eyebrow. "Let us hope they did then, for if the dragons hadn't changed nothing would have been left here, not even rocks"

Crassian nodded. "I know, I saw that first hand on the way here"

Aras sighed. "We have sent riders and pigeons to every city in the area, even to Twelve towers. The answer came earlier today in fact."

Crassian tensed up. "Yes?"

Aras got up and went over to a desk in the corner, picked up a small letter. He handed it over to Crassian who grasped it eagerly. "Thank you"

He did read it fast and his heart skipped a few beats. "Massive damage, great loss of life, huge attack?"

Aras nodded. "Yes, unfortunately. I spoke with the messenger, he had spoken to other messengers too and the king has tried to get a sort of picture of the situation, it is dire sir"

Crassian swallowed hard. "And there are no slayers left?"

Aras coughed, his face a bit red. "Oh there are plenty of wannabes, but they lack the expertise if you know what I mean? These dragons aren't that bad, they aren't even as bad as the ones fifty years ago but that doesn't mean they are harmless. You have got to know what you are doing and they do travel in packs, attack one and the rest gets you"

Crassian swallowed. "Do you know if the king has any knights left?"

Aras shook his head. "I am sorry, there are very few soldiers left and even fewer knights, they all died trying to protect the cities. Only those to the far south did escape the destruction, the dragons came in waves and the first ones were the worst, the devastation was absolute. They say the palace of Twelve towers burned and so did the temples. The cities are unrecognizable now"

Crassian felt his throat tighten. "And here in the rural areas, how is the situation?"

Aras shrugged. "Terrible, the villages are without protection, as are the farms and smaller cities. We don't have enough soldiers to go out there and fight. The high command does prioritize the inner cities, those important to them. The areas to the north are to be abandoned, there is no help coming that way for sure for the king doesn't have men to spare. And there is hardly anyone left up there alive after this"

Crassian sighed. "You are right, it is rather terrible, but we cannot think of those territories now. We have to focus on the farmlands. Do you have horses?"

Aras frowned. "Ah, yes? Why?"

Crassian swallowed hard, he felt a sort of resignation within, his duty before his own wishes. "I need hundred men, they can be squires, stable lads, even farmers but they must be able to ride and hold a lance."

Aras tilted his head. "I am sure I can get a hundred men as long as they aren't soldiers but what can you possibly hope to achieve?"

Crassian made a grimace. "Save some lives, I don't care how many. If the dragons stay here the winter will be the death of so many and not because of the beasts. People cannot leave their villages to gather food with dragons around and the beasts will devour the livestock. We have to do something"

Aras smiled, a very humble smile. "I will see what I can do"

Crassian smiled and got back up. "And I need a new horse too, the one I arrived on is worse than any dragon."

Aras had to snicker and turned to go out and find someone to order around. Crassian closed his eyes. He wondered where the group was, if they had survived. Now they would be needed, more than ever before. They had the skills and experience and they did also know how to teach others the art. Crassian would do his best, but he missed Phraan and the others and he would pray for their safe return. It was after all the only thing he really could do. He had lead a group of trained knights and soldiers north and he had been the only one to return alive, he had wanted to be a dragon slayer so now he would get the chance to see if he really could do the job well.

The group had reached the plains after a couple of days and it became rather apparent that the dragons had scoured the land free of life. There wasn't sign of wildlife anywhere and they even found a couple of dead trolls. Phraan was very quiet as they rode, Dhokay tried to cheer him up but it didn't really work and Thiana meant that he just needed time. He would return to his old self but it would take time. The land would also return to its former self, life would return and now the plains would be left alone, they doubted that anyone would settle there. They were not far from the city of Mudwall when they saw the first signs of life. It was a pack of orcs and Phraan was surprised to see that the old shaman was alive and well. He greeted them with respect and the orcs did go down on one knee to honour them. The old one was smiling. "You did it, I knew you would. Now our old lands are safe again and we will return to the lands of our ancestors"

Phraan nodded and felt a sting of pride. "Yes, the dark mages are gone"

Zaray was following them, she was limping but it was getting better and she would soon be able to fly again. The shaman bowed to her. "Daughter of flame, I have seen you regain what was lost, have no despair"

Zaray lowered her head. "I thank you old one"

The shaman stared at the huge pack of tiny dragons, they followed Phraan now and the queen had found a seat on the wide rump of Drake where she sat as if it was her god given right. "Little one, queen of many, you will make a true difference"

The tiny dragon purred and her crest did shudder, displaying her bright colours. Phraan did smile. "We are heading back south, I fear that we may be needed there now!"

The shaman nodded. "Yes, true slayers are really in demand, do not waste time with these lands, they were wild and wild they will remain. Man has no right to them, let them be. No, go south and help the population, get rid of the dragons."

Phraan did rein in Drake. "It will be a great deal of work"

The old orc winked. "It will, but you will love it"

He reached out and took Phraan's hand. "Don't forget those gone but don't let them rule your heart. Look ahead"

He bowed his head. "I will see the sacred lands before I die, that is my greatest joy. Go now, fate is not yet done with you"

Phraan wondered what the old one meant by that but he urged Drake on and they rode off. Mudwall was gone, the city burned to the ground and the same sad pattern could be seen everywhere. Villages and farms levelled with the ground and there weren't people anywhere.

But they did encounter packs of dragons and now they started doing what they came for. With Rivath and Drake Phraan became an even deadlier force than before and before long they fell into a sort of routine. They were cooperating and thus they became very efficient. They chased the packs and discovered that the dragons did gather around the rivers that made them easy to track and Thiana and Taurin used their gifts to awaken the forests and then trees and roots did their fair share of the killings.

Peter did learn more and more of Tersus and the two did their fair share of the work, they had discovered a sort of chemical which attracted dragons and now they used it shamelessly to trick the dragons into kill zones where they were disposed of rather easily. The two became very valuable now and since Tersus finally did live up to his name he could mingle with others like a normal person. He soon became infamous for knowing some drinking songs which were so explicit even the brothels at Twelve towers had forbidden them. Peter got freed from the spell which had been lain over him, he didn't have to serve for four years, Ivran made sure of that and the man swore that he would serve them for as long as needed, after that he would try to make a living making perfume and Tersus wanted to help him. It did seem as if Tersus in fact did see Peter as something far closer than a mere apprentice and now that he had gotten rid of the stink Peter didn't seem completely against the idea, he did seem to favour males and Tersus was if not a picture of beauty at least an interesting person. They would most certainly have an interesting life together, whatever they chose to do. They would most certainly go to Twelve towers first but then their future was open and Peter would probably learn a lot from Tersus, things both useful and not.

The group moved southwards, Zaray did manage to fly now, her injuries almost completely healed and she was doing her best to decimate the number of dragons left. Her flames and her claws did take care of the really large ones and she left the easier ones to the group. The winter moved forth as they travelled south, they had good equipment and didn't need much and all of them were hardy and tough. Ivran created small pockets of hot air where they camped and he also used his magic to get the horse's food and shelter. He was getting more and more confident and he was constantly practicing. When he returned to Oakfell he would demand to take the tests again and this time he wouldn't try to hide what he was, he was more powerful than any other mage, and he wasn't even trying to brag.

He would use his magic in the battles and sometimes he would take out whole packs on his own, he felt that this was a way more useful way of making a living than as a mere mage. Then they reached the first villages of the southern territories and learned that a crazy knight was fighting the dragons with a small army of farm boys and retired veterans and Phraan realized that it had to be Crassian, he was eager to meet the man and hear his story. This area was teeming with dragons and Dhokay did predict that there would be many years of work left for them there. Now the dragons were natural beasts once more and they would reproduce again and the numbers were very high in some areas.

Zaray did grieve the fact that she wasn't able to shift back to her old self, she scared the living daylights out of people when she was in dragon shape and even if it was very efficient she missed being able to be just herself. Then one morning she woke up with a start and realized that the ground was very much closer than the evening before and Ivran was snickering as she embraced them all, laughing with joy. He snickered even more when she hugged Phraan a little longer than the others. Dabin was giggling and Thiana and Taurin bumped their fists, of course hidden behind their backs.

Two weeks later they did meet the knight who by now was rather famous, Crassian was almost weeping with joy when he saw them and the group he had assembled was gaping and almost unable to move out of sheer respect. The two groups did become one and Phraan and the others did teach the men how to do this job. With Zaray being able to shift at will again they had a very good weapon in her and Ivran had even made sure that she could use her magical bow again, which she did with glee. With her magical arrows she could bring down many dragons and monsters very fast and she became very valuable for them since she could take the dragon shape when she wanted to now and could survey an area from the air before they entered it and thus warn them of any unforeseen dangers.

The king wanted them to come south to help rid the area around Twelve towers of dragons but Phraan declined, they followed their plan, going south at their own pace, clearing out the dragons one area at a time. Twelve towers had walls, the small villages didn't. They would camp under the canopy of large trees, spend the evenings resting and remembering the old times and Phraan felt a new pride and sense of purpose. The hunt was still dangerous, and they did lose some men in the beginning but they were doing a good job and soon these last remnants of the madness of the dark mages would be gone. He missed Vitile but he and Zaray was getting closer by the day and he was in a way glad they still had years of work ahead of them. Even with their efficiency the dragons were many and the realm vast, the area affected by the dragons was enormous

Ivran had warned the academy of the dark mages and their power, at first the high mages there didn't believe him but then they had to and a couple of men were revealed to be serving the chaos and they were promptly imprisoned and there was a huge process of making sure that nothing remained of the brotherhood. Afterwards the academy owed Ivran a lot and he was offered the title of high mage but refused politely. He was a dragon slayer now and that was in fact much better than being a mage.

Summer returned once more and the group had camped in a very lovely spot by a bend in the river. It was warm and pleasant and they had killed a pack of rather large dragons earlier that day. They had eaten and the king did provide them with everything they needed so good wine was easily available. Two more dwarves had joined them and one was a very charming female with a sweet spot for Dabin who acted like a man who doesn't really know what to do or say anymore. It caused some laughter since he started to stutter whenever she spoke to him, sometimes with hilarious results. There was singing and an atmosphere of joy and contentment and Shaluun had filled his glass for the fifth time when he did notice that Phraan and Zaray was nowhere to be seen. Dhokay just sent the elf a wry grin. "They haven't gotten far, I can hear them"

Shaluun tilted his head and listened and he went beet red. A human wouldn't be able to hear anything but he was an elf after all and his ears were very good. Dhokay did look happy. "It is good for him, he has been moping for too long. Vitile would have wanted him to be happy again"

Shaluun had to snicker. "Well, he does sound very…happy!"

Dhokay pressed his cup against Shaluun's. "Just like the good old days"

Shaluun grinned widely and returned the gesture. "Yes, cheers to that. Just like the good old days"

www.ingramcontent.com/pod-product-compliance
Lightning Source LLC
Chambersburg PA
CBHW070350030726
47504CB00001B/137